GW00503797

DEMA

DEMARA'S DREAM

Genevieve Lyons

LITTLE, BROWN AND COMPANY

A *Little, Brown* Book

First published in Great Britain in 1994
by Little, Brown and Company

Copyright © Genevieve Lyons 1994

The moral right of the author has been asserted.

A CIP catalogue record for this book
is available from the British Library.

ISBN 0 316 90365 5

Photoset in North Wales by
Derek Doyle & Associates, Mold, Clwyd
Printed and bound in Great Britain by
BPCC Hazell Books Ltd
Member of BPCC Ltd

Little, Brown and Company (UK) Limited
Brettenham House
Lancaster Place
London WC2E 7EN

*This book is for Sophie, Melina and Michele,
who also strive to realize their dreams.*

DEMARA'S DREAM

Chapter One

When her parents told Demara that they were going to send her away from Ballymora she thought her heart would break. Exile! That lonely state seemed insupportable to her.

It had never occurred to her that it would come to that. To leave this place of her soul, to separate her from this Eden that she had been born into seemed a cruel amputation. It separated her from the source of her energy, her hopes, her dreams.

Not that Demara consciously knew all that; she *felt* it in every fibre of her being, this passionate attachment to the Kerry land that bred her. Reason had little to do with it.

Áine Donnelly, her elder sister, was across the sea in England, that cold, pale place Demara dreaded though she'd never set foot there.

'Yer a country bumpkin, Demara,' her sister Maeve taunted her. Maeve was dying to go to England which she saw as a Utopia of bright lights and opportunity.

'An' what of it if I am?' Demara retorted angrily. 'At least I know where I belong.' She would run down the *boreen* between the shoulder-high border of crimson and cerise fuchsias, to the sea, tears in her eyes at her family's lack of understanding.

And then, invariably, she got angry. What did they know? They yearned for the security that came with industry and factories, money earned working shoulder-to-shoulder in dark places where the air was foul and there was no space. Didn't they know that there was no security in the whole wide world? Didn't they realize that it was only inside you that security could be found, knowing

1

what was valuable, revering it. Houses could be taken away, and God knew that in Ireland in the 1880s that was a common enough occurrence: jobs could be lost, cows and sheep died; it was natural. But the land was always there, beautiful and good. And she was part of that land, like the golden wheat they had been harvesting, she had her roots in the soil. The turbulent sea was her life's blood. The sturdy chestnut tree, old as Granny Donnelly, was her ancestor. They could not desert Ballymora, and neither could she.

Unless they forced her, her family, appealing for her help. They were part of the ordinary world, not part of her dream. Pierce Donnelly, her father, knew the depth of her love for him, and knew that, eventually, she would do as he asked, and exile was what he was asking. And while loving him deeply she hated him too for trampling on her feelings of compassion and love.

Killian and Galvin, her older brothers, had followed Áine across that cold, grey sea.

'The wrong way!' she yelled at her mother, Brigid. 'The wrong bloody way!'

'Ah sure now, America's too far for the likes of us,' Brigid replied. She always had her mind on other things. Demara often wondered what her mother thought about, what ideas or dreams drifted in and out of her brain, or whether she was simply preoccupied with planting and weeding, cooking and mending, milking the cow and all that pother.

'If they were in America we'd never see them,' her mother said.

'We never see them now!' Demara replied, exasperated. 'They haven't been home since they went. Surely there's enough Donnellys now in exile?'

She did not want to contemplate the thought of being banished, separated from all she loved best: her mam, her brother and sisters, the great wide Atlantic, the purple Kerry mountains, Duff Dannon with his strong wrists and his passionate eyes, Granny Donnelly and her ancient wisdom, and that huge giant of a man, a gentle man, a man she loved with all her heart: her father, Pierce Donnelly.

But most of all, more than anything in the world, to leave

Bannagh Dubh would surely break her heart. Bannagh Dubh, the enchanted stretch of land to the left of Ballymora Castle, off the Lester estate and reaching out into the Atlantic Ocean. It was a land so beautiful as to squeeze the heart and brighten the eye of the beholder. The air was never grey there, the light dazzled in shafts, illuminating the glories of the landscape. It would spotlight a small white cottage pressed close to the lea of the mountain, veiled by pale grey and mauve shadows and pearly clouds. It would shimmer on the blue lakes spotting the valleys, winking in the clear air. It was a place that soothed the soul, that stimulated the imagination and contented the spirit. It was a place she could not bear to leave.

But her father had not enough money to keep her at home and no matter how hard he worked and her mother, herself and Maeve helping Lady Lester up at Ballymora Castle, by the time the rent was paid, the rates and taxes, there was not enough to keep body and soul and family together.

When Áine had gone to London the year before last Demara had thought that maybe, just maybe, no one else need go.

'You'll send a percentage of your wages back home to us girl, to help your da,' Brigid Donnelly had instructed her daughter. But Áine had met Lorcan Brennan on the boat over from Waterford.

'She went all soppy over him, I expect,' Demara said angrily to her younger sister Maeve. 'Typical. All she ever wanted was to marry and be a slave like Mam. All the fellas knew it. She would have been satisfied with any one of them but they didn't want to take her on.'

'Sure the only men with enough money to marry here in Ballymora are old and ugly with bad breath and gappy teeth,' Maeve said despairingly.

'So she marries the first fella she meets on the boat, God help us, and bang go my hopes of stayin' home.' Demara felt the tears prick her eyes.

Áine had got married in London and had had a babby, a little boy, Seaneen.

'Much good she is to us,' Mam said angrily, thumping the dough. 'All the money they earn, her an' her husband, they need now an' a child there. She can't send any to us. 'Twouldn't be right.'

So there was nothing left for it but for Demara to go to London. Áine wrote glowing accounts of life in the capital city of the world and Mam decided that Demara should join her sister and get a good job and send the financial help Áine couldn't. Demara was strong and young and willing and she could earn enough to send them the money they sorely needed.

'If I could just once, just once get ahead of myself, God'n I'd rest 'asy,' Pierce Donnelly said on a sigh.

'Won't her husband, this Lorcan, mind me goin' to live with them?' Demara asked doubtfully. Her mother sniffed.

'An' why would he?' she said, biting off a piece of cotton and re-threading the needle. Her hands were never idle and Demara had never seen her mother at rest. 'Aren't you one of the family? An' families stick together. An', God help us, isn't *he* one of the family now, this Lorcan Brennan an' we don't even know him.'

They had never laid eyes on Lorcan Brennan, wouldn't know him if they passed him in the street. He was simply a name to them. But Áine said he was a grand man and very good to her.

' 'A course she'd say that,' Maeve muttered. 'An' she so relieved to be hitched.'

Galvin and Killian had gone to Liverpool last year and they had good jobs in the shipyards. They sent home money every week between them and most grateful Pierce was for it, but it didn't do the trick, he said, it fell short of covering expenses and paying Lord Edward. Now it seemed it was Demara's turn. There would only be Maeve, Dana and Brindsley left behind with Mam and Da after she had gone.

On the day her mother told her that she must go to Áine in London Demara ran to Bannagh Dubh like a wounded animal to its lair. Alone she stood and let the wind tear at her black hair. It stung her eyes and dispersed her tears and her heart lifted as it always did when she beheld the majesty of the place.

'Oh God,' she closed her eyes, then opened them again, 'oh spirits of this place, this ancient land, oh heaven, oh lovely, lovely earth, don't let it happen. Don't let me go into exile and forget you. Don't banish me from here. Don't let my poor heart break.'

The wind wailed and the sea roared and her shawl flapped about her. 'I'll get like Áine,' she thought. 'Áine wanted to be like Mam. And Maeve and Dana want romance, for God's sake. And the boys want wealth and Brindsley wants knowledge. But all I want is this place.'

'Ye can't own land,' her father always said. 'How can ye *own* something God made an' is His? Ye can lease it. Ye can sit on it an' *say* its yours. But it's not. Not really.'

Well, she wanted Bannagh Dubh and her da wanted to buy his cottage.

She sat on her rock looking out to sea. In the wild wet September evening twilight was hovering, nearly there. The clouds raced and changed shape, silver-edged and black as soot, and the sea rose up in waves of grey and broke into riots of sparkling foam, crashing on the shingle. The land was full of whispering shadows and bright shafts of light fell from behind the clouds onto the gilded water.

A great stillness descended upon her. The deep peace and serenity she always felt here slipped over her troubled spirit and soothed her. 'I love this place, I'll die without it,' she whispered and tasted the salt on her lips. 'Oh, if there were any way to build a house in this valley, to dwell within that house all my days, there is nothing I would not do to have it.'

A cloud raced across the sky blocking out the light and the wind gave a frightened moan.

'There is a way.'

At first she thought it was a trick of the wind and the waves. She thought the soughing air had whispered magic, but, looking in the direction the voice had come from, a little above her on a slab of stone she saw a tall cloaked figure facing out to sea.

'Did you speak to me, sir?' she asked, polite but nervous.

5

But the majesty of the scene, the grandeur of nature took away her nerves. The terror and fear she might have felt in another less imposing place was absent. The shrouded figure was mysterious. He was not a gentleman from the castle as she had first thought, nor a travelling man. There was something about him that set him apart, a lack of definition, a peculiar fluidity of movement. She was not startled by this strange man standing above her. She had been nurtured on dreams and myths and the land she lived in defied her *not* to believe in magic.

'I said there is a way.' The stranger did not turn to look at her. His black cloak flapped around him and he stood stiffly looking out over the horizon and she could not see his hooded face.

'How, sir?'

'You do not have to worry about that. That need not concern you.'

'Who are you, sir? What do you do here?' she asked.

'I am on my way somewhere else,' the stranger replied. 'Where, is of no consequence to you. But it will be a place where there are beaches and wild, wonderful stretches of unspoiled territory. Great and glorious uninhabited lands need populating. They need places where people can see the views and admire. They need hotels and castles where the rich can stay and marvel. Where they can hunt the animals and pick the flowers and cut down the trees for timber. Ah, there is a lot I can do to help mankind explore and conquer this marvellous world.' The wind flapped around the thin frame. 'If only I had more requests from people like you.'

'What do you mean, sir?'

'You will be given your house on this land. You will have it. That is my responsibility. But there are certain things you will have to understand.'

'What things?'

'There is a price to pay. There is always a price to pay.' His cloak billowed out like a sail in the wind and he laughed, a mellow sound, like gentle thunder.

'I'll pay any price, sir,' she answered firmly.

A house here! That tall white building that would stand

as she visualized it, shimmering in the sunshine, glowing in the moonlight.

'You are glib!' His voice taunted.

'I am sure!'

'Have a caution, miss. Think on it.'

'I have thought. Many a night I have lain awake thinking. I mean what I say.'

'Even though you will forfeit love? Even though you will forfeit happiness? Even though you will give up the chance to love a husband? To bear his children? Even though this land is all you will get?'

'If I get my house, here in Bannagh Dubh, there is nothing else that could matter more to me, sir. Nothing.'

'You will lose it the moment you decide you want something else more.'

'That is all right. I won't. I have nothing to lose.'

'Not even Duff Dannon?'

'Not even he.'

'Be careful. You must be sure.'

'I am sure. It is my dream. It has always been my dream.'

'Then you shall have it. But tell me once more for I would have you say it three times, then the bargain is struck and cannot be undone. We never pressure you. We like you to make your choice freely. Tell me once more.'

'I will pay any price, sir, for my house and this land in Bannagh Dubh.' She said it firmly.

'Then it is done.'

She narrowed her eyes and turned her head to where she would have her house built. It would be a house made of granite with silver speckles catching the sun's light. The lake was a pool of gold now, the sun was about to set and the curtain of clouds had parted to give her her moment of glory.

Demara knew the exact spot where the house would be: at the side of the lake, facing the sea and ringed by the protective mountains. Was there ever a place so sweet, so perfect? It was an enchanted place, a magic place. The air would always be fresh, smelling of the sea and heather, wild thyme and honey and broom. Each day the mountains would tell a different story and the brook

7

would sing a new song. Each moment would reveal Nature in her bounty changing her dress, her perfume, her looks. Demara sighed and drew her shawl closer around her shoulders.

'Ah, if only I could. But it's the idle dream of a fanciful girl, sir,' she said and looked around. But there was no one there.

He had gone, the tall stranger in his black cloak. Where did he go? He had said he was on his way somewhere else. Where, she wondered, was that?

She jumped up, shading her eyes from the molten glow of sunlight on the lake, but high or low he was nowhere to be seen. The valley curved and rose steeply, dark shadows spreading, but they were not dark enough to curtain the stranger and hide him from her view.

Where was he in the wild night? He could not have walked forward for the tide had come in and the apron of beach in front of the rocks was six feet deep in icy water crashing against the caves, filling them and then receding with a cruel gulp.

Perhaps she had imagined him. She sighed again and pulled her shawl up over her unruly hair, tucking the wayward curls under it and out of her eyes and off her forehead. She retraced her steps, looking back over her shoulder now and again to see if perhaps the stranger would suddenly reveal himself or appear standing behind a tree or on the curve of the road over the mountain, but he did not show himself.

She climbed the incline, bracken pulling at her skirt, waist-high in ferns, and walked along the lane to the cottage as darkness settled over all the land and the first stars pricked the sky.

A bush stirred and she jumped as Cogger Kavanagh leaped out, frightening her half out of her wits.

'Oh Jasus, Cogger, did ye have to do that?'

'An' where you goin', Miss Demara lamb?' he asked, grinning at her slyly.

He was Katey Kavanagh's son, she, reputed to be a witch, but liked nevertheless. She cured what ailed you, had herbs and remedies which, Demara's mam said, worked for sure. Katey's son Cogger was not the full shilling, a bit astray in the head and mostly he was all right but he had a cruel streak and could turn on a body unexpectedly so people kept out of his way. He carried with him the danger of the unpredictable.

He adored Demara though, worshipped her, held her innocently in his dreams and sometimes, to her annoyance, followed her. She liked walking the mountains and valleys, listening to her own thoughts, listening to nature, looking and savouring, and it was disconcerting to have Cogger pop up from behind a bush and realize that he had dogged her every step. She tried to let him impinge on her life as little as possible and treated him casually, lightly.

'Off to England, worse luck.' She gave him her brilliant smile and for a moment in his thick brain that was all he saw: her dazzling acceptance of him. Then the import of her words sank in slowly.

'Away?' he asked, sucking his one front tooth.

'Far away, Cogger.' She narrowed her eyes and stared at the purple mass of the mountains and the distant seething movement of the sea.

'Don't go, Demara lamb,' he pleaded. 'Don't go.' His wet tongue travelled around and around the tooth.

'I have to, Cogger. Mam and Da need the money.'

'I'll get ye money. I know where gold is. Aladdin's gold.' He looked at her sideways, knowingly. She laughed. Everyone knew Cogger mixed dream with reality, stories with fact.

'Oh, Cogger, don't be silly. Gold in Ballymora? That'll be the day. Even Lord Lester on the hill up there is poor as a church mouse, God help him.'

'But I would like to help you . . . to stay . . .'

'Don't be fanciful, Cogger. You're a dreamer like Brindsley, so you are.' He smiled. He liked being compared to her handsome brother. 'Your head is in the clouds, as my da says.' And she turned away from him. 'Bye, Cogger,' she called and she left him looking forlorn and near to tears, wringing his hands in the middle of the lane.

9

She hurried homewards for it was nearly suppertime and her mam and Maeve would be expecting her help. Dana was lazy and managed most of the time to avoid doing her chores.

As Demara turned the curve of the road her heart leaped for she saw Duff Dannon sitting on the three-barred gate staring out to sea. He dropped to his feet at her approach. He ran to meet her and grabbed her forearms in a hard, fast grip.

'Is it true then? Yer goin'?'

She laughed. 'God, Duff, everyone seems to know my business. Yes, I'm going, love. It has to be. Though for a moment there . . .' She stared over his shoulder into the moon and thought of the black-cloaked stranger.

'Demara, don't go. Don't.'

She looked at him. 'God'n I'm popular! No one wants me to go, Duff. Don't you know how hard that makes it? Don't you realize how you're pullin' me apart?' She looked over his shoulder again, then up at him. That dark face was as familiar as her own. It was as dear as her own. She could not imagine life without that face in it.

'Did you see a tall man, I think he was old, in a cloak? Did he pass this way, Duff?'

He shook his head impatiently. 'No. What are ye talkin' about, Demara?'

'Nothing. A man. He offered hope. I should have known it was a dream,' she sighed.

'Oh you an' your dreams! It's signs and wonders yer lookin' for. An' ye'll not find them in the fact and the harshness of life, Demara, never.'

'Well, ye don't know that for sure,' Demara said tartly. 'I have to go, Duff. Mam and Da need me to. Things is bad.'

'They're bad everywhere,' he said. 'But I could look after you if you'd let me. I could take care of you.'

He drew her into the safe circle of his arms and pressed his lips into her soft hair. She felt her body dissolve like dew in the sun and her will-power weakened.

'I know ye could, Duff.' She touched his cheek with sensitive fingers and he kissed the palm of her hand then took her chin in the cup of his hands.

'Listen, Demara. We'll go to Dublin city, just the two of us. We'll have a grand time.'

'It's not a grand time I want, Duff. That's Maeve, not me. I want to stay here. I don't want to go, oh, I don't want to go.'

He had never seen her weep. He put his big hand gently on her head, pressing it tenderly to his breast, feeling the dampness of the evening dew on her shawl.

'Then don't, heart of my heart. Don't. Stay here with me. You're my soul, my life, ye know that. Stay here and we'll share the hardships. We can carve a living for the two of us. We're young. We're strong. We can stay here, *alanna*, if ye want. I love this land as much as you do. Stay and together we'll help yer mam and da.'

She looked up at him, face drenched, wet lashes, trembling chin.

'How, Duff? In this place, how?'

He turned angrily away. 'Damn,' he said harshly, banging his fist against his thigh. He knew she was right. He knew that if they toiled all the hours God gave they could just about support each other, but to help the Donnellys would be another matter and quite out of the question.

'Damn. Damn. Damn. I don't know, Demara darlin', I don't know.'

'Let's leave it now, Duff. I've got to get back. Mam will need me.'

He pulled her into his arms. His kiss was passionate and warm and she drank in the taste of him, the smell of him; he smelled of all the things she loved and was familiar with, the scents that made her life: the earth, the grass, his maleness, the material of his old jacket and the sweet, sweet dew upon his face. She drew him to her and Cogger watched from the ditch and as they kissed he squeezed his eyes shut and bit his lips and waggled the tooth in his gum. He was embarrassed and at the same time excited and he was on Duff's side. He hoped Duff would win. Only one thing was important: he did not want Demara to go away.

11

Chapter Two

Maeve gave her sister a reproachful look as she entered the cottage, took off her shawl and hung it on the back of the door.

'The table's long set,' Maeve said, blue eyes snapping. 'An' where were you? Are the likes of you too grand now yer off to the lights of London to help the likes of us?'

'Oh, Maeve, don't be silly. You know that's not the case.'

Maeve put her hands on her hips. She was jealous that she was not going to the glittering capital city. She was angry that Demara, who obviously was not all that anxious to go, was being sent, and she had to stay at home and miss all the excitement.

'Oh I'm silly now, am I?' she cried.

'Sit down, Maeve, and hush up,' Brigid Donnelly snapped. 'All of you. Sit. Where's Brindsley?'

'Up in his room with his books, Ma, readin' his books,' Maeve said.

'That boy will be the death of me,' Brigid said severely, but there was a soft inflection in her voice when she spoke of Brindsley.

Katey Kavanagh said that Brigid was as hard as flint until it came to her youngest son.

'I'm comin', Mam,' Brindsley called from above.

The upstairs wasn't really a room. The attic was divided in half and then one half of it divided again. The large half held the conjugal bed. In it all Brigid's children had been conceived and born. One of the sub-divided halves was occupied by the girls and the other by the boys. They lay on duck-down mattresses and it was impossible to stand up straight; Brindsley read and studied hunched over like Mr Danagher the tailor below in Listowel. But they were luckier than most and it was due to Pierce Donnelly's industry and delicacy that they had so much privacy and space. Many of their neighbours kept their livestock in the main room which was also where they all slept together and Katey Kavanagh kept the pig inside in cold weather, not because the Kavanaghs wanted to, but because the animals were very valuable, sometimes more valuable than human beings, essential to their survival and no chances could be taken with their health. As for an upper room, the neighbours thought that a delusion of grandeur on the part of Pierce Donnelly.

'An' sure didn't he always have his head in the clouds, an' his mother before him, an' now Demara, God help us!' they said rather fondly.

People liked Pierce Donnelly for he had charm. But they deplored his restless ambition. It was a waste of time in this neck of the woods with rents and taxes on productivity so outrageous. What was the point of a man toiling when the more he produced, the harder he worked, the higher his rent and the more taxes he paid? It was self-defeating. It was bound to leave a man frustrated.

'Frus-ter-a-ted is all he'll get outa it,' Mickey O'Gorman said sagely over his pint of porter in Ma Stacey's pub. It was not, properly speaking, a pub but the Widow Stacey's front room where she made a living serving (at a price) porter and *uisce beatha*.

'It's no good tiltin' at windmills,' Mickey continued. 'None what-so-ever. Ye have te accept that here in Ballymora nature rules.'

'An' Lord Lester. Don't forget his Lordship,' Brian Gilligan reminded them.

'Ah sure he's all right is Edward Lester. He's the salt of the earth.'

'Aye, so he is.' The habitués of Ma Stacey's shebeen, in front of the turf fire, all agreed, shaking their heads in unison. It was a conversation they often had and everyone knew the cues and the conclusion; a comfortable and predictable exchange.

When the Great Famine had raged across the land near forty to fifty years before, they'd all survived, thanks to

Lord Edward and they had not forgotten. Although some of them had not yet been born, their families remembered and were grateful. The shebeen and the group of cottages that comprised the village of Ballymora were on the borders of the Lester estate.

It was hard by the domain of the Marquis of Killygally and they never forgot how lucky they were that it wasn't just across the river where that terrible landowner charged exorbitant rents and eviction for non-payment was prompt and inexorable. There were few tenants surviving on his land now for they had fallen like flies in that terrible time, unaided, while the flamboyant Marquis sported, hunting and shooting on the fertile land. The little group from Ballymora shivered when they heard that the prancing Marquis of Killygally, who was known as Bosie to his friends, was trying to purchase the river and their land up to the Five-Mile bridge beyond their cottages in Ballymora. This would make him their landlord and the mere idea caused them to cross themselves in fear and reassure themselves that Edward Lester, who hated the Marquis, would never allow that. Lord Edward called him a 'jumped-up tuppenny-halfpenny type of foreigner who raped the land and left chaos where before there had been order'. He had sworn never to let him have as much as one half-acre of Lester property. No, you couldn't fault Lord Lester. It wasn't his fault that the British Government levied taxes and penalized the working man in Ireland. Lord Lester was a kindly man, a just man. He charged them a fair rent which was more than could be said for a lot of his contemporaries. He did what he could for his tenants and the cottagers and tried his utmost to be fair.

'It's just that he shouldn't be there at all!' Mog Murtagh, a little leprechaun of a man, muttered, wiping the froth off his mouth with the back of his hand. 'What right has he to be there I'd like to know, sittin' on our land, callin' it his own, an' weren't there Murtaghs on that land long before his time an' no mistake.'

'He's there by the grace of King George of Hanover who gave away what he had stolen from us!' Miles Murphy the drover said, sweetly reasonable. 'It's not the poor man's fault, for God's sake, what his great-grandaddy did. Wasn't he hisself born here in Ballymora? All those transactions happened a long time ago.'

Mickey O'Gorman was scratching his head with the stem of his clay pipe, ruminating. He was not drunk yet. It was early days, as he said himself. Mickey O'Gorman did not always know when to stop. He beat his wife Carmel when he'd had a skinful and everyone in the little hamlet covered their ears with their bedclothes so they couldn't hear her screams.

'Now supposin',' he asked the assembled company, 'just supposin' His High and Mighty King George had given *my* great-granda a slice of Devon or Birmingham over there in England, d'ye think I'd give it up now? Never!'

'It's not the same thing at all!' Brian Gilligan was incensed. 'It couldn't have happened. We'da never tried to occupy England, God's sake. But, anyhow, can you imagine an English King giving an Irish peasant *anythin'*?'

'It's a tangle an' no mistake,' Dinny McQuaid rubbed the wispy hair on his chin. Like a goats it was and sparse so you could see his skin, white there, in contrast to the brown weatherbeaten face.

'But the son, Linton Lester, gawney!' Mog reminded them, and they shook their heads and said no more for the thought depressed them. Linton Lester was a different kettle of fish entirely to his father and the men of Ballymora did not want to live to see the day when the old man died and his son became their landlord.

'Ah well, sure there's no point dwellin' on it,' Matty O'Flynn tried to lift up the conversation from where it had fallen flat on the floor.

'Let me fill yer tankards,' Ma Stacey encouraged them. The fog of smoke from the turf fire and the clay pipes was powerfully thirst-making and she had a business to run. Her husband had passed on and she cast a bold eye about for another, but sure there wasn't an available man to be found anywhere near their part of the world. Except one. And Ma Stacey waited, hoped that one day Phil Conlon, the Lesters' Bailiff, would notice her and that people would forget his ugly job and let her have her way with

15

him. He was a gorgeous hunk of a man, an upstanding man and he had a knack of doing well that suited Ma and caused her interest. She had survived her husband's death and opened her shebeen and made her pennies any way she could that was respectable. She wasn't popular with the other women, but who the hell cared. Neither were any of the folks who tried to rise above the poverty of the place. Like the Donnellys. Jealous the cottagers were of them. Well it wasn't going to cause her any worry if she could help it. So she urged them to fill up and be merry.

Pierce Donnelly had left the men in the shebeen after his evening pint and followed his daughter, ten minutes after her, up the lane home. He liked Lord Lester and had reason to be grateful to him. It was because of him that he wanted Demara to go to London. He knew, like the others, that they could have fared much worse. Many was the place in Ireland had an absentee landlord and many another had a cruel one, and people went in fear. At least at Ballymora you could take your troubles, within reason, to Edward Lester in the sure knowledge he'd give you fair hearing. After the terrible depression that hit the land after the famine, in most places in Ireland the tenants were ruthlessly evicted. Pierce Donnelly's mother, old Granny Donnelly, remembered it well and Pierce was fiercely grateful she'd not had to leave as so many others were forced to do.

It was just that making ends meet was a hopeless job, Pierce mused. The only way to keep his head above water was to send his children to England. It pained him sorely but he could see no alternative.

The reason for Pierce Donnelly's anxiety was his desire to make himself and his wife and children independent of the system. Some years ago, pre-empting the Land League, Lord Lester had announced that they could buy their little cottages, thus freeing themselves from the spectre of eviction. They would feel secure, for no one could oust them if they owned their dwelling places. The fear of eviction hung over their heads like a pall, twisting their guts and loosening their bowels when there was talk of it abroad. The sight of the Bailiff or Agent putting

16

whole families out onto the street was shocking and terrifying. For some of them it meant death, for some the poorhouse, for most the break-up of their family, so Lord Lester's offer struck his tenants as a Godsend. Many thought it was prompted by the way his son Linton was developing. Linton Lester would have all the tenants off the estate and out of the area, away from Ballymora as soon as he could and Edward Lester wanted to prevent any such cavalier behaviour. He had given them an option – for a slightly larger amount monthly than their normal rent they could buy their cottages and smallholdings on instalments.

'Never mind as they're ours since the dawn of time,' Mickey O'Gorman was wont to sigh.

Some had a few crowns put by. Some had money from another source: a relation in America, an offspring in England, or extra work done at unseasonable times, like Pierce Donnelly who worked all the hours that God gave. He was in a fierce hurry to pay those last instalments. He scrimped and saved, sold what he could, though there was not much over once the family had been taken care of, and toiled his life away, laboured for a pittance and handed over the most of it to Lord Lester's Bailiff, Phil Conlan, along with the shillings Galvin and Killian sent from Liverpool. If Demara could send him as much as they did, regularly, then, maybe five years on they would own their own home. Think of it! Their own cottage. Then he could relax a little, watch the sun go down, talk to his son Brindsley and get an untroubled night's sleep. He was not sure exactly what he would do with the few free and golden hours, he just knew that it would be a Utopia not to have that sword hanging over his head, not to have to tote the heavy burden of rent and the possibility of homelessness. He felt his whole life had been a desperate gallop and when he owned his home the race would be over and he could rest.

When he came into the cottage that evening everyone turned to him, faces glad in welcome. Dana leapt into his arms, Maeve reached for him and Demara smiled. Brindsley had not come down yet from his little cubby hole.

'Sit down, Dana. Sit down, Meave,' Brigid cried, then pitching her voice up an octive she yelled, 'Brindsley!

Brindsley, leave them books and come downstairs this minute.'

Brindsley arrived seconds later, hair tousled, eyes sleepy, a half-smile on his face.

'Sit you down son, an' now Da you say grace.'

They blessed themselves swiftly.

'Name of the Father, Son, and Holy Ghost. For what we have on this table, Lord, we thank You. For those around it we ask your blessing.'

When he had finished speaking Pierce looked up, eyes bright, as he surveyed his wife and children. 'Ye all had a good day then?' he asked.

'Da.'

'Yes, Demara, what is it?'

'Do I have to go to London?'

Everyone stopped and looked at Demara and for a moment there was silence. Pierce shook his head.

'If ye won't go I'll not force you. If it's that painful then I couldn't ask you. But, Demara love, we need the money. The family needs the money.'

Demara felt the heart go out of her.

'Ye understand love, when we own the cottage we'll be in the clear. I have to get the money te pay the rest of it an' this is the only way.'

'Yer a selfish child, Demara,' Brigid said severely. 'Your da works all the hours god sends an' never a complaint. All he's askin' is ye give up five years of yer life to contribute. That's all. It's the least. . .'

Pierce looked at his strong-faced wife in surprise. He had not expected her to be so partisan, so loyal.

'Then can I go with her?' Maeve asked, startling them all. 'It'll halve the time. If we both contribute, if we both help, Da? Mam?'

Everyone's attention was riveted to the dark-haired beauty of the family, not least of all Pierce's.

'I want to go with Demara,' she said. 'Don't ye see the sense of it?'

Pierce stared at his daughter. Yes, he could see the sense of it and he wished he couldn't. Everyone knew she was his favourite. The family looked from one to the other quietly

18

expectant, awaiting a reaction.

Pierce would have dearly loved Maeve to stay in Ballymora. She was the child of his heart, but he knew too that it made sense to let her go with Demara. He was aware of the validity of Demara's argument; that Áine and Lorcan might not be anxious to share their home even with members of the family. Brigid had a far-fetched and extraordinary idea that in England, particularly in London, people lived in vast houses, were swish and *flaithiúil*, open-handed and quite unreal, like people in story-books. She thought that even of Dublin, God help her, poor ignorant woman. Pierce shook his head and smiled wryly. He knew, even though he had never been out of Kerry in his life, that poor people usually stayed poor, and that only the rich had space, and in cities there were a lot of the former and only a handful of the latter, a privileged few.

No, Áine might not welcome the arrival of her sister at all, and if that were the case, then it was well that Maeve was with Demara. Two together would be safer than a girl on her own. He knew too that Maeve had a talent. He could see it clear as day and he knew in his heart that she had to use God's gift to her and that he could not stand in her way.

Maeve would be lost to them if he let her go and that would grieve him sorely. People did not usually return to Ballymora once they had left. Demara, maybe, would come back; she had a dream. A house on the lake at Bannagh Dubh, but Maeve, no! His firefly, his moonbeam, his ray of sunshine would glitter and glow wherever she was and take on the colours of that place like a chameleon. She did not need to belong to any one place. She made whatever place she was in her own. He would lose her forever.

And how could he stop that? How could he stop a butterfly flitting into the sun?

He looked around the table. They were all waiting for his word. He nodded once and lowered his head over the potatoes in the middle of the table, ready to be served, so that the family would not see the tears in his eyes.

'Oh, Da . . . Da . . . Da. . .' Maeve jumped up to hug him but Brigid ordered her sharply to sit down.

Brigid had a great way with potatoes. She mashed them after she had boiled and peeled them, she added diced carrots and sliced onion and mixed them with the potatoes. She crisped the top in the oven and served the bake with a much-simmered gravy made from left-over bones. She served now and the plates were passed around and Maeve gave a little smile at Demara but her sister was gazing into space and did not catch her eye.

There was a statue of the Virgin Mary on the ledge over the turf fire. It had a red night-light always glowing before it. It was just like the ruby light that burned forever before the Blessed Sacrament in the church above in Ballymora. Demara stared at it until her eyes watered. She was trying to remember what the cloaked stranger had said exactly and how he had looked. He had been tall and thin she knew, but she couldn't recall seeing his face. What had he meant? She thought he had made a promise. He had told her she would get what she wanted. But how could that be?

It was obvious that she was going away, leaving all she loved behind. Da would not force her to go; he had made that obvious, but she couldn't stay knowing the family needed the money.

'God ye look fierce, Demara,' Brindsley said. 'Ye look as if ye've seen the Devil.'

'Mebbe I have at that,' she replied tartly and took a drink of milk from her mug.

'Jasus, don't say that,' Brigid crossed herself.

'What did ye see, Demara?' Pierce asked in his quiet, interested way.

'A man, Da, a tall cloaked man who told me I'd get my house in Bannagh Dubh, but I'd have to forget about. . .' she frowned, 'what did he call it? Happiness in love and . . . in life I think he meant and . . . oh, mebbe I imagined it.'

'God'n I hope so,' Dana said in a small voice. She was small and pale and slim, like a fairy child, Demara said. Her skin was white as snowdrops and her eyes big as the pansies in the Lesters' woods.

Brigid looked around the table at her family. The younger ones had Pierce's good looks. In earlier days, when they were first married, Pierce had taken her with fierce and lustful abandon and she had conceived Killian, Galvin and Áine. They looked like her, those three, long-faced and dour and they had none of their father's charm. But with the passage of time and the strains of making a living the urgent edge had gone off Pierce's desire and he needed the stimulus of her love to have sex. It was only in the late evening when something she did or said aroused a deep responsive tenderness in him that Pierce took her with a loving warmth and not wild need. Demara, Maeve, Brindsley and Dana had been conceived in this tender mating and their beauty astonished.

Brigid looked at her youngest. Dana would cling. She hung on her father, she leaned on Brigid and she would be weaned onto a husband whom she would elevate, poor man, to a God-like position. Dana wanted that man to be Duff Dannon. Brigid sighed to herself. Duff loved Demara and was in the eyes of everyone, her man. But Demara was going to London and, with the blithe faith of a child, she expected Duff to wait for her. The likelihood of that happening, Brigid knew, was remote. Duff was in the hot days, the time of his life when his manly drive was demanding, and Dana was tenacious. It could only lead to trouble.

Maeve was like a waterfall, a butterfly, mercury. She sparkled, she flitted, she was forever in motion. No one could catch her though God knew that all the boys in the place had tried. What would happen to her in London Brigid did not know. She could go either one way or the other; no in-between, no moderation for Maeve. London would either nurture her quick-silver temperament or kill it stone dead.

Brindsley was a dreamer and she worried about him. He lacked direction, had a too-vivid imagination and seemed incapable of knuckling down to sober hard work as his brothers had. He was all mind, was Brindsley.

And Demara. Demara was sensible, hard-working, vivacious and loving. She had a practical streak. She would make a success of life if only she would give up this ridiculous dream she had, that wild obsession to have her own house in Bannagh Dubh; who had ever heard of such a thing? It was not as if you could farm there; the land was too rocky and it was too close to the sea. But Demara had clung to this dream most of her life.

When she was about six or seven Demara had not returned from the village school one evening and they had been worried sick. Pierce and Brigid, helped by their neighbours, had searched for the little girl. Katey Kavanagh had even taken out the Tarot cards to see if they could help her fathom where Demara had disappeared to, but to no avail.

It was Cogger who led them to her and it was one o'clock in the morning and Pierce and Brigid distracted with worry and fear.

She had been sitting on a rock in Bannagh Dubh, oblivious of the danger of the black sea, the heaving, heedless waves breaking at its sea-weeded base. She looked tiny, sitting there, *her* rock she called it, in *her* valley. She had clung to it, the wind whipping her hair across her cheeks and she had not wanted to go home. Since that day she had hankered to have her own house there. It was an odd desire for a girl. Her sisters and their friends wanted nothing better than to get married and have children, for what else was there for a woman? Most of them wanted to get out of Ballymora, shake its red soil from their feet, and anyhow the provision of a house was a man's responsibility.

Maeve Donnelly wanted to be an actress like the pretty Rhoda Phillips in the Dublin Theatre Company. They toured Ireland playing melodramas and Shakespeare. Maeve loved to go and see the plays performed and she swore she could do better than the rather mature leading lady who *sounded* a superb Juliet but was, at forty-odd years, a little overweight and middle aged to be completely convincing as the fourteen-year-old heroine.

She stood there in her tawdry finery, her paste jewellery, her mock fur trimming and cried:

'I have a faint cold fear thrills through my veins that almost freezes up the heat of life. . .'

22

and Maeve, hands clasped to her breast, would whisper the words in unison. She was oblivious of the sleazy second-rate accoutrements of the touring company. All that she was aware of was the poetry and the tragedy. Her common sense dictated to her that she would never be as silly as Juliet, but her passionate soul and her temperament told her just as clearly that one day she would be up there with her hands clasped saying those exact words.

She had been educated in the church school. She had learned with her brothers and sisters to write and count. Pierce was a great one for education. Many another family in Ballymora did not bother to send their children to the school. Yerra sure, what was the point when they'd be labouring men and women all their lives? Sure who needs it? But Pierce was adamant and Maeve and Demara needed no prodding.

But all Demara wanted was to live in Bannagh Dubh. 'I'll learn me lessons, Ma, but here's where I'll stay,' she told her mother and when Brindsley asked her what she wanted to learn at school then she replied, 'Sure to open me mind like Da says. Just because ye want to stay at home doesn't mean ye have to be stupid.'

Brigid wondered what Pierce would say when he found out that she was pregnant again, at this time of her life, just when they thought her child-bearing days were over.

She knew what he would say. He would hold her close and say it was God's will and a child was a blessing and a precious thing. She remembered his joy when his first son Killian was born. He'd swelled up with pride, so much so that she'd thought he'd burst. And where was that first born now? Why in Liverpool city working, slaving for money to send home to his da. And as Demara had reminded her, they never saw him. Never saw Galvin either. The second son. Gone away. Learning strange ways and another way of talking and looking at things. Oh indeed she knew. They changed so they did, across the water. There was all that talk about Brian Gilligan's daughter in London. Brian was devoted

23

to Mother Church and his wife Della was always putting on the pious act, prostrating herself in the church as if she was a nun and hinting at other people what they should and shouldn't be doing to get to heaven, as if she was an expert. Well, for all their talk, Bryony, it was said, was up to no good in the Big Smoke.

Brigid shook herself. This kind of thinking was bad for her. She despised it in anyone else, so she changed the direction of her thoughts and thought again about the totally unexpected pregnancy.

Maybe this child was needed. With Killian and Galvin gone, with Demara and Maeve going, with Áine also gone, there would be only Dana and Brindsley left at home. Yes, maybe the babby was needed and maybe Pierce would agree. He would certainly say he thought it a good thing but deep down wouldn't he hate it? Wouldn't he be worried sick? Wouldn't the new life negate the extra money Demara and Maeve would send, please God, and force them to use it on the babby and not to pay Lord Lester? Another mouth to feed, God help us, another responsibility at the close of their days.

'Tell him to control himself, woman,' Father Maguire had said when she asked his advice in Confession, though how he could help her she had no idea. She went sadly away and talked no more about it. How could she do that to Pierce? When his arms drew her into his tender embrace and his body sought hers like a thirsty man sought a refreshing spring of water, how could she tell him to control himself? How indeed could she control herself? She blushed and said a little prayer for forgiveness for she was sure it was a sin to enjoy her beloved as much as she did, but she had never had the courage and was too modest to confess that to Father Maguire in Confession.

Ah well! What was done was done and there was no earthly good worrying about it now. It was as well that Maeve was going with Demara for the double wage would be essential now.

They had cleared the table and washed the dishes and tidied the room and now they all knelt at their chairs, facing the backs, elbows on the seats, hands clasped, fingers entwined and said the family Rosary.

Maeve loved the words. The Five Joyful Mysteries, the Five Sorrowful Mysteries, the Five Glorious Mysteries. The joyful ones comprised the Annunciation and the Birth at Christmas and the early part of Christ's life; the Sorrowful were His Death and the Glorious, His resurrection. Maeve loved the poetry of the prayers, she responded to their strong theatrical flavour that satisfied her soul. Brindsley grappled with the pros and cons of logic and proof *vis-à-vis* Faith and Trust and provable Fact. Dana and her parents were fervent, praying to God to help and guide them on their journey through life and in Dana's case to get what she wanted: Duff Dannon. Demara shivered and wondered if in fact she had made a pact with the Devil.

Chapter Three

cᵒᗩ ᗡᵒ

After prayers most of the family went to bed. They would be up between four-thirty and five a.m. and their days were busy and exhausting. Often at supper eyelids drooped and Brigid had to rebuke to keep them awake. Tonight only Demara slipped out. Maeve went to bed to dream ecstatically of London and fairy lights and handsome men in evening dress. Dana was calculating how long after Demara's departure she could safely begin her campaign to seduce Duff away from his preoccupation with her sister, and Brindsley simply wanted to do as he always did: read far into the night.

Demara left the cottage. The moon was out sailing in silver shafts across the sky. She ran fleet of foot down the slope to where Katey Kavanagh's cottage squatted in the moonlight.

She knocked on the door as many a boy or girl had done before her in anticipation of a miracle. It made Father

25

Maguire bitter to reflect that more miracles resulted from a parishioner's visit to Katey's cottage than a visit to the church.

The old woman called 'Come in' and Demara entered.

The room was exactly the same as their room at home but vastly different in contents and decoration. It was dark. No lamps illuminated, only the light from the turf-fire danced on the ceiling and clay floor. The walls were decorated with bottles of various shapes and sizes. They contained the ingredients of Katey Kavanagh's cures and potions.

Katey herself looked nothing like the witches in fairy tales. She was a rotund little woman with hard red cheeks, merry currant-eyes and neat grey hair caught at the nape of the neck in a tight bun.

'Oh it's yourself, is it, Demara Donnelly,' she said brightly.

'Yes, missus, it's me. An' how's yerself?'

'Well. Thanks be to God, well. Come in an' take yer ease. I was half-expectin' ye, so I was.'

'Were you indeed, Katey? Well I didn't make up my mind to come here till halfway through the rosary,' Demara said tartly.

'An' what's that got to do wi' it?' Katey Kavanagh was not in the least put out. 'Didn't the lad see you an' you talkin' to a tall cloaked man.'

Demara's eyes flew open wide.

'Did he, Katey, did Cogger? Truly? I began to think I was loosin' my wits, so I did. No one else saw him.'

'How would they an' he from the Other Side.'

'How do you know that?'

'Come here, Cogger lad.'

For the first time Demara saw that the boy had been crouched all the time in the shadows by the dresser. He emerged, a foolish grin on his face.

'The man you saw talkin' to Demara, Cogger, what kind o' man was he?'

'He was not there, but he was there,' Cogger said at last. 'In. Out.'

'What does he mean?'

'What he says.'

'Come from the sea an' air,' Cogger said. 'No face. Skull. Like you see at the bottom of the sea.'

Demara shivered.

'What'd he want wi' you? What'd he ask?' Katey's currant-eyes glittered.

'Y'know somethin', Katey, I can't remember exactly. But he promised me the house.'

'Oh that!' Katey sighed. Everyone knew about Demara's dream. People were used to her being in the valley every moment she was free, and the wild things she said about it.

'Yes that. It's what I want, Katey, and he said I could have it only I'd never have love and children and that stuff. As if I wanted it.'

Katey's face paled.

'Be careful, Demara love. Be very careful. Are you sure you know what you are doing?'

'*He* asked me that too. Of course I'm sure! I never wanted anythin' else. You know that, Katey.'

Katey shook her head, 'Yer too young to know what ye want. At your age people hold a dream too tight, they can't see its disadvantages. They can't see the price they have te pay.'

'But I think I imagined it. I'm going to London to make some money to send to Da. How can I have a house if I do that?'

Katey shrugged. 'You've started it in motion, Demara lamb. Only time will tell.'

'Well I hope time *will* bring me my house no matter what it costs,' Demara said, longing in her voice. Katey Kavanagh looked at her with pitying eyes. 'For your sake, Demara Donnelly, I hope not.'

'Don't say that, Katey.' She sighed and rose. 'I'm off now.' She smoothed her skirts and went to the door. 'I'll come and say farewell when I'm on my way to London,' she said as she left. Cogger followed her. He caught up with her in the lane. 'Demara lamb, why don't ye come wi' me an' I'll show ye the gold? Why not?' he asked reasonably.

Demara laughed. 'No, Cogger, don't be foolish now. But thank you for seein' the man.'

27

Cogger reddened and hung his head. When he looked up she was gone. He only wanted to help her and he couldn't understand why she seemed to spurn it. He knew the gold would help but he didn't know why. However she always refused to come to see it when he asked her. That was a pity. He never asked anyone else.

He had a lot of secrets. Not only the money but other things, beautiful things in the caves and out in the hidden cove where no one went and only the fishermen saw the siren singing on the rocks in the dead of night under the moon. He had found the treasures bit by bit on dark nights when he roamed the shoreline scavenging, combing the beaches and looking for the shells his mother stuck on boxes she sold at fairs and to the gypsies. The bigger shells he gave to Demara. He knew where things were hidden and he told no one. He liked secrets. He hugged them close; they were all he had.

The men laughed at Cogger Kavanagh. He made them feel whole and handsome so their laughter was without malice and his only consolation was that he knew things they didn't.

As Demara walked away from the Kavanagh cottage she saw a dark form in front of her and for a moment she thought it was the cloaked stranger. But it was only Father Maguire beating the ditches with his stick. He laid about him with violence to eject the lovers who got up to all kinds of wickedness in the bushes in the summertime. It was a bit cold for them now late at night but Father Maguire was intent on purging the countryside of all illicit passion, so he beat the undergrowth in spring, summer, autumn and winter, allowing youthful dalliance no respite at all.

Demara said, 'Goodnight, Father,' demurely.

Father Maguire looked up from his exertions and gave her a wintry smile. 'Good evening yourself, Demara Donnelly. An' I hope yer not up to any mischief an' you abroad in the night?'

'I'm off to say goodnight to my granny, Father.' Demara sounded virtuous.

'Comin' in the opposite direction to where your home is situated? An' where have ye come *from* I ask myself?' He gave her a crooked glance. It was a suspicious look that he bestowed on everyone for he was quite sure the whole human race was up to no good and he didn't trust one of them. 'I've thought, Demara Donnelly, an' I've come up with the answer.'

Demara gave him an amused glance, 'Well now, aren't you the clever man, Father Maguire?'

'Ye came from Katey Kavanagh's, didn't ye?'

'Yes, Father. Aren't you right. Aren't you *always* right!' she cried saucily. He let out a hoot of rage and she giggled to herself. She would be gone soon and Father Maguire's anger would not affect her. 'Twas an ill wind, she thought, and sped up the boreen to her granny's cottage.

She could smell the sea. She loved the black salty taste on her lips and she sighed with the pleasure that walking the valleys and the hills at night gave her. The stars were timeless and tranquil, illuminating the countryside that was so changeable. She could smell the hay as well as the ocean. The sharp warm perfume reminded her of the bread her mother baked and she smiled as she thought of Duff holding her, teasing her behind the hayricks. She stopped a moment and leaned over a five-barred gate. The moon had turned the field silver and she laid her cheek against the rough wood and wished again that she did not have to leave. Then she sighed and continued her walk to Granny Donnelly's cottage.

It nestled in a dell at the slope of the mountains, bathed now in the shining gleam of the moon. She found the gnarled and wrinkled old lady nodding before the fire. The room was full of shadows and a candle flickered on the mantelpiece, bathing everything in russet and gold.

People said Granny Donnelly did not go to bed at all but woke and drowsed and nibbled her days and nights away. She was rocking by the fire now, chair creaking, chin dropped on her chest, head back, when her grand-daughter shook her gently.

'Granny? Granny, it's me, Demara.'

The old lady came slowly back to life from the sleep she knew one day would be permanent.

'Ah, my flower, my sunshine, an' how are ye, darlin'?' she asked.

'I'm grand, Granny, indeed I am.'

'Aye-yi. Ah, Demara love, sit ye down where I can see ye. Yer a sight fer sore eyes, so ye are. Oh they all do their duty and come to see me but none of the others settle. They don't rest. That Maeve jigs about like she sat on a bed o' nettles. An' Brindsley is never here when his body is; his mind is rovin' somewhere else, posin' questions that have no answer. And Dana is a shadow. She'll only take on a decent flavour of her own when you've gone or when she gets wed.' Granny Donnelly squinted up at Demara, milky eyes seeing more than their semi-blindness allowed, her mouth twisted in a toothless grin. She was old and ugly and Demara loved her dearly. Her hair was sparse, soft as a baby's, grey to pure white and combed carefully back over the pink skull, secured by a black comb at the nape of her neck. Her skin was like crushed tissue-paper, criss-crossed by a hundred lines and wrinkles and her hands were like crooked twigs from a silver birch.

'How did you know that, Granny?' Demara asked. 'It seems everyone knows.'

'Yer sister Maeve came to tend me today.' They all took turns looking after the old lady. 'An' she said ye were goin' and she said she wanted to go too an' she was goin' te ask her da. I told her if she wanted to go that bad I'd tell him to let her. My son has always obeyed me, always. Mind you, I never asked him to do what he couldn't or something I knew he wouldn't,' she grinned, then glanced at Demara. 'Did she get her way? I'll warrant she did. Pierce could never resist that angel face.'

'Yes, Granny, she got her way, but, Granny, I must tell ye. . .'

'Well, get on wi' it, get on. Yer burstin' te tell me somethin' so get on wi' it, child.'

Demara related the startling happenings of the evening while her granny listened intently, rocking and nodding in the fire's glow, her little feet pushing on the iron fender.

'Ye'll scuttle yerself, Demara, wi' that dream of a house in Bannagh Dubh, so ye will. Whoever heard of such a

30

thing? A woman? Owning a house? An' a peasant woman at that! In this country? In any country for that matter!'

'D'ye think I dreamed him, Granny? The stranger in the cloak?'

'There's more in life than ye can imagine, Demara *alanna*. No, I don't think ye dreamed him. But I don't know. If ye didn't an' he was real, or as real as a being like that can be, then ye've had it; there's no goin' back over that path. What ye've done ye've done an' it can't be undone, so ye'll just have to live wi' it.' She looked at her granddaughter curiously. 'What made ye make such a promise? A store of trouble ye've laid on yerself an' no mistake.'

'I made it because I thought it would be worth it; to have a house in Bannagh Dubh.'

'Ah, lass, that's what ye think when yer young. I was the same, God help me. I'da made a bargain wi' the Devil for my brave soldier at the time, if I could'da. But I'd've regretted it all my life, I reckon. He wanted to take me to England, an' I wouldna transplanted at all. But me mam refused to let me loose. An English soljer in a red jacket! She locked me in my room for three days an' three nights. She only let me out when he was gone, gone, gone. For good.' Demara knew the story well, but she loved to hear it. She loved to sit by the light of the candle and the turf fire and listen to the old lady reminisce. 'The thing is, Demara, I hated her at the time, but she did the right thing. He'da left me in London after he'd had his way wi' me. I'da been dumped. Looking back, he was all flash an' no depth. But I couldn'a see it at the time.' She sighed.

'That's what I'm afraid of, Granny; that I'll not transplant.'

'Ah, yer made of hardier stuff than me, Demara Donnelly. You'll survive.'

'Well, you did too.'

'Half. I half survived.'

They both stared into the burning turf. Little piles of grey ash fell onto the brick surround and the flames leapt and licked the sods with greedy ruby tongues.

Granny Donnelly remembered the girl she once was.

31

She had been fleet of foot then in her red petticoat, quick in everything she did, and a head of thick blue-black hair on her head that made her the envy of all the other girls in Ballymora. Down to her waist it was and that waist a man could span with his two hands.

Her soldier was a British Grenadier. God Almighty but he looked beautiful up on his white horse, and she never got over him and she never would. She would have been tarred and feathered for consorting with the enemy if anyone had found out, but no one did.

They met in Bannagh Dubh and fell in love and he wanted her to go to London with him. But her mother found out from Katey Kavanagh's ma who was searching for mussels down by the sea shore. She saw them together clasped in each other's arms and they locked her up for three days and nights and her soldier left without her. He left her grieving and lonely all the days and nights of her life. Oh she had married a good man, Tom Donnelly, a grand man, but in her heart the red-jacketed officer remained enshrined and nowt she could do would unseat him. He had taken up residence in her heart and that was that.

Demara thought of the cloaked stranger and sighed. She saw that the ould wan had slipped into sleep or dreams and she tiptoed away out of the cottage, closed the door behind her and walked down the boreen.

The world was silvered under the full moon and the stars seemed to wink slowly, shutting one eye and then another. As she turned out of the lane into the road she saw Duff Dannon coming towards her, slapping his leg with a stick as he walked and whistling. When he saw her he hurried up to her.

'Been to Granny Donnelly's?' he asked.

'Aye. An' where are you off to this time o' night, Duff, may I ask?'

'Sure I'm down to Ma Stacey's for a dram,' he answered.

They stood looking at each other a moment. The pull was there, the almost irresistible urge to close the gap between them; to embrace fiercely, passionately. But neither obeyed their instincts. He didn't want her to go away. He was allowing her to know that. She didn't want to go, but had no choice. There was nothing to be said.

They looked steadily into each other's eyes and after a time Duff raised his hand and touched her cheek. She leaned forward and kissed his lips. Soft as a feather her lips were, and tender, but passionless and cool.

Neither knew it then but something had been decided in the silence of the night when both of them discovered they could walk away from each other.

Chapter Four

Duff could see the lights of Ma Stacey's from a long way off. They winked and glowed a golden yellow in the silver light of the moon. They beckoned him there, those orange lights. Not that there was any need to coax him. The meetings in Ma Stacey's were food and drink to him and he needed no enticement.

Charles Stewart Parnell. They would be talking of the great man in the shebeen tonight. That was why he was eager to get there. Charles Stewart Parnell. He was a man to look up to, a man to admire. He was the man who had started it all and Dillon and Davitt were driving forces.

The Land Leaguers, they called themselves, and their basic issue was the destruction of landlordism and the changing of tenants into peasant proprietors.

The Kerry branch had been founded in Tralee in 1879, and the whole idea inspired Duff. The other cottagers were cautious and Duff deemed it his duty to bring them round to his view.

Duff had heard about the meeting of tenant farmers at Westport and what Parnell had said. He had read it in the papers. He had learned that speech off by heart. It had fired his imagination and given his uneasy resentment a target: landlords. They were the target. Landlords.

He pushed into the warm, crowded and smoky interior of Ma Stacey's little front room. He ordered himself a small one and a pint. He was greeted on every side, had his back slapped and was looked to for confirmation and approval when people expressed opinions. Duff was, in spite of his youth, considered something of a leader. Granny Donnelly said it was because he sounded sure of his opinions and that led people to believe he knew what he was talking about.

'That's great news afoot, eh, Duff?' Dinny McQuaid asked, eyes slanted in sly enquiry.

'And what news is that, Dinny?' Duff asked. He was amused because Dinny refused to put anything concrete into words in case he could be contradicted, or, worse still, be found to be wrong and therefore ridiculed.

Dinny said nothing.

'It's Michael Davitt as persuaded him to lead the Land League. Parnell, I mean. We were talkin',' Brian Gilligan said to Duff by way of explanation.

'It's Michael Davitt as persuaded him. Isn't he the great man now?' Dinny spoke, on safe ground now.

They all respected and loved Michael Davitt. He was a Fenian and National Hero. He had spent years in British prisons for the Nationalist Republican cause. He it was who had persuaded the young Member of Parliament for County Meath, Charles Stewart Parnell, to make his famous speech to a meeting of tenant farmers in Westport.

'Yes an' Parnell had the guts to say it,' Mog Murtagh smacked his lips, relishing the talk and the drink and the company. 'Give it to us, Duff,' he demanded, eyes beaming at the young man. 'Sure you do it grand an' no mistake.'

Duff quoted obediently. He knew the speech by heart and it was an almost nightly occurrence that he was asked to repeat it in the shebeen.

' "A fair rent is a rent the tenant can reasonably afford to pay according to the times . . ." '

'That's it . . . that's the bit . . . "accordin' to the times" . . . that's it!' Mickey O'Gorman nudged Dinny in the ribs and gave him a drunken conspiratorial wink.

' ". . . according to the times",' Duff continued. ' "But in bad times a tenant cannot be expected to pay as much as he did in good times . . ." '

'See, Dinny, see? Not "pay as much as he did in good times" – isn't that the miracle? Isn't it though?' Deegan Belcher scratched his bulbous nose.

'Are you goin' to keep interruptin', puttin' the lad off his stroke?' Dinny asked peevishly.

'Aw shut up will ye an' let him proceed,' Mog Murtagh said sharply.

' "Now what must we do in order to induce the landlords to see the position? You must show them that you intend to hold a firm grip of your homesteads and your lands." '

'Ye hear that? He's tellin' us to fight back,' Deegan Belcher, who was a large florid giant of a man, shouted, banging his mug of beer on the counter. Cogger Kavanagh in the corner seat by the fire jumped at the bang but said nothing.

'I assed ye and assed ye te let the boy finish,' Mog Murtagh said in piercing command and there was instant silence.

' ". . . and your lands",' Duff continued. ' "You must not allow yourselves to be dispossessed as your fathers were in 1847 . . ." '

'An' how does he expect us to do that, eh?' Matty O'Flynn asked nervously. 'Sounds like aggression to me. How does he think that can be accomplished, eh?'

'It's easier said than done,' Shooshie Sheehan the fiddler agreed. 'We can't take on the likes of them an' their strength.'

'WILL YE LET HIM FINISH?' Mog roared.

' ". . . in 1847 . . . I hope that on those properties where the rents are out of all proportion to the times a reduction may be made and that immediately. If not, you must help yourselves, and the public opinion of the world will stand by you, and support you in your struggle to defend your homesteads." ' Duff finished to a burst of applause and shouts of approval. He raised his porter and downed it in one go.

'Who is he anyway? This Parnell?' Matty O'Flynn persisted.

'Sure he's an English Protestant, so he is.' Deegan Belcher stated scornfully. Loud jeers greeted this statement.

'But he's on our side an' he's a Member of Parliament, an' that's what counts,' Duff finished.

'Aye. Any port in a storm,' Mog nodded sagely.

'They're calling it the Land League,' Duff said. 'An' we all have to be part of it.'

'Ah now, that's goin' a bit far!' Dinny McQuaid muttered.

'But we don't need it, Duff!' Matty said simply. 'Lord Lester is not an unkind man. We have no problems here in Ballymora.'

'Until his son and heir takes over an' then we'll rue the day we left ourselves out. We'll have no protection then,' Duff said firmly.

'God'n yer always spoilin' things wi' statements like that,' Mickey O'Gorman said bitterly. 'Bloody spoil-sport!'

'Well, I'm tellin' ye that Edward Lester and Linton Lester are two different stories,' Matty O'Flynn said firmly.

'But this Parnell is an Englishman. Since when did an Englishman understand our troubles?' Dinny asked reasonably.

'Look, the Land Leaguers' top officials, except Parnell, are all Fenians, all native Irish. It's Ireland for Irishmen. Parnell is useful to them because he *thinks* he's Irish an' he wants the same as we do.'

'Well I wouldn't trust any of them!' Dinny said with finality.

Why don't they listen, Duff thought, as he ordered another pint, why are they so feeble under oppression? The years of occupation had sapped their energy and made them weak. Why were they so reluctant to fight? Accepting second-best, putting up with the Devil they knew because they were so shit-scared of the Devil they didn't know?

What would they do when Linton Lester's day came and under the present law he could throw them instantly out of house and home if he so desired? And it would come, inevitably, and sooner than any here expected. Lady Lester's maid, Eileen McGrath, was walking out with Brian Gilligan's son Peadar, and Eileen had told Peadar that Lady

Lester was very worried about her husband's health. Added to that Dr Martin from Listowel was visiting Ballymora Castle three times a week these days and everyone knew that Edward Lester had not needed a doctor these twenty years or more. It was serious whatever was wrong with him. It worried Peadar who told Duff and it worried Duff when he heard.

As if that was not enough, Demara was leaving. The pain he felt, the loneliness in his heart at the thought of it made him wince, but he felt it was not manly to care so, to feel so much. Women were for pleasure. They were the soft side of life, and for him to sicken like this because she was going to London was weak and feeble of him. But he could not seem to help himself. Everything he did, everything he planned was for her, for both of them when they married. It made him angry and frustrated not to be able to take charge of things. By rights he should be in command, he should help Pierce financially so that Demara need not go to London. His inability to solve the problem hit at his pride and diminished him in his own eyes.

He had not taken Demara's talk of a cloaked stranger very seriously. Demara was a dreamer, a girl who dabbled in ideas that Duff found incomprehensible. He was a man of action, she had her head in the clouds, was romantic and fanciful. Duff was quite happy to have her so; it was feminine and he made no effort to understand her. He would walk with her in the mountains or court her in Bannagh Dubh and not listen to what she said as she rambled on about the old days and the Kings and Queens of Erin. The *Shee an Gannon* and the *Gruagach Gaire* and Fin MacCumhail and the Fenians of old and the battles and loves and dreams of *Tir na n-Og*. She talked of the warriors lined up in the emerald fields and how the wheat would be splashed with the scarlet blood of the wounded and how the shields sang in Tara's hallowed halls.

He would hear the words but the meaning would not penetrate for his head was too full of the present; of the Land League, of Pierce Donnelly's problems, of his own smallholding and how it fared as each season turned and most of all of Demara, her beauty, her allure. He would sit with her on the mountain slope and watch her lips as she talked, soft ripe lips like poppies, intent on controlling his response to her desirability, watching the play of light and shadow on her breasts, the curves he could see above her bodice, the dark mysterious dent between those marble globes, the outline beneath the thin stuff of her dress. While she talked, tucking her skirt up to her knees, dangling her slim white ankles in the water, he would stare at her toes, plump and pink like sweetmeats, and as she pulled her shawl over her shoulders his mind was fully occupied with the curve of her thighs and the delicate complicated design of her ear, the firmness of her pale cheek and the tempting milky column of her neck.

How in the name of God could he concentrate when such bounty was on display? The fire of her lips, what her mouth did to him, how at her touch he became firmly ready to take her as he dreamed he would when they were wed, all that promise of her he had thought of as exclusively his was now to vanish from his life. His impatience to possess her, to roam freely through the depths, the nooks and crannies of her body, was held in check by the certainty of the eventual realization of his desires. Now all that was changed. All had become uncertain. Lord Lester was ill, and Demara Donnelly was going to London and the foundations of his life had been rendered shaky. Nothing was secure, nothing was definite, all was in doubt.

He saw a large ungainly hand on his knee and he looked up to meet Cogger Kavanagh's protruding eyes.

'We'll both miss her, Duff,' he said.

Duff nodded and sighed. 'Aye, that we will.'

'But she come back. The man from the Other Side said so, an' a man like that don't lie.'

Duff nodded again and looked into his empty mug and decided that the only thing to do that night was to get drunk.

Chapter Five

cᘏ ᘒ

Lord Lester lay propped up in bed with at least eight pillows and a bolster behind him. On his head he had a ruby cotton fez and he wore his wine-paisley dressing-gown over his nightshirt. His breathing was shallow and his handsome face livid. The bed was a high four-poster with heavy brocade curtains held back by gold ropes. A huge log fire burned in the grate and the room was lit by a couple of branches of candles. It was airless and stuffy but they had not dared to open a window for weeks in case his Lordship took a chill.

Kitty, his wife, sat at his side and held his right hand between her own. Every now and then she patted it as if in reassurance. It was precisely the way she had patted the little hand of their son Linton when she was saying goodbye to him. She had a faded beauty that her husband still found irresistible and touching and the gaze he rested upon her every so often was full of concern and love. What would she do without him?

He was a worried man. Healthy all his life, this sudden illness had alarmed him and taken him unprepared. He had not noticed the passage of time nor had he observed age creep up on him or Kitty; he had been too busy. The sudden collapse of the body he relied on frightened him. He had been active all his life and the forced inactivity irked him and made him irritable when he most wanted to be calm and patient.

But the real problem was Linton. Goddamn Linton he thought angrily, then felt his breathing become difficult. It always happened when he got agitated. He gasped, cursed himself for a fool and tried to relax.

Edward Lester loved Ballymora Castle. He had been born in the bed he now lay in, dying, and he had lived

39

most of his life within the castle grounds. He was content to do that, content not to stray very far from the familiar and beloved place.

He loved the mountains, the rivers and lakes and the verdant beauty of this corner of Kerry. He liked to feel too that he was like a father to the peasants, and he took his role of Squire to the smallholders and farmers in the vicinity and on his land very seriously.

He was a religious man, a good Protestant, conscientious in the performance of his duty. He hoped he was a peace-maker.

Ballymora Castle was not an imposing building. It was a muddle of styles, not nearly as big and pleasing to the eye as many of the other estates hereabouts. It was not as well cared for as perhaps it should be, due to Lord Lester's shortage of funds and the magnanimous manner of his treatment of his peasants. There were cobwebs in the darker corners of the rooms and halls. Slates were always missing from this or that part of the roof. The west wing needed attention and was hardly used nowadays and there was dry rot in the oak beams in the baronial hall. A vague air of neglect hung over the castle, but Edward loved its shabby comfort and dealt with the problems as they arose or when they appeared to be getting out of hand. They could not afford to have the repairs dealt with as promptly as they should have been, but that fact did not bother Edward unduly.

The problem, he thought, was Linton. His only son. His heir. Linton wanted to sell Ballymora. He cared not a fig for Ireland. He craved to return to England. He did not see the beauty of the place, did not give a hoot for the history and tradition of the Lesters of Ballymora, was indifferent to the responsibility they had to the tenants and dependants. Ireland was, after all, a colony of the British Crown and as befitted a powerful protector the representatives of that sovereignty should set an honourable example. Linton's father told him this but his son thought that was all hogwash and said so loudly and often, and Edward had to admit that his own righteous views were not widely held so that Linton found support among most of his social equals. The Marquis of Killygally in Stillwater was an absentee landlord who bled the country dry and treated the natives with brutal disdain. His example and that of others like him did not deflect Edward from what he saw as his duty, but it did not endear him to his fellow countrymen in Ireland who laughed at his strict moral conduct and resented him for showing them up and making them feel guilty.

However, he cared nothing for the opinion of others, but it worried him that his son should be at one with the short-sighted and heedless rakes and wastrels who took what they could and gave nothing back to this uneasy land. Edward had begun to realize that their days in Ireland were numbered and England was bound to lose this green and fertile island, this last stop before America, if they did not put their houses in order and stop riding rough-shod over a nation driven very near the edge of its endurance. Edward Lester was only too aware that if you pushed people too far they would eventually revolt. He knew all about the Land Leaguers and was on their side. He too felt that unreasonable rents and foul treatment by the landlords was untenable and reform was not only necessary but vital.

Linton did not agree. If he, Edward, died tomorrow he knew his son would lose no time evicting anyone and everyone who lived on Lester lands. He would promptly sell up and shake the dust of Ireland off his feet. Edward felt his heart pound at the thought. He had achieved a happy prosperity, a contented community and he was proud of what he had accomplished. To see it wiped away in one fell swoop caused his heart to rumble and dodge about unevenly in his chest, so he closed his eyes and tried to breathe evenly to get himself under control.

There was a knock on the door. Kilty, the old retainer, entered and whispered to her Ladyship that Vernon Blackstock, the Lester solicitor, had arrived and would Lord Edward be up to seeing him?

'Come in, Blackstock, come in. Don't hover. Hope you didn't find the journey too tiresome?'

Edward struggled against the pillows, propping himself

up and became short of breath again. Kitty tut-tutted. 'Calm yourself, Edward,' she said.

Dear Kitty, he thought, dear, sweet woman. He did not know what he would have done without her by his side these past thirty years. However, much as he adored her he did not feel he could trust her as far as her son was concerned. Linton could do no wrong in his mother's eyes.

'It's good to see you, Blackstock old fellow. Leave us, m'dear. Things to discuss.' He waffled on while he was thinking, trying to pull himself together and bring an energy into his voice where there was none. Kitty tut-tutted again, said something about him not tiring himself, but left the room without protest. The habit of implicit obedience to her husband was ingrained.

'Now, Blackstock, pour yourself a port. Rollicking stuff! Came from Lisbon. Smuggled, I think. Caves below were riddled with contraband in the old days, and, no doubt today. Though I must say I've seen no signs of it. However, I'm straying from the point. Come here and sit near me for I've got to leave things right and tight.'

'Good heavens, my lord, you mustn't talk like that,' Blackstock crossed himself swiftly. 'You are good for a long time yet.' He poured the ruby liquid into a cut-glass. He was a round butterball of a man, red-faced and globular, a fringe of grey hair decorated his bald pate and his eyes overbrimming with glee were surrounded by a complicated mass of pouches and creases all indicating a merry participation in life. He was energetic and alert and he sat beside the great bed in the chair that Kitty had occupied minutes before. He sipped his excellent drink, wiped his brow and crossed his fragile ankles and dainty feet and looked attentively at Lord Edward Lester.

'At your service, your Lordship. At your service,' he said, fixing bright eyes on the grey-faced man in the bed. Now that he was closer Vernon Blackstock could see the deterioration of this once-robust man.

'It's about my will, d'ye see. I want it watertight. Watertight.' Edward glanced at the little man. 'Y'know, Blackstock, that my son does not, er, like this place. He is a young man and has a young man's greed for the high life, for the fillies, for the cards and er, I'm afraid, the ladies. To put it bluntly, he's weak. He thinks life should be one great party and he does not look prudently into the future and his responsibilities. Thinks more of gratifying his base cravings than of doing his duty.'

Vernon Blackstock pursed his lips in disapproval, shook his head and took another sip of his port. Not that he was against the pleasures of this life. Heaven's no! But in moderation. Moderation in everything, and from what he knew of Linton Lester that word did not even glimmer at the edge of any consideration. Linton Lester was a young man to whom moderation was incomprehensible. There was only one man more immoderate than he and that was the Marquis of Killygally, who, God help us, didn't even know the meaning of the word.

'In short, London beckons and Ballymora bores,' Lord Lester finished.

'Oh dear, dear, dear me! Youngsters today, my lord, are quite appallingly rash and heedless.'

'I've made my will quite plain, Blackstock, but I'm not sure it's clear enough. I want all the loopholes blocked. I want the castle and the estate entailed. Kitty has the administration with my son. That's how it stands at present, as you are aware of. But I want now to change that and not give Linton any powers at all for some time yet. I want to insist that Linton does not inherit until he is thirty years of age. Does that strike you as unfair, Blackstock?'

The solicitor smiled, 'No, my lord. It strikes me as very prudent. Very prudent indeed. But if I may say, it will not strike Lord Linton as prudent, I'm afraid. Not at all. He cannot but consider it unfair.'

'Well, too bad. I cannot help that. If he had shown more filial respect and . . . that blasted Killygally, Blackstock. The man is a shocking influence.'

Vernon Blackstock heartily agreed. It was what he had been thinking himself. He did business with the Marquis, but that did not mean he had to like him. He shivered. He did not want to admit to himself his fear of the owner of Stillwater.

'You'll leave a board of trustees?' Blackstock asked.

'Yes. That's my intention. And a clause that my intentions cannot be queried. That if the will is disputed everything is frozen for a five-year period. Or longer if you deem it necessary. Help yourself to a little more port, Blackstock. Have the document prepared for me to sign by tomorrow morning. All right?'

'What document, Father?' Linton Lester asked. He had entered the room unheard and stood now looking at his father.

Whenever Edward saw his son unexpectedly he was always overcome by a shock of recognition, for he came face to face with himself. This was the young man he had once been, long ago. Young. Handsome. Vital. Ah God, so long ago. Linton had the same clear profile, the same amber eyes, the same wide smile. Yet there was a difference. Linton Lester's face was a weak face. Edward Lester's face was very strong. There was a discontent about Linton that his father never possessed. His son was restless where he had always been calm. His son was ruthless where he had always been openminded. And his son was cruel where he had always been kind.

Edward had hidden these facts from himself over the years, but now the truth seemed important and he had to admit to himself his son's true nature. He had kept hoping Linton would change, grow up, mature. So far his hopes had not been fulfilled.

He looked at his son now with clear eyes. 'Some papers Blackstock is preparing for me to sign.'

'It's your will, isn't it? You are going to disinherit me?'

Edward felt the pain of the insult, the unfairness. 'Don't be ridiculous, boy. Good God Almighty, what have I ever done to you to make you think that of me?'

'I know how you love this old heap of stones.' Linton Lester's eyes flickered around the room. It was faded grandeur and he hated it. He yearned for a smart, modern town dwelling in London. He did not want to live here, in this sleepy backwater drowning in purple mists, the land soggy with rain and full of complaining peasants and unfashionable women. Used to getting his own way, thwarted by his father, he itched to escape.

44

But there was not enough money for him to leave and set himself up in a suitably fashionable establishment in London and he had no intention of being penniless.

'Father, if you're changing your will, please remember that you'll be dead and I'll be alive when the terms are read.'

Again Lord Lester winced at the callousness.

'I am aware of that, Linton,' he said.

'What will it matter to you then if I do sell Ballymora? Do you think I'll run it well? Especially as you will have forced me against my will? Do you think Mother will be happy here without you? Don't you realize that she'll miss you dreadfully and she'll want to go to her relations in London, and not remain here mouldering, trying to cope with a crumbling old castle and a lot of hostile natives?' Edward closed his eyes. He felt a huge lump in his throat that prevented him from swallowing.

What Linton said was true. Forcing his son to stay, become a landlord, would not be a good thing at all. He would take it out on the tenants. He would not work, as he himself had done, to build up a good relationship between the tenants and himself.

'This place, Ballymora Castle, does not only comprise of us. This family. Me, your mother, you, Linton,' Edward tried to explain, although he knew it was no use. 'We have a responsibility to the people here. To our servants. Our tenants. The cottagers. They live here. It is our job to rule fairly. To be just and moderate.'

'Even when they are disloyal? Even when they plot sedition? Even when they revolt? Oh, Father, these people are not your friends. No matter how you see them as your children, your little flock, they see us as strangers. As aliens on their land.'

Once more Edward knew there was truth in what the boy said. But he realized too that Linton was saying it for the wrong reasons. It was not because he understood the situation, rather he was using this popular argument to get hold of Ballymora and sell it. The estate, the land needed a master, someone the people could relate to, and, hopefully, respect. If he left Linton no alternative other than to remain here in the land he hated, then God help the land. And the tenants. And Kitty.

Kitty had been his life, Edward thought. She loved him and because she loved him so much she put up with Ballymora. But when she spoke of 'home' she meant England. She would hate to be trapped here without him. She would become eccentric and talk to herself. She would be lonely and let things slide. She would stop going out and entertaining. She would become cut off.

He felt exhausted and depressed and he wanted desperately to cry. He had not wept since he was ten years old and he couldn't think why he had an overwhelming urge to burst into tears now.

At that moment Kitty returned.

'Out, out everybody. You've been here long enough. Oh, my dearest, look at you.' She ran to his side and laid a hand on his cheek. Then she turned to Linton and Mr Blackstock. 'Oh how could you have tired him so,' she said reproachfully. 'Leave him now, please. Leave him to rest.'

They left, Linton striding quickly from the room. Vernon Blackstock gulped the remains of his port before he put the glass on the table and hurried on his little fat legs after his host's son.

'Oh, my darling, have they exhausted you?' she asked him, pressing her cheek against his face. Her voice was fully of honey-warmth and he felt the pain in his heart again, this time from the love he wanted to pour out to her.

'A little, Kitty. A little.'

She tidied the pillows, made him comfortable.

'Kilty will bring you up some broth to give you strength. I'll tell them to prepare it for you.'

'Not yet, Kitty. Sit by me. Hold my hand. It helps me so much when you do.'

She felt the tears catch in her throat. He was so helpless, he who had been so strong. She was terrified of losing him. How she would ever survive without his dear presence she did not know and was too frightened to contemplate.

He was looking at her as if trying to memorize every nook and cranny of her face.

'I love you so much,' he said. 'You know that, don't you?'

She nodded. She was alarmed and tried not to show it. He must be dying, she thought, for he never said such things to her. Oh of course she knew he loved her but she had not heard him say so since their wedding night and it worried her sorely to hear it now.

She dampened a cloth with eau-de-Cologne and laid it on his forehead. 'Have I been a good husband to you, Kitty my dear? I've tried to be. It would help me to know.'

Her eyes were full of tears. 'You've been the best and dearest husband in the world, my darling. There has never been a day that I have not thanked God for giving you to me.'

She tried to control the quaver in her voice but did not succeed. He gave a sigh of great content.

'Don't fret, Kitty. Don't be distressed. It's good to know I haven't failed you.'

'Oh, Edward. Never.'

'Thank you, my dear. Thank you. Now I can rest,' he said and closed his eyes.

Chapter Six

cஇ இ

The following morning Vernon Blackstock arrived, prompt and cheerful as the sun rose over Ballymora Castle. He crossed the wooden humpback bridge, stepping daintily on his small feet, and leaning over its plaited side looked down upon the silver backs of fish as they darted and dove and fanned their bright tails from left to right.

'The trout will be leaping soon,' he muttered to himself, nodding his head. He wore a tall hat that was shiny in the early morning sun. 'Deed, it's market day,' he added when he saw Miles Murphy, the drover, honking and harassing his pigs to the market and they squealing on their dainty hooves.

Mr Blackstock looked down on his own gaitered feet

and giggled to himself. He admired his neat little shoes and the shine Mousie K, his servant, put on them. He liked the look of them under his gaiters and so did Moll, his wife. Moll was mad about his toes. He did a sharp little skip when he thought of Moll as he walked down the granite stone path past mossy statuary under arches of clipped yew. Moll was a roly-poly jammy pudding of a woman and he loved to have her for afters. He squirmed with delight as he thought of her. She thought him quite perfect, his feet delicious and the fun and games they enjoyed together he felt sure would make Father Maguire turn the colour of the underside of the fish in the stream and his eyes pop right out of his head at what he was missing.

'There are things, Father Maguire, you never even dreamed of,' Mr Blackstock chortled as he hopped up the path on his much-nibbled toes, 'that give such pleasure to a man an' if the good God above classes them as mortlers then I, for one, don't want to know Him for he's a terrible eejit.' Or, as he put it to Lord Edward, 'A good woman calms the aggravation in a man's breast and focusses his mind away from trouble.'

And Lord Edward had to agree. Lord Edward was a man with no axe to grind, unlike his fidgety son Linton. Well, Linton would be trussed up nicely, like one of Mousie K's chickens after she'd cooked it, sitting before him on the table waiting to be carved. He'd not be able to cross his father once this will was signed.

Vernon Blackstock came out into the lavender *parterre* at the side of the house and he danced around the driveway with little hop, skip and jump steps. He liked coming to visit Lord Lester. He was sure of a good meal, and he was a man who treated his stomach with consideration and respect, a fat fee, which he padded, of course, and expenses which he also padded. 'Rounded out nicely,' he said to himself. 'Rounded out. Can't bill the aristocracy four guineas and add to it one guinea and two pounds ten shillings when ten guineas sounds so much more professional and satisfactory.'

Kilty opened the door to his bell and Vernon's good humour vanished instantly. He knew at once that Lord

Edward Lester had died in the night. Kilty's face was blotched, red and white and he made no attempt to hide his tears.

'The master passed on,' he sobbed as Vernon stepped into the huge hall. Kilty took his proffered hat and wiped his nose on his sleeve. 'The poor master passed on last night, Mr Blackstock. Ah, sir, 'tis a sad day for us an' no mistake.'

A sad day for Vernon Blackstock too, for although he enjoyed the material benefits accruing from his work for Lord Lester, he was genuinely fond of Edward and Kitty and had a warm affection for them both.

But not Linton, and it was Linton who walked down the grand curving staircase now, dressed in his perfectly-cut riding breeches and jacket, tapping his whip against his thigh. The old house crumbled about him, ceilings flaking, carpets frayed and threadbare, but the young man himself looked the very height of fashion, fastidiously groomed.

'Ah, Mr Blackstock, nice to see you.'

Vernon's heart skipped a beat for the young man was the spit image of his father in the trembling light that flickered in mote-filled shadows and prisms and bright shafts of red and blue and gold through the stained-glass windows above.

'Nice to see you, Lord Linton,' Vernon Blackstock replied respectfully. No need to cross the young man yet awhile.

'I expect you have brought the new will with you, Mr Blackstock, to be signed?'

Blackstock bowed his head. He could look very imposing when he chose and he puffed himself out like a bull-frog but did not reply.

'Well, it will have to wait forever,' Linton Lester said with a smile.

It was typical of Linton to crow, Vernon thought. As Moll always said, 'Sweet manners bring sweet favours and sour returns sour.' Linton's father knew this and had a willing staff in the house and willing workers on his estate and in his fields, men and women who did not take every opportunity to sabotage their tasks for him because he rubbed them up the wrong way. The Irish were very good at this: bath water arriving tepid, food not quite right, performance unaccountably slow. Vernon Blackstock had always admired the way Lord Edward had handled his staff and got the best from them. The same could not be said for his son.

'I take that to mean that your father is dead,' Blackstock stated rather than asked.

'Yes. My father died in his sleep last night.' Vernon Blackstock was surprised at the sudden emotion in the young man's voice.

Linton turned his head away swiftly and struggled with some fine sentiment within him, then seemed to strangle and kill it.

'I am deeply distressed to hear it,' Blackstock said.

'Oh cut the crap, Blackstock. He was barely hanging on. It was time he shuffled off this mortal coil.'

'Ah, sir, Shakespeare.'

'Well, it may have been blasted Shakespeare but they're my sentiments at the moment. Time for new blood.' He smiled briefly, adding, 'Me.'

'I'll need to see you, all together,' Blackstock said. 'Tomorrow. The next day. At your convenience.'

'Why not now?'

Blackstock cleared his throat, 'I don't think that would be appropriate, my lord.'

The boy stood tall, pulling himself úp to his full height when Blackstock addressed him by his new title.

'Why not?' he asked, tapping the whip in the palm of his hand.

'Your mother, my lord, will hardly be in a condition to . . .'

'Oh I suppose you are right.' Linton Lester descended the rest of the stairs and stood beside the lawyer. There was a large portrait of Edward Lester over the giant stone fireplace in the hall. Vernon Blackstock glanced at it and the kindly face looked back at him, reassurance in the eyes.

'Although why we can't get it over . . .'

'I have not got the old will with me, my lord,' Blackstock countered.

'No. Of course not. You never expected to execute that one, did you?' he laughed. 'Well, come back tomorrow or the next day.'

'I can see you are very ignorant of death and its obligations,' Vernon said, then, seeing the hint of anger sparkling behind the amber eyes, he continued smoothly, 'and indeed why should you? Young people have no conception, no real experience of the grim reaper,' he sighed. 'I will inform Layde and Masters in Listowel and they will prepare the coffin. Your father left instructions as to the type of wood and the design and so forth, so that is all clear.' He saw a startled expression cross the young face beside him. 'Katey Kavanagh, Della Gilligan and the cottage women will lay him out, here, sir, in the great hall would be appropriate, I think. Give the villagers and his tenants and the staff opportunity to pay their last respects. Tip their fingers. Now, my lord, the next thing is tricky, Lord Edward, being Church of Ireland, is a Protestant. If he'd been a Catholic now there'da been no problem, no problem at all with Father Maguire below and the church handy. Of course you have the chapel here, but a C of I parson will be quite difficult to get aholt of . . .'

Linton was looking at him as if he were insane. 'Have you taken leave of your senses, Blackstock? If my father had been a Catholic . . . Good God, man, that's treason!'

'I meant, sir, the convenience with which the whole ceremony is to be conducted would be simpler.' Blackstock amended, 'No offence intended, indeed, my lord.'

'Look, Blackstock, I expect we'll have to deal with these undertakers in Listowel . . . if it is in my father's will?'

'It is, sir.'

'But I think we'll dispense with the lying-in-state you propose, Blackstock. Let us just get on with it.'

Blackstock decided not to take issue with Linton just now. He would deal with him through Kilty who would be implacable in this matter on behalf of his beloved master. Besides, and here Blackstock smiled to himself, Linton would have to deal with Katey Kavanagh who would arrive any moment now with her entourage from the village to perform the business of laying-out that was their prerogative. He would love to see anyone trying to come between Katey Kavanagh and a dead body. The thought was delicious, the scene would be irresistible.

He bowed to hide his expression, then asked to see Lady Kitty.

'She is with my dead father,' Linton Lester said. 'Kilty will show you up.'

'I know the way, sir.' The young man looked at him swiftly, a gleam in the amber eyes.

'Indeed you do, Blackstock, indeed you do!'

He walked past the solicitor, the heels of his boots clanging on the flagged floor, and pulled the old tassled rope-bell beside the fireplace.

'Kilty will show you up nevertheless,' he said firmly and sat in the carved Jacobean chair pushing his feet against the wrought-iron fender. 'And Blackstock,' he looked up, fingers clasped beneath his chin.

'Yes, my lord?'

'When this will is read I want you to leave Ballymora Castle for good and never darken *my* door again. Understood?'

'I'm afraid that won't be . . .'

'It is quite pointless trying to argue or persuade me to change my mind. I want, as I said, new blood about the place, which, incidentally I'll be selling, Blackstock, lock, stock and . . .'

'Well, my lord . . .'

'Here's Kilty. Will you please take Mr Blackstock to my mother, Kilty, there's a good man, and for heaven's sake stop snivelling and whingeing, it grates me, indeed it does.'

Blackstock followed Kilty up the stairs. The old man was unsteady on his feet and his bent back shook with silent sobs. The solicitor leapt two stairs and came level with the aged retainer on the sweep of the landing. There was a dusty Roman bust that leaned drunkenly sideways, barely keeping its balance on a little crooked pedestal in a niche. It epitomized for Vernon the state of Ballymora Castle; base chipping away barely balanced on *terra firma*.

Vernon caught the old man and put his arm clumsily around his shoulders. He felt the skinny bundle of bones collapse in his embrace and he put his other hand beneath Kilty's elbow, literally holding him up.

'Ah God help us, sir, it's sad, a sad day an' the master gone, sir. He was my friend,' he said simply.

'And hadn't you the grand life together, Kilty,' Vernon tried to reassure the old retainer. 'Wasn't it a great innings?'

Kilty nodded, drew his arm across his nose and eyes, gathered himself together and stood tall again, shrugging off Vernon Blackstock's helping hands.

'This way, sir,' he said with gracious dignity and led the solicitor down the wide corridor to the bedroom.

At the door, Blackstock turned. 'Get the women up, Kilty,' he said. 'Tell Katey Kavanagh not to let anyone stop her. Understand?' and the old man nodded in complete understanding.

The room stank. Vernon Blackstock took a deep breath which nearly caused him to faint and tried afterwards to breathe shallowly. Edward had obviously evacuated his bowels and he looked ghastly in death. There was nothing uplifting about the remains and Vernon turned his head from the sight. He did not want to remember his friend like this: eyes rolled back, milk-white in his head, mouth hanging open, a trail of saliva running down to the stubbly grey chin. This gruesome cadaver was not the warm vibrant man Vernon had known, worked for and liked. But his wife seemed totally unaware of the disagreeable state her late husband lay in.

Kitty sat by the bed holding a lifeless hand in hers. 'I don't want to let him go, Mr Blackstock,' she whispered as he came over to her and pressed her shoulder in his sympathetic grip.

'I know, m'lady. I know. But, if I may make so bold, his Lordship would not want that. Think what *he'd* want and stick to it. Leave him to the women. Kilty has sent for them. Come away with me now.'

'He's all I've got, Mr Blackstock. All I've ever had. He took care of me. He guided me. He loved me and looked after me. What will I do now, without him? I'll be lost.' She sounded so desperately alone.

53

'You'll . . .' What could he say? Recover? Get over it? It seemed cruel to even suggest anything like that so he changed the subject. Best keep her busy.

'Does the doctor know? Has he been informed?' he asked.

'I better send for him,' she replied. 'Doctor Martin was with Edward last evening until about midnight. I hate to disturb his sleep so soon. Edward passed away at that empty, desolate time, Mr Blackstock – three a.m.'

'So you were alone, poor dear lady.'

She shook her head.

'Ah no. There was someone else here. Maybe it was Kilty.' She thought, then shook her head again, 'And maybe not. I didn't properly look. He was tall. Wearing a black cloak.' She looked up at Vernon Blackstock, a puzzled expression on her gentle face. 'Now why would Kilty be wearing a cloak, I ask you?'

Behind her mild blue eyes an ocean of unshed tears threatened to spill. The corners of her mouth tried bravely to fight the oncoming deluge and her chin clenched and unclenched with the battle within.

'Ah, Mr Blackstock . . .' her eyes pleaded, 'tell me it's not true. Tell me he will smile at me again.' Then the storm broke and he led her sobbing from the room.

Eileen McGrath, her maid, was hovering about outside the door in a pother of uncertainty.

'Ah, there you are, m'lady,' she clucked as Vernon led her out. 'Come on with me, I'll look after ye. A tissane, nice and relaxing will help no end . . .'

'I'm so sorry, m'lady,' Vernon muttered ineffectually as Eileen McGrath steered her lady down the corridor.

'Oh, Eileen,' Vernon called after her and as the maid turned, 'There has been some opposition to the laying-out. Will you see that the women from the village are admitted and take care of Lord Edward, God rest him.'

Eileen McGrath's eyes snapped. She knew exactly what Vernon Blackstock was inferring.

'Oh don't you worry, Mr Blackstock,' she said, 'they'll be admitted.' Then she turned her attention to her weeping mistress. 'I'll look after ye now, dear lady, I'll look after ye.'

54

Led by Katey Kavanagh and Della Gilligan the women came from the village to wash and clean the corpse, but Brigid Donnelly was not with them.

She was bidding farewell to two of her daughters as they climbed into Mog Murtagh's cart on the first stage of their journey to London.

Chapter Seven

⁓ ⁓

They had not heard the news of Lord Lester's death or perhaps Pierce Donnelly would never have let them go into exile. Who knew how things in Ballymora would turn out now?

They had no luggage as such, only a knapsack each, holding an extra skirt and change of clothes, their rosaries and papers, a bar of crude soap and a screw-top bottle of Katey Kavanagh's medicine for all illnesses.

They walked to the crossroads half a mile from the cottage hard on the Marquis of Killygally's pastures and waited for Mog Murtagh to show up. He had been on a binge the night before and had slept on the straw in his cart. He could not tell them the momentous news for he had not heard it.

Pierce carried the knapsacks and held Demara's hand as if she were a little girl again. Brigid followed, her arm around Maeve's shoulder and Dana lagged behind trying to conceal her glee.

Mog Murtagh, straw in his pulverized hat, hay on his gansey, a rich stubble on his chin and a terrible odour of stale sweat and booze about him, appeared atop his cart.

'All aboard now,' he yelled, as if he were the captain of a ship.

Brigid wept as she held Maeve to her ample sagging breasts longer than was necessary. Maeve was slippery to get hold of. She was into the cart, swift as a hare, eager to escape.

Demara was stoic. She set her face north and refused to look back at the sea and the mountains. She was unyielding and hard as a tree in winter and she did not melt even when her father held her, tears in his eyes, whispering, 'Forgive me, *allana*, forgive me.'

Duff was there too, to hold her, a brief moment, look in the desolation of her eyes for hope and finding none, turn away to see Dana smiling sympathetically up at him.

Cogger watched from behind a tree. Everyone knew where he lurked. They could hear the hard ugly sobs that tore his squashed chest and his terrible pig-snorting and snuffling, but they left him in peace to expiate his grief in his own way.

'Forgive me, darlin', forgive me,' Pierce reiterated as he lifted Demara onto the cart.

Demara did not help him out of his guilt. She said no words of reassurance. She wanted him to suffer. She set her back straight against the grey fog that lifted in the east revealing, little by seductive little, the fierce glory of the rising sun, the dramatic sweep of the sage-green and purple mountains, and the glimmer and thrust of the mighty Atlantic, deceptively, sweetly Madonna-blue this fine morning.

'*Slainte a cairde*,' Mog Murtagh said, waving his whip and the cart gave a sort of a roll and pitch and jog-trotted up the boreen on its way to the station accompanied by the loud blasts of Able, the pony, farting as he trotted away.

Pierce's brother, their Uncle Peader, would get them on the train, standing up at the back in the luggage van, or with the cattle on the way to market. He wasn't supposed to do this, but he broke the rules right, left and centre and, as Pierce said, over and over, he'd get himself the sack if he wasn't careful. But Uncle Peader said, 'Fair game!' and ignored all such advice.

Jogging along in the cart, Demara could feel her heart twist within her. Butterflies danced in the buddleia, blue, yellow, soft brown, and the fuchsia, cerise and royal purple, hung their bell-heads against a verdant and fuscous bank of shoulder-high foliage.

And there, beneath, pink and white valerian, the herb

that Katey Kavanagh used too freely to soothe suffering, left its bitter smell on the heavenly air. To leave Ballymora was sad, to leave at this moment in nature was tragedy.

But then, Demara thought, no matter what minute, phase of the moon, second or season she left it would be a terrible separation. A little later, in full autumn this world would be draped in gold and russet and bronze, a glowing amber world where the workers sang bawdy songs as they harvested the bursting grain, the fruit spattered purple and black juice and the apples in Lord Lester's orchard had rosy skins and Brigid made jam and stocked the larder for the winter with flour for buttermilk-bread.

And in winter there was time for stories over the turf fire and the snow snapped fingers and toes and they wrapped themselves in many shawls, red-nosed and crisp-cheeked, giggling in church or running near the scarlet-spotted holly bush that leant with crooked branches and splashed red against the snow.

And tender spring when the lambs dropped and the leaves burgeoned and gave the air the gift of oxygen, and bluebells carpeted Lord Lester's woods, and cowslips, primroses and violets lurked there in clumps and the sun was butter-yellow hanging in pastel skies of salmon-pink, pearl-grey and azure.

Demara shut the door on sharp memories of poverty, of bare feet bleeding in the cold hoar frost, of hunger gnawing in the night, of hands swollen from picking and septic wounds that killed and maimed, and babies born dim-witted or malformed and some that died of hunger in a land of milk and honey. She thrust all such thoughts away and carefully selected the impressions that would sustain her in the long dark days ahead. She would produce them for nourishment when hope had gone and Bannagh Dubh and Ballymora seemed far away.

She had one last hope: that Uncle Peader wouldn't be able to get them on the train and they would be turned back at the station to retrace their journey to Ballymora, to return to the land she loved. But no such reprieve was forthcoming.

57

Uncle Peader was a mottled, whiskey-faced, whiskered sort of a man, bit and bellied and impressive in his uniform. He made them wait under the clump of trees at the siding until the goods train came in, then, with a lot of sly winking and dexterous manoeuvring they ran from the trees to under the foot-bridge, and from under the foot-bridge to behind the water-tank and from behind the water-tank into the last carriage where the cows hooved the shallow boards and turned lazy eyes on the foreign species suddenly erupting into their midst. No. Sadly, they were on their way.

Maeve irritated her sister by her exuberant optimism. Sitting on the floor of the cattle-car, tucking their skirts into their waist-bands to avert being soiled by the loamy, steaming cow-dung, all Maeve could do was babble on about the nirvana she thought London was going to be. Demara doubted such a Utopia existed anywhere outside a story book.

'God, will ye shut yer gob,' she admonished and didn't see, or ignored, the tears in her sister's eyes. She had her own pain to deal with and she was not going to be brought out of it by consideration for her sister.

Maeve was, in fact, bolstering her courage by persuading herself of the truth of the notion of London's irresistible allure. Already she missed her mother and the security of her home and she needed to assure herself that everything was going to be wonderful. Demara's cold face was no help to her and so she wittered on, her voice more plaintive as the old train chugged along with endless delays and many stops both between and at stations.

At last Maeve's monologue stammered and stuttered to a stop and she sank into a frightened silence as the train bore them, like swallows on the wind, into exile.

Chapter Eight

❧ ❧

They came up the dusty road like a flock of pitchy crows, or magpies in their black, bustling with importance, purposefully in step, elbows back, ram-rod straight, energetically on their way to work.

Dressed from head to foot in jetty shawls that covered their heads and fell to the hemline at the backs of their black skirts which swished in the dust, black unlaced boots on their feet, they came by hereditary right to lay out the body.

'A table, sur. A table in the room for us, Kilty,' their leader Katey Kavanagh demanded as they fanned out in the hall, then regrouped in sudden awe at the size of the place. Intimidated by the grandeur they saw about them they moved nearer each other in a tight little group and followed Kilty up the stairs. Halfway up they met the new Lord Lester. He had come in from his ride with every intention of being firm about forbidding a laying-out of his father's remains but the phalanx of stalwart proud-headed, black-clad matrons made him nervous and he had not the nounce to stand there and order them out.

'What the hell are these people doing on the front stairs, Kilty?' he did manage to say.

'This is the custom, my lord,' Kilty replied smoothly and Linton caught the gleam in the retainer's eye and determined to dismiss him at the first opportunity, and passing them he ran up the stairs and dived into his chambers.

Manny Flynn and Denmar the stuffy butler brought the table for the women into the late Lord Lester's chamber.

'Put it there, Manny,' Della instructed, delighted beyond measure to be able to order the stuck-up handyman about.

'Brought home the advantage of bein' a lady,' she said

59

afterwards to Katey.

The women washed the body in carbolic and lysol. They laughed and chatted as they worked, exchanging gossip and opinions and the burning topic of the Donnelly girls' departure for London. No one was allowed into the room as they worked for it would not be seemly. Lord Edward Lester was unceremoniously lowered onto the floor while the bed was stripped, then picked up and turned over with tenderness and casual competence as if he were a helpless infant.

'Sure an' isn't it just his carcase, God help us, that's here? Isn't his soul now with the Blessed Lord in Heaven above and with the Angels and Saints?' Brian Gilligan's wife Della asked piously and Carmel O'Gorman looked at her with large contemptuous eyes. One of them was black. The other women were sorry to see what Mickey O'Gorman did to Carmel but they dared not comment. She would kill them if they did, so they had to pretend it was not there and the cuts and bruises did not exist. It did not occur to them to interfere. Carmel was unlucky and had made a bad bargain, so she had no alternative but to put up with the beatings a drunken husband inflicted upon her.

'No, he is not,' Carmel said firmly, 'an' he a Protestant! Sure the Prods don't believe in the Virgin Mary!' She looked at the ceiling and crossed herself, 'Christ's sake! He'll only be in Purgatory yet awhile,' she finished confidently.

'What's Pierce Donnelly goin' to think of this catastrophe, I'd like to know?' Jinny, Mog Murtagh's wife, asked. 'Isn't it goin' to destroy him entirely!' They were bursting with an excitement that was hard to contain. It gripped them all, the self-importance of people caught up in momentous affairs.

'He'da never let those girls outa his sight an' he knew his Lordship here had gone to his reward,' Sheena McQuaid pursed her full red lips, ripe as blackberries in autumn and shook her head as she scrubbed his lordship's rump. Della Gilligan was rubbing his legs with lysol.

'Brigid always favoured Maeve and Pierce thinks of Demara like a son. They're goin' to be lost wi'out them.'

'Oh there'll be no containin' them when they realize what's happened.' Carmel O'Gorman was standing, hands on hips, inspecting the dead body. 'Aren't we all the same eventually,' she said rhetorically.

'Will ye look at the poor man now. Helpless!' Delia McCormack shook her head.

'Ah but he's a beautiful corpse! A beautiful corpse!' Sheena McQuaid put her middle finger behind the ball of her thumb and flicked at Lord Lester's private parts. 'Just makin' sure!' she giggled when the others all looked at her.

Della tut-tutted. 'Now, now, now,' she said. 'Less levity, more respect.'

Della Gilligan was head bottle-washer in the matter of corpses and the treatment of them. Her sister Maureen was married to Billy Layde, the undertaker, which gave her an authority, albeit at second hand, that the others did not feel she deserved. She, as Katey Kavanagh muttered, 'threw her weight around rather a lot', but they gave in gracefully, with an 'Ah sure why not?' attitude and bowed their heads and did as she instructed, always on the alert that she didn't overstep the mark and Katey Kavanagh's overall authority.

'Brigid and Pierce Donnelly are goin' to bust a gut when they hear about this,' she said. 'But what will Demara say, I ask you, when *she* finds out?'

'Sure it's all their own fault. Isn't it all because of Pierce Donnelly's fierce ambition? If he'da been content like the rest of us they wouldn't be on the train this minute on their way to cross the water.'

'An Brigid expectin' again,' Della said, with a wink and a nod.

Everyone stopped and stared at her. 'You sure?' Sheena asked. 'I never heard.'

'Oh Brigid hasn't said a word to a living soul, not even Pierce, I'd swear. But ye've only got to look at her.'

Jinny thought, conjuring up Brigid's face when last seen. 'Now that ye mention it . . .' she said, nodding. 'Now that ye mention it . . .'

'Yerra she's right!' Sheena said with certainty. 'The look of her. She's got that broody preoccupation in her eyes.'

Carmel O'Gorman shook her head. 'Ah now, ye better be careful, spreadin' scandal. . .'

'It's *not* scandal. Aren't they married in the eyes of God and the law, so what's scandalous about it?'

'I didn't say that. I meant it is scandal to repeat something that might not be true. . .'

'Even if it's *not* true Brigid Donnelly is married an' there's no scandal in her havin' a babby,' Della said with finality. 'We're *speculatin'* is all.'

'Well it's a fine kettle of fish, Demara and Maeve gone, Brigid pregnant. . .'

'We *think*,' Carmel O'Gorman amended.

'I'll strangle ye, Carmel, so I will,' Sheena said and continued, 'and Pierce Donnelly fair set to buy his little houseen an' no chance at all now.'

'Well, as you said, serve him, gettin' ideas above his station.' But Sheena looked serious, 'It's all very well to laugh,' she said piously, looking at the rubbery grey carcase before them on the table, 'at someone else's misfortune, but when all's said an' done, that's a good man there,' she pointed at the corpse, 'gone. Gone. An' I reckon when the new young master gets the bit between his teeth we may all have cause to worry.'

Chastened, the women paused and looked at the old man, naked before them. They shivered and proceeded with their work in silence, all levity gone.

Chapter Nine

ᢀ ᢁ

Brigid and Pierce Donnelly trudged back to the cottage to find the place deserted and everyone gone. All the men were away working or drinking but where the women had vanished to perplexed them. Then Brigid saw Ellie Murtagh, the crippled daughter of Mog and Jinny Murtagh, sitting in her box. She had been born twisted in the legs and they'd made her a wooden box with a thin leather thong to pull it along and a duck-down pillow in the bottom so that her poor little frame would not be bumped and jounced about. It was only two feet by two feet for she was a slip of a girleen and never properly grew or developed and looked now like a six-year-old instead of the twelve she actually was.

She sat in the box now, alone beside the oak tree and looked up at Pierce and Brigid Donnelly with wide and frightened eyes.

'Ellie, where's everyone?'

'Me ma . . . ma . . . ma . . . ma . . .' the little girl gibbered. No one spoke to Ellie Murtagh and she was rarely, if ever, asked like this to actually communicate a piece of information. Brigid resisted a desire to slap her.

'Calm down, Ellie. Take a deep breath.' Brigid placed her hand on the child's chest and felt the little ribs push out and collapse. 'Now another. In. Out. Good, good. Now think. Where are the other women, Ellie?'

Ellie pointed towards the castle and Pierce's heart plummeted and he knew at once what had happened. There was only one thing that would take all the women up to the castle and that was death. Pierce Donnelly grabbed Ellie's shoulder, 'The lord's dead? He's dead?'

The child squirmed and fidgeted, moving under his hands like a fish, unable to run from him, her eyes searching the horizon for help, finding none.

'Leave her be, Pierce. She most likely doesn't know,' Brigid sighed. 'But I guess you're right. Lord Edward's dead, poor man, an' the women have gone up to lay him out.'

Pierce turned to her, his face beaded with sweat, his eyes wild.

'Go up there, woman. Find out what's happened, God's sakes, we're ruined.'

They both knew Lord Edward was dead, but in case there was a smidgeon of hope that maybe, just maybe, it was a different catastrophe that had drawn the women of Ballymora up the hill, Brigid did as her husband wanted and trudged up the long road to the grey stone building atop the hill.

What she found there was what they expected and feared most; the dead Lord and the mourning women and Lady Kitty and Lord Linton at loggerheads already before the great stone fireplace.

Brigid did not understand what they said but she grasped the gist of what passed between them in short snappy sentences. Lady Kitty wanted things to remain as they were, Lord Linton didn't. That was the bleak news she told Pierce Donnelly when she came home and he sat before the empty hearth clenching and unclenching his hands in an agony of frustration.

What to do? What to do? It was too late now to stop Demara and Maeve. They were across on the water now and there was no stopping them. And up in the castle the stroppy young Lord was rarin' to escape the restrictions and limitations the tag of 'Lord of the Castle' imposed upon him. Pierce Donnelly feared the worst.

Chapter Ten

cᘐ ᘐ

Cogger climbed down the rocky path to the sea. The tide was out and the moon high. The beach Demara loved to sit and gaze down on was not a friendly place. Bannagh Dubh was dangerous. The tide came in quickly there, roiling and roistering over the rocky beach and sucking in and out of caves big as houses, halted in its tempestuous onslaught by the cliffs.

Cogger climbed down, secure in his knowledge of tides and phases of the moon and the signs and secret language of nature. He was far more in tune with that language than with the contradictory utterances of human beings. He found it difficult if not impossible to know when people were lying, or glossing over the truth, like when Duff Dannon's mother was dying and everyone told her she looked in the pink. He did not understand the games they played.

There was nothing really wrong with Cogger Kavanagh except his mind worked in a simpler, more direct way than others, and he had difficulty in verbal communication. If he had been able to read and write he might even have proved himself a genius like Sir Oliver Goldsmith up in Dublin a hundred years ago who 'wrote like an angel but talked like poor Pol'.

Cogger's thoughts were bright and shining and pure. Clear and simple. His soul was steeped and flooded by the beauty of his surroundings. As with Demara the grandeur of Bannagh Dubh and the land they lived on moved him painfully with a sweetly unbearable emotion.

His mother Katey, close to the land, shared her secrets with him, moving confidently through woods and up mountains, identifying poisons and healing herbs, the signs of good weather and bad, the evidence of storms or droughts or bad harvests, the secrets of the fox and the badger and the toad and together, without words, they nodded and picked and plucked, understanding all.

No, Cogger was no fool, he simply had difficulty expressing himself and the villagers didn't listen to his awkward mumbled speech, so he did not bother them with his findings.

He had tried to tell Demara because he loved her. She was the evening star, more beautiful than the statue of the Blessed Virgin in the church, more radiant than the midian sun, untouchable, nearer to nature than the others, and he revered her.

But she too did not heed him, did not hear what his clumsy mouth tried to enunciate and place before her like a gift. His teeth and tongue mangled the words, he could not bring forth the simple sentences others brought forth with ease.

If only she would stop for a moment and listen. But she had gone, left Bannagh Dubh and Ballymora and who knew when she would return?

He scrambled down the twisted path to the sea. It had been there since pirate days, the days of plunder on the

Spanish main and boats, defeated by the fierce Atlantic pitched up against the Irish coast. Kinsale and Dingle. Kerry and Galway and Cork. Half the Spanish Armada had foundered here and many an isolated ship laden with treasure detached itself – whether deliberately or accidentally, who could say? – and extricating itself from the fleet somehow landed on this coast-line and then disappeared, never heard of again. Those ships were heavy with gold plundered from some Aztec or Inca prince by bug-eyed, greedy Spaniards and when small dark men with foreign accents and little breeding set up in grand houses in Dublin or London or Paris and spent with a lavish hand, who bothered to do more than cursorily enquire the source of their fortunes?

Those days were past and forgotten and no brigand in gold braid and epaulettes came here now. Only smugglers still sometimes crept up the creeks along the coast with brandy or wine or tobacco. Mean little men of business and brutish thugs with respect for nothing but money. They did not use Bannagh Dubh, the rocks were too treacherous, the tides too violent in their to-ing and fro-ing, and Bocha Creek, up the coast, was a better way to land discreetly, undetected.

So Cogger had the beach to himself. There were seagulls there and an eagle, its eyrie high up in the cliff face. There were black rocks and you could see the shining backs of dolphins out there, in the distance, off-shore.

They watched from the headland, he and Demara, but she would never come down here, on the beach, with him. She stayed aloft on the high slope where the land fell and the tide came up more sedately and her rock was flat and grey in the moonlight, where the sand petered out and became turf and the grass was green as fresh mint and tasted sweet to eat. There was a lake beyond and she told him she wanted to build a house beside it and he could see no reason why not.

But she would never come down here.

If she did she would learn about the gold and she would be surprised and happy and perhaps she would listen to him then and he could serve her. It was what he wanted to

66

do. Be her slave, always near her, careful of her, devoted. He would tell no one else his secret. They hit his head when they passed him by and when he talked they cuffed him and treated him with indifference as if he were made of wood. He had tried once to tell them, in a moment of defiance, angry with them because they were so dismissive, deriding him when he tried to enunciate: '. . . old . . . old . . . eer . . . ege . . . G-g-g . . . o . . . old.'

And they paid no attention at all. And no one followed him to look when he beckoned. So they could go to the Devil for all he cared.

The wind was high. It was cold now at night, a chill sitting on the air that boded a bad winter. It would snow this Christmas, he thought, and the people would be freezing. Children would die. But the autumn would be golden, warm. The swallows had not gone yet. Preparations were under way, but they were still here.

His boots made a scrunching noise as he tramped along the beach to the cave under Ben Bannach. It ran for miles, that cave, deep underground, and far inside it, where the shimmering stalagmites and stalactites created an enchanted ice-world, a fairyland of silver and mother-of-pearl and opal, there were skeletons, the ancient bones of men who had drowned in the fierce tidal waves that sometimes swamped the cove, or sailors, lost, cut-off, sitting on treasure they would not live to spend.

And it was there, the treasure. The gold. Cases of it. All there. Smuggled a long time ago. Or wrecked. And Cogger opened the cases and stared at it, winking and blinking in the pale cold light and shook his head.

He knew he was surrounded by wonders, but to him everything in nature was wondrous, the sea no less than the precious metals, the moon no more so than the brilliant stones, the curving of the trees and the massy fuchsia, the graceful dance of the branches, and falling leaves were, if anything, more marvellous than the statuary here. It was all there, everything anyone needed was provided by the earth. She, glorious mother, yielded up food for hungry bellies and cures for sick bodies, and the treasures that lay here in the wavering aquamarine light were only an embellishment of her riches. There were mermaids out there on the rocks and dreams and magic and more mysteries in the earth, seas and heavens than anyone could dream. Cogger knew that. He knew that very well. 'St . . . st . . . t . . . oop . . .' he sighed, ' . . . ID,' he finished, whistling through his teeth.

He rubbed his eyes. There was a wavering light in the cave, a blue glow and he stared at the marvellous shapes carved from water and shook his head as he wondered. Then, like Ondine, he caught sight of his shadow, watched it leap as he moved, then made it leap. Slowly, then with more vigour he twisted and turned and clapped his hands and sang:

'Oh what I'd give for the salt-sea maiden,
Plaiting her hair in the pale moonlight. . .'

He danced around in a circle.

'Sat on a rock an' the tail of a fish. . .'

His dance was slow and clumsy but he enjoyed himself hugely.

'She stole my heart in the pale moon . . .' He did not stammer when he sang.

Sometimes he felt so full of life, of the love of all that was beautiful around him that he had to dance or sing. Sometimes both. But people did not understand and it frightened them. He knew his movements were awkward and startling, knew the villagers misunderstood. They thought the intensity of feeling had its roots in violence and not, as it was, love.

He knew also that his voice came out harsh and discordant and when he sang folk were silenced and ashamed for him. He often wanted to join in the singing in Ma Stacey's but knew better than to try. When in the long-gone past he *had* tried, the exuberance of the men there had died and a chill came over the place and he was left alone, isolated, looked at as strange.

So he did not sing or dance when there were folk around. He permitted himself expression here in the caves or at night on the beach when the tide was out and it was dark and no one could see.

He stopped when he had had enough and closed the trunks on the gold.

'St . . . t . . . t . . . oop . . . ID,' he stammered again and left the dripping cave, the harsh smell of seaweed in his nose. It was the time and the pods were popping and his mother would be harvesting the pungent weed for antiseptic and carrageen and for certain curative ingredients and many, many uses the rich gathering could be put to.

He emerged into the night and the remote light of the moon.

He saw the shadow on the beach, not his own, and stared at it. Then he looked up and there was the stranger, the cloaked vision who was here and yet not here, that Demara and he had seen that night before she left.

The tall man stood up on the promontory, his cloak flapping around him, his face concealed by its hood. Cogger tried to see his face but could not. It remained shadowed.

For a long time Cogger stared up from the beach at the still stranger, ram-rod straight, motionlessly staring out to sea. Then he lifted his hand and pointed.

He was pointing at the sea. Downwards. Cogger looked. He was pointing below where the sea was deepest and where the beach, that gully around the headland, was almost never dry. The tide was far out now, as far as ever it went, and Cogger could see, as the waves broke and sprayed over the sand, a huge pile of boulders of smooth granite stone, perfectly square, as if cut by a master stonemason. The squares were sprinkled with threads of shimmering silver. They lay in a huge mound almost out of sight in a place no one ever came to look.

The stranger still stood, pointing down from his perch on the headland and Cogger saw his hand had moved to his left, the finger bony and skeletal, was directed now to the inlet around the corner. That inlet was never empty of water. The sea always bubbled and thundered there, gurgled and heaved.

Cogger scrambled over the stones and onto one of the shining granite squares. There were hundreds of them and they were heaped up, he saw, in abundant piles and stacks and they stretched a long way and lay coldly bright in the clear-water pools. He leaped over onto another, then another, until he could go no further for the spray was drenching him and the water was becoming deep and the wind strong and he might lose his balance and he could not swim.

He looked up again. The stranger's thin finger, unwavering, indicated the deep gorge to his left.

He looked down, clinging to the rock-face, peering into the depths below. What he saw there took his breath away and caused him to tremble like a leaf in the autumn breeze.

It was like a workshop of statuary, a repository of beautiful sculpture, each piece matchless in its perfection. A white marble maiden exquisitely etched, gracefully holding drapery to partly cover her, but revealing her breasts, high and beautiful, her hair clinging, close-curled to her perfectly proportioned head and brow. Another warrior-woman in helmet and armour, holding a spear, stared up at him with empty stone eyes. There was the bust of a glorious young man with wings at his temples and on his heels; a thick-set sage and a noble bust with a laurel-wreath on his head. They all lay there, below the water, clearly revealed for moments as the foam-crested waves receded but never completely cleared the marble statue of a perfect naked youth who smiled at Cogger with the remote smile of the dead. The waves crashed over against the rocks and he could not see the graveyard of sculpture any more.

He clung to the rocks trying to work it all out. As far as he could see the statues, lying as if placed there by a giant hand, seemed to be protected from the ravages of the sea, pushed into the cave, higher up than the water, invisible to anyone on the headland. Yet they were seen by him from where he clung perilously as if through water. He remembered the tales about Roman conquerors, of Spanish ships laden with treasure, and the stories of sailors and fishermen who said that on the nights of the full moon they could see the siren who lived there, a naked woman who lured sailors to their deaths on the rocks below. She stood, they said, white as milk, high up in a cave, an eerie

70

sight, seductive and terrifying, suspended between heaven and earth, looking forever out to sea.

It must have been the marble statue of the part-draped Venus they saw, and as Cogger looked now, he could see her, standing there, gazing out to the horizon, ethereal and remote.

He moved back from the ledge, around the curve and she vanished from his sight. He looked at the slabs and squares of rock and smiled as he retreated. He glanced up and saw the black-cloaked stranger had gone. The promontory was bare, the wind higher now, moaning. Cogger grunted, nodded and smiled as he jumped back onto the pebbly beach.

It was all perfectly plain to him.

Demara's dream. Demara's house. The material was there, above and beneath the sea. It was all there.

But Demara was not. He had forgotten that. Demara had gone far away over the wild sea.

But she would come back. He knew her. He knew how strong her love for Bannagh Dubh was and she would return. She could not live otherwise.

Yes, she would come back and he would show her the glories the stranger had shown him tonight; that smooth silvered stone, those statues, and Demara would smile at him and kiss his forehead. He hummed another air beneath his breath as the tide turned and some dark clouds obliterated the light of the moon and all he could see was pitchy night around him. He began his journey home.

He was satisfied. He knew what was required; he would wait patiently. For him the darkness was irrelevant. He did not need light to guide him home.

Chapter Eleven

For three days Lord Edward Lester lay on a catafalque draped in crimson velvet and smelling sweetly of herbs but emitting an occasional whiff of lysol. He lay in the great hall of the castle on full view and people came from all parts to see him and bid him their last respects. They hoped too for a jar, a libation, a hope in which they were not disappointed, and a bite to eat, in which they were. Kitty couldn't be bothered to arrange it and Kilty had no influence over the kitchen.

Kitty was quite lost without her husband and Kilty was engaged in a silent malicious tussle with Lord Linton, deliberately misunderstanding the new young master's orders and doing nothing unless specifically asked. He had always pre-empted Lord Edward's commands when it came to the comfort of the household and its efficient running. Kilty was always there ahead of himself. But now, certain he would be dismissed, ᐟassured by Vernon Blackstock that there was a small annuity guaranteed in the will, he was enjoying himself enormously in a programme of cheerful disobedience, inaction and a monumentally protracted laggard execution of all his duties. Bells rang and remained unanswered and when they eventually were, 'Ah sure things are bound to be in con-fus-ion with the master barely cold,' Kilty would say. The breakfasts and baths were tepid, the staff suddenly clumsy and inefficient.

Brigid thought they had done a wonderful job on Lord Edward and that he looked pure beautiful, but her heart thumped within her with the dread and the worry of what would happen to them all now. She heard Lord Linton say it, there before the huge stone fireplace, the corpse of his father lying surrounded by candles a few feet away: 'I want those blasted cottagers off my land at once.'

She told the others what she had heard and they sat in Katey Kavanagh's and watched her turn the cards on the day the will was to be read.

'Can he do it, Della?' she asked, although she knew the answer.

Della nodded her head. 'It's the Lord's will,' she said. 'And Father Maguire will tell us to bow our heads to it.'

'It is *not* God's will for us, don't talk daft, it is *that* lord's will, him up there in the castle, bad cess to him,' Katey said and shook her head and gathered the cards together without revealing what she had seen there. 'It's all bad,' she said by way of explanation, 'nothing good there at all.'

'. . . *and so it is my wish and intention that Ballymora Castle continue to be run as it has been heretofore under my guidance . . .*'

Vernon Blackstock reading the will paused to clear his throat and Lord Linton jumped in: 'It does not say anywhere that I may not sell Ballymora Castle?'

They were gathered in the library. Kitty sobbed now and then and Vernon patted her hand to soothe her. He stood before the fire and, like Kilty, he took his time much to the irritation of the new young master.

'It is not a decision you are empowered to make,' Vernon Blackstock took great pleasure in informing him.

'But I thought the old will was . . .' Linton stammered, angry at his loss of face.

'You were mistaken, my lord, if I may respectfully say. Lord Edward never had any intention of allowing Ballymora Castle to be put on the market. Lord Edward has made Lady Kitty chief beneficiary and myself trustee and executor, m'lord.'

'Then why the new will?' Lord Lester asked, eyes snapping. 'Why was he in such a pother to get you up here to change it?'

Vernon Blackstock shrugged. 'Lord Edward wanted to add little codifications here and there. Bequests . . .' He remained deliberately vague. He had no intention of giving young Linton any ammunition. He knew the new

73

will provided for the tenants' security of tenure whilst the will he held in his hands merely suggested their rights be respected, but he was not going to volunteer that information. Lady Kitty's glance met his and her mild blue eyes were grateful. She knew what he kept back. She understood.

But what would happen, Vernon wondered, when Linton Lester discovered that loophole? Lady Kitty was no match for either her son's coaxing or his temper.

But for the moment Vernon was ashamed to admit to himself that he was filled with unholy glee at the spectacle of the frustrated Linton searching desperately for someone to blame or something to hit out at.

'Well, in any event, sir, *you* are not welcome here,' he stared at Blackstock. 'It gives me great pleasure to inform you I'll not be needing your services any more. It is my intention to employ a new solicitor.'

'Oh no, Linton dear, it's not . . .' Lady Kitty's eyes flew from her son's face to the face of the lawyer. 'Mr Blackstock has always been the soul of . . .'

'Be still, Mother, and mind yourself. You must remember who is Lord of the Manor now.'

Vernon Blackstock cleared his throat. 'With respect, m'lord—' he was hugely enjoying himself—'that is not possible.' He took his time. 'I am afraid you will have to put up with me, willy-nilly, for some time to come.'

Linton Lester was taken aback. 'Why so, sir?' he asked tentatively.

'Your father's explicit instructions are that I am to continue to handle your mother's affairs and Ballymora Castle. So, I regret, Lord Lester, that you cannot, em, dismiss me so summarily.'

'God's teeth, am I not master in my own home?' the young Lord sounded petulant.

Vernon Blackstock ignored him and went to Lady Kitty and kissed her hand. 'Let me offer my sympathies and help, dear lady, and permit me to take my leave now. You must be quite worn out.'

It had been a satisfactory interview from Vernon Blackstock's point of view and he left on a triumphant crest that he knew would not last long.

*

The funeral was conducted the next day. The Vicar of the Protestant Church of Ireland was in attendance. His services had been procured at great inconvenience and he was impatient to get the ceremony over and hurry back to the civilization of Galway.

Lady Kitty leaned on her son's arm. She was blinded by tears but her son's face remained stony. The cottagers, standing respectfully at the back, looked in vain for some sign of grief or gentleness or pity, but found none.

It was a strange ceremony. Words were muttered in the great hall with the servants, mutinous and sullen, the local dignitaries, Squire Slimon from Ballyterma crossfields and the grand and elegant Marquis of Killygally with his attendants yawning and fanning themselves and shooing away the odd bluebottle. The doctor and the cottagers lurked in the shadows near the door and, as Katey Kavanagh remarked later, it was a cold class of a service altogether.

The procession to the little graveyard close by the woods straggled along, mourning Lord Edward, and he was laid to rest there under grey Irish stone. The sun, an orange ball tinting the trees, made their eyes water, and the mourners not invited back to the castle drifted off, singly and in pairs.

A contingent from the cottagers waylaid Vernon Blackstock afterwards on the humpbacked bridge over the narrow part of the river. It was the bridge he had danced over only a week ago and now, he thought sadly, there was no cause to dance. The group was led by Pierce Donnelly and Duff Dannon. The men were white-lipped and tense.

'Well, sur? What's the news? For pity sake tell us.'

Vernon Blackstock shook his head. 'Easy, boys, easy. 'Tis all right so far. I've been, em, discreet about the ins and outs of it. I did not inform his young lordship of the lack of provision made for ye in the old will. Unfortunately Lord Edward passed away before he could sign the will wherein he had made that provision. Any honourable man would respect his father's last wishes on that score, but Lord Lester is, I'm sad to say, not an honourable man.'

75

The bronze leaves flurried down to the rippling water below, sailing on the transparent liquid flowing to the sea. They danced and drifted like golden fairy curraghs over the stones and around the whirling eddies. Vernon Blackstock removed his gaze from the anxious eyes of the cottagers and stared at the water below gurgling down to the sea. He sighed. 'I'm sorry, fellas,' he said defeatedly and shrugged.

'Listen, man.' Pierce Donnelly grabbed his arm. 'We've been made certain promises.' Mickey O'Gorman, Brian Gilligan and Dinny McQuaid nodded vehemently in agreement and Duff Dannon added, 'We bin payin'. Over the full amount. Regular. We contributed to our homes on the clear understandin' we were buyin' them.'

'Ay. That's so,' Pierce Donnelly agreed. 'We'd own them in the end. We was promised.' Pierce was almost in tears, his desperation clear.

'I'll help ye all I can, lads,' Vernon told them sadly and saw the relief in their eyes. Mistaken relief. He realized that because he was a man of letters, a solicitor, they credited him with powers he did not possess. There was nothing more he could do. 'Now let me pass please,' he said firmly and they stood back silently, respectfully, and he crossed the bridge, no bounce at all in his step this time. He went home to Moll, who was upset by his worried face.

'Ah, love, what is it?' she asked, removing his coat.

'There's going to be trouble up above,' he told her and smiled when he looked at her plump face, eyes twinkling, dimples dancing, curls trembling as she fussed about him.

'Always worrit about others dear, darlin' man,' she tutted. 'Always, always. Aren't you the selfless one. C'mere te me now, an' a hug an' a kiss wouldn't do ye any harm.'

Vernon Blackstock was not surprised, after a few days, to be summoned to the castle once more. He guessed that Lord Lester had found the loopholes. However it was Lady Kitty who greeted him. She looked tired, he thought, and black did not suit her; it drained her of colour and left her skin sallow.

It was a golden day but chilly, a pale wintry sun partly

76

concealed by a grey chiffon scarf of cloud. They walked in the rose garden where the full blooms gave off a powerful scent and the petals fell slowly, scattering on the gravel pathway.

'Let us sit here,' Lady Kitty, to Vernon's consternation, pointed to a carved stone seat. He knew that he would inevitably suffer from a bout of something; either sciatica or lumbago, awful aches and pains would strike him, engendered by the resting of his buttocks on the cold stone. But he had no choice, manners dictated.

'Now, Mr Blackstock, I have to talk with you. You see—' Lady Kitty settled herself, arranging her skirts artistically about her and he had perforce to sit on the chill, hard surface—'poor Linton is driving me mad with his plans and demands! It is his youth. He is impetuous, anxious to become a person of social consequence in London. For which ambition, dear Mr Blackstock, I cannot entirely blame him. Indeed no! It was *my* dearest wish until I met my dear, dear husband . . .' Here she paused and dabbed her eyes with a tiny handkerchief. '. . . to do the Season and shine in London . . .' She sighed and looked at him with tragic eyes. '. . . was . . . is a seductive thought, Mr Blackstock, and not one to be sneezed at. Oh no! I can quite see my dear son's point of view, and I must say I respect his aspiration; it is in no way dishonourable.'

Vernon wished she'd get to the point. It was with difficulty he refrained from jumping in and pre-empting her, but experience had taught him that allowing clients free reign to amble verbally paid dividends. Often they reached the conclusion he wanted them to arrive at all on their own and thought him a clever fellow because of that. Here was Lady Lester trying to whitewash her son because he wanted to opt out of his responsibilities. He nodded, feeling ashamed, but, after all, what could he do?

'So you see, well, he is a young man and wishes to pursue his own interests.'

'And what would they be, m'lady?' he asked after a pause in which she waited for him to speak. She lowered her lashes, then raised her eyes, blue and pleading to his. My God, she's flirting with me, he thought, and swallowed

77

rapidly once, then twice, and tried not to think about the chill creeping from his now numb posterior down his legs.

'Em – sowing his wild oats,' she said archly. 'Whatever it is young men do, Mr Blackstock.'

She was floundering and he should help her. Rudderless, bereft after all these years of her husband's protection, she simply did not know what to do now. She was blindly searching for someone, anyone, to help and guide her.

Her son should have come to her aid. If he had allowed his mother to lean on him now he would have become indispensable to her and she would have been putty in his hands. But he was far too short-sighted to seize his opportunity and preferred confrontation, argument and battle. He had, Vernon Blackstock decided, gladiatorial instincts.

Lady Lester laid her hand on his arm and he removed it, held it gently between his for a moment, then let it go. It hovered, anchorless, lost in mid-air a moment, then she let it glide into her lap like one of the petals falling from the roses. After a moment of silence during which a clock in the distance chimed, a seagull squawked and the soughing of the sea reached them like a whisper, he said, 'My dear lady, let him get it out of his system. Let him go to London and enjoy himself, obeying his father's wishes and leaving things as they are here . . .'

She was plucking at her skirt and he could see she was not happy at his words, but he ploughed on. 'Then perhaps, after a year or two, he'll have matured a little . . .'

'You make him sound like a wine . . . or a cheese,' Lady Kitty tapped his knee. 'No, Mr Blackstock, it is not as simple as that. He is not a child any longer. I cannot *order* him about.' Her eyes shifted from his and all sign of coquetry quite vanished. 'He has put it to me. We will sell all the land, from the moorland to the east down to the river . . .'

'But that is where Pierce Donnelly and the cottagers are and Lord Edward wished most explicitly . . .'

A man's voice interrupted. 'Sadly he is not with us any more, Mr Blackstock, and it is *not* in his will. It is *my* wish you have to consider now.'

Lord Linton had come upon them silently. His mother

78

sighed and her eyes filled with tears, 'Oh, Mr Blackstock, I do not like this any more than you do, but what alternative have we? There is no money in the coffers and if we sell to the Marquis of Killygally, he is prepared to give us a very good price . . .'

'A generous price if the land is cleared,' Lord Lester interrupted. 'He wants no tenants or the like on good farming and hunting country. We intend to call in the rents and evict. It is a hard life, Mr Blackstock, you must know that.'

'But to sell your land . . .'

'We have more than enough. It's only a corner of the estate . . .'

'And to a man like the Marquis . . .'

'His money is as good as anyone else's . . .'

'Could you not find another corner to sell?' Vernon Blackstock pleaded, hating to demean himself, but unable to rid himself of the memory of Pierce Donnelly's anxious eyes.

'No. Not bordering on the Marquis's land. He is only interested in those acres. Now go and tell those cottagers I want them gone by the week's end.'

Vernon Blackstock jumped to his feet, forgetting his frozen posterior, and even Lady Lester looked startled.

'A *week*? Dear God, man, it's their whole lives you are destroying! A week . . .'

Linton Lester turned away. 'I've quite made up my mind,' he said calmly.

'But it is not possible to do that. There must be a law . . .'

'*You* should know that there is not! The landowner's wishes are all important. Who I have on my land and for how long is my affair. No one has the right to contravene my wishes in this.' He waved his hand impatiently. 'We want to get started for London. I don't want to keep my mother here a moment longer than I have to. You have not considered, Mr Blackstock, how painful and lonely it is here for Lady Lester without my father. She has nothing here to beguile her, nothing at all.'

The charade was ridiculous and Vernon Blackstock felt his anger rise. Lady lester had never needed beguiling.

She had been happy all her married life here and Linton Lester's little ploy to throw the blame for his precipitate action on his mother's shoulders was unworthy and ludicrous.

'And, with respect, my lord, have you considered how terrifying it will be for those men and women and children to find themselves homeless in a week?' Vernon Blackstock asked coldly.

Linton Lester leaned forward and gave his mother his arm, helping her to rise. 'I have nothing more to say to you, sir,' he told the solicitor, who bowed.

'I'm afraid, Lord Lester, commerce with me is inevitable,' he replied with small relish. 'And I must tell you that it is your bailiff's or your agent's job to inform those unfortunate cottagers of their fate, not mine. I bid you good-day. Lady Lester.' He bowed formally to her. 'It is a sad day for Ballymora, madam. Your poor husband's wishes, his last intentions, ignored.'

'Oh, Mr Blackstock, I'm sorry.' Kitty was nearly in tears. 'I know my husband . . . my late husband trusted you, valued your . . .'

'Mother!' Linton Lester's voice was sharp. 'Come along. We must set the wheels in motion. You seem to have forgotten we have no choice. Good-day, Mr Blackstock,' he said and led his mother out of the rose garden.

Chapter Twelve

⊸ ⟞

The Kerry cows were coming home in the gloaming, plump and dainty from the mint-green fields and Ma Stacey's pub was crowded, the men sitting, gloomily sipping, the ebb and flow of the conversation ranging from anger to despair and back.

'We're done fer sure,' Dinny McQuaid moaned. 'Mi'as well drown our sorrows.'

'Shut yer gob, Dinny McQuaid,' Deegan Belcher banged his tankard on the wooden counter. Deegan was an angry man. He lived in a constant state of simmering aggression, spoiling for a fight. One side of his mouth was permanently lower than the other, as if he said Gwan! And it remained in this sceptical grimace constantly. 'The bloody landlords are the scum of the earth an' they'll be the ruin of us, that's fer sure.'

Pierce Donnelly looked at the big man with distaste, 'Now, now, Deegan, don't get into a lather. Now is the time to *do* what Charles Stewart Parnell is always advisin'.' He looked at them fiercely and they backed away, startled by the idea of action, amazed by the novelty of it. They had no experience at all in that direction and were for the moment stunned at the thought.

Truth to tell, Pierce was astounded at his temerity in suggesting it, but he happened to meet Duff Dannon's eyes and saw an answering gleam there.

'Well said, man,' Duff Dannon smacked his tankard down also. 'What have we got to lose?'

'Let's take Mr Parnell's advice, not snivel like slaves about our terrible lot!' Pierce cried. 'What odds, fellas?' he asked, hands out, palms up. What indeed!

Mickey O'Gorman was the first to answer. Carmel O'Gorman was pregnant and he had no mind to be on the roads with her in her delicate condition and winter on the way. He wiped his mouth with the back of his hand, rubbing his heavy moustache with his fingers.

'An' why not?' he asked rhetorically. 'Why not. Sure Lord bloody Linton'll have us on the road quick as a flash an' no alternative. We could make a stand.'

'Phil Conlon said even if we pay the new rent he can put it up again so's it's impossible to pay an' get rid of us no matter what,' Miles Murphy the drover complained. He had the meanest cottage and kept body and soul together somehow. Some said he poached but this was hotly denied by the rest of the cottagers.

Duff looked at Mog Murtagh who avoided his eyes as he avoided trouble. 'Waren't you the boyo as always wants to hear Charles Stewart Parnell's speech, Mog?' he asked softly. 'Was it only for the fine sound of the phrases then, an' not the meanin'?'

'Ah no, no,' Mog muttered in his beer. 'But I don't want con-fron-ta-tion. No. Ah no! That's out for me. Sure we'll survive somehow, Jinny an' me.'

'What about little Ellie?' Pierce asked.

'Ah isn't she a sacred child, looked after special. God'll take care of her, never fear,' Mog said complacently.

'Isn't it God's promise he'll take care of *all* of us?' Pierce asked.

Mog nodded vehemently. 'Ah yis, sure, only he'll take care of some more than others.'

'Lave the man alone.' Brian Gilligan didn't like the turn the conversation had taken. 'He means that God loves the afflicted. Sure we'll weather the storm somehow, Pierce, you'll see.' His innocent grey eyes were mild in his craggy face. 'Sure we'll weather it somehow, with God's help.' He scratched his ginger thatch. 'Mebbe the new lord will change his mind.'

'Well, if that's the best you can come up with, Brian Gilligan, I'm sorry for your trouble. Gawd Almighty, the man's an idiot.'

'Just who are ye callin' an idiot? Eh?' Deegan Belcher's face was red and belligerent.

'An' mebbe pigs will fly,' Miles Murphy muttered.

'Who are ye callin' an idiot?' Deegan repeated, his large stomach shaking with his anger.

'Ah shut up, Deegan. This is important,' Duff cried. 'You're so certain of God, Brian Gilligan, well, where is He now, I'd like to know?'

'Oh that's scandalous, Duff, so it is,' Brian looked shocked. 'Oh you mustn't talk like that. What would Father Maguire say?'

'I don't give a shit what Father Maguire says,' Duff was moved to insist.

The door of the shebeen opened and Vernon Blackstock entered, closely followed by Kilty and the Lester bailiff, Phil Conlon.

Duff stood searching the newcomers faces for some hope of good news, but he found none. The others waited, watching, their hearts sinking, for Vernon Blackstock ordered them all a pint and that proved he had some terrible news to impart. When they all had their fists around a tankard, their watchful eyes fixed on Vernon Blackstock, he cleared his throat uncomfortably.

'You've got to leave,' he said. There was a moment's stunned silence. The actual hearing of the news was shocking, even though they had half expected it.

'You're not serious, man.'

'Listen boys . . .' Phil Conlon spoke. He was not their favourite character – Lord Lester's man, a bailiff – but in this moment of crisis he wanted to let them know he did not approve of what was being done to them.

'It's not right,' he said. 'Not at all. Lord Edward'd turn in his grave.'

'I'm right in thinkin' that he is not following the letter of the law?' Pierce asked and Vernon Blackstock nodded in agreement.

'No. He is not. In fact he is breaking it. But no court in the land will find against him, and you cannot afford to challenge him. You haven't got the money.'

'So what you are saying is, he's going to break the law and there's nothing we can do about it?' Duff Dannon's voice was full of anger.

'That's what I'm sayin'. Except that it is debatable whether he *is* breaking the law. That would have to be argued,' Vernon Blackstock told them. 'But in any event, you couldn't afford to take your landlord to court.'

'I'll kill him,' Deegan Belcher thundered, his huge frame shaking in fury. 'I'll throttle him. I'll have his guts for garters.'

'Now shut up, Deegan. That will get you nowhere. You would have to kill them all and then the polis'd take you away an' lock ye up, and then what would ye do?'

'How long have we got?' Duff Dannon asked. 'How long, man?'

'You've a week . . .' Vernon said the words and a sudden silence fell. They stared in disbelief, trying to assimilate the actuality of what they had heard. It was no longer a dire happening scheduled for sometime in the future, it was, suddenly, an immediate event that stared them in the face.

'Ye've a week,' Phil Conlon corroborated Vernon's ultimatum. 'An' I want ye to know I'm sorely troubled about it. Sorely.'

'What'll I tell Carmel?' Mickey O'Gorman asked rhetorically. He knew what he would tell her and what her reaction would be. She would smile at him and say, 'We'll manage, Mickey love, an' we're together.' The thought made him wince in pain at her trustfulness. On the other hand, in the Gilligan family, the giant fisherman Brian was led by the nose like a pig to market by his wife Della, yet he too felt the drop of his stomach at the thought of eviction. 'What'll I tell Della? And the childer?'

And Dinny McQuaid, swallowing his pint in nervous gulps, thought of Sheena and her house-proud ways, her dissatisfaction at their lack of some of the things she craved for and he gagged on his jar. 'What'll I tell Sheena?'

And the angry man, the furious Deegan, fought back a wave of nausea and told himself it was not going to happen.

They all thought of someone who twisted their hearts; Mog Murtagh, fully confident that little Ellie in her box was God's exclusive child, nevertheless squirmed mentally, tears at the edge of his eyes at the thought of her adrift with him and Jinny in the wide cold world without a roof over their heads. Duff Dannon thought of Christie, his brother, and Christie's wife Mary and their six-month-old babby, Jessy, and his heart pumped anger worthy of Deegan Belcher. Pierce Donnelly thought of all he had done to their little home and how warm it was and sacred. He thought of Brindsley, serious over his books and given the great opportunity to study, how having to leave all that behind would destroy their whole lives. And Dana, who appeared so much more confident than she was, shadowed by her lovely sisters Demara and Maeve, out on the wild wet roads with him would die in a month. And he thought of Brigid and all the work and care they had put into the cottage, everything he had striven for invested in that homestead, now to be taken away.

'It's not right,' he protested angrily, voicing all their thoughts. 'It is not right. I've paid for that cottage; a lot it amounted to over the years, on a promise I'd own it. It is not right!'

Duff Dannon shot him a warning dart from angry eyes. 'We'll talk about it among ourselves,' he said winking and gesturing with his head towards Phil Conlon and Vernon Blackstock.

'I just wanted you to know I do not approve,' Phil Conlon said, catching the glance. He looked over the bar at Ma Stacey, gave her the benefit of a scorching glance, doffed his cap and turned to leave. But Mickey O'Gorman blocked his way.

'An' what's that supposed to mean?' Mickey asked. 'That ye'll go ahead an' evict us, but ye won't *enjoy* it? Eh? Ye'll turf us out but it'll give ye no *pleasure*? Don't approve! I ask you!'

Ma Stacey was behind the counter leaning her large bosom on its surface. She too added her halfpenny worth. 'Don't come beggin' at my door an' ye on the side of the landlords,' she told him.

'What do I have te do te change that?' he asked her.

She looked at him levelly. 'Ye know, Phil Conlon. Ye know.'

He nodded and turned once more. This time it was Duff who stopped him.

'Yer a funny man, Phil,' he said, trying to control his fury. 'Born and raised among us, on our side as 'twer, one of us, but willin' to do the boss's dirty work for him agin us. A veritable Judas you are.'

Phil Conlon surveyed them ranged against him in the dark snug. 'I'm makin' no apology,' he said. 'I'm doin' my job. If I don't someone else will an' mebbe someone not as kind as me. Lord Lester's been good to me all these years, so he has.'

'Lord *Edward*. Sure he's been good to us all. We owe him. But this young whippersnapper's a whole different story. An' how long, Phil Conlon, do ye think ye'll be in work now he's taken over? Sure he'll sell the place before ye can blink and frog-hop it across the water.'

'I'll wait an' see what happens. No point in hasty decisions.' Phil's lips were tight and he glared at them all.

'He can't sell Ballymora Castle,' Vernon Blackstock told them. 'It's against the terms of his father's will.' He spoke gently but they all looked to him and listened. He was a professional man.

'What do you think will happen, Mr Blackstock?' Pierce Donnelly asked him.

'I'll tell you. I think Linton Lester is set on going to London. He has done the deal with the Marquis of Killygally and the transaction is nearly completed. I think he'll try to get rid of you all before he signs the land over. I'm sorry for you all, terribly sorry. Lord Edward tried so hard to prevent this happening.' He cleared his throat and tossed off his whiskey. 'I'm truly sorry. I did my best for you.'

'Much good it did us,' Brian Gilligan muttered.

'I did my best, but I failed. Now I must go.'

'Home te yer grand house. No fear of you losin' that, not like us.' Deegan Belcher for once did not shout. He seemed strangely subdued. 'Jasus, it's well fer some.'

'Ah lave him be,' Dinny McQuaid said. 'Sure it's not his fault.'

'We know ye did yer best, sir,' Duff Dannon said stiffly. 'There's no hard feelings. So good-night te ye.'

They watched Vernon Blackstock pick up his cane and gloves from the counter and make his way to the entrance, followed by Phil Conlon. Duff glanced at his retreating back. 'Not like some I could mention,' he called after Phil. 'Not like some!'

Chapter Thirteen

⁘ ⁘

There was silence over that little group of cottages that night. The sun slipped behind the crouching mountains in the dusk but no one sat in doorways to gossip as was their custom on fine evenings, and though the night was mild and the moon hung low over the silvered mountains and there was a soft breeze from the sea, each house was shuttered and closed up tight.

Shooshie Sheehan didn't give them a tune on his fiddle before he turned in as he usually did when the evening was mellow, and Katey Kavanagh and Cogger were firmly ensconced and not abroad in the twilight hours. Only Granny Donnelly drowsed, and, blissfully ignorant, slept peacefully through all the excitement.

'We'll ask Father Maguire what to do,' Della Gilligan decided to her husband Brian as he lowered his nightshirt after he'd satisfactorily accomplished his marital duty. 'He'll know what's best.'

But he did not. Father Maguire implied that the whole situation was somehow their own fault and that they had brought disaster upon themselves by their lack of dedication to the Sacred Heart. He harangued them that Sunday from the pulpit. 'God is punishing ye,' he told them. 'Ye offend Him constantly. Ye disobey Him. Ye set yerselves up against Him. Ye anger Him with yer impure thoughts and yer driving ambition.' He glared at Pierce Donnelly.

No one would have been surprised if Duff Dannon, had he been there, had walked out, but they were astonished when Pierce Donnelly stood, scraping the bench back and saying loudly to his startled wife, 'Come, Brigid, I'll hear no more of this.' And he left the church followed by Brigid, blushing furiously, Dana, simpering foolishly, and

Brindsley looking triumphant, the cynosure of all eyes.

Mog Murtagh and Jinny with Ellie in her arms, Shooshie Sheehan, Deegan Belcher, always glad of the opportunity to make a gesture of defiance, Dinny McQuaid, then the most of them followed as they realized that in these times of crisis they could do strange things they normally would not contemplate. They were being pushed too far.

'Come back. Come back. Infidels, satanists, heretics!' Father Maguire screamed after them as they left the church. His face was very red. 'Ye'll go directly to Hell for this, children of Beelzebub. Ye'll burn forever in torment for yer disobedience. The Holy Mother'll weep. Haven't ye brought this on yerselves, unbelievers.'

But he had lost them. Eternal hellfire seemed arbitrary and remote when eviction was so close. The trouble they had was too near for his little flock to be worried by threats of possible damnation.

Next morning was the day marked out for the eviction. Katey was up at four a.m. before the dew had properly fallen and out she went into the Lester woods picking her herbs and mushrooms as usual, sniffing the air that passed the castle as if a whiff of it might explain things to her satisfaction. But no shaft of enlightenment came and when she returned to the little group of cottages at five, her apron full, her feet wet, it was to nod to the other women who had come to lean over their half-doors, staring into the middle-distance at nothing.

Pierce Donnelly had not slept. He had tossed and turned for a couple of hours next to Brigid who remained stiff as a poker beside him, awake also and full of fear.

Six o'clock of the morning came and went, the uncertainty growing, and Mickey O'Gorman had just patted his wife's hand and said, 'Maybe it's all just a bad dream,' when over the rise in the boreen, around the bend in the road, Lord Linton Lester appeared little by little; first the top of his head, then his face, then his bottle-green tweed jacket, then his fawn riding breeches, then his high-polished brown boots. Phil Conlon followed

him closely and behind Phil, Denmar the butler and
Manny O'Flynn the under-footman and the two stable
lads, Paddy and Ben, made up the procession.

It had not as much as entered Linton Lester's head that
there would be any resistance. He looked on the whole
event of the evictions as an inconvenience and the people
as nothing more or less than hindrances. However, he had
decided to accompany his bailiff, not trusting the job to be
done efficiently without his presence upon the scene. He
knew of Phil Conlon's sympathies and he wanted no
slip-up. He was in a hurry to get the whole business over
and done with and be on his way to London and a more
satisfactory social life.

Phil Conlon came to a stop in front of the cottages and
read aloud the notice: '. . . *hereby give notice to evict from these
premises, they being the legal property of Lord Linton Edward
Lester of Ballymora Castle of. . .'*

There was a lot more but these words were the only ones
the cottagers heard. They stood, some in doorways, some
in the boreen, some leaning on their spades on their little
plots, all bemused and stunned.

Then Lord Lester, who had been listening with barely
concealed irritation, waved his hand. 'Get on with it, man,'
he cried to Phil, who stood in the centre of the little group
of cottagers.

'Now leave quietly. All leave quietly,' Phil said firmly.
'One by one, out!' He gestured to Manny and the stable
lads who stood hesitating, uncertain what exactly was
expected of them. It was Denmar who walked into the
Gilligans' house and shouted to them as they knelt
praying, 'Out! Out! Out now!'

Brian hesitated, looked about him as if for heaven-sent
help, but nothing happened. Then he sighed and took his
wife's hand and rose up. 'We better go, *allana,*' he said.
'Take each other's hands, pets,' he told the children and
this they obediently did. They emerged into the amber
day, blinking, Della holding a sewing-basket over her arm.
It had not occurred to her to take anything else but the
sewing-basket and her rosary beads.

'Ah sure we all better do as the man says,' Dinny

89

McQuaid muttered as, without any prompting he pushed the hand-cart he had laden with goods and chattels and followed the Gilligans out to the boreen. 'Della Gilligan, ye shoulda got yer things together instead of prayin',' he shouted at the other family. Mog Murtagh, donkey trap piled high with household stuffs and little crippled Ellie on the top, joined the rest, followed by Shooshie Sheehan holding his fiddle and Mickey O'Gorman, sober this day, his arm tenderly around Carmel whose black eye was now purple. There was no sign of Duff Dannon or Katey Kavanagh or Deegan Belcher or Ma Stacey. Or the Donnellys.

It was the Donnellys' house Phil Conlon targeted next. He rapped on the lower half of the door with his riding whip.

'Out! Out! Out now!'

There was silence. Somewhere a lark sang its heart out. A dog barked. Phil Conlon rapped again, 'Out!' he cried.

'Get the hell away from my home,' Pierce's huge bellow shook the onlookers, friends and foes alike. The cottagers wending their way from their homes down the lane turned back and stood amazed at the noise. His voice reverberated around the hollow and sent waves to the mountains.

'And mine.' Another bellow from behind the closed door opposite where Duff Dannon, Christie and Mary Dannon lived.

'And mine!' A huge roar from behind Deegan Belcher's door raised little surprise.

'What the Devil. . .?' Linton Lester hesitated. This was not supposed to happen. 'What is it, Conlon?' he asked peevishly. 'What the Devil's wrong?'

'They don't want to leave, m'lord,' Phil Conlon said.

'Well of course they don't! It's your job to get rid of them without fuss.'

'Out! Out! Out now!' Phil shouted at the Donnellys' door. 'Come on out, Pierce Donnelly. It's time te leave. Ye've been warned.'

'Well I'm not goin'.'

'What . . . what . . . what did he say?' Lord Lester

90

queried, then drew himself up and shouted back, 'It's the law you're breaking. It is a prisonable offense.' He looked at Phil Conlon. 'What's the man's name?'

'Pierce Donnelly, sir.'

'Pierce Donnelly, are you there?'

Silence.

'Answer and come out in the name of the law!'

The Donnelly door suddenly burst open and Pierce stood there, his shoulders back, his twelve-bore shotgun in his hands, pointing at Lord Lester, Phil Conlon and the group around them. Then, as the group was digesting the sight confronting them the Dannons' door behind them similarly burst open and Duff and Christie stood there holding a rifle and a shotgun respectively, both perfectly polished and cocked, aimed at Lord Lester's heart. Then there was a roar and Deegan Belcher's sodden, moss-covered half-door bounced open and Deegan stood, naked to his trousers, a rifle held low and deceptively loosely, his eyes glittering in anticipation. He didn't say anything. He didn't need to.

'Good God, men, have you run mad?' Linton Lester's eyes were popping, amazed at this unexpected turn of events and distinctly nervous.

'No, Lord Lester, but what you are doing, sir, breaks the gentleman's agreement we had with Lord Edward Lester, your father, m'lord, and I, for one, do not intend to budge from my home until my case is heard at the next assizes. With due respect, m'lord,' Pierce Donnelly announced loudly and clearly.

'And without respect, I say,' Duff Dannon cried. Still Deegan said nothing, but smiled.

There was a cheer from the group standing poised for flight in the boreen and a hesitant shuffling move back into the little enclave.

'Me too, sir,' Christie Dannon said.

'We had a word with Mr Blackstock, sir, and he said we were entitled to a hearing.'

Mr Blackstock had told them they had no such entitlement but he had also told them that Lord Lester was pig-ignorant of the law and would not know that.

91

At the mention of Vernon Blackstock Lord Lester lost his temper which was a mistake. 'Go into that man's cottage, Manny,' he told the white-faced under-footman, 'and put a taper to the fire and set it alight.'

There was a gasp from the onlookers. They knew this was what happened when others had tried civil disobedience.

'Me, sir?' Manny looked at the angry lord, 'Me, sir? Set fire to the cottage?' he asked in trembling tones. 'But me da lives just up there!'

'Then, you, idiot, you,' Lord Lester shouted at the stableboy.

Lord Lester had made his second mistake. Idiot was a dangerous word to use. Every hamlet and village in the country had an idiot. Everyone knew who the idiot was and that person was sacred. No one else was allowed to cast aspersions and it was considered very bad form to damn with the epithet. Cogger Kavanagh was Ballymora's idiot and not the stableboy, Pat, and to call him so was both an honour he did not deserve and a terrible insult.

'Do as I say,' Lord Linton ordered, but now Pat and Manny stared at each other mutinously.

'Me mam an' me da are in there,' Manny pointed to the cottage furthest down the hill. 'Are ye askin' me to set fire to me own home?'

'You don't *live* there, you fool. You live with me! Now get on with it.'

'The man's stupid,' Pat, the stableboy, muttered to Manny. 'Askin' a man te set fire to his mam's and da's home! Never heard the like!'

'Get on with it!' Lord Linton shouted. He was getting nervous and this made him belligerent.

Manny was devoted to his job. He saw a wonderful future for himself in service. He had no desire to cross his employer and jeopardize his chances of getting a reference, but this was too much.

'No, sir! I will not. I will not set fire to anyone's home. Ask someone else to do it.' Manny's face was beet-red as he squared up to his master. There was another loud cheer, louder, less tentative, this time from the crowd. They were going back towards their homes and Lord Linton suddenly saw that the exodus had ceased and the chances of a quick elimination of the tenants was fading fast.

He looked at them, furious and uncomprehending. 'Very well. If that is the way you want it.' He drew himself up, glowering at the footman, 'You are dismissed from my service forthwith!'

If he had thought to embarrass the little man he did not succeed. Manny felt swaggery in front of his neighbours and with their cheers echoing in his ears he was carried away on a tide of bravado.

He slung his master's riding whip and cloak which he had been given to hold, in the dirt of the boreen in front of Lord Lester. 'Only too delighted to lave, yer lordship,' he chortled, with a gallant bow. He then turned his back and joined the crowd. Pat and Ben the stable lads scuttled to join him, one on each side of the under-footman, and the crowd pressed in around them in front of the cottages, cheering, but watching with wary eyes to see what would happen next. They were certain some dreadful nemesis would crash down on them, for no peasants had ever won in such a confrontation before.

Duff, Deegan, Christie and Pierce still held their guns aimed at Lord Lester and he stared at them and the crowd, taken aback, uncertain how to proceed. Turning this way and that in his fury he saw his bailiff, Phil Conlon. He gestured him over and when the big man sauntered to his side he yelled at him, 'Aim your gun at them, Conlon. Shoot any man who will not leave his dwelling. I take full responsibility. Do you hear me? Shoot them down like dogs!'

Phil Conlon let the gun he carried over his back slide off.

'Jasus, we're done for now,' Brian Gilligan muttered to Della and she slipped her hand into his and held him tight.

Phil Conlon looked around at the group.

'Shoot them, Conlon, if they don't go. Shoot them, you hear?'

Phil pulled the gun around under his arm, slipped it out, then very slowly he cocked it. He stood up straight and pointed it at Duff and Christie. Then Deegan, then Pierce.

Then he swung it to face his master, who gaped, mouth ajar into the dark muzzle.

Lord Linton Lester stood alone, all the guns there leveled at him. The crowd had never before seen anything like it. They held their collective breath.

'I'm with *them*,' Phil Conlon said, stepping back, smiling at the astounded young lord and earning a loud cheer from the crowd as he moved to become part of them.

When the noise had died down, Phil Conlon said, 'Your father, God rest him, Lord Edward, would never have allowed this madness to happen. These are human beings. You treat them without respect, without consideration. I cannot go along wi' it. It would be agin my principles.'

'You won't get away with it,' Linton Lester said as calmly as he could, trying to salvage what little dignity he had left. Drawing himself up, he looked at them, the angry faces, the amused ones, the defiant expressions all around him, the triumphant eyes. 'You'll have to go eventually,' he said, almost sadly. 'I'll win, you fools, I'll win,' he repeated, then turned and walked away down the boreen, back towards the castle. They watched him breathlessly, stunned by what had just happened, afraid to move. When Linton Lester reached the curve in the road, he looked back and heard a concerted roar of derision and victory which rose up and increased in volume. He turned away, rounded the corner and disappeared from view.

Chapter Fourteen

❧ ☙

Linton Lester was not a man who bore grudges. He was far too selfish. He was in a fever of impatience to get to London and anything that impeded him angered him.

So he decided to leave the problem in the hands of the

man to whom he had sold the land. Why make it his war when somebody else could deal with it? He would take his money and leave this benighted spot to enjoy himself in civilization.

He rode over to see the Marquis and told him what had occurred. 'For meself, old dear,' he said, 'I don't *care* a toss as long as I can get out of this cesspool of a place an' take meself to London.'

Linton Lester lounged in the wide-winged chair, one leg dangling over the arm.

'Take my advice, Bosie,' he told the Marquis, 'get Muswell.'

When he returned to Ballymora Castle he sent for Vernon Blackstock. 'I've suggested to the Marquis that he send for Muswell,' he told the solicitor. 'It's the only thing to do in the circumstances, Blackstock. And I must say I do not admire your part in all this. Rest assured I'll be shot of you as soon as I legally can.'

Vernon Blackstock bowed, but said nothing.

'This situation cannot be allowed to accelerate,' Linton said. 'It is dangerous. It's like the French Revolution, by God, an' it cannot be sustained.' He thought for a moment. 'Who *is* this Duff Dannon? He interests me. What is he?'

'He's a Land Leaguer, m'lord.'

'What on earth are they?'

'Your father thought. . .'

'I do not want to be told about what my father thought. I simply want that little clutch of people off my land. Off Bosie's land.'

'It might be better for you, m'lord, if you gave in now, left them alone. And the Marquis of Killygally. He too might be well advised to leave them be. I've heard terrible things. . .'

Lord Lester leapt to his feet.

'Never,' he cried. 'Never once do you seem to want to try to help me. Goddammit, man, I employ you. I pay your bills. Don't you understand that the peasants have no right to. . .'

'But they have, m'lord. They have rights. . .'

'You're on their side. You've made that plain. They were

using phraseology they could only have got from you, Blackstock. They mentioned your name. One of them quoted you. If you think I'm going to leave them alone, as you put it, back down in front of a bunch of morons. . .'

'You already have, m'lord!'

Lord Lester bit his tongue.

'How did the Marquis feel about you leaving the evictions to him?' Vernon Blackstock wondered. He had chosen his words carefully, for he nearly said, 'leave your dirty work to him'.

'He wasn't too pleased,' Linton conceded.

Bosie had told him he would give him a better price for the land if he got rid of the cottagers. 'However, old bean, I'll have to knock off something if I have to do the job myself. I have no qualms about evictions,' he had added. 'I announced that I wanted my tenants cleared in a week and I achieved it too.'

Lord Lester thought about it, and in the end decided a few sovereigns off was a worthwhile price to pay to rid himself of the nuisance.

The sooner he could get out of this God-forsaken corner of the world, get back into society and forget all about Ballymora, the better.

'What exactly is the legal position, Blackstock? Remember, you are paid to advise me.'

'I thought you had dismissed me, my lord,' Blackstock said sweetly.

Linton Lester shook his head. 'How excessively silly of you, sir. Until this business is over you know I cannot do that,' he said and straightened, kicked a log with the tip of his toe and stood up. He looked at Blackstock with glittering eyes. 'Don't underestimate me, sir. What about Muswell?'

'Muswell is a thug, m'lord. A thug and a villain.'

'Good. Then get him. Send him to Bosie.'

'Sir, please listen to me.' Blackstock tried to remain calm, remembering Moll's warning about his blood-pressure. 'If you let these men remain. . .'

'No peasants will get the better of me. . .'

'*Please*, my lord, listen. It could become a war. If you get Muswell there'll be bloodshed and I'm perfectly sure you do not want the blood of innocent people on your hands.'

'*They* started it. Dolts and idiots! How dare they, Blackstock! In any event I propose to be in London and the affair will rest in Bosie's hands. Now what I want you to do is draw up the bills of sale, the papers, whatever. I'll fill in the amounts. And Blackstock . . . tell Muswell he's needed at Stillwater. The Marquis will want to see him.'

Vernon Blackstock gave up. He left the library and found Kilty hovering about in the corridor. He asked to see Lady Kitty but she was in bed, Kilty said, with a slight indisposition.

'Is it true, sir?' Kilty asked him. 'That they defied his high and mighty? Oh tell me, sir. It does my poor heart good to hear. Phil Conlon has left, they say, an' Manny and Ben and Paddy did not return, an' the word is they've all told his lordship to go stuff himself. Oh I wish I had been there, sir, I do, that I do.'

'Well, I wouldn't be so happy about it, Kilty, if I were you. It is going to end in disaster, I warn you.' Vernon Blackstock shook his head. 'Those people don't realize. . .'

'Still I wish I'd been there, sir. Routed he was. Whipped. Defeated entirely.' Kilty's body shook with inner glee and Vernon said no more, kept his dire warnings to himself and took himself off to his home and wife and all the pleasures that they promised. One thing he was quite determined about: he was not going to send for Muswell. Wild horses wouldn't persuade him. Let Lord Linton Lester do his own dirty work. Vernon Blackstock had no intention of filthying his hands by any contact with that infamous agent.

Chapter Fifteen

⤏ ⤎

Demara and Maeve stood side by side staring into the black water. As the ship ploughed inexorably towards England Demara's spirits plummeted. Dark water, dark thoughts and miles and miles from home, they were adrift in the world.

'I'm not as keen as I was at home,' Maeve whispered to her sister, looking up at the taller girl, eyes wide with apprehension in the damp night that surrounded them.

'Ach, don't be a goose, Maeve,' Demara said briskly. ' 'Twill be all right, never you fear.' She lied to her sister, sounding much more cheerful than she felt. She had to. She lied to herself too or she would have descended into a deep pit of despair from which she might not be able to escape.

They disliked Lorcan Brennan on sight.

'He's a scut,' Maeve whispered to Demara who said 'Shush!' but silently agreed with her sister about their brother-in-law. He had no trouble recognizing them, fresh as they were from rural Ireland.

'Yiz'll have to get rid of them shawls,' he muttered, not meeting their eyes in the shoving, pushing crowd that swirled around them. There were more people there than they had ever seen, and the station frightened them though Demara would never have admitted it. Large and echoing, the hustle and bustle, the hordes of people, the terrible haste they all seemed in, the noise, the smoke, the hootings and blasting on steam horns, the paper-boys, the chestnut vendors, the saveloy sellers, the flower girls, all unfamiliar sights, sounds and impressions for the two girls from the country.

Lorcan Brennan was a young, irritable Dublin man with yellow horsy teeth and stiff black hair growing low over his brow. He seemed to be in a terrible hurry. 'Yiz are Demara an' Maeve. Follie me!' he commanded and hurried on before them and they had to run to keep up with him. An ill-mannered lout, Demara decided, used as she was to the exquisite courtesy of the peasants in Kerry. Their meticulous greetings and blessings, their courtly ways and good wishes seemed very remote at this moment. Perhaps it was not the way of the big city, which, thought Demara, would be a pity. She took for granted the polite and considerate behaviour of the cottagers. It was essential for them. It made life rich.

Lorcan Brennan seemed not bound by those rules. He did not introduce himself, or take Demara's carpet bag, or offer to carry it for her. He simply hustled them out of the great London station away from the steam and the roar like an angry sea, only less musical, and they emerged into the street.

It seemed to Demara even more crowded out there and she felt Maeve's arm snuggle through hers and her sister clung close, walking very near her side, demurely, eyes lowered.

'Come on! Come on!' Lorcan urged them. 'We gotta take a bus.'

Demara put her foot on the platform of a horse-drawn vehicle painted yellow.

'No, no, not that one,' Lorcan yelled and grabbed her shawl which fell in the stinking muddy street. 'No! Ours is blue!'

They followed him obediently as he pushed his way through the biggest crowd they had ever seen. Urchins tussled on the street, filthy as sin, yelling and screeching at each other. A street seller was crying 'Buy a Rabbit' and another 'Buy a Fine Table Basket'. The dogs seemed starved and they barked and sniffed Demara's skirts, and there were fine gentlemen and ladies in carriages passing by. A lamplighter was lighting the lamps with a taper, while a couple of sailors wearing the Queen's uniform were reeling drunkenly down the street.

Bewildered they allowed themselves to board the horse-bus indicated by Lorcan, get off it a little later and onto another, this time a chocolate-coloured one to Fleet Street, and finally they got off that vehicle and were led down a bleak little street to a small, dark house.

Whitefriars Street in the east of the city off Fleet Street was a sunless warren of damp houses, the rent only seven shillings and nine pence a week. When they had been built no thought had been given to fresh air, clean water, beauty or cleanliness, and the sight of the place chilled Demara to the soul.

Lorcan Brennan ran ahead of them into the house.

'He's a scut!' Maeve insisted and Demara silently agreed

as they climbed up the narrow stairs, watched with interest by the other tenants.

'I 'ope they're not stayin' long!' a little bird-like woman with a loud voice asked Áine through tight unwelcoming lips. Afterwards they found out she was the landlady, Mrs Box, who, when she collected their rent every Saturday morning, would take the opportunity to lecture Áine on her visitors.

'It's against the rules,' she repeated over and over.

Maeve and Demara could not understand what business it was of hers, and why, if you paid your rent, you couldn't have whom you pleased in your home. 'It's not like that here,' Áine sighed. 'You'll find out. There are rules for everything here, not like at home. An' anyhow everyone breaks them.'

Mrs Box smelled strongly of the peppermint she always sucked in a mouth dotted with rotten teeth.

Áine welcomed them tearfully, hugging them.

'Oh ye remind me of home, Demara,' she cried. 'Here, come inside. How's Mam and Da an' Brindsley?' she asked eagerly, leaving Dana out. She had never liked Dana. She seemed to smell, from Demara's clothes, the sea-breezes of Ballymora and the sharp scent of the heather and golden broom and she held onto her sisters fiercely, touching them every now and then for reassurance. They had reminded her, brought back sweet memories of childhood and the beautiful place she was born, a place lost to her now.

The nostalgia did not last, however, which was hardly surprising. Lorcan mooched around the room, then sat in a chair and read a newspaper, ignoring them.

Áine had made a comfortable home. It looked very much like the cottage in Ballymora with a table in front of the small fire in the little grate, and above it on the mantelpiece an effigy of the Virgin Mary, nose chipped, blue mantle scraped, with a night-light burning before it.

Áine followed Demara's eyes as she glanced about her home. She surveyed it with pride. 'Isn't it grand?' she asked her sister. 'Isn't it just like Mam's? The Blessed Mother, I mean. I got it in Whitechapel Market.'

She took the kettle off the fire and put some tea in it. 'A treat,' she said, 'te welcome you.' Her husband grunted.

'It's all grand,' Demara said, not meaning it. There was a hard lump in her chest, lodged there like a rock, and she couldn't swallow. How she was going to drink the tea she did not know.

She thought the rooms neat and tidy, sure, but they had a crowded feeling about them, not helped by their presence, and they had a tawdry, secondhand quality. The furniture was of inferior materials and everything looked worn and tired, as worn and tired as she felt. It was depressing.

'I know you think this place is bleak, Demara . . . ' Áine said, catching her sister's eye. Bleak! That was the word. They were bleak rooms. No matter how much Áine had tried to reproduce their living-room at home it had not worked – nor could it ever – here. The rooms were bleak indeed. They boxed you in so you felt suffocated. The windows looked out on bricks and mortar and no grass or trees were to be seen. The buildings were high, the street narrow and no space around them. Demara felt enclosed, restricted, weighed down by a feeling of doom.

'Don't be daft! What are ye trying to say? That this place isn't good enough?' Lorcan snapped.

'No, no. I'm not.' She didn't know what to call him so she avoided his name. 'Oh no. It's lovely. Áine has it lovely.' Demara hoped her protestations were not too vehement. 'And the Virgin Mary is lovely. Just like Mam's.'

'Yes. I got it in . . . oh I told you.' Áine was looking nervously at her husband. 'Not too far from here. Lots of Irish there. Irish and Jews. They say you could furnish a house, feed a family and plant a garden from Whitechapel Market.'

She needed to boast, Demara thought. Lorcan sucked in his breath as she spoke and blew it out through his nose, expressing disapproval of anything Demara might think.

'Now Áine, you have everything lovely here and you know it,' she said firmly.

Lorcan shook his paper and got up from his chair.

'I'll have to go in a minute,' he said.

101

'It's amazing the amount of irritation he can put into shakin' a paper,' Maeve whispered.

Lorcan Brennan worked in a bar, The Hare and Hounds in Bouverie Street. He pulled the pump, brought up the barrels from the cellar and earned good money. He worked most of the day and half the night dressed in his shirtsleeves and a huge white apron that Áine washed each night on his return, and ironed for him each morning.

Áine told them that on top of his weekly wage of two pounds seven shillings and six pence, when he broomed the floor each night and mopped it he always found the odd coin.

'Dropped from a careless or drunken pocket,' Áine said and Maeve and Demara wondered at a place where money could be found and swept up from a floor.

But he worked hard, opening up the bar, and cleaning up after closing time, at the beck and call of the boss the rest of the day. It was hectic and hard and at the end of a long day Lorcan Brennan appreciated his home and the few hours he could spend there in the company of his wife and child. He did not want these two strange females, his wife's sisters, intruding into his domestic bliss. He was a good husband and Áine was happy with him. There was only one fly in the ointment. Each Saturday night Lorcan Brennan came home drunk as a fiddler's bitch, his character completely changed. Áine never knew how he would be: amorous, argumentative, violent, or stupefied.

'. . . See the babby . . .' Áine was saying as Seaneen began to mule and Lorcan pulled on his jacket, kissed his wife and baby and left the apartment, slamming the door behind him and completely ignoring the sisters except to indicate his hostility to them.

'He doesn't like us here,' Demara stated rather obviously, feeling very awkward. Áine was busy showing off her baby and didn't reply. But it was a situation that was to become more and more uncomfortable as the days passed. Lorcan Brennan would burst into his home, beaming and exuberant, only to have his face fall into discontent when he became aware of the presence of Áine's sisters.

Áine thought herself blessed and a cut above the rest because the apartment comprised *two* rooms. All the other tenants lived in one. They shared the outside lavatory, keeping chamber pots under the beds, or the sofa in the case of Demara and Maeve. They washed in a basin kept in the Brennan bedroom which Áine put out in front of the fire once a week for her sisters. It was another of the luxuries Lorcan Brennan had to give up for he could no longer bathe naked in front of the fire in the living-room. Modesty forbade, and he had to make do now with a rub down in the cold bedroom. He resented the sacrifice which was necessary with the two sisters now camped there.

Áine made them welcome that day but she was to change quickly under the stress of their presence. Lorcan barely concealed his irritation.

And all Demara's fears were realized. London was a foul and fog-ridden city, the streets black with slime and soot, humans packed like ants into mean dwellings, and Áine, though she tried hard to make them comfortable, could not help but show them in a thousand different ways how she hated sharing her home with them.

Mrs Box, the landlady, resented them too. She said she was breaking the rules allowing them to stay there at all. She liked to look after the baby, Seaneen, and the sisters' presence prevented her the freedom of access she had grown accustomed to with Mr and Mrs Brennan out most of the day working.

'Mrs Box loves to look after him when I'm out at work,' Áine told Demara and Maeve, keeping one eye on the baby she cradled and the other on her husband's restless movements.

'But we can do it while we're here,' Demara said, unwittingly making an enemy of the landlady.

Áine was working for a 'jumped-up Dublin woman who thought she was Kitty O'Shea!' 'Honest to God,' Áine said, 'she thinks she's some kind of royalty just because she married a poor weed of an Englishman with more money than sense. Honest to God, there's no snob like an Irish snob when they get the bit between their teeth.' And she shook her head.

'Well isn't she the lucky one,' Maeve said. 'A house of her own, a husband with money, an' able to afford you to help her. Isn't that the grand life entirely!'

Áine snorted. 'Be her slave, more like, at twenty pounds a year! Oh she takes all her frustrations out on me.'

'What frustrations, Áine?' Demara asked. 'Sure what has she got to be frustrated about?'

'Well, her husband for one.' Áine was bathing the babby Seaneen who was gurgling and splashing the water in the tin tub in front of the fire. Strands of Áine's hair had come adrift and her cheeks were damp. Demara thought she looked very pretty. 'She married him for the dosh. Now she has to put up with him an' he's no oil painting.'

'I'd give value for money,' Demara said. 'A bargain's a bargain after all.'

Áine glanced at her sister sideways. 'Sometimes people can't help how they feel. Living with someone can be difficult.' She was blushing. 'Oh I don't mean Lorcan . . .' she stammered.

'I know what ye mean, Áine,' Demara said quietly. 'An' we'll be gone soon as we can find lodgings.'

Áine pulled a night robe over the squirming baby's head. He was a good, sweet-tempered little creature and they all loved him.

'Oh Mam'd kill me if she knew' Áine said awkwardly. 'But it's this place. It's too small for the four of us, to say nothing of little precious here. And Lorcan. . .'

'He has every right to be put out. Two strange women invading his home. . .'

'Oh you understand, Demara! I'm so relieved.' Áine had tears in her eyes and she tucked the cooing baby into the little cradle Lorcan had made for him out of half a barrel, cut sideways, that he had got from the pub. It rocked when the baby moved and lulled him, but it smelled strongly of wine.

'Indeed I do. Just give us time. Me an' Maeve are looking.'

It was not easy to find lodgings. A lot of places had signs up on cardboard notices in their front windows saying:

NO IRISH WELCOME or NO IRISH NEED APPLY, or simply NO IRISH HERE beneath the VACANCIES and ROOMS TO LET notices.

'How'd they know we were Irish?' Maeve asked. 'How'd they know if we didn't tell them?'

'Our accents, *amadán*,' Demara said tiredly after they had been rejected for the ninth or tenth time.

However, the work situation was good. Labour was at a premium and the sisters had no difficulty finding employment: Maeve, with her nimble fingers, got work in Whitechapel with a Jew, Arnold Goldstein. She did simple alterations and repairs on secondhand clothes for re-sale. Arnold Goldstein was a fair man and he provided a machine for the heavy work. She soon got the hang of pedalling and aiming the cloth evenly. But she spent a lot of time replacing buttons and turning suits inside out and re-stitching them. Hopeful white-collar workers with barely a farthing to their names bought these secondhand refurbished garments for a reasonable price and felt quite smart in them. Mr Goldstein was a jovial man and he did not work Maeve too hard, and although the hours were long he gave her fourteen shillings a week and she thought herself lucky. There were work factories in that area, sweat-shops where children slaved and mothers with babies at their hips worked until they dropped for half what Maeve took home each week.

Demara got a skivvying job in a large house in Eaton Square and Áine was furious because her sister was paid a whole pound more for doing much less. Mrs Benson, the tenant from the top floor, a piano teacher who went to the house in Belgravia once a week to give the young daughter music lessons, had told Demara that they were looking for someone to do menial work.

'And when I say menial, dearie, I mean *menial*,' she said. 'But if you want employment then no doubt you'll learn to tolerate it.'

It was the beginning of Áine's irritation with her sisters. She was furious that Demara had formed an acquaintance with anyone else in the house. It was Áine's considered opinion that that only led to trouble.

'Mrs Box is all right,' she said, 'but I don't want us to be on familiar terms with anyone else. We keep ourselves to ourselves,' she said. 'It's the best way.'

They had their full quota of servants in Eaton Square and Demara did not sleep there, but came to work daily. The skivvying was back-breaking and Mrs Benson was correct – Demara did only the most menial tasks, but she did not mind, beggars can't be choosers and if she had to spend most of the day on her knees, her back was strong and she was used to hard work.

She never laid eyes on the master and mistress of the house, nor even their son and daughter, for she was far too lowly to be allowed anywhere near them. She never went front of house at all and the only time she was allowed upstairs was when the owners were out or asleep.

The experience Demara had gained at Ballymora Castle stood in good stead in Eaton Square and her employer, the housekeeper Mrs Croxley, a severe but fair task-master, was quite pleased with her, correctly assessing the girl's efficiency and uncomplaining cooperation. The girl was quiet and didn't fuss; Mrs Croxley, like Lord Edward Lester, dreaded antagonistic workers with a chip on their shoulders, and unfortunately, with the birth of the terrible Unions, which wanted a fair wage for everyone, this was the most common type of applicant for jobs nowadays. So Mrs Croxley looked on her Irish skivvy as a treasure.

In Whitefriars Street the situation worsened. Lorcan Brennan liked to be master in his own home and Maeve and Demara cramped his style. Áine was tired of her sisters' perpetual presence. Mrs Box rarely got to see Seaneen these days and was vociferous in her proclamations that if the owner of the house were to find out the tenants on the second floor had two extra lodgers he'd put up the rent.

'I thought she owned it,' Maeve said.

'No. She takes care of it for the owner, a Lord Plummer, who owns most of the houses in the street.' Áine glanced at her sister. 'You know – like Lord Lester.'

'And the next, and the next, and the next street,' Lorcan Brennan announced bitterly. 'He owns the whole bloody

106

neighbourhood. Oh a fine day's work *he* does when he ambles into The Hare and Hounds and picks up his bag of swag – the hard-earned wages of the working men of this parish.' Lorcan Brennan was always talking about the exploitation of the masses. Demara thought the subject had a familiar ring to it and remembered then Duff Dannon and the Land League, and felt her heart pierced by a pain so sharp it took her breath away.

The sisters slept in the living-room on two saggy old sofas. Like most of the furnishings, Áine had purchased them in the Whitechapel Market. They often heard whispering and noises from the bedroom. It was embarrassing. Maeve would put the sheet over her head in an agony of distressed confusion.

Then one night they distinctly heard Lorcan ask his wife, 'How long more'll they be here?' and Áine's whispered reply, 'Not long, Lorcan love. Not long.'

'We'll have to find somewhere,' Demara muttered, making up her mind to renew their efforts to find lodgings.

Then something happened to force them to leave Áine and Lorcan's home for good.

It was bizarre, a freak accident, something that had no foundation in truth, but was bound to happen given the circumstances.

Maeve and Demara travelled singly or together to their respective employments on the horse-drawn omnibus. It picked them up and let them down in Fleet Street, close to the bottom of the mean little street the Brennans lived in.

If they were lucky the conductor was Bert, a cocky little fellow who knew all his passengers by name and treated everyone with relentless good humour. His fate was to love the whole human race and he never seemed disillusioned by even the crassest of bad manners. There was always an excuse on his lips for disgruntled behaviour and he was so full of the milk of human kindness that he forgave the cruelties and rudenesses he suffered, reiterating that everyone had their own little peculiarities and oddities. A microcosm of man and womankind travelled on his omnibus and he made allowances for the extraordinary diversity of the human race.

107

The other conductor who alternated with Bert was Fred, who crammed as many as possible into his vehicle, going out onto the street and grabbing people and pushing them onto his omnibus. He had no greetings for his passengers and all they suffered at his hands was rough usage. Chalk and cheese, people murmured to each other as they boarded the omnibus. Fred regaled his passengers with tales of the accidents that *could* and *might* occur if the company continued to be so parsimonious. 'The London General Omnibus Company is cutting corners!' he'd say, then repeat dolefully, 'Cutting corners! If you knew what that meant you'd not be on this vehicle now!'

That evening Bert would take the same passengers home. 'Safe as houses!' he'd cry happily. ' 'Ave you ever known us to fail? Take you home safely. It's our motto.'.

The girls loved to see Bert, who flirted outrageously but quite harmlessly with them and often let them ride free. They had put their shawls aside and learned how to dress and act in the town and their days were not without interest. The hustle and bustle of London excited Maeve, but Demara resisted its somewhat hectic charm. She could not acclimatize herself even though she made the best of the circumstances she found herself in. She agreed with Bert that the only way to live is to look on the bright side and she got on with her routine as best and cheerfully as she could. But she was disgusted with the dirty pavements, the foggy mornings, the murky November evenings. The sullen faces of the workers pushing to their employment alongside her in the dark mornings depressed her. The golden leaves of Ballymora were far away and all she could see were slimy black puddles under the gaslight on the shuttered grey streets. No more cheerful greetings from open half-doors, no more cocks crowed to awaken her, no more the sweet breezes from the sea freshened her spirit. No more the clean air of Ballymora filled her lungs. No more the glimpse of purple and rust mountains refreshed her. Their days were long and arduous and Demara noted that Maeve, once so volatile and full of life in Ballymora, in London had grown pale and drawn. She felt, Demara knew, crushed and subdued in the Brennans' home, unable to express herself.

They were both eager to leave. Áine complained incessantly about the Dublin woman, but Demara realized that her tirade was not really against her employer, rather about the sisters whom she felt she could not openly berate for messing up her life. Demara could not find it in her heart to blame Áine.

Lorcan's temper shortened with the days, and his drunken performance on Saturdays, their inability to predict what state he would come home in, Demara's conviction that their presence aggravated his drunkenness, and Áine's shame at the state her husband was in made it imperative for them to leave. Demara and Maeve longed to escape.

Then one Saturday it all bubbled to a head.

The stairs in the building were narrow and the landings leading to the rooms little more than a cat walk. The tenants tried to avoid each other when they met, shrinking into doorways or pressing themselves against the walls as they passed each other. The English did not like physical contact, Demara discovered.

That Saturday, Maeve, coming home from work late, met Lorcan with a few drinks on him. He scowled at her automatically, then as she drew near him he noticed in his inebriated fashion the luminous pearl-white of her skin, the violet of her eyes and the ripeness of her lips. He had spent a lot of time *not* looking at the sisters, studiously avoiding eye-contact in order to maintain remoteness from them and for fear they would worm their way into his sympathy. He had quite made up his mind that by keeping them at arm's length he could get rid of them sooner and in this he was right.

So he had never really *seen* Maeve's beauty, never been confronted by it, as he was now. Also, to give Lorcan Brennan his due, he loved his wife and was not a womanizer. But a combination of things: anger at the sisters' presence in his home, frustration at not being able to make love to his wife without considering the sisters in the next room, and the fact that Maeve's loveliness took him by surprise and that he was drunk, all conspired to

109

make him act out of character.

They stood, close on the stairs a moment, then he lunged against her and pushed her back against the wall. All his anger bubbled to the surface. He was filled with a desire to smash – but also to kiss – this dazzling beauty.

'Bitch,' he cried. 'Bitch.'

He grabbed Maeve's breasts under the thick gabardine coat and, as she struggled, the door of their rooms opened and Áine, Seaneen in her arms, stood looking at them, taking in the scene. She screamed a loud piercing shriek and there was an immediate clatter of doors opening.

'What's happening?' Mrs Box demanded.

Maeve struggled, pulling her hat straight and trying to tidy her clothes.

'Get out, Maeve. Leave now, y'hear?'

Demara had come out behind Áine and surveying the scene realized immediately the truth of the situation and also that Áine was right – they would have to leave.

'It was her,' Lorcan said, blustering. 'Listen to me, it was her. She's always after me. She won't leave me alone, Áine.'

'Get outa my home!' Áine screamed in a tight voice. 'Get out now!' She looked at Lorcan. 'And you get in!'

Demara glanced at her sister.

'Áine, don't be silly. You're not going to believe that of Maeve? You know it's not Maeve's fault. It's that stupid man. She just isn't like that. . .'

'Are you suggesting my husband made overtures to that slut? Why, she flirted with every man in Ballymora.'

'They were all after her, Áine, but she didn't encourage them, you know she didn't.'

Demara realized the futility of what she was saying and knew suddenly that reason and logic didn't count here. Áine couldn't afford to believe that Lorcan was guilty of anything and she would never take her sister's side against her husband. She could never be impartial in any argument concerning him.

'Get out, you sluts!' Lorcan was shouting at them red-faced. 'I never wanted you here in the first place. Cluttering up our home, always in the way.'

110

'What the Devil's going on up there. Will you be quiet. This is a respectable house. Bloody Irish! Never should have taken you in. Only for the baby . . .' Mrs Box now added her say.

'Keep yer oar *out*. Hear me,' Lorcan yelled at the landlady.

'Now see what you have done,' Áine was working herself up into a fine lather, partly to justify throwing her sisters out, to make her feel less guilty, and partly to let Mrs Box see she was getting rid of them.

The commotion on the stairs was reaching a crescendo. People stood in their doorways and watched breathlessly, occasionally shouting a 'Shut up' or a 'God's sake be quiet'. Maeve was crying. Lorcan and Áine were screaming at each other, at Maeve and Demara, and the baby was yelling. Mr Swift, the clerk from the shipping line who lived downstairs, was raising his voice in praise of peace, Mrs Benson, the piano teacher from the top floor, was leaning over the bannisters demanding in a piercing tutorial voice to know what was going on, and could they please keep their voices down as she was trying to teach her pupil the scales, and Mrs Box was telling them all to shut up.

Demara, while all this was going on, sighed and faced the inevitable, for they could not stay now, even if Lorcan apologized. She went quietly into the Brennans' flat and put their few meagre belongings in the carpet-bag, then whispering to Áine that she would call when they were settled to find out the news from Ballymora, she said, 'Come on, Maeve. We won't stay where we're not wanted.' She took her sister's hand and pulled her down the stairs, and leaving the inmates of the house shouting at each other, the two girls crept out into the dark, quiet street.

Chapter Sixteen

'What'll we do now?' Maeve asked her sister. 'Oh Demara, where'll we go?' It was dark and cold outside the house in Whitefriars Street, and quite deserted. Demara had no idea where they could go. They couldn't go looking for a room at this time of the evening and the streets looked bare and full of shadows. For the first time in her life she was afraid.

'We'll go to the station. We'll catch an omnibus there,' she said, making up her mind. There would be people around the station, there would be activity and if they took an omnibus they might meet Bert.

They hurried down the echoing pavements and turned into Fleet Street. There were others here and it was less scary, but the crowd had shuttered faces and kept themselves isolated from their fellow men. '*Dias Mhuire gut*' [God and Mary go with you] – Demara thought of the obligatory traditional greeting to strangers on the Irish roads and she longed to hear the friendly salutation. But no one looked at her and Maeve, no one met their eyes.

They had only travelled a short distance when it began to rain. 'Oh hell and damnation,' Demara muttered beneath her breath.

Maeve was shocked. 'Don't, Demara. Mam would be upset,' she admonished.

'Well Mam isn't here!' Demara retorted tartly as the shower became a downpour and she felt the water trickle down the back of her neck.

'I'm sorry, Demara, it's all my fault.' Maeve looked up at her sister's face. Hers was streaked with rain and tears.

Demara hugged her. 'Nonsense, Maeve. You couldn't help it. We've got each other, pet. Don't worry.'

'God and Mary will help us now!' Maeve whispered.

'Mam promised, so she did. Just pray to Mary, our Mother, she told me, an' she'll help.'

'Well, I don't know about that!' Demara was not sure that Mary, or even God, come to that, could hear anything from the crowded masses of London town, but at that moment they heard the tram in the distance and ran out towards it, hoping it would stop, but it was a long way off and Demara lost heart and stopped running. 'We've no money,' she said sadly. 'Even if we could catch it we couldn't pay.'

They could hear the clip-clop of the horses chippy and cheering, and the sound of its wheels rolling, scratching and scraping the street and to their surprise they heard it stop just behind them. They looked back to see Bert hanging out, holding onto the post, shouting and beckoning to them.

'Cor blimey! Wot you girls doing at this time o' night out in this kind o' weather?' he cried, hauling them inside the omnibus. 'Right, Mac,' he cried to the driver up front and Mac flicked his whip and the horses plodded slowly forward again. 'Don't you know it's not safe for young ladies?'

Demara had never been so pleased to see anyone in her life.

'We've been thrown out of our lodgings, Bert,' Maeve sobbed, turning a heart-broken face, damp violet eyes to the young conductor. 'We don't know what to do, where to go.'

Bert was as susceptible as everyone to Maeve's beauty and his warm heart melted. Besides he had lodgings near the depot. 'Listen, I think my landlady'll take you in 'slong as you don't say you're Irish,' he said cheerily. 'I knock off soon.'

Demara thought, same trouble everywhere: if you're Irish you'll have a reluctant landlord. The Irish and landlords just don't mix. She wondered why.

Bert was making Maeve laugh. She hadn't smiled that much recently and Demara remembered what Granny Donnelly had said about her: 'If Maeve's not given a wee bit of encouragement her light goes out.'

113

Demara stared out of the omnibus at the bleak streets as it lumbered on. She worried about her sister, but was careful when she wrote home to keep the letters cheerful and optimistic, enclosing half of all they earned.

They had heard nothing recently from Ballymora although her mam was in the habit of sending a letter written by Brindsley once a month to Áine. Demara was starved of news. Her homesickness got worse instead of better.

' 'Ere we are. Now let me take your bag. Not much, 'ave you?' Bert's snub-nosed, jolly little face crinkled in a worried look. He had a thatch of straw-coloured hair that he slicked down under his uniform hat and hazel eyes so full of sympathy Demara feared he was going to burst into tears.

'Now don't say you're Irish,' he instructed. 'I'll do the talking.'

'An' I can do a very good English accent an' I try,' Maeve piped up.

He looked at her doubtfully. 'Well don't try it out just yet.'

They couldn't see the house he led them to. He took out his key and they stepped into a tiny hall occupied by a vision in pink. This female person resembled a cake, Demara thought, a lavishly decorated wedding cake gleaming with shiny trimmings.

Mrs Desmond was enormously fat and dressed in a flowing flowered *peignoir* with little rose-coloured shoes on her small feet. The mules were adorned with puffs of swansdown. The *peignoir* had bands of swansdown around the sleeves and down the front and it was open, revealing what seemed like oceans of white lace and satin. She wore a white satin corset and her chemise was visible to all the world. She, however, was unembarrassed, oblivious of her immodest state. Her hair was the colour of red-currants in the sun and so were her lips and cheeks. Bert had told them she used to be an actress. Her breath smelled heavily of juniper berries and it was only much later the girls discovered that actually this was gin. Her gestures were large and dramatic but she seemed kindly of expression and warm-hearted.

114

Nevertheless her greeting was alarming.

'What is all this commotion?' she trumpeted, standing in the hall as Bert opened the front door. 'Merciful heavens, Bert, have you run mad and acquired a harem? *Two* strange females! You know it's not allowed. I might, just might, have closed my eyes if you had seen fit to bring home *one* female, but under no circumstances may you take *two* females to your room. 'Pon my soul, I think you've lost your reason!'

'No, no, no, dear lady,' Bert hastened to assure her. 'No. They're *customers* o' mine. Dear sweet working girls both. Sisters, they are, and *no*, dear lady, I would not *dream*! I'm quite put out that you should think such a thing o' me. . .'

Bert looked so forlorn that the colourful lady hastened to assure him that she had jumped to a dramatic conclusion. 'Because I am dramatic by nature,' she informed them, 'I cannot help myself.'

'They've been evicted from their lodgings and I found 'em roaming the streets, alone and wet. And frightened. I fear for their lives if they are allowed to wander the streets of London like that.'

Mrs Desmond shook her head and tutted and sympathy dawned in her large moist eyes.

'Well, well, come in out of the rain. Close the door, Bert, there is a most uncomfortably severe wind blowing into my hall. Thrown out of your lodgings, you say? Not through any impropriety, I trust?'

Bert shook his head emphatically. 'No, no, dear lady. Quite the reverse.'

It was Bert's recounting the story of the wicked landlord making overtures to Maeve that won Belle Desmond over. Demara realized that Maeve had told him what had happened, and Mrs Desmond, looking at Maeve, her violet eyes, her dimples, her clouds of black curls, did not find the story at all hard to believe, and it touched her warm heart. She called them 'orphans of the storm', pressed them to her ample bosom, and ushered them in.

It was a very warm house. Unlike the Brennans'. When they entered there was no chilly impersonality, only a cosy welcoming. It was also a cluttered house. The hall was full of theatre memorabilia. There were framed billboards, advertisements for plays and pantos covering every available space. Charles Keane presents *The Corsican Brothers* at the Princess's Theatre. Mrs John Wood presents *She Stoops To Conquer* at the St James Theatre, King Street. H.J. Byron presents *Ours* at the Prince of Wales, Coventry Street. And on each, Mrs Desmond's name was printed large beneath other illustrious names.

'Me, duckey,' she hit the pictures one by one with the backs of her fingers. 'All me! Oh I was famous in my day.' She pointed. 'See that? That's me in panto in the Brit in Hoxton. For Sara Lane, dear old gel. Dead now. Played principal boy there when she was seventy.'

A picture of Mrs Desmond in tights that revealed her figure in quite a shocking way was prominently displayed and Maeve was struck by another of her in a wispy costume striking a wild pose, her hands clutched in the hair at her temples, eyes rolled upwards in a frightening, crazed expression.

'Ophelia, dear,' she said, noting the direction of Maeve's glance, 'Sadlers Wells. I played Shakespeare for Samuel Phelps for three seasons. But I never did get on with Robert Edgar when he took over.' She sighed, gave over remembering and suddenly looked old and tired. 'And then the tragedy happened and it all went wrong,' she said softly.

'Now, now, Mrs D. Don't take on,' Bert ordered and the good lady pulled herself up and smiled, a flirtatious look in her eyes that they afterwards realized was a habit from past days of glory. 'Come on in and 'ave a cuppa with me in my boudoir.'

She drew the three of them into a pink, womb-like room, chock-a-block with cushions and tiny tables, more pictures, more playbills on the walls, ornaments, fans, bowls, every available space occupied so that the girls felt it a hazard just entering the room, never mind partaking of refreshment.

However, this was accomplished easily. There was an oil heating device flickering beneath a silver samovar on the only solid table in the room. Maeve was fascinated to see a circle of tiny hooks holding cups around the samovar, three of which Mrs Desmond selected, and, tipping the silver pot over, filled with steaming tea. Behind the table was a plump sofa covered in pale pink brocade in a pattern of full-blown roses. Mrs Desmond sat on this, pulling Maeve down beside her and lifting a fat, belligerent cat up and settling him on her lap. Demara perched herself on a tiny little chair at the other side of the room, and Bert hovered between, graceful as the cat, grinning delightedly at them all the time.

'I knew she'd take to you,' he whispered to Demara. 'I just knew.'

'Now, now, Cordelia,' Mrs Desmond said to the cat, 'don't fuss so. Some people come to see us. Ain't that nice?' She looked at them all, sweeping the room with her theatrical glance. 'She gets terribly jealous!' she stage-whispered to them. 'That,' she indicated the samovar, 'was a gift from an admirer in balmier days.' She chuckled, glancing at them coyly from beneath the unnaturally dark half-moons of eyelids and lashes. 'A Russian. Count, 'e said 'e was.' She shrugged. 'I don't know. 'Ad the dosh though. All that counted. That was, let's see . . .' She squinted. 'Yes, that was *As You Like It*.'

'Beg pardon?' Demara frowned, puzzled.

'The play,' Maeve explained to her sister. 'Shakespeare.'

Most of what this fat pink over-decorated lady in the over-heated, over-decorated room said was incomprehensible to Demara. She was glad she was not too near the blazing fire and wondered what the lady was talking about.

Mrs Belle Desmond, so proud of her diction, would have been horrified to discover that Demara Donnelly did not understand a word. Maeve, on the other hand, was in her element. She had never forgotten the touring company that had come to Kerry and Rhoda Phillips playing Juliet. She felt instantly at home in this place, with this woman, thrilled and excited by the fact that she was talking to a real live actress.

'I tend to date everything that happened to me by the play I was in at the time,' Belle explained, and suddenly her eyes were full of tears and her chin quivered and her bright cheeks shook. 'And most of all *The Drunkard*. That was when my darling . . . my pet . . . my dear one. . .'

Bert was instantly at her side, her fat pink hand in his.

She dabbed the corners of her eyes and took a deep breath, giving Maeve and Demara a brave little smile. 'But I mustn't dwell on that now. No. It would be impolite of me with guests here. Tell me all about it, my dears. What happened to you?'

Bert, who seemed very much at home in the little room, was now handing the tea around, manoeuvring easily between the chairs, tables and piano, Mrs Desmond, her cat and the girls.

'Well, first let me introduce you properly. This one is Demara. She skivvies for a grand house in Eaton Square. You know . . . one of the new ones.'

Mrs Desmond nodded. She was not interested in Demara. It was the other girl who took her fancy. She had sensed that Maeve was a kindred spirit. Something in the girl's open admiration, her obvious interest in the playbills, the ardent passion in her violet eyes, all led Mrs Desmond, correctly, to believe that the girl had Thespian leanings.

'And this one is Maeve who works for Mr Goldstein down in Whitechapel.'

'With *that* face?' Mrs Desmond screamed. 'With those looks? Those eyes? 'Ow times 'ave changed if such a face gets lost in the crowd!' She took Maeve's chin in her hand and tilted her face to the gas light. 'Perfect!' she breathed. 'Perfect. That face demands to be *seen*. To be shown off. To be paraded and gazed at with admiration and envy.' She finished with a flourish of her handkerchief and Cordelia leapt off her lap, stretched and yawned and settled down in front of the fire.

There were tears in Mrs Desmond's eyes again. 'You remind me of myself in earlier times,' she lamented, laying a hand on Bert's sleeve and another on her forehead and gazing into the middle distance. Bert stood on the other side of the sofa, patting the hand on his sleeve, and Demara sat, tea forgotten, staring openmouthed at this display of emotion. It was like being at a terribly interesting play, the performance of which has driven everything else out of one's mind, and she was hard put to keep up with events so far.

'I was a beauty like you,' Mrs Desmond informed them, smiling now. 'You would not think it to look upon me today, would you?'

She glanced around the room and Demara answered promptly, 'No, Mrs Desmond, you wouldn't.' But thankfully her words were drowned by Bert's affirmation that Belle was as beautiful today as she had ever been and as he was the only man present that was all the reassurance Mrs Desmond needed. Childishly hopeful she had waited optimistically to be contradicted. Bert always obliged.

'Admirers from all over the world queued to see me,' Mrs Desmond continued. 'Princes, politicians, earls and lords, all waited for a glance from my eyes.'

'Oh, Mrs Desmond, how wonderful. I've always dreamed of being on the stage . . .' Maeve stammered out her most secret ambition involuntarily.

Demara was shocked. 'Maeve! Holy Mother, what would Mam say?'

Mrs Desmond ignored her. 'Then you shall, my gel,' she told Maeve. 'The minute I saw you, I *knew*.'

'When?' Maeve's face was flushed and Mrs Desmond laughed.

'When you are ready. Oh you impetuous child! Patience. Patience.'

'No more Mr Goldstein. No more slaving over the discarded coats of poor people to sell them to even poorer ones. No *more*!' Maeve cried.

'No. But you'll work just as hard. Preparing,' Mrs Desmond waved a dramatic hand as if Maeve were Miranda cast adrift on a wild wet sea.

Demara half rose. 'Maeve . . . I don't think . . . it's well . . . a bit sudden and . . .' She paused, then blurted out, 'Yerra girl, what would yer mam say? What would Father Maguire. . .'

'To the Devil with Father Maguire,' Maeve cried hotly. 'Sure, it's all right for us to come here an' do menial occupations, skivvying and slavin' but get aspirations . . .' Maeve's eyes glowed and Mrs Desmond clapped her hands.

119

'Oh look at her. Look at that passion! That fire! Oh yes, Bert, she's a natural. And she's Irish!'

There was a sudden silence as Bert, Demara and Maeve stared at the old actress in consternation, expecting dismissal. But she smiled and explained, 'They are the *best* actresses. And actors. The Irish are gifted in the arts, m'dear, didn't you know?'

'I know, Mrs D. From the first time I clapped eyes on her I knew there was something about her you'd take a fancy to. Just knew.'

'Well, you were right, Bert. As usual. Bert,' she informed the girls, 'is usually right.' She smiled at Demara, handkerchief over her mouth. 'As for you, we'll find something much more, er, creative for you than skivvying for grand folks up West. Oh yes!'

'But Mrs Desmond . . . I'm quite all right doing what I'm doing . . . I could do a lot worse. . .'

'Now, now, no objections. It will all work out, you'll see. Now up to bed with you.' She stood, shooing them before her out into the hall, then up the stairs, standing behind them like a mother hen.

Whatever doubts Demara had, whatever reservations, vanished when she saw the room. It seemed to her that events had careered out of control, and her fate, hers and Maeve's, had been railroaded into a completely different direction before she had decided whether she wanted to take this road at all.

But the room clinched it. It was warm and cosy, and she had never seen anything so welcoming, so luxurious, so pretty before. There was a fire ready for lighting in the grate. A large bed, soft as sin, plumped-up quilts and pillows, a tallboy and a mirror. A mirror! Oh joy, oh bliss! Maeve had never even been close to a mirror before. There was a china jug filled with water and a basin scattered with roses on the tallboy. It was the most beautiful room they had ever seen.

'You'll stay here, my dears. This'll be yours.' Mrs Desmond seemed strangely subdued.

'Oh it's beautiful, Mrs Desmond.' Maeve clapped her hands.

'It was waiting. Waiting,' Mrs Desmond said and once more tears filled her eyes and she looked from one to the other.

'Ah now, Mrs Desmond, don't distress yourself. You know it's not good for you,' Bert soothed.

'My daughter . . .' Mrs Desmond wept. 'My daughter,' she repeated and Demara realized that her emotion was undeniably real and raw. 'This room was my daughter's. My Lucy. She disappeared. Vanished and I never saw her again.'

Bert came and put his arms around the huge woman who shook now from head to toe.

'There now, Mrs D. There now. Don't lose faith. She'll turn up one o' these fine days, never fear.'

He looked at the sisters. 'Never got over it, she didn't. Went out for some pork-pie, her Lucy did, to the pub on the corner. Never returned.'

Maeve impulsively ran to the sobbing woman and kissed her roundly. 'Dear Mrs Desmond, of course we'll stay if you are sure you don't mind having us here?'

Mrs Desmond shook her head. 'It'd be nice,' she said, 'to 'ave someone 'ere. Be nice.'

'We'll get on famously, you'll see. Oh don't cry. I can't bear it.'

Demara sat on the side of the bed, realizing events were out of control indeed. She felt the luxury of the eiderdown sink beneath her weight. She looked at the other three as if they were an alien species. The huge mountain of a woman, frilly as the ballgowns they wore at Ballymora Castle, weeping copiously, wrapped around by her sister and Bert both sobbing in sympathy left her puzzled. She shook her head, feeling out of the scene, as if it were all happening to someone else. She was worried about the whole situation, remembering what Father Maguire said about strolling players and how they were the spawn of the Devil and totally disreputable. But the bed would have tempted St Peter himself and she was bone weary and very far from home and familiar things. She decided to postpone any long-term decisions until the following morning – and by then it was too late. The bed had seduced her and she could not contemplate giving it up. Besides, to find a reasonable alternative to the comfort Mrs Desmond offered was an impossibility, so she shelved all thoughts of Father Maguire and agreed with Maeve to give in and live with the lonely, warm-hearted actress, as Bert advised.

After all, as Mrs Desmond had told them, Bert was always right.

Chapter Seventeen

৵৹ ৫৵

They soon settled into the little house in Soho Square. They learned to manoeuvre their way safely around the bric-à-brac and knick-knacks without knocking them down or falling over them, although that did happen once or twice. But Mrs Desmond was an amiable lady and did not scold them.

They were a jolly household, for the good lady's tears were like summer showers and one could be reasonably certain that the sunshine of her smile would quickly follow the rain. She was impulsive and, like Bert, incurably warm-hearted.

Bert's second name, they discovered, was Hockney, and both he and Belle made the girls feel welcome. It made a great change from the Brennans' melancholy menage. Their palpable desire to see the back of the sisters had, without Demara or Maeve being really aware of it, sapped their enthusiasm and good humour and subdued their zest for life in a most dismal way.

Mrs Desmond was not really a 'Mrs', they discovered. That was what appeared on the billboards. She had never married. It shocked Demara to discover that Belle Desmond had led a very active romantic life, unblessed by contracts with State or Church. Her loves were numerous, and Demara, when she found out this fascinating fact, stared at her as if she were some strange and wonderful species, for the Donnellys had never met anyone like that before.

Belle Desmond's lovers had provided her with the house in Soho Square, with her furniture, with her valuable jewellery and other *objets d'art* like the silver samovar. She had been frugal and careful with the money she had earned and the 'gifts' she had received for her favours. All of it had helped provide for her old age.

'It's only right a man takes care of you,' she explained to the girls in her parlour where she spent most of her time. 'See, we've got something they want. Something they want badly. Only otherwise available from a wife 'oo's probably cold, or reluctant, or considers it 'er duty, or is pregnant most of the time. Only other way is to get it from a prostitute down Whitechapel, an' a doxy, God 'elp us, is riddled with disease an in a 'urry. No joy there. No,' she shook her ruby curls. 'Give 'em a good time, I say, but make sure they provide for you. Seems reasonable to me. Looks don't last forever. Remember that, Maeve. And you, Demara. Get an 'ouse. Get diamonds. Get the furniture, the carriage, while you can. Make sure it's bought an' paid for an' in your name. None of this "revert to lease-holder if liaison terminated" lark, oh no! I got caught like that once. Little gem of a place in Chelsea. Young Duke, mad about me, 'e was. Well, when 'e had 'is fill, when he got tired as young blokes do, likin' a bit of variety, well, blow me if next day, *next day* mind, I'm *out*! Come 'ome from the theatre to find all my clothes, bags and baggage neat as could be in boxes on the pavement. I learned my lesson then.'

But everything had truly crashed for poor Mrs Desmond when Lucy disappeared. Bert told them the sad tale. It was quite common, children disappearing in London, and it made Demara shiver to think about it.

'Got 'erself in the family way, Belle did,' Bert said delicately. 'An' knock me sideways if she wasn't thrilled. Expect 'er to be down the back street gettin' rid of it, 'er in the theatre like, but no! Delighted she was. An' little Lucy was born. She doted on that little girl, doted. Loved 'er so much it was soppy. All the love that good woman was capable of, love she never gave 'er gentlemen friends she gave to 'er daughter. An' Belle Desmond is capable of a lot of love, I can tell you – you can *see*!'

They nodded. Indeed they could see Mrs Demond's eager ability to bestow love, to scatter it around abundantly on all God's creatures: on Bert, on themselves, on Cordelia the cat. 'All the love she is capable of was lavished on her child.' Bert sighed and shook his head. 'Used to get a pork-pie from The Horse and Hounds down the road for 'er mum. Everyone knew 'er. All loved 'er. All around the Square they'd call "good evening" to 'er. Safe as 'ouses we thought 'er. Well, one night she went out as usual for beer an' a pork-pie and never came back!' He spread his hands helplessly and looked at them sorrowfully. 'Vanished,' he continued. 'Not a sighting of her. She never was seen again.' He sat down and buried his head in his hands and the sisters sat still and waited. After a moment he looked up at them. 'Mrs D near lost her reason. Did really, now I come to think of it. Was out of 'er 'ead a year, I reckon. That was five years ago. Lucy'd be sixteen now. Little Lucy sixteen.' A faraway look came into Bert's eyes as he tried to imagine an older Lucy. 'Sixteen,' he whispered, then pulling himself together he added, 'Mrs D never set foot on the boards again. Never acted since. Said she 'adn't the 'eart. God's truth. Changed too, so she did.'

'How?' Maeve asked breathlessly.

'Well, she put on weight. She was ample but nice before, but she got stout, like you see. An' 'er accent slipped. Used to talk posh before, but it went with Lucy, the accent did. She cared about nothin' since. Till you came.' He looked at them seriously. 'I'm that grateful to both of you. It's good to 'ave you 'ere.' He held out his hands and pressed theirs in his firm grip. 'I keep looking for 'er,' he told them. 'Lucy. I stare at every face I see. On the omnibus, in the street, everywhere I go, everything I do, one eye is cocked to search the crowd in case she be there.' He looked at them, eyes glittering. 'And one day she will be. One day she'll be standing there.'

Demara insisted on going to Eaton Square and remained in that employment. She did not want to close all doors behind her and was mindful of Mrs Desmond's own advice to provide against misfortune. She was worried about the blind faith her sister had in the ageing actress, for although she warmed to the dear woman they did not really know if she was trustworthy and consistent. After all, Demara said, they had not known her above a few days.

'She could throw us out tomorrow, Maeve, an' then where would we be! The workhouse, like as not!'

'Oh she won't do that, Demara, not Mrs D,' Maeve reassured her.

'Well, we don't *know*. I'm going to Eaton Square, so I am, until I find another opening. Have you forgotten that we need money for Da? He's depending on us.'

Maeve sighed. 'No, I don't *forget*. You never let me. But listen, Demara, I'm going to make much more than fifteen shillings a week as an actress, you'll see.'

Demara hooted. 'That'll be the day. I'm worried, Maeve, at the daft ideas this woman has put in your head.'

But Maeve was not listening. 'Before this year is out, Demara,' she cried, 'Da'll have paid off Lord Lester an' you an' I'll be leading the grand life entirely.'

Demara shook her head. 'I don't *want* to lead the grand life, Maeve,' she cried. 'I want to go home. Home to Ballymora. Home to Bannagh Dubh.'

'Home? To Ballymora! That place? You must be daft, Demara.'

Demara did not reply. No one ever understood her, no one at all. Bert Hockney and Belle Desmond thought foggy old London was the hub of the universe. Áine and Lorcan had kicked the soil of Ireland off their feet with relief and so had Maeve. Her father and mother thought her fortunate to be away from their meagre existence, the daily toil, the hard grift. They did not see that working under the sky, out in the fields, or looking through the cottage window at the mountains was infinitely preferable to labouring in the dark hallways and toilets of other people's houses with never a glimpse of beauty, never a sight of God's creations. All of them ached for prosperity, financial security, financial gain. They said things like,

125

'When we get the money we will.' Well, Demara thought, suppose the money never comes? Does one wait all one's life in hopes? There was so much to enjoy without that. She courted insecurity. She craved the land with all its unpredictability. No one had ever understood or shared that dream. Even Duff didn't understand her. He talked of freedom and workers' rights and fair rents and how everyone would be happy *when* this state of things was made law. Well, suppose it never was? Why waste one's life anticipating? Putting off living until something happened? And what was all that about anyway, except money, and the good life, and security?

But she, she wanted Bannagh Dubh and the crashing waves, the huge mass of purple and green and burgundy mountains, the swans on the lake and the smell of the land, and a house – she could see it now – rising silver-stoned beside the cool green waters, beautiful white statues beside the trees and in the groves. She could see it all as she scrubbed the floors, scraping the stains with her nails, on her knees, her back aching. She could visualize each path and buttress, each room, each statue, pavilion, terrace, nut and joint, and it gave her the strength to go on, face to the ground, all day, every day. And that dream separated her from the others. Oh they laughed together, talked, and she slept in the same bed with her sister, but the others shared a common ambition, a common language, a mutual understanding, and when she tried to share her dream with them, she could see by their baffled faces that they did not understand her.

Maeve, on the other hand, was glowing with excited anticipation. Mrs Desmond was coaching her in the Thespian art. She was learning the tricks of the trade, how to move gracefully, and use large gestures, how to declaim, how to enunciate, how to project so that her voice would reach the back row of the Gods.

'Most important place, dearie, for if you don't thrill the Gods they stop the show. You have to bring the curtain down. That's how powerful they are.'

Maeve learned how to move an audience to tears or laughter at will.

126

Mrs Desmond lost her Cockney accent teaching Maeve and spoke in a grand and plummy voice that commanded attention.

'Yes. The Gods can bring the curtain down!'

'How, Mrs D, how?'

'Why, with booing and hissing and catcalls, that's how,' Mrs D explained. 'Oh the nobs is too polite unless it is really bad. Too stuffed they mostly are, after dinner, you know. But the Gods! You have to woo 'em. Win 'em. Now you try again, dearie.'

She taught Maeve how to use a fan to good effect – 'So's you can play Restoration comedy: Goldsmith, Congreve, Farquhar.' She breathed the names as Brigid used to breathe the names of the saints.

She taught Maeve how to laugh, which she said was the most difficult thing to do. 'Cold, on the stage, half-dead with first-night nerves, oh, my dear, you can tell the calibre of an artist by whether he or she can laugh out loud and sound spontaneous.' She taught Maeve to cry on cue. She taught her how to take an audience into her confidence, flirt behind a fan and she taught her how to get a laugh. She taught her about double-takes, slow burns. 'You gotta play to each member of the audience, duckie,' she told her willing pupil. 'You gotta make them feel you're talking to him or her alone.'

Maeve loved her tuition. She learned quickly. In fact Mrs Desmond said to Bert one foggy day in March six months after they had arrived, 'She's nearly ready. Oh it was a fortuitous day you brought the Donnellys here, Bert Hockney. Fortuitous day indeed!'

'I'll say it was,' Bert agreed and watched Mrs Desmond's face glow with good feeling. She had changed since the Donnellys had taken up residence in her home. She was less prone to tears, more to laughter these days. She looked forward to each day instead of dreading it. She had a purpose, an aim.

'You sound much more like your old self, Mrs D,' Bert said to her. 'And your accent is getting grander, posher, your voice, if I may say, is riper, like an organ again.'

Belle laughed. 'Well, it 'as to, dunnit,' she joked. 'How

127

can I teach Maeve how to enunciate if I talk like a fishmonger from Billingsgate?'

Bert himself felt life was sharper. It had more of an edge since the sisters came to Soho Square. And Maeve bloomed like a flower in May. Only Demara remained a problem.

She grew paler and thinner and seemed lifeless and despondent. Mrs D grew concerned about her and she sent Bert to the Smithfield slaughterhouse to procure a cup of blood for her to drink every day, to strengthen her and prevent tuberculosis.

'For she's in a very run-down condition and she'll get sick if she's not careful.'

Belle Desmond did not understand why Demara couldn't simply accept fifteen shillings a week to send to her father in Kerry. She was quite happy to pay that sum for the privilege, she said, of helping her protégée and they could pay it back out of Maeve's earnings, later, when she began to work.

'For she will, you'll see. And she'll make a great stir.'

But Demara did not feel so optimistic about Maeve. When she saw her sister standing in the parlour declaiming great speeches to Mrs Desmond she was full of misgivings and could not shake off the feeling that the old actress was living in a fool's paradise.

They both tried to persuade Demara to give up the skivvying but she refused and would not accept the money, saying it was not right. She trudged out with Bert before the first light streaked the sky, a thin figure, tired even at dawn.

Bert on the other hand was eager to get to work. He loved his omnibus and the three bays that drew it: Daisy, Molly and Toe. He loved his passengers and looked forward to greeting them each day.

But, worried about Demara. Being of a sympathetic nature he felt drawn to the weak and helpless so it was natural that he should be tenderly concerned about her. Maeve was so happy and seemed to flourish. She hardly noticed Bert now except as an audience in Mrs Desmond's parlour. She was completely tied up with her theatrical tuition. Demara looked so dejected, so downcast that the young man felt it his mission to cheer her, to bring a smile to her lips. He mistook her low spirits for weakness and felt her in need of protection.

Demara was not weak. She was homesick. Longing for Ballymora ate at her soul, gnawed at her spirit. On top of that she was desperately worried about her family. Maeve was too busy to notice the passing of time, but as the weeks flew by there was little or no news from the Donnellys in Kerry.

Demara could not seem to find out what was happening. Maeve went to see Áine for news, choosing times when Lorcan would be at the public house, and, she told Demara, after the first few moments everything was all right between them.

'It was all a misunderstanding, Demara,' Maeve said, after her first visit. Demara could not go for she worked all day. Maeve dismissed the past as if it never happened. She snuggled up to Demara in the warm bed, in her white flannel nightgown, close to her sister's warmth. 'Oh, she assured me it was merely a storm in a teacup.' Maeve's voice sounded musical and low, and Demara thought not for the first time how posh her sister's speech had become, how English. Like Lady Lester. She had also noticed how Mrs Desmond had lost her accent and rarely dropped an aitch or mispronounced her vowels. Both of them, Demara mused, got grander day by day, sounding mellifluous and just a tiny bit theatrical.

'Well, that's very convenient for her,' Demara remarked, and it never occurred to her that she too was picking up Maeve's accent and speech patterns. 'Still she'll be glad enough we're gone, I'll be bound,' she added.

After a long delay Áine gave her a letter from their mam. It was brief, she told Demara – all it said was that they were well and she hoped Maeve and Demara were happy with her and Lorcan, and that they said their prayers and went to Mass on Sunday.

'And that's all. That is what was in the letter. It was written by Brindsley, Demara, and it seemed all right to me.'

'Well, I think something is wrong,' Demara said.

'Ah no!' Maeve seemed positive. 'If there was anything wrong Mrs D says we would definitely hear about it. No.' Maeve screwed up her eyes. 'It's the post. That was what it was. The post.'

'Well, I only know that Áine said that kind of a delay never happened before.' Demara was still worried.

'She didn't look too good, Demara,' Maeve told her sister. 'She looked to me like as if, well . . . ' She hesitated, then glanced at Demara. 'I know it is silly to say, but she looked like Carmel O'Gorman.'

'You mean. . .?'

'Yes. I thought she had a black eye.'

Demara propped herself up on her elbow and stared at her sister in amazement. 'No, Maeve, you must have been wrong. I can't believe it.'

'Well, I'm only telling you what it looked like to me,' Maeve said tartly. 'That's all. I'm going to sleep now, Demara. Don't worry so.'

She smiled and Demara thought how very beautiful she looked, the lace at her throat, her cloudy dark hair framing her heart-shaped face, her violet eyes luminous and large. She looked very happy, very content.

'Oh, Demara, we're so lucky,' she breathed. 'So very fortunate. Mrs D is such an angel. Just think, we could still be with Áine and Lorcan in that awful place. It's so lovely here.' She stretched. 'So comfortable. So warm.' She snuggled down, seeing this room as the fulfilment of all her dreams. No yearning for the wild Atlantic disturbed her serenity, no dreaming of castles and lakes, of mountains and statues. She was perfectly content, at peace, and like a puppy, grateful to the person who gave her sustenance and warmth.

Demara sighed and wished that she too could live within the day, that she could stem this ache for her own land that tore her so cruelly apart, that she could put aside the dream that consumed her.

It seemed, however, impossible.

She decided to go and see Áine herself, although working in Eaton Square left her no opportunity. Then fate took a hand.

She had come home one night from her daily labour. It was Friday and she found Maeve and Mrs Desmond sitting in the living-room practising curtsies. Bert had gone out, they told her, to purchase eel stew and beer and they were looking forward to a delicious supper. They were startled when, in the midst of their happy chatter, Demara burst into a storm of tears. Their laughter ceased abruptly and Maeve rose in consternation from her curtsy and ran to her sister, knocking down some Limoges china from an occasional table.

Demara never cried.

'Oh dearest, what is it? Oh dear, dear Demara, don't cry, please. You frighten me when you do. You're supposed to be the strong one. Oh don't dearest, don't.'

But Demara's sobs continued, uncheckable, a torrent of pent-up frustration and exhaustion. Strong, tough even in surroundings she knew and loved, the strange stone city had sapped her energy and left her worn out.

Mrs Desmond took command of the situation. She stood up, her rouged cheeks shaking, her body quivering with emotion. 'Now you listen to me, my gel,' Belle said firmly, 'You are being stupidly stubborn and mulish. It is not doing you any good whatsoever skivvying in that place, you hear me?' She resettled her bosoms over her corsets comfortably, shifting them with her lower arm. '*Stiff-necked pride,*' she emphasized, 'never got *anyone anywhere*! You take what's offered in this life, for I'll tell you, without a doubt it'll not be offered twice. You can *die* in the poorhouse, your pride intact, I do assure you. I've seen it happen.' She sat down again. Demara had shut-up. Sobs shook her body every now and then and Maeve patted her on the back, but Mrs Desmond had her audience, 'Why Sally Letts, R.I.P. Sleeping in Highgate Cemetery she is now, God help her, "I'll take help from no man!" Sally used to say over and over again. I heard her with these very ears. We played together, *Love's Labour Lost* in Sadler's Wells. She said it to me more than once, waiting in the wings to go on. As if it were some wise and wonderful pronouncement. Bah! She disapproved of me. Thought I

131

was mercenary. Alas, she lived to realize I spoke only the truth. She gave her all for love. Never counted the cost. Refused help grandly. Never mind that he was a rogue and a swine for all that he was a handsome devil. Get a little something from him, I told her, but she scorned my advice. Well, he left her, so he did, when she got into the family way, and she died, she did, giving birth in the poorhouse down in Bethnal Green. Wouldn't ask for help. Wouldn't accept it. I would have helped. So would the rest of the company at the Wells, but no. Stiff-necked pride.'

'Mrs Desmond . . . Demara . . . you were saying . . .' Bert prompted, for Belle had fallen into thought.

'Oh yes. Beg pardon. I strayed. Still, it was to the point. Thank you, Bert, for reminding me.' Then she cleared her throat and announced, 'Little Mary Jacks.'

They all looked at her blankly.

'Little Mary Jacks as does for us here,' she explained. A little waif from the Convent of the Sisters of Mercy lived in the basement and cleaned the house for Mrs Desmond. She was sly, lazy and unappealing and Mrs Desmond had been known to repeat on many occasions that Mary Jacks was more of a hindrance than a help and that Mrs Desmond intended to send her back to the convent.

'Palms things, she does. The sisters warned me about her but she is worse than they said. Have to check her every time she goes out. Even then she slips out behind my back, cunning little chit, takes half the house. An exaggeration, my dears, but she would if she could and no doubt sell the booty in the market.' Belle had a fierce light in her eyes, 'Well,' she continued, 'I quite made up my mind to dismiss her and tell the nuns she was not up to scratch when I found her with one of my silver-framed photographs down her apron, and I wouldn't mind but it is a likeness of my lovely Lord Hunt who gave me the emerald ring, a kinder man you never met, and a more generous one would be hard to find, and that is the only likeness of him. . .'

'Mrs D . . . the job . . .' Bert prompted.

'Oh yes! Well. I hoped you wouldn't take offence, and no offence intended, only the best intentions mind, but I thought why not Demara for the job. I could pay you two pounds a week, if you do the job well, and I shall be quite a hard taskmaster—' Here Maeve burst out laughing, but Belle hurried on. 'You must be better value than Mary Jacks, an' I have to have a skivvy here, an' it might as well be you.' Mrs Desmond flopped back in her sofa and mopped her face with a large handkerchief. 'Well, what do you say? You must agree, an' it's reasonable to see that I need someone. I pay better than the skinflints up in Belgravia and the work will be more interesting. Housekeeping. Cooking. I'm getting far too old and fat for the execution of such duties and I'm too busy with your sister and I *need* someone, Demara. You would be here, in this house, cosy and snug with us, me and Maeve and Bert. Oh, I think it will suit famously if only you will agree.'

'How could you refuse, Demara?' Maeve demanded and her sister, in truth, could not think of one reason. It seemed churlish to refuse and she agreed with, truth be told, relief and gratitude. She felt confident that Mrs Desmond would demand less of her than of a convent maid but she would circumvent that by taking upon herself extra duties and more work than any maid would willingly do.

So she agreed amid cheer and congratulations. She wept a little and Bert wiped her tears, saying it was natural. She felt weak and emotional. She had been working too hard for too long, without the warmth of human intercourse, without friendship, and now in this companionable atmosphere she felt vulnerable because of the obvious affection felt for her, the concern shown.

She left Eaton Square. Mrs Croxley was grudging, not at all pleased that she had to find a new skivvy and very surprised that Demara did not need a reference. She rolled her eyes and asked in a sarcastic tone, 'Well for some! Find a nice gentleman to take care of you, did you?' Demara shrugged and didn't answer. She had not realized how much she had hated her work until she turned her back on Eaton Square and walked down Sloane Street, crossed the Park, feeling, for the first time in London, free.

Mrs Desmond suggested she take the next day off and go and see her sister in Whitefriars Street. Mrs Desmond was inquisitive by nature and added to that was her facination with every facet of the sisters' lives, therefore she felt that both of them would work better if their minds were at rest about Áine and the family.

'No one ever worked better with an anxious mind,' she told them. 'So you go and find out what's happening.' And she packed Demara and Maeve off to see their sister.

Áine was pregnant again. She told them in tones that suggested she was far from pleased, eyeing their pretty clothes jealously.

'Why are you unhappy about it, Áine?' Maeve asked gently. 'After all, Seaneen is a darling boy and you and Lorcan love him.'

'God, what's love got to do with it?' Áine asked bitterly. 'We can't afford it an' I'll have to give up skivvying in a few months. Jasus, then we'll have te feed another mouth.'

'Áine, don't worry. I'll help if I can,' Maeve cried.

'An' what can you do? Ye think ye'll have a career on the stage an' ye must be owa yer mind. You! On the stage? God, what a laugh!' She picked Seaneen up and began undressing him. She glanced at them and commented, 'You seem to have fallen on your feet.'

'You make that sound as if we shouldn't have good luck.' Maeve was becoming irritated by her sister's complaining.

'Oh no. It's just that ye always land cushy.'

Lorcan came in, and seeing the sisters there threw his eyes up to the ceiling and stormed into the bedroom. Áine looked frightened.

'At least we're wanted in Soho Square. Mrs Desmond *likes* having us around,' Maeve stated loudly.

'What news from home?' Demara asked.

'Oh, I got a letter. From Mam. Written by Brindsley.' Áine shook her head. 'It sounds odd though. Almost as if they are hiding something. But Mam says they are all right. Well, she says, they're all well. She put down a cross and so did Da. Everything, Brindsley says, is fine.'

'Then there's no call to worry?' Maeve sounded relieved.

'I don't know,' Áine was not going to give them peace of mind. 'I thought the letter sounded, well, worried.

That's all. But they said nuthin'.'

'I'd so love to go over there; make sure everything is all right.'

'What could be wrong, Demara?' Maeve asked. 'What on earth could be wrong?'

Demara stood, preparatory to leaving. She shook out her skirts, reluctant on this day that had brought a new beginning for her to dwell on depressing thoughts or speculations. She sighed, kissed Áine and took Maeve's arm.

'I really don't know,' she said. 'And perhaps everything is all right and we are just imagining problems where there are none.'

Chapter Eighteen

Lord Linton Lester rode over to Stillwater and drank a bottle with Bosie from the yard of claret laid down for the Marquis at his birth. At least that is what the Marquis claimed and Linton had to agree it had a superb flavour, a magnificent bouquet. The sale of the river property and land pertaining thereto, including the cottages, was quick and effortless. Linton Lester congratulated himself and wished he could enjoy his claret a little more but the presence of the buyer was off-putting and spoiled a chap's pleasure and made him feel uncomfortable.

The Marquis was a big man, his body showing signs of excess, but not yet flabby. His face was soft and jowly and his eyes were lifeless. Linton always felt he was looking into the eyes of a fish when he met Bosie's vacuous stare. But it would be silly to underestimate the Marquis's sharp mind. He had wheeled and dealed, amassing a fortune in, it was whispered, ways the fashionable world would not condone. However they were glad enough to help him spend it, having no scruples about that.

Linton Lester did not care how the money was come by provided he could pocket some of it. He was always a little nervous in the Marquis's presence, under the slippery gaze of those fishy eyes.

'Sorry I couldn't shift the *hoi polloi*,' he said flippantly, smirking man to man at Bosie.

'Don't worry, old chap, I'll see it is taken care of, never fear.'

'See Muswell about it. I would.' Linton advised rolling a mouthful of the claret around his tongue. 'Excellent grog, Bosie. Excellent.'

Having advised the Marquis to bring in Muswell, Linton Lester thought that he had done his duty. Besides the bottle was empty, so he rose to take his leave. 'Must be off, Bosie. Things to do.'

Bosie looked up at him uninterestedly. 'What things?'

'Well, I'm taking the mater to London *tout de suite*.' Linton laughed nervously.

'Take the papers into Aeronson down below in his office, Linton. He'll look after you.'

Aeronson was Bosie's bailiff and general manager of the estate. Linton nodded as Mrs Black the housekeeper entered. She waited until Lord Lester had gone, then as the door shut behind him she asked, 'Will you want to visit my lady today, m'lord?'

Bosie glanced briefly at her. 'Don't know yet,' he replied indifferently. He noticed that a frown crossed Mrs Black's forehead and he suddenly turned swiftly as a cat and hissed, 'I'll do what I wish, when I wish, Mrs Black. Is that quite clear?'

She curtsied swiftly. 'Yes, sir. Indeed, sir.'

'Then go to your mistress and tell her that.'

Bosie smiled his frigid smile and listened to the pacing footsteps overhead. He would not be ordered about in his own home. He pressed a bell near him and after a moment Melrose his butler entered. 'Tell Aeronson to come and see me, Melrose, would you? When he has finished with Lord Lester.'

'Yes, my lord.'

He could have asked that young whippersnapper Lester

to tell his manager to come up to the big house but Bosie did not like anyone speculating on his actions. Linton Lester's suggestion that Muswell clean up the cottagers was a good one. The man was ruthless and would do his dirty work for him. He smiled. Those stupid cottagers! Setting themselves up against the gentry. Fools! Didn't they know that they could not win? No one ever did against the power of money and influence. He smiled a cool mirthless grin and decided to tell Aeronson to send for Muswell and sort these cottagers out once and for all. It was a pesky business and he, like Linton Lester, wanted to return to London. Everyone who was anyone would be in town now and Bosie was nothing if not anxious to play the social game. His great weakness was his desire to be included in all invitations. No, he amended, to *have* to be included. He did not mind being loathed. In fact he quite enjoyed people's dislike of him, and when nevertheless they were obliged to invite him to the soirées, dinners, parties and social events that London was a-buzz with, it was, for him, the perfect combination, a delicious irony.

However, London would just have to wait. This business with the cottagers took precedence over his social life and he'd better set about it with the ruthless single-mindedness he was famous for. Bosie sipped his claret and waited for Aeronson, grinning in his chair beside the great open fire, listening to the footsteps above him, pacing, pacing, pacing.

Chapter Nineteen

ᔐ ᕬ

Phil Conlon, the Lester bailiff, was in limbo. Having turned his gun on Lord Lester, he naturally enough lost his job. He was suddenly a hero and the lads bought him porter by the quart and he was slapped on the back and made to feel the great one, the cock of the walk, until he

suddenly left them speechless by moving in with Ma
Stacey. Everyone was shocked and did not know quite how
to react. Illicit relationships did not happen at all in rural
Ireland, according to anyone you spoke to. Now here was
the bold Phil living in sin, brazen and open for all to see,
flaunting his liaison with the widow. It caused quite a stir,
and not a little consternation.

They all knew that Phil and Ma Stacey shared the same
bed. There was only one bed in the shebeen. That was a
shocking situation but what could one do? One could
hardly cold-shoulder a man who had saved you from
eviction.

'Landed on his feet has Phil Conlon,' Mog Murtagh
muttered enviously. 'But then his luck's always in.'

They all waited with breathless interest for Father
Maguire's reaction, and indeed it was not long before the
irate cleric made his feelings plain. He ranted from the
pulpit about the certain damnation of fornicators and
lechers and was put off his stride for a moment when little
Moll Gilligan piped up in a piercing treble, 'What's a
fornicator, Mammy?'

However there were other matters to worry about and,
whereas the Phil Conlon situation would have taken
precedence over all else in normal times, these times were
far from normal.

Duff Dannon called a meeting of the men in Ma
Stacey's.

'We have te have a plan,' he told them.

'What plan?' Mickey O'Gorman was on his way to
mellow content, alcoholically speaking, before the bel-
ligerency set in.

'What plan?' Dinny McQuaid echoed. 'In the name of
God, what plan? Sure how can the likes of us plan?'

'I told ye. Right across Ireland the people are plannin'.
It's a fact. They're risin' up against tyranny.'

'What are they plannin'?' Brian Gilligan asked
nervously.

'Jasus, how to save their homes.' Duff tried not to sound
impatient at their obtuseness, their timidity, their blind
optimism. They had nothing to lose so why the hell

hesitate? They were threatened with eviction yet they quibbled and dithered and were afeared to break the law.

'We can send for the moonlighters,' he said softly, determinedly.

A sudden silence fell and the men shifted uneasily. They put down their pints and waited breathlessly.

'Isn't that goin' a bit far?' Billy O'Flynn asked.

'Listen to ye. Will ye listen! A bunch of lily-livered eejits ye are.' Pierce Donnelly stood up and surveyed them angrily. 'They'll come with an army an' throw ye out. Evict ye. Or the polis'll come with Lord Lester. They'll come in force with Linton Lester. They'll come with bullet an' buckshot an' we'll be done for. All our investment obliterated, gone! Out on the road we'll be wi' our wives an' children. Winter an 'twill be bitter cold, Cogger says. Right, Cogger?'

He looked at Cogger rocking in the corner of the hearth in his usual place. Cogger nodded vehemently. 'Oh 't-t-t-twill that,' he agreed.

'Are ye men or what?' Duff Dannon asked them. 'Giving in all the time. Hopin' against hope something or some-one'll save ye at the last moment.'

'Did last time,' Brian Gilligan muttered. 'Like the hand o' God.'

''Twas Pierce Donnelly's gun, not the hand of the Almighty, Brian. 'Twas Pierce Donnelly's courage an' the threat of bullets that saved us, not God,' Duff Dannon insisted.

'Mebbe it's the same thing,' Pierce said gently. 'Mebbe God Almighty inspired us, Duff an' meself. Mebbe He guided us an' mebbe it was His Hand. Mebbe He's tellin' us this is the only way.'

'That's sacrilege, man!' Brian Gilligan was shocked.

'God an' Father Maguire are *not* one an' the same, Brian, whatever the Devil ye think.'

'Well, well, well, an' we get the moonlighters,' Mog burst out, 'an' we're in thrall to them. An' what can they do?'

'Keep us in our homes, man, that's what they'll do.'

'Like prisoners,' Deegan Belcher cried.

'They're terrible tough, that's what I've heard. On us as well as them.'

They'd all heard of the moonlighters who had become a class of folk hero to the tenants of Kerry and Clare. They brought a distasteful violence to the land but they kept the people in their homes. Not that they instigated the violence, but rather they met force with force and recognized no court of English persuasion.

'I'm goin' to list the advantages an' the disadvantages, fellas,' Duff said. 'The advantages are, they'll meet force with force, they'll help us with men an' guns.'

'A siege!' Mickey babbled. 'I know siege. Father Ignatius told us about the Siege of Drogheda. They all died there. All of them. Hundreds of citizens starved to death. I'd rather be alive on the road than dead inside the house.'

'Sure how'll ye die with the hens in the yard an' the cow outside? Don't be daft man. Drogheda was a town!'

'What are the other advantages, Duff?' Pierce asked.

'Well, the gentry's afraid of them. They strike terror in the hearts of the landlords. They stop everyone working on the land for the owners. Harvests are not brought in . . .'

'But we've brought in this year's harvest,' Billy objected.

'That's as maybe, but there are other things to be done, as you know.' Duff shook his head, 'No, no one wants to tangle with the moonlighters.'

The men gathered sat quietly digesting this information, then Pierce asked, 'And the disadvantages? Tell us about those?'

'Well, we're lumbered wi' em then,' Deegan Belcher said. 'They come here an' take over. I've heard about them. Yer life's not yer own any more. They tell ye what to do. They run things.'

Duff nodded. 'Yes. That's so. They'll ask us . . . no, tell us not to pay rent. We'll *have* to agree. They'll moider any one of us if we break their rules. There'll be no more choosin'. Choice is out the window. They are savage in that. In return they'll see we are not thrown out.'

'Why would they insist we not pay rent? I thought they were on our side?' Dinny puzzled.

'That way they have power over the landlords. Bargaining power. Withholding labour. Withholding payments. And it's unity of purpose, that's their strength. It's civil disobedience with everyone actin' in concert. Together. That's the way they can't hurt us at all.'

'I don't understand,' Dinny cried plaintively.

'It was like what happened to the Widow Leary last year,' Duff said. 'A band of moonlighters reinstated her in her home. Now, see, the landlord, or more likely the agent, that bastard Sam Hussey – him an' Muswell are alike as two peas in a pod – well he could come next day an' throw her out. Only he couldn't because everyone was together. They dug their heels in an' eventually the landlord gave in. They had paid no rent, an' when the tenants pay no rent the landlord loses.'

'Wouldn't that be grand, payin' no rent.' This last had appealed to Mog Murtagh. He was contemplating the rosiness of that thought but Duff squashed his delighted anticipation.

'Ye don't pay it *until* the situation is resolved an' *then* ye pay it all. Back rent as well. Anyone who didn't put it away would be a fool.' He fixed a severe eye on Mog who dipped his nose swiftly into his drink.

'We'll have to do as they say?' Pierce Donnelly asked. Duff nodded. 'I have reservations on that one point,' Pierce said.

'So have I, Pierce,' Duff agreed. 'So have I. They take things pretty far, God help us.'

Pierce sighed. 'So does Lord Lester.'

At that moment Phil Conlon pushed through the door bringing a flurry of red leaves and the chill of the wind with him. He surveyed the group in the pub and they surveyed him. They were used to seeing him as the Lester bailiff and his *volte face* had left them unsure how to treat him. This uncertainty was further complicated by his relationship with Ma Stacey. They were not used to such brazen lack of discretion. So they looked at him blankly.

'They've sent for Muswell,' he announced, and all thought of his amorous dallying and past authority vanished, and an ice-cold fear entered their hearts. Lips tightened. Eyes widened. Breaths were drawn in sharply.

'The Agent? Muswell?' Pierce Donnelly asked in disbelief.

They all knew who he was. His fame had brought terror into the hearts of tenants everywhere. Muswell the Agent who stamped out civil disobedience, a man of cold dedication, a greedy man who liked money, a bully who enjoyed the execution of his duty and did not care even if he had to kill. A heartless man. Cold-blooded and pitiless.

'I'm sorry,' Phil said. 'I only just heard. That bastard Aeronson told me. We met at the Stillwater boundary. This land, here, this side of the river, yer homes, yer houses, this shebeen, sorry, Ma, has been sold to the Marquis of Killygally.'

They stared at him in disbelief. Mog Murtagh muttered, 'That bastard', and Cogger, picking up their alarm, began to make little moaning noises.

'Lord Lester's gone to London with Lady Kitty,' Phil continued. 'It will be a fight to the death.'

'Then we'll send for the moonlighters,' Pierce Donnelly announced firmly, all doubts gone. The others nodded. Circumstances had changed. The Marquis was in a different league to Linton Lester. He would show no mercy. They knew that.

'Are you with us, Phil?' Duff asked.

The ex-bailiff grinned and nodded. 'What do you think, Duff? O' course.'

'Then we must keep stout hearts within us, boys,' Duff cried and the men in Stacey's bar banged their pints on the counter and on the beer barrels and the windowsill and cried out, 'Send for the moonlighters! Send for the moonlighters! Send for the moonlighters!'

Cogger joined in, relieved that the tension seemed gone. The cry arose and was carried on the wind like distant drums to Grandma Donnelly in her chair, slipping in and out of her dreams. It was carried to the women and children in the houses who listened fearfully to the cry and wondered what it meant.

Chapter Twenty

cᴏɕ ɕᴏɔ

The men sent for the moonlighters. The Marquis sent for
Muswell, and a week later seven strangers arrived in
Ballymora. Six of them were together. They looked
curiously alike, as if they had dressed purposely to seem
anonymous and because of this they were startling. They
looked, the cottagers thought, like clerks, and in the
country clerks apparel appeared incongruous. They
arrived off Mog Murtagh's trap, looking like crows in their
dark garb, then alighting outside Granny Donnelly's
cottage they walked in a tight little bunch down the sandy
boreen, gawped at by the cottagers.

Grandma Donnelly sat outside on this fine autumn day.
She sensed the excitement in the little hamlet and didn't
want to miss any of the fun. She missed Demara. Brigid
had told her that Demara and Maeve were with Áine in
London, both girls were working, Maeve in a clothes shop
and Demara in a big house in Belgravia, and Granny
hoped they were both happy, but doubted it. Maeve
needed to express her artistic talent and Demara needed
Ballymora. Granny looked at the arrival of the strange
men. They seemed to her like angels of death. She
shivered and asked Brindsley to take her back inside.

The seventh man arrived by brougham and went
directly to Stillwater. He was a very large man, square of
body, thickly built, like a tree, oak-sturdy, ruddy of
complexion with a high hectic colour and a map of veins
visible just beneath his tough, brick-coloured skin. He
leapt up the flight of steps to the door with energy and
purpose and as he ran up the steps the six men in dark
suits were walking down the dusty path between the
cottages until they reached Duff Dannon's door, where
Duff was waiting in the lane to greet them.

Their leader, indistinguishable from the rest in his suit and high white collar, black boots and hat, put out his hand to Duff. '*Dias Mhuire gut*,' he greeted Duff in Gaelic. They shook hands, and Duff opened the half-door where Mary and his brother Christie stood, gawping at the strangers, and the men one by one bent double and entered the cottage and disappeared inside.

The others made their way slowly from their spectator positions to Duff's cottage. 'How'll he fit them all in?' Della Gilligan wondered to Brian. 'They shoulda gone into the Donnellys',' she whispered in scathing tones. 'They'd find it grand entirely there, what with the extra space Pierce Donnelly built on. It 'ud accommodate them much better.'

Up at the big house the Agent Muswell waited in the hall, warming his toes before the fire. He stood with his foot on the fender, a huge iron-wrought piece. Then he scraped some dirt off the sole of his boot. He smiled mirthlessly at the little pile of dried mud that had fallen. Some of it stuck in the trellis and he thought that would be extra work for the servant. He pulled his fingers from their joints making a cracking noise, then stood to attention as the Marquis of Killygally came down the wide sweep of the stairs.

'Welcome, old boy,' Bosie sang out but did not proffer his hand or invite the visitor to sit. He, however, threw himself into a wide-winged chair.

'Good journey?' The Marquis showed no interest in the answer.

'Yes, my lord.'

'All set for action?' Bosie's face was soft, but not his eyes. His eyes were contemptuous and angry. 'Keepin' me here, this blasted business,' he said.

'Yes, my lord,' Muswell nodded. He was used to the gentry. He thought them mindless, arrogant children playing with fire. His disdain for them was only exceeded by his detestation of the peasants.

His job was unpleasant and people hated him and the landlords despised him but he was indifferent. Because he was indifferent to the opinion of others he was strong. He earned a lot of money; his fees were high.

'I'll need some of your workers, my lord,' he said. 'Men who are not squeamish.' He looked at the man sitting there on the other side of the fireplace. Could he be called a man? Muswell tried to keep the contempt from his eyes. He had heard about the Marquis of Killygally. Fop, seducer of little boys, he was not someone to admire. He was not the sort of tough, hard-drinking, fisty man that Muswell admired.

The Marquis nodded. 'You shall have them,' he said indifferently.

'And you give me a free hand? I don't want recriminations afterwards when it is too late.'

The Marquis laughed. His eyelids were drooping. He had drunk deep the night before and was drowsy now. A shaft of sunlight dappled with the colours of the stained-glass window opposite playing on his face made him feel lethargic.

There was a long silence in the hall. A bluebottle buzzed and slammed itself against the window. It was very hot. The sun blazed in and the fire burned high and the Marquis of Killygally fought sleep.

Then the door at the end of the great hall opened and Melrose entered to announce, 'Mr Blackstock, m'lord.' And Vernon, his boots squeaking, marched up and joined them, a roll of papers in his fist. His glance lighted on Muswell and he gave him a brief nod. Then he looked at Bosie and realized why the Agent was there. He suppressed a shudder and bowed to the Marquis.

'I brought the papers to be signed, m'lord,' he said.

'Then the transaction is complete?' the Marquis queried.

'Well, they should be signed by Lady Kitty . . .'

'I told you, Lady Kitty is only the trustee. Linton is the rightful owner of Ballymora. You won't find a court in the land will find for the lady. So don't bore me with such trivialities please, Blackstock.'

'Very good, my lord.'

'Good. Good. I'll attend to that now. Melrose,' he called, 'serve Mr Blackstock a sherry. Linton gone? Did you leave him with Aeronson?'

'No, my lord. He has gone to London with Lady Lester.'

'Lucky dog! Well,' he glanced at Muswell, 'depending on this gentleman, I should soon follow him.'

Muswell watched impassively as Melrose poured a sherry for the solicitor and handed it to him. Neither man, the aristocrat nor the lawyer, paid any attention to him. He smiled coldly to himself.

Blackstock sipped his drink. He had done all he could to prevent this disaster. He had told the Marquis he should have Lady Lester's signature and if he chose to ignore his warning then there was nothing he could do about it. He was afraid that the Marquis was right. In a court case the judge would find for Lord Linton against his mother, she being only a woman. He looked at the Marquis, who went to the end of the vast hall to a heavy Jacobean desk and, picking up a quill pen, glanced through the papers. Blackstock turned back to Muswell.

'Looking forward to your work, Muswell?' He sipped his drink and looked with contempt at the huge man.

There was a knock and the Manager Aeronson entered. He was a small man, a tidy little man, neat as the columns of numbers he spent his time adding, subtracting, dividing.

'My lord . . .' He bowed obsequiously.

'Oh damn it, Aeronson, cannot you see I'm busy?' the Marquis shouted down the hall.

'Yes, my lord.' Mr Aeronson turned to leave.

'No, no, no, where do you think you are going?' the Marquis inquired. 'Sit, man, sit.' Then as Mr Aeronson moved across the hall to join Blackstock and Muswell: 'No, no, no, man. There, there, sit there next the door.'

Vernon Blackstock looked at the small man. He obediently sat by the door in the big chair there. He was the picture of acquiescence, his demeanour deferential, yet Vernon felt that underneath that façade there surged a simmering resentment and a feline cunning that was waiting, ready to come to the boil at the appropriate moment. Vernon turned back to the Marquis. There was the sound of the pen scratching and a log falling in the fireplace. No one spoke until Vernon Blackstock, realizing that Muswell had not answered him, repeated the question.

'Looking forward to your work, Muswell?'

146

'Not precisely *looking forward*, Mr Blackstock. Just doing my job. Like you,' Muswell replied, cocking his head, peering at the plump little lawyer. 'I don't *pretend*, Blackstock,' he continued. 'You sell land for Lester. You take no blame for that. Carrying out the boss's wishes. I simply do ditto. Only my boss wants me to ask these people to leave. It is his right.'

'Ask?' Blackstock could not keep the incredulity from his voice.

Muswell nodded sagely. 'I will do that, Blackstock. I will give them fair chance. Then if they refuse I'll have to resort to . . . em . . . firmer methods.'

'Like Kenmare? Where you burned a whole village?'

Muswell shrugged. 'The Earl wanted rid of those little cottages. Eventually they would have to be demolished.'

'Just like Ballymora?'

'Just like Ballymora,' Muswell agreed indifferently.

Vernon Blackstock sighed. There was no point trying to reason with this man. 'Then you'll be pleased to hear they've sent for the moonlighters,' he said and slyly waited for the effect it might have.

Muswell drew in a breath sharply and Blackstock had the satisfaction of seeing him disconcerted.

The Marquis's boots clattered on the floor as he returned down the hall to them, waving the documents he had just signed.

'Here you are, Blackstock. Your copies. I've kept the originals for Aeronson. All right and tight, sir, finished and done with.'

'Unless Lady Kitty takes action.'

'Against her son? Don't be silly, Blackstock. There's a good chap.'

'I have just been informed by Mr Blackstock here, m'lord, that the villagers have sent for the moonlighters.'

The Marquis looked at the Agent blankly. 'What the Devil are you talking about? Moonlighters? Sounds like a masquerade or a troop of strolling players.'

'No, my lord. No. They are violent men who help these cottagers in civil disobedience . . .'

'Violent? I thought civil disobedience meant that no

violence occurred? Well, don't bore me with details. That is what you are employed to deal with and you are being paid enough, Goddammit. We knew it would be a war? Eh, Blackstock? So get on with it, man, and don't bother me.'

Blackstock could not prevent himself throwing a gleeful little glance at the Agent.

'I'll need more money, m'lord,' the man said stubbornly. 'If I'm taking on the moonlighters I'll be entitled to more money.'

'All *right*, Muswell,' the Marquis said impatiently, his angry eyes snapping. 'Talk to Aeronson about it.' He gestured with his head to the door where the Manager still sat. 'He'll settle a fair fee with you. As I said, don't bother me now.'

The Marquis slammed the roll of papers into the lawyer's hand and strode to the door, which Melrose opened. The men rose and followed him out into the grey day. Melrose placed a caped coat over the Marquis's shoulders as he walked. He bid them a curt 'Good day, gentlemen' and without further ado crunched over the gravel, shouting over his shoulder, 'Good luck, Muswell,' a small crooked smile on his lips.

But the Agent was not listening or paying attention. He was wondering how a tiny hamlet of ignorant peasants had managed to get themselves backed by the moonlighters and a job he had thought he could breeze through could suddenly look so daunting. He did not bother to bid farewell to the Marquis but hissed angrily at Aeronson, 'Well, let's get the arrangements over, Aeronson, before we go any further. We have a lot to discuss.'

Aeronson smiled. He was a patient man and he could see at a glance that Muswell did not possess this virtue.

'Certainly, certainly, Mr Muswell, come with me, my good sir, come with me.' And he led the Agent down through the glen to his office.

Chapter Twenty-One

Fleur could hear them downstairs, not what they said, but the deep rumble of their voices. The gallery where she sat, tapestry on her knee, skeins of silk in a basket beside her, was directly above the great hall.

When she came here first she had not been allowed to sit in the gallery. She had been out of her head then. Like her mother. Bosie told her it ran in the family. He had given her shots of morphine to 'quiet' her and she had become so deranged that he became worried about her and asked Dr Martin to come and see her.

Dr Martin was a nice man and she liked him. He gave her laudanum to keep her balanced. He said he sympathized deeply and felt for her in her confused mental state and told her that the drugs would do the trick.

She had been here at Stillwater for a very long time but she had never been outside. She had sat in her rooms since Bosie had married her and brought her here. The tapestry was almost complete now. It showed a hunting scene, mediaeval ladies with cones and streamers of floating gauze on their heads and falcons on their wrists and gentlemen in doublet and hose riding through a forest with birds above them and deer ahead. But all Fleur could think of when she stared at it was what lay beneath the thick undergrowth and trees. She envisaged their tangled roots stretching beneath the soil, the slime alive with creeping, crawling things that ate your eyes out when you were in your grave and slid into your ears and mouth and up your nostrils. Down there the world was dark and blind things groped and bumped and turned and twisted and reproduced and did that awful dance that Bosie forced on her so often in those other, blood-red days.

All that was a long time ago. Now that she was nearly

blind, her eyes covered with a white film, he did not torture her much any more. He liked her to keep out of his way, though every so often he came to feed off her like a great bat.

It was a woman's duty, her mother once told her, to submit to her husband, and her mother smiled as she told her, as if it would be wonderful.

Fleur tried to remember the past, before she had come to Stillwater. That other time was shadowy and difficult to recapture, the memory elusive. It was a mirage in the back of her mind. It was a time when her mother had laughed and her big brother had come home from India, and the world was full of light. Life then was, in her memory, packed with happy, joyous activity. There was music and flowers in rooms golden with sunshine and her father tickled her and carried her on his shoulders. But it was all so far away, so lost. Like something that had happened to someone else. They had had tea on the lawn and her dresses were white and everyone said she was pretty and called her a princess. There were fairytales and the princesses in them were always rescued by a handsome prince.

Then that world had collapsed. It had happened when her papa had died and her mamma had lost her reason. The Marquis had come then and taken her away and married her and no one had rescued her. No handsome prince had ridden up and saved her and her nightmare had begun.

She did not like to think about those days. He had brutalized her. He had wiped out all the gentle past and forced her to do things that seemed to her hateful and monstrous. She had begged for mercy, pleaded with him, but he had gagged her then 'quieted' her.

Sometimes he had brought other men back with him and they had all done things to her, invaded her body, used her. They were so big and she was so small and frightened.

'You are my possession, Fleur,' the Marquis had told her, smiling. 'In law I can do what I want with you. Never forget that. Like my horse. Like my dog. Only you are not as important to me as they are.'

Mrs Black came to look after her when she got so ill and

Bosie was angry and beat her. After Mrs Black came he had not bothered her so much, and he went to London and only came home occasionally. Mrs Black told Fleur that women had no rights. Your father owns you, she said, and then he gives you to your husband, and your husband owns you and it is up to you to obey him. You must do as he bids for he is your lord and master.

Now she stayed in her rooms, shut off from the rest of the house, except to come down to the gallery with Mrs Black in attendance to stitch her tapestry.

She could hear him with the men below. She hoped he would go without coming up to see her. She had heard Vernon Blackstock and Mr Aeronson. She knew their voices but she had never come face to face with them. The big giant of a man she did not know. He was a stranger.

Did anyone know of her existence? She doubted it. No one ever looked up at her windows in the west wing. Except one man. A man who came and stood and stared up at her. Sometimes she fancied that their eyes met, only now she was nearly blind that could not be. He reminded her of someone – who? Someone from that other life, far away. Someone from the past.

He came at intervals and stood near the elm tree's shadow and stared up at her window and she glanced back at him, puzzled over where she had seen him before. But she had no interest in pursuing the matter, he was probably a dream and anyhow it was a long time since she had imagined him, that kindly face looking up at her window.

No one ever came to Stillwater to stay and Fleur thought that it was probably because of her. He was ashamed of her. She was disgusting. He told her so. She was not to be shown off. A failure of a woman, she was a nonentity to be kept hidden.

She didn't care any more. Once she had cried all the time and tried to escape, and tried to kill herself. He locked her in her quarters and sealed her windows and told Mrs Black to guard her, watch her. He had said she could never get away because the law was on his side. She was his possession. He kept her up all night playing cruel games with her.

Then that stopped. She was so grateful, so relieved, and

151

now she kept well out of sight and far from the world with only Mrs Black for company. She did not think that the people who came here knew she was here at all. Mrs Black never went out and only Mrs Vargan – the frugal, cold and stony-faced housekeeper – and Melrose the butler moved between the world outside and the one she inhabited within the walls of Stillwater. None of them wanted to lose their positions here so they kept a complete silence on the matter of Fleur, and though people gossiped and speculated, the servants of the Marquis of Killygally held their peace.

Time had no rhythm for Fleur. She sat and dreamed, or slept in fitful spells, or chased nightmares in broad daylight and wandered in her head and wondered when the men downstairs would go. She thought she heard Vernon Blackstock leave. She went to the window but there was no one there so she returned to her seat. She embroidered with nervous fingers and twice she pricked herself.

'Rest asy!' Mrs Black admonished. 'Rest asy.' But when she heard the sound of boots on the gravel outside Fleur rose to her feet and went to the window again.

Yes. It was the lawyer and that other man. She narrowed her eyes. The outlines were blurred for she could only see imperfect shapes. She could usually tell, nevertheless, who the people were.

She began to pace the gallery. If he was going to come up it would be now. Soon. She heard his voice below but it seemed to be receding. Pray God he did not bid them farewell then think of her. Then he would come up and take her wrist in a cruel grip and drag her behind him to his room. She shivered and paced.

'Rest asy,' Mrs Black urged her.

He was pacing too, below her, and she heard him laugh.

'He pays the bills!' Mrs Black said, and nodded, rocking in her chair.

Fleur went to the windows again. She saw her husband in his grey cloak walking away. She knew now that he would leave her alone. She let her breath out slowly. She went to her tapestry and picked up the skein of silk and began again to work. He would not come. She felt as if a burden she had been carrying had fallen from her. She could feel the silence shrouding her again. The peace. The perfect, tomb-like peace.

Chapter Twenty-Two

The man sat at the head of the table where Duff's brother's wife Mary usually sat to dish up the potatoes. The others stood behind him. Five of them. The man's face was as cold as Muswell's but there was a fanatic's light in his eyes.

'Ye sent for us,' he said, and the cottagers nodded.

'What is your name?' Duff asked.

'Call me Clancy.'

His face was thin, the skin stretched, barely covering his bones. The cuffs of his shirt hung loose on his wrists. His mouth was a straight line. The others, Duff thought, could be his brothers. They all had the same withdrawn and self-contained energy about them. Two of them were very tall, one with wild curls low on his brow had the looks of a travelling man and was short, but they all had that sober, intent look; thin white faces, out-of-the-sun faces. They stood bunched around the seated Clancy, straight-backed, to attention, like soldiers.

The villagers stood before them, equally close together, for confidence, and because the room was small.

'We must close this gap,' Clancy waved his hand towards the cottagers and then back to the men behind him, indicating the space between the villagers and the moonlighters. 'Our purpose is the same.'

'What do you want us to do?' Duff asked and Clancy looked at him sharply, sensing his reticence.

'Why are you cottagers always so feeble?' he asked.

'Ah now, come on, no need to be offensive,' Mog

Murtagh muttered.

'You are quite happy to ask others to fight on your behalf, but you balk at doing it yourselves,' Clancy finished, staring at them through narrowed eyes.

'We do not wish to break the law,' Pierce Donnelly said in a firm voice.

'We are God-fearing men,' Brian Gilligan added.

Clancy threw back his head and laughed mirthlessly. The men standing behind him remained impassive. Their leader shook his head as if astonished at man's stupidity. 'But you don't mind us doing it for you? Like Pilate you are giving an order for something to be done that you do not approve of?'

There was silence in the cottage. No one could think of what to reply.

'The laws are not of your making,' Clancy said slowly. 'They are not democratically instigated by a majority vote by the people of this country. They are the laws of a foreign power occupying your land and these laws are not in your communal interest. Also, you have no right of appeal or redress, no opportunity to change or register your objections to this foreign power? Is that not so?'

The cottagers nodded.

'But that's an ould story,' Mog Murtagh ventured. 'An' there's nowt we can do about it.'

'That's where you are wrong,' Clancy said firmly. The black material of his coat was worn and shiny, Pierce noted, and he did not look as if he had eaten in weeks.

'Once we were a nation of heroes,' the man said, anger in his eyes. 'In the mythological mould, we had Sarsfield, Wolfe Tone, Daniel O'Connell. Now it's bloody Parnell, pussyfooting around like a goddamn politician.'

'But he *is* a politician,' Pierce said emphatically. 'He's a politician and he is determined we get just what you are suggesting – our right to govern ourselves.'

'Well, it's not doing you much good now, is it?'

His eyes were glittering dangerously and his glance flickered over the men assembled there, crushed into the tiny room, eyeing him doubtfully. 'Oh yes, he'll bring it up again in Parliament and again, and again, until they yield

154

eventually.' He stressed the word, then repeated it, '*Eventually.* Then Salisbury or Gladstone will reverse it and we'll be back where we started.' He shook his head. 'No, men. It will not do. It is not enough. If we want to achieve anything for ourselves then this is war. War.'

They were silent, reluctant to commit themselves, fearful of action, nervous of what would be asked of them, antagonistic to him now.

Clancy sighed.

'Them's fighting words,' Dinny McQuaid said fearfully.

'Are you men or what?' Clancy asked tiredly. 'Jasus, they're taking your homes offa you. Will ye lie down under that?'

'No,' Duff cried. 'No, no, no. I for one will not.' He glanced around at his fellow tenants. 'Well?' he asked.

'I'll not let them push me around,' Pierce Donnelly agreed. 'But then I decided that long ago.'

'The rest of yiz?' Duff asked.

'Well, I don't want to take to the road,' Mog Murtagh said reluctantly.

'Me neither. 'Tisn't right.'

'Well, are ye behind us then?' Duff cried.

'Yes, yes, yes,' they cried on a rising tide of agreement. They all joined in now yelling 'Yes, yes, yes,' working up their sense of grievance. Running with the pack.

'God, yer easily led!' Clancy muttered and sighed, then continued, '*We* have created our own courts, our own laws. We have our own rules that suit *our* interests and we are not answerable to any foreign power.'

'How can you do that?' Duff asked.

'By democratic vote. We did it. It is done. Up and down the land our courts are in session irrespective of other authority. Just because the English say we must be ruled by their laws does not mean we have to obey. What is legal or illegal in their country is not necessarily so in ours. And the taking by force of our homes across the country, the evictions and terrorization of tenants is certainly not in our interests. Did you know we have support all over Europe? Did you know that pressure is being brought to bear from

155

France and Germany, Spain and Italy for the English government to moderate their treatment of the Irish?'

'Jasus, is that a fact?' Deegan Belcher was impressed. 'They know about us over there then? In those foreign places?'

'Oh, indeed they do. Indeed they do. This land is ours. It is our heritage. It was wrongfully purloined. Why should we pay enormous rents for what belongs by rights to us? Just because they tell us that is the law?'

The tenants nodded, agreeing. 'Our forebears owned Ballymora until the King of England gave it to the Lesters who came an' told us we'd have to pay for the privilege of working it for them,' Duff Dannon said.

'What do you do then?' Mickey O'Gorman asked, needing to find out precisely what would be required of him.

'We set up our own court here. Decide what is right for us and abide by that. We also decide what is wrong.' Clancy stood. 'And from now on we pay no more rents. Understood?'

'Yes. Oh yes,' Mog Murtagh rubbed his hands together in delight.

'And we wait,' Clancy stated.

'Where? Like where will yiz be? All of yiz?' Deegan Belcher demanded.

'Ah yes. One man in each household where there is another male. We will not foist ourselves onto widows and women living alone.'

A groan went up. No one wanted a stranger in their homes.

'And a barn? A building big enough to hold court and meetings?'

'There's Lally Flynn's old barn,' Shooshie Sheehan volunteered. 'Lally's dead now. Went off her skull. It's down below. It's been empty now for years.'

'All right,' Clancy sounded indifferent. 'Get the women to tidy it. Fix it up. Make it presentable. We will make a sign that says PEOPLE'S COURT and put it where it can be seen. Is that understood?'

'Yes, sir,' Dinny McQuaid said, touching his cap.

'Do not call me sir,' the tall man told them. 'My name is Clancy and I am an ordinary soul like yourselves.'

'He walked to the door and stared out. The men spilled into the boreen where the women clustered, trying to hear what went on inside. Clancy looked for a moment, then turned back.

'We make our own rules and simply stick to them. We do not threaten. We do not instigate violence.'

Most of the men were relieved to hear that, except perhaps Deegan Belcher who loved a fight and was very handy with his fists.

Clancy's eyes had become cold as ice and he added, 'But if they threaten us, do violence to us, then we do have the right to strike back. And in that event we are lethal.' He let the word hang on the air. 'We shoot accurately. To kill or maim effectively. We do not threaten idly. What we say we'll do we *do*.'

He looked at the group of men and sighed again. Except for Duff Dannon and Pierce Donnelly all he could see before him was a bunch of indecisive people with no real backbone, little conviction, no purpose, no ideals. They were content to be left alone to tend their own patch and did not want to be drawn into political commitment. They were selfish and self-protective and cared not a jot as long as they personally were not threatened. They had no ambition for their land, none for themselves.

'Is there a sympathetic lawyer hereabouts?' he asked. He did not expect that there was but it was a chance and would constitute a bonus. He asked as a matter of form, not expecting a positive reply. To his surprise he was wrong. Apparently there was.

'A Mr Blackstock, sir . . . er . . . Clancy,' Pierce told him.

Duff nodded. 'Yes. Vernon Blackstock is on our side. Oh, he'll not do anythin' to jeopardize his position. But he helps us.' Same old story, Clancy thought; sympathetic to the cause but careful not to make his position public in case the powerful were angered.

'I'd like to see him,' he said.

'He lives below in Listowel. We'll send Mog in the cart to fetch him.'

157

Mog nodded, delighted to do this little errand.

'That is all then.'

Dinny McQuaid cleared his throat. 'Em . . . do we pay ye?' he asked timidly.

'We're not rich men,' Deegan Belcher added.

'Don't insult us, man.' Clancy showed some anger for the first time. 'We take no money, only a roof over our heads and simple food in our bellies.'

'God be praised,' Brian Gilligan sighed. 'For we're humble people and have little.'

'Why do you accept that?' Clancy asked him, throwing him into confusion.

'Beg pardon?' Dinny blinked.

'Why should you be so humble, have so little? Eh? You work hard, do you not?'

'All the hours God gives,' Dinny assured him. He sighed in a resigned manner and Clancy looked at him impatiently.

'There is nothing to be proud of in your attitude,' he told Dinny.

'If you stood up for yourselves you could be comfortable. Think of it, in America, working as you do now, you would be very comfortable indeed. Think on that.' He stood in the doorway looking at them. 'Ye've got to fight for your rights, not feebly give in.'

They stood around him, their heads bowed and he wanted to cry. 'Let's look at this barn,' he said and went out into the bright day.

Chapter Twenty-Three

໐ ໐

The days passed. In London Maeve and Demara were getting their bearings but here in Ballymora the leaves, gold, red, russet, bronze and magenta, blazed on the trees, then drifted down the river, or settled in soggy piles beside the fields. The mists were thick pearly swirls and hid the headland morning and night, and the air was chill and fresh.

The cottagers became used to the strangers in their midst but they never lowered their guard, they remained formal and distant. They were not unfriendly, simply not friendly. And the same applied to the strangers. They too kept their distance.

Clancy spent most of his time down in the barn where the men mended the roof and patched it up until it was habitable. The women polished it and decorated it, and a large sign was painted as Clancy had requested, PEOPLE'S COURT writ large for all the world to see.

Father Maguire had harsh words to say about the strangers. Denouncing them from the pulpit he deplored the tendency to go against authority.

'God did not put Englishmen in charge for no good reason,' he yelled at them. 'They are a superior race. They are *meant* to be the masters Look at Jerusalem in Christ Lord Jesus' time. The Romans were in charge then, were they not? Eh? An' what did He say? Render to Caesar the things that are Caesar's and to God the things that are God's. Eh? Well then, so much more must ye bow yer heads to the English overlords until God Himself takes a hand and crushes them underfoot. Turn the other cheek, bretherin, turn the other cheek.'

'Mebbe Christ's taking a hand by guiding us. Mebbe the strangers are Christ's messengers?' Pierce Donnelly called up to the pulpit.

There was a stunned silence. No one had ever done that before, shouted back at the priest and he in full flow in the church. The congregation stared open-mouthed at their priest. Father Maguire drew in a breath through his teeth. 'Yer a hard man, Pierce Donnelly,' he yelled from the pulpit. 'That's the second time ye've blasphemed in the house of the Lord.'

'The Bishops have agreed with us.' The voice they had, by now, all become accustomed to rang out and the congregation turned their heads to see Clancy standing at the church door.

'The Bishops, ye say? I doubt it, young fella-me-lad. Comin' here, bringin' violence an' discord. Spawn of the Devil.'

But the man in his black suit standing at the door was not to be disconcerted. 'Jesus Christ condemned oppression, Father. What do you say to Mr Muswell down now in the valley tryin' to cast Grandma Donnelly out of her home?'

Pierce let out a bull-bellow, leapt up and charged down the aisle towards the church entrance. Clancy stood there, his hand halting the angry man. 'Hush now. Softly. Softly. Come one, come all. In a battalion. Orderly.'

And, as the congregation rose in a body and stood, he led them out of the church to Father Maguire's cries of, 'Stop, stop. Come back here at once. I'm not finished wi' ye. The voice of Satan is calling ye and ye are damned that listen to his call.'

'My old mother is being manhandled, Father, and you are up there blethering about doin' nothin'? Are ye a human being or are ye a fool entirely?'

'If that is what God wants us to do then He's not a very nice person an' I for one don't want to know Him,' Brigid Donnelly said primly, and followed her husband as he left the church with the others.

In a moment it was empty and Father Maguire was left in the pulpit ranting to thin air.

They followed Clancy down the hill in orderly fashion, men in front, followed by the women and children. The day was bright and the air clear. The leaves scudded in flurries from the trees and clouds soft as puffballs raced across the cold blue sky.

'How'd you know what was happening?' Duff asked as he strode along.

'My men were on watch-out. They signalled me,' Clancy replied.

The people did not notice the weather or feel the knife-cold breeze from the sea to their left. They hurried along and all they could think of was Pierce Donnelly's mother being disturbed. They all knew her. They protected her in her old age. She should not be troubled by the rough hands of strangers. She should be left in peace rocking in her chair, her life slowly reaching its natural conclusion.

She was weeping. She was looking at the flames licking her roof and she was sobbing helplessly, bewildered, calling out her son's name.

When they reached that first cottage the crowd began to murmur. Anger bubbled and welled up in their hearts.

Muswell stood outside the neat little cottage, solid as a rock and as impervious. He had carried the old lady in her rocking-chair out into the boreen and set her down then set fire to her roof. She had taken nothing of her memories with her, no trinket, no memento was allowed her, even her shawl was inside the house.

There were six men from Stillwater and they stood behind Muswell looking vaguely shamefaced. With them were the policemen from the nearest town. They shifted from foot to foot, embarrassed and uncomfortable at the shameful action. It was their job to see there was no trouble, but they resented the task and felt it had nothing to do with them.

Muswell had waited until they were all at church. If Clancy had not warned them the whole village could have been demolished in their absence.

They looked at Clancy now for guidance. 'Calmly now!' he warned. 'Ye know what to do.'

'So it's you!' Muswell caught sight of him.

'Yes. It's me.' Clancy answered and he pointed to where his men, well drilled, were walking from the pump up the hill to Granny Donnelly's cottage. Each one was carrying a bucket of water. Quietly, efficiently, three other men were throwing damp tarpaulin ships' sails procured from Brian Gilligan over the flames on the roof. They lay on them, fixing them down, and the others passed them the buckets and they doused the sizzling sailcloth with the water. Under Clancy's direction the men went to their homes, tucked guns in their belts, got the buckets which were sitting in readiness behind their front doors, took them to the pump and, making a line, passed the full buckets up the line to the men on Granny Donnelly's roof.

'Get your men away from here, Clancy,' Muswell was shouting. 'In the name of the law!'

'We do not recognize that law here, Muswell. Evictions are not legal here. If you want to know what the law is here why don't you come down to Lally Flynn's barn and find out.'

Muswell snorted but in spite of himself he was disconcerted. This crowd was organized to an unexpected degree and it bothered him.

'Get those men away from the cottages, Clancy, or I'll . . .'

'Or what, Muswell?' Clancy asked, turning to the big man, 'Or you'll shoot the old lady? Just your style! She is eighty-one years, Jesus sake! Eighty-one!'

Clancy could hear the angry murmur of the crowd at his words. He knew the effect they were having on the neighbours. Also on the police who hated the situation they found themselves in.

The wind blew grey clouds of smoke inland and the acrid smell of burning thatch filled the air. Granny Donnelly wept helplessly, unable to understand what was happening. She had slipped out of the rocking-chair and onto her knees and she wrung her hands, white hair streaming in the wind, keening.

'Where's Demara?' she kept asking over and over. 'What's goin' on? There's men in the house – strangers. They're firin' the house. Oh, Pierce my son, my son, don't let the men hurt me.'

'Don't worry, Granny. Pierce is settin' it all to rights. There now. There.' Brigid held her thin shoulders so tightly in her anger that the old woman cried out in pain. Brindsley, who had been amazed by the sight that met his eyes, was charging now at Muswell. He was crying, unaware that there were tears on his cheeks, and he bounced off the big man who brushed him away as if he were an irritating insect.

'You scut! You slime! You shit!' he kept shouting but Muswell took little notice of him, shooing him until Brindsley slipped in the mud wet from the passing of the buckets of water and fell, struggling helplessly, frustrated and raging, trying to get up.

'Get those men away or I'll shoot.' Muswell had drawn his gun and he now beckoned the police to do likewise. As he ordered, as he turned, all buckets were suddenly lowered and the hands that held them were now around the barrels of guns. Guns of all shapes and sizes were now aimed at Muswell, rifles and shotguns, revolvers and muskets of ancient vintage, but at the ready, held steadily, pointed at him by the men on the roof, the men on the ground, Clancy's men and the cottagers, all facing Muswell and his men with angry eyes.

'No. We'll not leave here. We'll shoot and rid this land of its vermin, Muswell,' Clancy replied.

He saw the flicker in Muswell's eyes, the doubt and speculation there, and knew the man remembered the old score.

'Go on, Muswell, give me a reason to use this,' Clancy continued, giving his gun a small jerk. 'Oh you could kill me, sure. But you know that I don't really care and you know why. Sure you could kill one of us, or even two. But you'll go too. And you want to live, don't you, Muswell? Otherwise why are you putting all that money into a bank in Galway? Amassing a nice little fortune out of the evictions you supervise? Eh, Muswell? One move of your hand and I'll blow your brains out. With pleasure. And you don't want me to do that, do you, Muswell?'

For a moment everyone was still. Like a painting, no one moved. A bird sang fiercely, proclaiming its freedom and flew wild and graceful from the field behind Granny Donnelly's to the apple tree beside the smouldering roof, then away from the smoke and up again into the blue.

Muswell let his hand fall. He'd lost and he knew it. However, he was philosophical; there was always another day. He had the advantage. He was simply doing his job. They *cared*, and people who cared lost. They were made vulnerable by passion. It was life and death for the cottagers. He had no such emotional involvement. He was executioner, dispassionate and calm. Eventually he would win.

He turned away, jerked his head to the police and the men with him to follow him. They looked, as Dinny

163

McQuaid said afterwards, mighty relieved. Without a word they took themselves off.

Clancy's men tidied up Granny Donnelly's roof, laying a new layer of sailcloth over the last of the sparks and smoke, damping it, soothing it out. The women fussed over the old lady and cleaned the cottage and Brigid said that she would stay with her that night in case the shock caught up with the old woman and she had a nasty turn.

'No, no, no, I don't want to go in there,' Granny cried and pulled away as the woman tried to guide her into her home. Pierce told Brigid to take her back home with them.

'She'll have te stay wi' us, poor wee Mother – for a while – she's scared owa her wits.'

'I don't wanna go in there,' Granny moaned. 'The men'll come te get me.'

Brigid put her arm around the old lady and led her away from the smoke. 'Never mind, Granny, ye'll come wi' us. Pierce'll look after ye, never fear. Ye'll stay wi' us.'

Duff turned to Clancy, 'Well, we showed them, din' we?' he said triumphantly. 'We gave them the old heave-ho.'

'They'll be back,' Clancy said laconically, gazing in the direction they'd left.

'Wi' a cannon?' Dinny McQuaid sniggered.

'Don't overestimate us, Mr McQuaid,' Clancy said calmly. 'For God's sake don't underestimate them.'

Chapter Twenty-Four

∽◎ ◎∾

They gathered in the pub that night, celebrating. At first they were jubilant, and then, as the realization that this was a no-holds-barred fight dawned, apprehensive.

'What'll they do next?' Mickey O'Gorman asked fearfully, then looked at Ma Stacey who was leaning her vast bosoms on the counter. 'Fill it up, Ma, there's a terrible thirst on me, so there is.'

'It's the tension,' Mog Murtagh supplied helpfully. 'The tension plays havoc with the thirst.'

'Go asy there, Mickey, you want to keep yer hands offa Carmel these days, now don't ye?'

A look of fierce anger crossed Mickey's face and he opened his mouth to snarl something, but Ma had turned her back and he was yapping at thin air, so he subsided and stuck his nose in his pint.

'So what *will* they do next?' Shooshie Sheehan asked the room at large.

'They'll get reinforcements.' The voice from the corner was soft but penetrating. They had not noticed him there, Clancy, the moonlighter, who hardly drank at all, sitting in the corner, bearing a distinct resemblance to one of Billy Layde's corpses. He was sitting in Cogger Kavanagh's place and the latter hovered unhappily behind him, hopping from foot to foot, grinning inanely every so often, displaced.

'Wasn't it grand though?' Deegan Belcher smiled, eyes glowing at the memory.

'Totally routed them, we did. Had to surrender, so they did. Walk away with their tails between their legs,' Mickey O'Gorman gloated.

'Aye, 'twas a grand sight,' Brian Gilligan concurred, supping his black porter with relish.

'They'll be back,' Duff Dannon said.

'That's right, Duff, throw cold water.' Mog Murtagh looked to heaven and sighed.

'Aye, they will that,' Clancy nodded in agreement with Duff. 'But we'll keep guard,' he added. 'Take turns.'

'Why?' Brian Gilligan asked. 'We've won, haven't we?'

'Jasus, man, are ye an eejit or what?' Duff asked. 'They know we mean to give them a fight, so they will probably try to sneak up on us, use underhand tactics. We must be ready. The cottages should never be left unattended again. Night and day we'll have sentries.'

'I still think they've gone wi' their tails between their legs an' they'll not tangle wi' us again,' Brian Gilligan stated.

'That's wishful thinking, ye don't know Muswell like I do.' Clancy was firm.

'We'll be like a real army,' Deegan said, sounding excited.

Clancy threw him a withering glance. 'Ye'll have to enrol yer most reliable men.' The look he gave Duff showed he did not believe there were many such men in the hamlet.

'Aren't we all that?' Deegan Belcher banged his tankard down. 'Couldn't ye trust any one of us wi' yer lives?'

'Forgive me, but I'm not so sure about that. Tell ye the truth ye don't inspire me, but I have my men.'

Deegan went a dark shade of purple.

'Oh, I don't doubt your courage,' Clancy said. 'It's the discipline. My men are used to staying awake at night. I doubt if any of ye are. Besides ye have to get on wi' yer work.' Deegan nodded, slightly mollified. 'Doyle and Carmody are on watch now. Bogue and Pascal will take over at midnight till three of the morning. You like to offer for that, Deegan?' Clancy cast him a quizzical glance. All the bounce went out of Belcher and he subsided, shaking his head. 'At three I'll go on wi' Whelan till dawn. Daytime is not that much of a problem, so I want yiz lot to mount guard then.'

'I'll do anythin' ye say,' Pierce cried. 'Wasn't my old mother ousted from her home an' we at holy Mass?'

Clancy shook his head. 'Our experience shows,' he declared, 'that they try that first, out in broad daylight, bold as brass. Terrorizing tactics. Usually it works. People are scared. Too scared to fight. Too disorganized. A few people get killed or maimed, the cottages are set on fire.' His eyes narrowed. 'But when that fails, as it did with us there to stop it today. . .'

'Yeah, wasn't it gorgeous? There we all were, wi' our guns. Weren't we the big men, showin' them.' Mog Murtagh waxed enthusiastic, but Duff Dannon interrupted him. 'Don't cod yerself, Mog. Without Clancy here, an' his men, we'da been banjaxed. Bullet fodder. Our houses kindling for a bonfire! Crippled we'da bin.'

'Please, sir, Mr Clancy, continue,' Billy Flynn respectfully suggested. Billy was always deferential because Manny Flynn up at Ballymora Castle was his brother and therefore on the opposite side.

'Thank you. When that fails. . .'

'What?' Deegan Belcher asked, not keeping abreast with the conversation.

'What happened today, Deegan, are ye deaf or drunk or what? The evictions didn't succeed, or didn't ye notice?' Dinny McQuaid was heavily sarcastic.

'They will probably change tactics,' Clancy informed them. 'They may come at night. Try to surprise us. They may lull us into a sense of security. Wait a while before trying again. They know I'm here now with my men and so they know what they're up against.'

'Yeah, wild boyos! There'll be no stoppin' us. We'll pulverize them.' Miles Murphy the drover, a little the worse for porter, bounced up and down excitedly.

Clancy ignored him. 'They'll do nothing tonight. It's too soon and they can't organize it quite so quickly. So we can all get a good night's sleep. But I don't think they'll leave it too long.'

'He'll know too that the longer he leaves it the better we can muster support,' Duff Dannon said. 'There's many a boyo hereabouts would join a good fight when the word spreads.'

Clancy nodded. 'Exactly. Although that depends on the urgency. The Marquis is returning to London. Muswell might just let the whole situation go off the boil. I hope not, but that's what I'd do if I was in his place.'

He had noticed Cogger's jig behind him and now he waved him away as if he was an irritating fly and Cogger, who had had it in his head to confide in the stranger about the treasure and the gold, decided against it and slunk to the small draughty pew by the door that everyone avoided, for the man who sat there was overwhelmed by gusts of icy wind every time the door opened or closed.

'Listen to me now,' Clancy said, flexing his long nervous fingers. 'Make a list of men to keep a lookout. Not casually mind; our enemy is too canny. If we are watching for them, they'll be keeping an eye on us too, never fear. This is serious, fellas. This is war.'

'An' you're the man to lead us.' Miles Murphy cut another caper and clapped his hands and the others joined in as a great swell of gratitude overwhelmed them and they gave Clancy the palm of their hands and a cheer of congratulations. He stilled them with a calm and unemotional look.

'Don't be so fast with the praise, men,' he said. 'Ye'll be tired of us ere long.'

'Never, Clancy, never.' Mickey O'Gorman was effusive and unsteady. 'Eh, lads?' The rest of them cried out loudly that they would be forever grateful and another round was ordered.

'You'll soon be wantin' to be shot of me,' Clancy told them, a wry grin on his face, and they nodded but did not understand.

He stood up and pulled his black topcoat around him. 'I'll take a walk around the place before I get some shut-eye, for I'll need to be rested when I go on duty this night.' He turned to Duff Dannon. 'Will you accompany me?' he asked.

Duff nodded and the two men left the shebeen. Cogger scuttled to the vacated seat in the inglenook and the men returned to sup their porter and ruminate on events, mulling over and exaggerating every little incident with a '. . . did ye see. . .' and 'remember when . . .' as if they were events that had happened years ago.

Ma Stacey scrubbed the oaken counter vigorously, pushing her ginger hair off her forehead, hoping that the lads, as she called them, old and young, would take the hint and pack it in and she could close up shop. It had been a long and tiring day and evening and she had done twice her normal work, for events had driven the men inside the hostelry much earlier than usual and they'd stayed on, missing Father Maguires Devotions to the Virgin Mary at six o'clock, after the Angelus, for the thrilling happenings needed airing and alcohol to entrench them in communal memory in a satisfactory way.

But Ma Stacey had a man in her bed these days, and half her waking hours were spent thinking about the pleasures that awaited her between the sheets. She went about in a haze of physical expectancy, nerves all at the ready. It had been unexpected, the arrival of the bailiff Phil Conlon into her home; unexpected, but very welcome.

God'n he was a lusty man, she thought, mopping the counter with a sensuous motion, a passionate, needy man, and never before in her life had she had such satisfactory gratification. Her late husband had been an over-hasty lover, in and out, in and out and quick as a flash, all over before a woman could get the taste, God help us. Phil Conlon had opened up a whole new world of the senses to the widow and she wanted to get as much of him as she could before he tired of her and slung his hook elsewhere. She was after all no spring chicken, and she was a widow. There were pretty young girls in the village and Phil Conlon would be quite a catch for any of them. She shivered with pleasure at the thought of his husky, hairy male frame, his thick virile thighs and his arms so firm, so strong around her, and she wiped the counter enthusiastically and called out, 'Drink up! Drink up, lads,' although it was only nine o'clock of an evening.

They put their tankards to their lips and quaffed their drinks, then, banging them on the counter, took their farewells. Truth to tell they were one and all – except perhaps Mickey O'Gorman, who always needed another – tired out. It had been an exciting day, an exhausting day, a day unique in the sleepy history of Ballymora and a good rest was what they needed.

'God bless ye, Ma,' they called out as they took their leave, yawning and stretching. 'Peace be wi' ye tonight.'

Only Phil Conlon remained, and when she locked and bolted the door, before she had time to put the guard in front of the fire or turn out the lamps, he had his arms around her and, with a groan of pleasure, she turned into them and pressed her ripe and ready body to his. Her cleaning rag fell to the floor, and, knees weak, she sank after it, feeling his weight, heavy with passion, on top of her and there, in the amber glow of the flickering firelight, against Cogger's seat, Phil took her, bringing her to a climax that made her cry out loudly and raucously, and Cogger, wandering outside under the moon, ran home scared, thinking it was the banshee after him in the night.

Chapter Twenty-Five

ᑫᕮ ᕮᑫ

Clancy and Duff heard Ma Stacey's bellow but they paid
no attention. It was part of the noises all around them; the
scuttle of night creatures through the trees, the scrabbling
of moles and badgers and the patter of rabbits and hares,
the nocturnal business of owls and kestrels, the splashing
of trout in the river and the stealthy activity of Mog
Murtagh poaching whatever was available in the darkness
of the night. The men on duty shivered and pulled on
their pipes and cigarettes as if that way they would get
warmer and rubbed their hands together and blew on
them.

Duff and Clancy strode side by side down the boreen,
taking the pathway towards Bannagh Dubh.

'Ye feel strongly about all this?' Duff suggested.

His companion was silent, walking swiftly, eyes
narrowed against the wind. Then he stopped and nodded.
'Aye, Duff. I do that. I'm committed to the aims of the
Land League.'

'I thought ye didn't hold with Parnell?'

'Neither do I. He doesn't go far enough. They always
compromise. But the Land League, yes. A fair rent, yes.'

Duff smiled, thinking of what now seemed the far-off
days in Ma Stacey's shebeen and himself giving the speech:
'*A fair rent is a rent the tenant can reasonably afford to pay
according to the times . . .*'

'I want to help lay a more solid foundation for positive
Irish thinking among farmers and peasantry. That's what
I'm trying to do.'

'Ye know all about it?'

'I think of little else, Duff. It's my life. I have no other. It
was taken away from me.'

Duff wanted to know what he meant but didn't ask.

170

'See, I'm considered an extremist,' Clancy continued. 'Parnell shouts, is bellicose and fiery, but, at heart he is a moderate. What I see – what I dream of – is Ireland free of tyranny. Ireland free of England and its laws. Ireland with its own laws and language and culture. Those men in there . . . ' he waved back over his shoulder in the direction of the pub. 'They believe the propaganda by now. They really think that any Englishman, no matter how worthless or ignorant, is somehow superior to them. That is a terrible thing to instil in a man's mind.'

They walked for some considerable time in silence, and finally they reached the headland and stopped simultaneously. Clancy's steps had taken them to Bannagh Dubh.

He stared out over the restless Atlantic. It was black down there, over the cliff edge, and the moon sprinkled diamanté glitter over the crests of the waves.

'Just look at it,' Clancy commanded. 'It's so beautiful it hurts. You know, Duff, that's what this fight is all about: the land. It's all about the land. People covet it. We all want it. The ascendency, the peasants, Pierce Donnelly, yourself. Yet it belongs to no one. Only God has a legitimate claim to the land.'

Duff thought of Demara and her crazy dream. Land. Precious land. Clancy straightened and faced Duff. 'But it's going to be tougher than your friends think,' he told him.

The air sliced them icily and he shivered. 'It's not a schoolboy adventure like *Treasure Island*,' he added, teeth chattering, 'although they seem to think so. You'll have to warn them though. Ah, Duff, they don't seem to realize they might lose their lives.'

Duff didn't know what he meant by the reference to *Treasure Island*. He had never heard of it. But he did understand Clancy's assessment of his friends. Except for Pierce Donnelly they had an insubstantial grasp on events. So he nodded.

'I know,' he agreed. 'They think it's tit for tat and non-payment of rent is bloody wonderful and think of all the pints they can buy and the shawl for the missus against the cold and the extra food for hungry bellies this winter. Yerra ye can't blame them.'

'You must warn them to save that rent. It is to be withheld, not not paid. You'll have to see they understand.'

'I'll try. 'Twont be easy, but I'll try.'

'Do they know some of them might die?' Clancy asked.

'I don't think they've speculated on that aspect at all,' Duff replied. 'They talk airily of death but never fear it will happen to them.'

There was silence between them for a while, each man lost in his thoughts. Clancy was musing on the inefficiency of the peasants. He thought also he'd have to warn Pascal to keep his eyes, and probably his hands, off Dinny McQuaid's wife. There was trouble brewing there and there was nothing Clancy hated more than affairs of passion, misunderstandings with irate husbands to come between the men and their duty. Duff thought of Demara and her wild hair, her beauty, her spirit. He wished Brigid would write her the events that were shaping their lives here in Ballymora. She would come home then, he had no doubt. But her mother refused. She insisted on keeping Demara and Maeve in ignorance. Demara would grow sophisticated and uppity in London, he believed, then where would they be? But he loved her. With all his heart he wanted her, and now his great fear was that she would grow away from him, away from her own land.

The wind was whipping Duff's hair and Clancy pulled his cap down lower on his brow. A lone bird of prey, an eagle or a hawk, shrieked from the cliff and the mighty Ben Bannagh cast a heavy shadow over the landscape. They could hear in the night the sound of Shooshie Sheehan fiddling some sassy jig indoors, away to the east. A scarf of charcoal cloud slid across the face of the moon.

'Why'd you do this Clancy?' Duff turned with his companion to walk back to the village. 'It's a queer class of a life ye lead. Why'd you risk yer life for us?'

'A lotta reasons.' The tall man paused and kicked a stone, then leaned against a beech, old, gnarled, ghost-grey in the moonlight. 'I love this land. It is mine. I'm a Celt. I'm *not* English. As I said, I resent them and their laws here in what is my country. I resent them struttin' around tellin' me what to do.'

'You know, whenever men talk like that,' Duff said, 'they rarely *do* anything about it. They seem to need a spur. Something personal to galvanize them.'

Clancy sighed and nodded. 'You are right,' he replied. 'There was something else.' Duff could see the sinews of his face tauten and shiver under his pale skin. 'They came one day to where I lived my peaceful life. We were a community, like your friends, keeping out of trouble – anything for a quiet life – you know!' Duff nodded. 'That's why I understand them. Dinny McQuaid. Mickey O'Gorman. Mog Murtagh and the rest. Once upon a time I was like them. And, as I said, I lived quiet in my small place on God's earth when Lord Dover of Clare decided he wanted the land cleared. He sent Muswell to us and that bastard burned our cottages down. Fifteen of them. Burned to the ground.' He was quiet a moment and seemed to be struggling with himself. Duff waited quietly. 'We were out in the fields. It was harvest time. And we were not prepared. Unlike ye there was no one there to warn us, to help us. We didn't know what was happening. One minute we were a happy contented little community, the next the sky was ablaze with light and a torch had been set to our roofs.' He glanced at Duff and his voice was harsh. 'Do ye know how quickly dry thatch burns? Have ye ever heard the screams of people trapped in a blazing inferno? It's a sound I'll never forget. It's a sound that'll haunt me till the day I die. It's a sound that stops me sleeping. It's a sound I'll spend my life trying to shield others from hearing.' He cleared his throat and Duff saw the terrific struggle within the man. 'All the homes were gone in the twinkling of an eye. The men here – Doyle and Carmody, Whelan, Bogue and Pascal – all lost their cottages. And me. Only I lost my wife and child too. See, they were indoors for the child was sick. They were roasted alive in that house.'

He paused again and Duff saw he was wringing his hands, twisting his fingers around each other, hurting himself. 'The babby was sick,' his voice faltered. 'And Maura, the wife, had stayed home to nurse him. The rest of the women were in the fields. But my darlin' and the

173

babby were burned to death in that fire. D'ye blame me? Do ye?'

Duff laid his arm across the tall man's shoulders. His body was taut and unyielding as granite. They stood together and then he turned to Duff, eyes burning. 'I'll fight every poxy landlord in Ireland who tries to evict people like that. And I'll fight Muswell to the death. There's no place for the likes of him in our fair land. Brutal bloody bastard. I'll fight them until I find peace in death and see my dear ones again.'

He took Duff's arm in a fierce grip, staring at him. 'Go now,' he said firmly. 'Go. Be of stout heart. But keep this to yourself. I'll not have my war made their war and I'll not have my weakness bruited abroad for all the world to pick over and gossip about.'

Duff left him there, a shadowy stooped figure in the moonlight. He turned down the boreen towards his home.

Chapter Twenty-Six

ᴄᴏ ᴏᴠ

Duff had not gone very far before he saw Dana Donnelly, a moonlit figure leaning against Brian Gilligan's gate. For a moment he thought it was Demara and his heart tripped in his breast. As he neared her she let her shawl slip down from her hair and over her shoulders and he saw it was the younger sister.

'What are you doin' abroad in the night?' he asked her when he drew level with her.

She shrugged, ''Tisn't late,' she replied tartly.

'Waitin' for your sweetheart?' he asked. She had been plaguing him of late and he tried to indicate to her that he was not interested in her. At least not in that way.

'Now, Duff Dannon, you know you're the only man I ever fancied,' she said lightly, archly, and she moved towards him.

He looked at her as she moved nearer him, her hands on her hips, a mocking light in her big brown eyes. Her hair was black as midnight and her skin pearly as the dewdrops.

It was cold in the boreen, not icy as it had been on the headland near the sea, but enough to make his eyes water and his nose feel pinched. But the blouse she wore was low-necked and he could see her breasts rising from the white stuff.

In spite of himself he wanted to touch them, to see if her skin was cold or as warm and soft as it looked. She read the thought in his eyes. She moved nearer him, close enough to smell the whiskey on his breath and she stared up at him, bold-eyed.

'Well, why don't ye?' she asked.

'What?' He was startled and his mouth felt dry.

'Touch me,' she replied and he turned from her angrily and moved away from her up the boreen.

'Yer not yerself, Dana child,' he murmured crossly.

She slipped in front of him, blocking his way. 'I'm *not* a child,' she cried and pulled the blouse off one shoulder and with the gesture revealed her breast, round, warm, tipped with its raspberry-hard nipple, like an exotic fruit under the moonlight. 'Ye don't often get to look upon the likes of that, now do ye?' she asked softly. She was right. Life in the village was frustrating. Dilly McQueen serviced most of the lusty lads for a couple of pence down the valley and that was the best a fella could hope for. Father Maguire and the good Catholic mothers saw that nothing happened even between courting couples and here was Dana Donnelly, her breast bare as Venus under the starry sky.

'Jasus, Dana, what're ye doing?' he asked aghast and, feeling, to his horror, his body reacting to her brazen gesture.

He tried to dodge past her. He could go down to the river and plunge in the icy water to subdue his wayward body but he had to get past this temptress first.

Getting past her, he knew afterwards, should not have been all that difficult, but, to his horror, she pulled the blouse right off, over her head, her arms above her, both breasts free, taut with her stretching. She held the garment above her awhile, aloft, like a flag, and stood there, legs apart, her skirt on her hips, the long seductive slope of her body to her waist milk-white against the massy darkness.

He swallowed painfully, rooted to the spot. She did not seem nervous or afraid. She did not look around to see if anyone else was there. She took his hand in hers and laid it flat across her breast, rubbing his fingers against her nipples, and he found her skin was hot to touch.

He was lost and he knew it. 'Come,' she said and pulled him into the Gilligan barn, hard by the boreen. 'Come', holding his hand, 'Come' against the new-mown hay piled high against the barn door. The ripe smell of cattle was all around them, but they cared little for that. Dana wanted him. That was the reality. She had always wanted him. There had been no chance with Demara at home, but now she would have him, now she would hold him and damn the consequences.

He would have to marry her. Duff was an honourable man and he would be forced to wed her after tonight. She pulled down her skirt, standing on the straw. She took his face between her hands and guided his mouth to her taut, ripe nipple.

He drank her in. His body was on fire. He could not stop now even if he wanted to. A fleeting thought of Demara crossed his mind but vanished in a haze of lusty passion. It was the first time in his life he had a female cooperate in sex with him. Dilly had lain back passive, skirt above her head, and let him get on with it. But Dana touched him, slid her hands along his thighs till he could feel a million nerve ends tingling. She licked his skin as if she could eat him, kissed his nipples and his lips, avidly drinking him in, then she lay back and opened her legs and gently, possessively urged him on top of her.

For a moment he hesitated. His deep sense of responsibility, his promises to Demara, the teachings of his Church, the respect due to the sanctity of the family that his mother had instilled in him, all demanded a halt, a pause to consider before the ultimate action was taken, but she touched him with trembling fingers and 'Come', she urged and he plunged into her and found to his amazed delight that this entry was awaited, moisture-laden, that she rose to him, that she embraced him deep inside her, holding him as tightly there as her arms held his body, her hands stroking his buttocks.

And he came, blasting into her like a trumpeting bull. It was like nothing he had ever experienced before. No thought of Demara crossed his mind now. There was nothing in his head but this wanton woman and her bounteous body. So later, when she had uncoupled herself and put on her clothes, smoothing them down while he watched her, a wide grin on his face, he did not fully absorb what she said when she turned to leave the barn. He heard her words like water flowing over him, his body replete, his eyes heavy – he heard her say, 'Old holy Moses, Brian Gilligan'd have a heart attack an' he knew what was happening in his barn this night.' She was smiling at him. 'But sure why should we care, you and me, Duff Dannon, an' we'll be married in the spring.'

Chapter Twenty-Seven

Winter had arrived overnight and the countrymen and women paused as Demeter took herself underground to search for her daughter. The land was dead and unproductive, the autumn leaves lost their glory, shrivelled and died and the hoar-frost touched the brambles and withered the last blackberries. They had nothing to think about in the hamlet except the threat from the Marquis and they talked that subject to death in both the shebeen and the privacy of their cottages.

Except that there was no privacy any more. It became obvious as winter encroached that although the barn could

177

be used by day it was neither warm enough in the cold nights nor near enough in the dark evenings to keep a satisfactory watch from. So the moonlighters had to be billeted with the cottagers on a more permanent basis. Strangers penetrated the heart of their little world and their constant presence there was an irritant few relished. The Donnellys had Clancy in Demara's bed. 'He can sleep below in the cowshed,' Brigid said, but Pierce shook his head. 'No, pet. We'll put him in Demara's bed. It's only fitting.' Brigid sighed deeply, said nothing, and prepared to do as her husband asked. Pierce's word was law in his house.

Duff Dannon, his brother Christie and Mary his sister-in-law had Bogue in their barn. He was a monosyllabic sort of man who kept himself to himself. Nevertheless, they felt the intrusion and some of their ease with each other disappeared.

'It's like someone was listenin' in te our conversations,' Mary Dannon whispered. 'Puttin' us on guard, takin' away our free and easy chat.'

She simply voiced what they all thought. Brian Gilligan felt too intimidated to get his leg over Della's plump body, in case he was, God forbid, heard! ' 'Tis puttin' a terrible strain on us, one an' all,' he moaned about Carmody's unsmiling presence in his cottage.

The widow McCormack was furious that Clancy refused to delegate a man into her home, she being alone, but he refused to listen to her blandishments and she remained in a fever of frustrated fury that Sheena McQuaid was landed with the darkly smouldering Pascal.

Mickey O'Gorman and Carmel disliked Whelan, the moonlighter they were assigned. Mary Dannon nodded sympathetically at Carmel's obvious irritation and found nothing odd in her affirmation that, 'Whelan drives me mad, so he does, the way he sucks his teeth. Now I know you'll tell me my Mickey does that too, but I don't *mind* Mickey. He's got a kind of rhythm I'm used to. Whelan does it out of time and unexpected like, an' I find meself waitin'. It drives me mad!'

Mary Dannon understood perfectly. It was the small

irritations that got under the skin and only Sheena seemed quite happy with the dark travelling man.

Clancy could smell Demara as he lay in her bed. The scent disturbed him and made him restless.

One moonlit night he rose, ill-at-ease in his skin, and stared out of the tiny window into the wild dark night. The clouds raced across the face of the moon and the trees groaned and sighed under the wind. He felt the piece of paper under his fingers, unconsciously picking it up before his curiosity was aroused. He had taken it from on top of a pile of books in the embrasure and now he opened it up.

What he saw surprised him. It was a drawing, remarkable in that it had obviously been executed by an amateur, yet showed a knowledge that would have been worthy of praise in a university graduate and was thus astounding in a peasant. The drawing was signed Demara and headed 'Demara's Dream'.

It showed a manor house, unlike the local castles, more Palladian inspired. Clancy had seen such drawings in Trinity College up in Dublin, when he had gone there for talks with Sionshagh ni Brechnagh, a lawyer sympathetic to the Land League cause and in favour of the moonlighters. He had helped Clancy draw up the legal documents and laws, frame them in correct terms.

This peasant girl, the daughter of Brigid and Pierce Donnelly, had executed a sketch that compared well with any of the professional ones he had seen framed on the hallowed walls of the college. She had not only penned the beautifully symmetrical house, but had landscaped the gardens and plotted the plumbing. She had placed the pillared house before the lake, protected from the sea by regiments of lime trees and pines. She had put pipes from the lake to the house and statues at the head of walks and in a grove, and on the other side of the lake a gazebo where a weeping willow provided a refuge for the swans. This beautiful sight would be visible from the house.

He wondered at her ingenuity. He speculated on where she had seen the classic sculpture. How could she know such statues existed? He soon gave it up. His fellow

179

countrymen may have irritated him with their lack of stamina in their fight for freedom and the half-hearted way they accepted occupation, but they never let him down in the department of imagination.

He put the drawing back where it had lain and sighed. 'Land, land,' he murmured. 'It's all about land!'

Chapter Twenty-Eight

ɔ⊕ ⊕ɔ

The cottagers waited and Muswell did nothing. Life went on and time passed. Brigid and Pierce heard from Áine that Demara and Maeve were not with the Brennans any more. They had left and Brigid gathered there had been ill-feeling between the sisters. Then came the letter from Demara to notify them of their new address in Soho Square and tell them all about their new landlady, Belle Desmond, her kindness to them both and her determination to help Maeve to become an actress.

Pierce was none too pleased about this. However, he was a patient and philosophical man and there was nothing he could do about the situation from his cottage in Ballymora and, as he said to Brigid one night, 'I'd prefer to trust Demara and Maeve, *allana*. Surely they know what they're doin'? We brought them up good and honourably and they know right from wrong. I think we should be able to put our faith in them, an' not worry too much. This lady, Belle whatever-it-is, yerra she must be nice to have taken them in, an' I'm sure Demara an' Maeve wouldn't be led astray. They're good girls, Brigid pet, so quit yer worrin' and lave it be.'

Gossip had it that Muswell had gone back to Limerick.

'The Marquis has given up for sure,' Mog Murtagh said optimistically in the shebeen but Clancy shook his head. 'No. He's clever. He knows that's what ye'll think. He knows exactly what he's doin'. He's lullin' us into a sense of false security, hopin' ye'll get fed up wi' us and we'll go away. Then he'll pounce.'

'But ye could be wrong again? Couldn't ye?' Brian Gilligan said triumphantly.

'Meantime we're feedin' ye all, puttin' ye up in our homes. Lookin' after ye better than if ye were our own – oh a fine life ye have an' no mistake!' Mickey O'Gorman drew the back of his hand across his porter-soaked moustache. Everyone knew he had been beating Carmel again and the drink heavy on him and she expecting again.

The women were disenchanted too. They felt the moon-lighters had outstayed their welcome. It was a hard life in the winter and food had to stretch and the extra presence in their homes was not conducive to peace of mind and good humour.

The Donnelly household was bursting at the seams. Although Demara and Maeve had gone, Clancy and Granny Donnelly had taken their beds. Brigid had to admit, however, that Clancy was no trouble and he ate very sparingly, showing little interest in food. He was quiet about the place and helped Brindsley with his studies. He was also a great help when Brigid lost her child, for Pierce was distracted with worry, concerned about his wife's health, and Clancy did Pierce's work so that he could stay with his wife in her hour of need.

The evenings drew in and lamplight or candlelight became essential. Keeping watch had gradually become a bore, then a chore, then in the cold winter nights a hated duty foisted on them by outsiders. The command was very reluctantly obeyed. Finally the village men, when called to watch, simply turned over under their duck-down, went back to sleep and didn't show up.

Clancy called a meeting in the big barn by the river and warned that if the cottagers did not pitch up for their sentry duty he and his men would leave Ballymora.

'Just because it is winter and cold and uncomfortable doesn't mean we can let up,' he cried to his stubborn-faced audience. 'Don't ye see, that's exactly what they're hoping?'

'Who? An' who are we talkin' about?' Shooshie Sheehan asked. 'I don't see no one but us, so I don't.'

'We're talkin' about Muswell an' his lot,' Duff Dannon cried.

'Yerra they've quit!' Brian Gilligan shouted. 'Doesn't Father Maguire say so an' isn't his word the nearest we get to the Almighty's this side of Heaven.'

'I hope yer wrong about that,' Duff muttered, then stood beside Clancy. 'This man is right,' he told them. 'Think men – think. Can ye see the likes of Muswell quittin'?'

'Yeah! Why not? He knows when he's beat,' Mickey O'Gorman yelled.

'God, yer fools!' Pierce Donnelly shook his head and his storm-light rattled. They all carried lights and their shadows danced on the high walls of the barn.

''Tis all very well for ye to talk, Pierce Donnelly. 'Twas your mother they picked on. We can't be asked to guard our homes day an' night puttin' up strangers free gratis an' for nuthin', just to accommodate you!' Dinny McQuaid's mean little face glowed with resentment.

The slant to their thinking shocked Pierce and Duff.

'An' I heard somethin' up above from Kilty. He heard it from Lord High-an'-Mighty Lester before he went away!' Deegan Belcher said belligerently, thumbs hooked into his belt.

'What was that ye heard, Deegan?' Mickey asked.

''Twas that Clancy here has a mighty good reason to declare a war on Mr Muswell. Eh, Clancy? Am I right or am I?'

Clancy nodded but Duff answered for him. 'Sure he has. He told me about it right from the start. An' you would too if you were him.'

'What was that reason now?' Brian Gilligan inquired.

'Muswell was responsible for burning my wife and child to death when he set fire to my cottage.' Clancy's voice had that chill tone that Duff knew and there was a sudden hush in the barn. Perhaps, Duff thought, this piece of information might not have the effect desired by Deegan Belcher, but the reverse.

'I didn't tell ye because I can't bear to talk about it much. Ye understand.' Clancy said now, breaking the silence. 'An if I think about it too much I'll strangle the man with these bare hands.' He held them out before him and the cottagers saw they were trembling. 'An' that would do no good at all, an' I'd end up swinging on a gallows at Limerick. Then I couldn't halt the landlords in their tracks and stop the evictions.'

'He's sayin' that – it's all talk. Keep yer war outa here, Mr Clancy,' Deegan shouted.

'If I thought the Marquis or Lord Lester had it in for me alone, d'ye think I'd drag ye into this? De ye really believe that?' he asked them.

'No. O' course not,' Duff assured him.

'It's Pierce Donnelly too. It was his ma. It was his house,' Deegan persisted. The others were strangely quiet. Pierce Donnelly was always a bit above himself what with building rooms onto his cottage and his desire to buy it. He was an easy mark for them to blame and they wanted an excuse now, any excuse to get off this hook and stop worrying and get on with their lives.

'Sure how'd we know Deegan here isn't right?' Brian Gilligan asked. 'Mebbe the Marquis has it in for Pierce Donnelly here an' Duff an' they tryin' to buy their cottages, which is more'n the rest of us can afford to do. Mebbe Muswell's fight is with Clancy here an' little to do wi' us. And mebbe the Lesters and the Marquis's fight is with the Dannons and the Donnellys.'

'Will ye listen?' Clancy cried. 'I don't believe the Marquis of Killygally or Lord Linton Lester *know* Duff or Pierce here were buying their cottages and anyway that would be irrelevant to them. Don't ye see, it's not *about* that? The fight isn't based on anything so paltry, so small. They want ye off the land. It's that simple.'

'An' how do ye know that, Mister High-an'-Mighty Clancy? Who told ye? Anyone say it out? No! Ye think yer God, comin' here, tellin' us what to do!' Deegan Belcher's face was red as he shouted in righteous anger, eyes flickering right and left for corroboration.

Clancy waited for the noise to subside. 'Have ye forgotten *ye* sent for *me*?' he asked them, then when their angry voices died down he added. 'Have ye forgotten why?'

He had them and they knew it and they resented his victory.

'I'll lave ye to talk about it amongst yourselves,' Clancy told them. 'I'll abide by your decision.'

He stood and they felt themselves dismissed, like schoolboys. They left the barn, muttering, walking back to their peaceful homes across the fields and along the bridle-path, airing their grievances, aggressive voices loud in the quiet night.

There was a crescent moon hanging in the dark blue velvet of the sky. The stars, like matchless jewels, were cold, remote and brilliant. There was no wind, only a soft chill breeze that smelled of seaweed. The lights of their lanterns glowed orange and they could see the golden patches of welcoming light from their cottages spilling out into the evening.

'Sure 'tis peaceful as a nunnery,' Shooshie Sheehan mused, wanting to believe what Deegan Belcher and Brian Gilligan affirmed. The others nodded and they paused awhile in the stilly evening, casting around the resting countryside and finding nought amiss. They did not need to share their feelings of security nor verbal or physical communication to indicate what they were going to do. They were of one mind and they turned towards the wide open door of Ma Stacey's.

Chapter Twenty-Nine

In the barn, dark now that the lanterns were gone, Duff was shaking his head. 'They've forgotten,' he said. 'Already they've forgotten.'

'Not forgotten – rather put it behind them,' Pierce answered. 'It is what human beings do. See, they don't want to anticipate trouble.'

184

'Thereby making it impossible to combat it,' Clancy agreed.

The three men looked at each other in troubled concern.

'I'm afraid we'll be asked to go,' Clancy said. 'An' if you ask us, we'll have to leave. There's others who want us an' we won't stay where we're not welcome. We are a service and only remain where people feel we're needed.'

'We think you're needed here,' Duff said and looked at Pierce for agreement.

Pierce nodded vigorously. 'Aye. That we do.'

'Well, Pierce and Duff here do not constitute a majority,' Clancy said. 'You better follow the others and persuade them to let us stay, otherwise we're off and you're damned.'

Duff and Pierce left the tall man standing in the barn alone, looking isolated and bleak. They followed the little group of lamps bobbing in the dark ahead of them and saw them disappear into Ma Stacey's.

'Let's hope Phil's there,' Duff sighed. 'He'll back us up.'

'It still means we're only three!' Pierce remarked disconsolately. Duff was uncomfortable being alone with Pierce. Since his passionate encounter with Dana Donnelly he had been in an agonizing state of guilt and indecision. It seemed to him that Demara's face, reproachful and condemning, stared at him from the four corners of his room, that she sat in silent judgement at the foot of his bed, peered at him with an accusing expression from behind every tree and stalked him through the days, wagging her finger at him in disgust.

He had avoided Dana, ashamed of himself, for by now he had convinced himself that it had all been his fault. What had possessed him? Was he no better than the beasts of the fields that he should behave in such a way with a good Catholic Irish girl, and the daughter of a friend at that?

He looked back over his shoulder. Clancy stood in the barn door. He was a silhouette. He always seemed to be apart, an island, and very lonely. Yet, there was too about him something that forbade comfort or intimacy. He was

185

not a man to yield to a passing temptation. He looked then at his friend Pierce. Pierce had been a father to him since he could remember. His own father had been killed in a farm accident when he was eight years old and Pierce had taken the lonely boys under his wing. He had always been there whenever he or Christie had needed him. And now Duff had seduced his youngest daughter, an intolerable disloyalty. Jasus, he must have been out of his mind. He had not been able to sleep since that night and he felt acutely embarrassed to walk, like this, alone in the stilly night with Dana's father.

'Ye'll be weddin' our Dana, she tells me,' Pierce Donnelly's voice broke the silence of the night and Duff felt his heart pound and his stomach sink. Pierce stopped now, stood still and looked at Duff with frank and trusting eyes. 'I can't tell ye how happy that makes me, Duff. Though I allus thought 'twas Demara ye fancied. But with her goin' te England, I suppose . . . ' He faltered to a stop, looking at Duff curiously. For the other had gone pale as the moon and looked shocked and sick. Not the look of a happy man.

'Why, what is it, man? Did I say ought wrong?'

Duff quickly gathered himself together. He heard the voice, clear and sharp as crystal. 'We'll be married in the spring.' He drew a deep breath.

'No. No, Pierce! No indeed. Yes, me and Dana are . . . that is . . . we . . . it's like. . .'

Pierce guffawed. 'Jasus, man, is that what ails ye? Yer like a schoolgirl, so ye are. I never woulda thought the bold Duff would get himself in a twist over a woman. God'n isn't it wonderful how the stuffing is knocked outa the toughest fellas when marriage is in the air!' He was laughing and thumping Duff with rough affection. Then, when his laughter died he became serious again. 'I'm glad of it, Duff. I truly am. I'll be the first to welcome ye into the family. 'Twill do Dana good. That gal needs to be married. 'Twill make Ma an' the missus very happy.' He gave Duff an awkward bear-hug, then, as if all were settled, he strode onwards over the fields to the shebeen and Duff had to run to keep up with him.

Chapter Thirty

ဆဝ ၆ဝ

There were hot and heavy disagreements in Ma Stacey's that night. Duff was correct in his assumption that Phil Conlon would back himself and Pierce, but they were the only three against the others, all of whom wanted to be shot of the strangers. Mickey O'Gorman summed it up for the majority when he said, 'A pack of leeches they are, on our backs, eatin' our food, always present so we can't fart or have a private conversation at all. Jasus, the sooner they've gone the better!'

Useless for Phil or Duff or Pierce to warn them about the seriousness of the Marquis's intent.

'Isn't he in London?' Deegan Belcher demanded, eyebrows raised. 'Yerra he might never return. He might get killed in an accident!'

Phil Conlon shook his head. 'An' he mightn't!' he cried. 'God, yer fools!'

And so the argument was tossed about and the porter flowed and the night wore on.

Up the road in Sheena McQuaid's the women had gathered together to talk over the situation. They would not be asked their opinion but if they did not agree with their men then inevitably they got their way. An ultimatum delivered by any of the wives overruled most decisions by the men.

They squatted on milking stools before the turf fire, their shawls hugged close to their bodies, their boots stretched out to the blaze.

Katey Kavanagh was quite certain. 'Lookit, it's simple. When have the likes of the Marquis of Killygally ever allowed us to win? Eh?'

Brigid nodded. 'Yeah. He'll turf us out sooner or later. We know that. Fact is, we have no chance if Clancy an' his friends leave. The only chance we have is if they stay.'

'God'n they're a bloody nuisance,' Carmel O'Gorman shifted her large breasts with her wrists. 'Under our feet all the time. I'd give anythin' to have the place to myself again.'

They nodded in agreement, all except Sheena. The women glanced at her from under lowered lids, and noticed she had a glint in her eyes, and, as Brigid said afterwards, a sort of shiftiness about her. They had all noticed the buoyancy to her step that had appeared since the arrival of Pascal into the McQuaid household, and, as Katey Kavanagh pointed out, Dinny did not give the appearance of a man who would be a tiger in bed.

Jinny Murtagh had Ellie Murtagh on her lap, holding her, kissing her cheek every few minutes.

'I'm afeerd Muswell's men will come when Ellie is alone,' she said and the girl sank her face into the crook of Jinny's neck. 'They have no respect, they haven't. Your Pierce said it 'ud be a no-holds-barred, Brigid, an' I'm afeerd he's right.'

'Those eejits . . . ' Sheena began.

'Meanin' our husbands?' Della Gilligan inquired a little primly.

'Yeah – them! They'll get rid of Clancy an' the men. . .'

'An wouldn't that be the death of ye, Sheena McQuaid!' said Delia McCormack the widow, overbrimming with rage at her neighbour who had two men in her life now an' she had none.

'An' we'll be at the mercy of the Marquis, wait an' see,' Sheena finished, giving no indication that she heard Delia.

'Not if I have anythin' te do wi' it.' Katey Kavanagh drew herself up and jerking her head cried, 'Follie me, girls, an' let's tell them.'

They left the fire reluctantly and Jinny put Ellie into the cart-box and they all went up the lane to the shebeen.

The moon hung serenely in the changeless sky and all nature was still when the sound of Shooshie's fiddle broke the silence in a series of mournful half-notes and counter-harmony.

188

''Tis the end of somethin',' Brigid sighed. 'Mebbe we're too late.'

The men were drinking, the conversation heated, when the door slammed open and the wives of the parish of Ballymora barged in and confronted their astonished husbands. Tankards were halted midway to mouths, mouths remained open, chins dropped, eyes popped, Adam's apples bobbed and eyebrows jumped at the sight of the group of stern-faced women crossing the threshold forbidden to them. Ma Stacey, however, was not fazed.

'Welcome, ladies,' she said with great aplomb. 'Come in an' take your aise. Can I get ye a drink?'

The men in a body transferred their amazement to Ma Stacey. The mere idea that any of their wives might take the landlady up on her offer appalled them. But their minds were set to rest on that score. Katey Kavanagh shook her grey locks vigorously.

'No, thankee kindly,' she said. 'Now, me fine fellas, we have come te tackle ye about somethin' else.'

'Well don't,' Deegan Belcher growled roundly. 'We sorted it all out. Ye lave it to us.'

'Yeah, ye go home to where ye belong an' lave it to the men.' Dinny McQuaid's eyes glittered as he glanced at his wife, a fatuous grin on his face. He had caught the glances exchanged between his wife and the stranger and his blood had risen up in confusion and hurt pride, the more so because he could never catch them doing anything wrong. Not that he wanted to. Taking action was never a strongpoint of Dinny's and what he would be forced to do if he caught them did not bear thinking about. But now the object of his wife's glances would leave Ballymora, taking the torment away and Dinny could rest easy again.

His wife stood now behind Katey, shoulder-to-shoulder with Brigid Donnelly, and their purpose was clear.

'The men must stay,' Katey declared. 'Don't ye see, ye gombeen men, they're right?'

'Pierce?' Brigid had seen his face, bleak and defeated.

'They've been told to go,' Pierce said. 'Mog Murtagh went down a half-hour since an' told them he'd take them in the cart to Listowel.'

189

'Jasus! Holy Mother, yer fools.' Sheena McQuaid had gone pale and Dinny could not repress a gleeful smile.

'Couldn't someone follow them an' get them back?' Katey Kavanagh asked.

'Yerra on what woman? An' why, for God's sake? Won't we be private now an' just ourselves?' Dinny McQuaid looked at his wife who returned his glance with a stare so stony it made his blood run cold. He faltered to a stop.

'Aw, come on, lads. Let's drink up. It's right to celebrate. Shooshie play us a merry one, there's a good lad.'

It was strange, Duff thought, how within a week it was as if Clancy and his men had never been in Ballymora. Life resumed its normal routine, families settled in for the winter and people stopped referring to the strangers at all. Father Maguire sometimes spoke of 'the Devil's men we harboured in our midst', but most of the cottagers paid no attention to what Father Maguire said anyway.

It got so that they had to wrack their brains to remember the names of Clancy's men who had dwelt in their homes and eaten their food.

All except Sheena McQuaid.

And Duff Dannon.

And Pierce Donnelly.

Chapter Thirty-One

࿔ ࿔

Mary Jacks was sent back to the Sisters. That she returned at all surprised the Reverend Mother.

'We are very dissatisfied with you, Mary.' The Reverend Mother sounded dejected. 'You'll have to learn! Remember you were not our first choice. We were going to send little Rose to Mrs Desmond, but you implored us and we finally gave in.'

'I didn't know it would be so 'ard, Reverend Mother.'

Mary Jacks sly little face was creased with anxiety. She really looked as if she was telling the truth.

'Mrs Desmond is not a very hard taskmaster, Mary. Not from what I've heard.'

'Well, you 'eard wrong. Worked me like a slave, she did. I did my best . . .'

'Well, you didn't succeed. I feel that you've let us down and we cannot properly send you out to work again with the record you have until you change radically. Oh dear me, no. You'll have to work within the confines of the convent for the time being.' The Reverend Mother returned her attention back to her desk and missed the expression of satisfaction that crossed Mary Jacks' face. This suited her perfectly. Why she ever wanted to leave the convent in the first place she could not now remember. It had something to do with one of the seamstresses, a postulant, sent to the Sisters from the courts. The postulant was in the convent because she had been found whoring in Chapel Street and the judge sometimes sent relative newcomers to the oldest profession to a convent where perhaps they might gain some moral fibre and discover it was better to starve to death than lose your virtue. This postulant had painted a glowing picture of the benefits of nicking what one could from a house one was skivvying in.

'Nick it. Palm it. Sell it. Soon yer pockets'll be jangling,' she assured the openmouthed Mary Jacks who had then persuaded Reverend Mother to send her up the road to Mrs Desmond instead of Rose. The postulant hadn't known Belle Desmond and her habit of frisking the maids before they left the house.

Mary Jacks was an orphan and so the nuns tried to be kind to her and they allowed her to work for Mrs Desmond. They were quite relieved as it happened because they did not want to let Rose out into the metropolis.

Rose had no idea who she was or whether she was an orphan or not. She had lost her memory and couldn't remember what her name was or where she lived. She didn't remember anything about her past.

191

The nuns had found her in an alley, broken and bleeding and very near to death. They had brought her to the convent where they tended her. There was another orphan sharing the room with her, a girl her own age called Tilly Bywater and she had taken Rose to her heart and helped the nuns to care for her.

Rose recovered slowly but she never could tell them what had happened or how she had got into the state they found her in. 'God has mercifully drawn a veil,' the Reverend Mother said. 'I only hope no one is pining for her, missing her, she is such a sweet child. Dear God, it is a cruel world indeed when a child could be hurt so badly.'

Tilly Bywater loved Rose, and Rose, in turn, was nice to everyone. She was glad she had been found by the nuns and was grateful to them for helping her.

When Mary Jacks returned it meant that the nuns had to send someone in her place. Mary Jacks was glad she had been sent back to the convent because she would see Rose again and the work would not be as hard as in Mrs Desmond's house. She could fake a sickness here and the nuns were taken in by it. Mrs Desmond, that consummate actress, was never deceived. 'I've seen better than you try to fool me, Mary Jacks, so don't you put on that act with me!'

No, all in all she was glad to disappear behind the high walls of the convent. The nuns, the postulants and the children never left it except when they got a job somewhere else, and that was the way Mary Jacks liked it.

She hugged Rose and kissed Tilly Bywater.

'Gosh, it's good to be back,' she said. 'I didn't like it out there, God's truth I didn't.'

Rose was glad to see her. She was invisibly mending some bed linen for ladies in Mayfair who gave their custom to the convent, and Tilly was making lace. They sat in the cloisters under the chestnut tree in the quiet courtyard. The sun shone down, butter-coloured and cool, not hot at all, and Rose stitched and stitched, carefully pulling the thread and every now and then biting it off. Tilly tilted her frame and narrowed her eyes as she worked.

'And I'm afraid I'm home under a cloud!' Mary Jacks informed them.

'Oh my God, Mary, you botched it again! Oh, Rose,' exclaimed Tilly. She looked at her friend. 'They'll send one of us, bet they will. Oh dear.'

'Never mind, you're back, that's all that matters,' Rose laughed, speaking to Mary.

'How are you, Rose? You look pale,' Mary asked.

'No, I'm exceedingly well, Mary. You remember how pale I always am.'

She took the girl's hand in hers. 'Oh come and sit beside us and tell us all about it.'

'I hated it, Rose. The basement was dark and there was no courtyard like this, no chestnut tree to sit under and no time to sit. It was lonely. I didn't like Mrs Desmond. She could see right through you . . .'

Tilly laughed aloud. 'You mean she caught you thieving!'

Mary's eyes flashed. 'Well! Anyhow she dyed her hair red and wore rouge!'

'Oh fancy!'

'It's true. I didn't like the Donnelly girls what lived with 'er. They were nice, I 'ave to admit that, but they wanted things done all the time and I 'ave only one pair of 'ands,' Mary reflected, then added, 'The only one I *really* liked was a real good sport, name of Bert 'ockney.'

'And they sent you away?' Tilly asked.

Mary nodded, 'Oh I was a bad girl. But I'd listened to Gertie . . . remember?'

Rose smiled. 'Needed her head examined, did Gertie. Bound to end up in prison. What you do bad?'

Mary freely admitted her petty pilfering. 'I'm awful, I know, but the truth is I missed you both and the nuns and in a kind of a way I wanted them to catch me. Send me back 'ere.'

Rose patted her hand and smiled. 'Well, you succeeded. Here you are!'

'You don't think I'm awful? A thief?'

Rose shook her head. 'What right have I to criticize you? Or anyone? I may have been a thief. I don't remember. I

193

don't remember my past at all. The doctor said I might have done something terrible. I heard him tell Reverend Mother that it was best to keep me in here. He said I might be wanted for murder. He said I had been attacked and could have killed the attacker, and that was why I was covered in blood.'

'Oh, Rosie, then you 'ad good cause! No one would send you to prison for that!' Tilly sounded outraged at the very idea.

'The doctor said they would. 'E said that in law you can't kill someone defending yourself. Oh, Mary, I might have done *anything*. So 'ow can I blame you?' Rose shivered and Tilly took her hand and held it in hers.

'Oh don't start all that stuff again, Rose. Reverend Mother sent that doctor away with a flea in his ear. I was there, remember,' Tilly said. 'You were in a terrible state, Rose.' She looked at her friend with loving eyes. 'You were nearly dead. Someone had done something awful to you.' She kissed Rose's cheek. 'I know you,' she insisted. 'You couldn't hurt anyone! You're too gentle.'

'Yet Reverend mother never lets me outside these walls,' Rose whispered.

'Do you want to go?' Mary asked. Rose shook her head.

'There, you see then!' Tilly said as if that closed the matter.

But Rose had that lost look again, the one Tilly remembered. Sometimes she sort of went away, drifted into some mental distance, and didn't hear what you said.

Tilly shook her gently. 'Come on, Rose. We're here.' She glanced at Mary who gave her another shake. 'Is my room still empty?' she asked and smiled as Rose came back to them.

It was Tilly who answered. 'It's empty. Come on. I'll help you.'

The two of them left the cloisters and Rose went back to work. She narrowed her eyes and stitched and stretched and pulled and held the material out to make sure the thread blended and the stitches could not be seen.

Sometimes tiny things slid across her mind and she tried to catch them but she could no more hold them than you

194

could a moonbeam. What use was it anyway? Like Mary and Tilly she was happy here. It was the only world she knew. And if, sometimes, there was an ache inside her, an unbearable longing for someone, who she did not know, but someone from that blanked-out past, then she had learned to squash it, trample on it until it went away.

She could not imagine where she had been before. Had she parents? A mother who loved her? Tears came into her eyes when she thought about that and she got a funny feeling at the back of her nose.

But she might have had a terrible mother. It might have been her mother who had beaten her up. Or worse, maybe her mother hated her, wanted to be rid of her.

Rose sighed. She simply did not know and it was probably better that way. But something Mary had said teased her brain, and she didn't know what it was. Something Mary had mentioned. A name. A place. She frowned, thinking, but it was no use. She couldn't remember.

Chapter Thirty-Two

✂ ✂

Lucy Desmond was just eleven years old when she lost her mother, her past, and seemed to fall off the face of the earth.

She had gone for the pork-pie to The Horse and Hounds down the side-street off Soho Square. She was skipping along, merry as a cricket. She was a joyous creature and complacent in the way of children who have known only love and indulgence all their lives.

She was particularly happy that evening because Bert Hockney would be there for supper. She liked Bert. He made her and her mother laugh and he was very kind.

She reached The Horse and Hounds, humming the song the organ-grinder was playing and as she reached it a couple of soldiers and a gentleman rode up to the door of the public house.

She stopped a moment to stare at the wonderful scarlet uniforms. They looked so smart, so elegant up there above her on their steeds. She saw that the gold buttons on the uniforms had little leaves embossed on them. She thought how she would love buttons emblazoned like that on her shoes, and she pulled her cloak further around her and the hood over her bright blonde curls.

She did not notice how the gentleman riding with the soldiers scrutinized her also. He was drably dressed compared to the uniforms and did not catch her eye.

It began to drizzle, the sky darkened and the lamplighter came around to light the lamps. The activity recalled her errand to her mind and she turned to go into the tavern.

When the gentleman approached her it took her by surprise. She was startled and jumped.

'Sir? What, sir?' she asked.

He looked down upon her benignly. He was corpulent and to her he looked very old.

'I said you are a very pretty young lady.' He spoke softly.

She blushed. 'Oh I'm not a lady,' she hastened to assure him.

'We'll see you inside, Bosie,' one of the soldiers called, dismounting and tethering his horse.

'Tell them I want the upstairs room. We'll go in the back way,' the gentleman called to his friends and winked at them.

'Yes. If no one else has bagged it,' the other soldier shouted back.

'No one has!' the gentleman cried. 'Go on ahead. I'll catch up. I booked it.'

He turned to the little maid. 'Have you ever been upstairs in The Horse and Hounds?' he asked her in the same way Bert asked her to search for a present he had brought her.

She shook her head. 'No, sir. Only grand people go up there.'

'Yes. For private parties.' He bent down to her for she

was short of stature, small for her age. 'We are having a private party there this evening. It is a grand room.' He turned away from her, then as she went to move towards the entrance he looked back. 'Would you care to have a peek at it?' he asked conspiratorially. 'I could sneak you up the back stairs, then you could have a look, and hurry right down again. It is very beautiful.'

He was leaning towards her now and his breath smelled and she didn't like that, but she was curious. Lily and Ben Marks who ran the public house had often boasted of the grandeur of the room upstairs. 'It's a treat, so it is,' Lily had told Lucy time and time again when she came in for some beer. 'Real elegant it is, but it's not for the likes of you,' she'd say and fill Lucy's jug and give her carefully measured portions of pie.

Lucy wanted to see for herself how grand and elegant it was so when the old gentleman said he'd show it to her she trotted along beside him, around the corner to the private entrance and up the stairs in front of him. He was staring at her frilly drawers but she did not know that.

When they reached the room she was very disappointed. It was dark and musty, badly furnished with the upholstery coming out of some of the chairs and a loose spring under the sofa. There was a smell of stale alcohol and yesterday's tobacco. Her mama's front parlour was far grander.

She stood in the centre of the room, which was now strangely quiet. The soldiers had unbuttoned their uniforms and stood staring at her, drinking their drinks. The gentleman too was looking intently at her.

Suddenly she was afraid. Terribly afraid. She turned swiftly and began to run but the gentleman put his foot out and she tripped over it and fell. She knew he had done it deliberately.

'Got ya!' he cried triumphantly.

'Isn't it a bit dangerous, Bosie?' one of the soldiers asked. 'We don't know who she is.'

'Look at her! Stuff cloak, jug for beer! This is no lady, as she herself told me. She'll not talk, will you, little one?' Bosie asked, pinching her cheek, catching her by the shoulder, hurting her.

'Let me go,' she whispered. She was terribly frightened and her voice had deserted her. She could hear the noise from the pub below, a roar of conversation and activity. A piano plonking 'If you were the Only Girl in the World . . .', so when Bosie grabbed her again and Lucy cried out, they knew and she knew no one would hear her.

'Which of us first?' one of the soldiers asked, his voice thick.

'Well, who do you think?' Bosie was unbuttoning his trousers. 'Don't ask fool questions, Dominic. I got the gal up here so naturally I get first dip.'

Suddenly she could see his private parts. She had never seen a man naked before and the huge thing that escaped his trousers terrified her.

'Hold her,' he ordered and the two soldiers jumped on her and held her on the floor. One of them caught her by the wrists and held them above her head and the other spread her legs and pushed up her skirts. She struggled and fought but they dragged off her drawers and then the gentleman lay on top of her and she thought he would crush her to death. She begged, her voice choking, and she wriggled to escape, but she was powerless. He rammed that great big thing into her and she shrieked in agony and mercifully partially lost consciousness. In a haze of agonizing pain she felt him ram her repeatedly, her body protesting at every invasion. Then something happened to him, like a fit, she thought, and he fell off her and there was one of the soldiers over her doing to her what the gentleman had done. Only the pain was worse now and he made such animal noises and it became so unbearable that she blacked out. Then she felt a searing agony tear her body apart again and when she half-opened her eyes there were two of them on top of her, the one called Bosie pushing that great thing of his into the behind of the man who was ramming her. They were roaring, the three of them, shouting obscenities, doing these terrible things to each other. Their faces were mottled and throbbing and seemed to her like the gargoyles she had seen on buildings in the city. After a moment of excruciating pain she completely lost consciousness.

198

Slowly the pain drifted back. Lucy felt herself lifted up and carried. She heard their voices, soft now, speaking about her and treating her as if she were a discarded piece of rubbish. 'Throw her there. Someone will find her.'

She did not know where she was. She could feel the slime of the street below her. Her face was in something that smelled like horse-manure. She was bleeding. She could smell and taste her blood. She heard the dancing of hooves on the ground somewhere near and that was when she heard a voice calling, 'Lucy? Lucy? Lucy, where are you? Lucy? . . .' Darkness folded in on her and held her for days, weeks, months? She did not know.

A couple of nuns from the Convent of Good Hope found her. They brought her back with them and tended her terrible wounds. Tilly helped them and they kept her with them.

At first they tried to find out her name, where she came from. To no avail. She had forgotten. From the moment they found her she had no recollection of her past.

Eventually her body recovered. She never got her memory back and she seemed always a little vague in her mind. As if she was somewhere else.

The nuns grew to love her. Her sweet disposition won their hearts and eventually they ceased trying to persuade her to remember. They stopped badgering her about who she was, where she came from and what had happened to her. There was never an answer.

Chapter Thirty-Three

☕

It was spring and Maeve was ready to make her debut. According to Belle Desmond what she now needed was an audience.

'An audience is like an animal; a large, warm, breathing beast, to be tamed every night or it will devour you. All you've got to do is show it who's master.'

'Mistress,' Demara said.

'Oh fooey!' Belle hated her dramatic flow to be checked. She waved her arms, explaining, illustrating. 'You have to command their attention, hypnotize them, enchant them and they'll become your slaves. But if you fail – BOOM!' She clapped her hands together. 'They'll hiss you and boo you savagely and chase you off the stage. There's no compromise.'

They were in the overcrowded living-room. Everything shone, there was not the tiniest speck of dust. Demara was a superb housekeeper. They sat around the crackling fire toasting muffins Demara had purchased from Smark the muffin-man. It was a cold March day and the rain pattered on the window panes, but all was cosy and comfortable within.

Mrs Desmond sat, feet in the cinders, gazing into the leaping flames, then, as was her wont when she was, as she put it, inspired by an idea, she clapped her hands and cried out in a loud voice, 'Geoffrey Denton! Bless me, Geoffrey Denton.' She clasped her hands over her heart as if she had trilled out 'Romeo' or 'Abelard' or 'Hamlet' in a full theatre to a packed, admiring audience.

'Geoffrey Denton!' she repeated fervently.

Demara knew Belle Desmond by now well enough to decipher her line of thought.

'Is he an actor?' she inquired, feeling sure she was correct in her surmise.

'An actor!' Belle screamed.

'An actor!' Maeve stared at Demara in horror.

'She calls Geoffrey Denton *an* actor!' Belle cried in shocked tones.

'Oh sacrilege! Oh philistine! Oh ignoramus!'

Demara looked at Maeve for enlightenment.

'He is the greatest actor-manager in the world today.' Maeve sighed. 'He is Hamlet, he is Othello, he is Macbeth.'

'But what of Irving? I thought Henry Irving was the best,' Demara asked.

Belle Desmond shook her head. 'You would be wrong,' she declared. 'Oh, Irving is superb. He is magnificent. But

Geoffrey Denton has the edge. He is the genius. He is the finest artist.'

'It's like the debate as to whether Duse or Bernhardt is the greatest. Some say one, some say the other.' Maeve's little face glowed in admiration when she mentioned the names. Then she caught Belle Desmond's eye. 'In Europe,' she added hastily. 'The greatest in Europe. Not in England. In England everyone agrees Belle Desmond was far and away the best.'

Demara smiled to herself. How far they had come, how poised her sister was now, how diplomatic. She smiled too because she herself had changed. So much of what Belle had taught Maeve had rubbed off on herself. Not consciously but despite herself her manners had refined, as had her voice and her posture. Belle Desmond was a brilliant teacher. But as Maeve had devined, that was not what she wanted to be told.

'Well I *was*, dear child, I *was*. Now it is Ellen Terry or Mrs Pat Campbell.'

'Mrs Desmond has played opposite Denton,' Maeve whispered by way of explanation. 'She didn't act with Irving.'

'Oh I see!' Demara nodded.

'Irving at the Lyceum has Ellen Terry, but who has Denton got now that Catherine Hewett is dead?' Mrs Desmond asked rhetorically, then answered herself triumphantly, 'No one! He has no one at all!'

'Catherine Herett was carried off with the pox . . .' Maeve told Demara but Belle interrupted her. 'We don't know that for certain,' she said with some severity. 'She was on the generous side with her favours and her symptoms sounded very much as if she . . . ' Sighing Mrs Desmond put a hand to her head. 'Oh these gels!' she remarked. 'Think their looks and luck will last forever. Well, don't you believe it for it isn't true. We all have a time, a short time to make our mark, provide for ourselves, and if we waste it—' she clicked her tongue against her teeth— 'pfffit! It is gone and we are left, opportunity over, on the path to self-destruction!'

She stood, and brushed down her skirt. 'I'll go to see

Denton. He played my son when I did Lady Macduff "How will you live?" "As the birds do, Mother". Oh, he was so touching! I wept real tears. And he played Arthur to my Constance in *King John*.' She clasped her hands to her bosom and declaimed, ' "No, no I will not, having breath to cry". It was heart-rending, that! Yes, he brought tears to the eyes of everyone who saw him perform. "Must you with hot irons, burn out both mine eyes?" Ah! What an actor.' She smiled at Maeve. 'He'll see you, Maeve Donnelly, because I ask him to and then the rest is up to you.'

Maeve told Demara that night that she felt ill with apprehension. 'I'm *terrified*!' she confided, snuggling up close to her sister under the eiderdown. 'Suppose he hates me? Suppose he thinks I have no talent?'

'Well, he might hate you but he won't think you've no talent. Any idiot can see that you have!'

Maeve squirmed with delight. Demara had never complimented her before and coming from her sister the praise meant a lot. All during the long winter months of training Demara had not discussed her sister's talent or lack of it, so now Maeve rejoiced to hear the unequivocal statement. She had felt guilty, not working, behaving like a lady while her sister laboured at the housework, built the fires, cleaned the grates, cooked, washed dishes, washed clothes, starched and ironed, polished, scrubbed; she worked longer hours and twice as hard as ever she did in Eaton Square and all the while Maeve lived the life of a lady, was waited on hand and foot, did no household chores and simply took instruction in speech, deportment, comedy timing, the control and projection of emotion and other such accomplishments. If Maeve's application to these lessons Mrs Desmond had given her paid off, then it was all worthwhile, but if she was rejected then all her efforts were a sad waste of time and she was very aware of this fact.

The next day Mrs Desmond ordered a hansom cab and, dressed in their best, Maeve and Belle drove off to the Strand to see Geoffrey Denton at the Chandos

Theatre. Demara preferred to remain at home and prepare everything for their return, for if they were successful they would want to celebrate and if not they would need the consolation of good food and wine.

Maeve looked delectable in a pale blue linen suit with the new leg-o'-mutton sleeves. She had stitched her outfit herself and added lace at the throat and wrists. She had resisted Belle's attempts to paint and powder her and Mrs Desmond had to agree with Demara that she looked quite perfect the way God made her.

'Ach! You're right – why gild the lily?' Mrs Desmond sighed and hustled her young protégée into the cab. Telling the jarvey where to take them, she settled back breathlessly in her seat and sniffed hartshorn to revive her. She was a magnificent sight in crimson taffeta and black jet trimming, rouged cheeks and bright red curls framing her plump face. She was tightly laced into her stays and that, coupled with the fact that she scarcely ever left home these days, had put her in quite a pother. Since her little Lucy had disappeared she preferred to remain indoors in case her lost child turned up unexpectedly. No one had the heart to suggest that this seemed an unlikely occurrence and even now, before they left she instructed Demara, 'If a little girl pulls the bell, don't turn her away no matter what, but keep her with you until I come home.'

Demara assured her on that point, thinking, as she spoke that Lucy could hardly still be the little girl Belle remembered, and tucked a rug around the plump, bejewelled actress.

The cab took them around to the back of the theatre, to the stage-door in a little alley off the Strand. Maeve was wide-eyed with excitement and not at all put off by the lack of glamour and the dusty, dirty, tawdry chaos backstage.

Geoffrey Denton received them in his dressing-room. He sat before a huge wall-mirror and in front of him stood a table arranged extremely neatly with scores of sticks of various colours of make-up, jars of cream and grease and oil, black, blue and grey pencils, a gas-jet, false eyebrows, strips of beard and moustache. Elsewhere in the room were wigs, lace collars, scripts, quill pens, sheets of music, canes of various designs, cards, telegrams, messages stuck to the mirror, period shoes, silk hose, scarves, fans, swords and daggers plain and with jewelled hilts, bucklers, riding boots, breeches, embroidered tunics, gauntlet gloves, a sofa, a full-length mirror on a frame that tilted – indeed, the whole room was as cluttered in its way as Mrs Desmond's living-room.

The man sitting in front of the mirror with his back to them turned at their entrance and stared at Maeve with open admiration. He completely ignored Belle Desmond for the moment and she obviously did not mind but rather presented her protégée with outstretched hands as if she were some rare and breakable piece of china.

'Is she not perfect?' she inquired before anything was said.

' "Shall I compare thee to a summer's day?" ' Geoffrey Denton's tones were passionate and theatrical. ' "Thou art more lovely and more temperate. . ." Oh yes, she is perfect. But can she act?'

His bulk filled the room and so did his organ-resonant voice, yet he was graceful and his voice seductive. A commanding presence, he concentrated fiercely on who ever he was addressing.

He greeted the middle-aged actress warmly and if he noticed a change in her he showed no sign of it.

'Dear Belle, I haven't greeted you yet – how remiss of me. My dear, dear, dear girl, how are you? But need I ask? You too are lovelier than a summer day.'

'Oh, Geoffrey, you old rogue! An autumn day for me, I'm afraid. An autumn day.'

He kissed her on both cheeks then squarely on the mouth. 'She is everything you say,' he said, sitting again and scrutinizing Maeve more closely. 'Everything you say, but I ask you again, can she act?'

Maeve had been standing still, looking around her and at the great actor. She turned her back for a second, then, as the two stared at her she turned to face them once more, only she was different. Her enormous violet eyes were anguished, her face a mask of agony.

' "Alas, Iago, What shall I do to win my lord again? Good

friend, go to him, for by this light of heaven, I know not how I lost him." ' Her voice rang with passion, with the pain of loss. It brought tears to their eyes.

She paused, facing him, knelt before him, holding the attention in that little dressing-room with unerring authority.

' "Here I kneel – if ever my will did trespass 'gainst his love . . ." '

She finished Desdemona's heart-rending speech then stood, gathered herself together, a sparkle in her eyes replacing the tragic turmoil there, a smile curving her lips, and in lower, more vibrant tones she commenced, ' "Be kind and courteous to this gentleman; Hop in his walks and gambol in his eyes; feed him with apricocks and dewberries, With purple grapes, green figs and mul-berries. . ." '

They could *see* the fruit. Her intonation, the way she savoured the words brought the luscious spheres, their colour, their flavour acutely to mind. ' ". . . to fan the moonbeams from his sleeping eyes. . ." '

They could see the blue and silver shafts of light, feel the fatigue, and were transported to a magic place with this Titania. When she stopped there was a long silence.

'She can act! No doubt about it, she can act,' Geoffrey Denton whispered in awed tones. 'This is a great actress.'

There was no doubt in his mind. This slim little girl who hardly reached his shoulder had the power to paint him pictures, to move him, inspire him, make him weep.

Mrs Desmond wiped her eyes. 'I told you, Geoffrey. Do I lie?' The actor's noble face seemed hewn from rock yet clearly showed the play of his feelings and emotions with startling unselfconsciousness. Nothing was hidden on that transparent countenance. He turned now, a warm smile lighting up his large brown eyes. 'Dear Belle! 'Pon my soul, the beauty of your protégée, the brilliance of her performance overwhelms me.' He embraced Mrs Des-mond warmly, then turned with a flourish to Maeve. 'Maeve Donnelly, you'll be a star! Belle wrote to me about you – the letter is here somewhere.' He rifled through the correspondence on the long table before him. 'Ah! Got it.

Yes . . .' He ran his finger down the page. '. . . Here it is . . . *a child of great beauty and outstanding ability* . . . Well, I thought you were exaggerating, Belle, 'pon my soul I did, but I was wrong.' He looked long and admiringly at Maeve then turned to Belle. 'You were understating the case, dear lady. And how did you know, my dear, that I was looking for a Titania? Did you know that when you chose that speech for her to perform?'

'Of course I did, Geoffrey.' Belle burst out laughing. 'I'm not a fool!'

'You never were!' The great actor frowned and thought while they waited breathlessly. 'It would be a good part to start her on,' he said. 'She does not have to carry the play – Titania is not the focal character, it gives her the opportunity to speak the glorious verse without demanding too much emotional expression too soon.' He took Maeve's hand between his own and looked deeply into her eyes. 'My dear, welcome to the theatre. Welcome to the heartbreak and the triumph. Belle will read the play to you. We do *Cyrano* after this.' He flicked a poster which read '*Much Ado About Nothing*' with the back of his hand. 'I wish I'd met you in time for Roxanne.'

'She wasn't ready,' Belle told him.

'She'd have been much better than little miss lispy Doris Blake,' he shuddered. 'Where Fulton got her is a mystery! Why she is playing Roxanne is another. Money has something to do with it, I'll be bound. We open next week, start rehearsals for *A Midsummer Night's Dream* the next. Tell Fulton she'll be here then. Tell him Titania.' He turned from them, dismissing them perfectly.

When they were in the carriage Belle and Maeve hugged each other.

'Oh well done, my dear, well done.' Belle wiped her eyes, her bosom heaving with emotion. 'Not that I doubted you for a moment. But you know, there is always the moment when you perform for a stranger for the first time. . .'

'I didn't even think . . .' Maeve was astonished now at what she had done. 'I didn't realize what I was doing until I did it.'

'And we have a very good arrangement, my dear. I took you to Geoffrey not only because he is the best, but also because he is a generous employer.'

'Trust you, dear Mrs Desmond,' Maeve giggled.

'Oh indeed,' Belle replied tartly. 'I never sold myself cheap. And I'm not going to allow you to do so either. But as I say, Geoffrey always believed in paying for the best. He is a wise man.'

'Does he ever stop acting?' Maeve asked, and Mrs Desmond threw back her head and laughed, loudly and heartily.

'No, my dear, never!' she replied. 'Never!'

Chapter Thirty-Four

cso ͡ɔ

Demara watched her sister blossom. Maeve changed from a small shy violet blending with the landscape into a hothouse orchid proudly holding up its head the better to display its beauty. She had developed an air, a hauteur, a grand manner that perhaps was not as charming as her uncultivated freshness had been but which nonetheless commanded attention and admiration.

Geoffrey Denton put the finishing touches to Belle Desmond's work with rehearsals in a real theatre. In that empty vastness, on that echoing stage, Maeve developed her style.

A Midsummer Night's Dream was due to open at the end of March. As the great night neared Demara saw hardly anything at all of Maeve. She seemed to spend most of her days and evenings in the theatre. During the day she rehearsed *A Midsummer Night's Dream* and she stayed, she told Demara, in the evening in order to listen to Geoffrey Denton's delivery and phrasing. She was avid to learn.

Demara found herself coerced into helping in the theatre with the costumes and props. It had happened gradually with Maeve using her sister as a chaperon. Another consequence of Belle Desmond's loss was her conviction that no female, whatever her age, was safe abroad on the streets of London. So she insisted that Maeve be accompanied to and from work. Bert was a willing escort and Belle herself liked to accompany Maeve and see the theatre where she had once been a great star. She was not in the least jealous or nostalgic, for, as she said herself, she had reached the top of her profession and now was the time to make way for the young. She found the cab journeys too tiring and was over anxious she might miss her Lucy's return, however remote that possibility, so Demara's help was solicited. And Bert was especially useful in seeing Maeve home.

On delivering Maeve to the Chandos Theatre Demara naturally made the acquaintance of the cast and staff of the theatre and her gentle, competent manner inspired confidence. When they became aware of her skill as a needlewoman they began to ask her to do little jobs for them. She replied that she was afraid of offending the wardrobe mistress, but that lady was overworked and only too happy to have some help.

Demara made all Maeve's dresses for her and the company paid her. The money helped and she was able to send a little more to the family in Ireland.

She sent home money to Vernon Blackstock with religious constancy. Every month letters arrived from Ballymora: a tally from Vernon Blackstock, accounting for every penny they sent and a missive from Brigid written by Brindsley. It said more or less the same thing every month in more or less the same words: *Thank you for the money. All is well here. Hope it is there. We keep well and hope you do too. Ma and Da.*

It hardly varied except once or twice, when an odd little post-script was added, like: *We do not see why you should leave Áine and your own family for strangers.* And: *We do not like the idea of Maeve on the stage. And Father Maguire does not either.*

Demara explained everything in her letters to them, which were long and full of the type of information she would have liked to receive. She informed them, to the best of her ability, why the things they inquired about had happened; Áine's apartment was too small, she told them, and with the babby Seaneen they were crowded. She knew her mother would wonder why that mattered with family. She could hear her father ask the question. But they did not refer to it again. Maeve, Demara informed them later, was a very talented actress and she was with a very respectable company and they need not worry. Again the subject was not referred to and the letters came worded the same.

Demara asked for news. She asked questions that were never answered. And so, as time passed, she became used to receiving the few trite, unrevealing lines, consoling herself that no news probably meant that all was well, yet feeling deep inside her a nasty little certainty that it was not.

She polished her memories in bed at night in the dark when the lamp was out and Maeve's sweet sleeping breath fanned her cheek and no one could see her tears. She remembered the mauve mists, the veils that parted as she walked the country lanes to reveal the sublime majesty of the green land, the trees, the leaves and azure lakes scattered like jewels across the verdant swards.

One night as thoughts of the great swell of the mountains, the lowering Ben Bannagh and the crashing of the black sea against the red cliffs, the smell of the heather and the raucous shriek of seagulls threatened to overwhelm her, she thought she heard a sigh, a deep reverberating moan, and she turned to see if her sister was in pain.

A shaft of silvery light from between the curtains illuminated her sister's beautiful, sleeping face, and, relieved, Demara turned away and sighed and prepared to settle herself for sleep also.

But it came again, a groan that made her shiver and, propping herself up on her elbows, she looked about the room.

A shadow detached itself from the wardrobe. It seemed fluid to Demara, insubstantial, yet very real, a cloaked figure, hooded, moving against the dusk, part of the darkness, yet apart.

'Who are you?' she asked. 'What do you want?'

Strangely she was not afraid.

209

'You know me! You know the answers to those questions.' The voice was scarce above a whisper.

'No. I do not know what you want.'

'I want nothing. I have come to tell you that it is all there waiting for you.'

'What is?'

'The materials for your house in Bannagh Dubh. It is there. Your wish has not been forgotten. It has been registered. Our pact holds.'

Then there was nothing. The curtains blew. The door of the wardrobe fell open on its hinges. No one was there.

Had she dreamed it? Was it a spectre she had seen or a figment of her imagination? A ghost? A demon? Satan? All she knew was that she felt reassured. Her dream was reinforced by the vision. It *would* happen.

She gave a contented sigh and went back to her dreams of Bannagh Dubh, the mountains and the sea.

Chapter Thirty-Five

ぉ ∞

Demara went to Berwick Street Market to get beads for Maeve's dress. Her sister had told her how she wanted to look as Titania: 'All moonbeams and soft shimmer, Demara, not gaudy, not obvious.'

Wardrobe in the theatre had a costume made of gold thread which had been worn by another Titania and they were not prepared to pay for another.

'It's far too *heavy*, Demara,' Maeve complained. 'It is earthbound. Titania should look ethereal.'

'Then we must get what you want, Maeve.' Belle was certain. 'It is worth it. It is your first performance and you either stand or fall by it, so no expense must be spared. Very few actresses get a second chance and I don't want anything preventing you from giving of your best.'

'Demara can do it for me. She'll understand what I want.

Titania has to be fluid. A fairy queen, a spirit. Like water. She moves insubstantially. I want to wear gossamer.'

Demara decided to try chiffon and to sew tiny seed-pearls and sequins and beads like a waterfall in panels over the finest silk shift.

Áine told them that Berwick Street Market had a bead stall where she could choose from a wide variety at very competitive prices. So one fine spring morning Demara and Bert set out to make her purchases.

The day was chilly but fresh. Snowdrops pushed up from under the cold earth and daffodils nodded, pinched but bright yellow. The sun, pale primrose, washed a pearl-grey sky.

'It's on its way,' Bert said, confidently sniffing the sharp air.

'What, Bert?' she asked.

'The nice weather,' he replied. His face was red with the rawness of the day but his eyes twinkled with his good humour. Every so often he searched the faces of the passersby and Demara, who had asked him about this before, knew that he was searchiing for Lucy Desmond.

'I wonder why Áine is so pessimistic,' Demara mused. 'Honestly, Bert, she complains so much! She's so sure everyone is better off than she is and that's not true. It's such a pain!'

'There are people like that – see the bad side of everything. Give them silver, they'd complain it wasn't gold.'

'I suppose so.' She glanced at her companion in his best suit, shiny at the elbows, but neat and brushed. 'You know, Bert, I don't know what Maeve and I would have done without you. You changed our lives completely. I don't think we've ever thanked you enough.'

Bert's face turned redder, his hands in his pockets were tight fists and he kept kicking any substantial object his boots came in contact with in an agony of self-consciousness.

'Aw!'

'No, I mean it. Our life with Áine was tense, and, well, difficult. But you introduced us to Mrs Desmond, and everything changed.'

'All I did – like, all I did was introduce you. That's all!'

She tucked his arm through hers. 'It's not all, dear Bert. Without you there was no sunshine in our lives. Now there is a lot.'

He said nothing but there were tears sparkling in his eyes and a foolish grin on his face.

When they arrived at the market they were greeted by a cacophany of street cries, vendors selling 'Eels and crabs', 'Flounders', 'Oranges and lemons, twelve pence a peck'. There were stalls selling shoelaces and buttons, scarves from the Indies, fine leather pouches, carved ivory, tins and ironware. There were barrowboys, costermongers and street traders jostling each other for customers and trying to keep out the gypsies. There were also traders in repairs and services yelling at the top of their lungs, 'Brass pot or iron pot to mend?', 'Wood to cleave?', 'Old chairs to mend?', 'Knives or scissors to grind?'

Someone was playing a barrel-organ and the combined noises made conversation impossible.

Bert indicated a stall some way off and Demara hurried after him. He cleaved a pathway through the throngs, pushing and shoving to make his way and clear a path for her. The racket seemed louder the deeper they penetrated.

The beads, crystals, pearl and sequins, buttons and mother-of-pearl displayed on the stall by a costermonger who wore a costume made of mother-of-pearl buttons himself. They were so various as to take Demara's breath away.

'How lovely!' she cried. 'Oh, Bert, how delightful.'

'You make your choice, lady,' the man told her cheerfully. 'You'll get no better value the world over!'

'Demara? Demara Donnelly?'

She heard the soft inquiry at her elbow and turned to look into the face of a girl a few years older than she. She was extremely pretty and familiar in some strange, half-remembered way. Yet Demara was sure she was a stranger. The girl obviously did not think so and was smiling at Demara as if they were the oldest friends.

'Demara Donnelly, I declare! You do not remember

212

me?' The girl laughed. Her clothes were fashionable if a little gaudy and there was something a touch brazen about her that Demara found difficult to pinpoint. Bert was pulling her away.

'Look here, Demara,' he cried. ' 'Ere are just wot you are looking for.' He did not know what she was looking for and to Demara's surprise he seemed anxious to get her away from the laughing stranger.

Demara stared at the girl. She was very lightly clad, although in the pink of fashion. It was such a fresh day yet she wore a beige satin dress trimmed with chocolate-coloured velvet and she had a feathered hat like a cockade on top of her heavy dressed auburn curls. She had a fine Indian shawl over her shoulders, hardly enough to keep the chill out. And Demara noticed she was most definitely made-up. Her skin was very white and her cheeks and lips were brushed with rouge. A small black-clad maid, a girl of about fifteen years of age with a tiny pinched face and a white mop-cap, accompanied her. She was laden with parcels and purchases she had some difficulty in managing.

The laughing girl stared at Demara with wide curious eyes that suddenly became hard.

'You don't recognize me, do you? Oh heavens above, Demara, I'm Bryony Gilligan, Brian and Della from home—' she corrected herself – 'from Ballymora, I mean. Don't you recognize me?'

For a moment it did not sink in. Ballymora was so far away, another world, another life. In Demara's memory the people of her village were unsophisticated; the antithesis of Londoners. Their cheeks were naturally rosy, their eyes were bright, their garb drab; they were unpainted and natural. They were the exact opposite of the thin pale-faced workers and poor of the city, and the capital's dandies, rakes and fashionable upper classes were armed with all the artifice of the metropolis. To connect this elegant young lady accompanied by her maid with Brian and Della Gilligan seemed an outlandish feat and one that took several minutes to accomplish.

'Bryony? Bryony Gilligan? But . . . but . . .'

'Oh, Demara, don't be green! Lord above, I declare you sound witless, upon my word you do! I don't know whether to be insulted or flattered!'

'Bryony! Oh be flattered. I thought you were a fine, fashionable lady.'

'I *am*, Demara, I *am*!' The girl's eyes glittered and there was a cautionary look there that made Demara pause. 'And what pray are you doing here in London? I never thought that you, Demara, would be parted from your beloved Bannagh Dubh?'

'I came to earn some money to send home to Da so he can finish payments on the cottage,' Demara explained.

'Did not we all do that, Demara. Not send it to finish payments on the cottage that, my dear, was a Donnelly conceit. Only the Donnellys and the Dannons were uppity enough to aspire to *buying* their homes! But we all came to London to send money home!'

There was bitterness in the girl's voice. 'And your family? They are all well, I trust?'

'I hope so!' Demara replied politely, and Bryony gazed at her, trying to detect any derision in her childhood friend. 'My mother doesn't say much in her letters; the usual inquiries, the usual reassurances.'

Bryony's eyes widened and Demara smiled to herself. Constantly listening to Shakespeare and the other playwrights Belle Desmond used for Maeve's coaching had helped Demara's vocabulary, a fact she was conscious of and that she realized was not lost on the bright girl before her.

'Are you living with Áine?' Bryony asked.

Demara shook her head. 'When I came over I stayed there.'

'I did too,' Bryony smiled. 'When I arrived I stayed one night. It was enough.'

Something in Demara's eyes warned her not to say any more on that subject. 'No. We, Maeve and I. . .'

'Oh! Is Maeve with you then?'

Demara nodded.

A monkey in a smart red military jacket jumped on her shoulder and held out his tiny peaked cap for coins. He

214

was the organ-grinder's little assistant and with a laugh Bryony unloosened the strings of her bag and took out some silver which she tossed into the monkey's cap. The little fellow drew back his lips, gave a delighted cry then ran chattering away. Bryony's attitude was not lost on Demara. She showed a lofty generosity and the ability to be flash with money. Demara felt the gesture had been executed to show her that Bryony had plenty to splash around.

'Maeve is an actress,' Demara said. She did not know why she announced this fact and felt it was probably to show off. She was ashamed of her motives.

Bryony narrowed her eyes, 'An actress?'

Regretting she had given this information Demara hedged. 'Well, not quite yet perhaps,' she said. 'She is making her debut in a few weeks.'

'Ah indeed. In the Music Hall in Edgeware Road? There are a lot of Irish performers there. I suppose she sings?'

'Oh no!' Demara didn't know why she was shocked. 'Not there! She is playing in the Chandos Theatre in the Strand. She is Titania. In *A Midsummer Night's Dream*. With Geoffrey Denton.'

She detected a touch of the green-eyed monster in Bryony's eyes, which stared at her speculatively. 'And you, Demara? What do you do?' she asked, pressing a fragment of cambric edged with lace against her forehead with great delicacy.

'I housekeep for our landlady,' Demara replied in untroubled honesty. She had not yet learned to dissemble. 'I used to skivvy for Lady Carmichael in Eaton Square.' She saw Bryony's shiver of disgust and a look of horror cross her face. 'But I don't have to do that any more,' she concluded.

'Really, Demara, how awful for you! How appalling!' Bryony waved the handkerchief to and fro in front of her face, which had grown pale.

'Oh, it was not so bad really. We worked as hard at home in Ballymora, if not harder.'

Bryony looked at Demara with some distaste. 'I do not like to remember those days,' she said emphatically.

'Oh? Strange! I love to. Memories of home are all that sustain me in this foreign land,' Demara replied truthfully.

'My dear, you'd best forget all about Ballymora if you want to make progress in London,' Bryony informed her. 'Small villages and their lifestyle are a matter of ridicule in this place.'

'Then I am sorry for the ones who mock. They cannot be up to very much.'

Bryony laughed scornfully, but she laid her hand on Demara's arm. 'Listen, Demara, if you ever feel like, oh, earning *real* money, not having to worry about bills, having a good time, well, you could do worse than to come and see me.'

'What employment are you in, Bryony?' Demara asked innocently.

Bryony burst out laughing again. It was that harsh little tinkle like bells out of tune. Then she stopped and looked challengingly at Demara. 'I'm *not* employed,' she declared, keeping her eyes fixed on Demara's face, 'I'm kept!'

At first Demara did not understand and Bryony could see the bewilderment in her eyes.

'Kept?'

'Yes, Demara. Kept. I expect Father Maguire would say I was ruined!'

Demara suddenly understood. She had heard enough about the sinful and base impulses of men and the maidens who satisfied the bestial in the male sex. Their priest had pounded the pulpit often enough in near frenzied diatribe against such commercial exchange. Women who sold their bodies for favours sold their souls to the Devil. So said Father Maguire and Father Maguire, they said in Ballymora, was God's right hand.

'Don't look so shocked, Demara,' Bryony smiled. 'I'm protected. I have powerful protectors and I am looked after well. A girl who is ruined leads a comfortable life.'

'Where do you live?'

'Around the corner in Manchester Square,' Bryony said. 'I live there in fashionable luxury. I have my own servants. Bessie here is my maid.' The girl bobbed a curtsy. 'I would like it if . . . ' She faltered to a stop, then glanced up at

216

Demara with a suddenly vulnerable look. ' . . . if you could, perhaps, visit? Take tea with me . . . but perhaps you'd prefer not. . .'

'Of course,' Demara reassured her hastily. 'I'd . . . we'd be delighted to.' Demara impulsively took the girl's arm and leaned over and kissed her cheek. She heard Bert, who was hovering a little distance from them, hoot derisively and she glanced at him. 'This is my friend Bert Hockney, Bryony,' she said, 'Bert, this is Bryony Gilligan from my home town.'

Bert snatched off his cap and bowed awkwardly. Bryony did a little bob and said haughtily, 'Charmed.' Then she turned back to Demara. 'May I ask you then to drop in on me at number ten? Any Tuesday, Wednesday or Friday between the hours of three and six o'clock of the afternoon. I would be so happy to receive you.'

Bert hooted again under his breath and Demara nodded. 'I would love to, Bryony. You may count on me.'

Bryony smiled and leaning over returned Demara's embrace, then, calling to her maid, she hurried away, the crowd parting automatically before her as if she were someone of importance. Bert and Demara watched until she disappeared from view, then Demara rounded on him.

'Don't you *ever* show discourtesy to a friend of mine again, Bert Hockney, do you hear me?'

'Why . . . why . . . ' the astonished Bert blinked. He had never known Demara so angry. 'I'm sorry. I didn't mean to. It's just that . . . ' he petered out.

'Just that what, Bert?'

'It's just that, well, she seemed to be a lady of bad reputation, miss.' He always called Demara miss when he was nervous of her.

'And so what?' she asked crisply. 'Who are you to sit in judgement? By what divine right do you assume the mantle of our heavenly Father, God Himself? Dear me, Bert, you astonish me, that you do.'

'I'm sorry, miss, truly I am.'

'I will have you know that my friends are never condemned for how they live their lives or what their role in life may be. Rich or poor. Honourable or not. As the case may be. Sometimes, Bert, we cannot help the paths we are set on. And we have no right to condemn others out of hand.'

'I understand, miss. I'll never do it again,' Bert replied contritely.

'I should hope not,' she said briskly. 'Just imagine, Bert, if that is the profession poor little Lucy Desmond has been lured into? Would you condemn her in the same way as you did Bryony?'

This thought had never struck Bert before and he stopped, amazed at the idea.

'Now come along, Bert,' Demara told him. 'We must make our purchases and return home directly. Mrs Desmond will be worried if we are delayed, and we must not cause her anxiety.'

Bert nodded, relieved that she seemed to have forgiven him. She chose her baubles and trimmings from the stall and turned to leave, noting with a wry smile that no one troubled to get out of her way as she walked along. Yet the crowd must have known, if Bert did, that Bryony was a female of dubious reputation. She shook her head. How hypocritical people are, she thought, and, well satisfied with her purchases and with a lot to think on she left the market and returned home.

Chapter Thirty-Six

جو جھ

Demara did not think about Bryony again until after her sister's debut.

It was a triumph. Ethereal in her moonbeam dress, so exquisite the audience gasped at her entrance, her voice viola-mellow, Maeve spoke the words with humour and passion and thrilled both her audience and the critics, and all London declared itself at her feet.

It was heady stuff for the young country-girl but Maeve seemed to weather the storm of admiration, the accolades, the excesses of the crowds and the hordes of adoring people who swore that they were completely under her spell. She had Belle's influence to steady her and Geoffrey Denton was at pains to enlighten her about the fickle nature of the public.

'Enjoy it while it lasts,' he told her, 'because, my dear, it won't! They love to build you up only to knock you down, and if you believe them, if you let them know they have power over you, they'll despise you. If you let them seduce you they'll devour you. Be a realist and do not let these extravagances go to your head.'

'They love the new discovery. You are the fashion. If you wear a ribbon around your throat, they'll all follow. They'll laud you, adore you, and then when they've had enough they'll discard you,' Belle told her. 'But you are good. You are a first-class actress and when the new young darling emerges and you have to take a back seat you have the talent to continue in your career. I hope you have the sense.'

They sent Maeve flowers and presents, always within the bounds of good taste. Those that were not were returned. She received love-letters by the score. Everybody wanted to meet her. Society opened its doors to her. She was not stupid enough to imagine all the barriers were down but she felt herself welcome wherever she went. She was courted, fêted, elevated from obscurity to fame – and she kept her head.

Mrs Desmond then decided to write to the convent for another skivvy. 'It makes me feel quite ill, Demara, to see you on your hands and knees scrubbing and polishing.'

'Yes, Demara,' Maeve backed her up, 'I'm earning enough now for you not to have to work so hard.'

'But I do not mind,' Demara assured them.

'Well, it gives me palpitations,' Belle affirmed. 'Besides, as Maeve says, we can afford some help now.' She stopped Demara's protests with a commanding hand. 'No. I insist. You'll still have plenty to do, stitching and sewing and cooking. But for the scrubbing and such, we need another pair of hands. And you'll be giving some poor homeless child a home.'

'You did not do well with Mary Jacks.'

'Nor did I,' Belle agreed. 'But all the others I had from the Sisters were solid gold. And every barrel of apples has a bad 'un. Besides, poor Mary wasn't that bad. She stole, that's true, but perhaps I would in her position.'

'You're too soft, Mrs D,' Bert cried, 'an' I know why you does it. You 'ave a soft 'eart an' you like caring for people. That's why I brought Demara and Maeve here in the first place.'

Belle laughed, then turned to Demara. 'So you see, Demara,' she said, 'I'm quite set on it.'

She wrote to the convent and once more the Reverend Mother pondered on who to send. It was heartbreaking to have to make the choice. Mrs Desmond was a good woman and whoever went to her was bound to be happy. Mary Jacks was the first girl Mrs Desmond had sent back and who had not been happy there.

She had never met Mrs Desmond. She was a name on a list of women who needed home help and to whom the Sisters sent that help. The Reverend Mother understood that Mrs Desmond had a kind heart.

She looked out into the courtyard. The sun kissed the warm York stone and the statue of St Anthony stood on his pedestal serenely gazing down on the two girls below him. They sat on the stone bench which was warm from the sun. Rose inevitably sewing and Tilly Bywater beside her, knitting matinée jackets for the orphan babies below in the hospital. A little apart from them Mary Jacks was reading. Mary was practising for Father Brown. He wanted a reader for an old blind lady who lived in Frith Street, not far from the convent. Mary Jacks had set her heart on the job, and the Reverend Mother was glad they had found something that suited her so well.

The choice then was between Rose and Tilly. It was a difficult choice. She did not think Rose was really up to it. The girl was not strong and she had a weak chest. It worried Reverend Mother that since her arrival five years ago Rose had not been out of the convent. She had never even been out for an errand. She got panicky if it was suggested she go.

Reverend Mother looked again at the letter. If, as one of the girls had told her long ago, Mrs Desmond was an actress, then she probably had a loud voice and loud voices frightened Rose. She cowered and went into one of her trances. She could of course explain to Mrs Desmond that the child had had a frightening experience, but that would hardly be fair on either employer or employee. After all, Mrs Desmond had a right to expect the best.

Reverend Mother pondered. Should she take a chance? It might do Rose a power of good to have some commerce with the world outside the convent walls. But no. She shook her head.

It would have to be Tilly. She did not want to separate that pair. They were like sisters, but Tilly was the perfect choice, she had to admit. Nina Norris was pert. Sarah Kerr was plain stupid. Joan Planer had some very unpleasant habits. No, Tilly Bywater was the one, and the only things against the idea were that 1) Tilly was nervous and when she was excited she dropped things, and 2) she was devoted to Rose and Rose to her and it would be a shame to split them up.

Out in the cloisters Mary Jacks was finishing a page, ' " 'er . . . 'er . . . Her mother said, smiling." There. Got it.' She shut the book triumphantly.

'Do you miss your mother, Rose?' Tilly asked.

The Reverend Mother had opened her window preparatory to calling Tilly in, but she listened for the reply.

'Oh, yes. If I had one,' Rose said. 'You know, Tilly, sometimes I feel it *here*,' she pressed her heart, 'like a needle. I don't know if I want to find out whether I have one or not.'

'What do you mean, Rose?'

'Well, if I had a mother and she loved me, just think of all the pain I must have caused her. And if I hadn't, then think of the pain that will cause me. I don't think I want to know. And I'm so happy here.' She caught Tilly's hand, 'And I'm so afraid Reverend Mother will send me away. I'd die if I had to leave.'

221

Reverend Mother did not listen to any more. She called down to the three girls. 'Tilly? Tilly? will you come up here to me now, please? And don't forget to scrape your boots when you come in, there's a good girl.'

Rose's eyes filled with tears. The window closed and she held Tilly's hand in a fierce grip. 'She's sending you away, Till. Oh I'm going to be lost without you.'

'Oh hush up, Rose. I'll visit. Reverend Mother likes us to, so I'll come every Sunday, just you wait and see.'

'Well, I'll miss you anyhow,' Rose reiterated.

'And I'll miss you. I expect I'll be busy though. But I *will* come to see you.'

She ran indoors without scraping her boots and Rose sighed. It would be lonely without Tilly. She glanced at Mary Jacks who was practising her aitches, saying *HA HA HA*, spluttering on the exhale breath. Mary wouldn't replace Tilly in Rose's affections but she was better than nothing. She smiled at the girl. 'Would you like me to help you?' she asked, and Mary hurried over to her.

Tilly left for Soho Square that evening. Dispatched by the Reverend Mother, she took all her worldly possessions from the little room she shared with Rose. She left the convent, carrying a small holdall, and found Bert Hockney waiting for her outside to escort her to her new abode.

Demara liked her immediately. Her nervousness touched her and Tilly was strong and not at all work-shy, but willing and cheerful. She had a happy disposition and told Mrs Desmond that she was very glad to be there. She told Demara, much to her amusement, that she didn't understand how Mary Jacks could have said that Mrs Desmond was a slave-driver, for Tilly did not think she could accuse her employer of that.

Demara took the girl under her wing and together they shared the household chores and duties.

She still dreamed of Ballymora, but the dream lacked urgency, the edge had worn off her purpose. The house in Soho Square was very comfortable. They ate well. Their life was becoming more social. Maeve was sparkling: like an enchanted creature she twinkled brilliantly and the company she kept was interesting. Demara was getting

222

used to luxury and took comfort for granted. And then
Maeve met Sebastian Davenport.

Chapter Thirty-Seven

ᴄᴏ ᴏᴄ

Every night the theatre was packed. Geoffrey Denton was
vastly pleased. All London was queuing to see the
beautiful young Titania. Geoffrey was a very great artist
but not one averse to financial rewards. There was rivalry
between all the actor-managers and the advent of Maeve
Donnelly in the company had put him well ahead of Irving
and Forbes-Robertson.

Lord Sebastian Davenport, who would be the ninth Earl
of Malvern when his father died, was young, handsome
and a leader of fashion. He was also one of the most
eligible bachelors in England.

'If he takes you up, Maeve, you're made,' Geoffrey
Denton told her when he discovered the prospective Earl
had a box that night.

Maeve laughed, but thought nothing of what he said.
She liked Geoffrey very much. He was like her father,
strong, confident, a figure of authority whom she trusted.

She was happier than she ever dreamed she could be,
and men did not enter into the picture. She adored the
theatre, she loved Belle Desmond, she felt fulfilled,
cherished and secure. Everywhere she went she was made
much of. Her happiness showed on her face. Her eyes
dazzled. Her skin was luminous. Her energy and joy
sparkled like the bubbles in champagne.

Her days were full. She rehearsed in the morning. The
next production was *Othello* and she was cast as
Desdemona. She wanted more than anything for her
interpretation of the tragic heroine to be even better than
Titania.

'The critics loved you in the *Dream*,' Belle told her. 'Now

223

they'll be watching like hawks and if Desdemona isn't superior in every way they'll be only too pleased to crucify you. We want to deepen your voice; work on the lower register. The way you're reading those lines, Desdemona comes across as simply very sweet.'

'She *is* sweet!'

'Yes, but she's strong too. She defies her father. That took courage in those days. Belle waved enthusiastically, 'Listen: "*My downright violence and scorn of fortunes may trumpet to the world . . .*" Strong! Strong, Maeve. Her voice should ring with passion and strength! And later she's bewildered. But she is not weak! She *knows* she has done nothing wrong. She has the surety of innocence . . .'

'Oh, Belle, I wish I could have seen you in the part. You must have been magnificent!'

The innocence Belle talked of shone in her faded blue eyes as she coached her pupil and Maeve could see under the fleshy middle-aged body the young and beautiful girl, eager for love, on fire with passion, and saw what a great actress Belle must have been.

In the afternoons Maeve worked on her voice. Then, after tea, in front of the fire with Mrs Desmond and Demara, she rested until it was time to go to the theatre.

After the performance she was tired and she liked to return straight home. Belle was usually asleep by then but Demara, if she was not collecting Maeve, waited up for her. They talked. Demara got food from the public house, fish and chips, or cooked something herself for her sister. Sometimes she made soup like the broth Brigid used to make in Ballymora and Maeve listened while Demara talked of home, and very often Maeve nodded off as Demara reminisced, her yearning for her homeland in her voice, in her eyes, in every gesture she made.

Then the sisters went to bed and slept till morning's light. No more rising at four a.m. in the dark, for the milking. No more facing the freezing dawn in winter. No more labouring under the heat of the summer sun at midday in August. Maeve couldn't understand her sister's preference.

'Why ever do you want to go back?' she would ask

Demara in bewildered disbelief. 'Here we've got the cushy life, the warmth, good food in our bellies, and tasty food at that.' Her violet eyes sparkled at the thought of all their creature comforts. 'We have choice,' she added. 'Oh, Demara, the luxury of deciding what to eat, which dainty morsel we'll sample this day. What pretty gown I'll wear. The Liberty print or the India cotton. Oh, it's grand!'

'Oh, I appreciate all that,' Demara replied. 'But here people shut their doors against the world and I long, Maeve, for the half-door open to all, friend and stranger alike, and the turf-fire to tell tales around. Knowing everybody. Acquainting ourselves with travellers. Making them welcome. Ah, but much more than that is the sea calling to my blood and the wind in the trees. It's the colours and the mists and my dream of a tall pearl-grey house in Bannagh Dubh overlooking the lake and facing the wild Atlantic.

The firelight flickered on Maeve's rosy face. 'I've heard tell,' she said, 'of countries where the sun always shines and the sea is blue and calm and warm as this broth.'

'An' who wants that?' Demara asked her, puzzled. 'Who wants such an unnatural state, I ask you?'

'Well, I do for one.' Maeve said firmly.

When Demara did not accompany her sister from the theatre, Bert did. Bert loved to pick up the famous actress from the Chandos. Basking in reflected glory and feeling very privileged, he would strut forward and help her into her cab and fuss over her till she giggled and told him to stop, that she was not a ninny, and quite capable of operating under her own steam.

Sebastian Davenport had golden hair, like the knights in the fairy-tale books in Lucy Desmond's book-case, preserved against her return. Sebastian was tall and had brown velvet eyes and square shoulders and straight limbs.

The night they met, Maeve returned so late that the fire in Belle's living-room had gone out and Demara, who had fallen asleep, awakened with a shock, shivering in her chair, her feet in the ashes.

Demara looked sleepily at the clock and saw the hand pointed to three. Then she pulled her India fringed shawl around her and called out to her sister.

Maeve put her head around the door. Her eyes were like stars and her face flushed, and she wore an air of electric excitement about her.

'Oh, Demara. Oh, dearest, darling Demara! Oh what a time I've had.' She danced into the room, hugged her sister, waltzed around the furniture clapping her hands together.

'Stop, stop, Maeve. What happened? Where were you till this time? You shouldn't stay out so late. Where is Bert? Dear Lord above!'

'Oh, Demara, you're always talking of the wonders of Ballymora – well, who ever heard of staying out late there!'

'It's different and you know it! And hush up – you'll wake Belle.'

'Sebastian Davenport! He was in a box tonight. Mr Denton told me it would be a great thing for us if he liked the show. He sets the fashion in society, Mr Denton said.' Maeve sat down, then stood up restlessly and left the room. Demara followed. Her body felt tired and cramped. She stretched her arms and looked at her sister's radiant face, and a sudden shiver of fear spasmed through her. It was cold in the hall but Maeve did not seem to notice. She sat on the bottom stair and hugged herself.

'Oh, Maeve, be careful,' Demara warned her.

But Maeve was not listening. 'Geoffrey Denton brought me out in the interval to promenade in my pink silk robe.' She glanced at Demara, then jumped up and threw her arms around her sister. 'Oh, he's beautiful, Demara. He came from his box, so tall, so magnificent. His skin is so clear, his hands so perfect. He smiled at me. "I'm Sebastian Davenport," he said and I curtsied. He took my hand and kissed it. His lips were so soft. There seemed to be a smell of, oh I don't know, but it was a beautiful smell and it came from him. His smile is enchanting, Demara.'

Demara stared at her, trying to take in this long eulogy of praise. 'Oh Lord, Maeve, let's go to bed. We'll talk of this in the morning. I'm quite worn out and cramped.' She took the lamp and the sisters went up the stairs together. Demara put the lamp on the tallboy and turned it down. It burned low and the room was filled with rosy light.

'Now let me help you undress,' Demara said and unbuttoned the back of Maeve's dress, ridiculously pleased to see every tiny hoop of satin neatly around every tiny covered button. She knew her sister's toilet would not be so neat if the gentleman had taken advantage of her. Then she unlaced Maeve's corset, pleased to note ditto.

When they were tucked up in bed and Demara had turned the gas-light out she turned to her sister. 'So where were you? You still have not told me.'

'Well, during the interval he asked me to supper. He said, oh, Demara, it was so elegant, he said, "Will you do me the honour of supping with me?" Oh, Demara, if you could have heard it! I felt like the Queen.' She bounced around to face her sister. 'After the play he sent his carriage, which came from his apartments in Jermyn Street – he has a country estate in Berkshire, I think, can you imagine? Well, he just waited for this carriage and it took us to a wonderful restaurant. I didn't ask what the name was. I'm afraid I pretended I knew it. Well, everyone there knew *me*. They all greeted me – waiters, everyone. It was thrilling. We had champagne and elegant food that looked like pictures.' Maeve leaned on her elbow looking down at her sister who was fighting to stay awake. As there was no anxiety about Maeve's chastity Demara ached to sleep.

'Oh, Demara, it was the loveliest evening of my life. We talked and talked and he told me about many things. He stays in Jermyn Street and goes to the country at weekends. Then he escorted me home in the carriage.' Demara tried to keep her eyes open. 'In the carriage he was going to kiss me.' Demara opened her eyes wide and waited. 'Oh, Demara, I've never been kissed. You've been kissed. I saw Duff Dannon kiss you in the boreen . . .' Demara squirmed. Duff of the warm arms and thick thighs. Duff whose chestnut hair curled over the collar of his jacket. Duff, whose embraces, whose kisses she missed more than she could bear to admit. 'But I was too shy. It was too soon. You've known Duff all your life but I only met Sebastian this evening. I told him I did not want to yet. I knew he understood. He smiled at me and hit the roof of the carriage with his cane and the driver cracked his whip

227

and the horse increased its pace. So I'm here.'

Demara let out a relieved sigh and closed her eyes again. She was too tired to discuss the matter further. Tomorrow would be time enough to warn her little sister.

Now it was time to sleep. She said as much, or mumbled it to Maeve who bent over her and kissed her cheek, then snuggled down beside her and within minutes both of them were fast asleep.

Chapter Thirty-Eight

ᥱᥩ᷉ ᧚᷉ᥴ

She dreamed of him that night. How could she not? She had never met anyone like him before. Everything about him was exotic and rare. He came from a different species, someone very strange and utterly seductive.

His body had always been pampered. He had been fed the best food-stuffs since birth. Everything about him was groomed and perfect, not a hair out of place – the best barber saw to that. His nails were manicured yet he was also strong, physically in his prime. Beneath his clothes his body functioned with total efficiency, his whole being giving off an aura of perfect health. She had never met anyone like that before. The youths she knew at home were healthy and strong, true, but polished and groomed like one of Lord Edward's palominos, never!

So she dreamed, soft, sensuous dreams, dreams of love and undefined passion. She was as yet untutored and did not know exactly the shape her dreams could take, so she stirred restlessly and yearned for what would come and wondered what that would be.

He had been bowled over by the beautiful fairy queen in her moonbeam dress. She seemed to him to float a little off the stage like a real goddess. Her hair, loose in a cloudy cascade, threaded with pearls floating around her milky shoulders, seemed to him alive and full of stardust. The costume she wore revealed nothing, yet promised everything. It clung, appeared transparent, its draperies swirling out about the lovely young body, while in reality it was opaque. It drove him mad, this tantalizing suggestion of perfection, and he was determined to possess her.

Her voice too was seductive. Girls from the lower classes, his mother was fond of saying – and he found through personal experience she was right – had voices that grated. Their accents were common. It was something, his mother told him, that he as a cultivated man would have to make allowances for. Maeve's voice however was modulated and musical. He loved listening to her and he let her see his interest, his excitement, his desire.

She was entranced. Enchanted. He was a hero of old, a prince so glamorous she would happily have followed him wherever he asked her to go. She would have trotted after him barefoot to the ends of the earth if he so desired.

But she was modest. Her upbringing had bequeathed her a high sense of morality. She possessed an innate pride that prevented him from rushing in and treating her as he had treated actresses before. He had intended to. He was so sure she was a whore before he met her, he was sure that she could be bought. To his surprise she had a dignity that demanded respect, and the last thing he wanted was for that expression of adoration in her eyes to turn to contempt.

After he had left her in Soho Square, to his vast surprise unkissed, he returned to his apartments in Jermyn Street an astonished and frustrated man. The apartment was a bachelor's home and was used, in the main, for seduction. Its primary purpose was to lull, to relax, to dazzle the lady of his choice, to provide a setting both opulent and comfortable where sex could be indulged in both expeditiously and conveniently.

The food he usually served there was light, the wines heady, and the large bed behind a brocade curtain at the other end of the room was easily accessible. Candles flickered. The chandelier cast a muted golden glow that flattered the lady and relaxed her.

Tonight Sebastian Davenport was restless. He wondered

229

now why he had been so tardy. What on earth had got into him? He pulled the bell for his servant Hodge who had to button his waistcoat swiftly as he hurried to answer his master's summons.

His master must have been quick this night and he had been taken by surprise, off his guard and he was not ready to buttle. Perhaps, Hodge thought with amusement, the damsel had refused him. That would be a turn-up for the books. It had only ever happened once before and in the event the master had taken her anyway. Hodge had not liked that. The girl had come with his master to the apartment for supper and when he made advances she had taken fright. She had tried to escape but Sebastian, not at all used to being refused in this way, had mastered her, like an unbroken filly, he said to Hodge later, then sent her away weeping, her bodice stuffed with money. It had been Hodge's duty to get her a cab and lift the poor broken creature into it and send her on her way.

To Hodge's relief, that was not the case this evening and he found his master in high fettle, but nervous and edgy.

'She's a prize, Hodge,' he told his man. 'A rare prize and I'll have her, never you fear. We'll have supper here tomorrow night, eh, Hodge? Do your best. I want everything perfect.'

'Yes, my lord.'

'She is an artist, Hodge. A great actress. She is playing Shakespeare at the Chandos Theatre in the Strand.'

Ah, thought Hodge, that was why he did not force the pace. An actress was vocal and a personality that people would listen to if she chose to talk. One would have to be careful how one treated her if one did not want to be gossiped about.

'She loves me Hodge. She adores me.' Sebastian cried happily while Hodge thought, 'Poor bitch. Little does she know what she's letting herself in for.'

'I'm going to White's. I feel like play tonight. Be a good chap and fetch my coat and a hansom. I've sent Stephens with the carriage to the mews.'

So he would gamble, Hodge thought, face impassive, demeanour deferential. Gamble tonight and lose in the evening as much as he paid Hodge in a year. It was true what they said: lucky in love, unlucky at cards. That certainly applied to his lordship.

He closed the door, listening to the clip-clop of the nag's hooves down the street taking his master to the club. He thought about the actress, his master's latest plaything, then sighed and shook his head. Her fate was a certainty. If he had a bet on it, he was sure that, unlike his master, he would win.

Chapter Thirty-Nine

 భా భా

The next morning Belle Desmond was appalled at her protégée's quaint statement that she was in love with Lord Sebastian Davenport. 'In love? What do you mean, in love? My dear girl, actresses do not fall in love. It would be a disaster!' Belle sipped hot chocolate and puffed in distress. She liked her chocolate in peace and this disturbing news had thrown her into a flurry of frayed nerves.

She stared at Maeve, sharp-eyed. The child's behaviour bothered her and what was worse she was laughing at Belle's words. 'I am in love, dearest Mrs D. Why should it be a disaster?'

'Because, precious child, actresses believe themselves too good for the *hoi polloi*. But they are not. No aristocrat is going to *marry* an actress, and to fall in love with an artist requires a certain temperament. Falling in love with an aristocrat has no future. But I told you that before and you cannot be so foolish as not to listen.' Belle rubbed her hands on the cup, warming them. 'You must not see him again, Maeve, and that's final. Listen, my dear, your career is just beginning to blossom. You are going to be the most wonderful Desdemona. This man will take your mind off your work and that is dangerous.'

'But Geoffrey Denton *told* me it would be good if Lord

Davenport liked me. Sebastian leads society in London and what he likes everyone likes. They follow him. . .'

'My dear, you are good enough to be followed without anyone else doing the leading. And what Geoffrey is talking about is *liking*. To be praised by his lordship is desirable. To become his doxy is quite another thing. . .'

'But *you've* been a doxy. . .'

'No, Maeve, no! I never was that!' Belle Desmond shook her head. 'The men in my life made discreet arrangements. Everything was done with taste. And I did not fall passionately in love. It would have been disastrous.'

They were in the parlour. Demara had lit the fire and was crouched, listening to this conversation, coaxing the flames with a bellows. Belle had shaken Maeve's earlier composure and the young actress had two hectic spots of red on her cheeks. Her eyes were bright with unshed tears. She looked frightened now and on the defensive, like some poor beleaguered animal.

'I was never a doxy, Maeve. No man cast me aside like an old garment when he tired of me. I never gave them the chance. I was a mistress. I went into each arrangement with my eyes wide open. No talk of love and such nonsense. You simply cannot afford to dally with the young Earl in the mindless way you seem to imagine. Pshaw! What would people say? It is arrant nonsense.'

'You are being quite hateful! Oh, Belle, you *must* have been in love. Sometime. You must know how it feels. You cannot hurt me so.'

'I'm *not* hurting you. You do not know the meaning of the word love, my fine young lady. You will if you do not nip this unsuitable affair in the bud. Now. At once.' She took Maeve's hands in hers. 'Now listen to me, my child. I am telling you this because I love you and I do not wish to see you hurt. That young man is heir to a great title. His family is old and noble. I do not know what fairy-tale ideas you have in that romantic head of yours, but if you think his family would countenance an alliance with the likes of an actress you are mad. You have to keep your head. You have to be realistic.'

'He could marry me. He could. . .'

Belle shrieked and Demara dropped the bellows.

'No, no, no. You don't understand, Maeve, pet. You just don't understand.' Demara cried, joining in for the first time. 'Tell her, Belle.'

Maeve turned on them both with ferocity. 'You're ruining everything. You're spoiling it. I've only just met him. Only last evening. I spent a little time with him. Such a little time. He treated me like a lady. Why cannot you leave me be? Let me see what happens. He is taking me to supper tonight. He said he would see me after the show. . .'

'Send him away. He wants you for only one thing.' Belle was fanning herself with her handkerchief. The news had put her blood pressure up and she felt breathless and hot. 'Men like him make sport of girls like you. Poor innocents.'

'Oh, be quiet. How can you demean me so?' Maeve looked angrily at Belle then Demara. 'If in Ballymora Lord Linton Lester had truly fallen in love with me, then he could have married me. You know that's true, Demara, don't you?'

'Not here,' Belle was very firm. 'Not in London society. He *may*, though I doubt it, be able to marry a governess, even a peasant, but, Maeve, never, *never* an actress! Never!'

Maeve was weeping. Tears drenched her face. She sniffed and shook and sobbed. 'You are cruel and horrid!' she stammered. 'I've only met him. It was so beautiful. He was . . . you are . . . oh, how can you hurt me so? You must hate me! Why are you doing this to me?'

Demara went to her sister and pressed her into a chair. 'Maeve, Belle loves you. You know that quite well. That is the only reason she is saying these things to you.' She bent down and looked into her sister's face. 'Oh, little sister, she is right. She speaks words of wisdom.'

'Well I shan't listen!' Maeve was adamant. 'I don't want to listen! And I'll never forgive either of you for spoiling everything for me.' She looked up defiantly. 'And I won't let you!' she cried, fiercely determined. 'I won't let you. Send Tilly to the theatre to tell them I shan't be in this morning.'

Belle was weeping in the corner. She dabbed her eyes

with her handkerchief, muttering about ingratitude. 'She's terrible when she's in full flow!' she cried now. 'Oh, Demara, it's useless. An actress in full flow is unstoppable.'

Maeve snorted and flounced out of the room. Demara and Belle heard her run up the stairs, then the banging of a door, then silence. Belle sighed. 'She disappoints me,' she said. 'No true professional would behave that way. I know Ellen Terry would not.' She shook her head. 'Perhaps I have overestimated her talent. She behaves now like a pampered beauty rather than a great artist. Oh dear! Oh dear!'

'I don't think you underestimated her talent, Mrs D, I think both of us are rather underestimating how she feels about Sebastian Davenport.'

Demara seated herself beside Belle on the sofa. 'You've lived all your life in London, met the aristocracy, you're used to grand houses. You've been courted and fêted. . .'

'When I was young we were very poor, Demara. You cannot imagine the squalor we lived in, ten of us in one room. I stole. I begged. And worked.' Her eyes glittered, her hard determination showing clearly. 'I worked so hard for my success and I vowed I'd never be poor again.'

'Well, dearest Belle, if I may say, my sister's life was very different from yours, and I think we ought to remember how different your aims are.'

'How do you mean? You were not rich.'

'No, but we never starved. Life was hard – *is* hard – but healthy, and there was always food on our table and turf for the fire and Mam keeps everything clean as a new pin.' She put her hand over Belle's. 'You always saw the rich. They drove past in their carriages. You glimpsed their lives, the magnificence of their homes, through doors opened to receive guests, through lighted windows?' Belle nodded. 'Well,' Demara continued, 'Maeve has never seen the like. The only aristocracy we knew lived in Ballymora Castle – dear Lord Edward Lester – and sure wasn't he nearly as poor as ourselves, and all the money he had went on mending leaky roofs and repairs long overdue. Don't you see, Belle, how Maeve could be addled through ignorance? She has no idea of real class distinction, of society and its demands. She is an innocent abroad and ripe to fall in love with Satan himself if he is disguised as Apollo, as this young man seems to be.'

'Sebastian Davenport is a rake – your description is good, Demara, and I see what you mean. I'm an actress after all and my imagination is vivid. And yes, you are right, I grew up in the city catching tantalizing glimpses of wealth all around me, asking, 'why them, not us?' Maeve is a country-girl, with no knowledge of society or grand houses; she must be quite at sea here in London.'

'She has no rule-book to follow,' Demara agreed. Belle turned to her, her kind eyes troubled. 'Where did you learn such wisdom, such understanding?' she asked and added, without waiting for a reply, 'Oh, I hope she is not going to be hurt. I hope the poor child does not suffer too much in the learning.'

Chapter Forty

cₒ Gₒ

Next day Hodge was piqued by his master's pernickety attention to detail and his constant fussing and interference in Hodge's choice of clothes for him, casting aside this shirt as too starched, that as not starched enough. It was more than a good man-servant should have to bear.

Hodge was efficient. He worked swiftly, with a speed that looked slap-dash, but was not. Above all he liked to be left to himself to do his work unhampered. But on this day Lord Sebastian Davenport would not, could not seem to leave him alone.

Hodge was irritated. His master was at fever-pitch over this actress and he was behaving like an eighteen-year-old Lothario. Heaven preserve us all from such fevers, Hodge prayed fervently, and set about checking the menu yet again.

Hodge had lots of tricks up his sleeve, tricks that saved time and money (which he then pocketed). For instance he often bought the pies from the pieman and heated them in the oven, and none of his master's guests, or his master for that matter, realized the meat they ate was of dubious origin and certainly was not the pork they supposed they were eating with such relish. He and Mrs Banks the cook were hand in glove, which was only right and proper. Mrs Banks never stayed beyond six of the evening, being of a somewhat shockable disposition and a blabbermouth as well. It was better that she remained innocent of the activities her young employer got up to of a night. As Sebastian Davenport confessed to Hodge, rumours and gossip might do him irreparable harm in the moral climate of the day.

'A lot of humbugs they are, Hodge, you ask me. All milk and honey on top and a hive of hornets underneath. Folk today put on such pious faces and appear so virtuous – blameless husbands, doting fathers – but most of them have a second string to their bows and are capable of such devious debauchery as would raise the hair on your head and make it stand up straight. Shock even me, Hodge.'

'Yes, m'lord.'

'Well, I for one am honest. But I do not wish to flaunt my life-style too openly, Hodge, which I consider would be foolish. Mater and Pater would not like it and I do not want to be gossiped about overly. So it is well that there be only two of us here of an evening. Or three, depending on how one looks at it. You. Me. And the lady of my choice.'

'Yes, m'lord.'

'After all, Hodge, my brother would be only too delighted if he got wind of my activities.'

'Oh, sir, Lord Rudolph is not like that. Indeed, sir, he is most amiable.' Hodge was not going to let his master get away with that.

'Well, be that as it may, my poor mama would have the vapours and my father would call me to heel and keep me at home in the country – which I love, Hodge, with all my heart, but which is so deadly dull if one is confined there above a week.' And he would sigh and show his even white teeth in a grin of such charm that even Hodge would be drawn to agree with him.

Everything was finally to Lord Sebastian Davenport's liking that momentous evening that Miss Maeve Donnelly was to visit. It had not been easy. Maeve Donnelly had admired Venetian glass, so Venetian glasses had to be found and used. The little table for two sparkled with the silver and the crystal. She had said she loved gardenias too, so, out of season, from the flowerseller in Belgravia, Hodge purchased armfuls of the bright blooms, which were placed in vases all around the room.

Lord Sebastian was obsessed with this new young lady but nevertheless he had no intention of sitting through the whole play two evenings running. When the curtain rose on Act Two, Scene Two for Maeve's first entrance and she heard Geoffrey give her her cue: 'Ill met by moonlight proud Titania' she was, for a long moment, transfixed and still as a statue for the box was full of strangers and her lover absent. Poor Geoffrey felt that cold, empty feeling of fear that assaults all actors when, after a reasonable pause, their cue is not answered, and he was assailed by the customary anxiety that crept from the pit of his stomach up to his chest. To his relief, the reply finally came – late, it was true, but clear and vital: 'What, jealous Oberon! Fairies, skip hence . . .' and Maeve was in fine voice, until they exited. Then with a sudden sob she rushed past him down the dark, dusty corridor to her dressing-room. He followed her.

'What is it, little Queen?' he asked kindly from her doorway. He disliked any of his artists to be upset. It made for weak performances. Try as they might not to let it affect the play it always did. She looked at him, violet eyes made double their size by black eye make-up, tragic as Juliet.

'That is Desdemona, little one,' he shouted jubilantly. 'When you look like that, you *are* Desdemona. Perfect. Look at yourself in the mirror.'

'I am here weeping because my heart is going to break and you tell me I'm Desdemona and ask me to look in the mirror,' she wept, nevertheless peeking into the glass to see if what he said could be true.

237

'Those eyes. That is how you must look at me in Act Five,' he cried.

She stopped weeping and stared at herself and saw what he meant.

'But hold hard,' he pulled himself up, 'that is not the point. What is it, proud Titania, that makes you look like that?'

'It is Sebastian, Mr Denton. Lord Davenport, that is. He is to take me to supper and he is not out there. There are strangers in his box.'

Geoffrey Denton threw back his head and laughed aloud. 'Great balls of fire, madam, do you think the boy is a blue-stocking? Sit through the whole play again tonight? When he was there last night? Not on your life! I thought he did well to endure through one whole performance. The concentration of the aristocracy is of notoriously short duration, and Lord Davenport's shorter than most.' He took her chin in his hands. 'No, my girl. That he sat through all last night's performance was a unique tribute to you. You may be sure he'll be here to collect you at the fall of the curtain, or if not that, he'll send his carriage to fetch you.' He looked at her closely, her wide innocent eyes so full of hope and guilelessness, and a worried frown crossed his forehead. It wrinkled his skin and she could see his wig-join, which remained smooth.

'You must not allow your emotions such free reign, m'dear. It is not good either on stage or off. Particularly off because that eventually affects on.'

She pulled away from him. 'Oh not you too! Everyone seems set on spoiling things for me.'

'On saving you from heartbreak, Maeve Donnelly. Listen to your friends. They love you much more than he does.'

His voice was kind but she turned on him with such fury that he instantly made up his mind to include *The Taming of the Shrew* in their repertoire. He would play Petruchio once more before he got too old for the part. And what a magnificent Katerina Maeve would make, looking as she did now, scorn and fire flashing from her eyes.

'You don't know that! No one knows how we feel about each other. How *dare* you presume, you, Mrs Desmond and my sister. None of you have a lover,' she cried triumphantly, 'so what could you know about it?'

He looked at her again and this time his eyes were cold. 'Have you asked yourself why we have no lovers, Maeve Donnelly?' He paused, looking at her. 'Have you asked yourself that? Find an answer and you may understand what we are warning you about.'

He left and she tossed her black curls and looked at herself in the glass and wiped a tear from the corner of her eye. She shook herself a little, then smoothed back her pearl-sprinkled hair and smiled to herself. 'He'll be here,' she whispered to herself. 'He'll come for me. I know. And we'll prove them all wrong.'

Chapter Forty-One

ৎৡ ৡৎ

When he eventually appeared in the back of the box in Act Five, halfway through the Pyramus and Thisbe comedy, she knew he had entered even though, standing backstage in readiness for her curtain call, she could not see him.

Her heart leapt within her and she pressed her hands to her cheeks and peered through the curtains to make sure she was correct.

Yes, he was there. He stood at the back of the box, alone, tall and beautiful, the dim light turning his hair ripe gold. She drew in her breath and tried to calm her beating heart but she seemed to have no control over it. It bounded inside her as if it would burst her rib-cage.

As Puck sang his farewell song on the shadowy stage, Geoffrey took her hand. 'Steady, girl,' he whispered. 'Steady.' The strong pressure helped her.

She could not see Sebastian at the curtain and when she went to her dressing-room in a state of wild anxiety, he was there, waiting.

'Oh you must not see me like this,' she cried aghast. 'Stage paint is horrible near-to.'

He laughed in a relaxed way and said he would wait for her outside. She was all fingers and thumbs and she drove Polly, her dresser, mad with her fidgeting and haste.

'Do I look pretty? Oh, do I? I decided on the velvet, Polly. Do you think I'm right?'

'You look like a princess, ma'am, indeed you do,' Polly said fervently.

The velvet was midnight blue and cut to reveal the delicate curve of her breast. It clung to her waist and its graceful folds fell to her ankles. She looked quite superb and for the first time in his life Sebastian Davenport was rendered speechless and nervous when he saw once again her dazzling beauty.

He had intended to kiss her in the carriage but he could not quite pluck up the courage. Maeve had the assurance, the confidence of the prettiest girl in the village, and she had not lost that authority in London. It gave her a formidable hauteur that would make a prince of the blood wary of treating her with familiarity.

And she was blindingly beautiful. She glowed, she sparkled and the first thing she said completely disarmed him. 'They told me you were only going to use me as a plaything, Sebastian, but I knew them to be wrong,' she confided, and laid a hand on his arm, appealing to him that such an idea was ridiculous. 'When you look at me like that – oh, the way you are looking at me now – I know they were lying.' She gave him a dazzling smile. 'I *knew* you weren't – what they said you were – a rake!' She giggled and looked at him with naked adoration and trust. 'Oh, Sebastian, even if you were taking advantage of me and you were going to toss me aside when you were finished with me, I would not care. I love you so and their disapproval has only made me more determined. But, my dearest, I trust you completely.'

With those words between them how could he proceed with the planned seduction? She had given him a cue and he had to pick it up. Reassurances were in order and so he hastened to reassure her. She was dramatic and seemed to him in charge of the whole scene. 'Later,' he told himself. 'Later.'

In the apartment he was once more taken aback by her beauty. He took her cloak and proceeded to pour her champagne and serve the caviar, giving her covert glances, wanting to break all the rules and frankly stare at her. Her skin was flawless. The shape of her lips, the way they pouted slightly, the rich colour of them, the way the corners of her mouth turned up as if she was going to laugh. Her marvellous eyes. Violet. Black-centered, fringed by soft lashes thick as paint-brushes, curled upwards like fans, fluttering. The cheekbones were so delicately carved. Most of all her face was a mirror of her every thought. Laughter chased consternation, astonishment registered after surprise and enjoyment. She was a riveting delight to watch, like some rare and exotic animal.

'What do you do, Sebastian?' she asked him as they ate and drank, she with relish. The question was unexpected. It took him by surprise. No one had ever asked him that before. One of the things that most excited him about Maeve was the way she treated him as if he were like everyone else. All through his life he had been deferred to as the heir to one of the oldest titles in Europe. People gave him automatic preference and bowed and scraped quite brazenly to find favour with him. She called him Sebastian right off and behaved as though he were the boy next door.

He had to think for a moment how to frame his reply.

'I . . . er . . . I hunt and shoot,' he said.

'Like my father,' she commented.

'And I go to balls and parties. Gamble in White's and Tattersall's. I am a member of all the gentlemen's clubs.'

It sounded feeble, he had to admit.

'I meant *work*. Da hunts and shoots but that's when he has time to spare. It's not real work. No, I mean what work do you do?'

'Well, when I'm older I'll go to the House of Lords,' he told her.

'What will you do there?'

He frowned. He did not like the turn the conversation

241

had taken. 'I'll tell you the truth. I don't know precisely. I expect I'll learn when I get there. Make laws and things.' He gave a small, deprecating smile.

'And you don't work now?' she asked.

'No. I suppose not. Too much else to do. 'Course I help Father look after the estates. We own a lot of land in Berkshire.'

'My da says only God owns the land. People *think* they do, but they don't really.'

'Oh rot! That's hogwash!' he protested, sounding more vehement than he meant to. He wished this conversation about work would stop. 'Sorry, Maeve, my sweet, but that is rubbish. Very quaint. Very Irish. You just try to trespass on my land and you'll soon see who owns it.'

'That's what Da means exactly,' she cried triumphantly. 'People *should* be able to go where they please. Walk on God's earth. Why should you and your family have exclusive rights to acres and acres of land and prevent others from using it?' She stared at him, sweetly reasonable.

'I don't know, my angel, and I do not really care! Now let me kiss those rosy lips. Let me . . .'

As he brought his face close to hers she put her fingers against his mouth and he found himself automatically kissing the tips.

'Sweet, sweet,' he murmured. 'But give me your mouth – I want to kiss those lips.'

'You are sure?' she asked.

He did not know what she meant.

'Oh, yes,' he breathed. 'Oh, yes.'

Her lips trembled under his. He could feel her soft breath on his mouth as he held her close.

She nearly swooned under his kiss. That it could be like this ecstasy, the meeting of mouth on mouth, that he could turn her whole being into melting submission astonished her. She felt everything dissolve inside her, yet every nerve-end was alive and throbbing. Her mouth clung to his for moments, for hours it seemed. It was her first kiss.

When she drew away from him her eyes were tender, like velvet petals, and she said with an abandon he found startling, 'I love you, Sebastian. Oh, I love you. I want to be with you for ever.'

'Hell and damnation!' he cried, letting her go and leaping to his feet. 'Who talks of forever?'

She was breaking the rules. She was not supposed to declare her love for him and treat this situation as if it were a proposal of marriage. She was an actress, dammit. She was not playing the game correctly. She was saying the wrong things, making him feel guilty. She was thrusting a responsibility upon him instead of joining him in a game of love.

'I want to marry you, Sebastian. I want to be your wife,' she was saying now, face ecstatic, and he stared at her in horror. The faces of his mother and father flashed before his eyes and he shuddered. An actress from the Chandos Theatre at Malvern Castle! The Earl and Countess would think he had run mad.

Yet he wanted her so badly. She was looking at him, eyes damp with passion, lashes sweeping her damask cheeks, a glint of violets in a dark wood. There was such trust in those eyes that his heart plummeted, then leapt in delight at her dazzling beauty. He would cross mountains, fight duels, go bankrupt for her sake, but marry? Spend forever at her side at Malvern? With Mater and Pater? No and no and no! It was out of the question. That whole side of his life was separate. It was an ordered, public existence. Everything that happened was governed by routine and tradition and the only people welcome there were the chosen few who knew the rules and abided by them, were part of the tradition and above all were the right sort of people with the right sort of credentials.

Besides, Fanny was waiting for him. He had not exactly proposed but there was an understanding between their families that they would marry and he was perfectly happy to comply with their joint decision. Fanny was the ideal wife and there would be plenty of opportunities for the Maeves of this world when he was married to her. She would never fuss and would be quite content to remain at Malvern when he was in London and keep her nose out of his masculine world.

An actress! An Irish actress! Good God, his father would never forgive him. He'd cut him out. He'd pass him over in favour of Rudi. Dull, moral old Rudi, the younger brother who somehow seemed the older one. No, Rudi would not get Malvern Castle and he, Sebastian, would not marry an Irish actress.

But how to proceed now? Maeve Donnelly sat there on his sofa in her low-necked blue velvet, staring up at him, her perfect little face full of love and trust, radiant as the evening star. He'd have to get rid of her now, tonight, and think about what he was going to do next, what his next move in this game of love would be. He knew it would go on. This was certainly not the end. He must have time. If he took advantage of the girl it could spell trouble. He wanted no breath of scandal. So far he had escaped public notoriety and he intended to keep things that way. He would seduce her and she would be willing but he needed another strategy. He needed a plan of campaign whereby she would gladly throw herself into his arms without the formality of the marriage ceremony and he knew that, given time, he could think of something. But there was no time now.

He took her hands and drew her to her feet. He kissed her again, this time more thoroughly. She tasted of peaches and his resolve nearly left him in the heady aura of her passionate response. But he had not escaped scandal by being a slave to his own desires. He was not that weak.

He took her shoulders. 'Dearest child. You must let me send you home now. If you stay I'll forget I'm a gentleman.'

'There, you see!' she cried triumphantly. 'I knew you would never behave improperly. Oh dearest, they are all wrong about you.' She blushed and lowered her eyes. 'Shall I see you tomorrow evening?' she asked ardently.

He nodded, sighing, 'Of course. Tomorrow after the play I'll be at the theatre.'

'And we will discuss our plans? Our future?'

Again he nodded.

'Dearest Sebastian!' she sighed in complete content and

thought herself the luckiest girl alive. She decided her taste was impeccable, her instincts sound, for had she not fallen in love with the most beautiful and honourable gentleman in London?

Chapter Forty-Two

cᴓ Gᴓ

Dana informed Duff that the wedding would take place in the spring. She told him in a roundabout way, meeting him accidentally in the boreen, smiling coyly up at him. 'Remember, Duff. In the spring. We'll be wed then, won't we?' And she moved away from him before he could reply.

Since the moonlighters had gone things had slipped back to normal in Ballymora. It seemed as if none of it had ever happened. Sheena McQuaid sometimes lapsed into an abstracted daydream and had at times a wistful look in her eyes, and Dana Donnelly appeared to be walking out with Duff Dannon, and there was talk of a wedding, but no one ever saw the two together and the collective opinion was one of excited speculation and an acute desire to see Demara Donnelly come home for a visit.

'Then we'd see the fur fly!' Delia McCormack speculated gleefully.

'It's all decided,' Dana said bashfully to her mother and Katey Kavanagh. Those ladies exchanged mystified glances, for it was the first they had heard of it in any official capacity.

'Are you sure it's not wishful thinkin'?' Brigid asked her daughter, and was rewarded by a baleful glare and the stricture 'I'm tellin you, take my word.'

Duff was not at all sure how it happened. A man of fierce certainties about his country and his rights, about patriotism and ideals, he was an innocent where women were concerned.

Demara had been the only woman in his life. She was in

his blood, part of his existence, his very heart-beat. Now she had gone and she had left him no hope. There had been no engagement, no promises to wait.

Somehow, in a subtle, insidious way, her sister had crept into his life, like a burr under his sock, itching him, scratching at him, ever present, and try as he might he could not seem to get rid of her.

God knows he tried. He sought ways to put her off. He devised speeches which she never listened to. She had a way of twisting what he said and ignoring his intent. And she never intruded. It was impossible to grasp at anything she said or did. She slipped away from confrontation, direct discussion, anything at all that was solid.

Dana went to his sister-in-law, Mary. He did not know what was said but that evening Mary looked at him slyly smiling.

'So! Dana says the weddin' is in the spring.'

It was a statement, not a question. He vowed then to speak to Dana, to ask her by what authority she made such assumptions. But he said nothing to Mary at that time, something he regretted in retrospect. Mary assumed his silence denoted agreement and she spoke about it to her friends and soon his friends were making sly jokes and horny innuendoes and everyone took it as fact.

And all the time, guiltily, he remembered that fierce coupling in the barn. It coloured all his reactions and made him reluctant to challenge Dana about anything she said. It removed his one weapon from him; the weapon of innocence.

His guilt chafed at him. It embarrassed him to admit even to himself that she had seduced him. No one would believe it if he told them, and even if they did they would despise him for the whole sorry episode. He could imagine the contempt. Dana Donnelly had lured him into committing an immoral act. It undermined his manhood and made him look ridiculous.

He went about his labours diligently and people inferred that the information they had received was correct. There was laughter behind hands and innuendo was rampant, but at least it was benign, they were on his side, this was the sort of joshing all betrothed couples were subjected to. Whereas if they had known the truth of it the ribbing would be malicious, and for him there was no escape; he had to spend the rest of his life in this community. Yet never, in those months, did anyone, either by accident or design, ask him outright was he marrying Dana Donnelly. No one gave him a chance to say no and he wondered if he would have had the courage to deny it, and thought probably not. Dana Donnelly had him cornered and he knew there was no earthly way to wriggle out of marrying her.

If he refused to comply with her obliquely stated wish all she had to do was tell her father what he had done to her in the barn. She held this over him like a lethal weapon. She knew how he loved Pierce. She knew what Pierce would do. There would be an instant shotgun wedding in Ballymora. Pierce Donnelly would frog-march him up to the altar and Father Maguire would let him have it from the pulpit. But all that would be nothing compared to Pierce Donnelly's hurt. He would be outraged that his daughter had been sullied, but he would be horrified that the deed had been committed by a man who was like a son to him, someone he had trusted. Someone he loved. Duff could not bear Pierce Donnelly's disapproval.

He saw no way out of the dilemma and as the days and weeks passed into months he grew to accept the inevitable. Demara was far away and he could see no hope.

Spring came to Ballymora and the banns were read. Duff was as surprised as anyone else in the church when Father Maguire read them out. Dana Donnelly was nothing if not thorough in her plans. She bewildered him with her demure looks and sometimes he thought he had imagined the wanton who had seduced him in the barn. She smiled shyly across at him in the church when the announcement was made and he listened to the words: *If anyone knows any reason why these two should not be married will they please contact the church within the next month.* He wanted to shout, 'I don't love her. Is that not a reason?' and he decided it probably was not. The church was full of paradoxes and though it insisted that love was the greatest virtue it condoned marriages of convenience as perfectly acceptable. Ballymora was full of parishioners who had married for convenience as well as the few who had married for love.

The announcement brought smiles to the faces in the congregation. Mickey, Brian, Mog and Deegan, Dinny and Matty and Shooshie all nodded in silent approval at the suitability of the union, and with pleasure in their hearts at the prospect of the celebration. There was sure to be lashings of booze. The women dreamed of the ceremony and the cooking and the making of the dresses.

Only Brigid Donnelly and Katey Kavanagh had their doubts and looked gravely across at each other. Cogger Kavanagh kept shaking his shaggy head as if someone was making a terrible mistake.

'Duff is Demara's man,' Katey whispered under her breath. 'What is he up to? He doesn't love Dana!'

Sheena McQuaid murmured in a voice loud enough for them all to hear, 'What's *she* up to is more to the point. Dana Donnelly absconding with her sister's intended. Lord have mercy on us!'

Mickey O'Gorman congratulated Duff in Ma Stacey's after that first calling of the banns. After all it was the first official acknowledgement of the marriage, it put the seal on the contract so to speak.

'Yer well in there, Duff, so ye are. The match is good. Yer a lucky man. We may not like it but the Donnellys is advantaged, so they are. Congratulations, an' may ye have prosperity an' all yer childer sons!'

'I'll drink te that!' Dinny McQuaid cried and the others echoed him and poured the bitter black porter down their open gullets then sighed contentedly as the liquor hit their stomachs and, as one man, they drew the backs of their hands across their foam-flecked moustaches.

'God'n church whets the thirst, doesn't it?' Mickey O'Gorman asked the world in general. 'I get a terrible thirst on me in church, so I do.'

'Now another all round,' Phil Conlon cried and Ma Stacey pulled the pints with gusto.

'A long life to ye, Duff Dannon,' Mog Murtagh raised his tankard and toasted the prospective bridegroom, who looked gloomily on the proceedings. There was a repeat of the ritual, a couple of times more, and after a pause, when Miles Murphy ran the back of his hand down the side of his trousers, 'Ye've made the right choice, Duff,' he said, nodding his head.

'An' isn't it about time?' Deegan Belcher remarked.

Loud guffaws greeted this. Mickey O'Gorman was getting drunkenly belligerent. He gazed speculatively at Duff and hitched his trousers a little higher with the heel of his hands, and narrowing his eyes he declared in a portentous manner, "Tisn't everything yer right about, Duff Dannon. Ye were a might wrong about the moonlighters, weren't ye? Threw yer weight around about that, me fine fella, an' what happened? Eh? Nuthin'! Nuthin' at all.'

Duff shrugged. He knew that for a long time, with nothing happening in Ballymora, the men had wanted to gloat. It was only natural. Now was the time to clear the air.

'Ah sure we all make mistakes,' Mog Murtagh cried, slapping him on the back. 'Got to be mag-nan-im-ous,' he stated carefully. 'Sup up now. This is a celebration.'

'If ye think Duff was wrong then yer in for a powerful shock.' Pierce Donnelly had arrived, and now as usual he was spoiling things for them. A lull fell on the conversation.

'What are ye tryin' te do? Ruin the whole thing?' Mickey O'Gorman squeaked in exasperation. 'Why can't ye keep yer contribution OUT if it's goin' to be negative! God sakes man! Isn't it your daughter as is gettin' wed?'

Phil Conlon stood behind the bar, his arm loosely around Eileen Stacey's plump shoulders.

'I think he's right,' Phil said. 'I think yiz'er all mad!'

'Well, ye would, Phil Conlon, an' you the boss's man fer years!' Dinny McQuaid's pursed mouth was set in disapproval.

'That was when he was a good boss an' Lord Edward was. An' I'm not goin' to apologize fer that. He was a fine honest man. But yer dealin' with a devil an' yer underestimating him.'

'Oh go on! Yer all the same. Harbingers of doom and gloom!' Mog Murtagh smacked his lips. 'An' not payin' rent sure as hell has made things easier for the likes of us!'

There was a pause and everyone looked at Mog.

'Ye've kept it? Ye've saved it to cough up if ye have to?' Phil Conlon asked him anxiously after a moment. Mog's eyes got shifty in their sockets and he grunted non-committally.

'Oh Jasus, I don't believe it!' Phil sighed and shook his head. 'Yer mad if ye didn't. Stark ravin' mad!' He looked around the room. 'Did the rest of ye? Save it? Put it aside?' He threw his eyes to heaven. 'Or spend it? Ye didn't spend it, did ye? Yer not such gormless eejits, are ye?'

A curious uneasiness befell all the men in the shebeen with the exception of Duff Dannon and Pierce Donnelly. And of course Cogger Kavanagh, who sat in his nook and watched the proceedings.

'Ah sure we'll be all right!' Brian Gilligan said soothingly, 'Don't ye see – we don't know *who* to pay it to, Phil! Lord Lester's in London an' we don't know if he's still the man. An' so is the Marquis. We haven't even been told officially the land we live on has been sold.'

'Yeah! You're not expectin' us to *guess* these things, are you, Phil Conlon, an' you not on the job any more?' Miles Murphy said snidely and laughed and the others joined in. But Phil looked grave.

'Look, don't be fools, men. Put the money aside in case it's needed in a hurry. Legally,' Pierce Donnelly told them. 'Otherwise ye might find yerselves without a case.'

'Yerra isn't it all right for you with four childer across the water sendin' the money home?' Brian Gilligan asked.

'Well, listen to him.' Mickey O'Gorman couldn't resist the opportunity the sanctimonious man had afforded him. 'What about Bryony? Couldn't she buy and sell the lot of us an' she earnin' a fine livin' on her back?'

Brian squealed and, fists flying, went for Mickey who by now was none too steady on his feet.

'Ye bastard! Ye son of a she-devil! Filthy swine! I'll

250

knock ye into a tin hat an' pulverize ye!'

He danced around Mickey, screaming at him to put up his fists, while Mickey just leaned against the bar and laughed.

Phil Conlon took the rag from Ma Stacey and came around the counter, stood between the two men and began to polish it. He was much bigger than either of them, and younger and stronger. He eyed them, one then the other. 'Fellas! Fellas! Yiz are both on the same side, God's sake. What's all this about? Eh? Mickey, yiz are out of order here. Brian's daughter is a lovely girl an' mebbe yer a wee bit jealous. . .'

'I yam not!' Mickey stopped smiling and glared at Phil. 'Because, Mickey, yer daughter is only a skivvy in Liverpool!'

Mickey drew himself up, balling his fists, but Phil continued smoothly, 'We can all hurl insults around, easy! Now shut yer gobs an' behave like the civilized men ye are, and not like childer!'

A voice came from the back where Deegan Belcher belatedly took up the argument that had only just penetrated his fuddled brain, 'Much common sense they showed urging us to keep those vultures of moonlighters here, an' here it's spring an' not a peep outa his lordship.'

'Well, if ye think that's the end of it yer in fer a big surprise, that's all I can say,' Pierce Donnelly muttered.

'God! There ye go again, Pierce. Always bloody right. Always know best. Well all I can say. . .'

The argument swung back and forth, waxed hot and cold over the days and weeks and months and even Pierce Donnelly began to think that perhaps indeed they had been let off the hook and the powers that ruled their lives had more important things to think about than their small hamlet of cottages in Ballymora. They prepared for the wedding and as the days rolled by they became optimistic and their spirits brightened, and they went about their tasks with light hearts and easy minds.

Chapter Forty-Three

ᴄᴏ ᴏᴠ

The next morning after Maeve's supper date with Sebastian, Áine paid them a visit.

Demara and Belle had waited up for their dearest Maeve the night before, dreading heaven knows what eventuality. They were very surprised therefore to discover on her return home that Maeve was in a state of intoxication brought about not by champagne but by a kiss. She had been kissed by Sebastian, she informed them proudly, and no other liberties had been attempted. They were alarmed however by her wild protestations of his love for her and her talk of marriage and betrothal. Such wild affirmations, they felt in their bones, must be misunderstandings. However, as Belle murmured to Demara, 'So far, so good! At least he has not seduced her. But her head, my dear Demara, is in the clouds and she is, I'm afraid, a foolish innocent abroad.'

They went to bed and slept deeply for all three were exhausted.

Early next morning they were abruptly awakened by a loud hammering on the front door. Tilly hurried to answer it. She had proved herself a willing worker, but inept. When nervous she dropped things, and broke them, but she was a grateful little body and cheerful too, and, unlike Mary Jacks, Belle and all at Soho Square found her a pleasure to have around.

She answered the door that morning and was thrown into confusion by the sight of a poorly dressed woman, obviously working class, who had a black eye, a bruised nose, and a cut and bleeding cheekbone. There was dried brown blood blocking the woman's nostril and caked on her forehead and bottom lip. Tilly would have slammed the door in her face had it not been for the presence of

Bert Hockney behind her. Tilly had lived with the kind of brutality this woman was obviously a victim of. She understood that world and she didn't want it anywhere near her.

But Bert seemed to know the woman. He started yelling for Demara and Belle as he helped the battered woman inside and closed the door.

Demara came running downstairs, alarmed by the urgency in Bert's voice.

'Oh heavens, it's Áine. What happened? What on earth's the matter? Bert?' All past disagreements were instantly forgotten at the sight of Áine's pathetic state.

'I brought her in, Demara,' Bert was saying.

'You did right. What happened, Áine?' she asked her sister, putting her arm around her, but Áine seemed only half-conscious and unable to speak for herself.

Maeve and Belle arrived on the landing demanding to know what the rumpus was, and they too were horrified at the state Áine was in.

'I'll get the tub, miss,' Tilly cried. 'Bathe her. An 'ot bath should 'elp.' Rose had said the hot baths had helped enormously when she had arrived at the convent bruised and battered. This girl didn't look as if she'd been raped, but she sure had been beat up badly. And underneath the desire to take care of the hurt woman there was also in Tilly a quite selfish desire not to have the carpets and furniture spoiled by the woman's muddy shoes and soiled clothes because she would have to clean them afterwards. Demara sighed to herself and helped Tilly to fill the aluminium tub with hot water and a handful of borax and they both stripped Áine of her clothes. Demara felt her heart well with pity for her sister's clothes and underwear were of the cheapest possible quality.

Her body was covered with bruises old and new. Demara and Maeve bathed their sister tenderly, biting back their anger, while Belle brewed up a tissane and Tilly prepared bandages and dressings for her wounds. There was a bone sticking through the skin at her wrist and Demara bound it tightly and asked Belle to give Áine a stiff dose of laudanum. 'I lost the baby,' she told them. 'I lost it.'

'We'll let her have the little box-room beside you, Tilly,'

253

Belle said, and was amused by Tilly's instantly mutinous face. She was not at all happy to have her basement invaded by an invalid, but she did as she was bidden with alacrity.

Áine screamed with pain as they helped her into the steaming tub, but the hot water and the teaspoon full of borax soothed her wounds and relaxed her.

'Who did it to you, Áine? Were you attacked in the street?' Maeve asked. Demara and Belle glanced at each other over her head. They knew the truth instinctively.

'Oh, it was an accident. It was my own fault really,' Áine whispered.

'Don't be silly, Áine. It was Lorcan, wasn't it?'

Maeve gasped and looked in astonishment at Demara.

'He couldn't!' she cried. 'Oh the beast! The animal.'

'Don't you call him that,' Áine protested. 'It's only when he's astray in the head of a Saturday.'

'Drunk, you mean.'

'Well, he can't help it, an' all I know is, he's a good man, so he is.'

'Oh my God, Áine, how can you make excuses for him after what he's done to you?' Maeve was indignant.

Áine glared at her. 'He's a saint the rest of the time, so he is,' she cried, her voice feeble. 'An' I haven't forgotten what you tried to do to him, Maeve Donnelly, an' you my sister.'

'Oh, Áine, how can you say that? You *know* it wasn't like that! And you seem to have forgotten he was astray in his head, as you put it, that day too.'

Demara shook her head at Maeve and put her finger to her lips. 'Not now,' she said. 'Áine, pet, hush and let the water heal you.' She examined the girl's body, shaking her head. 'You look as if you've been in the wars,' she said. 'I don't know about him being good though. If this is good then I'd hate to think what is bad.'

'Where's Seaneen?' Maeve asked, sponging her sister's bruised back.

'Lorcan has him. He'll be all right. Lorcan adores him. He's never hurt him. It's just that I irritate him when he's . . . when he's had a skinful and . . . and. . .'

'An' he threw 'er out!' Tilly finished.

Áine glanced at her, eyes cold.

'How'd you know that?' she asked.

'I know what they do. I bin in the situation. Men are 'orrible,' she informed them. ''Orrible, 'airy creatures. Like to fight an' drink an' 'it each other. Like wars they do. Wimmen're not like that. You find an army of wimmen marchin' out to kill an' maim? Never! Men is 'orrible an' should stay in their place.'

'She's right. Women are not such fools, eh, Tilly?' Demara asked.

Belle was staring at Tilly. She had never heard the girl string more than two sentences together. The speech had taken her by surprise.

'We've got better things to do than fight,' she said. 'Now get out of that tub and get dry. Then Tilly'll give you some broth and then you can sleep. Tilly, make up the bed, there's a dear.'

''Ave done, mum.'

'You must be Mrs Desmond?' Áine asked curiously, and Belle nodded.

Why doesn't she thank me? Belle wondered, then decided the girl was probably too hurt and confused, though her eyes flitted here and there appraising everything. Belle couldn't warm to her as she had warmed to Demara and Maeve. She realized the girl was angry and she didn't blame her for that but there was something grudging in her acceptance of help, a lack of gratitude that was almost offensive.

'You've gone all posh – listen to ye!' Áine said derisively as Maeve patted her dry. 'Jasus, ye could hear yerselves!'

'I'm heating some soup for you,' Demara said quickly.

''Ere's a nightgown, miss,' said Tilly as she came into the kitchen with the garment in her hand. 'The bed's ready an' warm.'

'That was quick,' Belle remarked.

'I 'ad the ironing just done, mum, an' I put on the sheet. I'll wait till she's in an' then I'll cover 'er. Make 'er more comfortable.'

'Tilly, you are wonderful,' Belle told her. Tilly squirmed

255

with delight.

They put Áine to bed in the box-room off the kitchen and she was soon asleep. The combination of the hot bath and the warming soup and the relinquishing of responsibility all acted as an inducement to sleep and Áine succumbed.

'Tilly, bring us some hot chocolate in the parlour. Is the fire alight?'

It was and the three sat around it curiously silent.

'Your sister is having a rough time,' Belle remarked finally.

Maeve nodded.

'She'll want to stay,' Demara sighed and they heard the crash outside the door as Tilly dropped and broke a cup.

'Was it full?' Demara asked anxiously as the girl entered.

'No, miss. I put the chocolate in the silver pot like you told me.'

'What on earth's the matter, Tilly?' Belle cried at the sight of the girl's quivering face.

'She'll 'ave me out, Mrs, I can see it. It was in 'er eyes. It was there. She clocked me, wot I do. She wants my position for 'erself. She'll get me out an' take my place.'

Maeve and Demara had seen it too in their sister's eyes. Despite her hurts, her bruises, she had summed up Belle Desmond and her home arrangements, compared all of it to the Dublin woman she was skivvying for and decided this was a better job and she would wrest it from the orphan. They knew Tilly's fears were justified.

'She won't, Tilly,' Demara assured her quietly. She looked at Maeve who nodded to the unspoken statement in her sister's eyes.

'I promise you, Tilly, your job is safe,' Maeve said.

Demara looked at Mrs Desmond. 'Belle,' she said, 'we don't want Áine here. Oh, we'll take care of her till she's better, but she brings trouble with her wherever she goes. It's better she does not remain here.'

The older woman nodded. 'I could tell that. I'm psychic about things like that. But don't worry, Tilly, this is your home, dear. You are part of the family now.'

Tilly wished she could believe that. So often in her short

life she thought she had found a refuge only to be sent away, find herself cast out again into an unsympathetic world. Well, this time she would fight to stay. She loved Mrs Desmond and Demara. Their kindness to her had made her life very happy. She thought Maeve a princess. She would fight to keep what she had here and no slant-eyed opportunist, even though she was a sister, would oust her.

The sleep saw Áine much improved. Tilly knew that she was much better than she pretended to be, but she lay abed and feigned exhaustion. Belle also saw through the charade. She was too used to theatricals to be taken in by an amateur.

The next day a liveried footman arrived with Bryony Gilligan's card and an invitation to tea in Manchester Square. *I'll send a carriage for you at four o'clock in the afternoon.* Bryony had written on the back.

They were delighted to accept. It was a gloriously sunny day and the girls wore their sprigged muslins. Winter had not completely vanished and summer was definitely on the way. The populace was exchanging umbrellas for parasols.

The carriage, a brougham, arrived promptly at the appointed hour and the sisters were duly impressed. That the daughter of their neighbour in Ballymora was responsible for this discreet show of affluence amused Demara considerably and gave her a thrill of excitement. If Bryony could do it, so could she. She could fulfil her dreams. She could succeed.

They got into the carriage and the coachman cracked his whip.

'It is going to become very difficult, Dem,' Maeve said, and as Demara looked at her quizzically she explained, 'We'll have to be firm with Áine. We'll have to be very strong-willed with her or she'll spoil everything.'

The carriage rumbled over the cobblestones and Demara nodded. She was always surprised at the strength of purpose that lay beneath her sister's fragile innocence. That delicate face concealed a formidable determination. Belle often remarked that Maeve had to have an unyielding strength of character to work as hard as she did and become such a superb actress.

257

'It doesn't happen by accident, you know,' Belle was fond of telling Demara after a performance.

In the carriage Demara turned to Maeve. 'She was horribly hurt, Maeve, goodness knows, and I feel churlish to mention it but she *is* milking the situation for all it's worth.'

Maeve nodded. She knew exactly what her sister referred to. 'She was very cross for missing this outing. She is mad she could not come with us,' she said.

'Well, she dug her own grave,' Demara said shrugging. 'She made such a fuss every time we tried to get her out of bed, pretending to have the vapours, that she couldn't make a spectacular recovery when she heard we were going to tea with Bryony.'

Maeve got the giggles. 'Lord, what a dilemma!' she chortled. 'Oh, Demara, she would have given anything to have accompanied us. She was in a state of frustrated fury, not being able to.'

'Yes, well, I wouldn't mind any of that, Maeve. It is human nature after all, if she wasn't so . . . so . . .' She hesitated.

'Destructive!' Maeve supplied. 'She spoils things, Demara. She makes trouble.' She turned to her sister. 'And I don't want us to lose what we have, with Belle. With each other. Yet what can we do? We cannot simply pack her off back to Lorcan. That would be terrible.'

The carriage drew up and her queries remained unanswered. They had arrived.

Chapter Forty-Four

∽ ∾

The footman they had seen that morning ushered them into the house. It was much larger inside than it appeared from the outside. A staircase swept regally down into a black-and-white chequered marble hall. There seemed to be a lot of people about, all very fashionably dressed, moving around, going and coming, perched on small Regency chairs, or the staircase, milling about the rooms off the hall, waving to each other, greeting and smiling and calling out. They laughed a lot and there seemed to be more gentlemen than ladies, and those ladies they saw seemed a trifle less conservative than Demara and Maeve were used to.

A small black page took their pelisses and led them into a beautifully appointed drawing-room. It reminded Maeve forcibly of Sebastian's apartment in Jermyn Street. It had the same aura of opulence and sensuality.

Bryony received them in a dress so fragile it looked, as Maeve remarked afterwards, as if it belonged on Titania or one of her fairies. Its gossamer material revealed the high curves of her bosom, which at this time of the day was surely unseemly.

However, that obviously did not bother Bryony, whose flaming hair was studded with diamonds and who wore a magnificent diamond necklace around her naked throat.

She sat on a chaise-longue surrounded by dandies paying court, and she held out her hand to Maeve and Demara as regally as any queen. She greeted them warmly and introduced them to the young blades around her. Although they came in all shapes and sizes they yet bore a certain resemblance in manner to Sebastian, and Maeve was instantly at home as she and Bryony engaged them in lively and spirited conversation.

Demara hung back, as was her wont. She thought the room over-heated and over-decorated and the prattle risqué. She was not comfortable here. The ambience did not suit her as it did her sister. She was far too simple in her tastes and her need for classic minimalism was offended by the tendency of the decoration to be rococo.

She seated herself near a window overlooking Manchester Square and turned her attention outward. It looked peaceful out there. Nannies were wheeling prams and escorting girls and boys with large hoops in and out of the square. The cherry trees were in bloom and the watery sky was trembling between day and dusk. Hansom cabs were

259

coming and going and the flower-girls were shouting their wares. There was an organ-grinder playing for coins. It was a pretty and cheerful scene and she chided herself for always comparing. Why did she have to think of Bannagh Dubh and solitary walks and the wild and lovely coast, the remoteness of it all? Why couldn't she forget?

'Awaken, dreamer! Is he so beguiling that you long for him with such a yearning?' The voice was light and humorous and she looked up, startled, into the walnut-skinned, monkey-like face of a man staring down at her. His hair was grey, his grin puckish and his eyes, periwinkle-blue, were full of humour.

'It was not a man I was longing for, sir,' she answered truthfully, liking the man instantly.

'Well, well now. I thought young and beautiful ladies thought of little else.'

'Then you would be wrong, sir. I rarely think of men . . .' She immediately thought of Duff Dannon and her face flooded with colour.

'See! You fib. Oh, perfidious lady, why do you lie? There is no shame in dreaming about a man.'

'I do assure you, sir, that I was not, when you asked me, thinking of anyone. If you must know I was thinking, dreaming, what you will, of land.'

'Ah!' the gentleman sighed. 'Interesting. Very interesting.' He glanced down at her. 'By the way, I am Perry Dawkins, at your service, ma'am.'

Demara held out her hand. 'And I am Demara Donnelly,' she announced. 'Is it not most unseemly to introduce ourselves to each other like this?'

'Yes. It is. You are correct. But I won't tell anyone if you don't.'

'I promise,' she dimpled back.

'We can get Bryony to do the honours, then propriety will be placated, or, contrarily, we can do away with protocol and simply enjoy each other's company.'

She laughed and he joined her and his merriment was contagious. 'Did I detect an Irish lilt in your voice? And would the land you were dreaming about be your homeland?'

She nodded. 'How perceptive of you.'

'I am noted for being perceptive,' he lightly replied. 'But tell me, you are the sister of the young actress who is taking all London by storm?'

'Yes, sir.'

'Ah, so the pretty actress has a beautiful sister.'

'You are confused sir. It is my sister who is beautiful, not I.'

'No, no. It is you who are confused. Your sister is a confection. She is a *frou-frou*: dimples, pink cheeks, large eyes and curls tumbling riotously around her. Pretty, pretty, pretty. You, on the other hand, are classically uncluttered.' He looked at her face with detached interest, as if he were looking at a statue. 'Marvellously simple, pure lines. A mobile brow, smooth as silk. Fine clear eyes and a matchless nose. You, Miss Demara Donnelly, are beautiful.'

She did not answer but looked across the room at Maeve's glowing face. Her heart, for some unaccountable reason, overflowed at that moment with love for her lovely sister, her aspirations, her hard work, her application and discipline.

'To me she is very beautiful,' she told Perry Dawkins.

'You love her,' he replied, then sighed. 'At any rate, they say young Sebastian Davenport agrees with you. The rumour is that he is quite obsessed with her.'

'That,' she replied, 'is what half the men in London are rumoured to be.'

'But it is Sebastian she favours.'

'That is supposed to be a secret,' she laughed.

'There is no such thing as a secret in London society, my dear,' he countered.

She turned to him. 'What sort of house are we in?' she asked, and, seeing his startled look, she added, 'I'm curious, sir. As an outsider and a stranger to, er, London society, I cannot always correctly assess my surroundings.' She looked at his face, which was comical in its confusion, and she laughed. 'Oh, don't be afraid. I won't be shocked. No doubt they told you, I am a country-girl, sir, a peasant.' She smiled up at him. 'And proud of it.'

'Well . . .'

'Though I may be wrong, I have a strange feeling I know the answer.'

He laughed too. 'It is not the sort of house you should frequent,' he told her confidentially, 'but it is not a brothel, if that's what you mean.'

'But it is not respectable?'

'Exactly. I regret to have to inform you, it is not.'

'For ladies? But I take it, sir, it is respectable, even fashionable, for gentlemen?'

'Precisely,' he replied. 'I'm sorry.'

'Oh, it is no matter to me, sir,' Demara smiled. 'Whatever the house, if a friend of mine invites me, I shall accept, and I make it respectable.'

'Bravo!' he cried.

'Believe me, sir, I care not a fig for what is done or is not done in polite society. I believe I am lucky.'

'I believe you are, madam.'

'You do not despise me?'

'Far from it. I am of like mind.'

They were silent a moment, then she saw him stiffen and realized he was looking in the direction of the door. She followed his gaze and saw the tall, handsome man who stood there, the very prince of fashion, a sun-god, his blond head back, his eyes flashing. He was, she was suddenly certain, Lord Sebastian Davenport, and he was looking in horror at Maeve, who sat with Bryony in the circle of men, quite unconscious of the angry stare directed at her. Demara rose to go to her sister, to warn her, but Perry Dawkins put a restraining hand on her arm. 'No, no,' he said. 'It is too late.'

He was correct. Sebastian was striding towards Maeve, the light of battle in his eyes. When he reached her he uttered one word, 'Maeve!' and she looked up, startled. Then a flood of joy turned her cheeks rosy, but at the tone of his next words her smile froze. 'What the Devil are you doing *here*?' His words crossed the room and a hush fell, and everyone waited with baited breath to see what would happen. There was an air of avid expectancy in the place and Demara noted that Perry Dawkins had a look of faint disgust on his face. Most of the guests had heard rumours about the young nobleman and the actress. All were hoping for a scandalous incident so that they would have a juicy piece of gossip to carry to their friends.

Maeve was staring at him with wide, innocent eyes, but there was a glimmer too of anger. 'What do you mean?' she asked him. 'Be civil, Sebastian. This is my friend Bryony Gilligan. Bryony, this is . . .'

Bryony was giggling. 'Oh, Sebastian and I are old friends, my dear. We've known each other very well indeed,' she said, the inference obvious. She winked at Sebastian who turned a brick-red.

He towered over Maeve, his lips white with rage. 'Come away from here at once!' he demanded.

He caught her by the wrist, pulled her to her feet and hustled her out of the room into the hall. They were watched with eager curiosity by the others present.

'Don't worry, Maeve. He'll forgive you. He's a very forgiving man,' Bryony called after them, laughing.

Demara shrugged off her companion's arm, gave him a smile, then hurried after her sister. When she reached the hall Lord Davenport was pulling Maeve's pelisse roughly over her shoulders.

'Sir, sir, do not use Maeve so,' Demara cried. 'What is the matter with you?'

'And who might you be that you question me?' he asked her rudely. He turned flashing eyes on her and she had to admit to herself that he was indeed a most handsome young man.

'I am her sister, sir,' Demara answered.

'Ah! Then how could you have allowed a creature so innocent, so pure into such a house as this? It is beyond me, madam, truly it is.'

'Please calm yourself, Davenport, and act your age.' Demara recognized the voice as Perry Dawkins' and she turned to see him propping up the doorpost, looking quizzically at the scene in the hall.

'Perry! Blow me, I didn't see you. Anyhow, this is none of your business, so keep out of it, I pray you.'

'Listen to me, Lord Davenport,' Demara said, her voice soothing. 'I met Bryony Gilligan in Berwick Street Market.

She invited me to take tea with her. I accepted. Why not? I knew of no reason to refuse. We grew up together in Ireland. I have known her since we were babies. I brought Maeve with me to visit her, quite naturally, you'll agree. What kind of house this is is neither here nor there to me. It is of no consequence.'

'That is very foolish, madam,' Lord Davenport said thinly.

'Bryony is an old friend. I have come to see her. It is as simple as that. Nothing improper has occurred since we came to alarm or disturb, except, sir, your behaviour.'

Perry Dawkins clapped his hands and cried, 'Bravo!' at her for the second time since they met. Demara glared at him and continued, 'We will leave, sir, when we are ready, not before. And Lord Davenport,' she added, bristling with indignation, 'you are *not* my sister's master, so unhand her and do not presume to tell her where she may or may not go.'

Sebastian was nonplussed. No one had ever talked to him like that before. Not even Nanny Lenton. Ladies were usually his willing slaves. But here he stood, in a whore's hall, being lectured and put in his place by the sister of the most beautiful girl in the world. He did not know what to do or say.

Maeve however was equal to the situation. 'I am perfectly capable of taking care of myself,' she said tartly to Demara, then, looking squarely at Sebastian, her eyes smouldering, she said, 'What I would like to know, sir, is, what are *you* doing here? If this is a house of ill-repute, as you seem to imply, then why are you in it?'

Sebastian did not lose his composure. 'I came to collect my friend here.' He glanced at the smiling man leaning against the door. 'Lord Perry Dawkins. We plan to spend the afternoon at Boodle's over a game and dine there until it is time for me to call for you at the theatre.' Sebastian's face was cool and bland and he looked at Maeve so innocently that Demara knew he was lying. She glanced over her shoulder at Perry Dawkins and found him grinning in admiration, but when he caught her glance he smoothed his expression into one similar to Lord Davenport's.

'That still does not explain your acquaintance with Bryony, which she was at pains to underline for me.'

This however was too much for Sebastian. 'No chit of a gel will tell me where I may or may not go,' he affirmed, his voice sharp. 'I do not have to account for my movements to anyone.'

Maeve looked at him with withering contempt. She looked enchanting. 'Then, sir, you must accord me the same courtesy, if you please. I too must be allowed to go where I choose without having to ask permission, or otherwise behave like a child!'

A footman had arrived in the hall. 'The carriage is in the square to take you where you wish to go,' he told Demara. Maeve took her sister's arm. 'Come, Demara,' she said. 'Let us go home and rest. I am quite worn out what with being haggled over as though I were a bone and not the sensitive artist that I am.'

Demara realized that Maeve was enjoying the scene and the routing of young Sebastian had given her much satisfaction. She wondered that love could wear so many faces. Now Maeve looked up at him with melting eyes, soft as violets after the rain, and her warm red lips trembled. 'Oh, sir, you have done me a great disservice. You have assumed I had knowledge of something no maiden could be expected to understand. I assure you I cannot comprehend a great deal of what you are talking about and I have no wish to. You have presumed to harry me and chivvy me as if I were a greenhorn soldier. A novice recruit. A boy who is ignorant. It is ill-becoming, sir, and I a girl. Why should I be privy to things I do not know? In any event I am an actress, sir, and not a minion you can order about at will. Nevertheless, I shall be willing to grant you the opportunity, after the performance tonight, to reinstate yourself in my affections. Good evening, Sebastian.'

She swept out of the house. Demara was breathless with admiration. She had underestimated Maeve. She glanced over at Perry Dawkins who was staring at the front door and then at Sebastian who looked thoroughly confused. She followed her sister and got into the carriage. They

265

drove off and Maeve burst into a fit of the giggles that did not abate until they had reached Soho Square.

Chapter Forty-Five

ᵔᵔᵔ ᵔᵔᵔ

Áine was determined to prolong her convalescence. She liked the Desmond house, and she wanted to be part of it. Yet she poisoned the very atmosphere she craved. She injected tension and dissention into the comfortable tranquillity. Her sniping at Tilly, her songs of complaint to Demara and Maeve, her whine of self-pity to a less than sympathetic Belle all combined to ruffle the happy climate in Soho Square and make it turbulent. She ran Tilly Bywater ragged with constant demands, and only Tilly's dogged gratitude and love for Belle, Maeve and Demara prevented her from losing her temper or bursting into tears. Like a lot of people who lacked humility, Áine treated those she considered her inferior very badly indeed and many an evening Tilly went to bed in the box-room and wept into her pillow until it was soggy and damp under her cheek.

'Oh, the sooner she goes the better,' Maeve whispered to Demara when they were tucked up in bed deep under the warm covers.

'Well, we cannot throw her out into the street, Maeve,' Demara said.

Maeve sighed, 'No, we can't. Oh, Demara, what are we going to do with her?'

The question was answered for them quite unexpectedly. A few days after the incident at Bryony Gilligan's Lorcan Brennan arrived at the front door of the house in Soho Square. He was spruced up in his best bib and tucker, a contrite expression on his face, and asking for his wife.

Áine's condition had improved considerably. However,

she refused to consider herself cured and when she heard he was there she suffered a prompt relapse.

'I won't see him! I won't!' she wailed. 'I want to stay here with you.'

'Pull yourself together,' Belle instructed her briskly. 'He won't do anything to you here. Stop being so hysterical.'

Indignant at Lorcan Brennan's treatment of his wife, Belle nevertheless cordially disliked the third Donnelly sister and wished only for her departure. Yet she had no intention of foisting Áine on her violent husband.

'He'll beat me again, missus, so he will,' Áine wailed.

'Well you don't have to go back to him. You can get yourself a live-in job as a domestic. There is a great demand at present and it is easy to get a position in service,' Belle assured her.

This was not at all what Áine wanted. 'I'll help you,' she cried and Belle shuddered. 'You keep me here an' I'll *slave* for you.'

Belle said nothing and between them they got her out of bed and helped her to dress. She agreed to see her husband provided they left the door open while she was speaking to him.

Áine disappeared into the room and Belle hovered nervously about in the hall with Demara and Maeve. They could hear Lorcan protesting and Áine whining, but they were taken aback when, shortly after she had gone in, Áine emerged, smiling, all doubt erased from her face, arm-in-arm with a triumphant Lorcan who bore his wife off with promises of good behaviour and the turning over of new leaves.

'Áine, you don't have to go back with him, you know,' Demara told her.

'He's my husband,' Áine replied. 'I miss my apartment. I miss my baby. Lorcan is my man.'

'I don't know what got into me, deed'n I don't,' he protested sincerely. 'I musta been mad.'

'Well, *we* know,' Maeve said, relapsing into the Irish vernacular as she always did when speaking to her fellow countrymen. 'It was the drink as got inte ye, Lorcan Brennan, so keep away from it if ye don't want to see the end of yer wife.'

'Your accent, Maeve, your speech!' Belle muttered feebly.

Lorcan nodded his head, 'Yiz are right. An' I'll not do it again,' he promised and took his wife's arm.

'You be all right, Áine?' Demara asked.

'Yes, an' isn't it better te have a husband an' yer own place than be dependent on foreigners,' she said smugly and flounced off out of the house.

'She could have said thank you,' Belle remarked mildly.

'Ma'd kill her,' Demara said.

Maeve and Demara were relieved at Áine's departure, but nevertheless they were concerned for her welfare.

'She's a fool to believe him, he'll never change,' Belle said.

'She believes him because she *wants* to,' Demara remarked.

At tea next day Belle was still holding a post-mortem on Áine's departure. They had been mulling over it ever since.

'He'll behave himself for a while,' Belle ruminated. 'But once they beat you they don't seem to be able to stop. Nothing is reversible.'

'There's a man at home, Mickey O'Gorman, who is like that,' Maeve said. 'Carmel O'Gorman always has a black eye or a cut lip, God help her.'

'Yes, well, what could she do, poor woman, in Ballymora? She would have to leave her home, her children, her people. She'd be out on the roads and probably starve. Nowhere to go. But Áine can get herself a position here, all found, no trouble.'

'Ma always said we mustn't mind the odd beating when we married,' Maeve said ruefully. 'She said it was a small price to pay for a home and board from her man.'

Demara was outraged. 'Oh that's nonsense. No man'll beat me!' she cried.

'No man has ever dared to raise his hand to me,' Belle said.

'Well, we're not taking her in again,' Demara declared. 'I'm not having any more upset in your home, Belle. You're so good.'

At this moment Tilly came into the room bearing a tray of

tea things. Her face was flushed and she looked at them eagerly. ' 'As she gone? 'As she?' she asked.

'Yes, Tilly. Yes. You can relax,' Demara assured the girl. 'And as I said, I'm not taking her back here, no matter what. I'll pay her fare home if it comes to that. Send her back home to Ma and Da. They'll know what to do with her.'

'Tilly, these tea-cakes are delicious. Quite delicious. Hope you put a couple aside for yourself,' Belle told the delighted maid.

'Oh yes, mum. Thankee, mum,' Tilly squealed, and left them.

'How about your Romeo? How about Sebastian, Maeve?' Demara asked. 'How is he behaving these days?'

'Like a lamb.' Maeve's face was wreathed in smiles. 'Like an angel. He is all solicitude. I think we threw him into complete confusion,' she giggled, 'and he does not quite know what to do about it.'

Sebastian had taken her to supper every night, except Saturday and Sunday when he was in the country, since the incident in Manchester Square. But he had not taken her to the apartment.

He had taken her to the Café Royal, and to Verrey's in Regent Street. He took her to see the fireworks and fountains at Crystal Palace and Collins Music Hall in Islington which she disliked and felt was unsuitable for ladies. It was this type of reaction that confused Sebastian. Every so often she behaved just like a female cousin and he wondered how he could have dared offend her sensibilities.

He had felt it politic to keep away from the apartment. He was unable to deal with Maeve's sparkling repartee which outfaced him so, and her calm assumption of dignity and her verbal *coup de grâce* unmanned him. She had a way of parrying his mildest comments, leaving him gaping like a landed fish. However, he also had to admit he found her behaviour stimulating and it made him desire her even more. He had never met anyone like her in his life, and she was not in the least in awe of him. She was indifferent to his status, unimpressed by his prestigious name, did not show him the deference others did – in fact she treated him as she did her sister, her dresser, Geoffrey Denton: with a directness, affection and honesty he found both seductive and irritating.

She had him at war with himself. He did not know how to deal with her. He had given up his original plan of seducing her. He persuaded himself that *he* had made the decision. In reality he knew he had not. Maeve Donnelly would not be seduced. And he dared not force her. She had the courage of her convictions and she would destroy him. There would be a scandal. She had told him to his consternation she was not at all afraid of scandal.

No, force was out, although that was what his father had advised him in the past with girls who teased. 'Break 'em, mount 'em, then pass 'em on,' his father counselled, and Sebastian had tried to do as he suggested, but he rarely met with opposition from the opposite sex and the only time he had resorted to force he had not enjoyed it. There was something distasteful in rape. It was quite common among his friends, a sport, one might call it. They went out, bagged a filly, and broke her. He found it tedious and unfulfilling. He had no need to prove his power. He had no need to dominate. His father and his father's friend the Marquis of Killygally needed every now and then to assert themselves. Let the world, their friends and servants know they were the masters. They liked to kill. Wars, hunting, duels appealed to them. They enjoyed showing who was boss. They also enjoyed humiliating others. It made them feel stronger.

Sebastian was not like that. Sex became a functional thing for him when faced with battle. His best encounters were with partners who explored their sexuality with him. Who shared the experience. Who enjoyed it. Like Byrony Gilligan. Bryony was a wonder in bed. She did things in bed that melted a man.

Yet here he was now, besotted by a temperamental young lady who treated him with a mixture of adoration and a total lack of respect. She seemed to think she was his equal; an outrageous idea! She was not prepared to become his slave or his plaything, which he could understand, but, used as he was to a certain subservience, her independence was unnerving.

So, he took her dining, to soirées, parties, all the places where it was correct to bring a mistress, yet he was not making love to her. He was falling more and more in love with her as the days passed.

All this had not gone unnoticed. The town was buzzing with gossip. Everyone believed they were lovers. The glorious young actress in the full flush of her triumph on the arm of her handsome nobleman aroused jealousy and malice. Maeve and Sebastian between them had everything: beauty, talent, wealth, nobility and glamour. They could not be allowed to get away with it. To flourish unscathed, to flaunt such an abundance was not permissible, so society set out to destroy them. And the easiest way to instigate a break-up was to inform the parents of the young heir. It always worked. It was always effective.

They chose Bosie for the job. It was an obvious choice. No one relished actually doing the betraying and Bosie would enjoy it. Hints were dropped here and there. The duty of any right-minded member of society was to inform the Duke and Duchess that their eldest son had formed an unsuitable liaison. The Marquis of Killygally, who, incidentally, was notoriously malicious, was Maynard Davenport's friend, and was obviously the one to inform the father of the son's obsession.

Maynard Davenport was having his portrait painted. He sat in the great hall in Malvern wearing his Knight of the Garter robes, his lip curled in what he fondly imagined to be a rakish grin, but which was in fact more reminiscent of a fatuous smirk. Bosie, Marquis of Killygally, flushed with wine, wondered how best to dump his information in Maynard's lap and so spoil his day. Bosie may have been the Duke's friend but that didn't mean he liked him.

He decided on the direct approach. 'Your son is well?' he asked.

'Sebastian? Fine, s'far as I know.'

'In love, eh?'

'What?'

271

'Love! Sebastian seems besotted by this actress. Wondered how you felt.'

Now he had come out with it he felt a ripple of fear and the old habit of killing the messenger flashed across his mind. Maynard Davenport was a violent man, a man of the old school. He believed in duelling and did not hold with modern, more diplomatic settling of differences. However the Duke did not raise an eyebrow at the news.

'I was too. At his age. Actress called Kemp. Kitty Kemp. Delicious child. Unwillin' at first but I soon broke her. She got over it an' we were the best of friends. Were until she died. In seventy-eight. Blow, that was.'

Bosie drew a deep breath. 'Well, it seems that Sebastian has not broken her. Rather, she has broken Sebastian. He is her lap-dog.'

This time the eyebrows shot up and the Duke turned his head sharply. The painter muttered a curse under his breath and begged his sitter to remain still.

Bosie's heart thumped in the same way as when he held a winning hand in Boodle's or White's.

'What the Devil do you mean?' the Duke asked tersely.

'Seems she leads Sebastian by the nose,' Bosie replied, keeping his voice careless. 'All around London. He's seen everywhere with her. He's besotted. Quite mad about her. Mind you, one can't blame him. She's a raving beauty.'

The Duke thought about it for a moment. The painter's strokes on the canvas became confident, and Bosie knew a fall of disappointment. He was expecting an outburst but nothing happened.

The Duke decided it was a storm in a teacup and, keeping his pose, murmured rather smugly, 'Davenports always had good taste.' Bosie sighed. This was more difficult than he had expected. 'Hodge, his man, says the boy hasn't mounted her yet. Not got the necessary balls.'

The Duke let out a roar. The painter cursed through his teeth and Bosie continued, heart beating fast, 'She's not to be seduced. He cannot seem to achieve it. Poor Sebastian. Hodge says it's a very poor showing.'

'Don't believe it. No son of mine . . .'

'Oh it's a fact! And it's not lost on society. Everyone

thinks they are in the grip of a passionate romance. Certainly Sebastian gives every sign of it. He seems to have lost his senses.' Maynard growled. 'He's seen everywhere with her, as I've said. He brought her to Lady Weatherby's soirée, was with her at Ascot. And at the Duke and Duchess of Lincoln's Assembly. And every night she is on the stage of the Chandos Theatre in the Strand dressed in the flimsiest of costumes.'

Maynard growled louder and Bosie thought perhaps he had gone too far. The painter cried irritably, 'Oh, my Lord! Please sit still!' and the Duke snarled back at him, 'Go to the Devil!'

He shot out of the chair and strode out of the great hall into the library, followed a little apprehensively by the Marquis. 'What the devil's to be done, Bosie?' he asked, pouring a whiskey from a decanter on a small table in front of the fire. 'He's my heir. God forbid the place would go to Rudi. Fellow is too clever by half. 'Pon my word, I can't understand half of what he talks about. Reads French!' He looked at the Marquis incredulously. 'Believe it? Reads Shakespeare! And a fellow called Dante. Reads him in Latin! Great thunderin' Moses, it's beyond understandin'. How did I spawn a son like that? I ask you? Eh? We've never had a bluestocking in the family before. Can't think how we came by this one. Only that I trust Iris I'd swear she'd been up to hanky-panky with some ghastly bookish bore.'

Bosie could see that the conversation had lost its direction. Rudolph, the Duke's second son, was a favourite cause for complaint. He decided to bring the talk back to its rightful subject. 'If I were you I'd be more worried about the behaviour of my heir than about Rudi.'

'Well, you're not!' Maynard said coldly. 'And I don't know what's to be done. Best maybe, to let it lie. Opposition only feeds the flames of passion.'

Now where on earth did the Duke pick up that gem of wisdom, Bosie wondered. He shook his head. This was not what he'd come for. He'd thought of threats, mayhem, decisions to horse-whip. Perhaps, oh delight, a scandal, but not this inept pondering. Trouble with the Duke was that he adored Sebastian.

273

At that moment Lady Iris came into the study. She was a plain, horsy-faced woman with a loud, hectoring voice, given to commands. 'What the Devil you doin' here, May? This time o' day? Artist fella is hanging about the hall lookin' unseated, poor chap! You get fed up with him?'

'Ghastly news, m'dear. Sebastian blottin' his copybook.' He looked dolefully at Bosie. 'Go on. Tell her.'

'Sebastian is consorting with an actress,' the Marquis stated dramatically.

'Naturally. Quite naturally,' Iris said complacently. 'Nothing wrong with my son. What's the matter, Bosie?' she asked maliciously. 'Forgotten what it's like to be young?' He winced. 'All young fellas fancy actresses. They get over it. They grow up. They marry. Besides, I know my son and when it comes to Malvern he'll toe the line.'

'He talks of marrying her.' It was out before he could stop himself. He had needed a violent reaction and it had been denied him. He was angry at Lady Iris's talk of marriage, so he decided to deliver a *coup de grâce* even if it was not true.

Now he had their attention and they stared at him, shocked.

Only it was not true. No one had suggested Sebastian would marry the girl. The rapt attention he was getting forced him to stick to the lie. He decided to brazen it out. 'Hodge, his man, said Sebastian had told him that if he did not possess the girl soon he'd have to marry her.' He said it glibly and took a deep gulp of whiskey.

'What the Devil's the matter with him? If he wants her why don't he have her? Since when is a filly that difficult to mount? Land sakes! I don't know what the younger generation's coming to. Milk-sops, all of them.' The Duke rose again. 'I'm goin' to see Hodge,' he announced to Bosie's consternation. 'Sort it out.'

'No, no, Maynard. I'd not do that,' he cried.

The Duke and Duchess looked at him in puzzlement.

'Why ever not?' the Duke asked.

'Interference might upset things, Maynard.'

'That's precisely what I aim to do – upset things! We'll go straight to Jermyn Street, Iris. Sort this mess out.

Thank you, Bosie, for lettin' us know. Don't fret. We'll get it tidied up. Can't have Rudi in the chair.'

He hurried from the room followed by his wife, and the Marquis of Killygally sank into the chair and poured himself a very large drink, noticing as he did so that his hand was shaking.

Chapter Forty-Six

ৎৡ ৡৎ

When the Duke reached town next day he decided against going straight to his son's apartment. He did not want to precipitate a crisis and he thought it better to test the water before jumping in. So he went to Boodle's in St James's Street. He met Lord Dawkins in the hall.

'Evening, Dawkins. Seen my son?'

Lord Peregrine Dawkins' merry face broke into a grin. He had had a few drinks and was in a jolly mood. 'Seen him all over town with his actress friend, or should I say *amorata*, eh, what?' He smiled at Maynard. 'Met her sister the other day. Beautiful girl. Bless me if I've been able to think of anyone since. Lodged in my brain, she has. Tell Sebastian the sister's made a conquest.'

'Dammit, Perry, I mean, is Sebastian here? In the club?'

Dawkins nodded. 'Got good taste, your son. In women. Likes the good life. Appreciates it. Bloody Queen, God bless her, tried to shut us all down! But hasn't done a blind bit of good, eh, Maynard? Eh? Can't get rid of a tradition like the gentlemen's club that easily, can you?'

'What the deuce you talking about, Dawkins?' The Duke had no time for silly conversation now. He was single-minded and could not relax until he knew the truth about Sebastian. He wanted to get shot of this actress business, then perhaps he could settle down to enjoy a game of cards with some of the gentlemen who greeted him as they moved about the club's hallowed premises. It was packed this evening.

'Place is crowded,' he murmured to Perry, who waved his hand.

'Exactly,' he crowed. 'Just as I said. She didn't succeed. She hates gentlemen's clubs, Her Majesty does. Thinks all manner of wickedness happens here. Tried to have them banned, but she didn't succeed. This place is packed today in spite of her holier-than-thou attitude. Your boy, by the way, is playing bezique. Or faro. He's in the back.' He waved his hand. 'He's in the back. Losing. Was when I left a moment ago. But you know what they say – lucky in love, unlucky at cards.'

'Yes. Yes.' Maynard had to think a moment. He had not followed his old friend's reasoning at all and didn't know what he was waffling on about. He knew that the old Queen had become more and more straitlaced over the years and that she disliked the existence of men's clubs, especially the gambling that went on in them. Quite a few clubs had closed down in the past dozen years or more and men were feeling a mite threatened, but most of them simply operated with discretion.

Perry Dawkins now irritated the Duke still further by recounting the incident in the house in Manchester Square involving his son, the actress and her sister. The story was much embellished and Perry was nothing if not admiring. 'You should have seen your son's face as the girl rounded on him. She certainly put him in his place! She's got class and spirit. Sister, too.' His periwinkle-blue eyes were sparkling as he looked at the Duke. 'Want to come to the theatre tonight, see the *Dream*? Maeve Donnelly is divine in it, I do assure you, and it is well worth a visit.'

Maynard bristled with aggravation. 'Not on your life!' he protested. 'Wouldn't be found dead! Good Lord Perry, Shakespeare! Music hall's more my line.'

Perry reflected that his old friend Maynard was not renowned for his brain power. A man of limited intelligence and imagination, he avoided anything that needed serious thought. They bid each other a cordial farewell and parted on the best of terms. Men could agree to disagree, Maynard reflected, unlike the female sex who took umbridge at the drop of a hat and were not to be easily placated.

Dear old Perry was warning him. Sebastian was in social hot water and it was up to his father to set the young blade straight.

The Duke found his son at a faro table. Perry was right. Sebastian was losing. His father smiled wryly. He could afford to lose, thanks to his mother's fortune. She could refuse him nothing and gave him a quite ludicrous allowance.

Maynard had no money himself. His profligate father had drunk the family coffers dry. However, Maynard had married money and though it irked him that his wife refused to sign her fortune over to him, he did not try to make her.

He could have. The law gave him the right. However, she managed Malvern too well and he valued his peaceful relationship with her too much to upset her, so he contented himself with allowing her to pay all the bills and keep their sons in pocket money while he spent his time hunting, shooting, gambling moderately and being a gentleman about town. This arrangement suited him. He had no worries. He had everything he wanted. He was content.

Sebastian greeted him civilly and guessed quite correctly what his father was doing in London. He took the wind from Maynard's sails by pre-empting him. When the Duke got him seated comfortably in the reading room with a large whiskey and soda in front of him, and commenced by clearing his throat preparatory to opening his mouth to make a speech, his son said: 'I suppose you've come about Maeve, Father?' His father stood with his mouth hanging open and Sebastian continued, 'Dash it, Father, people have been quick. Well, it's no use. I'll not listen to anything you say about her until you meet her. Can't say fairer than that, can I?'

'See here, Sebastian, you must see that your mother and I . . .' Maynard was floundering and he knew it. Sebastian held up his hand for silence. 'I mean it, Father,' he said. 'No talk of Maeve until after you have been introduced to

277

her. After all, how can you criticize someone you've never met?'

'Very easily, Sebastian. There is a type of person you simply do not bring into our society no matter how wonderful they are. You know that...'

'Father, stop!' Sebastian stood. 'I meant what I said, Father. I'm taking Maeve to dinner tonight. I thought the apartment would suit. I'll expect you there and you can meet her away from public stares. Until then I'll leave you to your own devices and wish you a pleasant evening. My mother is well?'

The Duke nodded. 'Extremely well. Rude health, your mother, but worried about this . . . gossip.'

'We'll talk about that later. I'm glad she is well. I bid you good evening.' He bowed to his father and left him nursing his whiskey and grumbling to himself about the youth of today.

The Marquis of Killygally joined him later and Maynard thought Bosie seemed uneasy.

'Sebastian insists I meet the filly,' he told him.

'Where? Café Royal? Sablonière? Kettner's?'

'No, Bosie. Sebastian thought that might be a little indiscreet, don't ye know. I appreciated that courtesy. Can't say I blame him. Shows he is no fool. Decided we meet in the apartment, in private. Don't want the world and his wife looking on, eh? His man is perfectly capable of providing a first-class meal and seeing we're left in peace.' He glanced at the Marquis with twinkling eyes. 'Sorry you'll miss the show, eh Bosie?'

Bosie's heart sank at the mention of Hodge and he was upset by the Duke's inference that he wanted a ring-side seat for the meeting. He was right of course, Bosie would have loved to have been a witness to the meeting.

'Well, I must be off, Bosie. Wish me luck.'

The Marquis of Killygally watched the Duke make his way through the tables, nodding to this one, greeting that one. He wished he could feel as confident as the Duke. Care little or nothing how the world held him. The Duke's lineage gave him an assurance that bordered on arrogance.

The Marquis wished, not for the first time, that his title was a more imposing one. It had been bestowed on his grandfather by a grateful king for his services subduing the restless natives in Ireland and it was slightly amusing. To the less well-informed it often seemed bogus. People sniggered at the title as if it came from some Gothic novel. It filled him with impotent rage that it was held in such low esteem.

He was a social climber, a snob, and he ached to frequent, by right, the homes of society's most exclusive leaders and become their dearest friend. But he had to work at it. Unfortunately his ambition showed, a fact that he was aware of. He tried to conceal it and failed. He saw their contempt for him in their eyes and writhed under it. Like just now, that remark that the Duke had made. And they hated him when they remembered Fleur. Those who knew.

However, he had something most of them needed. Money! He had a lot of money. He bought and sold land. He built factories. He gambled and was always lucky, unlike Sebastian. His stocks and shares multiplied and increased in value. He held on to Stillwater. He did not want to lose the source of his title. He wanted to be able to point to it on the map and say, that is my estate and I own the land, two hundred acres of it. He wanted to increase his holding. Increase his land assets. He was playing a waiting game with Linton Lester, knowing full well that the money he had given him for the river-bank property in Ballymora would not last for ever and sooner or later the young Lord would come to him for more. That young man wanted money more than he wanted anything else in the world. Bosie saw himself master of all the land from the borders of Waterford on the one side to Bannagh Dubh on the other and all the Lester land between.

He was generous to his friends in high places. He would often foot Maynard's bills, for everyone knew Iris held the purse-strings and chaps must stick together. There were many men of high degree who tolerated Bosie because of his habit of footing the bill. He did this with a sly smile, and they accepted with a casual nonchalance that made him wince. He told himself they'd change their tune, learn to respect him, look up to him, when . . . when. . .

When something happened that would make them envy him. He was certain this would happen some day. He would be on a pinnacle and people would bow to him. They would fight to be his friend. They would vie to be included in his company. Some day. Some day.

He had, unfortunately, by his sexual tastes, effectively cut himself off from one sure source of advancement. His reputation was an impediment and nice women disliked his company. In the puritanical world of Her Majesty Queen Victoria people of quality were not too happy to welcome him into their homes. And he could not produce Fleur. He had to keep her far away from public gaze.

He had unfortunately boasted of his sexual conquests, and realized too late he should have kept his mouth shut about them. He was a carnal man, his sexual appetite large, and with his wealth he had the wherewithal to indulge himself and pay for any mistakes he made. He had seen no reason to restrict himself.

From the beginning he had plundered all the women he could get, lustily and indiscriminately, from duchesses to their maids, virgins to whores. He boasted that there was not a woman he had ever coveted that he did not eventually have. Whether this was true or not was debated hotly but it did not endear him to respectable people.

His tastes had eventually become specialized. He had not wanted it so, but that was what happened to him. He liked youth. Only the young would do. Life became more dangerous. Gossip had suggested that to him a pretty fellow was as tempting as a pretty wench and there were unpleasant tales of young people being bent to his will, orgies that involved fledglings.

He tried to keep the gossip at bay but moral indignation was the favourite virtue of the times and people wore it with gusto.

So he had to scrabble and scheme to stay aboard the overcrowded vessel that was society. He was only too aware that even members of the best families could find themselves, through misfortune, debt, scandal or misalliance, shoved out into a troubled sea. They were forgotten quite quickly and that was a fate he did not want.

Bosie, Marquis of Killygally, was not, in spite of his money and land, a happy man. He was sick with ambition, greed and envy. He could not rest, and the secrets he kept hidden and feared would be discovered ate at his soul like a canker.

Chapter Forty-Seven

೧೨ ೧೨

Hodge greeted the Duke that night and told him that his master requested he wait for him as he was collecting Miss Maeve Donnelly from the theatre and would be back directly. The Duke questioned Hodge closely and discovered his instincts had been right and that that bounder Killygally had lied for effect.

'I knew it,' he said to himself, drinking some of Sebastian's excellent port wine. 'He means to stir up trouble. Bank on it.'

Now the threat of marriage had been disposed of he could safely leave his son's affairs alone. The boy was a Davenport and quite well able to deal with his women without help from his father. The Duke did not want to aggravate his son into taking a defensive attitude about his actress and perhaps being forced into a position he did not really want. Like Romeo and Juliet. If everyone had left those starcrossed lovers alone there would have been no tragedy, Maynard was sure of that. The one time he had seen the play he had been hard pressed not to interrupt the performance with his advice to the parents. He kept whispering to the actors on stage, 'Leave 'em alone! Leave 'em, I say. Can't you see she'll be bored with him in a month?' But they were kept apart and that was the nub of the matter. The Duke resolved to stay out of this whole affair of the actress and decided to look forward to the evening and make sure he had a cracking good time.

When Maeve entered, her beauty, her vitality, her sparkle quite overwhelmed him and it was a merry party around the dining table that evening. The old man was completely seduced by Maeve. The girl was beautiful. Everyone said she was talented. She had charming manners and was better acquainted with etiquette than a lot of the daughters of the aristocracy.

Maeve Donnelly never overstepped the boundary lines of propriety. There was about her something that forbade the taking of liberties. One could not be risqué in her presence, and what most surprised the Duke was her charming innocence.

She was not forward, but neither was she backward. With unerring good taste she trod the tightrope of conversation with the two men, and Maynard was suddenly aware of the terrible danger she could be. However, there was nothing he could do about it at that moment and he did not want to precipitate a critical situation so he kept his peace. He did however remark on her beauty and Maeve accepted the compliment with dignity and without coquetry.

'You have a sister equally pretty, I hear,' he remarked.

'Oh, sir, my sister is far more beautiful than I,' Maeve assured him earnestly.

'Is that right?' It was impossible not to be enchanted by her. 'It seems that Perry Dawkins is very taken by her.'

Maeve looked blank. 'I'm afraid, my lord, you have the advantage. I know no gentleman of that name.'

'They were introduced at the home of a Miss Bryony Gilligan, I believe.'

There was no embarassment at all on Maeve's face and she looked at him guilelessly. 'Yes,' she replied cordially. 'We were there. We visited Bryony, who comes from our home town in Ireland.'

'Kerry, I believe?'

'Yes, my lord. Ballymora, between Killygally and Bannagh Dubh. The nearest town is Listowel,' she dimpled. 'Oh, to you it would be tiny, but I am a country-girl, sir, and to me Listowel is big.'

'I am a country boy, Miss Donnelly, and I know precisely what you mean.' The Duke frowned. 'Tell me, do you know the Marquis of Killygally? He must live adjacent to you.'

She shook her head, a merry glint in her eyes. 'My lord, I come of peasant stock.' She glanced at Sebastian, smiling. 'I know I am not supposed to say it, but the truth is I would not be in a position to be acquainted with the Marquis.' Her eyes gleamed. 'Being far too lowly to be worthy of his notice.'

'Well!' The Duke was quite impressed by the girl's honesty and lack of pretension. 'Perhaps you and your sister would like to dine with Lord Dawkins and myself?' He glanced up. 'Oh, and Sebastian of course.' He smiled roguishly at her but she returned his look with modesty and charm. 'I would be delighted, my lord. Unfortunately it will have to be at a late hour because of the play. Perhaps you would care to attend a performance and we could all dine together afterwards?'

'Oh dear me, no!' the Duke refused hastily. 'Shakespeare is not at all my, er, cup of tea, my dear. Dear me, no!'

'We will collect you from the theatre as usual, Maeve.' Sebastian, pleased by his father's obvious liking for Maeve, was only too happy to be accommodating. 'And I'll get Hodge to bring your sister from Soho Square.'

'Not a good address, that!' the Duke muttered.

Maeve did not hear him. She was saying, 'Demara will come to the theatre. She often does that. To keep me company.'

'It is arranged then!' the Duke said and tackled his navarin of lamb.

They dined on the lamb with fillets of sole before and plum tart afterwards. The Duke was quite sorry when the evening came to a close and he bid them both good-night, retiring to the guest room. Sebastian sent Hodge for his carriage in the mews and when the servant left the room he took Maeve in his arms, folding her tenderly to his breast.

'I love you, Maeve Donnelly,' he said. 'You're like the

moon and the stars.' He smiled down at her. 'I didn't mean
to, you know. I meant to have you as a mistress.'

'Oh, I would never have consented to be that,' she
replied. She stood on tiptoe and took his face between her
hands.

'I love you too, *acoushla*,' she told him and kissed him full
on the lips. The kiss was deep and passionate and they
were both shaken by it. When it was over she stared at him
and to his horror tears sprang into her violet eyes. 'We are
in trouble, my love,' she said breathlessly. 'Do you realize
that?' She was trembling.

He nodded. 'I know,' he whispered.

'Your father will never consent to our marriage,' she
told him, 'and I would never be your mistress. So what will
we do?'

He took her in his arms again and held her to his heart.

'I don't know,' he said. 'I only know I cannot bear to lose
you.'

They heard the carriage outside and they smiled
tremulously at each other. He kissed the dimple at the
corner of her mouth, then as Hodge came to the door he
released her. She would have fallen had he not held her
arm firmly as he took her out of the room and guided her
down the steps and into the carriage.

Chapter Forty-Eight

ᘓ ᘔ

Holborn Restaurant was crowded with fashionable diners
and Hodge escorted Demara and Maeve to the table where
the Duke sat with his son and Lord Peregrine Dawkins.
The other women there were aglitter with jewels, in
contrast to the Donnelly sisters; Demara in black and white
satin with a black-bowed bustle and Maeve in a watered
silk that exactly matched her eyes were innocent of
jewellery. The lack gave them an aura of modesty and

unpretentiousness beside the more stylish ladies there.

'We have met already, I believe,' Perry greeted Demara with obvious pleasure.

'Indeed we did, sir,' she replied, taking the seat beside him as indicated by their host.

By the time supper was over the Duke was further confused. He had relied on pointing out to his son his actress friend's lack of manners. Or her scant knowledge of social graces. He assumed she would show a certain brazenness or a forwardness of manner that would automatically exclude her from appearing socially at Sebastian's side. But no, blow him, try hard as he might he couldn't find a blessed fault in either of the sisters. They were almost too decorous and well-mannered. If Hodge were mistaken and Sebastian did indeed entertain thoughts of marriage, the Duke realized he'd have to fall back on the fundamental objections: breeding, money, and land. All three were necessary in a bride for the heir to Malvern.

Maeve was subdued. One of the reasons the Duke found her so socially acceptable was because she was not her usual buoyant self. A faint, cold fear overwhelmed her and for the first time it occurred to her that for Sebastian and herself there might be no way out.

She was an optimist. She was also a realist. She had been sure that there was an answer if they looked hard enough for it and if their love was strong enough, but she had begun to realize that there might be an unsolvable problem.

Society was difficult to change. It was an intricate and complex ediface which had no logic. Its walls could not be breached without permission.

'Have some lobster,' Perry Dawkins advised Demara. 'The lobster here is very good.'

'Sebastian is my heir,' the Duke said quietly to Maeve, allowing Sebastian to order for them. 'He will be head of the family when I die. He'll run the estates, be in charge of almost one thousand human souls, their welfare.'

It was daunting to think about and Maeve felt herself pale.

'Whoever he marries will take on that task with him. It is a heavy responsibility best undertaken by someone with experience. Someone born and bred to it.'

She of course got the message he was trying, not so very subtly, to convey to her and when she looked into his eyes she saw no malice there. He did not dislike her. In fact it was obvious that he admired her. He regretted she was not a suitable bride for Sebastian, and he was telling her that her dream of an alliance between them was impossible. He sighed and her heart sank and a feeling of great dejection overwhelmed her.

Demara, on the other hand, was enjoying herself hugely. She loved the large and crowded place, the waiters rushing about as if the Devil were at their heels, the smell of food, the clink of glass and cutlery, the laughter, the noise. She enjoyed the meal; the lobster was excellent. And she liked the company. She found Perry Dawkins an entertaining companion who had a very low opinion of society and whose comments made her laugh a lot. His quips were merry and made at the expense of the elevated personages present.

'Take themselves far too seriously,' he told her. 'See their faces, all puffed up with pride and power. Idiots, most of 'em. Wouldn't know how to solve a problem if it came up and bit them. Have some of the roast lamb, my dear. This season's lamb is quite delicious.'

Perry Dawkins was fascinated by the 'Irish question' as he called it and asked her a million things about what was happening in her country.

'I'd be clapped in irons in the Tower if they knew what I think about Ireland,' he told her. 'Bloody cheek, we have, sitting on lands that do not belong to us, that we took by force. And starving the populace. Just because we have a far superior army, half of whom are, in the event, Irishmen.'

They ate the lamb, which was, as Perry said, delicious, though Maeve hardly touched hers. She was staring at Sebastian, wondering how she could live without him.

'What is it, my darling, my sweet?' he asked her, covering her hand with his. 'You look sad and I cannot bear it.'

'I'm so troubled, Sebastian. So confused.'

'Why, dearest heart? Father loves you. Anyone can see that.'

'He may love me but that does not mean he thinks I'm suitable for you. He is sad because he can see no future for us. Oh yes, Sebastian, he likes me, but he knows my place will never be at your side.'

Sebastian gasped. 'Just because something has not happened before does not mean it is impossible. You will be the first Duchess of Malvern who comes from common stock and it will give an infusion of new blood into our old, in-bred family.'

He was doubtful even as he spoke. He realized the pitfalls, the risks it would entail if this alliance took place. And he was not simply thinking of his own position. Maeve would be hurt too. People would be cruel. Maeve was vulnerable. Her feelings were easily bruised.

Maeve was shaking her head. The title she had heard him call her had made her shiver. Duchess. It sounded like some great part she had been chosen to play, a part that would tire her, and unlike a role in the theatre, not one that would end when the curtain fell.

'Oh, Sebastian, I don't know anything about the running of an estate.' She thought of Lady Lester coming down from the castle with calves-foot jelly when one of the cottagers fell ill, of how the cottagers disliked her charity. Charity took your dignity away. Charity humiliated. It kept the poor in their place and gave the rich power over them.

Maeve thought of the castle. Eileen McGrath once told her how Lady Kitty was having new curtains made, and was also decorating the guest room, organizing a ball, working out a menu for important visitors. A hundred skills she, Maeve, did not have, would not know how to begin to deal with.

'I could never be a mistress, Sebastian,' Maeve whispered, her throat constricted.

'Shush, my darling,' he told her, aching to hold her in his arms and promise her the moon. 'We'll find a way around it, I promise you.'

They had treacle tart and Perry assured them it was the best treacle tart in England.

287

'You will come downstairs to dance with me, Miss Demara Donnelly?' he asked and when he took her in his arms for a waltz he said lightly, 'The Duke may find your sister unsuitable for his heir, but I find you fit for any position in the world you chose to aspire to. Perhaps even, if I am lucky, if you could bear to, the position my late lamented wife left vacant when she passed away seven years ago.'

At first Demara thought she had misheard him or misunderstood what he meant. But when she looked into those twinkling blue eyes the message was there.

The crowd swirled around her. People were laughing and sweating and putting all their energy into the dance. The fiddlers were swaying and the orchestra leader was smiling and 'Tales From The Vienna Woods' was being played slightly quicker than was usual in Belgravia.

Perry was an energetic dancer. He was also as old as her father. She loved Duff Dannon, so there was no more to be said. She wished she didn't like him so much.

'You are very kind, sir,' she told him, turning her head sideways to see his face.

'Oh I'm not being kind,' he replied. 'Far from it. I would be indulging in gross selfishness and that's the truth. But you know, Demara, a man finds out as he gets older that duty can be a trap set by people who want us to do the unpleasant for them. I said, can be. A man must do his duty for his family of course, that goes without saying. But for the rest? Church? State? I'm not sure.' He had stopped and was looking at her more seriously than was usual for him. 'My father told me, when I was twenty, that it was my duty to marry Lady Ellen Richards, a lady of impeccable breeding and lineage who was also, I'm afraid, a malicious little person with no sense of humour. Oh, Demara, far be it for me to speak ill of the dead, but it's no use, my late wife was a sore trial to me. Then I was told by the powers that be that I must go to India and fight the enemy. So once more I obeyed. I saw my friends killed. I saw the enemy die. The corpses of enemies and friends are very similar. Suddenly I couldn't understand why I was killing. What was it all about? The Indians led their own peaceful existence in their own land – what was I doing there? Why were we killing each other? It made no sense. Since then, duty as it is instilled into us, I question.'

He had steered her to a table and ordered lemonade. They drank thirstily. She understood what he was saying and was in sympathy with him. They looked at each other and his blue eyes seemed to her infinitely reassuring.

'The moment I clapped eyes on you I wanted you. I said to myself, at once, mind, "If that young lady'd consent to be my wife I'd be the happiest man alive." And for once I'd be doing something to suit myself.' He looked at her earnestly. 'Don't say anything now,' he pleaded. 'Think it over.'

He took her elbow and guided her back to the dining-room. Demara was bewildered. In her wildest imagination nothing like this had ever happened to her. She liked Perry Dawkins. She liked him a great deal. But she loved Duff Dannon. She could not understand why Lord Dawkins had proposed to her. It had been totally unexpected. And impossible. She was going to marry Duff.

Somewhere at the back of her mind she heard a voice, like the voice of someone dead, say, 'No husband. No love'. She knew that was from a dream, a nightmare.

She would explain to Perry tomorrow why it was out of the question. She was going to marry Duff, build her white house in Bannagh Dubh. Who could stop her?

On the way home both sisters were subdued. When they got there a letter from their mother awaited them. It was written, as usual, by Brindsley. It was the same letter as always – it told Demara nothing, simply asked if she was well and Maeve was well and assured her they were all well. With that she had to be satisfied.

Chapter Forty-Nine

૭૭ ૭૨

No one in Ballymora felt the spontaneous delight that usually accompanied a wedding. The marriage of Duff and Dana seemed contrived. Everyone was sure they had not heard the whole story and of course they were right.

'There's more to this than meets the eye,' Della Gilligan said, echoing the thoughts of everyone in the little hamlet.

Ma Stacey shook her head and muttered something about there being no joy there. 'It's like cat and mouse,' she whispered to Phil Conlon and they in their big comfortable bed of sin.

'Which one is the cat?' Phil asked, his hand fondling her large, soft breast.

Eileen Stacey giggled. 'Ah, there ye have it. Hit it right on the nail, Phil. *She's* the cat. Duff Dannon, though meself I'd never have believed I'da live to say it, Duff Dannon is the mouse! I wonder what she has on him? It's the only explanation,' she mused, then shrieked with delight as Phil turned over onto her and they dismissed Duff and Dana from their thoughts and conversation, which very quickly became lewd.

Brigid and Pierce were reticent about the forthcoming nuptials. Pierce even thought he might ask Duff if he was quite sure he wanted to marry Dana. It seemed strange to the Donnellys, and they too felt there was something odd about the whole procedure. Duff Dannon hadn't formally asked Pierce for his daughter's hand as was customary. Pierce was puzzled at the way events were progressing.

There were rumours that the Marquis of Killygally had returned from London and was even now at Stillwater, but whenever Pierce tried to talk to Duff about it the latter avoided him or said little, glancing at him sideways with the eyes of a bull at bay.

'I canna help remembering he's Demara's fella,' Brigid whispered to her husband in bed in the night.

'Nor can I, pet. And there's something fishy about Duff these days. He's more like a hunted man than a bridegroom.'

Pierce slipped his arm under his wife's shoulders and held her loosely in his embrace. It was a familiar, comfortable position for both of them and they snuggled close together as they talked.

'And an angry one,' Brigid mused, then smiled. 'Not like us, *alanna*. Remember?' She glanced up at him.

'I was that keyed up, pet,' he whispered. 'Like Shooshie Sheehan's fiddle when the strings are too tight. I was in a fever. And your eyes were like stars.' There was a lump in his throat at the memory and he kissed her cheek. 'I hate to say it of our own but our Dana is a hard little *ubh*. You're right, woman. There's something more to this than meets the eye and I'm damned if I know how to find out.'

He could feel the want for her grow in him. She did too. Regretfully she shook her head. 'It's only nearly since I lost the babby,' she told him gently. 'Oh, Pierce, it's too soon.'

The seeds were scattered and sown, the harrowing done, and the weather grew softer. Seasons were not measured in days and months and years, but rather by the rhythm of the land. Blossoms appeared on the trees like lace and tender new leaves burst out. The young lambs gambolled and the cows dropped calves and all the babbies appeared behind proud, fat mothers. Groups of perky little chickens ran about mindlessly, ducks fanned behind their parents on the lake and cygnets hid in the reeds beside the river. The rain was soft as silk and the sky a washed madonna blue.

Eventually the wedding day dawned. They had decorated the cottages with blossom and every window held a bouquet. From early morning Shooshie scraped his fiddle and the young girls giggled and swayed in their freshly starched white petticoats, red skirts and their best and most decorative shawls.

291

The men lounged around the cottage half-doors, uncomfortable in their best blue suits, their waistcoats brushed, their brown boots polished so high you could see your face in them.

The women put tressle tables together out under the trees a wee way away from the cottages. They paused anxiously, searched the sky for clouds that might foretell rain and spoil everything. Seeing none they sighed contentedly and wiped their hands on aprons and tucked stray locks into the nest each one wore at the nape of her neck. They laid out the feast to which everyone had contributed, each according to his means, but the atmosphere was uneasy. There was unrest in the air. Everyone felt in their bones that this was not a usual wedding.

Jokes were made and Mary Dannon caused poor Brigid's heart to skip a beat when Katey Kavanagh called out to her, 'How'd ye fancy Dana Donnelly queening it in yer kitchen, Mary Dannon?' and Mary pushed her mane of red hair over her shoulder and sauced back, 'Let her just try, Katey Kavanagh! Let her just try!'

'More like a war breakin' out than a weddin',' Carmel O'Gorman sighed.

' 'Tisn't goin' to be an easy passage for you, girl,' Brigid whispered to her daughter and was startled by the light of battle in her youngest daughter's eyes.

'She doesn't stand a chance, Ma,' Dana replied, looking at Mary Dannon coldly. 'Not a hope in hell against me.'

Dana looked pretty in her white dress. It had been Brigid's own, given to her to wear at her wedding by Granny Donnelly, who had worn it at hers. It was trimmed with Limerick lace that some forebear had brought home from their travels, and Dana had a veil with a halo of waxen orange-blossom holding it on her head. The flowers, which had once been pure white, had aged and were now a pale cream and one or two of the blossoms were broken. But that was all right for the lace had faded too and they matched each other.

Duff wanted to run away. Now that the day had dawned he found himself in a state of terrible confusion. He had no idea how the whole situation had come about.

Mary Dannon was in fact furious with her brother-in-law. She would not have minded almost any other girl coming to live with them. She was good-humoured and gregarious and liked gossip and friendly crack, but she disliked Dana Donnelly intensely and the thought of sharing the cottage with her filled her with dread.

'If only ye'd waited for Demara to come home,' Mary said. 'Some men! Don't have an ounce of patience. Like bloody bulls, ye are.' She glared at Christie, her husband, who had got her pregnant six weeks after Kate was born so she'd lost it and since then she'd never felt right, and so gave Christie the back of her tongue whenever she was disturbed.

She wiped Kate's bottom now as Duff rounded on her. 'Now, sister, you know I'll not have ye talk about it,' he blustered. It was how he behaved these days; uncomfortable in his own skin.

'Or Maeve,' Christie sighed regretfully. 'Yerra there wasn't a man in Ballymora good enough to marry Maeve Donnelly, accordin' to that high and mighty father of hers.'

'Duff, put on yer navy blue,' Mary hectored him. 'An' here's a white shirt. Stop hanging around. It's yer weddin' day, more's the pity.'

'She was more beautiful than the moon,' Christie murmured, still thinking about Maeve.

'Unless yiv changed yer mind,' Mary still badgered Duff. 'An, yiv decided to leave yer bride waitin' at the altar.'

For one moment the idea seemed so attractive to Duff that he nearly decided to run away. Then he thought of Pierce Donnelly and came to the conclusion it was not a very good idea.

'There'll be rivers of stout flowing this day.' Christie Dannon licked his lips in anticipation and Duff had no option but to dress and put on a high white collar and his bowler hat and his polished boots.

'Get *on*, Duff. Yer late. Father Maguire'll be waitin'!'

Duff did as he was told and eventually they got him ready. He walked up the road with Christie and Mary. Shooshie Sheehan in his stuff suit and bowler danced behind him scraping his fiddle and the other men fell into place behind Shooshie as Mary left the men. Deegan Belcher, Dinny McQuaid, Brian Gilligan and his sons, Cogger Kavanagh, Miles Murphy the drover and his son, Mickey O'Gorman hugging a hangover, Mog Murtagh, the Flynns, Phil Conlon and Brindsley Donnelly. All the male cottagers came out into the boreen in their best and followed Duff up to the church. They would sit one side of the altar and their womenfolk, who followed the bride, would sit on the other. All the men followed Duff except Pierce who stayed behind to escort the bride.

Shooshie doubled back when the men reached the church and stood before the Donnelly cottage, fiddling energetically, and moments later the bride emerged into the spring sunlight in her white dress and veil. Shooshie danced before her, playing his heart out and she put her arm into her father's and walked with purposeful steps along the boreen, following Duff's footsteps but much more buoyantly, doing what she would be expected to do through their lives together after today.

The far from shy bride was followed now by Mary Dannon, Katey Kavanagh, Ma Stacey, Carmel O'Gorman, Sheena McQuaid, Della Gilligan and all her daughters, Jinny Murtagh and poor little Ellie, Delia McCormack and everyone except Granny Donnelly, who remained indoors and quiet in front of the fire where Brigid had settled her, tucking a rug around her thin old body.

Cogger Kavanagh came back from the church. They could see him as they walked, lopsidedly running back, and for a moment Dana's heart stopped in case something had happened to stop the ceremony.

'Donna do it! Donna do it! Donna do it!' he chanted at her, dancing along the dusty lane in front of her.

Dana brushed him away. 'Lose yourself, Cogger,' she cried angrily, but he thrust a sweaty face under hers and yelled, 'I'll tell Demara, so I will. I'm thinkin' that I'll tell Demara.'

'Go ahead, Cogger Kavanagh, see if I care,' she hissed at him and held on more tightly to her father's arm.

When they had nearly reached the church and were at

the crossroads, the exact spot where Pierce had bid
Demara and Maeve farewell, so long ago it seemed, their
progress was halted by a carriage, a landau with luggage
strapped to the back and the Lester arms on the side. It
came careering down the road in a cloud of dust, swaying
like a ship on a turbulent sea, listing as if it might topple
over at any minute. The procession drew to the side of the
road, into the cow parsley, and as they watched a head
came out of the window and shouted something at the
coachman who reigned in the horses with a resounding
'Whoah!' The landau pulled up and to the women's
surprise the face that was stuck out of the window
belonged to Lady Kitty. She asked loudly what was going
on, who was marrying who. Pierce Donnelly removed his
hat and bowed and explained that it was his daughter's
wedding day.

'The first of your beautiful girls to wed?' Lady Kitty
cried and Pierce shook his head.

'Ah no. Me eldest, Áine, is married away in London,' he
told her but she was not listening. She was fishing about in
her purse and she scattered some coins into the road.

'I wish you every happiness,' she cried blithely and
nodded to Pierce then gestured to the coachman who was
holding the beautifully matched bays. They were
shuddering and quivering and pawing the dirt, and now
with a shout the coachman urged them into action again.

'Isn't that queer?' Katey Kavanagh whispered to Brigid
Donnelly.

'I thought she'd gone to London for good.'

'Well, she's back, that's obvious,' Delia McCormack said.

'An' with enough luggage for a while,' Della Gilligan
remarked.

'Mebbe . . . mebbe she'll take over Ballymora,' Carmel
O'Gorman remembered the cold dead body of Lady
Kitty's husband the day they laid him out up at Ballymora
Castle.

'Wouldn't that be grand,' Sheena McQuaid sighed.

'Then all our troubles would be over. She's a lovely lady,
God bless her.'

'Don't be more of a fool than ye look,' Katey Kavanagh

sneered, 'Jasus, didn't the Marquis *buy* the land offa the Lesters an' ye can't undo that the way ye'd unravel a jumper. An' will ye lookit Dana, grovelling in the dust for a handful of coins! Why couldn't she have handed them to her?'

'Oh aren't ye the hoity-toity one, Katey Kavanagh. Turn up yer nose at the bounty of a lady.'

Dana had picked up the scattered coins. 'Wasn't that luck for ye, Dana?' Pierce smiled at his daughter, wishing he loved her more. He would have died for Demara or Maeve and he loved his youngest son with all his heart, but Dana and Áine he only barely liked, a fact that troubled him.

'Oh, if the luck isn't there, Father, I'll make it,' was his daughter's retort.

The procession reached the church and the women filed into their seats all in a body and Pierce handed Dana, with relief, to Duff at the altar. Then he took his place beside Brindsley and the other men.

Father Maguire turned to the altar and began, '*In nominee patre, filii, spiritue sanctus . . .*'

Holy Mass was said and then the marriage ceremony took place.

Duff stood there in a dream. He could not believe it was really happening. It was as if some other being occupied his body and he had no choice but to follow this through. Vows were taken. The sun slanted through the little stained-glass windows of the church and the song of the birds outside could be heard above the coughing and sighing and occasional sob in the congregation.

Dana could feel her triumphant heart beating a tattoo against her chest and Duff, whose mind had gone totally blank, tried to catch hold of what was happening, but it seemed impossible to grasp and slipped away from him like a dream.

'We'll be wettin' our whistles in a mo',' Mickey O'Gorman whispered to Phil Conlon beside him. 'I've a terrible thirst on me.'

'Oh, it's goin' to be a great day!' Dinny McQuaid muttered, licking his lips in anticipation.

296

'Rivers of stout will flow this day,' Mickey eulogized. It was as he said this that Mickey noticed a queer listening look on Phil Conlon's face. The ex-bailiff had an ear cocked as if he was trying to hear and it made Mickey prick his ears up and look at Dinny on the other side of Phil. Now Phil's body had become tense and he turned his face to the door. The men beside him turned too and they spread their tension, their awareness that there was something unusual happening outside. Each of the men, all of the women became alert, one by one, as Father Maguire blessed the couple in front of him. Even Duff looked around, face vacant of expression, and a rustle passed over the congregation like wind over a field of ripe corn.

What was it, that sound from outside, that distant commotion? What did they hear, so far away that it was almost an instinct? Something was happening, they could feel it in their bones. Like distant thunder. it foretold a storm.

They tried to shake off their foreboding. Had Lady Kitty sent some servants with wine and food from Ballymora Castle? Was that it? Their blood told them it was not. Deep inside they knew something terrible was happening out there, something to dread, something to fear, and each man and each woman stood in the church, alerted, transfixed smiles on their faces, reluctant to move, desperate to escape as Duff and Dana walked down the aisle.

The bride and groom had left the church and still no one moved. Usually the crowd surged after the new-married couple, eager for a jar, for the party to begin. But no one moved this day. They stood as if turned to stone, and some heard the echoes of another day when Clancy had stood at the back of the church and warned them of danger. Well, Clancy was not there any more and there was no one to warn them.

They were not surprised when Dana screamed, but it broke their immobility, and now thoroughly alarmed they hurried to the door, full of rising panic.

Dana's scream had been sharply horrified and it was

closely followed by a terrible shout from Duff and, as the congregation reached the door, they were assailed by the acrid smell of burning.

They saw in the distance smoke rising from their cottages, huge black billows disfiguring the sweet spring air. Like a volcanic eruption huge clouds of charcoal grey shot with lurid flame belched into the pale sunshine.

'Granny!' Brigid screamed and ran down the road, her skirts held up, her bare legs pumping under her, her hair losing its moorings and flying out about her like a banner. 'Granny! Granny!' she screamed as she ran, her heels hardly touching the ground.

'Ma!' Pierce's voice was knife-edged with panic, and fleet as a deer he followed Brigid down to the cottages.

The others, horrified realization dawning on them, ran after. Their voices rose, curses and prayers jostling for utterance, as moaning and gibbering in consternation they ran at breakneck speed, and as they got nearer they could see their worst fears were justified.

The man Muswell was seated on his grey mare. He saw them coming, and he wheeled his horse and galloped away, a flaming torch in his hand. He urged his mount forward and was followed by three other men, strangers to the cottagers, and they too were carrying torches.

They stood still as the horsemen disappeared, trying to absorb the scene of devastation. Their homes were furnaces, they could smell the smoke which lay heavy on the air. Charred particles fell from blazing roofs and walls. Furniture had been pulled out of some of the houses and set on fire separately. Sheena McQuaid fell weeping over her ruined loom and Della Gilligan searched frantically for her statue of the Virgin she so treasured in the pile of smouldering debris that had been the contents of her home.

Brigid had tried to rush into their cottage but she was defeated by the flames. Duff pulled off his shirt and gave it to Pierce who put it over his face, and, calling his mother, he ran through the inferno while Brigid stood outside wringing her hands and calling, 'Don't, Pierce, don't. Granny . . . oh, Granny love. Don't, Pierce, don't.'

298

Her throat was dry from the smoke and no one heard her.

Dana was crying helplessly. She was angry enough to kill. That this should have happened on her wedding day filled her with fury and Katey Kavanagh tried to soothe her.

'Yer da was right after all,' she muttered. 'About the landlord bidin' his time. We were wrong sendin' Clancy away.'

Dana turned on her fiercely. 'Much good that's done him, being right. Where'll we go now? What've we got? Oh a fine weddin' I'm havin' an' no mistake.'

Pierce emerged carrying Granny Donnelly carefully in his arms. She was a charred bundle and Pierce was crying. A gasp went up from the crowd.

'Ma! Ma! Ma!' he sobbed. His face was black and the tears made two white pathways down his cheeks. He laid her down tenderly on the grass and asked Dana for her veil. There was something about him that warned her not to say anything but do as he asked. She took it off and he laid it over the body of his mother. When he stood the small bundle looked like a patch of snow and the others forgot the wedding and the loss of their homes in the man's terrible grief.

Chapter Fifty

⌒⌒

For a while people were too numbed to fully comprehend what had happened. In a trice they had lost everything. It was like the end of the world for them. Their homes and all they possessed had gone. They wandered around lost and bewildered, stumbling among the ashes, poking in the wreckage, confused, not knowing what to do next.

Under the trees the wedding feast was laid, ready to eat. Children sobbed, picking up their parents' fear, babies wailed and ould wans keened, moaning, their grief hanging on the air as the day moved on into chaotic evening.

There was little to salvage. Muswell must have doused the cottages with paraffin or some inflammable substance for them to ignite and burn so quickly. He had done his job well.

'Let's go after him, the whore's spawn, the bastard, and crucify him,' Deegan Belcher bellowed and a few of the men took up the cry. 'Yes, let's kill him. Kill him! Let's string him up! Let's cut out his liver and lights!'

But Duff Dannon calmed them and indeed their bravado concealed so much grief and fear and bewilderment that it was not a real possibility.

'He'll be waitin',' Duff told them. 'That's what he'll be doin'. He'll be up there waitin' for us to do somethin' like that. Nothin' he'd like better. Give him an excuse.'

'Well, an' why not?' Deegan Belcher asked. 'I'd like a crack at him.'

Duff sighed. 'He'll have guns. He'll be waitin'. If we go up there now we'll find ourselves arrested. Even if we are peaceful. We'll end in gaol. Or wounded. Or dead. Best keep our peace. . .'

'Jasus man, ye talk of peace an' our homes gone!' Mickey O'Gorman was squeezing his hands together, not knowing what to do. He kept turning into his doorway, which was all that was left of the cottage, as if to go home, and there was nothing there but a pile of rubble, smoking walls and a fallen and charred door. 'Carmel,' he cried like a frightened child. 'Oh, Carmel, what'll we do?' and he turned to his wife who still bore the marks of the beating he had given her. But she, her face full of sympathy, opened her arms to him and folded him to her bosom.

Everyone's home was in the same state of demolition. They were devastated and turned, like animals, to their lairs, their burrows, their earths, the places they had marked, their own territory, that they had scented and claimed. But their homes were gone and they twisted and turned as if hoping the earth would swallow them up, consume them as their homes had been consumed.

Brigid was keening over the body of her beloved

mother-in-law and the women gathered around lamenting her loss as their own.

'At least we're all alive,' Sheena McQuaid said, looking on the bright side.

'Much use that an' we've no place to go,' Dinny told her.

'Lookit Cogger,' Brindsley said. 'Lookit Cogger. What's he tryin' te say?'

Cogger was leaping up and down in the boreen and pointing.

'He's pointing to the barn. Old Lally Flynn's barn. The one the moonlighters used.'

At the mention of the moonlighters a hush fell over the crowd. Katey Kavanagh raised a blackened face to the horizon and sighed. 'If only . . . ' she murmured.

'If ye'd listened to my da none of this woulda happened,' Brindsley shouted at them. He was shuddering with anger and outrage. No one should be allowed to do this to another human being. No free man should be so treated and humiliated. All his books were gone, the collected wisdom of the ages, dust and ashes now. And Granny. His Granny, a fixture in his life, a wonderfully assuring permanence, someone that he loved and cherished. There she lay, a charred bundle of bones covered in Dana's wedding veil, on the earth, dead. He shivered with hate and impotence. Nothing to do about it. Nothing to be done.

'Listen, lad, yer father was right. Phil Conlon was right. An' Duff Dannon was right. If we'd listened this couldn't have happened. But it's no good thinkin' like that now. If we do it'll drive us mad.' Katey Kavanagh touched Brindsley's arm, looking around at the men who avoided her eyes, hedging and dodging in their minds the acceptance of her statement. They tried to avoid any admission of culpability although it was patently obvious that what she said was true.

'Now listen,' she cried, her ugly old face red and blotched with the emotions she was feeling. 'Listen to me. What Cogger is tryin' to point out in his way, which if ye don't mind me sayin' so seems to me at this moment wiser 'n any of yiz, is that we use the moonlighters' barn as a temporary shelter for tonight.'

'An' what about me? What about my weddin'? What about that?' Dana shouted angrily.

'Shut up, you. It's just too bad, but ye've got the rest of yer life to celebrate. We have a crisis now an' we have to deal with it, so listen to me, all of yiz. We have to go on. We can't let them beat us. We have to decide, each an' every one of us, what te do. Well, I suggest we take that food . . . ' she pointed to the tressle table under the trees, 'an' take it down to the barn.'

There was a cry from Brigid Donnelly. 'Talkin' about weddin' food an' Granny dead at my feet . . . ' She was shaking, her body racked with sobs, her face streaked with tears. More terrible however was the torment in Pierce's eyes, the raw pain there.

Dana piped up, 'Shut up, will ye. This is my weddin'. We'll eat at the tables like we're supposed. . . '

Pierce hit her. He took the back of his hand to her and for the first time he struck one of his children. He didn't speak to her and she staggered away dazed. Duff did not come to her aid but went to her mother and it was he who soothed her and agreeing with Katey said, 'She is right, Brigid. She is right. We must eat. We have to keep our strength up, for this is not the end of the battle.' He helped her to her feet. 'God knows, an' you do too, how much I loved Granny Donnelly, but Katey is right. We have to go on. It is our duty, eh, Pierce?' He appealed to the silent, suffering man.

Pierce Donnelly shook himself, then lifted the charred piece of wood he had picked up, looked at it a moment then cracked it over his knee. It broke with a sharp bullet-like noise that made them jump. He turned to Duff, a piteous expression on his face, and the younger man nodded and stared at him, trying to pass him some of his strength in a look.

Pierce took the burning glance, absorbed the support and faith there, allowed it to seep into his being. 'Yes, you're right,' he said. 'We must not let them beat us.' Pierce had trouble with his voice, but he cleared his throat and it gained strength. 'That's what Clancy said. 'An' he was right. He was right about everything. We have to shake ourselves out of our indifference and fight the bastards. That's what he said. And the only way to do that is to survive.' He struggled, for he had a near overwhelming desire to fall on the body of his mother, curl up beside her as he used to when he was a little boy and go to sleep. He had striven for so long for each little advantage and now it had all been taken away from him and he was very tired. But that way lay defeat, death, abandonment and misery. He took a deep breath and, crying still through the words, unaware that he was, he repeated, 'We must survive. Cogger's idea is a very good one. We must go to the barn tonight. It solves our immediate problem of where to sleep. And what Katey suggests is right and proper. We must eat. We'll get the young people to carry the food down. We'll have to store some of it. Food now must be on ration. We don't know how long it will have to last.'

'We should mebbe divide it equally between us . . .' Delia suggested.

'No. The men need more,' Jinny cried. 'Our Ellie eats like a bird. Brindsley Donnelly needs more'n she does. . .'

'Will ye shut up, woman. Can't we discuss that later,' Mog admonished her.

'Yes . . . well, I was only sayin' . . . ' She looked at Pierce for comment but he had sunk to his knees and covered his face with one arm and was rocking himself to and fro. All they could see of his face was his mouth stretched open in a grimace of agony.

'Lave him be a moment,' Brigid said quietly. 'He loved his ma.'

Dana, standing in her wedding dress, shivered, then squared her shoulders. She walked over to her husband and took his arm. 'Let go,' Duff cried involuntarily, shaking off her arm. 'Brindsley, you get Joseph Gilligan and the other lads to collect all the stuff up above and mind ye don't drop any of it. We need it, not the birds.' Ignoring Dana at his side, he continued, 'Katey, get some of the women to bring anything they can salvage, even if it looks useless, anything that can be of any use at all and bring it to the barn.'

'There's nettles here for soup,' Sheena McQuaid cried.

'An' we won't run short of kelp, thanks be to God.'

Dinny was over with the boys, who were rolling the keg of porter down to the barn, and Sheena looked at Ma Stacey. 'Don't ye think we should send for the moonlighters?' she asked.

'God'n yer a brazen hussy, Sheena McQuaid,' Ma Stacey marvelled as she stared at her.

'Shush!' Sheena put her finger to her lips, but Cogger had heard and he cried out, 'Let's send for the moonlighters, l-l-lets s-s-end. . .'

And the others took up his cry, as if they could shift the responsibility onto someone else. As if by crying out for Clancy and his men all their troubles would be over. 'Let's send for the moonlighters. Let's send for them.'

Duff Dannon sighed. No one would ever forget his wedding day, this nightmare day. At least he would not have to see his bride alone tonight and wasn't that a queer thing for a bridegroom to be grateful for? He smiled wryly to himself. A bridegroom should be eager for the consummation of his marriage, yet Duff's blood ran cold as the breeze from the sea at the thought of it and he could summon up no desire to embrace Dana. He put it out of his mind and got on with more urgent things.

There was an optimistic air as the boys carefully removed the tables of food to the barn and Dinny, Mickey and Phil pushed the barrel of porter down the hill. People ran around salvaging oddities here and there. Someone found a chamber pot and someone else found the spirit to crack a joke. Della found a hoe and Delia found a blanket that had been washed and hung out to dry and then all the women went to their clothes lines and down to the hedges where the washing was draped and gratefully retrieved what they found there. Brian found a Bible that had fallen out of a window with only a few pages scorched and Brindsley said he would take care of it. A spirit of solidarity had been born.

They all had something to do now, a plan of campaign, and they set about it with a will, though sometimes the awful reality penetrated and someone or another would break down and weep while the others comforted.

They would have the cheek to send for the moonlighters, Duff realized as he listened to what they were saying. They would do that without turning a hair. They seemed to have completely forgotten how they had turned on those men. Did they not remember how they had insulted them, called Clancy and his band of men parasites and alarmists? Oh, the human being is a strange creature, a contrary creature, he thought, and adapts its ideas to suit its purposes. He heard Mickey O'Gorman shout to Dinny McQuaid as the barrel reached the bottom of the hill, 'I think a little medicinal alcohol would benefit us all now, don't ye agree, Dinny, me ould friend? Eh?'

Chapter Fifty-One

✂ ✂

They had a grand feast that night and afterwards settled on the straw and fell into an exhausted or drunken slumber.

Some hours afterwards Duff felt a hand over his mouth and another on his very centre, and, opening his eyes wide, saw Dana's pale face above him. She pressed her body against his and in a fury he shoved her roughly away, and all the while desire grew in him and he was ashamed.

Dana was cat-angry. She wanted to claw and spit and snarl but she could not bear the humiliation of the others finding out she had been rejected by her new husband. So she slid silently away from Duff and nursed her resentment.

The next few days were fraught with tension. In the terror of the realization of their loss they helped each other, consoled each other, and fought and quarrelled. Old grudges were resurrected. Ma Stacey yelled at Mary Dannon to keep her babby quiet and Deegan Belcher belligerently picked fist fights with anyone who crossed him. Trivial misunderstandings abounded and were likely to explode into life-and-death dramas. Dinny McQuaid sobbed and jittered in a blue funk until Sheena hit him over the head with a fire-blackened pot. Dinny had decided that Deegan Belcher was going to creep up on him in the night and kill him because he had borrowed his rake and not returned it and Mickey O'Gorman, drunk as a skunk, wanted to fight Mog Murtagh because he said Jinny had taken a hand-span more room in the barn than she should and therefore the O'Gormans had a hand-span less. But before the fight got properly started Mickey had collapsed in a drunken stupor.

'He can't hold it any more,' Phil Conlon remarked to Ma Stacey.

'Well, it's an ill wind,' she replied. 'Gives poor Carmel a breather after all these years.'

Brian Gilligan said he and his family would not remain in the barn if Phil Conlon and Ma Stacey slept together an' they not man and wife. He was told to shut up and go if he felt that way about it, but he didn't go. He just kept muttering on about the sword of the Lord falling on the adulterer until Brindsley Donnelly said in a loud voice, 'Let him who is without sin cast the first stone,' and Brian Gilligan abruptly shut up.

Then Mickey O'Gorman came to and attacked Carmel but Duff pushed him over with two fingers and he fell backwards on the hay.

'Yer a beast Mickey, ye know that? In fact, that's flatterin' ye! I don't know a beast that batters its mate, do ye?'

Mickey was squealing on the ground like a stuck pig and Carmel sobbing and the children howling when Pierce Donnelly banged the empty oil-drum and silenced them with the noise of it. 'Shut up the lot of ye,' he cried. 'Yer like a pack o' children. Listen, we have te live in this place together for the moment, so for God Almighty's sake let us be peaceful together and make a few plans an' organize ourselves.'

'Isn't it typical! Typical of the Donnellys?' Deegan Belcher spat. 'Organizin'! Even homeless they're tryin' to be uppity.'

'Oh shut yer gob, Deegan. When have ye ever tried anythin' con-ster-uc-tive?' Ma Stacey shook her head. 'Whatd'ye expect the man te do? Ask yer permission? Drop dead wi' shock?'

'Yeah! At least he's tryin' to do somethin'!' Phil Conlon agreed. He was rolling a barrel out. Ma Stacey had rescued, with the help of willing drinkers, quite a few after the fire. She had had them stored below ground in the cellar she had specially built so the fire had not got to them.

It was strange, Duff thought, how everyone disliked the Donnellys. There seemed no reason for this collective intolerance. Only Ma Stacey, Phil Conlon and possibly Katey Kavanagh actually liked them. The rest were irritated by Pierce's honourable, uncompromizing attitude to life. He worked harder than anyone and that they found aggravating. He never short-changed anyone. He refused to poach as the rest of them felt entitled. He added rooms to his cottage. He saved. He saw that his children had a good education. He showed the cottagers up and they saw themselves through his eyes and did not like what they saw. His behaviour illuminated their flaws and they hated him for that.

His girls were beautiful. That was another irritant. And Brindsley was clever. No, Duff mused, Pierce Donnelly was not an easy man to like.

But they turned to him in a crisis. He was the strongest of them all and they knew it. He was the wisest. Without him they would be scattered to the winds by now, strewn the length and breadth of Ireland, wandering witless along the highways and byways, homeless and afraid. No. Pierce Donnelly would lead them, keep them together, guide them, but he must not expect them to love him.

Father Maguire came down to see them and arrange about the funeral.

'It's God's will, Pierce *a cairde*, God's holy will.'

Pierce drew in a hissing breath. 'There I cannot agree with you, Father,' he said through stiff lips.

'Now, now, Pierce Donnelly, it behoves us to be thankful for our lot in life whatever that might be and accept God's will for us in all things.'

'Why, you smug bastard!' It was Carmel O'Gorman who spoke, rising up from the hay she lay on, nursing her bruised body, her newest child at her breast. She stood before the frocked priest, waving her free arm while she held the babby with the other. Her eyes blazed like fire-crackers. 'Don't you *dare* to presume to speak for your Master, you old humbug. Isn't it easy for ye to talk! Dinin' on lamb and beef while we make do with tatties. Oh, ye know what God thinks, indeed, an' you that close to him, suppin' the communion wine of an evenin' alone there in yer house all warm an' cosy!'

'Ye'll repent this day on the day of judgment,' Father Maguire shouted, trying to control his fury. He turned to Pierce.

'Ye'll come down tomorrow an' we'll carry her up to the graveyard wrapped in a sheet,' Pierce told him. 'It's the best we can do, Father, for we can't afford Billy Layde for the coffin. Not now. But she'da want to have you walk beside her in the holy vestments and to lie at rest above in the churchyard. So if it would be convenient we'll say tomorrow then, an' I'd go, Father, if I was you before the people here get angry.'

Father Maguire opened his mouth to protest but Pierce Donnelly urged him, 'Go now, Father, or you'll regret it.'

And the priest fled.

The next day Vernon Blackstock came to see them. He was shocked by what had happened and, he told them, Lady Kitty was too.

'It's a tangled mess,' he said, touched at their offers of refreshment when he knew how little they had and that they did not know when, if ever, they could afford to replenish the already dwindling supplies. He refused politely and asked for spring water, and perched on an upturned barrel he examined the toes of his boots and sipped the sweet water.

'It's very tangled,' he said. 'A legal nightmare.'

'Can you tell us what you mean?' Pierce asked.

Vernon Blackstock frowned, 'Well, it is like this. Linton Lester should not have sold your land to the Marquis.'

There were gasps and people pressed nearer, the better to hear.

'You see, the late Lord Lester left Lady Kitty in sole charge. In other words her signature on any bill of sale is required by law.'

'Well, that means we can have our cottages, what's left of them, back?' Duff Dannon asked eagerly. 'We have the land at least.'

'The right to be there,' Pierce Donnelly added.

Vernon Blackstock shook his head. 'The problem is,' he told them, 'she refuses to compromise her son. She will not bring matters to a head.'

'What does that mean?' Miles Murphy asked.

'What it means, simply, is this. The legal document Linton Lester signed with the Marquis of Killygally giving him your site is valid unless Lady Kitty contravenes it.' He peered at Miles. 'Unless she says it is illegal, and she will not do that.'

'What Mr Blackstock is saying, Miles, is this. It is all going to happen as we feared unless Lady Kitty goes against her son, and she won't do that.'

'The money was paid over for your piece of land, into Lord Linton Lester's hands, and he sadly appears to have got through most of it. So even if Lady Lester exerted her right to veto her son's selling the land, all the money would have to be repaid and there is no earthly chance of that, so once again the Marquis would insist on the land in lieu of the debt.' He shook his head. 'As I said, it is tangled and would take years of litigation to sort out. I'm afraid there's little hope for you.'

'And in the meantime . . . ' Delia McCormack inquired.

'In the meantime you have the Marquis determined to remove you from what he considers his land. He is a ruthless man, I don't have to tell you, you have seen it for yourselves.'

'But he's *got* us off. He's burned our cottages. You must have seen an' you passed them on the way here?' Mog Murtagh said.

'So what's he want now?' Deegan asked.

'He wants you out of here,' the solicitor said sadly.

309

'Outa here? Outa this barn where we only took shelter an' we homeless?' Brigid was incredulous.

'And I wouldn't pit myself against him if I were you,' Vernon Blackstock warned them. 'He is a cruel and vicious man.'

'We can send for the moonlighters again,' Duff Dannon said quietly.

'You turned them out before,' Blackstock mumbled.

'Would Clancy come back, do you suppose?' Pierce asked.

'No. He'd never. We insulted him,' Duff said but Vernon Blackstock held up his hand.

'I think he might,' he corrected Duff. 'He does not expect love or popularity. He says people are always glad to see him come, then glad to see him go. He expects to be disliked. Mebbe he'll return. He's your only hope, I'm afraid. Will I try to find him for ye? He was in Limerick last time I heard.'

Duff glanced around the circle of faces for permission.

'Ye all agree?' he asked. They nodded. Some sullenly, some eagerly, some doubtfully, some gladly. Sheena McQuaid with a smile on her face.

'Any disagree?' he asked. No one moved. Dinny wanted to but he chickened out. There might have to be an explanation.

'Right then, Mr Blackstock, let's send for Clancy.'

Chapter Fifty-Two

∽ ∾

The funeral was a sad affair. Brigid and Pierce, followed by Dana and flanked by Duff and Brindsley, walked slowly after Father Maguire to the churchyard. Little Des Gilligan in a white surplice and swinging a censer walked beside them in the spring rain up the hill.

The birds sang and the young leaves drank the fog of

rain gratefully. The flowers raised faces to the shimmering drops and gathered the moisture into their very centres.

Granny Donnelly looked like the branch of a tree, a bundle of twigs wrapped in a sheet, held in her sons arms. Pierce wept as he walked, his face wet as the flowers below the trees.

They stood around the grave, the earth soggy beneath their boots, and Father Maguire intoned about 'green pastures' and the Lord being their shepherd. Dana tried to hold Duff's hand but he moved fractionally away every time she made a tentative gesture. He had not touched her in the days and nights since the wedding except to push her away when she tried to embrace him. Bitter and angry she hissed at Katey Kavanagh, 'Yer wrong, ye ould witch, yer wrong.'

'What about?' the old woman asked, peering at her, thinking to herself that Dana Donnelly's nose was out of joint and she didn't look like a happy bride.

'Ye said, I remember, that fellas once they're roused cannot stop themselves. That they have no control. Well, yer wrong!'

'So!' Katey smirked. 'Ye've tried to rouse Duff an' failed, is that the whole of it?'

'It is not,' Dana replied tartly, furious that she had been so indiscreet. 'An' if ye breathe a word to anyone I'll put the evil eye on ye, d'ye hear me?'

Katey believed the girl. Dana Dannon would do just that if she felt inclined.

Katey never did say anything to anyone but somehow word spread that Dana Dannon couldn't get her new husband to perform his marital duty. They all said it was because of Demara. And they all whispered that the Donnellys had brought bad luck on their little community.

'If Pierce Donnelly had not been so ambitious then Demara would have stayed at home an' married Duff an' the poor man wouldn't be so afflicted,' Miles Murphy was heard to confide in Mog Murtagh. 'But no. Demara went off to earn money for her father's cottage, an' look what happened to that. Burned to a crisp, it was.'

'Yeah! An' that scheming sister Dana angers the good

Lord in heaven by persuading Duff to marry her and everyone knows he is Demara's fella. This scandal brings down the wrath of God on the whole lot of us,' Brian Gilligan told the men over a rationed jug of porter and they nodded. It made sense to them. 'It's all laid at the Donnelly door,' he said sagely. 'An' insultin' Father Maguire an' showin' disrespect in the house of God is askin' for trouble.'

All the past was dredged up now. All avenues led to the Donnellys.

'An' didn't Dana say Demara spoke to the Devil up on Bannagh Dubh and she made some ungodly pact wi' him, God help us,' Sheena McQuaid told her husband.

'Cogger said he saw the spectre,' Katey Kavanagh told Della Gilligan, who crossed herself. 'He came back sayin' she was talkin' to a shadowy thing that was there an' not there. That's what he said.'

There was a lot of talk and rumblings of discontent, and the talk was speculative, but as it was repeated it gathered the weight of fact.

But no one told Duff. And no one told Phil Conlon. And no one told Pierce Donnelly. And that silent man, face stoic and rain-wet now, watched his mother laid to rest in hallowed ground in the church yard and in his heart a knot of hatred tightened and became strong.

Chapter Fifty-Three

No one was more surprised than Demara when a bouquet of flowers arrived for her at the house in Soho Square. They were used to Maeve receiving lavish tributes: flowers, bon bons and even the odd piece of jewellery that Belle insisted she send back to the giver.

'It assumes you are prepared to give your favours, and that I do not imagine you want. More's the pity,' she said.

It did not occur to Belle or Demara, Bert or Tilly that the huge bouquet could be for anyone other than the actress.

The card however stated otherwise. It informed them that Lord Peregrine Dawkins of Hanover Square would be honoured if Miss Demara Donnelly would be willing to dine with him that evening. His servant would wait for a reply. If Miss Demara Donnelly agreed, he would send his carriage for her at curtain rise at the Chandos Theatre, as he knew that she usually accompanied her sister there each evening. After supper the carriage would pick up her sister and deliver them both home. Or if her sister had another engagement, then the carriage would take Demara home to Soho Square directly. There was something he wanted to discuss with Demara and he would be enchanted if she would agree to dine with him.

Demara was flattered but apprehensive. She had only met Perry Dawkins on two occasions. She had not taken his proposal too seriously. She imagined he was looking for a wife and once she told him she could certainly not wed him, then they would never see each other again. But she felt uncomfortable about dining with him.

'See him and find out what he wants,' was Belle's advice.

Demara had not told either Maeve or her landlady about the proposal. 'He is a very powerful man, Demara. Not to be underestimated.'

'The servant is waiting,' Maeve called to them. 'What should Tilly tell him?'

They all watched Demara who stared at the beautiful pink roses. 'I prefer wild flowers,' she said absently and Maeve exclaimed with irritation 'Oh, Demara!' as she watched her sister flick the card between her fingers.

'Oh, say I'll go,' she laughed finally. 'I'll expect his carriage at the theatre . . .'

'You must borrow my blue watered silk,' Maeve told her. 'It suits you better than it suits me and he has seen your striped satin.' Her sister's lack of interest in clothes sometimes irritated Maeve who considered what she was going to wear before anything else. Demara seemed indifferent to what she wore and still had a habit of searching for a shawl when she left the house, for all the world, Maeve admonished her, as if she was still in Kerry and on her way out to milk the cows.

'I wish I was,' Demara would infuriate her sister by replying. Maeve simply didn't understand her sentiments.

Demara wore the blue watered silk. It had a bustle and the low neck was filled with Brussels lace. Belle lent her a necklace of crystal that circled her throat like a collar and earrings that hung like dew-drops from her ears.

Peregrine Dawkins was waiting for her in the carriage. His man Harding came to Maeve's dressing-room where Demara was waiting, and when he brought her outside the middle-aged face, eyes twinkling, was grinning at her from the landau. She smiled the moment she saw him and realized how comfortable and at ease he made her feel.

'I've never fetched a lady from the theatre before,' he told her, helping her inside.

'Well, I've never dined alone with a man before tonight,' she said, settling her skirt and smiling at him.

'Well then, I have a big responsibility to see you enjoy yourself,' he told her. 'And you must call me Perry.'

They were both silent as they rolled along, the horses' hooves clopping on the cobblestones. The silence was neither intimidating or embarrassing, nor did she feel she should break it. It was the sort of silence that fell between old friends. It felt relaxing sitting beside him, in the dark, the familiar smell of leather and horseflesh in her nostrils. It reminded her of another place, another time.

The Café Royal was crowded. It was a glittering place, and Perry was greeted with great deference by the maître d'hôtel and shown to a table most comfortably positioned. They were then fussed over by a crowd of minions whose exact tasks Demara was not sure of. There seemed to be one whose main concern was the wine, another who hovered over a display of pastries, another pushing about a silver platter on wheels that held a crispy-skinned goose cooked to a turn, a batch of capons and chickens. There was another with a huge side of roast beef and yet another with a succulent ham decorated with apples and cherries. All of these persons were overseen by the maître d'hôtel

314

who conducted the whole proceedings with majestic authority and a haughty expression on his face.

Demara giggled. 'He takes it all very seriously,' she said and her companion laughed.

'Here, my dear, he is King. He rules his subjects with an iron fist. Now . . .' as yet another waiter handed her a huge menu in French '. . . what do you like? No. Do not pay any attention to that. I shall order for us both and I hope you eat your meal with great appetite. Anything you don't like we'll send back. That should wipe the haughty expression off his face.'

She obeyed him gladly and tucked into her food with enjoyment. An orchestra played 'Just a Song at Twilight' and they talked lightly and companionably about all sorts of things. The goose was excellent, the ham tastier than anything she had ever eaten before.

'I'm afraid he'll have to be allowed to remain haughty,' she said. 'Everything is perfect.'

She stole glances at him every now and then and she approved of what she saw. His skin, tanned and crinkled around the eyes, was soft and well cared for. His wrists were strong and his bright blue eyes kind. He had a gentle, authoritative manner and she felt safe with him.

When she had sampled the cheeses and polished off a delicious chocolate *bavarois*, delicate lady fingers and almond tuilles and he had chosen a perfect pear for her to finish with, she turned to him curiously.

'Why did you want to dine with me, Perry?' she asked.

He looked at her squarely, hands folded beneath his chin. 'You know why, in part,' he replied and without preamble, 'Do you know a man called the Marquis of Killygally?' His lip curled as he pronounced the name. It took her by surprise, this question. 'You see, my dear, Bryony told me where you came from. I mean, the exact address.'

'Yes, yes,' she said.

'You love your homeland, don't you, Demara?' he asked her.

'With all my heart,' she replied simply. 'There is a plot of land there called Bannagh Dubh. It is wild and glorious. I

315

want to build a house there. It is my dream.'

'Then don't let anyone try to stop you,' he told her.

'I won't, Perry,' she replied firmly.

'Bryony told me the Marquis of Killygally lives near you.'

'Yes. The Marquis's estates border the land our cottages are on.'

Perry Dawkins raised a delicate eyebrow. He had been right in his surmise that Bryony and the Donnelly girls knew this Marquis, or at least knew of him.

'Do you know him?' he asked.

She shook her head. 'No, Perry. I'm afraid I've never laid eyes on him. I've seen his carriage pass by and I've seen him in the distance on his horse, out riding.' She looked at him with candid eyes. 'You see, he is gentry. We work the land. He would have no time for the likes of us.'

'More fool he!' Perry remarked, laughing.

She touched her pale cheek with her finger and he thought how beautiful she was, how her lashes shadowed her eyes and her face had a lovely tranquillity. Yet too, there was mystery there. The dream perhaps?

'Oh, I did see him once on his big charger.' She glanced up at Perry. 'I kept away from him though.' She looked a little uncertain. He gave her an encouraging glance. 'We heard things about him, you see. Unpleasant things. Frightening things. My father warned us not to have anything to do with him, to run away if he came near us.' She threw him a swift smile. 'Of course it may have all been gossip. Villagers, living as we do in the wilds, have little better to do than embroider the truth.'

'I'm sure you do no such thing,' he smiled at her. 'I'll bet your papa was strict with you and did not tolerate idle chatter.'

'How did you know that?' she asked, surprised.

'It is obvious, little one. I know you and Maeve. I think he did a quite extraordinary job.'

'The Marquis . . . is he a friend of yours? I hope I haven't said anything . . .'

He shook his head and a little twisted smile crossed his lips. 'No. No, I think those rumours you heard were true.

They were based on fact.' He frowned. The solemn expression on his face was strange. He looked at her intently. 'If ever you hear of him in Ballymora, what he is up to. Or your family does, I would be grateful if you would let me know. About any activity. You see, I do not know myself what I am looking for.'

He stared at her and his blue eyes had a steely cold look that frightened her. 'No matter how trivial it seems. No matter what it concerns, please let me know.'

'But I am here, Perry. I am not in Ballymora.'

'Your family is. Your papa is. Just tell me if there is anything about him. You have my card. My address is on it.'

She looked at him curiously. 'May I ask why, sir?'

His face split into a wide, warm grin and the expression in his eyes softened. 'You may not. Not yet at any rate. And you, my fine young lady, keep away from that man. Remember your father's words, Demara, for I promise you I have never heard anything good about the Marquis.' Now his eyes were twinkling again. 'And it is not sir, my sweet lady. It is Perry, *please*.'

Demara ate her pear in silence and Lord Perry Dawkins watched her with pleasure. Her movements were graceful and economical. When she had finished and put down her fruit knife she wiped her hands on her napkin, then leaving it beside her plate she gave a contented sigh and turned to him again. 'That was perfect,' she said.

He leaned back in his chair, looked at her speculatively and remarked, 'You are the most satisfactory girl. You never flirt. You never act the fluttery female and you enjoy your food. Most satisfactory.' Then he straightened and looked at her intently. 'The other thing ... have you thought about it? Will you marry me?'

She stared at him in astonishment. 'You meant it?' she asked. 'I thought you were joking.'

'I never joke about serious things,' he replied.

'But why, Perry? Good heavens, why?'

He burst out laughing. 'That's one of the reasons,' he said. 'You make me laugh. I don't suppose you realize how important that is. Laughter is a wonderfully benign activity, Demara.'

'You don't ask someone you hardly know to marry you because they make you laugh,' she said.

'Oh I don't know. I think for me it might be enough.' He looked at her quizzically. 'There are quite a few more reasons actually. I need a wife, as I said. The upper-class English girls bore me to death. Most of my acquaintances are deadly dull and predictable. You are not. You are beautiful,' he ticked his reasons off on his fingers. 'You are warm. You are original. You are natural. You are spontaneous. When I saw you that day with Bryony I, well, fell in love with you at first sight. Simple as that.'

Demara stared at him. 'You did mean it,' she said. 'I didn't imagine . . .'

'Demara, don't say anything now. As I said before, there is no hurry. Think about it, that's all I ask.'

'But I couldn't marry you, Perry,' she said. 'And, oh dear, I hope I did not do or say anything that led you to think . . .'

'No. No, you did not mislead me in any way. But are you sure? You may change your mind. I can wait.'

'No. No, Perry. You don't understand. Oh, I'm very flattered. I like you very much and you are good company. But you see, Perry, I'm promised to another. In Ballymora. Duff Dannon. He is waiting for me. Oh, I'm sorry.'

He felt his stomach lurch in disappointment. He could see her distress and he hastened to reassure her.

'It's all right. I beg you, Demara, do not distress yourself. I'm sorry I disconcerted you. I promise you I would do nothing to cause you a moment's anxiety. Now, let's change the subject.'

But the evening was over. They were now awkward with each other. Demara was embarrassed and Lord Dawkins in his efforts to right things only made them more strained.

As they had in any event reached the end of their meal he ordered his carriage and in order to spare her blushes and alleviate her confusion he told her he was sending his man Harding home with her. Maeve had said she would be dining with Sebastian.

'You are not angry with me?' Demara asked.

'No. No, of course I'm not angry with you, dearest child. Far from it. It is you who should be angry with me.

Importuning you like that. I have had the most agreeable evening. Thank you for your charming company.' He kissed her hand and added, 'And don't forget you have a job to do for me. When you go home to see your beloved, you must keep your eyes and ears open for me and tell me what the Marquis is up to. Eh? And remember, if you change your mind . . .' She held up her hand but he continued, 'I only say, *if* you change your mind, or need my help, I am at your service.'

'Thank you, Perry. Don't think I'm not grateful. I'm very flattered, indeed I am.'

Harding saw her safely home. There was a letter from her mother waiting for her. She saw by the date it had been delayed. She opened it and found the usual message there, the usual questions, in the usual words. But it had a post-script which stated baldly: *Duff Dannon is to marry our Dana at the weekend.*

The date on the letter was two weeks ago.

Chapter Fifty-Four

cᴼꙅ ꙅᴼꙅ

Katey Kavanagh told them that Demara was coming home. Cogger executed a wild dance when he heard. Katey said she saw it in the cards, and Cogger danced around the barn and they stared at him as he lifted his knees up to his chin in funny jumps and capers and twirled on his toes and clapped his hands. His eyes and mouth were damp with excitement and he made a grunting noise deep in his throat. That was his idea of singing.

'What's she going to say when she finds out Dana married her fella?' Sheena McQuaid asked Brigid who promptly replied, 'She knows. I wrote and told her. Least, Brindsley did.'

'Maeve comin' too?' Sheena asked, but Brigid shook her

head. 'No. She has to be in the theatre every night.'

She frowned. She did not understand the life her daughter led, could not visualize it. She had no conception of what theatre was, never having gone to the performance that had so beguiled Maeve all those years ago.

Vernon Blackstock came to see them on the day Katey Kavanagh foretold Demara's return. 'How are ye getting on in here? Can't be easy?'

'What d'ye think, Mr Blackstock?' Pierce asked him sarcastically.

'He claims he told you to leave, gave every indication you should remove yourselves last autumn.'

'He wrote us nothing. He sent messages, but he never made it official in writing,' Duff volunteered.

'He didn't think you could write.'

Deegan Belcher snorted. 'God'n what does he think we are?' Never heard of the village school? Never heard of the hedge-priests? Never heard of the Irish love of learnin'?'

'So he thinks he gave us fair warning?' Mog Murtagh asked angrily. 'So what do we do next?'

'I have two things to tell ye. One is that Lady Kitty is very put out about all this. She wants to help in any way she can.'

Mickey O'Gorman lay on his straw made mindless by the drink. He bestirred himself now to comment, 'Oh gawd! Lady Kitty help us? Jasus, that's nice of her.' And he collapsed back into his maggoty dreams.

'Yes, it *is* nice of her,' Vernon said.

'How'd ye make that out? Only for her we'd still be snug in our little houseens,' Delia McCormack cried bitterly.

'Only for her son. Only for Lord Linton Lester. It is not her fault her son decided to ignore his father's wishes.'

'Then let her get the land back. Tell the authorities he had no right to sell.'

'I've explained to ye why that's impossible. Lady Lester will not cross her son. But she could ignore what has happened. She could claim that it was none of her business. She doesn't choose to do that. She has a suggestion which is more than kind of her.' He crossed his little ankles, neat and precise, and looked at them. He had their wrapt attention. 'She is prepared to let you have the land by the woods, above near the church. It belongs to the Lesters. She says she'll not let her son sell it. You'll be taking a risk, but it's worth a try.'

'You mean build new homes around the upper acres near Dead Man's Pool?' Pierce asked, delight breaking over his face. 'Ye mean that lovely fertile stretch?'

'Yes. You'd be on Lester land, you see.' Vernon smiled at him.

Pierce felt a great weight lift. He knew they were in a hopeless situation, but if Lady Lester was on their side, then that made a huge difference.

Duff was nodding vigorously. 'Yes. Yes,' he breathed. 'We could do that. We could build in a semi-circle. We're still near the river, only a little upland. We could start again. What's past is past. We canna change that. But we could make a new home for ourselves.'

'Wi' what?' Mog Murtagh squealed.

'Wi' what?' Dinny McQuaid asked.

'Wi' wattle an' daub. Wi' muck an' water. Wi' spit an' stones if necessary,' Duff cried angrily. 'Oh, ye make me sick! Yer complaints are unending. A lament that goes on day an' night. But let someone point a way out an' ye find a hundred reasons to reject an answer! I despair of ye.'

· He sighed and his head fell on his chest. It was Dana, his wife, the new spouse he had never made his own who smiled up at him and told him, 'I'll help ye. Brick for brick. Stone fer stone. I'll build wi' ye an' make us a houseen up there.' She put her arm through his and he did not shake her off. He was touched by her words. At that moment he surrendered, accepting his responsibility on a sudden, swayed by her attitude and her submissive look. He did not realize that he had.

'Me too. I'll build next to ye, Duff Dannon,' Pierce Donnelly cried and Brigid nodded.

'We'll start at dawn, won't we, Phil?' Ma Stacey asked. 'I'm fed up wi' this arrangement. Outa my own place. Not chargin' for porter.' She indicated the rest of the cottagers, 'An' them lot, watchin' us like hawks to see what we do, deep in the night.'

Phil gave a shout. 'Yes – an' – yes – an' – yes!' he yelled.

'We'll have a go, yes. Sure, what have we got to lose?' Brian Gilligan asked.

Della, his wife, nodded her head. 'There's reason in it,' she agreed. 'An' the boys will help.'

Dinny and Mog and Shooshie caved in and the others followed without much enthusiasm, but bowing to the inevitable and beginning to glimpse a ray of hope for them in their plight. The men still continued to complain and mourn for the homes that were gone for ever, but the women were glad that there were tasks ahead, work to do, jobs to perform.

'By the way, I've sent for Clancy and the moonlighters like you asked,' Vernon Blackstock said. There was silence. They looked at the solicitor, not sure how they felt about the news. Not sure how the man beside them felt. Not wanting to go against the majority.

'Do ye think we need them now?' Dinny asked and rested his front teeth on his bottom lip and looked at Pierce.

'We better have 'em. We want to make sure we do as much as we can to protect ourselves,' Pierce said.

A sigh rippled around the room. Pierce Donnelly laying down the law again.

' 'Tis all very well for you, Pierce Donnelly, an' you happy to work the hours God gives, slavin' an' labourin'."

'That's the man's own business, not yours.' Vernon Blackstock was surprised at the animosity in Miles Murphy's voice. 'What's it got to do with you? If a man works hard. . .'

'Doesn't he send his family out to earn money an' don't they have to live across the water in the pits of hell so's he can have his extra rooms an' fine food on the table?' Miles was heated.

Vernon Blackstock looked at him in astonishment. 'I don't know who has been gossiping in your ear, Miles Murphy, but I think ye've got the wrong end of the stick.'

'Let me answer, Mr Blackstock,' Pierce said calmly. 'I'm quite capable of tendin' my affairs, thank you.' He turned his attention to Miles who looked nervously about for some way to escape the man towering over him. He snorted, wiped his nose on his sleeve and stood on one leg like a stork, wishing he were anywhere but in front of an angry Pierce Donnelly.

'I sent my childer over the sea to London and Liverpool to get money to help us, surely,' Pierce told him evenly, but his eyes snapped. 'I work hard, an' if I save my money agin a crisis then that is my right, an' no man can deny that. All my money is gone now. Eaten up in flames ye'll be glad to hear. Now have ye anythin' te say te that?'

The drover shook his head so vigorously that his cap fell off.

'Well then, I'll thank ye kindly to keep yer mouth shut about me an' mine.'

At that moment Cogger Kavanagh rushed in yelling. His face was scarlet and he was whirling about in a terrible state, stumbling over children, falling over the creels and boxes and casks they had been using for furniture.

'Demara's coming! Demara's coming! Demara's coming!' he chortled, no lisp now. 'Demara's coming. Demara's on her way home.'

Chapter Fifty-Five

She walked away from the stage carrying her carpet-bag. She raised her face gratefully. She could feel the sea breeze on her scalp like fingers loosening the tension there, unbinding her braids and curls, freeing them, caressing her long black mane. She shook it free and stepped off the road and into the boreen, eager to get home.

She passed the church. The ferns were waist high and the cow-parsley was a sea of lace. There was a smell of grass on the wind and the faint clover scent she loved so much. But there was also a smell of burn. Burnt something? What? There was smoke drifting up into the pale grey sky and she could not see the chimneys of the cottages. That was odd. Always, coming from the crossroads, she could see first the little church, where she stood now, then the smoke from the turf-fires snaking upwards from the chimneys, mushroom dark against the green of the fields and hills and mountains.

Where were they? The chimneys? She moved forward and felt a curious apprehension chill her, but she shook it off. She was being foolish. She would round the bend and there they would be: the little group of cottages, the hens and chickens scrabbling in the yards, the odd pig or two grunting small-eyed in its pen. The flocks of Canada geese, the wild ducks from Siberia, and the sheep. Katey Kavanagh would be leaning on her half-door. Ellie Murtagh would be sitting in her box on wheels at their gate. Ma Stacey's head would emerge from the cellar which had an exit in the back yard.

But when she rounded the curve in the boreen, the rise and fall in the lane, she stood stock-still in horror and fear and loss at the sight that met her eyes.

There was nothing. Charred ground where once the cottages stood. Burnt remains, ashes blown where cowslips bloomed; where the gillyflowers proliferated, scorched and blackened earth; and where the cottages had rested deep in the rolling green, nothing remained. Just piles of destroyed beams. All was raized to flat scrub and roasted plants, a devastated waste that had, when she last saw it, teemed with life and beauty.

Shocked, she stood there, hands at her cheeks, feeling them cold, now burning hot, now icy again. Cogger came bounding up, uttering crow-like cries of welcome, raucous shouts of joy and saying her name over and over. 'Demara. D-d-d-d-emara. Demara.'

'Cogger. Oh, Cogger.' She threw her arms around the awkward body, holding him tight. She was so pleased to see him, so ridiculously happy to see that grotesque face and welcoming eyes, that touching joy at her return.

When she disentangled herself from his bear-like embrace she stared at him a moment, lips trembling, then

324

swept her hand in a wide gesture over the land. 'What happened, Cogger? In God's name, what happened?'

He stared at her, eyes bulging, now taking in the details of her appearance.

'Demara! Demara, y-y-yer voice! Oh J-j-janey. Oh Jesus, Mary an' Joseph, oh, Demara!'

Suddenly she wanted to shake him. She tried to curb her impatience. Had she forgotten already the gentle, patient way of the country?

'Cogger,' she said, as calmly as she could, while his eyes darted from the feathered hat in her hand, her smart travelling dress, her neat point-toed boots, the lace at her wrists and throat, the cameo at the neck of her lawn blouse. 'Cogger, listen to me. Where is my family?' No reply. 'Where is my family, Cogger? Where?' Still no reply and Cogger gazed at her as if she were an apparition. She shook him gently, 'Cogger, where is my family?' At last he spoke. He turned and pointed down to where the river flowed to the sea and Lally Flynn's barn sat ugly on the skyline. 'There. Down there, Demara. A-a-all together down there. I d-d-don' like it there, no I don'.'

'Who did this? Lord Lester?'

'No'm. He's dead. Old Lord Edward is dead. D-d-died day you left.'

'Then who did this?'

'The M-m-marquis . . . ' He pointed up to his right, over her shoulder to where Stillwater lay.

Demara shivered and had a fleeting vision of Perry Dawkins, his kind eyes cold as he talked to her of the Marquis of Killygally.

Suddenly she saw her father in the distance as he came up from the barn and her heart swelled near to burst. 'Da! Da!' she cried and stretched her arms out as she had when she was a little girl. 'Da! Da!' and she ran to him, ran to the safe embrace, ran to find an explanation and an answer to all her questions.

Chapter Fifty-Six

ᕬᕠ ᕢᕬ

Demara was aching to get to Bannagh Dubh. As always she wanted to run away, escape to her wild place and think. There was such a turmoil in her mind and there she could find peace and solitude and sort out her thoughts and emotions.

Now that her worst fears had been laid to rest and she found Brigid and Pierce and Brindsley well and unharmed she was dying to escape from the claustrophobic curiosity of the barn. She wanted to tackle her grief over Granny Donnelly's death alone with God and the sea and the sky, not here where eyes peered at her, some with hostility, some with friendliness, some with jealousy and some with avid curiosity.

They had all gathered around to gaze at her new, smart appearance and fashionable clothes. Suddenly she was a stranger in their midst.

There was no sign of Duff or her sister Dana and she was grateful for that. Neither did she ask after them and no one brought the subject up. The conversation settled on the events in Ballymora over the last weeks and what they intended doing about it. That Dana and Duff were married she knew, for everyone was at pains to tell her that the tragic events occurred while they were all up the hill at the weddin'. That was all they said about it, but it was enough.

'Why didn't you write what happened the first time, Ma?' she asked. 'Why didn't you, Brindsley?'

'We didn't want te trouble ye,' Pierce replied.

'Ye'd just gone, an then 'twas over an' they went away,' Brigid said.

'But they came back,' Demara said bitterly and the ring of faces nodded in unison.

'Ye must have known they would,' she cried in anger.

'Yer Da said they would but no one would listen te him.' Brigid said.

She turned on them, her face bright with anger. 'What were ye doin' then? Well, answer me. You know my da has all the brains there is in this place. God, you disgust me. Ignorant eejits.' The anger and outrage she felt over Granny Donnelly made her fight for breath. She felt as if she was choking and her need to get out of there grew until she turned to her father. 'I have to go to Bannagh Dubh, Da, Ma.'

They were not surprised, they knew her well. Since that night all those years ago when they found her on the rocks they were used to her running to that spot for comfort. Whenever she needed consolation she fled there.

'You understand, Da . . . ' Her vision was blurred and her eyes pleaded with him for tolerance.

'Ye were close to yer Granny,' Pierce said. 'Ye'll need a bit of privacy.'

She was too preoccupied to notice the stares of hostility that were turned towards her.

'Always lookin' for privacy, the Donnellys,' Delia McCormack muttered. 'Think themselves too good for the likes of us.'

'Oh, give it a rest, Delia,' Ma Stacey growled in her ear. 'Yer jealousy'll kill ye one of these days. It'll choke ye, ye mark my words.'

Demara pushed her way through the crowd standing and squatting around the entrance and went out into the fresh air. The barn had appalled her more than she would have liked to admit. She had forgotten the dirt, the sweat, the earthiness that cottagers lived in. She had forgotten the reality of it and had become civilized and out of touch during her exile. I have become spoiled, she thought. I'm the sort of person that I would have despised. Oh, God help me.

The fresh air tasted sweet. It had begun to drizzle, a fine scarf of moisture that clung in iridescent drops to her hair and lips. She raised her face to receive it.

This was what she missed in the crowded streets of London. She let her eyes drink in the silver luminescence of the rain over the purple and gold of the mountains. They rose majestic and timeless against the lavender-tinted sky. The chaffinches chattered in the blue and white periwinkle. The yellow catkins of goatwillow and the soft grey catkins of aspen shimmered with glimmering drops and the golden gorse patched the mountains like rays of sunshine.

The fields stretched out around her and as she hurried along the lane Cogger Kavanagh took up his place behind her as usual and jogged along, trying to keep up with her hurrying footsteps. There were tiny blue jack-the-hedge, lacy white cow-parsley, evergreen alkanet, marsh violets and bilberry along the way and the painted lady and the brimstone butterfly shook the sparkling drops from their wings and she saw every tiny thing with a grateful heart.

She wanted to reach Bannagh Dubh. Like an addict she craved the sight of it, the smell of it. Cogger hoppity-hopped behind her. He became breathless trying to match the speed of her steps.

She could see the sea now, heaving, crashing, spewing great flags of spray high above the tar-black rocks.

She was crying and she did not know it. Granny Donnelly, that lovely old woman, had been burned alive and Demara's heart was pierced with pain. And the wave of pain would recede like the waves below her and a huge tide of exaltation would overwhelm her. Her grief would change to fierce joy. I am here, her heart cried, I am home. I am in the place where I belong. At one with the sea, the sky, and the earth. And then the pain would take over again, squeezing her chest in a vice so that she bent over double with the agony of it.

Her home gone! All their homes gone! The lovingly tended furniture, the crockery her mother had washed and dried and polished with such care. Crockery was not easily come by in Ballymora. All their possessions, so cherished, gone. Burned. Consumed by fire. But worst of all, that dear old lady, astray in her head since the first time they had been threatened, had met a violent death. An undeservedly cruel death. All at the order of the Marquis of Killygally.

That name. Anger shook her and her slim body trembled. How dare he! The gulls were screaming and she shouted out, 'How dare he!'

Then there was Duff. She had to gain enough courage here to face Dana and Duff. She had lost him and she could not bear to face the actuality of it, or him. She did not want to see him face to face, yet it was inevitable. She did not want to turn a corner and confront him knowing his arms were forbidden to her, that she would never lie in their safe circle again. That her own sister had taken the gift of his body that she so wanted and needed, that someone else had tasted his sweet flesh, oh it was a bitter homecoming. Heart-splitting.

Yet here in Bannagh Dubh her heart lifted in spite of herself. Here it was timeless, nothing had changed. It was healing, a bounteous balm. A solace. Here in Bannagh Dubh, her chosen place, she could find comfort.

Cogger watched and waited. He guarded her and the birds screamed as they rode the wind, calling to each other.

Suddenly Cogger was alert. The stranger had not been there, Cogger knew, and now magically he was. The headland had been empty and bare and Demara had stood alone on the cliff staring into the distance, the wind tearing her hair, her shawl held tight around her. And now, out of nowhere, there he was. The tall stranger standing close behind her, his cloak flapping in the breeze like black sails. As before he was faceless and when the hood of his cloak stirred in the wind it looked like a skull underneath but you could not really see. Skulls belonged to dead men, Cogger reasoned, and this man was not dead. He moved quickly and there was energy in his movements.

They stood there on the cliff, the tall man's cloak billowing out and Demara's hair streaming in the wind and Cogger watched. He could see Demara listen, then ask something. She did not look at the stranger. He saw the figure raise his arm and point down. Again Cogger thought the finger looked dangerously bony. He followed the direction of the finger and gave a little cry of recognition, for the stranger's finger pointed out the hidden bay with the stones and the statues.

Cogger lay down on his stomach and leaned over the edge. Yes, they were there, the square-cut stones, the marble statuary dumped there by some long-lost pirate ship? Or Spanish galleon? Or some architect of Roman times who overestimated the climate? One of them, someone, had come to Kerry, maybe on a summer day, and built a house on the headland with plundered booty or stones cut from his homeland and never guessed how cruel the winter could be, how wild the wild Atlantic here on the coast of Bannagh Dubh.

Cogger looked back and the stranger was gone. Just like that. Vanished. Disappeared. Where had he gone? How had he left the scene so swiftly, so completely? Cogger could not figure it out and he looked up at Demara but did not approach her. He simply lay there watching as she stood perilously near the edge. She was staring with fascinated intent at the narrow gully where the stones and statuary lay waiting for her. He wished she would not stand so near the edge. She seemed in a trance, staring down.

And then Cogger saw Duff making his way up the hill towards her. He wondered what to do, whether to warn her, to call out to her, and once more decided to let nature take its course. He knew that nothing he did would affect anyone in the long run so he lay on the grass, not trying to hide, just resting on his stomach, leaning his chin on his hands. Waiting. Watching. Protecting Demara.

Chapter Fifty-Seven

∽ ๏๛

The stranger had a curious hollow voice. He said to Demara, 'Do you remember our pact?'

She let her arms fall but did not turn around. She nodded.

'You have not forgotten?'

She shook her head.

'It's all there.' He pointed to the thunderous cauldron of waves below them. She followed the direction of his arm, the cloak concealing it so that it looked like a bat's wing. She saw, noticed for the first time, the inlet. The sailors had mentioned it and the pale siren who perched high on the rocks there, luring men to their death. But she had never explored it. Familiarity had made her incurious and she was only interested in her bay, the land around it, the lake. Inlets and caves down the headland held no charms for her and the people, particularly the fishermen, thought them dangerous and kept away.

She moved slightly and stared down into the gully. She saw there the stones, the statues, everything she had dreamed about, everything she visualized for the building of her house.

Only it was resting in disorder beneath the sea. She stared down mesmerized by the fact of it, astonished by the pristine beauty of what she saw, amazed by the unexpected vision. She stared, then turned to ask the stranger to explain it to her, to ask how it came there and how she could raise all that beauty out of the sea, but he was nowhere to be seen. The cliff was empty of humans except for Cogger Kavanagh who had resumed his role as her shadow.

She turned back and stared down again at the treasure. She would have to get it up somehow from its resting place in the deep. Cogger would help her. She could take it around the headland bit by bit. They would have to work when the tide was out. It would be difficult, well nigh impossible, but they would succeed. She knew that and she knew too that the stranger had drawn her here, that it all had some mysterious meaning. She shivered and drew her shawl closer around her shoulders as she remembered the exact terms of the pact. 'You will forfeit love. You will forfeit happiness. You will give up the chance to love a husband, bear his children.'

Duff was married. That was part of the pact, the fact that she could never have him, her dark and beautiful love.

331

She straightened and looked out to sea again. Around the headland they would be gathering kelp and burning it off, drying it out. She could smell it sharp and strong. She licked her lips and tasted the sting of the salt. The wind had blown the soft rain away and was picking up strength. It caught her hair and blew it back like a flag behind her.

She felt the hands on her shoulders, pressed there suddenly, and she did not jump. She knew who it was. With a little moan she turned and looked up at him.

'Duff.' The cry tore her throat. 'Why?' she asked him, 'why?'

He looked angry but said nothing, just pressed his cold cheek to hers.

She shrugged his hands away and they fell to his side and hung there awkwardly.

'Demara . . . you left me!' he said finally, dully. 'Have you forgotten? I thought you would never return.'

'You knew I would! Don't lie to me, Duff. You knew I'd come back here.'

He turned his head from left to right in an agony. How to explain? What could he tell her? He could not tell her the truth, it would be unseemly, disloyal to her sister, his wife. And it would not change the fact that he was married to Dana. She saw his torment. 'I was to blame,' she said sadly, after a pause.

'No. No. How could you be?'

'That last time, when we said goodbye, I gave you no hope.'

'Nevertheless I should have waited. I should have been able to resist temptation.'

'Aha! So she set her trap for you and you, eejit that you are, fell in.'

'No. Don't speak of her like that. It is wrong.'

'But I am right. You could not help it, I suppose. But it is a pity. A great pity.' She looked at him sadly. 'Oh, Duff, you were my heart's blood. Everything in me, good and bad, was yours. We belonged.'

His face twisted in anguish and suddenly his arms were around her and his lips on hers, the soft sweetness burning them, the pain piercing their souls. They both knew they belonged here, together, wrapped in embrace. They both felt the rightness of it, like music, like the tides, like the rising of the moon and the setting of the sun, his rhythm was her rhythm. Their pulses beat as one and they both realized with dawning horror that they had violated something natural and right that should have happened between them. They had disobeyed a natural law that had married them, and each in their own way had denied it. It was like flying in the face of God. They had rejected a gift of great value that had been offered to them and now they would have to pay the price. Their kiss had been bitter-sweet but now, guiltily aware of their mistake, they sprang apart and stared at each other aghast.

'Oh, Duff, what have we done?' she asked piteously.

'Demara, what have *I* done?' He looked at her and his eyes were bleak as winter.

Cogger watched, glancing every now and then, as was his wont, at the path from Ballymora.

Now in the distance he saw Dana walking along, an angry tilt to her head, her arms crossed over her breast. And in the distance he heard a laugh. It was a male laugh. It was not Duff. And there was no one else there. It was a strange, wild, mirthless class of a sound and frightening. He would have guessed it was the stranger's but he was nowhere to be seen.

Cogger ran up to the pair on the headland and, taking Demara's hand in his and pointing down the hill to where Dana could be seen marching purposefully towards them, he pulled her away. Duff held onto her for a moment, but Cogger cried, 'Look there!' as he pointed to Dana. 'Come. Come quickly,' he said to Demara and held onto her more tightly.

He guided her swiftly down the flight of steps cut in the cliff face, so that she lost sight of Duff above her and was saved from a meeting and an anger Cogger knew she could not deal with at that particular moment.

Chapter Fifty-Eight

❧ ❧

'It is a state of affairs, Mr Blackstock, I cannot countenance,' Lady Kitty Lester told the solicitor as he toasted his feet before the big log fire and sipped his port appreciatively. 'What Linton thought he was doing is beyond my comprehension. Every time I think about it I distress myself dreadfully.'

The roses had returned to her cheeks and though she still wore the marks of grief and had certainly aged since her husband's death, she looked, Vernon Blackstock thought, much more bright and cheerful despite her words.

'Then you must not think of it, dear lady,' he replied.

'But it is my duty,' she said. 'What would dear Edward have said!'

'Unfortunately there is not a great deal we can do now,' he told her. 'And your kind gesture has without doubt improved everything and made up somewhat for the Marquis's brutal act.'

'Give them the land near Dead Man's Pool, over by the river,' she told him. 'Let them have some of the materials they need from my woods, the estate. They can have produce from us in the mean time, poor souls, and I'll back them in any way I can.'

'You are very gracious, my lady,' he said, sipping his port, 'and I have already told them they can rebuild. I've imparted your message to them and they are only too pleased to avail themselves of your generosity.'

'Why do you sound so cautious? Well, Blackstock?'

'Do not let them take advantage of you, my lady. They can, you know. It is in their character.'

'I'm well aware of that,' she said briskly. 'And thank you for your warning. I'll keep it in mind.'

'Not the Donnellys or the Dannons but some of the others.'

'Yes, well, we'll deal with that when it arises. Meanwhile you must keep me apprised of the climate of opinion.'

'Yes, my lady. You are so kind. I'm afraid some of the cottagers do not realize how generous you are being.'

'Oh, my dear man, how you do waffle on,' she said, smiling at him. 'But I see you are still worried. What are you afraid of?'

'I am afraid of the Marquis of Killygally. He is not a man to be trifled with.'

She frowned. 'I know,' she said fervently. 'He has a wicked reputation and has done some vile things in his life.'

She glanced at Vernon Blackstock who blushed. 'Indeed, my lady, one hears all kinds of tattle . . .'

'Tattle, my foot! The man is evil and most of what they say of him is true. In fact, I'd go so far as to say the man's the very Devil and what they say of him is not nearly as bad as the actuality.' She paused and glanced at Blackstock's worried countenance. 'Is his wife still prisoner at Stillwater? Eh, Mr Blackstock?'

Vernon Blackstock jumped. 'Wife?' he cried. 'Wife? I knew nothing of a wife! At Stillwater, you say? Indeed I have been there, Lady Kitty, and I have seen no wife! A prisoner, you say? 'Deed you intrigue me, my lady.' He leaned forward eagerly to hear what she had to say and Lady Kitty bustled a little importantly with this piece of gossip the solicitor had obviously not heard.

'Oh yes, indeed. She is a prisoner in that great house as assuredly as if she had been incarcerated in the Tower of London! But I am not surprised that you have not heard about it, few know that she is there.'

'It is a useful piece of information to have,' Vernon Blackstock mused, then asked, 'Who is she? When did he marry? Why does he keep her hidden?'

'Ah, Mr Blackstock, well you may ask. If you have the time I'll tell you all I know, though I would rather you did not spread it all about . . .'

'As if I would, my lady,' he protested. 'It would be

unprofessional of me, to be sure, to break your confidence.'

'That is, unless you need to! I certainly give you permission to use it to our advantage.' She looked at him, her eyes glittering. 'Eh, Mr Blackstock?' He nodded.

'Well,' she said, 'when the Marquis was still quite young his parents tried to arrange a suitable match for him. They were very bourgeois, a fact he never got over, poor man. They were always an ambitious family and they worked hard to bring about this alliance. It was advantageous; she was the exceedingly wealthy daughter of an old and honourable family. The Lascales. Iris Lascales. Married Maynard Davenport after the Marquis had been turned down by her family as exceedingly unsuitable. Marrying Maynard was a much better match for her and I believe they are tolerably happy. Quite comfortable together, I hear. He's had a string of mistresses but Iris never complains, sensible woman. Thank God I never had that trouble with dear Edward, though in seventy-nine or was it eighty there was this . . .'

'But about the Marquis?' Vernon Blackstock prompted her.

'Ah yes. Well, Bosie never forgave her for turning him down. He is quite vicious although she was, even then, a trifle old for him. He likes young flesh, I believe.' She wrinkled her nose. 'Oh dear! I don't want to go into that. It is all most distasteful.'

He nodded, agreeing heartily with Lady Kitty. Some things it was better not to talk about.

'Well, the Lascales had friends, bosom friends who lived quite close to the family. There was a girl, Iris adored her. Sweet child, but at the time only sixteen. The family were first bewildered at the Marquis's interest, then appalled. They were firmly set against him. Would have nothing to do with him. The father chased him away with a horse-whip, it is said. However, the old man was barely holding his estate together. He was deeply in debt. Everything he had was mortgaged heavily.' Vernon Blackstock shifted in his chair. 'Would you like a little more port?' Lady Kitty asked him and when he nodded

336

she indicated the decanter and he replenished his glass. After a moment she continued. 'Well, to cut a long story short, Bosie bought up the mortgage and the bills and held them against the old man. The upshot was that he shot himself. Damn silly thing to do for it left the females unprotected. The child, Fleur, held Bosie in revulsion. His attentions were deeply unattractive to her, but he married her, poor little thing. The mother had gone batty when the father shot himself and the elder brother was in India so the child had no way out. Or so it seemed to her. On her seventeenth birthday.'

'How could he do that to her?'

'Easily. Abducted her. Took her to Scotland and wed her. The mother was quite crazy and no one seemed to know what to do to prevent him. Caused quite a scandal at the time.' She glanced at Vernon. 'I've told you. Mother was quite do-lally. Father dead. Brother away in some God-forsaken land. People in England don't interfere. It's the mother's fault too. And the father's. They should have thought about her. Really. Caving in like that, forgetting their responsibility. Moaning minnies, I call them. All milk-and-water and not an ounce of backbone to be found! Can you imagine allowing something like that happening to your child?' Vernon Blackstock, having no children, couldn't, but tactfully nodded. 'If it was Linton I'd follow him to the ends of the earth rather than let him be abducted,' she told him earnestly. It would be a hardy adventurer who would abduct Linton Lester, Mr Blackstock thought, but kept his mouth closed. 'If that had been me, I'd have got the child back and *then* had my breakdown.'

'So what happened?'

'Well, the poor girl was left to her fate, which was Stillwater.'

'Wasn't there anyone else at all?'

Lady Kitty shook her head. ' 'Fraid not. Fleur's brother came home and found it was too late. Fleur had sunk into a depression. He tried to get Bosie to give her up but he refused. Said the law was on his side which was true. She was his wife. I don't know any more but I believe the brother talked to her and couldn't budge her. She remained at Stillwater and God knows what goes on there. People have forgotten all about her. Dr Martin attends her and although he is bound by professional etiquette not to discuss his patient, he looks very grave when her name is mentioned, and shakes his head like this.' She did a fair imitation of the old doctor shaking his head with profound gravity. 'It is very sad,' she concluded.

At that moment Kilty came in followed by the maid carrying a tray.

'Ah, tea! Will you join me in a dish, Mr Blackstock? Or would you prefer to stick to the port?'

'Port, my lady, if you don't object,' he replied. He felt warm and benign sitting there, content with life and very glad he had been spared so much of the suffering others had to bear. The cottagers and the burning of their homes. The struggle to survive that beset the Lesters. Lady Kitty's loss. The Marquis of Killygally and his appalling, evil tastes. The shadowy Fleur only half alive, her life spoiled.

Somehow, perhaps because his desires were modest, he had always had everything he wanted. He was happy with what he had and felt no cause for complaint. A good education, an open mind, a satisfactory but not over-ambitious practice, a good digestion, his plump Moll, all these things kept him in the pink. Life for him was extremely pleasant.

'Let me know what the cottagers decide to do,' Lady Kitty was saying. 'Give them my assurances of help. Now you see why I have no desire to see the Marquis of Killygally succeed at anything.' She sipped her tea, was silent a moment, then said, 'There is only one worry I have. It preys on my mind, dear Mr Blackstock. Do you think my Linton could fall under Bosie's spell and turn out like him? Do you think it possible?'

Vernon Blackstock thought it possible. But he was not going to upset her so he decided to lie.

'Dear me, no!' he cried emphatically. 'The Marquis has an evil soul. He is ruthless and cunning. And he has amassed a fortune. None of these things apply to your son.

Linton's only fault is that he wants the money to live the life of a young gentleman-about-town. He'll develop. He'll mature. He'll grow up.' He crossed his fingers as he spoke and hoped devoutly that what he promised was true. Lady Kitty was reassured.

'How kind of you to say so, Mr Blackstock. How very kind.' She smiled at him fondly. 'But then, you are very kind. A very kind person, are you not? Dear Edward, God rest him, had very good taste in the people he chose to associate with.'

Vernon Blackstock drained his port and, glowing with satisfaction, sent up a silent prayer of thanks for his good luck.

Chapter Fifty-Nine

ꙮ ꙮ

The next day Clancy and his little band of men arrived back in Ballymora. Once more they marched down the lane but this time there was no welcoming committee, nor curiosity. There was also no cheerful curl of smoke rising from thatched cottages snugly resting in the softly undulting countryside. Clancy noted the burned patches of earth, the blackened, desolate areas where once the little houses had so prettily nestled. His dark eyes were angry and his fingers twitched as he strode purposefully to the barn.

The cottagers were nervous of meeting Clancy and his men, remembering how they had told them to leave and not concealed their mistrust, but Clancy gave them no call to feel embarrassed. He was simply anxious to hear all that had happened and he and his men sat on upturned barrels and listened without interruption as they were informed, at first tentatively then in an outpouring of all that had come to pass.

'We truly thought it would be all right,' Dinny McQuaid

339

scratched his heavy moustache. 'Truly we did.'

'But at the weddin' an' all of us up beyond in the church, Muswell came, bad cess to him.' Deegan Belcher spat on the sawdust on the floor.

'Can ye take him out, Clancy? Can ye?' Mickey O'Gorman asked.

'Can ye top him? Can ye?' Deegan Belcher urged.

'I can do no such thing unprovoked,' Clancy said bleakly.

'An' what de ye call what he done te us if not provoke?' Mog Murtagh asked angrily.

'What do ye propose te do then?' Brian Gilligan demanded.

'We'll all have to muddle in here, I suppose,' Pierce Donnelly ventured. 'We have no homes yet for ye to share.'

'An' that's suppoꞃed to be a dig at us, Pierce Donnelly?' Deegan Belcher inquired heatedly. 'Ye gettin' at us because we din' take yer advice?'

'Oh, sit down, Deegan, an' save yer fury for another time,' Pierce told him. 'I'm too heartsore, man, mourning my old mother to think about digs an' gettin' at people.'

'We were sorry to hear of yer loss, Pierce Donnelly,' Clancy said, and Demara thought how driven the man was. Hands twisted, his forehead constantly furrowed, his narrow mouth clenched, he was sinew-taut from head to toe. He was bedevilled by ghosts, her father had told her, and, looking at him now – his sharp bones, his burning eyes – she shivered, for he let off a quivering air of suffering and obsession.

'And that's what I am going to be like too,' she thought, 'if I go on this way. Oh, I'm not like him yet, not all burning up, unable to think about anything else, but my dream could make me like him eventually. It could take me over, lock, stock and barrel, obsess me to the exclusion of all else and eventually burn me out! Oh God, what have I started?'

She suddenly felt very frightened and pulled her shawl tight around her body as she sat, cross-legged on a milking-stool with Brindsley, watching the others as they were watching her.

'We will stay with ye and help ye build yer houses. Mebbe it will stop anyone gettin' ideas about tearin' down what ye

340

build. Mebbe it will make them think twice,' Clancy was saying, the oil-lamps flickering and casting his giant shadow onto the wall. 'We will help protect ye and when yer done an' safe an' the houses built we'll go.'

The cottagers were angry at the anticlimax. They had visualized a wonderful scene of retribution, of vengeance and now they were disappointed. What was the use of these men coming here if all they were going to do was offer their labour? They looked at each other with furtive eyes and were surprised when Pierce Donnelly, who had more to avenge than anyone, meekly welcomed their suggestion.

'Thanks,' he said, 'We'll be glad of yer help. An' yer protection.'

Clancy's men found vacant clearings to lay themselves down. Each of them had brought a roll of bedding, like the travelling men, and they wrapped themselves up warm and closed their eyes. Clancy went outside and Pierce followed him. Duff rose and was about to leave the barn when Demara heard her sister's voice call him back. She heard him curse but he remained inside.

'You are good to return,' Pierce told Clancy in the still clear night. 'After the way ye were treated here.'

'I don't care how ye treat me,' Clancy said. 'I'm not interested in personal slights and insults and neither are my men. We are fighting a great battle. We are involved in a great struggle. We want the land returned to our own people, the people of Ireland. Petty things like the whims of ignorant people do not bother us.'

Pierce was suddenly filled with hope. He could not think why. Nothing Clancy had said was exactly reassuring, but, he thought, they were going to build new homes and they had help. There were people who thought their cause a just one. One of those people was Lady Lester and she too was going to help. It would be a new beginning.

And Demara was home.

She was a wonder to behold, was his daughter. Even in his sorrow she had warmed him. He felt his heart swell with pride as he thought about her. Lovely, she was, a jewel.

On his way back to the barn he nearly bumped into Sheena McQuaid who seemed to be hiding under the bushes. He opened his mouth to greet her but she put her finger to her lips and looked at him with pleading eyes so he went on his way without a word. A little further on he saw one of Clancy's men . . . Bodie? Was it? Or Pascal? He was scurrying towards the copse of larches and he called a quiet 'Yoo-hoo' out into the darkness.

So that's how the wind blows, Pierce thought, and entered the barn quietly so as not to disturb the sleepers.

He nearly stumbled over Duff at the entrance. He was fast asleep, snoring quietly on his and Dana's mattress near the barn door. He had a blanket wrapped around him, one of the ones Lady Lester had sent down. His face was turned away from his wife and he had his back to her. Dana sat, arms around her knees, facing away from her husband. She was staring into the darkness, lost in her own dark thoughts. Well, she was Duff's concern now, Pierce thought; he did not have to worry about her any more. He was glad.

He tiptoed past her and went to where his wife and family were sleeping, all except Demara who was writing with a pencil and a roll of paper she had brought with her from London.

'Are ye all right, *allana*?' he asked her softly.

She nodded. 'Just writing a message to a friend, Da. I've already written to Maeve.'

'You've not alarmed her, pet?'

'No, Da. No. I'd not do that.'

'No. 'Twould be no point an' she separated from us by an ocean. Ye understand?'

'I do, Da. I do.'

He slipped under the quilt beside Brigid, who grunted, then turned automatically into his arms.

Demara had written a note to Perry. It said:

You asked me news of the Marquis of Killygally. He killed my Grandmother and burned down our houses. To the ground. I hate him. You can see why. I send you greetings with a good but grieving heart. Demara Donnelly.

Demara had sealed her letter to her sister. In it she had told Maeve that Granny Donnelly was very, very ill, *But she is an old lady at the end of her life.* She also said that Lord Edward Lester had died, *but do not be alarmed, dearest sister, for Lady Lester has given all the cottagers a new place for their homes which they will build themselves. We will have better buildings, more space and light. All is well here,* she continued, *Brindsley sends a kiss and Ma and Da are well and cheerful. And it is true. Duff married Dana. But do not grieve for me, Maeve. I have quite made up my mind to survive the blow, and tomorrow I start to build my new house at Bannagh Dubh.*

Chapter Sixty

⤬ ⤬

The Duchess of Malvern knew exactly what she was doing. She said to her husband, having listened to him rave on about this little actress, Maeve Donnelly, that her eldest son was so smitten with, 'Then have Sebastian invite her to Malvern, Maynard. Let me cast an eye over her. It can't hurt, after all.' So her husband duly issued the invitation. Sebastian was to bring Maeve to Malvern on Saturday night after her performance and stay with them until Monday's midday meal, after which they would return to the city in time for Maeve's evening show. Sebastian suggested that they not travel such a long way on Saturday night. The play was tiring, the journey fatiguing, but his mamma insisted so he had no choice but to agree.

She had her reasons. She wanted to see what Maeve Donnelly, who she was pretty sure must be a Roman Catholic, would do when put in the position of being a member of the lord of the manor's party in the Church of England chapel, a service which she knew would be considered a grave sin to attend by her priests. She wanted to see what the ambitious little baggage would do when she found herself in the overpowering magnificence of

Malvern. She wanted to see how the cheap little upstart behaved surrounded by the aristocracy and fashionable society. 'I'll show her up,' the Duchess decided. 'I'll cure Sebastian of her for once and for all.' So she was determined to make the weekend as uncomfortable for Maeve as she possibly could. 'All in the name of his happiness,' she told herself. 'It is for his mamma, poor boy, to extricate him from this temptress's snares.'

She gave instructions to the servants that they saw through and understood the purpose. This weekend was all set to impress and intimidate.

She decided that Maeve should stay in the largest and most overpowering guest-room. The maid in attendance was chosen by the Duchess for her manner, which was that of an angry sergeant major. Masters was a formidable woman who had once been in attendance on the Princess Royal and had been instrumental in putting off many an unwelcome female guest at Malvern. One had to be very confident to survive Masters.

Iris ordered a large formal meal in the banqueting hall for after church on Sunday and suggested that her guests went riding before church. She invited some awe-inspiring people including the Bishop of Millford whom she instructed to wear full regalia. 'And you have my permission to embellish your outfit with whatever paraphernalia you choose, dear man,' she told him, well aware that the Bishop adored dressing up. 'I want you to impress. This little upstart needs to quake in her boots. I will teach her a lesson and send her home, I hope, with her tail between her legs. Can you imagine the heir to the dukedom wedding an Irish Catholic peasant?'

The Bishop screamed a loud protest and let his hand fall in consternation at the thought of such an outrage. He decided on purple and cerise, with a touch of gold and perhaps some chains.

Maeve and Sebastian arrived late on Saturday night. Maeve was far too exhausted however to be intimidated by anything as banal as an imposing room. She fell into a deep sleep and did not awaken until Masters brought in her early morning tea.

What Lady Iris had not taken into consideration was the fact that Maeve Donnelly was a consummate actress. Anyone who had seen her Titania could not doubt that, and what the Duchess had left out of her calculations was Maeve's ability to play brilliantly whatever role she was cast in. Chameleon-like, she managed always to fit in with her company. It was what she did best. So this morning she woke up in a grand and ornate room to see an imposing servant standing before her and she drew subconsciously on the work she was immersed in at the moment. She was immediately Desdemona (or she could have been Juliet), and Masters was immediately Emily or the Nurse. Thus she treated Masters with instant familiarity, as if she were the young mistress of the house, and totally disarmed her, for Masters recognized authority when she came across it. She also capitulated to Maeve's charm – another attribute the Duchess had overlooked. Actresses without the power to enchant do not reach the position of leading lady on the London stage.

Maeve allowed the maid to bathe and dress her in silence. She did not feel the need to converse. Masters respected the young girl's reticence and was quite amazed at her poise.

Lady Iris had instructed Masters not to lay out the young girl's riding habit. Masters complied with her mistress's instructions, as she did not want to be dismissed, but she doubted that this young lady would be disconcerted. My lady, she thought to herself wryly, has bitten off more than she can chew.

Dressed and ready in her flowered muslin, Maeve descended the staircase and, finding the enormous hall deserted, waited with composure for someone to come and tell her where to go.

When the major domo, a very imposing personage who knew exactly what her ladyship was up to, was asked by Maeve where she should go, he pointed her towards a door on her right. He had decided to be very careful. He had no wish to offend Maeve and one never knew who might become the next Duchess of Malvern no matter what lengths Lady Iris decided to go to. Maeve, he had to admit, looked more like a duchess than Lady Iris. She looked enchanting, and when he opened the sunny breakfast-room door and guided her inside everyone turned to look and they could none of them find fault with her.

Maeve was not disturbed by the scrutiny. She was used to stage entrances, pausing so that everyone could take her in, and this was what she did now. She waited tranquilly for someone to speak to her and eventually Maynard recollected his manners and rushed to her side.

'Forgive me, my dear. Sebastian is not down yet. Such a laggard! How radiant you look.' He stood holding her hand, agog with admiration, and Lady Iris saw with sinking heart what she was up against. She cleared her throat and as she came towards Maeve the latter noticed that she was the only one in the room not in riding dress.

Maynard introduced them and almost at once the gentlemen surrounded the actress and introductions were effected. The men greeted Maeve Donnelly with delighted appreciation, the women less enthusiastically.

A young man was sitting in the window embrasure eyeing her speculatively.

'This is my other son, Rudolph,' Maynard told her, and the young man, so like Sebastian but with a narrower, more intellectual face, bowed over her hand and smiled at her. 'No wonder Seb dotes on you,' he said gleefully. 'She's a Fildes, she's Reynolds' "Theory", she's a Murillo Madonna.' His eyes danced. 'You must call me Rudi. Everyone does.' He lowered his voice and leaned towards her. 'Don't let them get you down,' he whispered, smiling at her.

'Lord Peregrine Dawkins.' Maynard introduced the guest.

The eyes twinkled at her merrily and she felt herself blessed.

'We have already met,' he said loudly, then added quietly to Maeve, 'I received a curious missive from your charming sister. I would welcome the opportunity of discussing it with you.'

She nodded just as Sebastian came into the room, seeming flustered to find her already there. Maynard then brought her over to where a tall angular lady stood.

'Maeve, my mother,' Sebastian said, and Maeve found herself being scrutinized by cold, clear eyes. They were unfriendly eyes, inhospitable eyes, and Maeve knew that there was nothing she could do to win this lady over.

'Oh, dear me,' Lady Iris said to her. 'You're not in riding clothes. We like to go for a canter here before breakfast. You would know that, of course, if you were brought up hereabouts. But of course you do not ride. Actresses don't, I believe.'

'I have a habit in my dressing-case. It will take me only a moment to change,' Maeve laughed. 'Actresses can change very quickly, Lady Iris.'

She left the room and ran upstairs where Masters waited, half-expecting her. 'Oh help me, dear kind Masters,' Maeve begged and Masters readily complied. She was quite won over by the young lady's delightful manner. Within five minutes Maeve was tripping merrily down the stairs again, booted and spurred in her neat little jacket, her serge skirt hooked to her finger. As she reached the bottom she heard Sebastian calling and she looked up to see him leaning over the bannisters, grinning at her.

'You don't have to, you know,' he told her. 'I came to tell you you needn't.'

'Well, I'd like to,' she replied as he ushered her into the breakfast room again. 'There!' she cried triumphantly to the assembled guests and they clapped and laughed with her. Her face was flushed, her eyes sparkling and it was impossible not to be affected by her vitality.

They drank some hot chocolate before going out into the morning air. When there was a lull in the conversation Lady Iris, who had been waiting for a chance to make her next move, remarked quite loudly, 'What a delightful diamond pin you are wearing in your stock, my dear. Is that a present from my son?'

'Dear me, no!' Maeve laughed. 'It is only theatre paste, I'm afraid. I have no valuable jewellery, Lady Iris.'

347

'She refuses to accept anything from me,' Sebastian informed them all. 'Goodness knows I've tried to shower her with presents but she is scrupulous as a nun and will accept nothing but flowers and bon-bons.'

There was a hoot at the door as a stout lady stared through her *lorgnette* at Maeve. 'This is the Countess Ginsborg,' Lady Iris said to her guest, but before Maeve could say how-de-do the lady was loudly proclaiming, 'In my day, Iris, *actresses* were not allowed in respectable folks' homes. If they were allowed inside at *all* they had to use the servants' entrance.'

'Oh, Sabby, it's so nice to see you again.' A pretty young girl of about the same age as Maeve detached herself from the Countess's side and laid a hand on Sebastian's arm. She had a nice face, nice teeth, nice figure and was discreetly dressed. Maeve liked her instantly. She had a guileless face and that strange quality: goodness.

'You are more beautiful than they say,' the girl said as she turned to Maeve.

'This is Fanny Ginsborg,' Sebastian introduced them. 'We've known each other all our lives.'

Maeve, glancing at the Duchess, knew instantly that this was the girl Lady Iris wanted her son to marry.

'Let us ride,' the Duchess said and left the room, the others following. Their horses were waiting, saddled in the driveway. Everyone went directly to a mount and Maeve looked questioningly at the Duchess, who nodded to a beautiful black stallion. He seemed mettlesome and fiery and Maeve saw at once through the Duchess's little game.

'You must not let Maeve ride Black Prince,' Rudi said, looking at his mother in astonishment. 'That damned horse is not for a slip of a gel.'

'Nonsense,' Maeve laughed. 'I can manage.'

'Mother, it's a bit thick, really,' Rudi persisted.

Sebastian came over to them. 'Mother, you don't seriously expect Maeve to ride Black Prince?' he asked.

'Oh, Lady Iris, Black Prince is a bit frisky for Maeve. After all, she's an actress,' Fanny said. 'I'll take him.'

'No, Fanny. You stick to Queen's Angel. Leave this to me.'

348

'Whatever you say, Sebastian,' Fanny replied compliant-ly. She adores him, Maeve thought, amused at the dispute that had broken out.

'Give her Nune. Nune's a sweet bay and I'll take Black Prince,' Rudi suggested.

'Maeve, you wait in the library and we'll return presently,' Sebastian informed her.

It was precisely what the Duchess wanted, but once again she was thwarted.

'No. No, I'll ride him,' Maeve gave the statement her large stage voice. 'Don't fuss so!' And before anyone could stop her she had put her slim foot in the groom's clasped hands and was sitting side-saddle on Black Prince. The stallion's ears went back and he rolled his eyes and reared, but the girl never faltered. She leaned over the reins clasped between the gloved fingers of one hand and with the other she patted the horse's neck, ran her fingers through his mane and whispered to him in Gaelic.

Black Prince shuddered with pleasure and was suddenly very still. To Lady Iris's fury a little burst of applause led by Rudi greeted Maeve's achievement.

'How did you do that?' he asked her later. 'I never saw anything like it.'

'I could ride before I walked,' she told him. 'The gypsies taught me. They steal the horses but only if they can quiet them first, and they showed me how they do it. It works like magic.'

'Oh, I see.'

'We lived beside Lord Edward Lester and he sometimes let me ride his horses.'

'Oh? His son will be here tonight.'

'Oh, will he?' Maeve remarked lightly. Perhaps Lady Iris was cleverer than she thought.

Church was also a success for Maeve. Never very religious, irritated by Father Maguire's strident lectures and his lack of charity, Maeve was pleasantly surprised by the gentle service conducted in the castle chapel. It was in fact very little different from the ceremony she was used to in Ballymora, for the Davenports were High Anglican. But the protestant service was very mild compared to Father

Maguire's rather violent and abusive authoritarianism. Once more the Duchess's intention was frustrated, for Maeve joined in the service enthusiastically and with fervour.

Lunch was a sparkling affair. Maeve, egged on by Rudi, regaled them all with tales of the theatre but without once ever exceeding the bounds of propriety.

'Quite lovely, ain't she?' Maynard incensed his wife by remarking. All she could do was harrump angrily.

Perry Dawkins was one side of Maeve and Rudi the other.

'Don't mind Mater,' Rudi whispered in her ear. 'You'll win her over with no trouble at all.'

'Who is the pretty girl beside Sebastian?' she asked him.

'That is Fanny Ginsborg,' he replied. 'I thought you were introduced.'

'Oh, we were. But I want to know . . . are she and Sebastian. . .'

'Look, you mustn't bother your pretty head over Fan. No one seeing you could look at anyone else.'

She looked at him in surprise. 'Why, Rudi, you're trembling!' she cried. But he laughed and she thought she had been wrong.

'No,' he said. 'I just could not imagine anyone preferring Fanny Ginsborg to you.'

'Is it true what your sister writes?' Perry Dawkins asked her just then, taking her attention away from Rudi.

'I'm sure I don't know what she told you, sir,' Maeve replied.

'Well then, what is your news from home?'

He did not want to ask her outright about the events in Ballymora, for he guessed, shrewdly enough, that Maeve was not aware of the death of her grandmother. He had heard her speak of the old lady with genuine love and he knew she would not be here and in such a light frame of mind if she knew the truth. The girl had tender sensibilities and was not capable of indifference.

'Well sir, it appears that Lord Linton Lester,' she nodded to where the young gentleman sat, totally unaware of who she was, 'has sold, quite without permission, my

350

family's cottage to the Marquis of Killygally.' She looked at him swiftly. 'But it is all right, Perry. Lady Lester has given all the cottagers another piece of land to build on.'

'I see,' he said musingly. 'Do you know when your sister returns to London?'

Maeve shook her head. 'No, I don't. And I wish she would return. But I'd not be surprised if she never came back.'

He looked at her, surprised, and Maeve continued, 'You see, Perry, Demara has always had a dream and now she can rest content that I am with Belle and earning such a lot of money.'

He laughed. 'You must not say things like that,' he cried.

'Why not, sir. It is true.'

'Nevertheless, it is indiscreet.'

'Oh well. I expect she'll stay in Kerry,' she finished.

'I know about her dream,' he said, surprising her. 'I'd forgotten. I should have guessed.'

'Our father used to say, "It is not a dream for a woman, Demara. Women dream of marriage and babies." That's what Da used to say. I think it is a peculiar dream myself. Ma used to say it would elevate her into anxiety.'

'Your mother may be right, Maeve, but no matter how peculiar a dream is you must follow it. Don't you think?'

Maeve frowned. 'I don't know, my lord. If a dream is inappropriate' – she glanced over at Sebastian whose head was close to Fanny as they both laughed at something – 'then perhaps one should remember the proprieties.'

'In that event we would still believe the earth to be flat and Joan of Arc would have died of old age and Mary Wollstonecraft would never have written *A Vindication of the Rights of Women*. Innovators cannot think primarily of the "proprieties" or we should make no progress whatsoever.'

Maeve threw up her hands. 'Very well, my lord Dawkins, you win, truly you do. You speak very like Demara and I think it likely she is fulfilling her dream at this moment and not thinking about us at all. Although I cannot imagine how she intends to actually build the house. She said in her letter she was going to begin at

351

once.' She glanced at the man beside her. She liked his clear, nut-brown skin, his twinkling eyes. He had an amused air that reassured. She said, 'The boy she was . . . well . . . spoken for, I suppose you'd call it, Duff Dannon by name, well, he has married our sister.'

Perry Dawkin's face lightened.

'She said she didn't mind too much because she was starting the house. So I expect she already has.'

'Perhaps I should go and find out,' Perry Dawkins said softly.

Chapter Sixty-One

ᮥᮥ ᮥᮥ

Maeve had taken her script into the library to study quietly. She thought the room was empty, pushing open the door tentatively, peering in before she actually entered and settled herself at a table near the window. Where she could raise her head every now and then and see the peacocks strutting up and down the velvet lawn and the primroses clustered around the chestnut trees.

She was very sure of Desdemona now and was studying Juliet. On fire with love, just as she was and just as unsuitably, Juliet was not daunted, she thought, as she read and savoured the lines.

Gallop apace you fiery-footed steeds towards Phoebus lodging. . .

It had a round and grand and desperate ring to it, a passionate urgency that she had to convey vocally as well as visually. The audience had to hear every word and relish them as she did. She whispered them, then called them out. Her voice reverberated through the library.

'She was such a fool, Juliet.'

The sound of the voice from the winged chair startled her and she jumped.

'Imagining love would triumph. It never does.'

A head turned and looked at her. She knew who it was. Bosie, Marquis of Killygally. She did not like him. Knowing him only by sight she shrank from him. His face had an unpleasant pallor and the expression in his eyes was malicious even though he was smiling. He looked at her impertinently.

She rose and made for the door but she had to pass him to get there and as she did his hand shot out and he gripped her wrist. 'You think Sebastian will marry you. You think that you will win over his family and they will accept you, open their arms to you. You think, my dear girl, that you are irresistible.' His words were uttered lightly, sibilantly. 'But like Juliet you'll find that you'll not succeed and all you'll do is alienate his parents and cause terrible trouble in the family.' He looked up at her, his eyes mocking. 'Selfish people like you, oh yes, and Juliet too, never take into consideration the terrible rifts they cause in the family of their loved one. You'll tear the Davenports apart but you're too selfish to care.' He let go of her wrist and stood up, blocking her way to the door. He was very close and she could smell his breath and see the sweat on the mottled pores of his skin. 'Why do you *want* to marry him, little actress? He'll bore you very soon. And he'll live to curse you for turning his mother against him. And you'll have to give up your career. And you don't want to do that now, do you? For what? You'll recover. People always recover from love. I'll wager if you break it off with Sebastian he'll be engaged to Fanny Ginsborg within the month.'

'He would not!' Stung by his words she cried out the denial, then stopped. She did not want to argue with him. She would make up her own mind.

'One hundred guineas says I'm right. I am so sure of winning that you need not cover it.'

'You are wrong!' she cried firmly, passionately.

'Think, my young friend, think. You would live here all the year around. Can you imagine it? Your work would be running this cold, unfriendly place, not acting to adoring audiences every night. The staff here would be hostile because you would not know what to tell them. The one thing a staff hates is inadequate management. Sebastian would go to London, go to his clubs, the play, but he would not want his wife to accompany him. Oh no. You would be stuck here with the likes of me and Maynard chasing you around this old pile of stones. You would have Fanny and the Countess as your nearest friends. Oh, a jolly crowd to amuse you. All the flock you met today. The county's best, I do assure you. And no more acting. That would be unthinkable. A Davenport on the stage. No! Never! Lord, madam, you'd die of boredom in a week.'

'Why do you want me to refuse Sebastian so very much?' she asked.

'I have my reasons,' he said.

She moved away from him. 'What reasons? You seem very anxious to prevent my boredom.'

He smiled. His full red lips were wet and she looked at him with distaste.

'Ah, madam, there you have me. I'm sure in my whole life I have never wished anyone well, so I promise you I have no notion why I'm taking this trouble over you.'

She gave him her most regal and contemptuous glare. 'Excuse me, sir,' she cried. 'I wish to leave the room.'

He grinned at her. 'I'm not stopping you,' he said, standing squarely in front of her. He suddenly grabbed her. 'You're a pretty thing,' he said, and planted a wet kiss on her cheek. She had turned her face just in time.

'If you touch me again I'll scream and my scream is so loud it will pierce your eardrums. I shall tell the Duke of your behaviour.'

He let her go abruptly. 'The Duke knows me well,' he said. 'He would never believe you.'

'On the contrary, sir. If he knows you well then he'll certainly believe me.'

He stepped back but only marginally and she had to brush past him. Her body shrank from him but he was enjoying himself hugely. In that moment she loathed him.

She escaped and went to her room but she could not rest. She felt defiled. She scrubbed her cheek where his lips had left a damp trace and, taking her cloak, she hurried out into the afternoon sun.

She chose to walk down the avenue of lime trees to the deer park. The does clustered under the trees with their fawns, heads gracefully poised on slender necks, and the stag, a little apart, watched her with alert eyes. 'Let anyone threaten them,' his look said and she thought of the Duke and his family and knew, deep in her soul, that however well-disposed towards her he seemed, he, like the stag, would die for the honour of the Davenports.

The worst part of that meeting in the library, she grudgingly had to admit, was that what the Marquis said made sense. She leaned on the gate and stared at the stag.

'You are beautiful,' she told him and his ears twitched. 'Only it is a pity you have to be so terribly proud.'

Chapter Sixty-Two

∽ ∾

As Masters dressed her for the ball that evening Maeve realized grimly that life here would not be to her taste. It would be uncomfortable. There was so much fuss and formality, so little that was friendly or convivial. Clad in white satin and lace, her hair piled high on her head and studded with Belle's pearls, a pearl collar at her throat, she looked breathtakingly beautiful.

'It's an honour to dress you,' Masters told her and was kissed warmly on the cheek for the compliment, something Masters was not at all used to.

As she glided down the stairs that evening Maeve heard the Countess Ginsborg remark, 'Of course she is beautiful, but coarse! A little fortune-hunter who I'm afraid won't wear well!'

Impervious to the gasps, the quite natural interest in this famous performer's entrance, Maeve bit back her tears and continued her descent. She knew the Countess wished her to hear and she gave perhaps her best performance that evening by allowing no one to see her hurt.

Sebastian was waiting for her and her heart lifted. He took her in his arms, drew her towards the ballroom and led her into the waltz.

The setting was opulent and romantic. The music swelled seductively. The women and the men were elegantly dressed. They laughed and chatted about things she did not understand. Jewels glittered, punch was drunk from silver goblets. Chandeliers gleamed and a thousand candles dazzled. They danced all night with flying feet and Sebastian looked at her with love.

'I love you, sweet princess,' he whispered in her ear as he led her to a chair to await him while he fetched her some punch.

Yes, everything was perfect. Yet she was not happy. Bewildered she asked herself why? She suddenly felt sick and frightened. What was the matter? Why did these painted people seem to her much more mercenary than the whores in Bryony Gilligan's house? Something in these rooms chilled her. There was no love here. She had become gradually aware during the evening that they did not only dislike her, they disliked each other. The sense of competition was strong. They competed.

At home in Ballymora if anyone had told her that she would be dancing with the handsome son of a duke in a castle, looking beautiful in white satin, drinking punch and eating caviar and pâté de foie gras she would have said that must be heaven. The reality was quite different. Beware of what you pray for for you might get it. Ah, yes. She smiled, hearing Father Maguire's voice, a voice she loathed, yet in this case being accurate.

What was missing from this place, she decided, was warmth. The warmth she took for granted at home in Ballymora, the warmth she took for granted in Soho Square, the warmth she took for granted in the theatre. She had been spoiled up to now. She remembered her father's voice telling her, 'You won't always be loved, Maeve. It will be a chastening day when you meet people who do not like you.' Well, that day had come.

'Maeve, may I present Lord Linton Lester. He will look after you while I am getting your punch.'

'I know I am not on your card, but may I ask the privilege of this polka?' Linton Lester asked her and she did not show by as much as the flicker of an eyelid that she recognized him. Her training was too good for that and she thought to herself that she had done more acting this weekend than in a week's rehearsal in the theatre.

He obviously did not have the slightest recollection of ever having met her before. Sebastian waved to her from across the floor and she smiled at him then turned to Linton. 'Thank you, sir,' she replied. 'I would be charmed.' And she stepped into the dance with him.

It was curious to hold his hand and have his arm around her, to be so near him. All her life he had been lord of the manor, a being so remote and above her that to touch him would be like touching a god. Yet here she was tripping merrily, his arms encircling her, his hand in hers. She repressed a giggle and thought of Demara and wished she were here and they could laugh together over what Mickey O'Gorman or Brian Gilligan or Deegan Belcher would think if they could see her now. But she had no one to share her humour with, and no one here would think it funny anyway.

Linton Lester was a good dancer, if a trifle energetic. But then the polka was nothing if not vigorous. He had a weak face, a petulant mouth, she noted, and, she was amused to see, he was nervous of her.

'You are a very great actress, I believe?' he said respectfully. 'I have not been to the play, I regret to say, but I have heard rapturous reports of your performance in it.'

She smiled at him. 'Do you live in London, sir?' she asked.

'I have an apartment in town,' he told her, and added, blushing, 'my estates are in Ireland, I'm afraid. A little place you will never have heard of. No one in fashionable London has!'

Why is he ashamed, she wondered. The lively dance prevented more speech and they threw themselves into it with abandon. When it was over Linton Lester bowed to her and left them as Sebastian returned to claim her. She

357

looked around for Perry Dawkins but she could not see him. She asked Sebastian where he was.

'Oh, I think he left. Went back to London,' he told her. 'He's an odd fish, Perry. I don't think he enjoys this kind of bash.'

For some reason she was sorry he had gone.

'Did you enjoy your polka?' Sebastian was asking her. She nodded and he continued, 'Linton is a nice fellow. Gambles dreadfully though. He's in deep to Bosie, I believe. He'll end up in trouble if he continues.'

'My sister writes that he sold part of his estate without the trustee's signature,' she remarked.

'Oh, dear me. How ungentlemanly of him.'

'The part of the estate he sold just happened to have our cottage on it,' she said. She glanced at Sebastian and to her surprise he was looking embarrassed. 'You see, the Marquis of Killygally owns the estate on one side of the river and the Lesters own the land on the other. Linton sold the land to the Marquis. Apparently Lord Lester needs the money.'

'Yes. Look, Maeve, I don't think we need to go into that just now.' He looked at her severely. 'Oh, let's not be too serious. Come, my sweet love, the air outside is balmy, the stars are out and I want to kiss you.'

He was deprived of his kiss, however, for at that moment the gong sounded and the fifty guests were summoned to supper.

Maeve was seated very far away from Sebastian and she found herself flanked by the Bishop on one side and Linton Lester on the other. A rotund and apoplectic Earl opposite her was complaining about the number of beggars on the streets of London while he tore at a chicken – for all the world, Maeve thought, as if he were Henry the Eighth.

'Can't go anywhere without bein' besieged,' he complained.

'Should do some honest work instead of importunin' gentlefolk like us,' a small beaky-nosed woman beside him commented.

'I do so agree with you, Lady Rice,' the Bishop

remarked. ' 'Tis such a sign of laziness – begging. You would think we had nothing to do with our money but give it to the poor.'

'I thought that was what Christ suggested we do,' Rudi Davenport on the other side of the beaky-nosed lady commented mildly.

The Bishop's jaw dropped and the Earl desisted from his chomping and stared at the young Davenport while Maeve smiled covertly at him.

Linton Lester scrutinized the young man opposite. 'You are really quite extraordinary, Rudi,' he said. 'If I didn't know you so well I'd think you were batty and belonged in Bedlam. These people should find work and not resort to lowering themselves to accepting charity.'

'I think Rudi is right,' Maeve remarked. She looked at Linton. 'And do *you* work, my lord?' she asked him sweetly, then looked at the Bishop. 'Truly it *is* there in the Holy Bible,' she told him.

'My dear little gel,' the Earl said, wiping his chin with his napkin, 'you do not know what you are talking about. These people are the dregs of humanity.' He searched for an appropriate word. 'They are . . . hooligans. They roam the streets, gangs of them, demanding money from hardworking gentlefolk. Frightening them out of their wits.'

'Oh, I'm well aware the streets of London are crowded with thieves and criminals. But not all beggars are like that. Some of them are so poor they have no homes, no food. There are some very sad cases, you have to agree.'

'Actress!' Linton Lester informed them dramatically by way of explanation. 'She is an actress and a woman. Softhearted.' He shook his head, dismissing her.

'I'm not. I very nearly ended up on the streets of London, homeless and hungry,' she told an astonished group of diners. She was not allowed to continue. A burst of conversation ended the discussion and everyone turned away from her. She realized she had committed a gaffe. Only Rudi winked at her, his intelligent eyes full of encouragement.

'We get the society we create,' Rudi said, but no one was listening.

'This is all very sordid,' the Countess cried. 'It is not appropriate talk for the dinner table.'

'I wonder how it started?' The Bishop cast an accusing eye at Maeve.

Maeve smiled down the table at Sebastian. He smiled back at her. Lady Iris saw the exchange and was filled with impotent rage. How dare this little baggage come here and purloin her eldest? She had to admit she liked the girl. She admired her spunk, but as a wife for the heir to Malvern? It simply would never do.

Maeve sighed and returned to her food. She had lost her appetite even though the dessert was a triumph of ice cream, meringue and cherries with a hot cherry sauce. No one spoke to her and she acknowledged to herself that she did not want to talk to them.

Again she wished that Demara was with her, but Demara was hundreds of miles away. She had begun work on her house in Bannagh Dubh and, knowing her sister, Maeve realized she would have little thought about anything else.

It was a long meal and at last it came to an end. As they rose from the table Rudi moved towards her.

'You did well, Maeve,' he said. 'You are a pretty nice person.'

She was surprised and touched. She was used to being called beautiful. This was a nicer compliment.

She smiled at him. His face was so like Sebastian's but lacked the symmetry that made the elder boy's face perfect. Rudi's face was stronger, Maeve realized, his eyes shrewder, his nostrils wider, more ardent, and although he was not as handsome as his brother his face was compelling and intelligent with a lot of humour lurking in his eyes and at the corners of his mouth.

'They talk of the poor as if it was their fault,' she told him.

'It is their excuse for doing nothing,' he replied. 'Don't let it worry you that they are fools.' He looked at her curiously. 'Yet you seem quite happy to accept living among these people.'

'You do,' she replied.

'Sometimes,' he said. 'But I'm not chained to Malvern, thank God.' He came closer to her. 'If you ever get bored with Sebastian, I am always available,' he said, smiling at her. 'But you are aware of that, are you not?' he speculated. She did not reply as just then Linton Lester and the Earl hurried off to play cards, and Sebastian appeared suddenly at her side.

'Come out onto the terrace,' he urged her, and he bore her away leaving his brother staring after them.

Sebastian was torn by his feelings. He felt like an idiot, a dolt, a greenhorn. All the men thought Maeve was his mistress. They envied him and he dared not tell them the truth. The trouble was that he was in love and his heart stuttered in his chest every time he looked at her or touched her. It was like a sickness and he could not breathe when he saw her suddenly, or thought about her. And, worse, he could not stop thinking about her. She haunted him. He was ashamed of the fact that he had not seduced her. How his friends would laugh if they knew. They would urge him to break the filly in, tell him that was what she really wanted and that underneath all, a refusal was a female desire to be mastered. But when he looked at her, the trust in her eyes, he just could not do it. To his horror he found he respected her wishes, which made him a fool.

She smiled up at him now under the moonlight. 'It is very big and magnificent, your home,' she whispered.

'So my mother is at pains to show you,' he remarked bitterly.

She placed her fingers on his lips. 'Hush! She loves you, Sebastian. She is only trying to protect you.'

'From a sweet little thing like you? I don't need protecting. You saw what she was trying to do, then?' he asked her, surprised. He had thought he was the only one who had divined his mother's purpose.

'Oh yes. I'm not a fool. But she does it because she adores you, not because she hates me, my love.'

'Well, she did not succeed,' he said emphatically.

'In one way she did.' Maeve gazed at the stars thickly sprinkled over the mantle of the night. 'She made me realize how small I am. Like one of those stars. She also made me see how very much a full-time occupation being Duchess of Malvern is.'

Sebastian said nothing. He was afraid to, and for a while they both leaned silently on the parapet and stared at the vast canopy above them. When she turned to him her cheeks were damp and her eyes full of tears.

'Oh, what are we to do, my love?' she asked him, fearful as he. 'I cannot be your mistress. It is not in my nature. I cannot share only one side of your life and be closeted away from you the rest of the time. I cannot live in shame, don't you see?' She was wringing her hands now as she paused for breath. 'Nor can I marry you and live here. Your mother is right, Sebastian. I am not up to it. I would not want to be.'

'But, my darling heart. . .'

'No, listen, let me finish. I am bored by these people who are such snobs. They are only interested in *who* someone is, not what they have achieved. They respect people with power and money and despise those without. They admire me because you have fallen in love with me and I have achieved success on the stage. They don't *like* me. They don't know me and at my first mistake they would crucify me. I could never be happy here surrounded by these people. I could not give up my career. And you, my love, could not have a Duchess of Malvern acting on the London stage. The gentry would never stand for it.' She smiled bitterly. 'So what are we to do?' She had her hands out, palms up, pleading with him. 'What can we do?' she begged.

There was no answer but he would not accept that. Not now. Not yet.

'We'll find an answer,' he replied with the confidence of youth. 'We *have* to find an answer.'

But she knew he would not. The gap between them was too great. Love was not enough. She felt a wave of sadness overwhelm her and she almost drowned in desolation. For a moment despair gripped her and she thought, If I was standing on a cliff now, if I was in Ballymora, I would jump. Jump into the sea and end it forever.

Sebastian pulled her into his embrace. He held her to him, his arms wrapped around her as far as they would go, and pulled her fiercely to his breast. He wanted her there forever, close to his heart-beat. She could feel his body trembling.

'You mustn't leave me,' he cried. 'We mustn't let go. Without you I will die. I'll wither into an old man at twenty-five. Life would be too long without you. Don't abandon me. You are my life's blood; without you I am lost.'

She knew he meant every word he said, but she also knew his words were not true. He would not die.

She ran her hands through his hair, then caressed his cheeks, looking at him tenderly. Then she kissed him. Her whole soul was in that kiss. He trembled with desire at the passionate intensity of it and he held her even tighter as if by crushing her he could make them one.

Then she pulled away from him. Her knees were weak and she nearly sank to the ground.

'Tell your mother she's won,' she said and as he felt the loss of her body, he leaned forward and stretched out his arms with a groan to hold her again, to clasp her to him, but she slipped away and was gone.

He stood on the balcony staring at the cold silver stars in the velvet sky. The sound of laughter came to him on the balmy air. A terrible sadness overwhelmed him. What she said was true, how could he deny it? His duchess could not perform on any stage. She would have to give up her career. Would Maeve Donnelly with all her talent do that? Had he a right to ask her? Would she be happy if she did? Could he ask her to spend all her life with the county society she so disliked? Boring snobs, she called them, with little kindness in their hearts. Why could he not have been Rudi? Why did he have to be heir to this place?

And as he asked himself this he knew in his soul that he was glad to be the heir. That he was fiercely ambitious, perhaps as ambitious as Maeve. He wanted to be Duke of Malvern. He liked the title, the power, the honour, the wealth.

He turned as his mother came onto the terrace. When

she looked at him all she could see was her first-born, his face wet with tears he was not even aware he was shedding. She put gentle arms around him.

'There, there, my son,' she soothed him. 'There, there. Everything will be all right.'

Chapter Sixty-Three

The Duchess sat in her drawing-room, a rug around her legs and a warming-pan in her lap. The rooms in Malvern Castle were enormous and quite impossible to heat.

It was tea-time the following day and all the guests had gone.

'I still think the gel's a delight,' Maynard was saying.

'Here, here, Pater,' Rudi agreed. 'She's a bonnie girl if ever I saw one, and fun too.'

'She simply doesn't come up to scratch,' Lady Iris insisted and sighed. 'Oh, if only you could understand.'

She knew they wouldn't believe her no matter what she said. In her heart she had to admit that she had liked Maeve Donnelly, admired her beauty, but more than that she had been impressed by the girl's spirit. However, she knew that Maeve would be quite the wrong choice for her son.

Sebastian needed a wife who would be dedicated to Malvern Castle, someone who would ensure that it ran on oiled wheels. Dear Sebastian, typically male, thought it all happened by accident. That beds got changed, meals served, flower-beds weeded and laundry done all without premeditation. Maeve would struggle to try but would not be able to deliver and the servants would take advantage of her ignorance. No, he needed someone who would be adept at that role and someone who loved the place and the people who were their neighbours and friends. Someone like Fanny Ginsborg.

Sebastian and Maeve were obviously in love, but in Lady Iris's opinion their love was not sensible and would not endure. The wear and tear of life would erode that first rapturous passion. It was all this modern free choice business that had, in her husband's opinion, 'buggered it up for everyone'. Of course she would not put it so crudely but it did sum up what she felt. Gone were the days when spouses were chosen for suitability. Fanny Ginsborg was eminently suitable, so why couldn't Sebastian marry her and have the actress as a mistress? Lady Iris could not understand why this was impossible.

Lady Iris could see why, in the short term, her son preferred Maeve. The actress was the type to drive men wild. That in itself, in her opinion, was a bad thing and usually led to jealousy and all those uncomfortable emotions one read about in the novels of Ann Radcliffe but fervently hoped one would never experience oneself.

Fanny would never arouse jealousy. She was far too well bred. Her father's estate, Henly House, bordered Malvern and she had 'come out' at Court and been presented to the Queen. She knew how to deal with servants, her mother had seen to that. Fanny was the sort of girl one grew to love and appreciate, and therein, Lady Iris concluded, lay the difference.

The huge log fire shifted noisily in the hearth, its heat quickly dispersed in the chilly room. Maynard had his muffler around his throat. A drop of moisture hung from his nose and he was reading the *London Gazette*. 'Still think she's a peach!' he said.

At that moment Sebastian burst into the room. He was sweating, his hair plastered to his forehead.

'Thought you'd gone back to London,' his father remarked mildly, cutting the pages of the magazine with a silver paper-knife.

'Oh, I went all right. And I came back.' He threw his gloves on the small table beside his father.

'I say, old fellow, watch it! Don't knock my tea over.'

Sebastian gave a whistle of irritation.

'Why was that, dear?' his mother asked. Something was up and she didn't know and couldn't guess whether it was good news or bad. She dreaded a breach with her son.

'Well, you did it, Mother, didn't you?'

Her heart skipped a beat. 'What did I do, dear?'

'Maeve doesn't want to see me any more,' he announced.

Lady Iris sucked in her breath. The girl was indeed no fool. She was playing her trump card. Lady Iris felt a twinge of regret that she would not have her as a daughter-in-law.

'She told me she would not be a suitable mistress of Malvern, Mother,' Sebastian cried furiously. 'Now I wonder just who put that idea into her head.' He marched around the room, banging into the furniture, hitting his fist in his palm and kicking the chairs as he passed. He was in a thundering bad temper.

'I say, steady on, old chap,' Rudi murmured.

'I *expected* my mother to make my dearest love feel wanted. I *hoped* my *own* mother would persuade her that she would be an asset to Malvern. Mother! Any fool can see she'd be an asset anywhere.'

'She would that, my son!' Lady Iris said.

'But no! My own mother tries to show her up. Make her feel uncomfortable . . .'

Lady Iris wished now with all her heart she had not resorted to those rather cheap tricks. She felt ashamed, but she had no intention of allowing anyone to see that.

'She did *not* feel uncomfortable, Sebastian,' she said firmly. 'That is the whole point. I *tested* her and she passed with flying colours. She made the decision. Not I.'

'You did everything to make her feel awkward.'

'Look, sit down and tell us what happened.'

'I thought she was wondrous!' Maynard looked up from his reading. He glanced at Rudi and was surprised to meet a look of such excitement that he wondered if he had missed something.

'Maynard!' His wife admonished. 'Sit down, Sebastian, do! Drink a cup of tea.'

Sebastian sat down abruptly on a narrow upright chair.

'How can I think of tea right now, Mother?' he said despairingly.

'What happened? Keep askin' but no one takes a blind

bit of notice,' Maynard grumbled.

'Well, last night at the ball . . .'

'Yes, wondered about that. She went off to bed early . . .'

'Father, please! Let me finish. Well, she told me our love was hopeless, I think she called it. Of course I didn't believe it.'

'Why not, Sebastian? Maeve seems to me a girl who means what she says,' said Rudi, looking at his brother in surprise.

'Well, she's a girl, isn't she. Has silly ideas and sensibilities, don't you know.'

'No, I don't,' Rudi protested. 'There's nothing in the least silly about Maeve.'

'Rudi, let your brother finish! Heavens above, it's impossible to get an answer in this house.'

'Well, I thought it was the vapours,' he glared at his brother and then shifted his fierce stare onto his mother, 'because of the crass way she had been treated. But no. She told me on the way to London that she never wants to see me again. Never!'

'Perhaps she'll change her mind?' Rudi suggested gently.

'No. I received a hand-delivered missive this morning telling me, no, instructing me not to contact her again. It was heartbreaking. All about how she loved me but it had become obvious to her that she could never be my wife.'

'Can't think why you couldn't have taken her as a mistress. That's what I would have done.' Maynard blew his nose, then returned to his reading.

Sebastian buried his face in his hands and Maynard looked at Lady Iris. 'Young love!' he remarked. 'Terrible thing! The very devil!'

'It's not Mamma's fault, Sebastian,' Rudi spoke quietly. 'Maeve is a bright, intelligent girl. She decided to put a stop to her involvement with you not because Mamma was beastly to her—' Lady Iris huffed and Rudi glanced at her — 'Although you were, Mater, you can't deny it—' he looked back at his brother — 'Or because she was intimidated by this great pile of stones, because she was not. I think she decided on the break because she did not

367

see herself giving up her career to run this place. Because she found it uncomfortable and she found us deadly boring! And that's the truth of it.'

'We are *not* boring!' Maynard declared angrily. 'Stuff and nonsense.'

'It is not uncomfortable,' Lady Iris said stony-faced.

'Oh, Mater. It's freezing! Look at us all. Shivering as if we were out there in a gale force wind!' Rudi pointed to the windows.

'That is not what Maeve said,' Sebastian cried.

'Of course it is not. But that is what she meant. She simply found Malvern not to her taste.'

'Are we boring?' Maynard asked. 'Must say I never thought so. But are we?'

'If the cap fits, Father, wear it.' Rudi stood up, holding his book to his chest. 'She is quite enchanting, Sebastian, and the loss is ours. No wonder the aristocracy is stale, flat and unprofitable. We live off the toil of others, we contribute nothing and when an opportunity to enliven our introverted and unimaginative world is sent to us by the gods we search for every means in our power to shut it out. Reject it. Oh dear me, what fools we are.'

'What is the boy talking about?' his father asked. 'Damned if I can understand one word in three.'

'I am going to the library. Dead genius is better company than the tedious and dull living.'

He was gone before his mother could object. Sebastian ground his teeth. 'I will *not* do as she asks. I love her too much.'

'If you love her as much as you say then that's exactly what you'll do – what she asks,' Lady Iris stated.

Maynard looked over his son's bent head at his wife. 'Opposition only strengthens love,' he said. ''Fraid you blew it, Iris old girl. Made matters worse!'

'Oh shut up, Maynard,' Lady Iris so far forgot herself as to snap.

Sebastian stood up and strode to the door. 'I'm returning to London,' he said.

'But you've just come down,' his father cried.

'Well I'm going back. Got to *do* something. Got to see

her.' He bowed briefly, 'Mater. Pater,' and turning on his heel was gone.

'Oh dear me, dear, dear me. What a pother. What a fuss. Told you, Iris, to leave them alone. It would blow over. Told you, least said. Didn't I? Told you you don't understand men. Gel herself is too intelligent to marry him. I could have got him a willin' filly. Once he was satisfied he'd soon go off the actress, though must say she is a perfect pippin. Now you've fixated him, Iris. Challenged him. The Davenports could never resist a challenge. You've put an obstacle in his way and now he's . . .'

'If you do not stop this instant, Maynard, I shall scream!' Lady Iris announced. He looked at her and saw she was serious, so he picked up the *Gazette* and began to read the latest article about Home Rule in Ireland.

Chapter Sixty-Four

cᴐ ɠᴐ

Maeve's lovely face was swollen from crying. Her tears flowed, Belle was glad to see, in a torrent. Belle didn't approve of tight-lipped acceptance; she preferred the dams to burst and thereby bring relief.

'And she has nothing to show for it,' she moaned to Bert. 'No jewels, no little advantages. Dear me, what a waste.'

Belle's own rouged and raddled cheeks were damp, as was the bodice of her black bombazine where Maeve's cheek had lain every day now for a week as she returned from rehearsals and lay weeping on the older woman's bosom.

Tilly made tea and kept the samovar topped up while Bert brought them food from The Horse and Hounds. They lived on pork pie and eel stew and savaloy and mash. Tilly stewed tripe and onions, but no one had much of an appetite and they subsisted on tea and Mariott's Luxury Biscuits.

Maeve refused all contact with Sebastian. She returned his flowers and his notes unopened. Belle was bewildered.

'Why can't you be his mistress?' she asked reasonably.

'Don't you see? I love him too much to have only one part of him. I couldn't share him.'

'At least you'd have half of him,' Belle said. 'I would have thought that that would be better than nothing. This way you'll not see him at all.'

'His mamma will marry him off to Fanny Ginsborg and she will be a perfect Duchess. She will make him an excellent wife.' Maeve was beating the pillow as if it was the enemy. 'She will play their games with them, but oh, Belle, I would be so bored!'

'That is why you'd best be his mistress,' Belle stated calmly.

'No. No. No. You don't understand. I love him too much. I couldn't bear the thought of him going to her bed! I would poison her, scratch her eyes out. Kill her. Oh, don't you understand?'

Belle sighed and shook her plum-red curls which trembled near her cheeks in clusters held by pink ribbons. She didn't understand.

'I do,' Bert said. ''S not right, bein' a mistress, oh beggin' yer pardon, Mrs Desmond, dear. Maeve's been brought up a Christian, even if she is a Catholic, God help her, so's she knows the right from the wrong.'

'I don't see anything *wrong* in it,' Maeve cried, 'I just don't think I could bear it, that's all!' And she fell to sobbing again.

'Does no one any harm as I can see,' Belle muttered. 'Does a lot of people a lot of good 'smatter of fact.'

'Well, maybe it's not for Maeve,' Bert said tactfully.

They all missed Demara. It was only after her departure that it became obvious how untiringly and uncomplainingly she had laboured for their comfort. Tilly tried very hard and was willing, but, as she told Belle, 'Demara must 'ave 'ad the constitution of an ox and the stamina of an 'orse. No matter 'ow 'ard I try I just can't manage it all. Not the cookin' an' the ironin' an' the cleanin' an' the sweepin' an' the polishin' an the dustin' an' the layin' of the fires an' the cleanin' of the grates an' the sewin' an' the mendin' an' the shoppin' . . .'

'Stop it, Tilly, stop! Bless the girl, she makes it sound like a litany.' Belle pressed her hands to her bosom. 'Your sister was a marvel,' she told Maeve.

'I know,' Maeve agreed and hiccupped and trembled and a sob rose in her throat and her head sank on Belle's shoulder and she was off again.

'We could get another girl from the convent,' Belle said over her head to Tilly. 'To help you.' She soothed Maeve's thick hair with plump fingers. Tilly's eyes lit up.

'Oh, I know just the one. Rose is her name. She is my friend. She nearly came to you 'ere 'stead of me but the Reverend Mother can't bear to part with her. Oh, that'd be great, mum.'

'Yes, well, we'll see. Meantime we have to get this young lady ready for the theatre.'

Surprisingly enough (or not, depending on how one looked at it), Maeve found she could give splendid performances, grief or no grief. She channelled her pain into her new role, one eminently suited to her frame of mind.

Belle had gone to see Geoffrey Denton. She explained what had happened and the actor-manager was relieved for he had been able to glean only from gossip what was happening to his leading lady.

'She has been working on her nerves, Mrs Desmond,' he told her. 'On a knife edge. I have been worried. I care about my artists, and Maeve is a very special creature.'

'I think, Mr Denton, that your next production should be *Romeo and Juliet*.'

'But the publicity already promises *Othello*,' he told her. 'I think it is too late to change now.'

'If you do it now you'll get a performance from Maeve Donnelly that will electrify London.'

Geoffrey Denton's eyes lit up. 'I think I see what you are getting at. I noticed in rehearsal that she is using the grief she feels in the role . . .'

'And Desdemona is not in the same category as Juliet, is she?'

'I get your point . . .'

'And she has been reading it. She knows the lines.'

'Madam, you are most probably correct. I'm a trifle old for Romeo, but I'll have one more crack at it.'

He decided to take Belle's advice and the play was acclaimed a triumph, Maeve's performance as Juliet forcing the critics to run out of words to praise her. As far as they were concerned it was the greatest Juliet in the history of the theatre. The reception was rapturous.

Still Maeve grieved. Deep down inside her a tide of loneliness and sorrow threatened to overwhelm her. She had never been unhappy and the experience was new. She examined it to see how it worked so that she could draw on her experience for her acting.

She had allowed herself to fall in love with Sebastian and, innocent that she was, she had been sure that somehow or another it would work out, that they could surmount all obstacles. But the game of truth and consequences had begun and she was too truthful not to face the consequences.

The hardest part was keeping Sebastian away from her. She wanted so desperately to run into his arms and ask him to make it all go away. Give in. Give up. She knew if she relented and went to him she would end up in his bed. It would be inevitable. And then the pain she suffered now would be as nothing compared to the agony she would set herself up for. In the eyes of society she would be ruined; a girl like Bryony with a reputation to match and she could never change it. She would have set her foot on a path there was no leaving. She felt no moral superiority about this, just knew she would feel cheap and cheated.

She loved him so much. Everything in her ached for him. She thirsted for him as a traveller in the desert thirsts for water. She was glad Demara was gone for her sister's sake, for at night she threshed and turned about, her limbs restless, her body on fire.

But she did not go to him. Did not see him. Kept her word. Her determination, that strength her parents had bestowed upon her, that dedication that helped her achieve success in the theatre gave her the courage to remain inflexible.

Sebastian bombarded her with flowers, letters, bonbons. He came to the theatre every night. She could see him in the box, his pale, intent face leaning on clasped hands as he stared at her fixedly.

When Romeo first sees her:
'It seems she hangs upon the cheek of night
Like a rich jewel in an Ethiop's ear—'
she could hear Sebastian sigh and she heard the words again as if he and not the ageing Geoffrey Denton spoke them. And when, in the balcony scene, Romeo said,
'. . . for stony limits cannot hold love out—'
she could see her lover sit up, straighten in his seat and she would look out into the darkness at his face and cry,
'Dost thou love me? I know thou wilt say Ay:
And I will take thy word: yet, if thou swear'st
Thou may'st prove false—'
and her voice would break, then soar with longing:
'Oh gentle Romeo, If thou dost love, pronounce it
faithfully—'
and the audience nightly heard him groan and all of London talked about Lord Sebastian Davenport in his box playing Romeo to Maeve Donnelly's Juliet. They came in droves to see the superb performance on the stage and the drama enacted in the box.

The role exhausted her. She put so much of herself into it. When she got to the chilling scene in the tomb of the Capulets –
'I have a faint cold fear thrills through my veins, That
almost freezes up the heat of life—'
she indeed felt the freezing fear and ached for him again and the terrible emptiness that opened up, grave-like in his absence. But she remembered too the little peasant girl in Ballymora listening to the touring actress speak the lines and she knew she had come a long, long way and had gained too much to lose now. She would not end up in a grave.

At the final curtain the audience saw that both Juliet on

the stage and Lord Sebastian Davenport in his box had tear-stained cheeks and that they could not tear their glances from each other. All London marvelled and gossiped and even the cynics were strangely moved.

Sebastian broke down the dressing-room door. She had refused to let him in to see her, so eventually, some weeks later, he used brute force to come face to face with his love.

She reached for Polly. She would have fallen if her dresser had not caught her in a firm grip. Maeve's face was white and her eyes looked bruised and hurt. She had lost weight and she stared at him helplessly.

'Oh please,' she implored him, clinging to Polly, 'please! Are you trying to kill me? If you love me, stay away.'

Her voice was so despairing that he was cut to the quick and he left with the words he had planned to say still-born on his lips.

After that it was easier. He came no more to the theatre. The box stayed empty and while each night she looked for him and was filled with despair when she saw he was not there, his absence took away the sharpness of her pain which in time became an ache.

She missed her sister terribly but in fact Demara's sympathy would only have impeded her recovery. Belle was brisk. She did not advocate moping over men and her common sense attitude helped the young actress enormously.

Geoffrey was delighted that Belle had talked him into doing *Romeo and Juliet*, and he now decided to shelve *Othello* and commence rehearsals for *The Taming of the Shrew*.

'She cannot sustain another emotional role, Geoffrey,' Belle had told him. 'Katerina will perk her up. The part is great fun and you can always do *Othello* later in the year.'

The actor-manager agreed with her advice, and rehearsals started. Maeve threw herself into her work and asked the famous Signora Montecelli to give her singing lessons. She filled her days with work, gave brilliant performances each evening and eventually, weeks later, when at the beginning of June she read in the society column of *The Times* that Lord Sebastian Davenport had announced his betrothal to Lady Fanny Ginsborg of Henly House, she did not break down. In fact she was surprised how calmly she took the announcement. She had mourned her lost love and now it was over. She put aside her childishly unthinking trust, decided to be more philosophical about life and worked even harder.

Chapter Sixty-Five

༄ ༄

Ballymora was a hive of activity. Earth, clay, stones, thatch, carts, nails and brick, breakneck toil, back-breaking labour – everyone was absorbed. Quarrels broke out, petty disputes, anger, slights, jealousies and covetousness, envy and pride. All the vices made an appearance, giving Father Maguire justification in his own estimation to rail about man's sinful nature. Dinny McQuaid was sure Mog Murtagh had a better site than he had for his cottage. It worried at him day and night. It spoiled his appetite. It even helped him forget his suspicions about Sheena's odd absences from the building site and the barn. Shooshie Sheehan demanded his cottage face the sea so he could sit of a night and watch the evening star, but where he ended up he faced the hills. He felt fenced in. He was dissatisfied.

Delia McCormack faced the sea and she didn't like it. But she wasn't going to let Shooshie have it, in case there was a snag to Shooshie's bit of land that was not at the moment apparent. She sensed a trap in it and refused to swap. They fell out about it, to nobody's surprise. Almost everyone was on bad terms with one neighbour or another.

They were building the cottages in a circle and Duff Dannon remarked that they had better put the doors at the back as none of them would be speaking to the others by the time they were finished.

They were agreed on one thing. They all of them

resented the Donnellys. Pierce, as usual, was efficient and set about building his new home energetically, therefore his building progressed and flourished and was well in advance of the others. There was no time off for skiving down to the barn for a jar and Brigid and Brindsley worked in a dedicated fashion and did not complain. The other cottagers hated this example. The Donnellys did not play the game.

Demara did not help her mother and father. Demara was not there with them. She was at Bannagh Dubh.

'Did ye see Demara Donnelly beyond in Bannagh Dubh wi' a spade in her hands an' she diggin' the earth like a labourin' man?' Delia McCormack asked the aghast villagers.

'She's diggin' a better house than any of us,' Deegan Belcher muttered with disgruntled pessimism. 'Who the divil does she think she is?'

'Do ye *want* a bigger house, Deegan?' Clancy inquired as he was passing by, a bucket in his hands. Deegan looked confused. 'There is nothing to stop you or anyone building a house the size of the castle if you choose to, Deegan,' Clancy added.

'Well an' I don't know about that Mr Clancy,' Deegan said with a surly glare at the moonlighter.

'Clancy, please.'

'An' here comes the grand man himself, Pierce Donnelly.'

'Will ye give over, Deegan! There's nothing the Donnellys father or daughter can do that ye can't. So stop yer complainin' and blamin' all yer problems on Pierce and Demara. Give over!'

Clancy had raised his voice and spoke loud enough for most of them to hear him. It would not do any good, he knew. They were resentful by nature, wary, suspicious and frightened. They took nothing for granted and expected the worst. They liked everyone of their group to conform and it was Pierce Donnelly's dedication and his daughter's enterprise that they looked on with distrust.

Pierce Donnelly smiled at Clancy. 'They compare!' he said. 'They blame themselves for not keeping up when one of us seeks better things. They look on it as a reproach and think they should try to do the same.'

'They'll not rise above the mire then. None of us would if there were not the likes of you to show it can be done. But don't expect them to like you for it.'

Pierce shook his head and Clancy looked at him intently. 'But your girl now!' he frowned, drawing his beetle-brows together. 'What the divil is she doin' out there in the wilds of Bannagh Dubh an' she a woman an' a young 'un at that?'

'She'll do what she'll do!' Pierce replied laconically. 'No one can tell Demara what to do.'

'Well, good luck to her,' the moonlighter said and proceeded to his task.

The cottagers were grateful for the help the moon-lighters gave them. Now that they had a different source of resentment the moonlighters were welcomed and their help building the cottages was found invaluable.

Demara was up to her neck in mud. The month of April had been wet and May promised more rain. The peach-blossom behind Ballymora Castle was dressing the trees in pale clusters of pink and the daffodils beside the river nodded their heads in the breeze, shivering and shaking off the raindrops that trembled on their petals. But it rained.

At first sight the task Demara had set herself seemed impossible. It would have defeated an architect with armies of helpers. But she remained undaunted. She tackled the job with determination and optimism.

'If we have to take up the stones one by one, Cogger, we'll do it,' she told him and Cogger rolled his tongue around his tombstone teeth and nodded eagerly, saying nothing. He knew that the stones were too heavy to be moved by himself and Demara but he knew too her dogged intent.

Help came from an unexpected quarter. Lady Kitty Lester, out riding one day, came upon Demara, fisherman's wellingtons on her feet, the hem of her mud-covered skirt tucked up into her waistband, digging the foundations of her house with Cogger Kavanagh in close attendance.

'What on earth are you doin', girl?' she asked, reigning in her dark brown mare. 'You'll not find mussels here. It's too far inland, don't you know. And anyway the ditches you are digging are far too deep.'

'I'm building a house, my lady,' Demara replied, straightening up and licking the raindrops off her top lip. ''Tisn't mussels I'm after.'

'I thought the land I allocated was at Dead Man's Pool, near the river?' Lady Lester remarked.

'This is not your land, my lady. It belongs to nobody. And I have chosen to build here.'

'Away from all your friends?'

'Yes, my lady.'

'But are you serious? It's a cold and windy place and I doubt you'll succeed. Are you quite sure?'

'Yes, my lady. Quite sure. I've always dreamed of having a house here.'

'It's a wild stretch and no mistake,' Lady Kitty shook her head.

'It's the garden of the world to me, my lady,' Demara told her.

'Have you seen Phil Conlon recently?' Lady Lester asked.

Demara nodded. 'He is down below helping Ma Stacey to build her shebee . . . her house.'

'Tell him I'd like to see him. Oh, and in case he gets uppity tell him I want him back. I have no one to help me and if we want to frustrate my wayward son's wilder intentions, then I'll need his help. Tell him I said so.' She smiled at Demara. The girl looked rooted in the earth, part of it, her clothes stained with soil, her bare legs poking out of the boots caked with mud. 'Tell him the coach horses are running wild in the fields and I cannot find the groom. Such a state of affairs could not exist if he were there. Tell him that Topthorn has cast a shoe three times and the smith says if he goes on like this there will be no hoof left to get a nail in! Everything is in a muddle and I need him. Tell him that, please.'

The image of the girl toiling in the mud, flanked by the

village idiot working with her, stayed in Lady Kitty's mind. When she reached home she changed her habit for a light wool day dress and came downstairs to the drawing-room where she had ordered tea to be served.

Her guest entered the room moments after she had seated herself in front of the fire and begun to pour the tea. Vernon Blackstock had just taken the cup from her when she looked up as the door opened and her visitor came into the room.

'Evening, Perry,' she greeted him warmly. 'Come in, come in and join us for tea.'

'Was it beastly out?' Lord Dawkins asked.

'Not in the least, Perry. You've become soft, living in London. Here you are, your tea. Milk? Sugar? Lemon?'

'Lemon.'

'No, my ride was very enjoyable, thank you. You know Vernon Blackstock, our solicitor? Lord Peregrine Dawkins.'

The men shook hands.

'I saw the most amazing thing just now, Perry. Quite extraordinary! Down in Bannagh Dubh. It looked like a painting by Constable. A scene from a hundred years ago.'

'What did you see?' Vernon Blackstock was stirring his tea.

'A girl. Quite a beautiful girl. You know how they are hereabouts, a mane of black curls and huge blue eyes. Her kirtle was tucked into her waist and her legs and skirt were caked with muck. She had that idiot fellow with her. He was helping her. And do you know what she was doing?' she asked and continued without waiting for a reply. 'She was digging the foundations of a house she said she was going to build! There in Bannagh Dubh. Can you believe that?' She shook her head incredulously, 'Even now I'm inclined to think I imagined the whole thing. Do you know who it could be, Mr Blackstock?'

'Yes. I know who that is. It's Demara Donnelly.'

'I asked her about Phil Conlon. I want to entice him back here. I declare I can't do without him and, you know, Mr Blackstock, now that I've decided to stay here . . . Perry where are you off to?'

Perry had put down his cup and saucer and was leaving. He glanced back at Kitty.

'I think I'll go for a ride,' he said. 'Before it gets dark. You are right, Kitty. I've allowed myself to stagnate in London and I suddenly feel the desire for exercise. If you'll excuse me?'

'Of course, dear man. Take Barabas.'

Peregrine walked to the door then turned. 'Bannagh Dubh? Where is that?'

'Down near the sea. Below the house and to the west. Dinner is served at nine, Perry.'

'Expect to see me then. Oh, and may I bring a guest? Will that inconvenience you?'

'Not in the least, Perry.'

Lord Dawkins left the room.

'Will you stay to dinner, Mr Blackstock? I would love to have your company. The coach can deliver you home later.'

He told her he would love to. He was most blest of men. His Moll would not mind. She was such an amiable creature and always urged him to accept stray or casual invitations. 'And chart everything to tell me later, for I'll quiz you, pet, you know I will,' she would tell him roguishly.

They sat on either side of the log fire sipping their tea and nibbling whiskey-cake. Then Lady Lester brushed down her skirt and smiled at the solicitor.

'I missed Ballymora so much when I was in London,' she told him. 'You cannot imagine how much I wanted to come home to this old pile.' She gave a little laugh. 'You know, Mr Blackstock, I really thought I would love to be back in the thick of things again, the theatres, the fashion, the wonderful parties, but I was wrong! Linton, bless him, had me persuaded. But the town has changed so since I was a gal. It is so crowded now and dirty. Some parts are quite shocking. And the poverty there is appalling, 'pon my word it is.'

She picked up her embroidery but left it lying in her lap. 'There was fog too. Ugh!' She shuddered delicately. 'No. I did not like it in the least, Mr Blackstock, and all my old friends seem to . . . how shall I say . . . lack grace. They seem overly fearful of the approach of age and dress most improperly, as if they were still in their girlhood. There is such a race to keep up with the fashion that within a month I was quite done up. So I said to myself, let Linton stay. Dear boy is having a top-hole time enjoying himself, cutting a dash around town. I told him, sell the house in Curzon Street, get yourself a bachelor apartment. Much cheaper. Toss your hat over the windmill, m'boy. Told him to have fun. Not much time for that later, eh, Mr Blackstock? Youth flies so fast. Blink and it's gone.'

Vernon Blackstock felt very doubtful about the wisdom of leaving Linton Lester loose in the fleshpots of London and giving him such advice. He hoped Lady Kitty had kept a tight reign on some of the stocks and shares she had inherited from Lord Edward and had not signed too much of the estate over to her son.

Then he gave up worrying. The heat of the fire, his full belly, the comfort of the winged and padded chair all conspired to relax him and remove all earthly considerations. He nodded off.

Lady Kitty smiled when she saw the slow decline of chin onto chest. Dear old friend, she thought. How I miss Edward!

She rose eventually and as dusk fell and the shadows lengthened she tiptoed from the room. Vernon Blackstock would awaken when he was rested.

Chapter Sixty-Six

∽ ∾

'Hello there!'

Demara heard the voice. For a moment she thought she had dreamed it. Perhaps it was a figment of her imagination. Like the stranger.

'Demara Donnelly!'

She turned, ankle-deep in mud, and looked up. She had discarded her fisherman's boots and was barefoot. The boots had filled with muck in the rain and they slowed her down.

He sat there on top of his black hunter, monkey-face wrinkled up in a smile, his blue eyes sparkling and dancing, looking at her with amusement and admiration.

'Perry!' she yelled, absurdly glad to see him. She pulled herself out of the muck as he slid from the saddle. He hugged her, lifting her off her feet, swinging her around.

'Perry! You'll get yourself filthy! I'm all covered in . . .'

But he swung her around again and she threw back her head and laughed, laughed for the first time since she came home. The ribbon binding her hair slipped off and her hair floated free around her.

He put her down eventually. ' 'Pon my soul, it's good to see you,' he said. Then he looked around and took it all in: the sea crashing and thundering on the tar-black rocks, the purple and gold mountains, the lake, slate-grey, tall reeds standing sentinel around it and the swans bending over their own reflections. The sheer grandeur of the spectacle took his breath away. They stood for a moment, side by side, absorbing the beauty.

'So this, Demara Donnelly, this is the magnificence you dream about?'

She nodded.

'Ah, Demara, it is a worthwhile dream,' he said. 'Though for myself I prefer it houseless.' He frowned. 'The landscape is wild. It will never be tamed, I do not think. A house here is . . . superfluous.'

She flushed. 'Oh, Perry, don't spoil it. I want it so much . . .'

'How the Devil, Demara, do you expect to do it?' he asked.

She looked at him slyly, as if wondering whether to confide in him or not. Then, making up her mind, she took his hand in hers. 'Come with me,' she said, drawing him around the lake and down to the cliff-face. Cogger hopped behind, waiting. Watching. Who was this well-dressed stranger? Cogger was wary but hopeful. Duff's defection had confused and perplexed Cogger. He could not imagine how Duff could choose to marry Dana. Cogger's loyalty was passionate.

Demara had come home only to find her lover had betrayed her – this was how Cogger saw it. Now a stranger had arrived on the scene. Not like the other one, not remote, insubstantial, strange, but a flesh-and-blood man with expensive clothes and smiling eyes.

But he was older than Duff by at least a decade. Not old like Granny Donnelly, but older than Demara, nearer her father's age.

Cogger decided to keep a close eye on things. He liked this man, his steady hands, his air of calm authority. And he had made her laugh. She had been pleased to see him, that much was obvious. But she had been hurt. He had seen her weep. He would not let such a thing happen again; he would protect her. He would die for her.

All he wanted of this life was to watch over Demara, be her guardian angel.

'Look, Perry,' she pointed. 'Down there, below.'

They knelt on the cliff and peered over. He stared, rubbed his eyes and gasped. 'Great heavens above!' he cried. 'Demara, it's Ancient Greece. It's Rome, it's Augustus. How the Devil did that get here?'

'I don't know,' she said, grinning at him, her teeth chattering now in the coldness of the wind from the sea. 'I don't care. I don't bother with questions like that.'

'Great heavens above!' he cried again in astonishment. 'It's a treasure! It's a bloomin' miracle.' He looked into her sparkling eyes. 'And how do you mean to get it up to the lake?' he asked.

'I don't know,' she replied, laughing. 'I just know I will.'

He stood, then leaned down and held out his hands to her. She put hers into his firm grasp and he drew her to her feet.

'Demara, you are a wonder!' he said, then added, 'Let me help you.'

'Would you?' Her face became serious. 'I am in earnest about this, you know, Perry. I mean to do it, with or without anyone's help.'

'I know,' he replied.

She smiled again. 'My father always says that it is a foolish and short-sighted man who rejects help because of his pride, and my father is a very wise man,' she told him.

'It sounds like wisdom to me,' he said.

'Then I accept your offer of help with gratitude.'

He looked at her and began to laugh, still holding her hands.

Cogger stood at a respectful distance and watched.

'What is so funny?' she asked.

'You! If your friends in London could see you now . . . you look like a gypsy or a horse thief.'

She was not disconcerted. This man never made her feel uncomfortable.

'What friends?' she asked him. 'Maeve has seen me like this many times. Bert and Belle would not care a hoot. Belle is an actress and therefore unsurprisable. Bert is good. A good man is never critical of his friends' state of dress.' She peered up at him. 'And I don't have any other friends there,' she said. 'Not really. Just a lot of people I know. And you know, Perry, out of all the people I met there the one I'd go to if I was in trouble, Bryony Gilligan, is not what you might consider a paragon of propriety, is she?'

He nodded, and she continued, 'Maybe those people might learn something from the way I look now, Perry. Maybe they would see that I'm a deal happier like this than all swanked up in corsets and frills.'

'Well, do you think you could bear them for one evening?' he asked her. She looked surprised. 'Could you change into halfway respectable clothes?'

'And why would I do that?' she asked him archly.

'Why? Because I ask you. And because I should like to call on you this evening about eight o'clock and take you up to Ballymora Castle as Lady Lester's guest for dinner.'

She swallowed. She had been used to elegant company in London, but this was different. She had grown up a peasant girl on Lester land. She had skivvied in the Lester castle. She had bobbed to Lord and Lady Lester when they rode past and her father touched his cap to them. To go there as a social equal to sit at table with them was daunting.

384

But she did not hesitate for long. 'I would be delighted,' she said.

'Then it is decided. Where shall I find you?'

She could have told him she would meet him at the crossroads. She could have arranged a rendezvous near the church, but she had a desire to be totally honest with this man, to let him see where she came from, to hide nothing. She also wanted him to see what had been done to them.

'You follow the boreen to the east from here, down past the church. On the right you will come to a burnt-out wilderness. Even the trees don't grow there any more. That is where we used to live. Our homes were burned down there and my granny died in the flames. The houses were set alight, as I told you, by a man called Muswell on the orders of the Marquis of Killygally.'

She stared at him and her eyes were cold. 'I hate that man, Perry. I hate him so.'

'I know,' he said. 'I know.'

'How could you?' she flared. 'What has he ever done to you?'

'He married my little sister,' Lord Dawkins said slowly. 'And he destroyed her.'

Demara digested this. She had wondered why he had sought information about the Marquis and now she knew. It was another bond between them.

'I will tell you about it later,' he said. 'Tell me how to find you tonight.'

'When you are in the wilderness where once we lived, you'll see ahead of you, towards the sea, a large barn. That is where we pig it,' she said angrily. 'That is where we have to pack in together like cattle for the fair. Oh, the injustice of it.'

He nodded, not saying anything, holding her hands, letting her sense his sympathy.

'I have been so sad, Perry. I have been grieving for my grandmother until now. Since I came home I have been yearning after an old passion. Someone I . . . lost.'

'Duff Dannon.'

'How do you know?'

'You told me, remember? When I asked you to marry me.'

She blushed and drew her hands gently away from his and turned her face to the sea.

'And your sister filled in the name.'

The sun had reached the horizon and shone, a brilliant bronze shield. She squinted in the light.

'And you remembered the name?' she said softly.

'I remembered it,' he paused. 'I remember everything about you. Everything you ever said. Everything Maeve ever told me about you.' He stared out at the shimmering sea, then asked, 'You lost him?'

'When I came back he was married to my sister.'

'Then he was not worthy of you,' he said firmly and with finality. 'I'll go to the barn at eight o'clock. I will have the carriage.'

He leaned over and kissed the corner of her mouth. His lips were gentle and soft and sweet. Then he turned and strode back to his horse, mounted it and galloped away. She watched him, hand shielding her eyes until he disappeared over the horizon.

'Come on, Cogger,' she cried. 'We have at least another hour before it gets too dark to work.' And her voice sounded more cheerful to him than it had since her return.

Chapter Sixty-Seven

༄ ༄

Demara had to bathe herself in the cold stream that evening. The water was icy and she could not help but yearn for the hot tub available at all times of the day and night in Soho Square. However, there was no other way to clean the mud and sweat off her body. There was no tub, no way of heating water, so she had to plunge into the icy depths to shift the muck she had acquired about her person during her working day.

In the barn she dressed herself and tried to remain impervious to the curiosity and jealous jibes and teasing that went on all around her at the sight of her elegant dress.

She looked regal in the blue-black silk and velvet frock trimmed with beads and sequins, aware that she looked incongruous in the crowded, smelly barn.

'Gawny, lookit Demara Donnelly! Thinks she's the Princess Royal!' Delia McCormack taunted her.

'God'n she's a great sight entirely,' Carmel O'Gorman sneered. 'Far too grand for the likes of us.'

'I made it!' she told them. 'I stitched every bead myself.'

But that passed over their heads, so intent were they on their derision. After all, who did she think she was, aping her betters?

'Be careful, Demara Donnelly, or ye'll trip over yer pride,' Della Gilligan remarked.

'Don't mind them, love, it's jealousy,' Brigid whispered.

But the women heard. 'Ooo! Hark at that. We're jealous of Lady Muck here. Up to her armpits in mud in the day an' puttin' on airs and graces of an evening'.'

'Notice she's not sayin' a thing to us! Far too grand!' Jinny Murtagh sniffed.

Demara looked up, and met her sister's eyes. She flinched from the malevolent glare Dana directed towards her, watching her motionless from the end of the barn. The sisters had not exchanged a word since Demara's return. Dana had assiduously avoided her and Demara had no intention of seeking her out.

'Oh, the Donnellys is always gettin' above themselves.'

The words rang out strong and clear and there was real venom in Delia McCormack's taunt. Demara turned away in disgust. But she made no reply.

And then she was ready, her hair piled high on her head, stockings on her legs and dainty shoes on her feet. The taunts had died down and the women were now gazing at this regal and stunning creature in their midst, as if she were from another world.

The door flew open and Perry Dawkins stood there in his high-polished shoes, his evening dress, his top hat and his black cloak lined with crimson satin, a silver-topped cane in his hand.

'Good evening to you,' he cried.

'Perry,' Demara greeted him gladly and, picking up her pelisse, made for the entrance.

Duff stood near the door and Dana rose and stood beside him. He glowered at the strange man. Perry took Demara's hand and tucked it through his arm. They left the barn and a stunned silence behind them.

In the carriage Demara collapsed in laughter. 'Oh, that was worth a sovereign!' she chortled, her laughter so infectious that Perry had perforce to join in although he did not know what he was laughing at.

'Did you see their faces? No, of course you didn't. Oh, it was priceless. Some of my neighbours are jealous cats!'

Perry's face became serious. 'Be careful, Demara. Emotions like that can be very dangerous. Remember violent emotions produce violent reactions.'

'I've got Cogger,' she said.

'I saw him today, near us on the headland.'

She gave him a conspiratorial smile. 'He'll be hanging out of the back of your carriage this minute, I'll be bound.'

'Why did you ever lose that glorious accent when you were in London?' he asked her.

'Didn't we have to? Maeve to be an actress, me to be acceptable. You English think, when you hear the accent, that we are inferior beings. Did you know that? And it is quite difficult to get work, or lodgings. Or anything for that matter. Let us say, it was expedient for me to lose my accent.'

He nodded. 'There's a hierarchy everywhere, Demara. Every member of the human race feels superior to someone else. It seems the idea of equality makes us nervous. We like having someone to despise, to look down on. But did it ever occur to you that the people we deride are usually those we are jealous of? They are people who have something we would dearly like to possess. Like those people in the barn. They want your enterprise; they are jealous of your beauty, your spunk.'

'But the English don't envy the Irish. They think we are

stupid. It has even been suggested in Parliament that our brains are smaller.'

'That is guilt. Excuses because they have stolen your land. They are forever trying to justify themselves.'

He turned to her as the carriage rolled over the gravel of the drive. 'But do not let us be too serious tonight,' he said. 'I want you to enjoy yourself, my dear girl; you have grieved enough. The time has come now for you to have a good time, and if I can bring a little happiness into your life then I'll count myself privileged.'

She smiled back at him. 'Oh, Perry,' she replied, 'you already have.'

Chapter Sixty-Eight

∽∾ ∾∾

'What a delightful gel! Where did you find her, Perry, you clever man?'

Lady Lester, resplendent in purple taffeta, rose to greet Demara and her guest from London.

'In your backyard, Kitty,' Perry Dawkins told her.

Lady Kitty put her eye-glass to her eye and exclaimed, 'Why it's the ragamuffin from Bannagh Dubh! Well, m'dear, I must say you scrub up beautifully.'

'May I present Miss Demara Donnelly, Kitty. Don't you think she is quite a discovery?'

'Ah! You are one of Pierce Donnelly's beautiful girls, eh? Yes, I've heard about you. We hear everything up here, y'know. Are you acquainted with Mr Vernon Blackstock?'

Vernon Blackstock nodded and smiled before Demara could reply. 'Indeed, my lady, I know Miss Donnelly well.'

'Well, sir,' Demara dimpled, 'I of course know you, but whether a person of your importance was aware of my existence seems to me unlikely.'

Lady Kitty clapped her hands. 'She is joshing us! Oh,

what a pretty wit. Delightful! Are there many such more surprises to be found among the cottagers?'

'The gulf, my lady, is almost unbridgeable,' Demara told her. 'You must be aware of that.'

' 'Deed I am, and I consider it deplorable and a waste to boot,' Lady Kitty said succinctly.

Vernon Blackstock rose from his chair, 'You must excuse me, Miss Donnelly, for being improperly dressed for the occasion, but Lady Lester was kind enough to invite me . . . er . . .'

'At the last moment, poor man, giving him no time at all to go home and change. I have been assuring him that it is perfectly all right in the circumstances, quite proper, and we will forgive him.'

'Of course. Don't give it another thought.'

Demara found that she was enjoying herself hugely. Perry caught her eye every now and then and gave her an encouraging nod. Lady Lester did everything in her power to make her feel welcome and relaxed. There was no snobbery or condescension in her manner and between the four of them they had a merry evening until after the meal was over and they had repaired to the blue drawing-room, where the conversation turned serious.

'We will not send you men off to smoke by yourselves unless you insist, Demara? I do not mind a little cigar smoke, do you, child?'

Demara reassured her on that point, giggling to herself as she thought of the barn, and Kilty brought in the humidor. The men selected their cigars and sat back at some remove from Lady Lester and Demara, who rested on the couch so that the smoke would not cause them any discomfort.

If Kilty found Demara's presence peculiar he did not show it. Except for one moment at the beginning of the evening when he had realized whom he was serving and nearly dropped a plate. Nearly, but not quite. And Lady Lester whispered, 'Well done, Kilty,' to his great discomfiture.

'You must have been shocked, dear child, to come home and find your cottage burned to the ground.'

'Indeed I was, Lady Lester.'

'And you must be aware that I would not have permitted such a thing to happen if I had known about it.'

'What could you have done to stop it, Lady Lester? Nothing, I think,' Demara said.

'I saw it tonight, Kitty,' Perry told her. 'It is a disgrace. That such a thing could happen is barbaric to say the least . . .' He shook his head.

'And most of the tenants are up to date with their rent,' Vernon Blackstock mused. 'It is, strictly speaking, against the law to do that, but then, in the heel of the hunt, the landlord has, eventually, the ultimate right to do as he wishes. He has, er, em, the last word.'

'It was kind of you, Lady Lester, to give our people this new area to build on,' Demara said.

'It is what my late husband would have wanted. The very least I could do. Oh dear, everything is such a pickle since he died.' Quick tears sprang to her eyes. 'I miss him so.'

Demara leaned over and took her hostess's hand. 'I understand,' she said.

'Demara lost her grandmother in the fire,' Perry Dawkins told her.

Kitty sniffed. 'How such things can happen in this enlightened day and age I cannot imagine. Why, they tell me that child labour is being outlawed and that women are looking for the vote.'

'Well, I hardly think, dear Lady Lester, that anything so bizarre is likely to happen. However, it should not be possible to evict people and burn down their houses. It is not civilized.' Vernon Blackstock's jowly face was a rather alarming shade of red and Lady Kitty feared for his blood pressure. She made a little motion of her hand to Kilty who took the port decanter with him when he left the room.

'Have you heard any news of Fleur?' Lady Lester asked Perry.

He shook his head regretfully. 'No, Kitty, I have not. I saw Mrs Black, the nurse and companion who looks after my poor sister, but she had little news for me, as usual.'

'The Marquis abducted Perry's sister when he was serving in India and married her against her will,' Lady Kitty explained to Demara.

'I saw her once at our father's funeral,' Perry said. 'I came home from the East to attend it. I'd never really been close to her. I loved her, of course, but I was abroad most of her life. She was a fragile little thing – you know, one of those young girls, so innocent, so sheltered, so unprepared that you feel she must be protected from the harsh realities of life. Mother doted on my father. His death hit her hard, and I'll always blame myself that I did not notice how hard. I had to get back to Jaipur and I'm sorry to say I didn't worry too much when I didn't hear from the family. I guessed my mother was not in the humour to write and in any event the post was very unreliable. When eventually our family lawyers, who were very concerned about the state of my mother's mental health, got word to me, it was too late. Fleur was incarcerated in Stillwater, legally married to the Marquis of Killygally, and there was nothing I could do. He would not allow me to see her. I have not set eyes on her since my father's funeral, except glimpses I have caught of her through Bosie's window.'

'Oh, Perry, I cannot imagine how awful that must be for you.'

'I come here, every so often,' he told Demara. 'Kitty has been so kind to me. I try to see Fleur. Sometimes I catch sight of her at her window at Stillwater. I have grown to know where her apartments are situated.'

'Have you tried breaking in?' Demara asked. 'That's what I'd do. No one would stop me.'

'I'm thinking of Fleur. He would make her pay. The doctor here, Dr Martin, who attends her, is a very nice man. He is worried about the balance of her mind. He strongly advises against all shocks. He has also told me that whenever I try to see her or make a fuss, that terrible man . . .' He lowered his head, struggling with himself. After a moment he continued '. . . damages her. As in law he is entitled to do.'

He looked at Demara across the room and she murmured, 'That changes things.'

392

'I've tried to see her,' Lady Kitty said, 'but have never succeeded.'

'One day I'll make him pay for his cruelty,' Perry said, deadly serious. 'But I do not want to end up in gaol because I have broken the law. *He* is in the wrong, not I.'

'He has done so much damage hereabouts,' Lady Kitty sighed. 'Burning your cottages! Oh no, it was too much.'

'It was what your husband feared, Lady Lester,' Vernon Blackstock said, and she nodded.

'He was wise, my husband, a very sound man,' she told Demara. 'My dear, I cannot bear to think of you in that barn. I've been thinking, ever since you arrived this evening. Why don't you stay here with us? I would love to have your company, you have cheered me up so much tonight.'

Demara started to protest, but Lady Kitty held up her hand. 'No, no, let me finish, my dear. From all points of view it would be wonderful to have you here. I am very lonely and I would appreciate the company at meals. You would be more comfortable. It is much more convenient to Bannagh Dubh and you could use our amenities here to help you build your house. And, lastly, Perry too would love to have you here, I'm sure.'

'I would relish it,' he said. 'Your presence would be delightful, Demara, and you know it. And it would, as Lady Kitty says, be much more comfortable for you. Oh, do say yes! I could help you with the work.'

'Well . . . if you really think . . .' Demara hesitated.

'I do. And that's decided.' Lady Kitty smiled.

'I think though I had better take you back tonight,' Perry said regretfully, and stood up to stretch. 'We don't want to give your fellow cottagers anything to gossip about.'

He tucked her into the carriage. She felt well-fed for the first time in days. Since coming home she had been made aware of how monotonous and scarce their food now was. She felt warm. And she felt needed. Content. Privileged. This was how life should be.

She would be glad to get a change from neeps and tatties, the parsnips, oat-cakes and cabbage. She would welcome privacy again and being able to bathe in warm water. She suddenly realized that her nerves had been as taut as the violin strings on Shooshie's fiddle. She let out a long breath and leaned her head on Perry's shoulder. In a minute she was almost asleep.

When they reached the barn he handed her out and watched as she slid inside, turning only once to wave farewell to him before she disappeared.

Chapter Sixty-Nine

⊷ ⊶

Demara's arrival back at the barn was observed by two men. Cogger Kavanagh had, as she had guessed, got himself a ride up to Ballymora Castle hanging onto the back of Perry's carriage. On their arrival there Perry had had a word with Kilty, and Cogger found himself welcomed into the kitchen where Mags Moran had given him a bowl of soup, a large slice of ham and some pickled onions.

'Sit ye down, boy, an' fill yer belly,' Mags had instructed him, and he had done just that. Then when he had reassured himself that Demara was safe and happy, for he could hear her laughing in the dining-room, he had gone back to the vicinity of the barn and waited for her to come home.

He saw Duff come out and walk to the five-barred gate near the Lesters' meadow. He leaned on the gate and Cogger was going to go to him when he saw Dana leave the barn and walk timidly and uncertainly towards her husband.

'Come to bed, love,' she said. Cogger could hear her words clearly. The night was very still. He could hear the geese down near the river hissing at a fox, the splash of trout and the cry of the curlew in the distance.

'Lave me be!' Duff's answer was rough.

'Ah, Duff, stop this nonsense, won't ye? Yer my husband now. Why won't ye bed me like yer supposed to? Why d'ye hate me so?'

'You ask that?' He looked at her incredulously. 'It's wonderful how wishful thinkin' can become a reality for some! Oh, Dana, lave me be. I never wooed ye an' I'll never bed ye. My heart wouldn't be in it. Don't ye know that?'

'I'm all ye've got! I'm all ye'll ever have.'

'Ye don't know me, woman. I don't want to touch ye. I don't even want to be near ye.'

Dana drew in a sharp breath. She loved him. She had always loved him. She had done what she could to get him. All right, she had tricked him, but everyone knew that all was fair in love and war and she had gambled high.

She had thought she'd won when they got married. The peak moment in her whole life had been when she walked, leaning on her father's arm, from their cottage in the veil her mother had worn on her wedding day.

But she had lost. Lost more completely than if they'd never been married. She could stand anything except this terrible coldness, his disgust, his refusal to speak to her, to communicate with her in any way at all.

She looked at him with longing, not believing even now that she could not win. Then she took his hand and kissed it. 'I love you, Duff. I'll always love you.'

He pulled his hand away, wiped it on his jacket as if she had contaminated him.

'Lave me, Dana. I've nuthin' to say to ye.'

'It's Demara, isn't it? It's Demara. Only for her you'd love me.'

'Yes, Dana. I love Demara. I've always loved Demara. You knew that. It was common knowledge.'

'Well, I've fixed it so that you'll never have her,' Dana cried triumphantly, hating herself for saying it, wishing she could stop herself, seeing his loathing for her grow in his eyes. 'That night . . . you didn't have to . . . you didn't *have* to take my body, Duff. Ye liked it well enough that night.'

'Go away, Dana. Leave me be, for God's sake.'

Cogger saw her leave him and walk back to the barn. He

felt sorry for Dana. She loved someone she could never have. He understood that. He too loved the unattainable. He wished he could tell her what to do, but Dana was prickly. He would explain that the only thing to do was serve. Give love and expect no return. Devotion without reward. Giving without expecting anything back gave its own reward. You got something wonderful, but he did not know how or why. You felt a great warmth inside, a spring of joy, a well of content. He did not understand it, it was a mystery quite beyond his comprehension, and he knew Dana would never accept the premise even if he could explain it to her, which he could not.

He was going to speak to Duff when the carriage arrived back, Demara and Perry alighted and Demara went into the barn. Duff watched her. Cogger could not see the expression on his face but when she disappeared he turned back to the gate and leaned on it, his head in his hands. Cogger lay down under the hedge and closed his eyes.

Duff had seen a vision, someone he did not recognize. It was not the girl he had once walked out with. This was someone sophisticated and unreachable. Demara in that dress was a stranger to him. She was far above him, above them all. She was out of his class, remote as a star.

Was that all it took? Clothes? It did not matter, Duff mused, he would never wear the garb of a gentleman. He would be uncomfortable. Unlike Demara he could not wear fashionable finery. He had no desire to do so even if he could. He was ill-at-ease in his Sunday suit, the one he wore at his wedding, so he could imagine how he would feel in stylish clothes.

She had always had that crazy dream. A big house by the lake in Bannagh Dubh overlooking the sea. He had never shared that dream or even had sympathy with it. He had gone along with it but he had never understood it.

Demara's head was in the clouds. She was out of his grasp, slipping away from him, and there was nothing he could do about it. Her ambition far surpassed anything he might envisage. He was suddenly aware of the yawning chasm between them and with a despairing shrug he let her go. He gave up. The fight was unequal and he could not win. Married to her sister, poor as a tinker, homeless and with no prospects, he had absolutely nothing to offer, whilst she, in the full glory of her beauty, determined to build herself a home more imposing than anything he could imagine, polished with the gloss she had acquired in London, smartly dressed and groomed, she had the world at her feet if she wanted it.

He let his shoulders fall. All the energy left his stalwart frame and he bowed his head in defeat.

Chapter Seventy

⤴ ⤵

Tilly took a letter to the convent. She was told to wait for Reverend Mother in the cloisters. Rose was there, stitching as usual. She stood up when she saw Tilly, dropped the linen she was working on and ran to her friend.

'Tilly, Tilly, oh, how are you? And do you like your new home? We miss you here, really we do. Is your new mistress nice? Oh, tell me all, please, I want to hear everything.'

The June roses were out and the quiet arbours were full of their scent. The sun heated the stone flags beneath their feet and the girls sat together in the balmy day, their confidences bubbling over each other.

'She is kind and good,' Tilly said in answer to Rose's questions. 'She puts up with my awful clumsiness. You remember how I broke things, how awkward I am?'

Rose laughed. 'Oh, you were not too bad,' she replied and began to cough. Tilly looked at her closely. Rose looked pale as the linen she mended and there were deep shadows, like bruises, beneath her eyes.

'Have you been indisposed?' Tilly asked her, alarmed by her friend's pallor.

'I've not been very well, but I am better now,' Rose

replied, then, catching sight of Tilly's face, she protested, 'Do not look at me like that. I had a little cold and it went to my chest. Oh, it was nothing much and now it is nearly gone. They've been fussing over me here, feeding me calves' foot jelly and spinach soup until I am so full I cannot move.' She patted Tilly's hand. 'But why are you here? You haven't been sent away like Mary Jacks?'

'Not on your life! I've come to ask the Reverend Mother if she can let Mrs Desmond have another girl. You remember I told you that Maeve Donnelly, a great actress, lived with Mrs Desmond?' Rose nodded, listening to her friend with great attention. 'Her sister was the housekeeper. Well, now she has returned to Ireland and they don't know if she is coming back. She did a lot of work, Rose, worked like a 'orse, she did. There's too much for me, now she's gone. So, Mrs Desmond 'as written a letter to Reverend Mother asking for another girl.' She clasped Rose around her waist. 'I was 'oping they'd send you.'

'And so we would. So we would, Tilly my dear,' the Reverend Mother stood behind them. 'How are you, Tilly? Mrs Desmond says, now let me see,' she looked at the letter she held in her hand, 'Ah, yes. She says here "Tilly has been a god-send!" There now. Isn't that grand! Well now, as I was saying I would send Rose, but she has been far from well. We have been anxious about her and I truthfully do not think she is strong enough yet to do the work well.' She glanced at the letter again. 'Mrs Desmond says here "I need a girl with a strong back". So I thought of Angela.'

Tilly made a face.

'Why the face, Tilly?' Reverend Mother asked. 'Angela is a good, honest, truthful girl. She is a hard worker.'

'But she is such a gloom, Reverend Mother. She sees the black side of everything.'

'Then you must cheer her up.'

'Oh, I suppose she'll be all right. It was simply I wanted Rose so much.'

Everyone wanted Rose, the Reverend Mother reflected, including herself. She had never let the girl out of the convent because she was so terribly fond of her. So was everyone else.

She had given them a hard time this winter. She had been seriously ill and the doctor had warned then that her chest would always be weak, so she had a very good excuse for not letting her take up employment outside the convent.

But the Reverend Mother knew that part of Rose's malaise was the fact that she never went out. She was cut off from life and that was not good for her. She had not chosen the veil. She was, Reverend Mother thought, in limbo. Neither of the world or out of it. She said a silent prayer for guidance and then, almost involuntarily, she came to a swift decision. 'You may take Rose back with you to Soho Square, Tilly, and tell Mrs Desmond I'll write to her soon and that she is always in my prayers. Tell her also that Rose is not as strong as she perhaps hoped.' She smiled at them. 'Now, you girls have some lemonade together and a nice long chat while I get Rose's few bits and pieces together.'

Rose stared at the Reverend Mother as if she had lost her reason. Her face showed a mixture of dread and excitement. 'Leave here? Oh, Reverend Mother, do you think I should?' The Reverend Mother sat beside them a moment. 'My dear,' she said to Rose, 'I'm afraid I have been selfish, nurturing your delicacy, keeping you here all to ourselves when, in all fairness, I should give you a chance to find out what the world outside is like. I think I have been over-protective of you and this is the perfect opportunity. We have had only good reports of Mrs Desmond. Tilly is with her and she'll look after you, won't you, Tilly? See that she is well-treated, and if she is not, return her to us safe and sound? All right?' Tilly nodded emphatically and the Reverend Mother patted her hand. 'Good child. You will be perfectly safe, Rose, so do not worry, and you can come back here any time you want.'

Rose nodded. 'Very well, Reverend Mother.'

The Reverend Mother stood up. 'And now, children, I'll get Sister Agnes to prepare everything for you and Sister Monique will get you your drink.' She was about to leave them when a fit of coughing shook Rose's small frame. They both looked at her.

'She'll never manage the heavy work, Reverend Mother.' Tilly shook her head. 'Never. She is too frail. I don't think it would be fair on Rose or Mrs Desmond.'

'I just thought Rose should be given a chance to see the world outside,' Reverend Mother sighed.

'I'm happy here, Reverend Mother. Perfectly happy here.' Rose looked at the Superior, her eyes full of trust, and the Reverend Mother realized that perhaps after all she had been hasty in her decision.

'You'll take Angie then,' she told Tilly. 'I think it is better, don't you?'

Tilly had to agree. Rose's cough left her weak and Tilly did not want to find that she had to do all the heavy labour. Mrs Desmond had told Tilly that the new person could do the real skivvying and Tilly would be elevated to the position of maid: preparing the meals, the tea, doing the light work, like beds and ironing and washing. Tilly was only too happy at this promotion, but if Rose came, and taking into consideration Mrs Desmond's soft heart, *she* would be given the light work, not Tilly, who would find herself down with the scrubbing, the coal, the really exhausting chores.

'Yes, well, maybe Angela would be stronger.'

Reverend Mother nodded. 'I'll get Sister Agnes to help me pack Angie's things, then.'

She left them and in a little while the French novice brought them lemonade. The roses were white and pink and their heads drooped as if they were tired. A bee humming around the lemonade jug fell in and drowned and Tilly fished it out with her finger while Rose warned her it might sting.

They talked in desultory fashion and it was nearly seven of the evening when Tilly left the convent. She hugged her friend, realizing how thin she was beneath her dress. 'Take care of yourself, Rose, for you know how I love you,' Tilly urged.

'Come to see me when you have a chance,' Rose begged, then added, 'Sometimes I think I'm not really here at all. That I don't exist. I belong to no one. I have no memory of my past. I am a burden.'

'Oh, don't say that, Rose. You're not a burden to me. Or the Reverend Mother. Please don't think that.'

Rose shook herself. 'I'm sorry,' she said. 'I didn't mean to sound ungrateful. It's just that. . .'

'I know. It must be awful at times. But don't think about it now. I'll be back to see you very soon, I promise.'

Angela had arrived carrying her bag. 'Oh, come on, Tilly. It will be dark soon and we'll be set upon by thieves and vagabonds.' Tilly glanced heavenwards and Rose giggled.

As Tilly and Angela left they heard Reverend Mother in the cloisters calling to Rose, 'Come in, my dear. It is getting cold and we can't have you catching a chill.'

'I hope she'll be all right,' Tilly murmured and Angela said, 'I don't expect she will! Chests are delicate things. Not like heads. Headaches go but once your chest is feeble then it never goes back on itself, if you see what I mean.'

Tilly looked at her in exasperation. 'I *don't*,' she said, dragging her along. 'And I'll thank you to shut up about it.'

'Oh, all right,' Angela cried mutinously, 'but I've never known it to happen. Most of the girls I knew with bad chests died!'

Tilly pulled the girl along behind her and wished for the hundredth time that it was Rose going with her to Soho Square.

Chapter Seventy-One

⤨ ⤪

At first she thought it was Sebastian in the box. In her fevered state she faltered when the curtain rose and she saw the figure there.

'Now who calls?' she spoke her first words as Juliet before she entered. The Nurse, onstage, called off to her in the wings, 'Your Mother.' Going onstage Maeve cried,

'Madam, I am here . . .' and stopped, frozen centre-stage, looking at the box and its occupant, terror overwhelming her.

She had recovered somewhat from her broken love affair. She had come to accept the break-up and as long as she did not see Sebastian she could bear it. She had become accustomed to the empty box, but now, seeing the man standing there, her heart stopped and a knife-thrust of pain pierced her heart.

The man leaned forward and she saw that it was Rudi, Sebastian's brother, and to the relief of the Nurse and Lady Capulet who were waiting apprehensively for her to continue, she became her character again. 'What is your will?' she said sweetly, and the play continued.

Belle was anxious about her. 'She's nervous as a kitten,' she told Tilly. 'She's all wound up.'

'Some people never get over a broken 'eart,' Angela remarked dolefully.

'She has lost too much weight,' Belle worried.

'She jumps like a mucher on the job,' Angela said.

'What would you know about men who rob drunks?' Belle demanded.

'My dad, God rest 'im, was one, that's 'ow,' Angela replied and Tilly glanced at Belle and they both raised their eyes to heaven. But they liked Angela, for all her depressive observations delivered in sepulchral tones. She worked hard and made a great difference to Tilly's lot.

Rudi Davenport came every night after that. Audiences were disappointed that it was not Sebastian. They had been titillated by the sight of the beautiful actress on the stage and her lover, the heir to Malvern, in the box. They experienced the universal vicarious pleasure of voyeurs watching the beautiful and the famous revealing their weaknesses in public. But Maeve's performance was so raw, her passion so naked, that they soon forgot everything except the play and Juliet, and they stayed to stand and cheer.

Geoffrey Denton, however, was also worried about his new star. 'You're giving away too much, Maeve,' he told her. 'You can't keep it up. You'll break down. You'll wear

402

yourself out and that is unprofessional.'

'Let *me* worry about that, Mr Denton,' she said, and the following night she exhausted herself with another performance of the same searing intensity.

One evening when she came off after the curtain (she had received a standing ovation as usual for her performance), Rudi was waiting for her in her dressing-room. He was sitting, immaculate in his evening clothes, a carnation in his buttonhole, and smiling at her.

She did not know what to say to him. His connection with Sebastian, the fact that he had been there that fateful weekend, the weekend she had ended her involvement with his brother, brought back so many memories that for a moment she could not speak. She sat at her dressing-table and stared at her white face in the mirror, ignoring him. Polly stood beside her, waiting, glancing uncertainly from her mistress to the gentleman lounging in the visitor's chair.

'If you have come with a message from your brother I really do not wish to hear it,' she said eventually.

'Oh no! Sebastian does not know I am here,' Rudi replied calmly.

She tried to read his eyes but the expression was enigmatic. He was smiling but deep under the smile was speculation and nervousness. What that meant she did not know, could not hazard a guess. She was much too tired.

Nowadays she came off the stage utterly exhausted. She put her face in her hands and sighed wearily. 'What do you want?' she asked him.

'To take you out to supper and talk to you and make you laugh again. To help you if I can.' She opened her mouth to answer but he put up his hand to stop her. 'I'm not here to make any demands on you, Maeve. I would just like to explain my brother to you – my family, our life.'

'I *do* understand, Rudi.'

'Not entirely. Give me the opportunity. I think it might help you to talk to me. Clear the air.' He uncrossed his legs and sat up straight and continued, 'I've watched you, Maeve. I've been to the play every night now for weeks.'

She nodded. 'I know,' she said.

'You are an inspired Juliet, Maeve. I don't come to see you because of Sebastian or because I know you,' he said. 'I come because what you do on the stage every night is the highest possible manifestation of art. You transcend make-believe. You *are* the part. You are Shakespeare's Juliet *par excellence*. I have read the play, savoured the poetry, but I never dreamed I would see Juliet so brilliantly realized or the verse so passionately spoken. It soars.' He stared at her, his eyes shining, and she could not help but be pleased and flattered. 'But you are destroying yourself. Anyone can see it. You are consumed by your suffering, it is burning you up, and you must not allow yourself to be destroyed. I want to talk to you to see if perchance I can help.'

He was right, and she knew it. His assessment was absolutely correct. Geoffrey Denton had warned her. He had said very much the same things to her. Belle too had warned her and inside her little alarm bells rang urgently. She knew she could not go on like this much longer; knew she would destroy herself if she did not deal with the whole wretched situation.

'Is it worth it?' he asked. 'To waste your talent? Your life? Your future? For what? An unworthy passion for a man who gets himself betrothed a couple of weeks after he separates from you? Oh, Maeve, you can do better than that. You are made of sterner stuff.'

'All right!' she nodded, making up her mind. 'Yes. You are right. I'm being weak. Stupid. I'll dine with you.'

She supped with him that evening. Then every evening for the next week. She talked. He listened. She put her case eloquently, but whenever she romanticized or glossed over some harsh reality he forced her to see the truth.

'He stood up for me. He stood up to his mamma. His papa.'

'He then did what they told him.'

'He loves me. He said he would always love me.'

'But he is marrying someone else.'

'He told me he'd never be happy without me. I'm sure that is true. He may be marrying Fanny Ginsborg but he is miserable without me.'

'He was out riding with her last weekend and they came back to the house laughing together.'

'He was laughing?'

'He was laughing.'

He told her, 'The great love stories show weakness, not strength. People don't die of love unless they choose not to be brave or to face up to things. They are lazy, self-centred people intent on their own gratification. Think how silly it all is. You die because someone rejected you. Hurt pride! Wounded ego! Not love. Oh, it excites our pity, but then what is pity if it is not based on superiority. I am sorry for you because you are less than I, have less than I. There is always a *soupçon* of "there but for the grace of God go I" and consequent gratitude for personal immunity.'

He talked to her as no one else ever had, never underestimating her ability to understand. He made her laugh. Took way a lot of the drama inherent in the situation, lightened it for her. He alleviated her pain, diffused the knot of self-obsessive concentration on the state of her emotional life.

'I see you are doing *The Taming of the Shrew* next,' he said.

She nodded, 'Yes. Mr Denton scrapped *Othello* for the moment.' She smiled wryly. 'He said I was emotionally drained after Juliet and he did not wish to see me crack. Katerina will help me to let off steam.'

'He is a wise man. You've had your heart in Juliet, now put your fury into Katerina. Feel her flaring anger, experience her sheer bloody-mindedness. It will help tremendously.'

He told her about Malvern and explained his parents. 'They both like you,' he said. 'Mother admires your spunk.'

She looked at him quizzically. 'My spunk?'

'Your spirit. Father admires your beauty and charm. But they are not very bright. They are appalled because I like to read, because I love literature. Mother wonders where she went wrong with me. She feels awkward with me, like a school-child fearful of committing a gaffe. She adores Sebastian, who is exactly as she hoped her heir would be. That should tell you something.'

'What?'

405

'Well, think about it. You, I think – I could be wrong, mind – but I feel that the way you speak Shakespeare's verse, the grasp you have of it, your intelligent interpretation of Juliet, all of these attributes indicate to me a superior intellect. I think you fell madly, passionately in love with Sebastian, just as Juliet did with Romeo.' He paused and looked at her consideringly. 'Did it ever occur to you that Juliet would have become very bored with Romeo if their love had not been thwarted? Think about it tonight in bed.'

She did. It was amazing to discover what a bore and bungler Romeo was, under the waterfall of words. She dissected him, analysed him and found, as Rudi suggested, that he was not in fact the most fascinating man ever written about. What a spoiled, ineffectual youth he was, and from that conclusion she could not but compare him with Sebastian. He had Romeo's glamour and beauty, but he too, when the cards were down, showed little enterprise and tended to lose his head.

In a way she did not want her picture of Sebastian tarnished. She wanted, even though it caused her pain, to hold on to the old romantic image, but the thoughts Rudi had put into her head had changed her perception of him forever and she was forced to accept that she had been in love with an immature boy.

'You see, it has nothing to do with age,' Rudi told her when she shared her discovery with him. 'It has to do with intelligence. My dear girl, you would not have been happy for long with such a shallow fellow.' He glanced at her swiftly. 'Don't run away with the idea that I do not love my brother. Indeed I do, never doubt that. But I see him as he is. He is far happier than I am in his unconcerned heedless way and he will most likely have a far easier passage through life.' He leaned forward towards her. 'Can you imagine the long years you would spend with him if you married him, long years of tedium, no career, dreary dinner parties, stuffy people – and Sebastian, beautiful as a statue of a Greek god and just as mindless.' He leaned back in his chair. 'You see, Maeve, I think he is perfect for his role in life. He will be a wonderful *grand seigneur*, and

406

manage the estate well. He has no imagination. Fanny will make him a perfect wife.' He smiled at her. 'Mother and Father are right. Sebastian is right. They are all correct in their assumption that, like fire and ice, their eldest would melt and disappear completely under the heat you would generate. Do you understand?'

'Yes, Rudi, I think I do.'

'You are worthy of a more intelligent mate,' he said. 'One who is your weight. Mentally, I mean.'

He was right and she began to feel whole again. Yet some sentiment still tugged at her heart and one night, some weeks after Rudi first started taking her out, they were supping at the Café Royal when the thing she most dreaded happened and she discovered that the pain could, even now, be as sharp and immediate and unreasonable as it was when she first broke off with Sebastian.

Chapter Seventy-Two

൦ ൭

He had stayed away from town as much as he could because Maeve Donnelly was there. At any moment he might see her. She could not be overlooked. She was famous in London, a person of consequence, and he could not hope to avoid mention of her. He was terrified of being teased about her, in the clubs, in society, but most of all he was frightened of meeting her.

When he went up to London on business he stuck mainly to places where he could rest assured he would not meet her, and his sullen face warned his friends not to mention her name. The all-male bastions he frequented were the places he could be sure that whatever the circumstances chaps stuck together and did not torment him for explanations or reasons. The undoubted superiority of the male assured him of that.

But Sebastian and his father, the Duke, up from the

country, came across the Marquis of Killygally in cahoots with young Linton Lester in Drones in St James.

'Thought you were in Ireland?' Maynard said to Bosie and managed to make it sound an unfortunate place to have to be. 'Hear the natives are restless. Lookin' for Home Rule or somesuch and Ulster says never.' Maynard tossed off his brandy. 'Quite right too. Can't have these wallies gettin' ideas above their station.'

'No, I'm not, as you see, in Ireland,' Bosie smiled ironically at the Duke and his lips were tight. 'But I am returning quite soon. My business there is satisfactorily concluded.'

'So glad.' Maynard noted that Bosie swayed on his feet. Both he and the young Lester were heavily under the influence. 'Well, come along, Sebastian, let us push through this crowd. This place is going down. Lets in all sorts of riff-raff these days, eh Bosie?'

'I hope you are not referring to me?' Bosie sounded belligerent.

'Don't be silly, old chap.' Maynard looked surprised, but the Marquis was looking at Sebastian and there was a glint in his eye that the Duke did not like. Bosie was hell when he was riled.

'Well, Sebastian,' Bosie said, slurring a little, 'I hear that congratulations are in order. I'm glad you have quite recovered from your, shall we say, obsession with the beautiful Donnelly girl.' He narrowed his eyes and stared at Sebastian. 'Did you suggest your brother take over where you left off?'

Sebastian lunged towards him, causing an alarmed scuffle to break out as strangers were pushed willy-nilly. But the Duke caught his son's arm and swivelled it behind him while Linton Lester put a restraining arm across Bosie's corpulent body.

'Now, now, now. Peace, gentlemen. At all costs do not let us forget who we are,' Maynard said firmly.

'You cad! You liar! You bounder!' Sebastian hissed through his teeth.

Bosie smiled at him. The smile was triumphant and dangerous. 'I may be a cad, Davenport, and I may be a bounder, but I assure you I am not a liar. Rudi is at this moment having supper with your ex-mistress at the Café Royal in full view of half London.'

Sebastian rushed headlong out of the club before his father could stop him.

'Very much obliged to you I'm sure, sir,' Maynard said peevishly to Bosie. 'Now look what you have done. Hell and damnation, do you *have* to behave like a snake? Dammit, man, did no one ever tell you how intolerable your scheming is?'

'Scheming? What on earth are you talking about?' Bosie's stomach sank as his mind sobered. He knew he was cordially disliked and he hated any reference to the fact. And he could not afford to make an enemy of the Duke of Malvern.

'You are loathsome, sir. Everything you touch you contaminate. No decent person is comfortable with you. You rejoice in the unhappiness of others.'

'Steady on, Maynard, what have I done? Really I must protest at your . . .'

'Shut up and let me finish. I have wanted to say this to you for a long time now. I do not wish to receive you ever again at Malvern.'

This was a terrible insult and a disastrous social rejection.

Bosie drew himself up a trifle unsteadily. People near him were disassociating themselves from him. 'How dare you insult me so? If you were younger I would challenge you, sir.'

'And I would not accept your challenge. I do not fight duels with my social inferiors. Good-day to you, sir. Or should I say, goodbye.' The Duke turned on his heel and followed his son.

'Oh, what a lot of pother about nothing,' the Marquis laughed, but his laughter concealed his inner panic. People were slipping away. 'Now come along, Linton, and let us peruse those bills of sale.'

He clapped his hand on the boy's shoulder and propelled him to the reading room. He was seething. Like snakes coiling and curling inside him the rage he felt was almost uncontrollable. He tried to concentrate on this idiot boy beside him. He pushed him into a chair and sat opposite him, eyeing him with distaste. A greedy child interested only in the fleeting pleasures of the flesh, without a thought in his head for his heritage.

He would fritter it away. Bosie knew Lady Lester as trustee would fight his right to possess the land, but it would not stop him, with Muswell's help, staking his claim and occupying the land. Possession was, after all, nine-tenths the law.

Linton Lester was twenty-four years old. He was only too happy to hand over the title deeds his father had bequeathed to him in Lady Lester's care for the large sums of money the Marquis of Killygally gave him in exchange. And the Lesters had no way of refuding that money.

The Marquis had obtained the land near the river. Now he coveted the land between the road and the river, beside the dried-up reservoir they called Dead Man's Pool. There were acres of meadowland there, and woods.

Muswell had told him that the cottagers he had burned out were rebuilding on this land and he wanted them gone. It infuriated him that Lady Lester had given them permission to set up there. Something about that little band of cottagers tenacity enraged him and he had made up his mind that they had to be destroyed.

Linton Lester had taken out a roll of parchment documents. 'The woods,' he said. 'Acquired in eighteen twelve. The meadows to the east and the waters of the trout stream . . .'

'All right, all right, Linton. I have here a banker's draft made out to you and I think you'll agree that the sum is generous. I don't need to go over the documents again. I know them by heart.' Bosie could barely keep the irritation out of his voice.

'Don't we need Vernon Blackstock's signature?' Linton Lester asked, his eye on the banker's draft. He did not want anything to prevent him pocketing that this evening.

'I do not see why, Linton. You have reached your majority. I have here a document for you to sign. I can always get Mr Blackstock's signature, if I deem it necessary. Then it will be up to you to tackle your mother, Linton. If your mother wants it back she'll have to pay handsomely for it.'

'Yes, yes. I can manage my mother, Bosie, you know I can. She dotes on me.'

'Yes, well I hope so. But if she proves difficult then I don't want to hear about it. Tell her to contact Everard Blanchards, Seaton and Casson in Lincoln Fields, eh, Linton?'

He called the waiter and ordered another bottle of brandy. 'Drink up, Lester. Tonight we go to Whitechapel. There is a whorehouse there where all sorts of things are possible. Things you have never dreamed of. I need—' His face tightened and a wild look crept into his eyes— 'I need to dominate.' He glanced at the young man. 'I promise you, Lester, tonight you'll be amazed.'

Chapter Seventy-Three

రస్తు ౿ు

Sebastian hailed a hackney and his father, following him, missed him but caught another.

Sebastian felt like crying. He wanted to rail and kick and scream like a child whose favourite toy has been taken away.

No one should have her if he could not. No one should dine with her, especially not at the Café Royal where they had so often eaten together. But especially not his brother.

How could Rudi? What did he think he was doing? And what on earth did she want with Rudi? Rudi was terribly boring and high-brow and no fun at all.

Was she his mistress? He would never forgive his brother if he had succeeded where Sebastian had failed. But no. No, that seemed unlikely. She had refused him so it seemed unlikely she would allow his boring, not so handsome brother any favours.

He tried to calm himself but it was no use. He kept knocking on the roof of the hackney, yelling at the driver to hurry.

He had put Maeve out of his mind fairly successfully over the past month, and being in Malvern helped. Fanny had been very helpful too. She was true blue, a pal, just wonderful, and he felt totally at ease with her. Unlike Maeve she did not cause him confusion, uncertainty and that terrible breathless excitement that so unsettled him.

The cab stopped. It had arrived at the Café Royal. Sebastian paid the driver and raced into the lobby. He hurried straight to the dining-room and as soon as he entered he saw them.

She was wearing oyster satin and pearls and her dress was the new body-clinging design. She had never looked more lovely. Tiny clusters of curls had escaped her coiffeur and clung to her neck and temples. There were crystal drops in her ears and she was laughing. No longer pale and tragic, her rosy face was dancing with enjoyment and delight. He was infuriated by that. How dare she laugh. And Rudi was also laughing.

He marched over to the table before he had collected himself and instantly regretted his haste as he stood before them speechless, his mouth opening and closing like a fish.

'Hello, Sebastian,' Rudi greeted him unperturbed. 'Do please join us.'

Maeve thought she would swoon. Her hands shook so she clasped them together in her lap. Her heart was beating sixteen to the dozen and her stomach was doing somersaults. Her throat was so dry she could not swallow.

She stared at Sebastian and noticed he seemed in the same case.

'What the Devil are you doing here?' Sebastian managed at last. The other diners were riveted. Sebastian's precipitate entrance, Maeve's ex-lover as they thought, striding angrily to the beautiful actress's table where she was dining with his brother caused a flurry of interest, and they so forgot their table manners as to stare rudely and await what would happen with bated breath, forks poised in mid-air.

'Sit down, Sebastian,' Rudi commanded coldly, taking

412

charge of the situation. There was no chair so Rudi clicked his fingers and indicated what he wanted. A chair was provided for Sebastian forthwith. The diners, disappointed, returned to their food but kept a curious eye on the Davenports and their actress.

Within moments another frisson of interest rippled through the dining-room as the Duke of Malvern arrived, cast an eye around the room then bee-lined over to his sons. A chair was provided for him also.

All three stared at each other, and the other diners stared at them. The Duke was apprehensive, Sebastian was irritated, and Rudi was amused. Then they all looked at Maeve. She was pale as moonlight and a little quiver at the corners of her mouth alerted Rudi.

'What precipitated this sudden desire to dine here with us?' Rudi asked, his voice light.

'How *dare* you, how *dare* you . . .' Sebastian faltered, stumbling over his words.

'How dare I what, Sebastian? And I entreat you to remember that this place is full of avidly curious people. Maeve never had a more riveted audience.'

'I will not have it,' Sebastian protested.

'Rudi is right, Sebastian,' the Duke said softly. 'Please don't make a scene. We are overlooked.'

Rudi threw back his head and laughed and Maeve, catching his mood and looking at Sebastian's ludicrously irate face, began to giggle. Sebastian and the Duke stared blankly at them. Seeing the incomprehension on their faces only increased Maeve's giggles and turned them to laughter. Rudi caught her eye and they both broke into gales of hilarity which they did their best to control, thereby making themselves worse.

'This is absurd,' the Duke said.

'I did not come here to be laughed at.' Sebastian sounded pompous and Maeve could not help thinking how ridiculously outraged he seemed as she dabbed her eyes with her handkerchief.

'Oh don't be so stuffy, Sebastian,' she cried.

'Father, let us go. This situation is intolerable and I will not sit here and be insulted.'

413

'You are *not* being insulted, big brother,' Rudi said lightly. 'If you must go, you must. You should remember that you interrupted us. Maeve and I were having a friendly supper and you and Father came barging in uttering whoops of "how dare you" and "will not" and "I don't" to the absolute fascination of a roomful of strangers. Truthfully, Sebastian, I don't know what you are huffing and puffing about, really I don't.'

'You *dare* . . .' Sebastian began again and Maeve relapsed into giggles.

Rudi shook his head. 'There you go again. I entreat you, Father, take Sebastian home before he explodes.'

Sebastian opened his mouth but the Duke said firmly, *sotto voce*, 'Shut up, Sebastian. We have no place here. Get up and smile and bow to your brother and his guest and let us go.'

Sebastian obeyed his father precisely. They left and the diners lost interest and returned to their food.

'I've dreaded that happening so much,' Maeve told Rudi.

He covered her hand with his. 'You did well,' he said. 'And I do not think it will ever be so bad again.'

She looked at him with grateful eyes. 'No,' she agreed. 'It will never be so bad again.'

Chapter Seventy-Four

෧ ଚ

It was glorious weather in London. The markets were full of fruit off the boats in the docks and the girls in the streets of London cried out their wares. 'Fine duke cherries' and 'Fresh stawberries', as well as, 'Grapes, white and red grapes from the East' and 'Oranges and lemons. Buy oranges and lemons'. They sold bunches of lavender and pinks and Sweet William.

At Belle's their routine had settled down again and

Angie had settled in. Bert escorted Maeve to the theatre now, or sometimes Tilly did, but it was always Rudi who saw her home. 'Look upon me as your best friend,' he told her, his face serious. She was grateful to him for helping her. He was good company and entertaining and they laughed together a lot. He had a lively wit and understood the plays and literature she constantly explored. He helped her with Euripides and Socrates, with Webster and Goldsmith, with Farquhar and Congreve.

She came to rely on him more and more and when, at last, Sebastian's wedding day dawned, Rudi put in an appearance at the church then slipped away to Soho Square and whisked Maeve off to the country for a rustic lunch beside the river at Richmond. He had taken the precaution to pack a basket with cold chicken in aspic, poached salmon, French cheeses, strawberries and champagne.

'Do you mind about Sebastian?' he asked her. His face was so serious that she laughed.

'Not really,' she told him. 'Not now. You opened my eyes,' she added. Then leaning back against the bark of the willow that shaded them she sighed and said, 'I fear the pain I feel now is merely wounded pride. Oh, Rudi, I was a child-like Juliet, and looking back now . . . no, I don't mind at all about Sebastian.'

The sun cast dappled shadows where they sat on tartan rugs, the basket between them. She held the wine glass near her nose as the bubbles popped and smiled at him.

'At first,' she told him, 'I wanted to die. You knew that. I was sick with love and nearly went into a decline like those ladies poets write of.' She sighed again and glanced at him. 'You've helped me enormously, Rudi,' she said. 'Thank you.'

He ran his hand through his soft brown hair. He looked like a poet, she reflected, wings of hair falling over a pale forehead. But he was much more fun than any poet she had heard of.

'Oh don't thank me, I beg you. I have quite selfish reasons for my behaviour.'

She tilted her head sideways and looked at him from under her lashes. 'And what might they be?'

He had a wide generous mouth and it narrowed now as he bit his lower lip, then sat up and gazed at her, a quite new expression in his eyes. 'Can't you hazard a guess, Maeve? Your company for one thing. Your devastating smile for another. All London is at your feet and you ask me why I help you.'

She said nothing, lowering her glance, feeling the warm rays of the sun on her cheeks. She held her breath, waiting.

He took a deep breath, then announced, 'I am madly, totally, utterly in love with you, Maeve. I fell in love with you the first moment I saw you. I was ashamed, knowing you loved my brother, but I talked to you and then I realized you would never be happy with him. But still I couldn't do anything about it. So I waited – you have to admit I've been patient. You cannot accuse me of improper behaviour.'

'I wouldn't dream of it, Rudi, indeed I wouldn't.'

'I loved your bright, brave spirit, Maeve. You are so independent. You'd never have tolerated the closed world of Malvern. It would have stifled you. The petty jealousies, the protocol, the endless, pointless back-biting.'

She laughed again. 'You are right, Rudi. I could not have borne it,' she agreed.

'And Sebastian would bore you to death in six months.' He took her hands in his. 'So I waited. And courted you eventually in my own fashion. I love you, Maeve. I love your sharp, questing mind, your beauty, your talent.'

'Your family would be shocked.'

'You miss the point. Relieved would be a better word. Eventually. At first they'll be shocked. Yes. They'll say you are determined to better yourself, or some such rubbish. But they'll get used to the idea in time. As I told you before, they like you. And in the end it was because Sebastian is the heir that they were against a union between you two. I am the second son and my wife will not be hampered with duties. Fanny will be pleased if I marry a girl with a career who will not interfere with her running of Malvern. And you, my dear, are quite a catch. Every man in London wants you. You are an asset at parties.

Someone as rare and sought-after as you will draw people to Malvern. My mother and dear Fanny will not have to worry about their balls and soirées being successful. People will flock to see you whether you are there or not. Oh, we'll be famous you and I if you will only marry me.'

Maeve could see patches of blue through the delicate quivering leaves of the willow. She could hear the water lapping the riverbank at their feet. In the distance the countryside was spread with bluebells that matched the sky. She would always remember that afternoon, the birds warbling, the splash of the fish, the smell of grass.

He allowed her time. He waited.

'I'm not in love with you, Rudi,' she told him and his heart sank. 'If love is that sickening quivering of every nerve, then I never want to be in love again. What I feel for you, at this moment particularly, is a warmth that is spreading everywhere through my whole body, right down to my toes.' He felt her hand on his hair and she lifted his face and, bending her head, she kissed his mouth. The kiss, suffocatingly sweet, tasting of strawberries and champagne, was so gentle, so tender yet passionate that he could not breathe, and his arms enfolded her, infinitely welcoming. Her heart rose triumphantly and he pressed her tighter to him, then let her go. He stood up and let out a holler and a whoop of delight that frightened all the birds away and capsized a punt, the lad in it losing his balance and falling waist-high into the weeds.

Chapter Seventy-Five

৵৹ ৫৹

Tilly had told Rose all about Maeve, how talented and famous she was. Now, with Angela to do the hard work Tilly had more contact with Belle and Maeve, and since Maeve had asked for her company on the way to the theatre each evening she had seen several performances of the play.

She loved it. She seemed to find no difficulty with the poetry and ended up in tears after each show.

Belle had always allowed the girls she got from the convent to visit the nuns at least once a month. Tilly went weekly.

She sat with Rose one Saturday after she had left Maeve at the theatre for the matinee. She was telling her over again, for the hundredth time, all about Romeo and Juliet.

'She makes me cry, Rose,' Tilly told her friend.

'How terrible!' Rose shook her head. 'I don't like crying. It sort of hurts your chest.'

'No, Rose, it's not like that sort of crying. When your 'eart breaks and you don't want to live. Nah! 'S'not like that.'

'Wot then?'

'Sort of melancholy. Sort of like waiting for Christmas. Thinking about lovely things. I don't know, soppy mebbe, but it's not awful.'

'You said they're all dressed up?'

'Yeah. In dresses like the nuns, only rich. Like pictures of Queen Elizabeth in the 'istory books. An' the lights are on 'em all the time.'

'Lights?'

'Yeah. Not candles, oil. 'Undreds and 'undreds of 'em. Oh, I wish you could see it Rose – the play.'

Rose's eyes glowed. 'I wish I could too,' she said.

Next day Tilly told Maeve about her friend Rose in the convent.

'You say that since she came to live there she has never been outside the building?' Maeve asked incredulously. 'Why, even the nuns leave.'

'Well, she had some terrible experience before she came to live there. I remember the night she was brought in. She had been beaten bad.'

'Oh, how sad.' Maeve thought of Áine.

'Could I take her to see you act one night, Miss Maeve?' Tilly asked a little apprehensively.

'Of course you may, Tilly. We will arrange it.'

'We'll 'ave to pick 'er up. She'd get lost let loose in town. She'd loose 'er bottle. We'd 'ave to take 'er there and bring 'er back,' Tilly cautioned. 'Be a big undertaking.'

Maeve, supremely happy herself, wanted everyone else to be happy as well. 'We'll get Bert to drop me at the theatre early, then take you in the carriage to the convent, Tilly. I'll ask Lord Davenport to allow you to sit in the box for the performance.'

'Oh, Miss Maeve, you're so kind. So kind.' She grabbed Maeve's hand and kissed it but Maeve pulled it away. 'Now, Tilly, don't. I'm not at all kind as you well know for you've seen me in a pet and you know how beastly I can be.'

'Oh, I'll not hear a word against you, miss. You're an angel.' She gave Maeve a hug. 'I'll arrange it next Sunday when I go to the convent.'

Rose was both excited and apprehensive when she heard the news. 'You'll not leave me? Will you? I'll not be left alone? Will I?'

'No, no, Rose. Don't get into a pother. I'll be there all the time. I'll not leave you for a second. Don't fret, Rose, you'll be perfectly safe with me. Don't fear. But you're glad about it, aren't you?'

'Oh, I'm that pleased, Tilly. A theatre! I ain't never been.'

They decided on the Tuesday. Maeve was dropped at the theatre and she instructed the hackney to take Tilly and Bert to the convent.

They rang the bell in the arched door in the wall that was the entrance, and presently it was opened by Sister Agnes, her face nervous, holding Rose by the hand as if she were a child of six.

'You're sure she'll be all right?' the Sister asked anxiously. 'She's very dear to us and you were always flighty, Tilly.'

'Oh, Sister, you'll alarm her if you look and talk like that. O'course she'll be all right,' Tilly assured her.

Bert stepped from the shadows. 'She'll be fine,' he promised. 'I'll see to that.'

Rose had stepped onto the pavement, but now she stood, frozen to the spot, her mouth half-open, staring at Bert and clutching Sister Agnes's hand tightly in hers.

'Let me go, child,' the nun cried and Rose released her

suddenly. 'Now off with you. And have her back not too late,' she called as she shut the door behind Rose. 'Not too late,' she reiterated and they heard the key turn in the lock.

Rose seemed to collect herself and she climbed into the coach after Tilly and Bert and sat between them as they rode back to the Strand.

Something in her memory was stirring. Something buried deep was trying to struggle to the surface. Perhaps it was the hustle and bustle of the streets. Perhaps it was the noises, unfamiliar, yet not unknown to her. She was a little scared. The convent was so quiet.

However, she felt safe with Tilly. She looked at Bert. There was something about his face, his open countenance, his freckled nose, that recalled something to her, as if in a dream.

All of that evening was an enchantment for her. She felt as if she had been led into fairyland. It was a foreign country, filled with smiling people, perfumed and bejewelled, watching a fabulous story on the stage.

She sat in the box with a gentleman called Rudi who plied her with sweetmeats and a glass of champagne in the first interval. She listened to the words, understood the story, was carried away by it, utterly immersed in the tragic tale. When Romeo tried to reconcile Tybalt and Mercutio and when his sword killed Tybalt by accident, she cried out 'Oh no!', aghast. As Juliet lay in the tomb she shivered in sympathy so that the gentleman called Rudi gently put his cloak over her shoulders. At the end she clapped until her hands were sore, totally unaware of the stir she was causing in the auditorium.

Everyone was wondering who the drab in Rudi Davenport's box was and what the new situation entailed. But Rose was oblivious to them.

They came out into the Strand and Rose felt as if she was floating, dazed, dreaming, in another world, when out of the past, out of hell, out of the mire of that buried horror a gargoyle face loomed. Came at her leering, came at her like a monstrous obscenity, came at her like those paintings she had seen in the convent, copies of the

420

nightmare imaginings of great artists, visions of Hades, of Hell, of Lost Souls and the Damned. She was assaulted by most foul memories that washed over her, immersing her in disgust. She could see them again, grinning, sweating men with stale wine-breath and brutal hands. She remembered gruesome obscenities committed casually, mindless cruelty and blood.

She looked at the man who was sauntering along the Strand with another and knew him to have been there in that infernal region, knew him to have been the prime culprit in that nightmare where horror lived and her soul had died.

'Beg pardon,' the Marquis of Killygally, fresh over from Ireland, tipped his hat to the wild-eyed girl in his way, not because she deserved his consideration but because he had spied Rudi and he desired to patch up his differences with the Davenports.

Rose slipped to the ground unconscious.

Bosie moved on, turning to his companion whose monocle had dropped in surprise at the girl's swoon.

'Quite an effect you have on women, Bosie,' he said, laughing. 'Who is she?'

'Some drab. Never clapped eyes on her before tonight, dear fellow. Come on up to the club. Need a little tincture before we go to see Bryony in Manchester Square.'

Bert and Rudi lifted Rose into the carriage.

'I have to see Maeve,' Rudi said. 'Can you look after her? Deliver her to the nuns safely, Bert? Without me, I mean? I can come along if you think you need me.'

Bert had a funny look on his face, so Rudi turned enquiringly to Tilly.

'I'll look after 'er, never you fear, sir,' she assured him. 'Bert an' me, we'll manage. Won't we, Bert?' She shook him and he looked out of the carriage at Rudi.

'Wot? Oh yes, sir. We'll take care of 'er, don't worry.'

'Do you need me?' Rudi asked again.

Tilly shook her head. 'No, sir. We'll manage.'

Bert was silent on the journey and Tilly gave up trying to engage him in conversation. Rose remained semi-fainting in a corner. Tilly put her arm around her but she shrugged it off. She was mumbling and murmuring to herself as if she were dreaming, having nightmares. Every so often she shuddered and sat up, then swooned again.

Tilly was worried. She could not understand what had happened. Rose had enjoyed the play. She had been ecstatic until they reached the pavement, then suddenly this! Perhaps she had been scared by the crowds? But no. She did not think that was it. It was something more, something horrible that she caught a glimpse of. Tilly remembered the state Rose had been in when the sisters, Agnes and Emmanuel, had brought her back to the convent. Could that man have had anything to do with it?

Tilly gave up.

When they reached the convent Bert had great trouble rousing the nuns. With Compline at four-thirty a.m. they tended to sleep soundly when they could. There was consternation when they saw the state Rose was in.

Bert carried her into the little courtyard behind the door and across to the house. There he followed Sister Emmanuel's fat frame up the stairs and into a small monastic cell, clean and bare, and laid Rose on the narrow cot.

'You may go now, young sir,' Sister Emmanuel said and turned from him, blocking his view of Rose. He hesitated a moment then turned and left the room.

As he began to descend the stairs he heard a soft voice calling him. He turned and saw a tall nun standing above him. She was wearing a thick flannel nightgown and her head was covered with a nightcap. She had a white shawl held closely around her. Bert would not have known she was a nun except that he could see that under the cap her hair was shorn.

'What happened, boy?' she asked.

'She saw someone . . . she loved the play . . . she was so happy . . . excited.'

'Over-excited? Is that what brought it on? I should never have allowed her to go . . .'

Bert shook his head. 'I don't think it was that. I'm sure it wasn't.' He frowned. 'I think it was the man she saw. When we left the theatre. A man wot upset 'er.'

422

The Reverend Mother examined him closely. His face was turned to the light she held and clearly visible.

'There is something you are not telling me,' she said. 'Spit it out, boy.'

Bert frowned again. 'I'm not sure . . . I don't want to jump the gun . . .'

'You can tell me. I'll decide whether what you say is jumping the . . . er . . . gun or not.'

'See,' he stared at the tall nun and gulped. 'See, I think I know 'oo she is,' he said softly, eyes wide with fear. 'I was watching 'er all night. Staring at 'er. But I daren't say. It'd kill the mistress if I was wrong. Can I come and see 'er tomorrow, mebbe, the next day?'

The Reverend Mother nodded. She did not ask foolish and unnecessary questions. They would find out soon enough if it was the good Lord's will. If it was not – well, they could deal with that another day. Meanwhile there were herbs to brew to make a tissane for Rose. The tissane would sooth her, take away the nightmares.

She nodded to the young man and turned away. He hurried down the stairs and when he glanced over his shoulder she had disappeared.

Chapter Seventy-Six

⤺ ⤻

Bert was in a quandary. If he told Belle his suspicions he might give her hope, and then, if he was wrong, she might never recover.

But he did not think he was wrong. That face. Those eyes. The little pointed chin, so like Belle's. No, it was Lucy Desmond. Lucy had had a flat disc of skin near her ear. So had Rose. Surely that was enough of a coincidence.

She hadn't recognized him. That had confused him. What had happened to her? How had she ended up in a convent? The girls the nuns cared for were waifs and strays from the streets, orphans mostly, or children whose parents didn't want them. They were the rejects of society. The nuns took them in and tried to heal them and make them as whole as they could.

Belle Desmond had loved her child. Lucy had been the light of her eyes, so how had she turned up there, in a convent, with the homeless ones?

What should he say to Belle? How much should he tell her? He twisted his fingers together, screwing them around each other as the cab clattered along the streets in the darkness.

Tilly kept chattering, tormenting herself about whether it was all her fault and what she could or should have done, but he didn't listen to her.

The only one who could help him was Maeve. He came to a decision swiftly and when the cab dropped Tilly in front of the house in Soho Square he retained it and sent her indoors with strict instructions not to wake her mistress.

'You're a wee bit heavy-handed, Till, so take it easy! I got a bit of business needs takin' care of.'

'It's about Rose? In' it? I know there's somfink.'

'Don't fret, Till, and don't say anything to Mrs Desmond. Just go to bed, there's a good girl.'

He ordered the cabby to take him back to the theatre. The driver cracked his whip, said, 'Oi don't mind if oi do,' and they clip-clopped back the way they had come.

Their journey back to the theatre was swift. Bert figured that the trip via the convent and Soho Square had not taken too long, so all in all Meave had not had that much time to take off her make-up and costume. He hoped.

She was still there. She looked very lovely in her cream satin evening gown, diamanté in her hair. She had changed, he thought, and was now another person from the little skivvy he had befriended in those early days. She had always been beautiful, but now she was assured and elegant. She was very poised and a little intimidating.

She turned as he came into her dressing-room. She was clasping a glittering bracelet around her wrist. Rudi, Bert noticed, was lounging in the only other chair in the room.

424

Bert liked Rudi and was glad that he was here tonight. He was practical and would not hinder. Sebastian, Bert thought, would have been a hindrance.

'Why Bert!' Maeve cried. 'What are you doing here? Is something wrong? You look quite pale.'

Rudi rose, untangling his long legs. 'You look quite done-up, old fellow. Here, sit down. Give him some brandy, Maeve.'

Maeve kept a tray of glasses and decanters in her dressing-room for visitors and she poured a drink for Bert and handed it to him. 'Get that down you,' she told him. 'It will steady you. Then tell us what's the matter.'

He tossed the drink back and she waited for him to finish, then said, 'Please tell us what is wrong, Bert. What happened to upset you?'

Rudi, looking at him intently, stated, 'It's something to do with that child tonight. Isn't it?'

'Tilly's friend? The one Rudi says fainted?'

Bert nodded. They watched him expectantly. 'I think . . . I think . . .' He stopped and there was silence.

'What do you think, Bert?' Maeve's voice was curious. Bert was usually so calm, so down-to-earth; she could not fathom what could have upset him so.

He looked up at her. 'I think that girl – Tilly's friend from the convent – is Belle Desmond's lost Lucy.'

Maeve gasped and dropped to her knees in front of Bert. 'Oh, Bert, are you sure? Oh, how wonderful that would be! Oh, Rudi darling, I think I told you . . .'

He nodded, 'Yes, she lost her daughter. I remember. What makes you think Rose is the one?'

'When she was born she had a little patch of smooth skin, about the size of a florin, like a burn on her scalp. The hair never grew there. It was behind her right ear. Tonight, when she fainted, I saw it distinctly.'

'Then it must be,' Maeve clapped her hands together. 'Didn't she recognize you, though?'

He shook his head. 'No. Tilly says she's lost her memory. The nuns found her in a terrible state, bleeding and beaten, cowering in an alley. She'd been raped.'

'Oh my God.' Maeve crossed herself.

'I'm sorry, Maeve. I shouldn't 'ave been so coarse-spoken.'

Maeve shook her head impatiently. Used to Shakespearean language and the more outspoken expression of that time she had little use for the prudery of the day.

'Oh, we haven't time for niceties now,' she said sharply.

Rudi was staring at Bert. 'Why did she faint?' he asked and there was a sharp suspicion in his eyes.

'She saw someone. That man who bowed to you, I think.' Bert's eyes flew to Rudi's face. 'She saw him and I thought she would scream. Such a look of 'orror crossed 'er face. 'Oo was that man? Do you know him?'

'That man was the Marquis of Killygally,' Rudi said. Maeve gasped. 'The Marquis? Oh my God, Rudi, the Marquis!'

Rudi nodded his head. 'If what I think is true then it all makes sense. How old was she when she disappeared?'

'Eleven,' Bert replied. 'It was almost six years ago, sir. Six years.'

'Oh, my dear God,' Maeve shivered. 'The devil! The monster! The diabolical monster!'

'The man is vile,' Rudi said, his voice soft with contempt.

'What is it?' Bert asked.

'This man is known for his preference for children, Bert,' Rudi told him. 'He is a perverted beast.'

'The Marquis of . . .?' Bert inquired.

'Killygally,' Maeve supplied. 'A place near my home, Bert. There were rumours there too. Oh, the man is foul.'

'But all that must wait till later,' Rudi cried. 'First things first. We must tell Belle. Tomorrow, first thing. Then the child will have to be prepared. With medical attention available. It will be a shock, albeit a pleasant one. But primarily we must sup and then go home and sleep.' He smiled at Bert. 'Like soldiers before battle, one has to eat and sleep even though they are the last things one wants to do.'

'I'll take myself off then.' Bert rose but Rudi stopped him.

'Indeed no. You must eat with us. There is much you

426

have to tell us about the girl, much we have to discuss. No, Bert, you must join us.'

'Oh no, sir. I cannot. I've never been . . .'

'That is enough, Bert. You'll come with us and that's final.'

Bert shifted from foot to foot awkwardly. 'But, sir, I'm not dressed proper.' He indicated his clothing. 'And you'll be going to some grand place not suitable for the likes of me.'

'Don't talk nonsense, Bert. And never fear, we will not embarrass you. We'll go into Chellini's by the back door. I've ordered a private booth.' He glanced at Bert. 'They are like small private rooms, so no one will notice you.'

'If you're sure, sir?'

'I'm sure. Besides we need to talk to you, old fellow. You know all about this affair and we know little. Your help will be invaluable.'

Bert swelled with importance. All apprehension left him. He felt comfortable and secure. He also felt perfectly sure that the girl was Lucy Desmond.

Chapter Seventy-Seven

It was as Rudi told him. They went to the restaurant, arriving by the back stairs, and were shown to a small curtained cubicle with little more than a table and four chairs. Rudi ordered steak and kidney pudding.

'It's cooked in porter,' he told Bert.

He ordered beer all round and they settled down to eat and drink and discuss the situation and their plans.

'The more I think about it, sir, the more I'm certain that Rose is Lucy Desmond,' Bert told them.

'Call me Rudi, Bert. Don't stand on ceremony.'

Bert liked being there with them. They asked his advice and listened to what he said.

427

He had been feeling a bit wonky recently because there was talk of combustion buses and trams that ran on rails. It scared him, made him feel insecure, in case he was made redundant. But this evening he was fed like a prince and spoken to as if he were a person of importance. He enjoyed his moment of glory.

Also he was filled with joy that he had found Lucy. He could repay all Belle Desmond's generosity to him, her warm acceptance of her lodger as part of the family. She had done him a million kindnesses and now he could, in part, repay her.

He began to fidget. The apple turnover was delicious but he wanted it to be morning so that he could break the news to Belle and see her glad face.

'She'll be so pleased,' Maeve said to him as if she knew what he was thinking.

'I'll bring the carriage around,' Rudi said. 'In the morning. I'll be there, for she'll want to go to the convent instantly.'

Neither Maeve nor Bert slept much that night. The former tossed and turned and wished Demara was beside her so that she could share the good news. The latter did not even try. His eyes were bright as he sat on the side of his bed, wide-awake, and counted the hours till morning.

They were both down early, too excited to eat.

They could hear Tilly in the hall prattling on about the theatre and Rose's fainting. 'I'm sure it was my fault, ma'am.'

'She's down,' Maeve whispered to Bert. 'Oh, Bert.'

'Oh, I wish I knew what it was I did as upset 'er, ma'am,' Tilly was saying.

'There now, Tilly. I'm quite certain you're mistaken and that it was caused by something else. Probably Maeve's genius hit her a little late.'

She came into the room, her rose-coloured *peignoir* floating around her in a pink cloud. 'Why, my lambs, you're early risers and no mistake. Tilly's been telling me about the *contretemps*. Do explain.'

She kissed Maeve absently and watched Tilly pour her hot chocolate then glanced up and saw Maeve's expression, glanced at Bert, saw his. 'Why, my dears, what is it?' she asked, slightly apprehensive.

'Well, it's like this, Belle,' Bert said. 'I don't want to get your 'opes up . . .' he was suddenly uncertain. Suppose, just suppose he was wrong.

'My hopes up?' Belle queried, thoroughly alert now, glancing from Bert to Maeve and back again.

'Yes. But Belle . . . I think . . . that is, I'm nearly sure,' he gulped, 'that we found Lucy.'

Tilly dropped the plate of oatcakes and Belle's hand shook so much that she spilled her hot chocolate. She put the cup down, disbelief, hope and a terrible raw pain flitting across her face. 'Oh God,' she cried, putting her hand to her heart. 'Oh God! Let it be! Oh, Bert! Oh, Maeve! Oh my God.'

'I'll get a cloth. I'll wipe it up. Lucy, your daughter. Lucy. Oh! Oh! Oh!' Tilly was running around in little circles as if she had lost her head and Belle stood up, then sat down again.

'Stop, everyone. Stop,' Maeve cried.

'I'm not *sure*, mind,' Bert was saying. 'I'm not absolutely sure.'

The doorbell rang and Maeve rose. 'Rudi's here,' she announced, throwing them into further confusion. 'He's come to take you to the convent, Belle.'

'And me in a state of undress,' Belle cried. 'If it is Lucy . . .' She began to sob and Maeve put her arms around her. 'Oh if it is my daughter – oh, I don't think I could bear the joy. Oh, Maeve,' her rouged lips quivered, 'Oh, Maeve, I'll die of happiness if it is.'

'Much good that would do Lucy! No, you will not die of it, Belle. Stop being dramatic and go upstairs and dress yourself. I'll help you. And Tilly get the door. Show Lord Davenport into the parlour and get him a cup of chocolate. I'm sure he would love some.'

Belle took herself off, telling Maeve she was quite capable of getting dressed by herself. 'Send Tilly to help when she has given Rudi his drink.'

Tilly did as she was bid.

'Oh Lord, I 'ope I'm right, Maeve.' Bert looked worried.

'Wot if I'm wrong?'

'I don't think so, Bert,' she reassured him. 'It all fits.'

'Anyhow, we'll soon see,' Rudi said as he entered. 'Why did you banish me to that cold, unfriendly room?' he asked them. 'It's lovely in here.'

'Belle is out of her mind with excitement,' Maeve told him.

'Naturally,' he said, then, 'I went to the convent early this morning. I know the nuns are early risers and I thought it would be diplomatic to prepare everyone . . . we don't want . . .'

Maeve looked at him tenderly. 'You're a lovely man,' she told him. 'Thoughtful. It was most kind of you. We don't want people rushing about emotionally out of control.'

'They have it all planned,' Rudi said. 'The Reverend Mother saw me. What a remarkable woman she is. You know, Maeve, when all this is over I would like to make a donation to that place. They do such wonderful work. You have no idea . . .'

'Oh yes I 'ave,' Tilly said firmly. 'We'd all be on the streets only for them there . . .'

'She said Rose had been very disturbed, but if, as Bert thinks, Mrs Desmond is her mother, then such a wonderful discovery can only do her good.'

Belle Desmond never remembered the exact sequence of events. The day was strangely unreal, unrelated to any other day she could remember. Time was no longer measured as it usually was, it reeled about alarmingly, dragging out to seem endless, then speeding up as if the hours were seconds.

The ride to the convent in Rudi's carriage took weeks – years. It seemed the longest journey of Belle's life.

They waited in the visitors' parlour, each moment an hour, and then the Reverend Mother arrived and took Belle upstairs.

The nun did not waste time in polite greetings. She knew how anxious Belle must be to see her daughter.

'We have much to be grateful to you for, Mrs Desmond,' she said. 'You have placed so many of our girls with you and it is good to meet you at last under such happy circumstances. I hope your visit is fruitful. It would be divine justice if it were.'

Belle was too preoccupied to hear her. When they reached the room she pushed the nun aside in her anxiety to see, and there she was, no mistaking her, her Lucy, staring up at her from the pillow, eyes wide and fearful. Belle held her breath a moment and clutched the lintel to steady herself.

The girl's face changed slowly. At first her fear became puzzlement, then a look of wondrous hope illuminated her countenance. Her eyes shone as if they were two lamps dimly lit that someone had turned up to their full brilliance. She moved forward, leaning towards Belle and, stretching her arms out, waited confidently for them to be filled.

A sob tore through Belle and she rushed to enfold her child, hold her in her hungry embrace. She held her as if she would never let her go. Reverend Mother closed the door on them, a warm smile on her lips.

It was a rare occurence for any of the waifs in her care to find happiness or so sweet a reunion. But when it happened it made all her hard work seem worthwhile.

Chapter Seventy-Eight

∽∞ ∞∾

The celebrations that night in Soho Square, the reminiscences, the congratulations, mutual and general, the thanks poured on the Almighty, the rediscovery and reunion were confused and jubilant.

No one mentioned the Marquis. Belle did not ask what had happened all those years ago and why Lucy had disappeared. There was a whole lifetime ahead for that. They contented themselves with talking about the past, the 'do-you-remembers' and the 'when-wes' and 'did we' and 'how we were'.

It was a happy group of people who rejoiced. Belle never let go of her daughter's hand and Lucy held on tightly to Belle. Her memory had flooded back and every so often she smiled at her mother who kissed her cheek, or touched her to make sure she was really there, or hugged her in an excess of affection. Lucy cried 'Mamma, Mamma' over and over again and laid her head on Belle's ample bosom and pressed the plump hand that held hers to her cheek.

Rudi sat beside Maeve on the chaise-longue, smiling, lending charm and warmth to the proceedings. Maeve realized with a kind of awe how nice Rudi was, how much he genuinely cared for people and how well he fitted in anywhere. He was totally accepting of circumstances and people whatever their position and was equally at home in Soho Square, the Chandos Theatre or Malvern. His prime concern wherever he was seemed to be the welfare of others and an acute interest in the human race. She could not help thinking what fun life would be with him and slipped her hand into his as they watched the newly reconciled mother and daughter embrace yet again and Belle wipe her eyes with her soggy handkerchief and blow her nose and sigh and smile.

Bert was the hero of the hour. Everyone praised him. Belle was effusive in her gratitude and Lucy profuse in her thanks. He stared at the returned daughter, proud of her, basking in the holiday mood.

Tilly made tea, ran out to get pork pies and eel stew, stuffed capons and jugs of beer and they all set to with relish and tears and laughter.

At last Lucy, emotionally exhausted, asked to sleep in the big bed with Belle. 'Like I used to, Mamma, it all comes back to me now. Oh, darling Mamma, how could I ever have forgotten you?'

'Don't worry about that now, dearest child, oh you're not a child, are you, but to me you'll always be one. My dearest child.'

'I shall move out of your room, Lucy,' Maeve assured her. 'I was only keeping it warm for you.'

Belle looked flustered. Maeve however smiled. 'Dearest

Belle, I'm only too happy to let Lucy have her room back . . .'

'But I don't want you to go,' Belle protested.

'I'll have to leave in any case. Rudi and I are marrying.'

'We'll be househunting, Mrs Desmond,' Rudi told her. 'I'm going to find a suitable establishment for my bride. And you will be welcome there any time.'

'Oh, you'll visit us often. I'll see to that. And you, Bert,' Maeve told them, and Bert knew they would be welcome. Maeve was very loyal. He shook Rudi's hand, 'Congratulations, sir, I'm happy for you. You're a lucky man. I 'ope you realize that.'

Rudi nodded. 'There is only one thing left to do,' he said softly to Maeve. 'Only one piece of unfinished business and short of ending up in prison I'm damned if I can think of how to go about it.'

She raised her innocent face to his. 'What's that?' she asked.

'The destruction of the Marquis of Killygally. Killing him would be too easy. Destroying him in society would be the real punishment. My father has gone some considerable distance towards that. Somehow it has to be finished.'

'Oh, Rudi, don't sink to his level,' she told him. 'Tit-for-tat never brought happiness. Leave him to heaven.'

Chapter Seventy-Nine

࿊ ࿊

The news drifted into Ballymora. No one knew where it came from, whether the wind blew it over the sea or it fell with the rain. Certainly no human agency told them, yet they knew that the Marquis had bought the land.

The Marquis of Killygally was still in London. Lady Lester had not been in touch with her son recently, but the whisper started and grew and with it came panic. The Marquis of Killygally was buying or had bought all the land from the boreen to the Killygally moors. It was told one to the other that Lord Lester had sold the territory to the Marquis on his own cognizance. He had the authority as Lord Lester of Ballymora Castle. They said it was all up for the cottagers; they should stop building because very soon their homes would be once more in jeopardy. In fact, for sure, they would soon be rubble.

Panic gave way to stoicism. The cottagers became fatalistic. They could not win. It was no use Clancy saying they should stand their ground and fight. An awful acceptance overcame them and they slid into apathy.

June drenched the land in sunshine. Roses bloomed in Lady Lester's rose garden and the rushes were thick along the river bank. The air was alive with the buzz of bees.

'Yer givin' in wi'out a fight,' Clancy admonished them in the barn, which was also, if rumour was true, part of the sale.

'It's not your home,' Mickey O'Gorman said sullenly. There'd been no booze available so his mood was foul.

'We're not talkin' about my home,' Clancy answered. 'We're talkin' about yours.'

'The rats have deserted the sinkin' ship,' Brian Gilligan said mournfully.

'If ye mean by that who I think ye mean, there's no desertin' in it.' Clancy was fed up with them picking on each other, losing sight of the real enemy. Lady Lester had given the Donnellys the gatekeeper's cottage and the cottagers could not get over it.

'Pierce Donnelly'll come to our aid in our hour of need,' Clancy told them. He cast a severe eye over them and there was silence a moment. Brian Gilligan broke it. 'Is it the grand Pierce Donnelly himself yer talkin' about? An' what has he got to lose? Might I ask? Isn't he livin' off the fat entirely? Isn't he up in the gatekeeper's cottage wi' his family? An' Demara as grew up barefoot wi' Bryony an' Brenda an' Rosheen is up in the castle itself, lordin' it with the gentry and buildin' herself a house wi' naked statues all over the place? Sure Father Maguire is scandalized, so he

434

is! He's after sayin' it's a sacrilege.'

'An' Phil Conlon gone back to the bailiff's cottage,' Dinny McQuaid cried. 'Takin Ma Stacey wi' him an' workin' for the Lesters again an' them the ones who caused all the trouble in the first place. Sure only for the Lesters wouldn't we all be tucked up cosy as chickens in a boiler-room in our own houseens?'

'Listen te me, will ye?' Clancy shouted, wiping his forehead.

The day was hot. Working on the cottages was hard in the sun. The impetus driving them on to provide shelter for themselves and their families was sapped by the heat. It did not seem as urgent when the weather was clement.

The stench in the barn was terrible. People treated the place as temporary accommodation and therefore carelessly. It did not warrant the meticulous care they might have lavished on their own homes.

Clancy looked at them, lying about drenched in their own sweat, listless and morose. Sometimes he felt his fellow-countrymen didn't need the English – they were hell-bent on destroying themselves without help. The stalwarts were gone. The survivors. The stiff men, unbroken, proud, ready to fight for freedom, for their rights. Pierce Donnelly and Phil Conlon were not here any more.

Duff Dannon was. But he was an angry and bitter man now, followed everywhere by his wild-eyed Donnelly wife.

'Listen to me,' Clancy cried, angry with himself and them. 'Listen. We have te fight. Don't ye see? If ye let them win now ye'll lose everything an' yer pride. It's just not right. It's just not right!'

'Save yer breath, mister.' It was Deegan Belcher, ugly in his jealousy. ''Tisn't up to you to tell us what te do 'bout our situation – or Pierce Donnelly either,' he taunted. 'We toil, we work, and what do we get for our pains? Nothing! But others prosper.'

They all looked at Dana Dannon. She hadn't opened her mouth in weeks, and she stood there now, surveying them, cat-eyed. 'Others prosper,' she cried. 'Deegan is right. Ye toil, as Deegan said, an' so do I. We help each other. Look there—' she pointed at Della Gilligan— 'Della is feedin'

435

Sheena's baby while she draws water. Duff is out choppin' wood an' he'll give ye all some, you know that. So is Shooshie who hasn't had his fiddle under his chin for a month. But my family – I denounce them!' There was a cheer.

'Yer a jealous bitch Dana,' Sheena cried.

'Listen,' Dana overrode her, 'if my father had not tried to make our cottage larger the Lesters wouldn't have noticed us cottagers and nuthin' would've happened. Neither would the Marquis of Killy-bloody-gally.'

It was arrant nonsense what she said but it was what they wanted to hear. They needed a scapegoat and the Lesters and the Marquis were too remote and untouchable.

Clancy shrugged his shoulders and walked out of the barn in disgust. He'd leave them to stew in their own juice. There was no use trying to work on men who had lost sight of the objective.

Outside he met Duff. He greeted him. 'Good day to ye, Duff. Did ye get the wood?'

Duff nodded. His face was becoming set in lines of discontent. He eased the wood off his shoulders onto the ground.

'Walk away up the boreen with me, Duff. I'm sure worried about the situation, that I am, an' I need yer advice.'

Afterwards Clancy wished he had not gone away from the potential source of battle. Perhaps if they had stayed there outside the barn they could have prevented what happened, but he wanted to escape from the oppressive atmosphere and the opinions riddled with stupidity pouring from narrow, spiteful minds.

'I'd like te talk to ye, Duff,' he said, guiding Duff away from the barn. 'Clear the air. God knows it's clouded enough at this moment. I'd like to plan some sort of strategy. The people above are so muddled they are seeing the enemy in their midst and not focussing where they should at all.'

Duff nodded. 'They want to put a face on their trouble,' he said. 'The Marquis is remote. Muswell is hard to catch and they don't know where to look. All they can see is the Donnellys' good fortune and focus their hated on that.'

'People have always hated their own kind who make good. They see it as a reproach to them for not doing the same.'

They walked down to where the river widened. The reeds were waist-high and the bulrushes swayed in the breeze. Every now and then there was the plop of a fish and the shining dart of a dragonfly. Clancy threw a stone in the water.

'There's plenty of room for everyone. This country is hardly overpopulated. Since the famine there's hardly any of us left. Look at it.'

He swept his arm in a circle embracing mountains, the sea, the fields and meadows, the woods and trees as far as the eye could see. 'Look at it. In all that space, in all those acres, the two families, Killygally and the Lesters, Father Maguire, and us. Our little community. All that space an' no room for ye! It doesn't bear thinkin' about.'

There was a shout from the barn.

'What's that?' Duff asked, alarmed.

They were about a quarter of a mile away down towards the sea and they turned to look up.

What they saw alarmed Duff even more.

The cottagers were leaving the barn in a body, walking across-country, westward. They were waving their arms and seemed to be shouting. Their black figures silhouetted by the sunlight moved across the horizon. From where Duff and Clancy stood it was obvious they had a purpose and that their intent was evil. There was something frightening and menacing about them.

'Oh my God,' Duff cried. 'Where are they goin'? What the Devil are they up to?'

'They seem to be going towards Ballymora Castle, and, by the looks of them, they're up to no good.'

'That damned woman,' Duff cried. 'Dana. She is out in front with Deegan Belcher. Jesus and Mary what the . . .'

'Up in the barn she was ravin' on about her da and Demara, sayin' they caused all the trouble,' Clancy said.

'Oh holy Mother of God,' Duff cried, panic in his voice. 'Demara. She has it in for Demara. That's where they're goin'. We've got to stop them. She is full of poison, she could do anything.'

Duff was running after them now. 'Come on, Clancy. Jesus, man, cut across the fields and try to get there fast!'

They raced upwards towards Bannagh Dubh. Duff was a fit man, used to hard labour, and he soon pulled ahead of Clancy who was not. Clancy could feel his breath tearing at his chest as he tried to keep up with the younger man, unable to understand what had so alarmed him. He tripped and fell a few times, then picked himself up and hurried on.

Now they could hear a chorus of anger roaring on the air. They turned a corner, topped the rise, rounded the headland and looked with startled eyes at the sight that met them.

Beside the lake the four walls of a house rose up in silver stone, sparkling in the sunlight. The stones were perfectly cut and beautifully balanced but the building was not finished. The roof had still to be laid.

A gravel pathway led around the lake and down to the sea to what would be the entrance to this shimmering house.

There was a horse standing in the driveway and a low dray upon which was a cranking device and ropes like the sort used on boats. Held by the ropes were four large hunks of the silver stone with which the house was built. To Duff it looked like a pulley.

But most remarkable of all, around the lake and flanking the gravel drive, were life-sized statues of naked women and men. They stood proudly in their pagan nudity, a shocking sight for all to see.

Demara Donnelly was approaching this half-built house, her hand on the plough horse's bridle, and on the dray with the four blocks of silver stone sat Cogger Kavanagh.

Demara stopped in surprise. She was standing, shading her eyes with her free hand, looking to where the cottagers, a tight group led by her sister, had stopped in the driveway.

'Whore!'

Demara stared at her sister as if bemused, shaking her head gently to and fro. Clancy blinked. The word bewildered him. It was out of place here. Out of context in their battle.

'Whore!' The shrill cry came again.

'Oh Christ, no! The bitch!' Duff was striding towards them muttering, his boots crunching the gravel. He would have to go around the lake to reach them.

Clancy started to follow him but his eyes were drawn back to the group. What he saw spurred him on and he turned and ran after Duff.

Dana had lifted a stone from the pile near the bank. She raised it over her head, a look of venom disfiguring her face, and she threw it at her sister. 'Whore!' she screamed.

The stone glanced off Demara's forehead, cutting her. Demara looked at first surprised, then horrified. She put a hand to her forehead and realized she was bleeding. She looked at the blood with uncomprehending eyes.

Dana picked up another stone and threw it. She was shouting obscenities now, screaming and yelling. The others, carried away by their anger and the sight of blood, were following her lead. They were picking up the stones and throwing them at the helpless girl as she stood in front of her half-built house.

She did not try to defend herself. She just stood there, arms at her sides. Then a stone hit the horse and it reared.

Another hit Demara, then another, then a shower battered her slight body, forcing her to her knees, pain running through her like knives.

'Whore!' 'Bitch!' 'Filthy heathen!'

The naked statues had given some the excuse they needed and now they pelted her with fury and someone plucked the word 'witch' out of the air and all the insults merged into that one word.

'Witch!'

Duff had raced up behind them and was trying to prise the stones out of their hands. He was screaming at them. 'For pity sake, what are ye doing? Have ye lost yer minds?' But they pushed him away, faces black with the hatred that was bubbling up inside them, anger at their hopeless plight, their fury at someone was was not suffering as they.

Their aim was improving. The strength of their firing

439

increased. They advanced, hurtling the stones at Demara who knelt before them, her face pouring blood.

As Clancy ran the last distance to join Duff and try to stop them he saw Cogger, who had been standing on the dray jibbering in mindless fear, gather himself and leap from the cart. He ran out in front of Demara and, turning his back on the crowd, placed himself like a shield in front of her.

It did not stop them. Led by Deegan Belcher and Dana nothing would have stopped them now. They kept up the terrible onslaught, only Katey Kavanagh now joined Duff and Clancy in trying to halt an appalling assault.

Duff's face was cut and Clancy had a bruise on his cheekbone and his hands were covered in blood, though whether the blood was his own or another's he did not know.

Their violence accelerated now and they could not stop. They were one body, one heart, screaming with one voice intent on destruction. In a frenzy they pelted the pair until the back of the idiot's jacket was dark. Cogger held Demara in a tight embrace as he protected her and his body went numb and his poor heart, never strong, was bursting through his chest. Still they continued, Deegan Belcher crashing a huge hunk of stone into Duff Dannon's temple so hard he fell into the hedgerow. Clancy gripped at sleeves, caught bodies and jackets, sobbing, 'For God's sake, please.' But the bloodlust went on and still they screamed for more, curses hailing down, and pelted the bloody couple who lay in a crumpled heap before them.

There was a yell and loud gun-shots pierced the shouting. They stopped, faltering, stones in fists, sweat and saliva dribbling from dazed faces and mouths, breath tearing their chests, eyes filmed and clouded with hate. They stopped, confused for a moment, as if they were in some strange trance in an alien place far from home and they had been roused from a dream.

The man who had fired the gun, a small man with a walnut brown face, was marching down to the lakeside from Ballymora Castle and Lady Lester was right behind him.

'Are you animals?' he cried and his voice was cold with fury.

They stood blinking in the sun, trying to recall what this was all about, what they had been doing, and why. Like many a violent gesture the reasons seemed trivial in retrospect.

Katey Kavanagh ran to her son, echoing the Englishman's cry. 'Animals! Animals!' She forgot that she had been one with them until her son tried to defend their target and thereby became a victim himself.

'Leave them alone,' Perry called firmly, barking his command. 'Don't you dare touch them.'

'I'm his mother,' Katey cried.

'I don't care who you are. You should not have allowed this barbarity to happen.'

'Are they . . .?' Lady Kitty did not finish. There was real concern in her voice and suddenly the cottagers began to feel the beginnings of a creeping shame.

Lady Kitty had grown to love Demara over the weeks, finding solace in their friendship.

Perry was gently prising Demara and Cogger apart. Cogger was moaning, his arms stiff around Demara's body, his head on her shoulder.

'Here, you,' Perry called to Deegan Belcher, but Duff and Clancy stepped towards the Englishman.

'Not him,' Duff cried and bent down to the injured pair.

'Not you either,' Dana cried and strode up to her husband and tried to pull him away.

He stood and turned. He looked at her a moment then struck her across the cheek with the back of his hand.

'You sicken me,' he said. 'Leave me. Leave this place.'

Clancy had Cogger in his arms. 'Poor little man,' he said. 'Poor, gallant little man.'

He turned, holding Cogger's limp body as if he were a child. 'Look-ee-here! All of ye. Look at this man,' he shouted to them. 'This is a man. A man worthy of that name. He is brave and strong and he did what a real man should do. He tried to protect the weak, the innocent. I hope ye are proud of yerselves.'

'Up to the castle,' Lady Kitty instructed Clancy. 'Bring

him up to the castle.'

'He's my son, m'lady. I'm sorry – I'm so sorry but could I . . .'

'Come with us then,' Lady Lester told Katey kindly.

Perry was lifting Demara.

'Is she all right?' Duff asked.

'I don't know,' Perry said tersely. 'I pray to God she is.' He lifted her in his arms and followed Clancy and in that moment Duff would have given a king's ransom to be Perry Dawkins.

The cottagers watched them walk up to Ballymora Castle. They stood then, for a while, uncertainly. Some still clutched stones which they seemed unconscious of. They dropped them surreptitiously when they became aware of what they held.

They were alarmed now. Embarrassed. Like people discovered with no clothes on. They did not know where to look and settled for the ground. Only Deegan Belcher lifted his large head and roared loudly at the sun and threw the stone he held in his hand at the statue of Venus.

They watched Clancy with the unconscious Cogger in his arms and Perry cradling Demara, followed by Lady Lester, all going towards the castle. They saw Katey Kavanagh follow. They saw Duff wipe his forehead, his hands scratched and bleeding, turn then and point to the gatekeeper's cottage.

'I have te tell Pierce and Brigid,' he said. 'They are her parents. They have te be told.'

They watched him with furtive eyes as he hurried down to the little house that looked so peaceful in the distance. They moved apart, away from each other, nervous of each other, parties to a crime, disgraced.

They began to drift back to the barn where they were trapped together, where there would be no escape.

Their anger had not gone, was not dissipated. There had been no lancing of the boil. The poison simmered dangerously just beneath the surface and Clancy knew that before the air was cleared there would have to be a catharsis.

442

Chapter Eighty

∽◦ ◦∾

Duff covered the quarter mile to the Donnelly home and arrived breathless. He burst into the main road, shattering the peace there. Pierce, who had been cleaning and polishing his scythe, was sitting on one side of the room and Brigid, pressing the pedal of her spinning wheel, was fingering the wool with her hands. She loved the harsh feel of it that turned with her fingering to softness. The fire was low for the day was hot but they needed it for the kettle which sang on the hob. Its merry whistling drowned out the low drone of the bees.

Brigid looked up. 'Ah, it's yourself, Duff. Come in, wet yer whistle wi' a cup o' tea. 'Tis grand days are here now an' no mistake.' She busied herself with the kettle. 'Who would ever have thought we'd end up here in this lovely—' she broke off as she caught sight of Duff's face. 'Why, what is it, Duff? What's the matter?'

Pierce rose. The sun had been shining through the half-door into his eyes so at first he could not see Duff's face. 'Welcome, Duff, welcome—' then his vision cleared and he too stared at Duff, suddenly apprehensive. 'What is it, Duff?'

'It's Demara—' Brigid shot to her feet, eyes widening. 'No. No. Please don't . . . she's all right? She's . . .'

'She's hurt,' Duff said.

'Oh Jasus, Duff, what happened?' They were all talking at the same time, their sentences overlapping each other.

'Don't worry. She's been hurt, but she's up at the castle. Lady Lester's sent for Doctor Martin . . .'

'The doctor . . .' Brigid cried, alarmed.

Pierce had left the cottage. Brigid pulled Duff after her as she grabbed her shawl and hurried after her husband.

443

Pierce strode ahead, almost running in his anxiety to get to the castle.

'What happened, Duff? Tell me what happened.' Brigid panted as she hurried along beside Duff. 'She hurt herself on those stones? Didn't she? They're too heavy for a slip of a girl like her to try to shift. I told her . . .'

'The *amadáns* attacked her,' Duff told her angrily. 'Oh, she was hurt by stones all right, but not the bricks she was building the house with. Oh no! They stoned her, those bastards . . .'

Brigid stopped in her tracks and stared at him. 'Our own? Our own kind attacked her? Yerra, Duff, I don't believe ye.' She gazed at him incredulously.

'It's true as I'm standin' here,' he told her. 'Jasus, Brigid, I'm ashamed to call myself an Irishman this day.'

'Stoned? Stoned, you say? Like primitive times? Like savages? I can't believe it.'

'It's true, Brigid. I'm afraid it is true. They were mindless.' He shook his head. 'Mindless bloody violence.'

'Sheena? Della? Delia and Jinny?'

He nodded. 'An' the men. Don't forget the men. Oh, they were a grand bunch, stonin' a woman. Except me an' Clancy. His men were not there. They're guarding the site. That was how it was.'

'Jesus!' She began walking again. 'Who started it?' she asked.

She knew. It came to her sudden and sure. It had to be. Those people had to be led, God help them. They didn't have it in them to start something like that on their own. They had to have been egged on to violence. And it was her own family that had turned on itself. She waited for him to reply and heard what she expected.

'I'm sorry, Brigid. It was Dana.'

She hurried on. They were near the castle now. They could see Pierce disappear indoors.

'You should mind your wife, Duff,' she said coldly and trudged up to the great door after her husband. 'You should mind your wife.'

Chapter Eighty-One

❧ ❧

Pierce stood looking down at her still form in the bed. He did not take in the room: the pretty furniture, the flowers, the chaise-longue, the cushions. He saw only Demara, his white swallow, head bandaged, face bruised, lip cut, pale as a lily, her eyes closed, her breathing harsh.

'One of her ribs was hurt,' Doctor Martin said. 'Thank God it is not broken. She's been lucky. Unfortunately I can't say the same of poor Cogger Kavanagh. A stone hit his head – must have been very large. I'm afraid he's very bad. Very bad indeed.'

'He saved your daughter's life,' Perry said softly.

'What?' Pierce looked at the man who stood near the doctor by Demara's bed. He had a kindly face, an open, honest face with bright clear eyes.

'He saved your daughter's life,' the man repeated. Then he held out his hand. 'I'm Perry Dawkins, Mr Donnelly. I knew you at once. Your daughters are very like you. She'll be all right. Thanks to Cogger Kavanagh. The doctor has promised.'

Pierce shook his head absently. He believed this man.

Brigid had come into the room. With a cry at the sight of Demara's pale face and the bandages which alarmed her, she hurried to her daughter's side. Perry drew a chair over for her and she sat, taking Demara's hand in both of hers she held it against her cheek, then kissed it, then pressed it against her heart. 'Demara,' she whispered. 'Demara, oh my baby.'

Pierce did not touch his daughter. He knew if he did he would lose his fragile hold on both his tears and his temper. 'I'm going to the barn now, te tell them what kind of trash they are.'

He looked around the room, registered for the first time

its grandeur. Perhaps they had been wrong, he thought, to rise above their neighbours. 'Thou shalt not covet thy neighbour's goods' he murmured and wondered if he had been guilty of breaking the Commandments. He didn't think either he or Demara had but he was not sure. They simply wanted better than they had, better than the one-roomed cottages their neighbours had. They had provoked this violence and he asked himself if they perhaps deserved it for their temerity.

Even as he thought this he angrily rejected it. No, no and no. No one deserved this violence done to them. Violence was intrinsically bad. It solved nothing. It proved nothing and violence produced violence. It set off a chain reaction that had to burn itself out before it ceased.

'I'm goin' te the barn to tell them te stop. We have to stop it. We have te.' He looked up, his face clouded. 'But first I have te see Cogger.'

Cogger lay very much as Demara, bruised, his lip cut, his head bandaged. Every now and then he opened his eyes and his swollen lips moved, but he was only half-conscious and his words were slurred, so he did not make sense.

Pierce saw that Lady Lester was wiping his face gently with a napkin, for Cogger appeared to be feverish. On the other side of the bed, in an attitude of abject dejection, Katey Kavanagh ran her rosary through her fingers.

'Hail Mary, full of grace, the Lord is with Thee, blessed art thou among women and blessed is the fruit of thy womb, Jesus.'

The words sounded reassuring and familiar to Pierce and he looked for a while at the battered face of the poor idiot of Ballymora who was dying so that his daughter might live.

'I'm goin' te the barn te tell them,' he stated again.

'Are you quite certain that's wise, Mr Donnelly?' Lady Lester asked.

'Ye'll not do somethin' mebbe ye'll regret?' Katey interrupted her rosary to look up at him. 'Don't add yerself te the people who'll dread the dawn.'

'No. I'll not do that.' Pierce said.

446

He left the room and the castle, his face set in cold lines, determined, his eyes angry. Walking did not cool him, nor did he pause until the cottagers skulking in the barn jumped as the door was kicked open and Pierce Donnelly stood there silhouetted against the setting sun.

They were all there. Mog and Jinny Murtagh and little Ellie in her box. Brian Gilligan and the family and Della. Mickey and Carmel O'Gorman, Dinny McQuaid. Shooshie Sheehan, the Flynns, Miles Murphy, all of them, except Sheena McQuaid, and Pierce guessed that Sheena was out there in the gloaming consorting with Clancy's right-hand man. Their eyes blinked in the sudden light and they peered at him apprehensively. They watched him, wary, fearful and ashamed.

'Well, are ye proud of yerselves?' he demanded.

No one spoke.

'Are ye, ye tribe of foul, dishonourable men an' women? Are ye?'

''Twasn't our fault, Pierce,' Brian Gilligan cried. 'We got carried away.'

'Wasn't that what they said, those that crucified Jesus? Eh, Brian? Wasn't that what Pontius Pilate did when he washed his hands?'

'Demara's all right. We never meant te hurt her,' Miles Murphy said.

'Well now, Demara may be all right, Miles, but poor Cogger Kavanagh, as never harmed anyone in his life, is dyin'. Did ye know that? Cogger is above in the castle an' he's not long for this world.' He stared around with withering contempt. 'So I ask ye, are ye proud, pickin' on a woman an' a poor harmless fool? Are ye?'

'We din' start it, Pierce. No. We din' . . .' Shooshie Sheehan stammered, but looking up into Pierce's clear gaze he could not continue.

'Well then, who did?' He looked around. 'Who was the spotless one who cast the first stone?'

There was a sullen silence. No one wanted to tell Pierce Donnelly the truth of it.

'Who?' he repeated.

Dana stepped out in front of her father.

447

'I did,' she said.

They watched him, agog with curiosity. They saw his disbelief. They saw his sudden realization, and they saw his horror.

She stared at him defiantly. She did not cringe before him. She did not care what happened now.

He looked at her with disgust in his eyes. It was the same look she had seen on Duff's face.

'Get yer shawl,' he told her.

She was suddenly anxious.

'What're ye goin' te do?' she asked.

'Yer leavin'. Yer outa Ballymora forever. Yer not part of us any longer. I'll march ye to the parish boundary and then yer on yer way.'

'Leave? Leave here? Yer mad! I'll not leave.'

'Ye'll go. An we'll escort ye. Get yer shawl.'

'I want Mam. Get me mam.' She looked around wildly for help but the faces around her were cold and unsympathetic.

'Yer mam is up at the castle wi' Demara. Now get yer shawl.'

'Now? This minute?' She couldn't believe her ears. Anything else she could have borne. A beating. All the extra work. If they had cast her out but let her live here, near Duff, she could have managed somehow. But to be thrown out of the community, to be cast out into the wilderness, was more than she could bear. And the worst of it, the unbearable part would be not ever to see Duff again. Oh God, she prayed, not that, never that.

'I'll not go,' she cried. 'I'll do anythin' you say. I'll slave . . .'

'You don't stay. You broke the most fundamental law of our land today, my girl. Ye turned on yer own family. Yer own blood. Ye tried to kill yer own kind. Get your shawl, woman. Now.'

She was shaking now and she knelt before him, begging him, but the face she looked into was the face of a stranger.

'But Mam . . . Da, Mam won't want me to leave. Ah please, Da, please.'

He was implacable. 'I am not yer da. And she is not yer mam. No more. Never more. Yer not my kin. Yer not our kin. Get yer shawl.'

She rose with sudden dignity and went to the mattress she shared with Duff, the mattress upon which she had hoped he would make babies in her, the bed which had never been used for lovemaking, and she took her shawl from the quilt. She wrapped it around her shoulders. She glanced around the barn, the hateful barn where her love had been unfulfilled, unrequited, poisoned. She drew a breath and walked out into the twilight.

Her father had never loved her. He had given all his love to Maeve and Demara and Brindsley. There was nothing left for the rest of them. Nothing for Galvin and Killian in Liverpool or Áine in London. Nothing for her. They had worshipped him and he had held himself aloof from them, never giving them the love they craved. Now he had judged her as the hanging judge in Limerick would do.

She walked up the boreen. Pierce followed close behind. After him the cottagers moved in twos and threes, like shadows dodging in and out of the shade. They passed the church and they noticed an audacious lilt in Dana's walk. Only once she turned and looked at her father, but there was no kindness in his eyes, no leniency at all.

They came to the crossroads from where Demara and Maeve had left what now seemed a lifetime ago.

Dana stopped and turned. She was smiling and she looked at them defiantly.

'I only did what yiz all wanted to do,' she cried. 'Only ye hadn't the courage. And ye followed my lead, didn't ye? Well, goodbye. An' may ye all go te hell.'

She couldn't think of anything worse to say and there was a break in her voice at the end. Pierce heard it but did not relent. They stood in a semi-circle and watched her walk away down the empty road. They watched her until she disappeared into the darkness over the horizon.

Chapter Eighty-Two

⊷❧ ❧⊶

They returned, back down the same road, silently following Pierce, each of them immersed in their own sombre thoughts. As they neared the barn they saw one of Clancy's men, Carmody, running towards them waving his arms like windmills.

'It's the houses, they've done something to the houses,' Dinny McQuaid squealed apprehensively.

Carmody, acutely aware of the importance of his message, cried out loudly as he neared them, 'Muswell an' his men are firin' the cottages. They came chargin' outa nowhere. Oh hurry. Hurry.'

'I knew it. I knew it,' Dinny cried. 'An' we nearly finished.'

'Mine *was* finished,' Mog Murtagh exclaimed. 'I was movin' in next week.'

'All the women, get back te the barn. We don't want ye here. 'Tis no place for ye. Look after the childer.'

The women obeyed. They covered their heads with their shawls and set off to the barn, glancing back every now and then until the men were out of sight.

The cottagers followed Clancy. Clancy followed his men upstream, then across country until, once more, the terrible glare, the bright ominous orange glow on the horizon met their eyes.

The sight was followed swiftly by the acrid smell of smoke. It was familiar now, this smell, they'd experienced it before.

Pierce let out a bellow worthy of Deegan Belcher, and Dinny McQuaid, panting as he hurried to keep up with the tall man, whined, 'An' what's yer interest, Pierce Donnelly, an' you snug above in the gatehouse?'

Pierce stopped dead in his tracks and turned to stare at

the little man.

'Ye fool, Dinny McQuaid, ye dumb fool! D'ye think any of us are in this alone? Can't ye see the dangers? God help us, man, Muswell is the Marquis's man. 'Tis the Marquis is buyin' up the Lesters' land. 'Tis one an' the same enemy we all have and that enemy is not me! Jasus, man, yer a fool.' He looked at Dinny with barely concealed contempt, then around at the others, and, raising his voice, he shouted, 'Have ye forgotten me mam? Have ye? Isn't she above in the graveyard? Don't talk te me about what my interest is. Don't talk te me about bein' snug.' And turning from them he strode along ahead of them.

He knew what had happened. He knew before he saw the new, nearly completed cottages. They were burned to the ground. He knew who had done it and wondered what Clancy would say.

What he was not prepared for was the battle they came upon suddenly as they rounded the bend in the road.

Some of the cottages were on fire it was true, but not all. Muswell's men were endeavouring to set fire to the rest. Their torches flamed and leapt as darkness fell, cloaking the world in purple shadows. They looked like leaping devils as they ran hither and yon but they were chased by Clancy's men, and those men were putting up a brave fight. With a whoop the cottagers joined in.

The fight had been uneven. There were about twelve men with Muswell against Clancy's. Clancy's men were however bigger and more experienced and although Muswell's boys had arrived on horses most of them by now had been unseated. The horses were rearing and screaming and rolling their eyes as the acrid smoke belched from the cottages. Two of them were gutted, a third was on its way, another six relatively untouched. The cottages had not been thatched and were therefore harder to ignite.

Clancy's men were doing a grand job. They pulled the riders off the horses and, fists flying, were sorting out Muswell's gang with all the energy their hatred instilled in them. A fine laddo was reeling about in the centre of the circle of cottages, blood pouring from his nose. Another was bent double, hands gripping his groin where he had been kicked. There were two more struggling on the ground on their backs, having been demolished by Pascal and Whelan respectively, and Pascal was trying to pull one of the horsemen off his mount. As Pierce watched he succeeded and dragged the howling rider to the ground, gripping his waist, slowly forcing the torch back towards the unseated man's face. The crackling of the burning cottages mingled with the grunts and yells of the men as they fought, and when the new arrivals joined in there were shouts of encouragement from the Clancy contingent and the fray became more violent. The cottagers had something to erase. Their behaviour earlier had shamed them and now they saw a chance to retrieve their tarnished reputations.

Pierce looked around. The man he sought was not there. He could see that Clancy's men were well and truly ahead now that the cottagers had joined them. They had no need of him. He began to walk towards the trees.

Muswell must have come this way. He would have had to if he came from Stillwater, and certainly he had not arrived on any other road or they would have seen or heard him.

'Came chargin' outa nowhere,' Carmody had told them, so it must have been from the bridle-path through the woods.

Pierce left the struggling heaps of tangled bodies pulverizing each other and struck towards the thick, verdant mass of trees. As he reached the copse he heard voices. Someone cried, 'Don't be a fool . . .' and he knew it was Muswell's voice.

Muswell was screaming. Screaming at someone. The same way that Dana had begged Pierce, Muswell was now begging someone else. 'Don't! Don't! Don't!'

Then Pierce heard shots. One. Two. Three. He broke into a run and plunged into the wood. As he entered the green shade the light was cut with a suddenness that startled and confused him for a moment, and darkness fell all around him. He looked around him but could see nothing. There was the usual nocturnal rustlings and scamperings and little underground noises. The place was shrouded in dense gloom. Then that voice again. 'Don't! Please don't!' Then a weird disembodied scream, then a moaning that lasted moments. Then silence.

Suddenly Clancy stood before him. Like a ghost he had appeared from behind one of the trees, moon-white, lips back in a death-like grin, hands holding a smoking gun.

'Ye'll find him in there,' he told Pierce casually as if he were talking about a horse or a farm animal. Pierce stared at him.

'I gave him one for your mother,' Clancy said. 'One for my wife, one for my child and one for your mam. It's done, Pierce, and there's a great calm descended on me this night in the doing of it.'

'Well, yer great calm will soon disappear if you don't get outa here, Clancy,' Pierce warned him. 'Or they'll have ye for murder. Get goin', man. Get goin'.'

'They can't prove it.' Clancy stood there calmly.

'They don't have te.' Pierce shook him, trying to instill some urgency into him. 'The Marquis'll find some way of twistin' things te have ye hang. They'll bribe someone to swear they saw ye pull the trigger.'

Clancy's eyes were peaceful for the first time since he had come to Ballymora. His expression was at last free from inner turmoil. He looked steadily at Pierce.

'I don't care, man. Don't ye know that yet? Since my Maura died I've never cared for anything. Only one thing kept me alive and that was to get *him*.' He gestured with the gun back into the green density. 'So you see,' he smiled, 'there is nothing to live for now so it does not matter what they do to me.'

'Think of the men.' Pierce's voice was urgent. 'Your band of moonlighters. They'd die for you.'

'They'll find another leader to fight for justice in Ireland. Pascal is quite a man. He has vision and drive.'

Pierce caught Clancy's wrist and tried to take the gun away.

'What are ye doin'?' the moonlighter asked. 'Lave me be. I have another task to complete before we go.'

'What's that, Clancy?' Pierce gave up. The man was not to be hurried.

'Ye have te ask?' Clancy looked at Pierce incredulously and Pierce stared at him blankly. 'We have te show the Marquis above in Stillwater that he canna go around burnin' down Irish homes on Irish soil.'

'And how are we going to achieve that?' Pierce asked.

Clancy spread his hands, the gun still held loosely in his right one. 'Why, Pierce Donnelly, nuthin' could be simpler. We're going to give that bastard a taste of his own medicine. Then I'll go quietly wherever they take me.'

'What are ye goin' te do?'

'Why, set fire to Stillwater o'course!'

Pierce gasped. 'No, no, no, ye can't do that,' he cried.

'An' why not? What's sauce for the goose is sauce for the gander. What he can do with impunity, we can likeways do.'

'But not with impunity,' Pierce told him. 'Not with us. Don't ye see, man. The law says it is all right for him to do it to us, but not for us to do it to him. And until that law is changed we canna break it. We'll end up in gaol. I've no mind for that. Defend ourselves, ye said. That was the contract. Not murder and arson. The moonlighters have not been arrested, up to now. Because they act more or less within the law. They help the people defend themselves. Killing Muswell is murder. Setting fire to Stillwater is arson. We'll go to prison for it and I don't want that, Clancy. I don't want that.'

Clancy's face was like a strange white lantern in the leafy darkness. He sighed. 'Ye have yer family. So go home. Tell the men. We'll finish this ourselves. The moonlighters'll finish it. Go home, Pierce, in peace. And goodbye. Yer a good man.'

Pierce put out his hand and the moonlighter transferred the gun into his other hand and clasped Pierce in his firm grip. They smiled at each other.

'Thank you for that,' Pierce jerked his head backwards.

'Goodbye, friend,' Clancy said, then added, frowning, 'Go to the castle to enquire after your daughter.'

'Why?' Pierce asked. 'She must be sleeping now.'

'God man, yer an innocent. For an alibi. For witnesses. They'll have te believe Lady Lester, then no one can implicate ye.'

454

They shook hands again, then Clancy nodded and loped away. Pierce went back to the clearing. They had done well. The bodies of Muswell's men lay here and there, most of them out cold. A horse fretted and tossed its head, stirrup loose, upwind of the circle of half-built cottages. They had only succeeded in burning down two. One belonged to Dinny McQuaid who nursed a bloody nose and one belonged to Deegan Belcher who was grinning although his cheek was cut and he held an arm that looked strangely crooked. Miles Murphy was cutting a triumphant caper and holding aloft a jacket he had filched from one of the unconscious men. Brian Gilligan was looking strangely exultant, an expression of almost religious ecstasy on his face. Mickey O'Gorman and Mog Murtagh had bruised hands and black eyes and Shooshie Sheehan, clothes torn to shreds, was unhurt, as were most of Clancy's men. Dishevelled true, garments muddy and in some cases singed and torn, they nevertheless looked as if they had got the better of the encounter.

'It's a breeze when the cavalry come chargin',' Pascal told Pierce, brushing himself down. 'Up there on their horses they need a field, space, and they can only descend, God help them, te *terra firma* wi' a thump! Yerra it's a terrible disadvantage.'

Clancy was striding towards them now, and Pierce saw he was not holding the gun any more.

'Listen, lads,' he said when he reached them, 'we'll have to tie up that lot, that scum there who'd burn the houses of their fellow countrymen for money.'

His men nodded.

'Where's that blackguard of a leader?' Mog Murtagh asked.

'Yeah! Where's Muswell?' Mickey O'Gorman enquired.

'He's ... er ... gone! Enough said,' Clancy replied firmly. 'Now we have not much time to lose. I want ye lot to go back to the barn. Ye have te live here so I don't want ye to break the law. Here ye were defendin' yer property, or Lady Lester's—' he winked at Pierce— 'An' that's within the law. But I don't want ye here for the next phase.'

'An' what would that be?' Brian Gilligan asked.

455

'Me an' my men are up to Stillwater an' put the fear of God in the Marquis of Killygally.'

'We'll come too! Janey, we can't miss that,' Miles Murphy cried.

'Sure, we'll sort him.' Deegan Belcher sounded punch-drunk.

'Aye, that we will,' Mickey O'Gorman returned.

'No, ye won't! D'ye want te end in gaol? If ye don't mind, then come along by all means an' take the risk. Me an' my men here are used to gaol. But think carefully before ye join us.'

They were tying up Muswell's men using neckcloths, belts, shoe laces and anything they could find. It was to delay them only, the bonds were not meant to last, but Clancy did not want any of them getting word to the Marquis about what had happened.

Pierce turned away and started to walk back. He would take Clancy's advice. Like the women he glanced back over his shoulder once or twice and saw most of the other cottagers were doing likewise. They would all have dearly loved to go but no one wanted to be a martyr. They were moving one by one down to the barn, travelling slowly, and they too looked longingly back at the men of action. They probably ached all over, Pierce thought, from the fight. The atmosphere among them was different too, it had undergone a change. The shame, the hangdog avoidance of each other had gone. There was a comradely unity about them that had been missing earlier. This fight had been worthy and they obviously believed that they had redeemed themselves.

The moon had come out and it spilled pale silver light over all the land. Pierce strode along and there was in him the temptation to go directly home. It had been a long and anxious day, a day of unusual activity and he was bone tired. But he was a cautious man. He thought of Clancy's words. He stood a moment, the wind lifting his dark hair from his brow, then shaking his head he decided to take the moonlighter's advice and he turned his steps towards the castle.

Chapter Eighty-Three

∽ ⌒⌒

Kilty answered his knocking.

'They're all retirin', Pierce,' the old retainer told him. 'It's been a long day, sir, an' not without incident.' His dry voice cackled.

'Who is that, Kilty?' The voice was English and Pierce saw in the hall behind Kilty the man he'd seen before, the man with those bright, sharp blue eyes called Dawkins. He would do, Pierce decided, he would be a reliable alibi.

'Excuse me, sir, for disturbin' ye. It's just that I've come te make sure my girl is all right.'

'Good God, man, come in, come in. Where the Devil have you been? Your face is black as a chimney sweep's.'

Pierce had not expected this. He entered and stood, shifting from one foot to the other.

'Some brandy, Kilty. Two glasses.'

The Dawkins man strode across the hall, beckoning Pierce to follow. He led him into a large comfortable room with a huge fire burning. He threw himself into a winged chair and indicated the one opposite. 'Now sit down, man, and tell me what's afoot.'

Pierce Donnelly had never been in a room like this in his life, and he certainly had never sat in one. He stared at the man in confusion. 'Sit? Sir? Me? Here?'

'Yes, yes, man, sit, sit,' Perry said impatiently. 'Ah, here's Kilty. Pour us a large one each.' He watched as Kilty did as he asked and Pierce Donnelly watched too in fascination.

'Good, now then my good fellow, drink that. It will do you good.'

Pierce obeyed him. The brandy made a fiery passage-way down to his stomach. He was not sure what he was doing here. Perhaps this man thought he was someone else. But no, looking into those shrewd eyes he was aware that Perry Dawkins did not miss much.

'Well, what happened, Mr Donnelly? You didn't come by that blackening out in the green fields of Kerry.'

He did not know what to tell this man about the events of the evening, but, as the brandy imbued him with a certain relaxation of his natural caution he decided to tell the truth. In any event he knew it would not be wise to lie to this man.

As it happened Perry Dawkins had already guessed. 'Don't tell me the Marquis has tried to burn you out again?'

Pierce nodded. 'Aye, sir. I'm afraid so.'

'Good grief, has the man no morals at all?' Perry asked.

'Morals is not a word in the Marquis's vocabulary,' Pierce volunteered.

'Ah. I see now where your daughter got her quick wit,' Perry grinned.

'Well, he's within the law, sir. They say young Lord Lester is sellin' him great acres of this land. No doubt he owns our patch by now so he is within his rights.'

Perry frowned. 'He may be legally entitled, but there is also, Mr Donnelly, a humane law that one doesn't transgress.'

'Well, as I said, sir, I don't think the Marquis of Killygally would be worried about humanity at all.'

'What has he done this time? Did he cause much damage?'

Pierce shook his head. 'No, sir. Not this time. It was the new cottages, sir. The ones Lady Lester gave us permission to build.'

'But that is her land, is it not?'

'Well, sir, as I just said, we think the Marquis has bought it from young Lord Linton.'

'Ah, I see. Damme, the man is vile. So? The damage?'

'The moonlighters were guarding the hamlet, sir, an' they warned us, an' well, we routed them, sir.'

'Well done!'

'They only managed to fire two cottages, I think, sir, an' partly damage another. An' now the moonlighters are goin' to . . .' The smile faded from Pierce's face. He had gone too far. It had slipped out. His weariness, the warmth

458

of the fire, the brandy had all conspired to make him indiscreet.

Perry Dawkins eyes had sharpened. 'What? What are they going to do?'

'Nothin', sir. I spoke out of turn. I beg pardon, sir.'

Perry Dawkins was staring at him intently. 'Is it something to do with Stillwater?' he asked. 'You've got to tell me, Donnelly. You've *got* to.'

'I'm sure I don't know, sir.'

'Donnelly, listen to me. Listen carefully. My sister is in that house. Everyone has forgotten her existence, but not me. I have been trying to get her out for years. You talk of the law.' He snorted. 'Well, in her case the law says that bastard has total authority over her because he is her husband, but I who love her have none.' He stared at Pierce. 'Now, if those moonlighters as you call them are planning anything that will endanger her you *must* tell me. Otherwise don't worry. I'll not bother you for information that is none of my business.'

At first Pierce could not understand the man. It was all too sudden. Was the sister a guest? Or a servant? His wife? But the Marquis did not have a wife, everyone knew that. Then he remembered Brigid and the women whispering about a female up at Stillwater, a prisoner there. The Marquis's wife. He looked at Perry.

'You'll not get the polis? You'll not . . .'

'The last thing I want is the police. Listen, man, I want to get my sister *out*. I'll be breaking the law if I try to. The Marquis could have me arrested for abducting her.' He smiled grimly. 'Mind you, I don't think he will, but you must see, I will be like the moonlighters, outside the law.'

Pierce was still doubtful. 'Well, I don't know, sir . . .'

'I'm going anyway. I have to get there, but I'll be glad of your help. And afterwards I'll deny ever having been there. I hope you'll back me up, eh, Donnelly. But if they are going to damage Stillwater my sister may be hurt.'

'They are, sir.'

'What are they planning?'

'A taste of his own medicine, sir.'

Perry jumped to his feet. 'Burn it! Of course. They're

459

going to burn it.'

He was striding to the door. 'Come on, Donnelly,' he cried. 'We have to get there in time.'

'But, sir, I don't want to get put in gaol.'

'Rubbish, man. I'll vouch for you. Have no fear.'

Pierce gave in. How could he refuse to go with the man? He followed him out and around the corner to the stables.

'We'll ride over there, Donnelly, you and I. You lead the way.' And glancing over his shoulder at Pierce's anxious face Perry added, 'Do not look so worried, my good fellow, I guarantee your safety. Mount up and follow me.'

Chapter Eighty-Four

෨ ඁ

They rode through the night under the pale moon, the wind in their hair. Pierce found himself enjoying the challenge. He was protected. What a powerful thing that was, to be protected. What a grand feeling of security it gave one. He felt like a child again, beside his father, knowing he was in safe hands, that he would be taken care of.

He could only do good. He would try to stop those fools committing arson. He would try to help Dawkins' sister.

The neighbours would hate him. He would have to reconcile himself to that unpalatable fact. He was not with them, he was against what they were doing. But then, he had never been popular. He had always done things because they were right, not because he was on one side or another. The cottagers did not understand that.

There was the sound of pounding hooves behind them and Perry Dawkins turned to look around, not for a second slowing his pace. Pierce glanced over his shoulder too and saw Phil Conlon racing to catch them. His horse was galloping flat out and he came alongside Perry and Pierce but said nothing.

Afterwards he told them he had seen the smoke from his cottage up above the castle and had decided to investigate. As he rode down he saw Pierce and Lord Dawkins and decided to follow them even though they were not travelling in the direction of the smoke, but towards Stillwater. 'It's my job, after all,' he said.

Pierce nodded to him as he joined them and he rode along beside them, urging his mount forward.

They could see Stillwater under the stars long before they reached it. As they came through the trees, there it was, on its hill, elevated above the surrounding countryside as Ballymora Castle was all those miles away to the west.

At first the big house seemed asleep and the threesome reigned in their horses.

'What's happened? Why're we here?' Phil Conlon asked breathlessly.

'Clancy's goin' to set Stillwater on fire. Show the Marquis what it's like,' Pierce said.

'Jasus, no!' Phil whistled. 'Shag it!'

'He sent Muswell to burn the cottages again but Clancy was waitin' an' they were routed!' Pierce told him with relish.

'Good on! Did they do any damage?'

They were whispering and Pierce didn't know why.

'Oh my God! Look there.'

There was a sudden burst of activity around the big house. From a window on the ground floor came a sudden crash, a tinkling, splintering of the French windows, and glass burst out, like a shower of stars spraying out over the lawn in tiny glittering fragments. The scattering of glass shards was followed directly by an eruption of orange flame, great tongues of red-gold fire surging up around the house from the windows on the east side. At the same time there was a clarion call of 'Fire!' 'Fire!' 'Fire!' and Clancy and his men could be seen charging around the house, yelling and shouting, warning people.

The east wing was now blazing, the flames consuming everything in their path. Then out of the house, emerging into the night in various stages of undress came Melrose in long combinations, Mrs Vargan, a blanket wrapped around her pink flannel nightgown and screaming as if the Devil himself was chasing her. They could see Mr Aeronson the bailiff running down the hill, one leg of his breeches on and him holding the other leg in his hand as he raced to see what was happening. Phil conlon burst out laughing, slapping his thigh.

'Well done, me boyos,' he yelled. 'Now that scum knows what it feels like to be fired.'

Perry Dawkins looked at him, and Pierce answered, 'It is not a laughing matter, Phil.'

Perry urged his horse forward and Pierce followed him. Clancy saw them coming. He was still yelling, 'Fire!' and waving his hands to his men, ordering them to get out.

'Go on, run, fellas, now, run. Out now, out. Ye don't want to be caught now, do ye?' He looked at Pierce. 'I just want te make sure everyone's out.'

'We'll be off then, sir,' Bogue said. 'Away like the wind.' And he galloped off.

'We'll shake the dust of this place offa us,' Whelan cried. 'Say goodbye to the community for us.'

And the men split up and were gone, into the shadow of the trees. Only Clancy remained.

And that was what they had always been, Pierce thought, shadows. Tall, dark, men who were almost intangible, and it was only Sheena McQuaid who had grown to know one of them. They had shared their homes, shared their battle, but no one had really known them.

The fire was spreading, flames leaping, licking the walls up to the second floor now and Pierce realized that Perry Dawkins had dismounted and hurried to join him.

The front door was flung open and the Marquis, struggling to don a brocade dressing-gown, coughing his lungs out, reeled into the drive. He steadied himself against a pillar, spluttering, trying to draw in great gulps of air.

Perry pulled at Pierce's sleeve. He pointed up to the second-floor window in the west wing. There behind the

462

glass a small white face appeared, like a reflection of the moon.

'Fleur,' Perry whispered, keeping to the shadows and out of the Marquis's line of vision. 'Quickly,' he urged. 'Come on. Don't attract attention. Phil, take the horses around the back, this side, and wait for us there.'

They hugged the wall of the house, around the back where Perry found the door to the kitchen open. They hurried through and emerged into the hall. Pierce's heart beat fast. They could see the Marquis standing, back to them, in the doorway. He followed Dawkins up the stairs and, turning to the right, they reached the upper gallery. They ran down the corridor and Perry flung open the door at the end.

Fleur's startled face was turned towards them and her eyes, almost blind, were cataract-filmed. She stared, milk-white eyes turned to them, gazing into some distant place only she could see.

'Get outa here! Yiz are not allowed here.' A stout lady in black put a protective arm around the girl, or woman, standing near the window, staring at the blurry outline of the men who had suddenly erupted into her cloistered world. Fleur had a youthful body and movements yet on closer inspection she appeared middle-aged.

This was no fairytale awakening. No prince kissed the cheek of a young and beautiful princess, for the woman had the face of an aged nun. It was with pity in his heart that Perry looked upon his sister closely for the first time in twenty years.

She did not recognize him, that was obvious. She probably could not see him, he thought sadly, when he had stood below in the grounds, hoping for a sign from her.

She shrank from him now and the woman, Mrs Black, spoke to her softly as if she were a child. 'There now, lamb, don't worry. There now, *acushla*.'

'The house is on fire, madam,' Perry cried. 'You must leave immediately.'

Mrs Black stared at him as if he were mad. 'Don't tell lies,' she replied. 'This is a plot. The Marquis warned me. If you've come to get her you'll not succeed.'

'Listen, madam. There is not much time. Look out of the window if you do not believe me.'

But the woman was not to be shifted. Stubbornly she stood her ground. 'You'll not take my lamb,' she reiterated.

Pierce Donnelly came forward. He went to the woman and took her arm. 'He tells the truth,' he said, 'The man is not lyin'. The whole place is ablaze. Stick yer head outa the window an' see.'

'I cany. They're sealed,' she said.

They realized that what she said was true and Perry hurried on. 'Is there a back way out of here?' he asked.

'You'll not take her anywhere. She is the Marquis's legal wife.'

'I am her brother, madam, and have only her welfare at heart.' Perry's mouth was tight and he had trouble keeping his impatience in check. 'If you do not believe us, go to the door. You can smell the smoke.'

Before they realized what she was going to do she had run to the door and down the gallery calling, 'My lord, my lord, my lord, come quickly, come quickly.'

Perry moved swiftly. He swept his sister into his arms and strode out with her. Pierce ran ahead, opening doors, trying to find an exit.

They found the back stairs and hurried down the stone steps, feet clattering. Fleur was weightless, as light as a child, and she whimpered like a small animal in Perry's arms. She did not struggle even though she must be bewildered and cold. He should have brought a shawl or taken a cloak but there was nothing he could do about that now. He pushed open the door at the bottom of the steps and found himself outside. He saw with relief that across the gravel under a chestnut tree Phil Conlon waited with the horses.

Perry turned to Pierce. 'Mount up, Donnelly,' he ordered. 'Take her. Take her to Lady Lester at Ballymora Castle. Ride fast, man, as if the Devil were at your heels, and guard her with your life.'

Perry took off his cloak and wrapped it around her and Pierce did as he was instructed, putting Fleur across the saddle. Turning his mount swiftly he galloped away to the west.

Perry went around to the front of the house, Phil Conlon close behind him. The Marquis, speechless with rage, was hopping up and down in the driveway. Clancy stood in front of him, arms akimbo, and they caught the drift of what he was saying.

'. . . you know what it is like! This is not your country. Ye can't come here an' take our land, burn us out, cheat Lady Lester . . .'

The Marquis found his voice and yelled with impotent rage. Threats bubbled from him but Clancy paid no attention and neither Melrose, old and venerable, nor the cook nor Mr Aeronson had any notion of interfering with this tall avenging angel.

'Bastard! Scum! I'll see you swing if it is the last thing I do.'

'Catch me first!' Clancy cried, then putting his foot in the stirrup, he mounted his horse, turned her head and galloped away.

The Marquis threw his head back and, looking at the moon, raised a clenched fist to heaven and shook it at the blue velvet sky.

Perry Dawkins gestured to Phil and they crept away from the house, mounted their horses and left.

As they stole back however, Phil could not prevent a shiver of fear coursing through his veins. The Marquis's rage was a terrible thing to see. Someone, Phil knew, would have to pay.

Chapter Eighty-Five

∽ ∾

On his return to Ballymora Castle Perry went straight to Demara's room. She was glad to see him.

She was restless and could not sleep. Dr Martin had told

her she had a wonderfully healthy constitution and she should recover quickly.

'It seems,' she told Perry, 'that the hard life of a working girl is far healthier than that of a lady.'

She was, however, shocked by what had happened. She still could not believe that her sister, her neighbours, the people she had known all her life could have stoned her so cruelly. Surely it had been an illusion.

But the sad truth was that they had meant to kill her. They had desired her death, she had seen it in their faces. Horrified and disillusioned she turned to Perry for explanations, for understanding.

'Why, Perry? Why? I've known Jinny Murtagh and Della Gilligan, oh and all the others all my life. I've cut the harvest with them. I've sown in the fields alongside them. I've helped deliver Sheena McQuaid's babby, I've . . .'

'I know, Demara,' he said softly, soothing back her hair from her bandaged forehead. 'I can guess. But that was a crowd, not individuals. That was a mob. They – plural – had turned into singular: *it*, a wild, many-headed beast, a monster.'

'I cannot believe it, even now. Why, Perry? Why? What did I ever do to them?'

'You did nothing. You didn't have to. They are jealous of you and your father. They need something, someone to hate, because of the oppression they live under, because of the insecurity. They need a scapegoat and your family is it. You have improved yourself, you see. You have ambitions.'

She smiled tremulously at him. 'You are a great help, Perry.'

'People behave well when they are treated well,' he said. 'Poverty and fear bring terrible consequences.'

She looked at him with tender eyes. He had been such a support. He never questioned her. He had found the crane for her, had it sent to Bannagh Dubh. He had worked alongside her, shoulder to shoulder and when the weather had turned hot he had not given up. 'India was much hotter than this,' he said. They had, with local help, raised the stones and statuary and built the walls bit by bit.

There was something binding in working like that, sharing the toil with another. Her mother and father had shared a common purpose. They had created together something good, and they had worked hard to improve their lives and it had brought them very close.

That is what happened to herself and Perry as they toiled in Bannagh Dubh together, and now, lying on her bed in Ballymora Castle, she turned her trusting eyes to Perry because she had learned he was dependable.

'Was it because of my dream, Perry?' she asked him. 'Did that cause it?'

'It was partly that. You are showing them up. They imagine that you think their way of life is somehow inferior whereas the truth is you probably don't think of them at all.'

'I don't.'

'I know.'

'Oh, Perry, is my dream so terrible? Is it wrong to want something so badly?'

He shook his head. 'Of course not. You know that.' He frowned. 'Only one thing though . . .'

'What's that?'

'A dream can become an obsession. When your dream leaves no room for love, then that, I think, is not ideal.'

'Oh!' She digested this, then looked at him anxiously. 'How is Cogger?'

His face was grave. 'He is not well, Demara. He is very sick. Dr Martin does not hold much hope for him.'

'Oh, Cogger.' A sob tore her bruised and tender chest and she winced and tears trickled down her face. 'Oh, Cogger! He saved my life. He protected me. Oh, poor darlin' Cogger.'

'I know, Demara, I know.' His voice was soothing and infinitely understanding and she turned her cheek onto his hand.

'I must see him.'

'No, my dear, not yet,' he told her gently. 'You are not strong enough. You'll not last five minutes if you get out of bed now. You'll collapse and that will be no use to Cogger. Sleep now and when you awaken I'll take you to him.'

She was glad enough to obey him. She ached all over. Every movement was agony. It felt as if every bone in her body was broken – but Dr Martin had said that Cogger had saved her from the worst of the onslaught.

She slept fitfully. Perry never left her side except to share a bowl of broth with Lady Lester who kept vigil in Cogger's room.

'I simply do not feel like eating,' she told Perry. 'But one must keep one's strength up.'

'We'll eat heartily when Demara shows improvement,' he said.

'You'll be relieved,' she sighed. 'We'll all be relieved.'

Perry suddenly stopped supping and shuddered. He put his head in his hands. Lady Lester leaned over and patted his arm, then, in a moment, he took a deep breath and glanced at her. 'I thought they had killed her,' he said. 'When I saw her lying there, Cogger covering her, her clothes, her face covered in blood – oh, Kitty, I thought she was dead.'

'You love her very much, don't you?' she asked.

'Oh yes,' he replied swiftly. 'Oh yes. But she's in love with Duff, Kitty, and he is young and he is handsome. Why would she want me?'

'Demara Donnelly loves you Perry, only maybe she doesn't know it yet. But I can promise you she does.' Kitty gave him an amused glance. 'And as for Mr Dannon, he is not made of strong enough stuff for her, Perry. Oh, he is a simple man, a good man, but Demara confuses him and she'll realize that in time.'

Perry smiled. 'I hope you are right,' he said doubtfully.

Lady Lester thought how much she liked him, then remembered what it was she had wanted to say to him.

'Your sister, Perry. Mr Donnelly told me all about it. I've put her in the yellow room.' She chose her words carefully. 'She's a . . . frail creature. She'll need . . . a lot of . . . help.'

Perry sighed wearily. 'Can you imagine what it must have been like for her all those years?' He glanced at Kitty. 'I thought, you see, that she saw me when I made my yearly pilgrimage to stand outside Stillwater and watch for her face in the window. I thought she could see me and she was telling me not to interfere. I was so sure she'd send me a sign if she needed my help. But she was blind. She couldn't see. Oh, Kitty!'

'My dear man. Try not to think about what is past. Drink your soup. You must eat.'

The next morning Demara insisted on going to see Cogger. 'I can't rest properly until I do,' she told them.

Any movement was painful, but with the help of Kitty, Perry and Kilty she managed to get out of bed, struggle into her robe and, supported by the men, make her painful way to the room where Cogger lay.

As she came in Katey Kavanagh rose from her place beside her son and shrank into the darkness near the wall. She was ashamed to face Demara, but Demara had forgotten she had been among her attackers.

It hurt her to see Cogger lying there, broken and bandaged in the great canopied bed. His eyes were closed and his arms lay at his sides, like an effigy.

She sat beside him and picked up the large, lifeless hand. She put it to her cheek. His eyelids fluttered then his eyes opened.

'I could smell ye, Demara,' he whispered. He knew her scent. He recognized her touch above all others.

'Don't try to talk, Cogger,' she said, her eyes filling with tears. 'Just rest. Ye'll be all right.' She patted his hand and looking up met Dr Martin's eyes across the bed. He silently shook his head.

'Cogger, thank you. Thank you for savin' my life.'

'Ah sure, Demara, why wouldn't I an' you always an angel to me.' His voice was hoarse and faint. 'There's something though. I have te . . .'

'What is it, Cogger?'

'The cave . . .' he whispered.

'Yes. The stones. Where we got the statues. You knew they were there, Cogger, didn't you?'

'No. No. Not the stones. The other cave. Where the cliffs are high, in a cave . . .' His face was anxious. It was his parting present to her. His gift of gold and treasure.

'I'll look, Cogger, I'll look.'

'Promise me.' His hand tightened in hers.

469

'I promise,' she pledged.

Immediately his hand slackened in hers and his head fell to one side. She laid her forehead on his shoulder. She felt incredibly weak. The room seemed to suddenly fade and dissolve. She felt her head close down as if a light had been shut off and she slid to the floor before they could reach her.

Cogger never regained consciousness. One half-hour later he died in the great bed, his mother beside him.

Chapter Eighty-Six

∽๑ ๑∼

Perry Dawkins arrived in London a week later. There was a message from Lord Rudolph Davenport to meet him at White's any day of the week between the hours of four and six p.m.

Perry changed and hurried over to St James's Street and asked where the devil Rudi was. On being told he was in the small smoking room he made his way through a crowd of welcoming friends and shouted, 'Rudi, Rudi, dear old fellow,' as he caught sight of the young man. He clapped him on the back and demanded to know what was so important.

'I'm marrying Maeve,' he told Perry. 'Can you believe my luck?'

Perry laughed. 'Our interests are identical,' he said. 'For I fully intend to marry her sister.'

'Then we'll be brothers-in-law,' Rudi cried. 'What a splendid arrangement.'

Perry sighed. 'Whether the lady will agree is another matter.'

'There is something else, Perry,' Rudi told him. 'Remember Belle Desmond?'

'Yes, of course.'

'Remember she had a daughter who disappeared?'

Perry shook his head. 'I don't think I ever heard about it. What happened?'

Rudi told the whole story from the beginning. 'It's a terrible tale I have to tell, but I thought it would interest you because it concerns the Marquis of Killygally.'

Perry gave him a swift glance, but held his curiosity and listened to what Rudi had to tell him.

When he had finished and the two men sat before the fire in the golden light, both sickened by the tale, Rudi added, 'Maeve drew the whole story from the girl bit by bit. I guessed in the street that I was right. You should have seen her face when she laid eyes on Bosie. He abducted the child, raped her, brutalized her . . .'

Perry leapt to his feet and banged his cane on the floor muttering, 'Damnable. Damnable.' He began to pace.

'It does not bear contemplating,' Rudi said. 'The poor child lost her memory. She was in shock when the nuns found her, broken. Tilly, Belle Desmond's little maid, told us the rest. Hell, Perry, the man must be punished.'

'It is not only that child that he hurt,' Perry muttered. 'He did the same to my sister.'

'Your sister, Perry? I never knew you had one.'

'Oh yes. Bosie abducted her before you were born.' The memory of Fleur's eyes, her bewilderment, was too painful for him to think about now. He knew he had left her in good hands at Ballymora Castle and that Demara, when she fully recovered, would be glad to have her close. 'I came from Ireland because I want Bosie taken care of,' he said coldly.

Rudi opened his eyes wider. 'You mean . . . kill him?'

Perry shook his head. 'Oh no. That would be too easy. He does not deserve to be let off so lightly. Besides, Rudi, I do not make a habit or murder.'

'Then what?' Rudi's eyebrows shot up. 'Castrate him?' he whispered. 'Oh, that would do very nicely.'

'How bloodthirsty you are, young Davenport,' Perry said smiling. 'What would Maeve say if she knew how barbarous you are?'

471

Rudi laughed. 'Oh she's much worse than I,' he said. 'If you heard what she planned for my lord Bosie, why it makes castration attractive by comparison.'

'Well, I'm not thinking along those lines, although if my idea does not work, why then perhaps we'll try it.'

'What lines are you thinking along?'

'Pride, Rudi. His pride. His burning ambition to climb the ladder of social success. He has gone a certain distance, held on and is making his way slowly now to the top. He is invited to most of the important parties already, but there are some still closed to him. So my plan is to clip his wings, dear Rudi, so that he cannot fly at all. Don't you see what an abysmal nightmare that would be for him?'

Rudi was staring at the man opposite, understanding dawning. He sipped his wine, savouring both the vintage and the thought of ostracizing Bosie.

'My God, if he were dunned out of high places . . . oh, Perry, yes!'

'You see, Rudi, I dislike the thought of resorting to violence. I do not see why I should have to lower myself to that beast's level. I also dislike breaking the law. One never knows how embarrassing the situation one might fine oneself in. But can you imagine the satisfaction of having that man banned in society? Why, it would drive him insane.'

'But how to accomplish that, Perry? It may not be easy.'

'Neither will it be too difficult,' Perry reassured him. 'For it I need the help of your mother and father, Rudi. So I hope you are currently on good terms with them?'

'The best,' Rudi smiled. 'At first they were a bit miffed about my intention to marry Maeve. They thought I was trying to compete with Sebastian. As if anyone wouldn't marry Maeve given the chance.'

'I wouldn't,' Perry remarked drily, 'I love her sister much better.'

'Yes, but you are distinctly odd, Perry old fellow. Anyhow, Demara is enough like Maeve for me to understand your passion.'

Perry decided not to tell him that Demara was infinitely more beautiful than Maeve. He decided Rudi was blind on that point and therefore the best thing would be to let the boy think he had the prize when any idiot could see that he, Perry, had.

'What do you want Mamma and Pappa for?' Rudi asked. 'They don't like Bosie any more than we do. He offended Papa somehow, I don't know the ins and outs of it, but Papa calls him a bounder and won't have him in the house any more.'

'Are you sure they are quite happy about your marrying Maeve?'

'Oh yes. Mamma has seen the advantages. You know how she adores her position as leader of society and dearest Aunt Maud told her that to have Maeve Donnelly on your guest list absolutely ensures a successful evening. Aunt Maud . . .'

'The Dowager . . .'

'Exactly. As Aunt Maud is in London and at Court, although nothing much goes on there these days as you well know – it's deadly dull . . .'

'Nevertheless . . .'

Light dawned and Rudi sat up and his mouth fell open. ' 'Pon my soul, Perry, I see what you are gettin' at, damme if I don't.'

'Exactly! Your mother, Rudi, your aunt and dear Bryony Gilligan are the three who can cut him out. Completely. And, wonderful thought, the Duke, your father can ruin him in the clubs.'

'Strap me, you're right. Why, Perry, you're a genius. Although the truth is I would dearly love to wield a knife to that man's parts and make a soprano of him.'

'You would end up in Newgate and accomplish nothing.'

'He wouldn't be able to commit those crimes again.'

'Tell your mother, tell your aunt, tell Bryony the truth. About Lucy Desmond. About my sister. Everything. They are women and none is hard-hearted. They will be shocked and so they should. Tell them our plan. Say we mean to disgrace him. Tell them we need their cooperation.'

'And Pater?'

473

'Tell him the truth too. But the clubs won't banish a man for such misdemeanours, so I think we will have to drum up a cheating accusation.'

'Oh, Perry, Bosie would not cheat . . .'

'Strange the society we live in Rudi, where a man is drummed out of a club for cheating and not for rape,' Perry sighed. 'I know, dear boy, that Bosie would not cheat. We'll lie! It will be our only sin. We will lie blatantly, you and I. We will not tell your father about it though. He must think the accusation is genuine. And that, on top of what he will have heard about the Marquis from you, ought to do the trick.'

Chapter Eighty-Seven

〰 〰

Bosie was in a foul temper when he arrived back in London. The damage to Stillwater was considerable and he had reported the matter to the local constabulary who had not given him the reaction he sought. Far from sympathizing with him they stared at him with hostile eyes and gave him polite replies that were generally unhelpful. The truth of the matter was, Bosie mused angrily, that people these days were allowed to get away with murder and the bloody Irish stick together. Allegiance to the Crown was a joke to them and because he was English and a gentleman they had no intention of putting themselves out to help him.

'You have heard of this man, I take it?' he had asked the officer in charge.

'Oh aye! We know him. Isn't he the one who goes around Ireland helpin' people who have been unfairly evicted?' The constable's face was all innocence. The Army officer said much the same thing when he reported to the Army, having got no satisfaction from the police.

'Ah, Clancy, yes. We don't like to tangle with him. He

doesn't break the law, you see. Keeps well within it. And he usually has good grounds for his actions.' The young English officer glanced sideways at Bosie. 'What did you do to cross him?'

'Never mind that now. I want him arrested.'

'Hold on, sir. That's the province of the police.'

The Marquis gave up. He fumed over the incompetence and laziness of government bodies, particularly in Ireland.

His frustration was increased when, before going to London he tried to get help repairing the damage the fire had done to Stillwater. All he got were refusals and messages to inform him that no one was available. The same excuses were made in Listowel, Tralee and the environs of Killygally, Ballymora and Bannagh Dubh. Eventually Mr Aeronson told him that every available man in Kerry was working.

'Aren't they all in gainful employment at Ballymora Castle working for Lord Dawkins. An' won't it be the grandest house in Ireland. Pillars and columns an' statues all come out of the sea!'

The Marquis did not understand the drivel the man his bailiff had brought to see him was spouting. His mind was wrestling with the fact that Perry Dawkins was building a house in Ballymora. It had given him a nasty turn when he discovered Fleur's disappearance. He knew Perry must be behind it. Now, not content with sneaking his milksop sister away – Bosie's own legal wife – he was building a home in Kerry just down the road, you might say, from Stillwater. Well, let him take one step out of line and Bosie could slap an injunction for abduction on him. The Marquis thanked God that he could take Perry to court in the civilization of London and not in this barbaric land where they broke the law and closed their eyes to crime when it suited them. Bosie ground his teeth and decided that he would not take Perry to court just yet. He would hold that card up his sleeve.

He eventually had to settle for a team of builders who would repair the damage to Stillwater at twice the going rate and with astronomical travelling expenses because they had to come from Limerick. The work would mean

475

that Stillwater was uninhabitable for some time to come so Bosie took himself off to the fleshpots for some recreation.

When he arrived it was exactly a week after the conversation Perry had had with Rudi in White's. He stopped at his rooms in Cavendish Row and dropped off his trunks and changed for the evening. Then, aching for some civilized entertainment and the company of men his own class who would give him a sympathetic ear and perhaps a game of chance to cool his temper, he set off towards the clubs. He gave himself up to some pleasant speculation as to what he would eat that evening, having been at the mercy of his Irish cook in Kerry, and the vintage wine he would sup, and, eventually he thought he would find himself some street urchin for some fun to calm his frayed nerves.

He arrived at Drone's full of warm anticipation. Well known there, a regular guest, he was a little disconcerted when, on his entrance into the hall, a sudden silence fell. No one looked at him. No one greeted him or paid any attention to him. A hush settled over the place for a few moments, then the buzz of conversation recommenced.

He noted Benjy Newsetter talking to the Earl of Doncaster, both friends of his, and he went towards them, hand out in greeting, but at his approach they seemed to melt away and he was left, hand outstretched, walking towards the wall.

He shrugged it off. He was tired. He had been travelling. The journey had worn him out. Added to that his blood pressure was high from the ordeal he had been put through by those sons of bitches across the water.

He went to the gaming room. Again that sudden silence on his entry. Then the buzz of conversation, the pointed avoidance of eye contact, the shifting away of anyone he approached.

Something was distinctly odd or else he was imagining things, having hellish delusions, and it occurred to him that he had not eaten properly in days, not since before the fire at Stillwater, so perhaps he was having hallucinations.

He left the club, hailed a cab, and, feeling shaken but not seriously worried, he went to the Café Royal.

It was early. The crowds had not arrived yet for dinner

but nevertheless the place was full of acquaintances. He sighed with relief. Sanity at last.

He did not notice the odd look the cloakroom attendant gave him as he left his coat, but he began to feel distinctly uncomfortable once more when a hush fell over the foyer and the lounge as he walked through. Dammit, it was as though he was wearing a funny costume, or had the wrong clothes on.

He shook off the feeling. Determinedly he set himself to combat this mental delusion he seemed to be suffering from. He made his way to the dining-room and beckoned the *maître d'hôtel*. The man did not hurry over as he usually did. Bosie waited. The man was elusive. He *must* have noticed him standing at the entrance to the room gesticulating. It was his job to do so. He knew the exact importance of everyone in London, their status on the social scale and where to seat them. Bosie had always rated pretty high.

His temper was shortening moment by moment. He could feel the ball of rage growing within him and he tried to control it in order not to do or say anything he would regret later. He was good at that. He had spent years successfully swallowing his anger in order to assure his place in society. He had climbed to his secure position, welcomed in the highest circles, because he had control over his wayward temper. He promised himself that when his place in society had become unassailable he would then tell a few people what he really thought of them. But for now discretion was the better part.

At last he decided to take the law into his own hands. Blow the *maître d'hôtel*. He walked through the tables, a few of which were occupied, and confronted the *maître d'hôtel* halfway down the room. The man stared at him as if he were an insect, giving him no sign of welcome.

'I would like a table, André, if you please. I'm newly arrived from Ireland and am most monstrously hungry.'

The *maître d'hôtel* seemed to catch a glimpse of someone over the Marquis's shoulder and to Bosie's *chagrin* he dodged past him. The Marquis was now marooned, directionless and alone in a sea of tables. This did not happen even to the most humble diner. A few of the customers at the tables glanced at him with supercilious superiority. They conveyed their contempt at his inability to get himself seated.

The *maître d'hôtel* was greeting a nobody, in Bosie's opinion, as if he were an honoured customer, giving him the red-carpet treatment, whilst he, one of the Duke of Malvern's best friends, was being overlooked. It was intolerable and he strode out of the place in a furious rage, planning to himself how he personally would ruin the Café Royal.

'I have been treated monstrously here this evening,' he hissed to the hapless cloakroom attendant. 'I fully intend to inform all my friends of your incompetence. This place will be out of fashion in a week.'

He left, his head simmering with pain, his teeth grinding, his stomach a knot of fury.

He decided to walk down Regent Street, then Oxford Street, then turn into Soho and make his way to the Clarien. The walk calmed him somewhat. He was tired and hungry, he told himself, and he was allowing the unimportant to ruffle him – and that, as Maynard often pointed out, was a waste of time. There was probably some simple explanation: the king of some obscure eastern European country was arriving and had booked to dine at the Café Royal and André had allowed it to affect his judgement. Well, he would show André. Next time he would invite the Duke of Malvern and the Earl of Cress and Sturrage and a few other cronies of high degree and disconcert the *maître d'hôtel* – perhaps even refuse to allow him to serve them. He imagined himself surrounded by very important people saying in grand and ringing tones, 'We do not wish to order until this man has left.' How satisfactory that would be.

He entered the Clarien in a much better mood than he had left the Café Royal. The restaurant was half-full. He saw a group he knew at a table by the window and waved. No one returned the salute. He told himself not to be imaginative, that they probably had not seen him, but he suddenly felt very cold. A chill ran down his body as he asked Mr Clarien for a table. Mr Clarien looked at him in the same way the men in the club and André had looked at him and it was a terrible look.

'My lord, we have no vacancies this evening,' Mr Clarien stated firmly. Bosie could see his book and there were only about six bookings written there.

'This is ridiculous,' he cried.

'I'm afraid, my lord, there is no table for you here. Now if you will excuse me.' And the owner walked away and left him standing there. There was no 'Come back later, my lord, and we will fit you in', no regret, no apologies. Such a thing had never happened before.

Bosie crossed the room to where his cronies sat. There was a spare chair at the table.

'Evening, Gerald, Richmond, Carruthers. May I join you? Seems this place is more popular than I thought.'

The men at the table turned the same expression on him, that awful look in their eyes that he had in so short a space come to dread.

'If you don't mind, Bosie, we're expecting somebody. Sorry, old chap. Can't sit here.' And they turned their attention away from him. Cold-shouldered him.

He stood there, hesitant, unable to grasp what had just happened. Then full realization dawned – he had been cut. He felt that chill again tiptoe all over his body, icy digits slipping down his back, across his chest, over his arms, and suddenly his knees were weak.

At the table the three men had recommenced their conversation as if he did not exist and he stood staring at them in disbelief, aware that they were snubbing him, unable to move away. Then young Richmond glanced up at him and gave him a look of such withering contempt that Bosie turned tail and fled.

He felt ill now. He hailed a cab and sat hunched in the corner until it reached Cavendish Row. Then he got out and paid the driver. His man in London, Termick, was slow to answer his bell. Bosie was too frightened now to be angry. He sat in his panelled study looking at the unlit fire, shivering and bewildered. Termick eventually answered.

'Termick, I don't quite know how to ask you this, but I

have to know, have you heard anything about me in my absence?' He glanced up at his man and was surprised to see an expression of withering insolence on his butler's face.

It was now that Bosie realized he was in terrible trouble. Something appallingly damaging had been attributed to him while he was away. He had to find out what it was, then he could put it right. Then things would go back to normal and his friends would greet him and not treat him as if he had the plague. He had, in some way, been maligned, and he was sure that once he knew what had been said or done he could rectify the situation, correct the erroneous information and things would go back to normal.

'I have had some very strange er . . . reactions since my return, Termick. There must have been some terrible mistake. Please tell me what you have heard, then I can explain it away.'

'My lord, I am simply come to give you my notice. I'm sorry, sir. I am leaving.'

The Marquis of Killygally was shocked. Termick had been with him now for nigh on five years. Things must be very serious for him to leave. Positions were not easily come by. Most gentlemen's gentlemen hung on to their jobs and vacancies did not occur often. Gentlemen got used to their butlers.

'Termick, what is happening here? What have I been accused of? I've been condemned without a hearing,' he cried petulantly.

Termick did not bother to reply. 'If you'll excuse me, my lord.' He left quietly and without much ado. Bosie realized as he undressed for bed, by himself, without any help at all, that something weird was going on. He was bewildered. He truly could not guess what he had done to deserve such monstrous treatment.

Before he retired he checked the post as usual. The pile of letters on his desk in the bedroom was minuscule. Usually when he returned to Cavendish Row there were stacks of invitations to sort through, some to accept, some to regretfully reject. Tonight there were no attractive gold-edged requests for his company at Lady Berwick's on the first, nothing from the Countess D'Abru who, he knew, was having a ball with fireworks on the seventh, no invitation with Sebastian's personal message, 'Do give us the pleasure of your company, Bosie'. No invitation from Veronica Bainbridge to the monthly soirée she always held in the summer but which was strictly by invitation only. The post contained a bill from his tailor and his wine merchant. Quite unnecessarily insistent on settlement. It was this that unnerved Bosie more than anything else. Tailors and wine merchants did not mind waiting for their bills to be settled when their debtors were the height of fashion and in demand in society. But, at the first breath of scandal, the vultures swooped. Tomorrow he would have to find out what it was all about. Yes, that was it. He would deal with it tomorrow. He would clear the matter up and things would return to normal. He would get invitations again, they would arrive by the bucket. He would be greeted everywhere, 'Evening, Bosie', 'Afternoon, Bosie', 'Morning Bosie'. And he would not forget those who had snubbed him during this most ghastly day of his life. He would make them suffer for their impertinence. He would see that the Café Royal and Clarien's went out of style, he would change his tailor and his wine merchant. He would get a new manservant. And he would cut those upstarts he had spoken to in Clarien's out of his visiting book.

He was cold. Termick had not lit the fire nor warmed his bed. He was hungry and frightened. He knew that eventually he could correct the whole ghastly situation and told himself so. But it did not improve his comfort. He climbed out of bed and went downstairs to the wine cupboard and got the bottle of brandy that was there. He didn't know where the glasses were so when he got back to bed he drank from the bottle. When it was finished he fell into a fitful slumber. He was not a man who dreamed, but tonight his sleep was full of spectres. He lay there helpless while horror overwhelmed him. Circles of faces sneered at him. A queue of his friends walked up to him and spat at him full in the face. A crowd reviled him, yelling insults at him. He tossed and he turned but could not make them go away.

Then into the background faces slowly appeared, faces that he only half-remembered, faces from the past. They stared at him with pain-filled eyes, eyes wild with anger and hurt. He did not know who the faces belonged to. They were familiar yet he did not know them.

They frightened him. They made him want to run away but he lay heavy, pinned to his bed. Things spun about. The faces mingled and formed a screaming ring. There was a ringing in his head. Someone was crushing his brain. All the faces were hammering his head. They would not stop until his brain was a bleeding, soggy, bloody mass of pulp.

He screamed.

Chapter Eighty-Eight

ఆ ౷

The next morning was the most unpleasant and uncomfortable of his life. There was no hot chocolate and rolls, no smells of cooking from the servants' quarters, no dressing-gown and slippers laid out, no hot water, no one to shave him or look after him, no paper for him to read, nothing.

In a fury he dressed himself to the best of his ability and, leaving the rooms, went out and hailed himself a cab which took him to St Martin-in-the-Fields. He went into the Orange Street baths and for two pence procured himself a hot bath and a clean towel. Feeling marginally better he then went to the barber in St James where he was shaved. Emerging later he strolled down the street, feeling far more the thing and, convinced he had imagined most of the previous day's slights, he wandered into White's. To his disgust the first person he met was Perry Dawkins. To his vast surprise the man took his arm and propelled him willy-nilly into a small ante-room usually reserved for dignitaries and non-members who had to wait. There were periodicals on a small round table and a fire crackled in the grate. Bosie was glad of the warmth for he still felt the chill he had endured during the night.

Perry Dawkins pushed him into a chair on one side of the fire and seated himself in the other. Bosie was outraged and sputtered his objections, but under his anger there was a small knot of fear.

Someone else had come into the ante-chamber and he saw to his surprise that it was Rudi Davenport. Rudi closed the door behind him and leaned against it, and there was something menacing in his attitude.

'Morning, Rudi,' Bosie began, hoping to cut the hostile atmosphere. 'Morning, Perry. Let's order a little toddy. Start the day right, eh?' he suggested.

There was silence in the room. Bosie bore it, nerves stretched until he could bear it no longer. 'Oh well then, I'll order outside,' he cried, jumping to his feet. Suddenly he did not want to be here, did not want to be near these cold-eyed men who stared at him so impudently, but Perry's whiplash command stopped him in his tracks.

'Sit down!'

He sat.

'If you order outside your order will not be fulfilled,' Perry told him. Bosie remained silent. He did not want to hear any more, but Perry continued. 'From now on, Bosie, you are no longer a member of White's. You are no longer a member of Almack's or the Reform or—'

'What are you . . .' Bosie stammered. This was too much.

'You are no longer welcome in any fashionable home. You have no place any longer in London society.' Perry glanced over at him. 'Do you understand? I hope for your sake, Bosie, that you have cultivated other friendships, for I doubt the Irish will welcome you at Stillwater.'

'So that's what this is all about! You set me up because you are in league with Lady Lester over my land.' Bosie was outraged. 'Well, let me tell you . . .'

'No. Let us tell you,' Rudi said slowly and emphatically, speaking for the first time. 'This has nothing whatever to do with land. This has to to with cruelty to children.'

Bosie looked startled. 'Well, 'pon my soul I don't know what you're talking about,' he cried.

It dawned on Perry that he really did not know what he had done. 'You have committed terrible crimes, Bosie, and the time for payment is due.'

'You are mad! Your sister is my wife. I can take legal proceedings against you to get her back.' Bosie's threatening tones were a cover-up for fear. They were entering territory he preferred not to discuss.

'Do so by all means,' Perry replied calmly. 'And I shall bring my sister into court and let them judge as to her state and your treatment of her.'

'She is my wife. There is no law that says . . .'

'There may be no law against cruelty to wives, Bosie, but there is one against rape.'

Bosie stared at them in surprise, and Perry leaned forward.

'We have others. Others you despoiled and broke and cast away when you were finished with them. They have voices, Bosie, and will speak against you.'

Bosie remembered the faces in his nightmare but pushed them away. He had never thought those waifs mattered. They were the scum of the earth, not to trouble one's head about and no one would take an urchin's word against that of a gentleman.

'Listen, Perry, listen, Rudi,' he began, a reasonable man asking for a reasonable response, man to man. 'We are all men of the world here. What is this all about? No, I mean really? I come back to London to find myself set upon by all me friends—'

'And so it shall go on, Bosie. You are *persona non grata*. You are doomed. Your deeds are now known to one and all. A light has been directed onto your most sinister acts and all has been revealed. So many of your comrades-in-arms betrayed you for less than thirty pieces of silver. You must know, Bosie, you have terrible taste in friends.'

'You should never be guilty of doing things in the dark that cannot stand the light of day,' Rudi said and added, 'and Bosie, you have been cheating . . .'

Bosie leapt to his feet, an expression of outraged innocence on his face. 'I *never* cheated. Never. I'm not that stupid.'

Rudi crossed the room and pressed him back into the chair. 'But I *saw* you!' he said. 'Perry too. And my brother Sebastian. And my father.'

'The Duke?'

Rudi nodded and Bosie knew instantly that all was lost. The game was over. The Duke's word would never be doubted. He was destroyed, ruined. Everything was gone.

'You better leave now, Bosie,' Perry said quietly and Bosie rose and with the walk of an old man he went to the door. He looked at them, standing there, but there was no mercy in either face so he left because there was nothing else to do. Rudi threw himself into the chair the Marquis had vacated.

'Well?' he asked Perry.

Perry nodded. 'The man is beaten most effectively,' he said. 'Don't you agree?'

Rudi nodded again.

'I take no pleasure in it though,' Perry continued. 'The man does not even realize his cruelty. He will probably end his days ignorant of the extent of the evil he has done.'

Rudi stood. 'Let us go and have that toddy,' he suggested. 'This room has a bad smell in it.'

Chapter Eighty-Nine

cᴖ ᕐᴗ

Rudi purchased a delightful house in Grosvenor Square. He told Maeve she must have it furnished and decorated as she desired and she set to with childish delight, making frequent trips to Liberty in Regent Street, Peter Robinson in Oxford Circus and Whiteley's in Queensway. She bought fabrics, chose paint, and went to auctions to procure exactly the furniture she wanted.

The Taming of the Shrew opened and was a resounding success. The part of Katerina was far less emotionally demanding than Juliet and the heavines of spirit she had suffered disappeared and the light-hearted buoyancy returned.

She was falling more and more in love with Rudi. He was such a delightful companion, such a stimulating and lively person to be with, and day by day she was increasingly enamoured of him.

She loved his touch, his laugh, his strong hands, his shy smile. He did not tell her what to do, did not expect her to pretend to be other than she was. He appreciated her art, encouraging her and sharing everything with her as her friend.

'Do you mind me being an actress? Truly?' she asked him at dinner one evening.

He shook his head. 'No,' he said, 'no, I'm proud of you, dearest girl. Times are changing,' he added. 'Women will not long tolerate their slavery. It is as Mrs Pankhurst says and I agree with her. But,' he leaned over and covered her hand with his, 'you must not tell Mamma and Papa that I hold such radical views.'

She giggled. 'I promise,' she said.

He looked at her seriously. 'You see, Maeve, you are the first girl I have met who is not playing a game. Pretending to be less clever than they actually are. I dislike demure misses who – whether actually or artificially – seem to find me invincible, hang helplessly on my every word and elevate me to the position of a god. I want to have a partner who'll tell me I'm a fool if I'm acting like one, who'll exchange ideas with me, who'll learn with me, laugh with me, be my friend, my lover – and it just happens that you fit the description. Being an actress is part of that, part of the you I love.'

'But I don't want your mother and father to disapprove of your choice.'

'They've become used to it.'

The story of Lucy Desmond had shocked the Davenports and Iris, who was inclined to close her eyes to the indiscretions of the male aristocracy, was forced to look with open eyes at the pathetic case. She was surprised in an unexpected way by the fact that her son was so shocked by the actions of the Marquis of Killygally. He could so easily have condoned his behaviour – he had after all been brought up to believe that people in high places had the right to treat women as playthings. But Rudi was fairminded and respectful and she was secretly very pleased.

All society had swiftly closed its doors on the unfortunate Marquis who had nowhere to hide himself, nowhere to go but slink back to Stillwater, the builders and the workmen.

And as one door closed another opened, and society warmly welcomed Maeve in. Its members opened their arms to the lovely actress and took her and her talent to their hearts.

Sebastian had also come to terms with his brother's betrothal to Maeve. He had, he told his mother, been infatuated with the actress and he was far happier with his dear Fanny, who made no demands upon him and had only one desire: to make him happy.

'I did not like all that churning inside,' he told his mother. 'Most unpleasant sensation. I hate suffering, Mamma, and I suffered all the time when I was with Maeve. Rudi is welcome to that turmoil. See if I care. No, Fanny's the gel for me.'

Bosie returned to Stillwater to find that nothing had been done. The staff was gone and he was greeted coldly by Mr Aeronson. The house was freezing, the grounds unkempt, the horses running wild in the fields. It was a sorry state of affairs.

He procured new staff but they were ill-trained and incompetent. Anyone with talent and experience did not wish to go into service with him; his reputation had, as they said, gone before him.

He wandered the house, railing against fate and Rudi Davenport, but mostly against Perry Dawkins. He began to blame Perry for everything that had happened to him. He rode the hills furious with himself and all the world and to his everlasting surprise he missed Fleur. Just the fact of her not being there in the house, weaving her tapestry, gave him a feeling of loss.

He was utterly confounded by the swiftness of his rejection by the only people who mattered to him. He took to the brandy bottle, at first simply to get warm, then increasingly for company. He drank to drown his problems but his problems learned to swim. Then he drank because he needed the stuff to get him through the long, pointless days and nights. Then he drank because he had to. He was drunk most of the time and the only person he saw was Mr Aeronson his bailiff.

But Mr Aeronson, that precise and accurate man, would only discuss pounds, shillings and pence, half-pennies and farthings. He reported dutifully to his master. He actually did not notice people that much. Figures were his thing. He did not relate to other human beings, which explained why he had never married. He related to money and long lines of figures written in his meticulously neat hand. So he did not really see the Marquis. His head was too full of numbers to have room for the state the Marquis was in.

However, when he realized that his master, who used to be so astute in money matters was losing his grip, had become careless and showed little interest in the profits and losses – was in fact indifferent to the point of carelessness – he began his first game with numbers. He enjoyed this game so much that he improved upon it. It was such fun, gave him so much satisfaction, that it became the driving force of his life. Rearranging the figures. To suit himself. So that he benefited.

His master, the Marquis, could at any time query anything he wished and an essential part of the game for Mr Aeronson was waiting to see if he would. His blood pounded in his veins, his heart thumped, but the Marquis never did. He signed page after page, bill after bill without seeing, without checking. Once he would not have allowed a farthing to go unaccounted for, but times had changed and with them the fortune of Mr Aeronson.

He decided to up the stakes. His juggling from one column to the other had started in the last column and now was in the first, right next to the pound sign. He began to float in two digits. He became mesmerized by his game. He knew that as this progressed he would have to disappear. He had no intention of being caught.

He would go to Germany, he decided. No one would find him there. He spoke German fluently. His mother had been German. She had married an Irish sailor on shore leave in Hamburg. He had jumped ship and they fled to Ireland where their only son was born.

He would go to Hamburg and see the place his mother hailed from.

He smiled through his steel-rimmed spectacles at the Marquis of Killygally who smelled so revolting and looked so peculiar, as if he was about to pass out, and he slid another paper across the desk at him.

'My lord, here please . . .' he said politely and bowed his head so that Bosie could not see the smile on his face.

Chapter Ninety

As Maeve rushed about London choosing fabrics for curtains and occasional tables for the drawing-room and mirrors for the hall and escritoires for the bedroom, she was filled with a sense of well-being and joy. Life was radiant again.

They often dined with Perry and he talked about Demara.

'Has she got her dream?' Maeve asked one evening as they sat sipping champagne in Kettner's.

Perry smiled. 'The house is nearly finished. I think it will be finished by your wedding. But I think she is in for a surprise.'

'She's accepted Mamma's invitation,' Rudi said, 'so you will see her, my darling. I know you miss her.'

'Yes. She wrote and told me she would be here.' Maeve smiled across at Perry. 'And when is your wedding to be?' she asked.

'I try not to be impatient,' he replied, 'but there is something she has to find out.' He sighed and shrugged. 'When she'll have me,' he finished.

'I know when that will be,' Maeve told him.

He looked at her curiously. 'Oh? When?'

'When that house is finished. She's been obsessed with it as long as I can remember. And I've got a theory.' She bit her lip. 'Want to know what I think?'

'Absolutely! Please tell me.'

'Well, I think that when she finishes that house she won't want it any more. It was an ideal. A dream. Not for reality. The way Sebastian was in love with me. What she wanted, what he saw, were insubstantial illusions. Mirages. I think when it is finished you should ask her to set the date.'

Perry threw back his head and laughed. 'Strap me if I don't think you are right, Maeve,' he said. 'She wanted to do it all by herself, you know.'

Maeve nodded. 'I know. She might have taken years and wasted her life if you had not got help for her.'

'You mean she was building this house with her own hands?' Rudi asked in disbelief. Maeve and Perry glanced at each other and nodded.

'Oh yes,' Perry said. 'When I saw her, the first time I stayed with Kitty Lester after I had met Demara, she was up to her knees in muck and up to her elbows in dirt and she had nearly finished digging the foundations. And that is quite a job.'

'I like this family more and more,' Rudi said. 'That takes real dedication. What an amazing bunch you are.'

Perry leaned forward. 'The only thing that alarms me, Maeve, is . . .' He frowned and wrinkled his brow in thought. 'Oh, I don't know how to say this but, the only thing is, the house is not very attractive. I hope I haven't shocked you. But I have to say it.'

Maeve was not in the least disconcerted. 'I didn't imagine it would be. Attractive, I mean. Demara is not an architect, after all. Are the realizations of dreams ever nice?' she queried. 'Without expert advice? Without professional plans and specifications? I doubt it. It will be a hodge-podge of everything she has dreamed, you mark my words, and as I said, she'll lose interest as soon as it is finished and she has proved that she can do it. Then she'll marry you.'

'I hope you are right,' Perry sighed.

Maeve smiled at him affectionately. 'You belong in the family, Perry, so it will happen. Don't you agree, Rudi?'

Rudi nodded. 'You are such a close family, Maeve. You are very lucky, you know.'

Maeve didn't say anything. She thought of Áine and was ashamed. She had not bothered to check up on her sister since Áine had left Soho Square. Maeve had excused herself on the grounds that work and the demands of her career left her no time. Now however there was a break for August – the theatre was closed for the month and the new production was ready for its opening in October. Geoffrey Denton was doing *Cyrano* in September so that Maeve could have a month off for her wedding and her honeymoon. She had been rehearsing *As You Like It* during the day and performing Katerina in the *Shrew* in the evenings and her Rosalind was, Geoffrey Denton assured her, the most delightful performance of the part he had ever seen and was going to be another sensational success.

Áine had been far from Maeve's mind. She was enjoying her freedom. It was such a change for her to have the evenings off. August was warm but not too hot, and London was deserted for everyone had gone to the cooler air at the seaside or up to Scotland to the mountains.

One day Maeve went out accompanied by Tilly to shop. Lucy was not at all comfortable yet sallying forth into the town without male protection and Belle would not in any event allow her. The noise scared her. The rush of people caused her to panic and whoever was with her would have to hail a hackney and take her directly home. She only felt safe with Bert.

Maeve and Tilly went to Bond Street. Maeve wanted to go to Tessier's to order silver cutlery for her new home. They sauntered along, Tilly carrying the bibs and bobs Maeve had purchased on the way, and she was feeling carefree, untroubled by time. She relished the luxury of being able to dawdle and the knowledge that she could afford to buy what she wanted. It was a wonderful sense of achievement that her diligence and hard work had entitled her to and she was proud of what she had accomplished.

She hugged her happiness. Rudi adored her, London was at her feet, there was nothing she could wish for that she had not got. She wondered what she had done to deserve such happiness and hoped Demara would soon be finished at Bannagh Dubh and might discover what bliss there was in loving someone as much as she loved Rudi.

As she walked she noticed from the corner of her eye a beggar-woman with a baby of about eighteen months to two years wrapped in a shawl that bound them together. The woman sat on the street around the corner of one of the little side streets.

Maeve did not look directly at the woman, but stopped, opened her reticule which was hanging at her wrist, took out some change and bent to drop it in the woman's lap. She always gave to beggars. No matter how undeserving the poor might be they were welcome to what she could afford. When people in the great house cried out that they were parasites and sloths she tartly replied, 'If you find one of them who refuses to change places with you, why then I'll forbear to help them.'

The woman was strangely quiet. There was no 'God bless ye, ma'm' or 'Oh thankee, m'lady' and she glanced down and saw the woman's face, hidden in her shawl, was turned away so that Maeve couldn't see it.

It was the baby she recognized. Seaneen.

She dropped to her knees in front of the woman. 'Áine?' she asked, gently pulling the shawl back from the face and saw that indeed it was her sister. 'Áine!'

She was crouched on the pavement shivering. She looked angry but her cheeks were stained with tears.

'Oh, Áine, why didn't you let me know?'

Her sister said nothing, but looked mutinous and Maeve turned to Tilly. 'Go to Piccadilly and hail a cab.'

The maid rushed off to do as she was told and Maeve turned once more to her sister. 'Here,' she said, 'give Seaneen to me.'

'If ye say anythin'—' Áine warned through tight lips.

'I'm not going to say a word.' Maeve retorted. 'All I want to do is get you up and out of here.'

She helped her sister up off the pavement. Áine had some difficulty rising, as if her limbs and joints pained her.

'Here, take my arm,' Maeve told her, holding Seaneen in the crook of her arm. 'Hold on, come with me.'

She led Áine down Bond Street and out into Piccadilly. Tilly had a hackney waiting for them beside the curb.

The drive back to Soho Square took no time at all. When they arrived there, though Belle's heart sank at the sight of the only Donnelly she disliked, she was moved to tears by the state the girl was in.

Angela and Tilly filled the tub with steaming hot water and they peeled off the filthy rags that covered Áine's body. The tight line of her mouth, the suspicious glint in her eye, warned Belle and Maeve not to ask questions.

Lucy came in asking who the stranger was.

''Tis my sister, Áine,' Maeve explained.

'Oh, poor woman, what happened to you?' Lucy asked. Up to now no one had dared to inquire.

'Me husband! The bastard! Beat me so he did an' I left 'im.'

'Oh you poor thing.' Lucy's eyes were full of sympathy and Áine responded to the girl's warm-hearted concern.

They bathed her and patted her dry with soft towels.

'Where'll we put her?' Belle asked. Maeve now slept in a small room beside Lucy, who had her old room back.

'She and the baby must have mine,' Lucy said firmly.

'Oh no, I can't do that,' Âine protested, but her objection was feeble.

'Yes, you can,' Lucy was adamant. 'I want you to. I'll sleep with Mother.' She glanced at Belle who nodded. She was perfectly happy to share her bed with her daughter.

'Well then, that's decided,' Lucy cried.

Áine, they quickly discovered, was very ill. Her chest was weak and she coughed up blood and sometimes fits shook her whole frame as she desperately gasped for breath. She had lost a lot of weight and was woefully thin and emaciated.

Strangely enough it was Lucy who helped her most. The

493

young girl took to Áine from the beginning and seemed to consider it her mission to tend her and nurse her. It was to Lucy that Áine confided what had happened, though Belle and Maeve had already guessed.

Lorcan had behaved himself for a while after he had brought her home from Soho Square. Then, inevitably, he got drunk again and began once more to beat her. She had been badly hurt but was too proud to go back to Soho Square and admit failure. So she had stayed in the apartment, scared and humiliated and had made up her mind that, as her father always said, she had made her bed, so she would have to lie on it.

Lorcan had continued to beat her and his attacks got worse and worse.

'An' then,' she told Lucy, who sat swabbing her forehead with lavender water, 'and then he hit Seaneen. That was the last straw.' Her face was whiter than the pillow, an eggshell tint of blue in her skin, and there were dark circles under her eyes. 'My poor little babby,' she wept. She wept easily and weakly and Lucy bathed her tears with infinite tenderness.

The baby was in Lucy's old cradle at the foot of the bed. He was a curiously apathetic child, and they were worried about him too.

'He hit Seaneen,' Áine said. 'That poor wee mite that never hurt anyone and has only us te look after him. Bastard hit him.' Her tale was interspersed with violent fits of coughing that seemed to tear her apart.

'I had to leave. Seaneen was cryin'. It was his feed. It's natural for a babby to cry. He didn't mean any harm. Then Lorcan picks him up an' throws him against the wall. I screamed an' Lorcan hit me. He kept sayin' "make 'im stop, make 'im stop." As if I could.' She sighed and Lucy wiped the cloth across her mouth. 'I left 'im. Wi' nothin', I roamed the streets that night. I was so scared. A copper asked me if I was all right. I told him I was an' hurried on, as if I had somewhere to go. But I didn't. The streets were dark an' I was cold. Oh, you don't know how cold it can be, right through your bones, into the heart of you. I kept askin' myself if the danger out there wasn't a whole lot worse than what was waitin' for me in the apartment. But I knew one thing. I couldn't go back. Anyway, I found a doorway an' we sat there for the night. It was damp an' freezin'.' Her speech was interrupted by a fierce fit of coughing that near ripped her lungs apart. Lucy remembered. She knew that feeling. She knew the cold of the London pavements.

What Áine was telling her helped her to remember all that had happened to her. It had come back slowly. There was still a fog over some of the experiences of that terrible night. But as Áine spoke she remembered that she too had crouched in a doorway shivering and deadly cold, and a fearsome chill that had crept through her limbs and paralysed her. She remembered. Oh, she remembered.

Coughing fit over, Áine continued. 'Cold and lonely. Frightened I was, an' sick wi' worry about Seaneen. When morning came there was nowt to do but beg for charity, so I stuck out my hand. Jasus, 'twas the hardest thing I ever did. Me da's face kept comin' before me. Oh, the shame of it. An' when someone drops a couple of farthings to me I wanted to throw them away. Me pride hurt, see? But I didn't. An' that's how it's been since.'

'How long, Áine?' Lucy asked.

'Couple weeks. First I was down near Smithfield's, but I saw Lorcan. Roarin' drunk he was, reelin' up the street. I was scared owa me mind he'd see me. He'd murder me, see. Do it. Regret it later, but it'd be too late for me. Couple of nights I stayed in a place for the likes o' me, in Whitechapel Road, but it was scary there an' someone stole the few shillings I made that day. Took it owa Seaneen's swaddle. So I came west, to where the toffs are.' Her half-smile was bitter. 'An' ye know somethin'? The toffs are mean. It's the poor that give what little they have.'

She looked feverish and Lucy told her to hush up and rest.

'You can tell me the rest later.'

For the first time Lucy was preoccupied with someone else. She did not now have time to think about herself at all, she was so busy nursing Áine and looking after Seaneen, playing with the little boy and helping him to talk.

'Do you think it's all right, Lucy run off her feet with my sister?' Maeve asked Belle.

'Well, my dear, it seems to be helping her, and me personally, I wouldn't like to try to stop her.' She gave Maeve a tremulous smile. 'Oh, Maeve, you'll never know how wonderful it is to have her back. I missed her so dreadfully when she was away. I have to fight a desire in me not to let her out of my sight. In case I lose her again.'

Maeve clasped her in a warm embrace. 'She'll be all right, Belle. She's happy nursing Áine.'

'Yes, and while she is she'll not stray,' Belle whispered.

'Bert is spending all his time with her, Belle,' Maeve ventured. 'I noticed, did you?'

Belle smiled. 'It's what I've hoped and prayed for most. Bert and Lucy.' She looked at Maeve. 'Oh, Maeve, he's like a son to me. And he loves Lucy, he always has. He never stopped looking for her when she was away. And he found her. It was Bert who put two and two together and worked it out, otherwise, oh, Maeve, she might still be in the convent. And Lucy trusts him. They are both simple, gentle people. Oh, I would be so happy if they wed.' She glanced away, then back with a sly smile. 'Eventually,' she added.

Bert took Lucy, her hand in his, for a constitutional every evening. They walked around the square and down Frith Street. They sometimes drank a coffee in the coffee house in Dean Street before they strolled back home.

At first Lucy was nervous, but Bert kept her hand in his, covered by his big firm paw, and she often thought that no one could be nervous with Bert's hand over theirs.

She clung to him, relying on him to guide her and take care of her and he never let her down. She was someone rare and fragile in his life, someone he wanted to take care of. To him there was a mystical quality about Lucy. She had been stolen away, cruelly hurt. She had disappeared behind high convent walls and there she had lived her sheltered existence. And all the while he had been searching for her. He had stared into the face of every passenger on his omnibus, every pedestrian he had passed in the street. Always on the watch for her he had finally found her and now he knew he would never let her go.

But he did not want to startle or frighten her.

One evening when Áine was sleeping and Maeve was waiting in the parlour in her evening dress for Rudi to come for her, Lucy was sitting by her mother on the sofa, leaning her head on her shoulder, when Bert came in. As he entered Lucy jumped up, her face flushed, appealing to him, 'Isn't Maeve quite the most beautiful woman in the world, Bert? I think she looks like a bride already.'

'She is beautiful, certainly,' Bert agreed.

'Would you like to be one of my attendants, Lucy?' Maeve asked. 'I would buy you the loveliest gown you have ever seen.'

Lucy thought a moment. 'I would love to,' she said finally. 'But I would be awkward in such grand company.'

'Nonsense.' Maeve was adamant. 'There will be four of you carrying my train.'

Belle's eyebrows shot up. 'Train?' she exclaimed. 'Train? Oh, we are grand.'

'Yes,' Maeve nodded tranquilly. 'Train. I am hoping Demara will come over in September. Perry said she will and, Lucy, Demara will look after you. Sebastian's new wife, Fanny, will be another.'

'Why, Maeve, how clever of you.' Belle looked at her in admiration.

'Well, it is better to make friends in the family, don't you think?' Maeve remarked lightly, then looked at Lucy. 'Oh, Lucy, you must. You will be with Áine and your mother will be there and Bert. So you see . . .'

Lucy smiled, 'All right. If Mother and Bert are going to be there.' She gave him such a trusting look that Bert's heart skipped a beat. He took her into the Square that evening. It was mild, bright as day, and there were quite a few young couples strolling arm in arm in the pleasant square. He sat her down on a bench and suddenly dropped on one knee, surprising both of them.

'Lucy,' he said taking her hand and ignoring the derisive giggles and ribald remarks called out by the passersby. 'I can't 'old it to myself any longer. I 'ave to look after you. Will you marry me?'

497

'Oh get up, Bert,' she cried. 'Everyone is staring.' Her face was flushed and she did not seem to know where to look.

'Please answer me an' then I'll get up,' he told her firmly. The dampness of the grass was penetrating the knees of his trousers and he hoped she wouldn't keep him there too long.

She leaned forward, her face near his. He could see the delicate sheen on her skin, the ebb and flow of her blushes.

'I can't marry you dear, dear Bert. And you know why.'

There were tears bright as diamonds in her eyes.

He shook his head. 'No,' he cried, 'I don't know.'

His heart had plummeted deep into his stomach and he felt sick. He got up off his knee, eliciting a round of applause and a hoot from the people about. He sat beside her on the bench.

'Why?' he asked her. 'Why?'

'Oh, Bert, don't look like that. I can't bear it. Bert, you *know* why . . . of course you do.'

She was watching him gravely. He shook his head.

'When a man marries he has a right to expect . . . well . . .' She hesitated.

'What are you talking about, Lucy?' he asked.

'Well, a man has a right to expect his bride to be . . . intact.'

She hung her head, staring at her clasped hands.

Relief flooded Bert and he leapt to his feet, 'Oh blow me! Oh is that all? Oh great heavens above! Why I don't care a fig for that.' He sat down abruptly. 'Oh no. I didn't mean it was nothing. To you, what you felt, what you suffered, that was, well, shocking. But my little angel, you was hurt very bad an' I want to look after you. Make it up to you. I don't want you just for that. I love being with you. I want you to be my wife. I want you just the way you are, see?'

'But, Bert, I don't know if I could ever let anyone . . . any man . . . do, like, wot he expects, wot he should be entitled to . . . I just don't know . . .'

He took her hands in his. 'Listen, Lucy. I want to marry you to protect you. Look after you. Like you was my child,

498

see? Now if that is all you want, fine. That's all right by me. If you do come to love me in that way, well, that's all right too.' He smiled at her and touched her face. 'I don't want anything from you. I just want to give.' He stared at her a moment. 'When we're married, you can sleep anywhere you want. But you might like to sleep in the same bed as me. I'd just hold you, careful-like, in my arms – would you like that?'

She nodded eagerly. 'That'd be nice, Bert. That'd be very nice. It's just . . . the other . . . I don' know if I could after . . .'

'Then you don't 'ave to.' He held her face between his two huge hands and kissed her on the lips. 'You don't 'ave to do anything you don't want to do ever again.'

Chapter Ninety-One

୧ଓ ଜ୬

They broke the news when they returned to the house. Belle was overcome. 'Oh my dears,' she cried, clasping them in her arms. 'Oh my dears. Marriage is in the air.' Then dabbing her jowly cheeks with a mangled handkerchief she bustled them into the parlour. 'You'll live here with me?' she insisted. 'I can't rest until you agree. I would die without you.'

'Of course we'll stay with you,' Lucy said. 'Won't we, Bert?'

'Whatever you want, my dear.' Bert couldn't stop smiling. 'Whatever you desire.'

'Well, I'd like to get married in the convent,' she told him. 'Reverend Mother will be so pleased and I'll be with everyone I know.'

'That, my dear, I think can be arranged,' Bert said.

The only one with reservations was Áine. She whispered to Lucy that all men were brutes and monsters and that any woman who trusted one was a fool.

Lucy nodded and agreed, 'Yes, I expect they all are,' she said. 'Except Bert. Bert is dependable and kind, Áine.'

Áine was sinking. None of them realized how ill she was. She could not stop coughing and she continued to lose 'weight. The weeks spent out on the cold pavements had taken their toll and nothing Belle or Maeve or Lucy could brew up, no treatment the doctor recommended seemed to help her get well.

'I blame myself, Belle,' Maeve confided. 'I should have checked up to see if she was all right when she went back to Lorcan. Or stopped her going back. But truthfully I was only too glad to see her go. Oh, I'm a terrible person, truth be known.'

'You couldn't know,' Belle exclaimed. 'And interfering between married people is not to be recommended. Listen, Maeve, nobody could have prevented what happened, and Áine could have come here for help if she had swallowed that damned pride of hers. As it is, you've done all you could.'

Áine slipped away one warm night at the end of August as the two weddings approached.

'It is God reminding us,' Tilly cried.

She found the body, cold and stiff in Lucy's bed in the morning when she went to bring Áine her morning drink and medicine.

'Hold your tongue, Tilly,' Belle cried, and Maeve could not help but think how, even in death, Áine managed to make others feel bad about themselves.

'I should have been with her,' Lucy mourned.

'She never wanted others to be happy,' Maeve said sadly to Belle. 'She resented happiness because she didn't know how to be happy herself.'

'She loved you, Maeve, she told me,' Lucy said. 'She just felt you were so far above her that you would never understand her problems.'

'That was silly,' Maeve said, abashed. 'We all have the same problems.'

Maeve wrote and told Demara and enclosed a letter to Pierce and Brigid. She also knew that, no matter how she dreaded it, she would have to go and see Lorcan and tell him what had happened.

She asked Bert to accompany her. She had not been down into that part of London since they left, she and Demara, the day Lorcan had thrown them out. It seemed like years ago and it sent a chill down her spine to turn into that dark road, gloomy even on this sunny day. There were lines of laundry on cord stretched across the street. Top and tailed sheets, darned combinations, threadbare vests, patched petticoats flapped about in the sooty air and it reminded Maeve of her past poverty and made her feel guilty she had not been a little more help to her sister.

They climbed the narrow stairs to the Brennan apartment. Maeve had forgotten the smell, that stale stench of booze and urine, the acrid aroma of cooking and rotting refuse and poverty. Had the stairs always been so narrow and dark and had they always smelled so badly?

She had been so excited, so full of hope when she first arrived in London that she had not noticed the terrible decay of the place. But Demara had. Expectancy dulled Maeve's sight and sense of smell, but Demara had always been clear-sighted. But then, Maeve mused, lifting her skirts and picking her way delicately over the rubbish, Demara's dream had always lain elsewhere.

The door to the Brennans' rooms was open. They stepped gingerly inside and Maeve gasped as her eyes became accustomed to the gloom.

The curtains were drawn against the light of day. The place reeked of alcohol and the mess was appalling. Everything was in chaos, dirt and neglect everywhere. Piles of crockery caked with ancient food lay in the sink. Pots and pans, foul and burned, dirty clothes in discarded piles, stains marking the room that Áine and Lorcan had been so proud of and kept spotless. As Maeve recoiled from the scene before her. Lorcan came reeling out of the bedroom. He stared at her angrily and for a moment she felt frightened, then she drew herself up.

'What yiz want?' he demanded.

'Lorcan, we've come with bad news.'

'That bitch left me. Took the babby and went. Lookit this place—' he gestured around the room— 'Like a pig-sty. Man needs a wife – keep house.'

'Lorcan, I said I have some bad news.'

But he wasn't listening. 'I gave her a good life. Nice home here. Food. I gave her everything. And what's she do? Lave me. Lave me alone here, alone. All alone.' His voice trailed off.

'Maybe if you hadn't hit her . . .' Maeve began, then bit her lip. Bert laid a restraining hand on her arm.

'She say that?' Lorcan moved unsteadily to the sofa. One of the castors had broken and the sofa leaned sideways. 'Bloody lie. Gave her everythin' . . .'

'Lorcan, she's dead.'

Maeve hadn't meant it to come out like that but her patience was stretched and she could not bear to listen to his whining a moment longer.

It was as if she shot him. His body jack-knifed and with a cry he collapsed on the sofa. 'Ah Jasus, no, no, no, no, no!' The cries came harsh and agonized. 'Ah Jasus, no, no, no . . .'

She found herself against all reason sitting beside him on the sofa comforting him. He rested his face on her bosom and cried out his grief, uncontrollably, like a baby.

Some time later, they talked. All the swagger gone, Lorcan was torn with regret and guilt. Everyone around Áine felt guilt, Maeve thought, everyone except Lucy.

'I loved her, Maeve, honest to God, but I hit her. It was the drink talkin'. You was right an' it was awful. How could I do such terrible things to her? But . . . but . . . an' I'm not tryin' to excuse myself, but she seemed to *ask* for it, y'know? Like she deserved it. Like she'd goad me, lookin' at me, darin' me, like an' I'd hit her. Ah Jesus, how could I know I'd lose her? It was like we was in some kind of awful game. Locked in together. An' now she's dead an' I can never make it up to her. Ah Jasus.'

The funeral was a sad affair. Lorcan, his suit hanging loosely on his emaciated frame, wept all the way through the ceremony. Pierce and Brigid did not come. It would take too long, they said, they would never reach London in time, and besides they had too much to do with the finishing of the new cottages. These were brick and they were proud to say were superior in every way to the old ones. The Donnellys could stay in the gatehouse or live in the one Brindsley and Da had built with the neighbours, they had not made up their minds yet. Everyone sent regards. Little about Áine.

Demera did not come. She and Perry were staying at Ballymora Castle and she was completing her house in Bannagh Dubh, she said. *I have had prodigious help from an army of men that Perry provided,* she wrote, *and soon it will be over. Somehow it is not turning out quite as I imagined, Maeve. In my dream it floated, was part of the mountains, part of the lake, part of the sea and the fields and the woods. Like* Tir na n-Og. *A magical part of the landscape. I imagined it nearer to one, then the other. Sea, sky, hills. Oh, Maeve, it was movable in my dreams. But in reality it is very solid and I feel sometimes that nature is rejecting it.*

It squats by the lake and refuses to be managed. I expect it will take time to settle into the landscape.

But now I know I can do it Maeve, and I'm sure you understand, for you too accepted the challenge life offered you.

Then she continued, *I'm sorry no one from here will be at Áine's funeral. But even if I left here instantly I would not reach London in time. That's an excuse, you will say, and you are probably right. I suppose it is because I was never close to Áine and I wonder if anyone was, even Lorcan?*

I'll be over for the wedding next month, dearest girl, and until then take care of yourself and give my love to Belle and Lucy, whom I long to meet, to Bert and everyone in Soho Square. And my regards to your Rudi.

Maeve could not dwell in sadness knowing her wedding was so near. She did not want to grieve for her sister, she just wanted to forget. She knew it was selfish of her, but she decided not to pretend to emotions she did not feel.

Only Lorcan, she thought, mourns her. Only Lorcan. Even little Seaneen seemed to forget her and was quite happy.

After the service Lorcan collected the baby.

'I'm goin' back te me mammy in Dublin,' he told them. 'She'll help me with the babby. It'll be all right, never fear.'

'Let us know how you get on,' Maeve told him, feeling

fairly sure they would lose contact. He promised and left.

They quickly shook off the residue of pain and gloom he left behind and set themselves to prepare for the weddings. Only Lucy made the long journey to Highbury to Áine's grave and laid a bunch of fresh flowers there every week.

Chapter Ninety-Two

⁓ ⁓

There was celebration in Ballymora. The cottages were completed high up inland, out of the direct line of the ocean's winds. Only Brigid mourned Áine when she had time, and she did not have much of that. London seemed far away and her imagination could not take her there, she had nothing to compare it with except the high and mighty interior of Ballymora Castle which made her feel awkward and clumsy. So it remained in her mind a kind of exulted place where only the very brightest and best were accepted and the ugly and stupid were cast out into darkness. Poor Áine therefore was a failure while Maeve and Demara had succeeded. And that was the way of the world.

It was not totally unfair. Maeve, Demara and Brindsley had worked hard all their lives to learn, to be educated. They had never avoided lessons or tried to duck out of study of an evening when they had to rise next morning at four-thirty a.m. for the milking. Áine had never bothered and she and Dana had escaped their lessons whenever they could. Killian and Galvin were remote figures to Brigid and she rarely thought about them.

Truth to tell it was Granny Donnelly she missed most. The old lady had given her ballast, her presence had made Brigid feel strong.

She also wanted desperately to see Seaneen. She was the child's grandmother and she yearned to hold him in her

504

arms. She had Brindsley write to Lorcan Brennan at the Dublin address of his parents asking him to come and see them in Ballymora and bring the babby. She had a cordial reply saying Lorcan would visit them in the spring. He did not want to lose touch with Áine's family. He missed Áine dreadfully and he would like them to meet Seaneen. He told them he had a job in a pub in Sackville Street and that maybe when Seaneen was a little older he might send his son to Kerry for the summers.

Brigid was delighted. 'We can put all the trouble behind us now,' she remarked to Pierce, sitting in the kitchen of their new cottage. They had decided to leave the gatehouse and live in the new home. It was better that way.

'We can get on wi' our lives now without the worry of an eviction in it,' Brigid continued, kneading the dough with her fists.

Pierce nodded. 'Aye. 'Tis grand how it all worked out,' he answered. 'Clancy was a great help – and haven't the girls done well for themselves?'

'Yerra, sure I suppose they have.' Brigid was doubtful. 'In my heart, Pierce love, I'da rather Demara'd married Duff Dannon. Isn't he more her own kind?'

'Duff Dannon'd never have satisfied Demara,' Pierce said. 'She's too ambitious.'

Brigid sighed. 'That she gets from you, Pierce love,' she remarked.

'Aye, well mebbe she does, an' it's no bad thing. Ye have te stretch upwards, don't ye? An' he's a fine man, Dawkins. A nice fella.'

Brigid had to agree. 'So he is,' she said. 'An' Maeve a big success in London. Marryin' a person of importance. This Rudi.' She stopped bashing the dough and crossed her arms over her ample bosom.

Pierce shook his head. 'I'm not too sure about the stage. 'Tis said to be the Devil's profession an' Father Maguire's dead set against it.'

'Father Maguire's dead set against everything! Never mind him.' Brigid looked at her husband. 'Remember the evictions?' she reminded him. 'Where was the bold Father then? That man is a shockin' disappointment when ye need help. An' anyhow, Demara says this Rudi is grand and Maeve is happy.'

'Oh well, she may be grand and happy but Demara says she's not goin' to church in that heathen land.'

'Isn't it funny now how yer interested all of a sudden in the Catholic Church, Pierce Donnelly,' Brigid cried, 'when 'twasn't long ago yer were stridin' owa the chapel above in protest.'

'It was in the heat of the moment, Brigid love,' he replied.

But she shook her head, 'Oh no, 'twasn't,' she told him firmly. ''Tis because Maeve is a girl that yer worried about the church-going. You think it'll keep her in her place. If it was Killian or Galvin in Liverpool ye wouldn't give it a thought.'

'Religion is a woman's business,' Pierce said. 'A good woman goes to church an' it helps her stay outa trouble an' be a good wife an' the mother of her childer. Men is a whole other kettle of fish.'

'An' is that what ye think kept me a good wife and mother all these years, Pierce?' She smiled at him and shook her head. 'Have ye forgotten, love? Well, have ye?'

He gave her his sudden smile and she felt her heart surge with love for him. But she could not speak about it, this overwhelming tide that washed over her when he smiled at her that way. So she changed the subject: 'Katey Kavanagh was tellin' me only the other day that Sheena McQuaid was seen with Clancy's man down in the rushes near Bannagh Dubh.'

'You don't tell me.' Pierce wasn't really interested in Sheena McQuaid's goings-on. In his opinion Dinny McQuaid deserved what he got but he was not going to say that to Brigid. Women were like children. There was only so much that was healthy for them to know.

'Yeah. An' Mary Dannon said they were naked as sheep on shearing day.'

'You don't tell me.'

She glanced at her husband and saw his indifference, but it did not stop her. 'Katey misses Cogger somethin' dreadful.'

'An' I miss me mam,' Pierce said, tight-lipped.

506

'Ah, I know, love. So do I. We lost two precious ones.'
Brigid sighed. 'An' it all happened in a year. A year, 'twas.'

'A year next autumn,' Pierce nodded. 'Aye, 'tis so. An'
who would have thought his lordship the Marquis of
Killygally would be drinkin' himself to death up in
Stillwater?'

'Well, we've got our new homes.' She smiled at Pierce in
satisfaction, glanced around the cheerful room and
returned to her kneading with a vengeance. 'The new
cottage is a treat,' she said, smiling. 'It's only beautiful,
Pierce.'

Chapter Ninety-Three

So the little enclave at Ballymora settled down, pleased
with itself, perfectly unprepared for what happened next.

The wave came from nowhere. Deep in the sea's
conflagration of tides and currents, it burst onshore. From
the fierce underwater jetstreams, dredged from the deep
where the salt-weed swayed and the great whales played, it
gathered itself up, roiled and swirled, and, mustering the
freak impetus it had accrued, it hurled itself in fury at the
shore.

And as it rose it gained momentum and size. Unusual
and bizarre forces fostered its gigantic enormity. Its huge
swollen bulk reared into the air, forty feet high,
proud-headed, foam-tipped, its shimmering crest silver in
the sun as it flung itself landwards. A huge sheet of raging
water, blotting out the horizon, curtaining the world.

It was a tidal wave of such magnitude as had never been
seen in the land before.

It all happened so quickly that it was over before anyone
realized anything at all had occurred.

During that sun-filled afternoon the sea had kept its
mystery and showed no sign of anger or revolt. Only its

surface was constantly shifting. Restless waves had crested and crashed when they reached the cliff-base, and the mist-hung rocks had scattered the spray. The sea was sucked into sand-strewn caverns and hurtled itself up the shore, breaking on the beach, rushing violently up the creeks and coves.

It took only one moment, the drawing-together of all the powerful forces great Neptune possessed, and it gathered up into a monstrous high wall of saltwater, opened giant spume-speckled jaws, and, surging forward, literally took a bite out of the land. The raging sea sucked into its gargantuan belly everything that lay in its path. It greedily consumed a herd of cattle, it devoured Lally Flynn's barn, lock, stock and barrel, it gulped down the sheep on Matty O'Flynn's lawn and the cattle Miles Murphy would drive that evening. It rushed in, sweeping everything before it in its fierce, fast journey. It stole Cogger's treasure trove from within the caves where it had lain for so many years. It greedily claimed the gold and jewels of princes, sucking them out to sea. It claimed Mr Aeronson's cottage with Mr Aeronson in it and all his savings so carefully hoarded over the years. It claimed the Stillwater papers and deeds and signed documents. It claimed Mr Aeronson's piles of filched gold and it claimed the books Mr Aeronson had so carefully kept, totting and adding and subtracting for over a decade. It consumed the remains of the old cottages, the ones that Muswell had burned, strewing seaweed and shells and cracking the branches of the trees in its path. It engulfed Sheena McQuaid and Clancy's man lying on top of her in the dunes and rushes of Bannagh Dubh and both of them reaching orgasm. They were clasped in violent embrace and it soldered them one to the other for eternity as they floated out into the deep, cradled in the billows, together forever.

And it enveloped Demera's dream. It stole the house, the stones, the statuary, the beautiful Apollo and Diana. It reclaimed its property that had for so many hundreds of years lain tranquilly in its bosom. Now it was sucked back home.

The mighty tidal wave flooded the land and swept it clean. One moment of violence, then perfect peace, perfect calm. Tranquillity restored.

High up in Stillwater the Marquis of Killygally stared drunkenly into the empty grate. He did not feel the cold, the brandy saw to that, but the intermingling of his days and nights drew him into a world of hallucination. He raised his eyes to the window and saw the crest of the wave demolish Mr Aeronson's little house and the sheep from the pastures and he blinked and thought it was the onset of madness, and he was afraid. The alcohol he imbibed to sooth his nerves in fact aggravated them and he could not eat or sleep or be easy any more. He lived in a nightmare peopled with ghosts. They came at him screaming for vengeance every time he closed his eyes, so nowadays he did not close them.

He shivered when he saw the crest for it was alive with images of his demons and he ran from them in terror.

He ran to the room Fleur had occupied and, fully dressed, he burrowed into her bed and pulled the bedclothes over his head. He took the corner of the tapestry and put it near his nose and around his thumb and nursing it in his arms he tried to hide.

The cottagers watched the wave in disbelief then relief as they slapped each other on the back and blessed their good luck.

'If Pierce Donnelly hadn't had great dreams and ambitions and drawn the attention of young Linton Lester on him, sure we'd never have been asked to move. An' then wouldn't we still be in those cottages below?' Miles Murphy asked, crossing himself.

'Deed'n we wouldn't!' Matty Flynn cried. 'Wouldn't we be washed away out to sea now. There wouldn't be hide nor hair of us to be seen ever again.'

'Did ye see it?' Shooshie Sheehan marvelled. 'As tall as the Tower of Babel reaching up to the sky. As we escaped its maw, thanks to the bold man hisself – Pierce.'

'Yeah! There's no doubt we're blessed,' Brian Gilligan breathed. 'It's a miracle that saved us. If that wouldn't renew yer faith in God, nuthin' would.'

509

'Yerra what's God got te do wi it?' Deegan Belcher inquired. ''Twas a much earlier magic so 'twas that saved us. Didn't Miles say that his brother over Dingle way heard the siren screechin' from the rock below where Demara Donnelly's been yankin' the stones and those terrible obscene statues owa the sea for her house?'

'An' didn't I see a gaunt black figure, like the Devil . . .'

'Isn't the Devil the Marquis above drinkin' himself to death in Stillwater, for God's sake?' Matty O'Flynn asked. 'Jasus, some people is born wi' more than they know what te do with.'

'Didn't I see him, standin' on the headland, his arms stretched, the cloak on him billowin' out like sails in the wind an' him wi' the hood up. But when he turned didn't he have the face of death. A skull!' Deegan Belcher breathed. ''Tis Demara Donnelly's fault an' her stealin' the secrets of the ocean. An' talkin' to the Devil. Didn't Cogger Kavanagh say . . .' Deegan faltered to a stop.

'That kind o' talk cost my son his life,' Katey Kavanagh cried, outraged. 'Haven't ye learned yer lesson yet? Jasus, didn't ye find out at least that blamin' others is neither a help nor a solution. God, yer fools an' no mistake.'

'Still it's quare. Demara Donnelly takin' the stone and those pagan statues owa the sea an' that great wave takin' it all back.' Delia McCormack shook her head. 'Ye've gotta admit it's quare.'

But Mickey O'Gorman was dwelling on pleasanter things. ''Twas well now that Ma Stacey . . .'

'Mrs Phil Conlon,' Carmel O'Gorman interrupted him. 'Don't forget or ye'll upset her an' she'll not serve ye.'

'Oh Jasus, that'd kill him!' Deegan howled.

'Well I firget betimes. Mrs Conlon then – wasn't it well that she didn't rebuild the shebeen on the site of the one that was burned?' Mickey contemplated the tragedy of all those barrels of porter floating out of reach on the briny.

Christie Dannon nodded. 'Swept away, they'da been.'

'I'll be glad when she opens again,' complained Mickey O'Gorman, sourly sober. 'Sobriety doesn't suit me.'

'Ye'll end up like his lordship the Marquis above,' Della Gilligan remarked.

510

'Yerra don't fret, Mickey. 'Twon't be long now an' her doors'll open,' Matty Flynn consoled him.

'Isn't she the lucky one?' Brian Gilligan asked. 'Makes a fortune owa the shebeen an' married now te Phil an' him pullin' in a bailiff's wages.'

'Ah, ye don't begrudge her that?' Mog Murtagh asked. 'Ah, surely not.'

They were a self-satisfied bunch that night, sitting outside their nice new cottages watching the moon come out over the bay. There was a sweet freshness in the air after the tidal wave and they puffed their clay pipes in contented contemplation. Their wives were indoors cooking the spuds for the evening meal. They had been saved by a fluke from the most terrible wave which if they had not had to leave their old cottages would have swept them all away. They blessed themselves and gave thanks to God and decided to go to early Mass in the morning.

Perry and Demara had at first been unaware of what had happened. They were sipping tea in Lady Lester's drawing-room, talking of Maeve's wedding and the fact that it was September already.

Then they heard a noise like the rushing of angels' wings and they hurried out onto the terrace.

It was warm out there, a sultry heat. Then almost instantly a cold mist from the sea curled its way up and the light became crystal clear and they saw the sheet of ice-blue water rise below them. For one moment it was poised there, its wide arms reaching over Demara's house, hovering like a giant silver butterfly. Then, as they watched, it swept inwards and collapsed in a foaming cauldron, then receded and left behind it – nothing. No house, no statuary, no sign that anything at all had ever been there.

Demara looked at Perry. 'It's gone!' she breathed. 'It's gone.'

'Oh, my dear, you must not fret. You can build it again.'

Demara shook her head. 'It wasn't meant to be,' she said.

'What do you mean, child?' Lady Lester asked.

'I don't know,' Demara said. 'I'm relieved. I don't know why, but I'm relieved.'

511

Kitty looked at Demara. 'I suppose you'll want to begin the whole thing over again?' she asked in a resigned voice.

'No,' Demara said. 'No.' She looked at Perry, 'Perry?'

'Yes?'

She took his hand in hers. Her touch was tender. 'Perry, does your offer still hold?'

'Which one?'

'Your offer to marry me?'

His eyes smiled and he enfolded her hand between his two. 'Oh yes. Why?'

'Well, I accept.'

'Dear lovely girl, are you sure?'

She nodded, 'Perfectly.'

'I'll buy you a house hereabouts,' he offered. 'I've come to love this country.'

'But not down there,' she pointed down to Bannagh Dubh.

'No. Maybe that's best left as God intended.'

'Are you sure you want to live here, Perry?' she asked.

'Yes. It is perhaps the most beautiful place I have ever been,' he replied. 'But we'll go to London for the season and to see Maeve's plays.'

'I'd like that.'

'On the other hand,' he said, 'when I'm here I wouldn't care if I never saw London again. Look at that.' He pointed to the view that lay before them.

The sky looked as if it too had been washed by the wave. It spread its wisteria-blue canopy over the sea, at peace now, hiding its tempestuous heart under a deceptive calm. The mountains were golden and mauve and purple and brown, dappled with light and uneasy darkness.

'Well, I'll not have you making choices,' Demara was adamant. 'We'll find a place here and go over there in the dark months.'

'Maybe we can get Stillwater from the Marquis and consolidate our position,' Perry said.

'We'd have to see what Fleur thought about that.'

Mrs Black had come to look after Fleur. Despite her odd ideas she was devoted to her charge and, most importantly, Fleur was very fond of her.

'We'll look after her, Perry,' Demara assured him now. 'She will live with us when we marry.'

He pressed her hands. 'Say that again,' he asked. 'Please say that again.'

'When we get married,' she repeated and he kissed her gently.

'It sounds so wonderful, but it will take me a little time to believe my good fortune.' He took her face between his hands. 'I love you, Demara. You know that.'

She nodded. 'I know, Perry.'

'Are you sure you have no . . . regrets?'

She smiled. 'You mean Duff? Oh no, Perry. I'm far too grown up now to settle for Duff Dannon.'

He kissed her then and his kiss was deeply satisfying. She felt the response of her body to his grow and draw them closer in their embrace. Then he let her go.

'I long to have you completely, Perry,' she told him, surprising him. 'I feel a deep hunger for you, a need only you can satisfy.'

'Oh, my dearest.' He held her to him again. 'Oh, my dear, dear one.' Then he smiled at her and said huskily, 'I wanted you the first moment I saw you. Saying what you just said makes me want you more. Oh, my love, let us get married very soon.'

'Very soon,' she promised. 'Very soon.'

'Maeve told me to ask you to marry me when you had built your house. She said you would say yes then.'

'Well, she was right, wasn't she? Except that *I* asked *you*.' She kissed him lightly on the lips. 'Now, my love, I need to go down to Bannagh Dubh and be alone for a moment.'

He nodded, kissed her cheek and went inside.

Demara left the castle and made her way down to her special place. She passed the site where she had built the house. It had completely disappeared. There were one or two blocks of stone which lay like the ruins of a once great building and the statue of Diana rested on its side near the headland. A piece of green seaweed had caught between her fingers. As Demara walked across the springy turf the thought came to her that the land looked better without her house, that the wild naked coast had a virgin beauty

513

that would have been spoiled by the alien stone and statues plundered from the ocean's depths. Perhaps, she thought, they had been used long ago by a pirate, an artist, a rich man, and the land and the sea had conspired to destroy their audacity in thinking they could improve on perfection. Perhaps that was why the stone had been lying at the bottom of the sea for her to find and try again. And fail again. And in years to come some other would try. And fail.

Those statues, that stone belonged somewhere else, in a sunnier clime, where their purity fitted with the landscape, not here where the wild Atlantic breakers and the echoing mountains favoured a more rugged and hardy style of architecture. 'Our cottages fit perfectly into this land,' she thought to herself.

Dusk was falling. She stood on the headland where she had stood that night last November before she and Maeve left for London. She tried to remember how she had felt; angry, she thought, afraid and lonely. So much had changed since then. Cogger was dead. And Áine. And her darling Granny Donnelly. She and Maeve had both realized their dreams. Maeve was fulfilled by her artistic career and was marrying a man she loved. They would be happy.

And Demara had found that the realization of her dream had not satisfied her. She had needed much more than mere stone to content her. She needed her man. Not the handsome young blade she had been so crazy for before she left and went across the water, but a wise man, a mature man, a good man. A man whose body and soul she wanted to embrace. A man whose every desire she wanted to gratify. To this man she wanted to devote her life.

He was worth it. He was open and generous and she loved him.

As she stood, the wind catching her skirts which danced around her ankles, blowing her long tresses from her face, she realized how much she loved that man. Then she heard the voice again:

'So you rejected the offer. My offer.'

'I did not reject it, sir. The land rejected it.'

514

'Nature is not always on my side.'

She looked at him as he stood, face away from her, black cloak billowing out, hooded, tall as a tree.

'I don't want the house,' she told him.

'A pity. A great pity.'

'There are more important things,' she said simply.

'You did not think that before,' he told her. 'You thought then the world would be well lost for the fulfilment of your dream.'

'I've grown up,' she said. 'I've become wiser, that's all. I've learned that people, not buildings, are the stuff that dreams are made of.'

He laughed and the wind caught his laugh and tossed it about. 'There are many who never learn their lesson,' he said. 'Luckily for me. Goodbye, Demara. We'll not meet again.'

'I'm sorry to disappoint you,' she said.

'Oh, you must not be. I win more than I lose. Ah well, I have appointments to keep. There are people all over the world waiting eagerly for me.'

The wind picked up and a cloud darkened the sky and when she turned her head he was gone.

She could see her father's house up the incline to her right. There were lights twinkling in the cottagers' windows and she could hear faintly on the wind the sound of Shooshie Sheehan playing his fiddle. Behind her on the hill the Lester household prepared for dinner and down beyond the trees in a new public house Ma Stacev, now Mrs Phil Conlon, was pulling her first pint.

She drew a deep breath of the cold salt air. She remembered what her father had told her.

'No one can ever possess the land, Demara. It belongs to us all. It is God's gift to us.'

She turned and began to climb back up the hill. As she neared the house Perry Dawkins came out on the terrace. When he saw her he came to meet and she stretched out her arms and ran to him.

Little, Brown now offers an exciting range of quality titles by both established and new authors. All of the books in this series are available by faxing, or posting your order to:

Little, Brown Books,
Cash Sales Department,
P.O. Box 11,
Falmouth,
Cornwall,
TR1O 9EN
Fax: 0326-376423

Payments can be made as follows: Cheque, postal order (payable to Little, Brown Cash Sales) or by credit cards, Visa/Access/Mastercard. Do not send cash or currency. U.K. customers and B.F.P.O.; Allow £1.00 for postage and packing for the first book, plus 50p for the second book, plus 30p for each additional book up to a maximum charge of £3.00 (7 books plus). U.K. orders over £75 free postage and packing.

Overseas customers including Ireland, please allow £2.00 for postage and packing for the first book, plus £1.00 for the second book, plus 50p for each additional book.

NAME (Block Letters) ....
ADDRESS ....
....
....

☐ I enclose my remittance for ....

☐ I wish to pay by Visa/Access/Mastercard

Number ☐☐☐☐☐☐☐☐☐☐☐☐☐☐☐☐

Card Expiry Date ☐☐☐☐